Praise for

HOSTAGE OF EMPIRE

"Intricate, elegant, and sharp as a blade—*The Throne of the Five Winds* is sweeping political fantasy at its finest."

—Tasha Suri, author of *The Jasmine Throne*

"Emmett's worldbuilding is sophisticated and captivating."

—*Publishers Weekly*

"With a deliberate pace and fine attention to details of dress and custom, Emmett weaves a masterful tale of court intrigues."

—*Booklist* (starred review)

"Brimful of thrilling palace drama and menacing court intrigue."

—Kate Elliott, author of *Black Wolves*

"Action and intrigue [take] place within a layered and beautifully realized fantasy world that will appeal to readers of Evan Winter's *The Rage of Dragons* and K. Arsenault Rivera's *The Tiger's Daughter*."

—*B&N Sci-Fi & Fantasy Blog*

THE
BLOODY
THRONE

By S. C. Emmett

HOSTAGE OF EMPIRE

The Throne of the Five Winds

The Poison Prince

The Bloody Throne

THE
BLOODY
THRONE

HOSTAGE OF EMPIRE:
BOOK THREE

S. C. EMMETT

orbitbooks.net

Copyright © 2022 by Lilith Saintcrow

Cover design by Lisa Marie Pompilio
Cover illustration by Miranda Meeks
Cover copyright © 2022 by Hachette Book Group, Inc.
Map by Charis Loke

Orbit
Hachette Book Group
1290 Avenue of the Americas
New York, NY 10104
orbitbooks.net

First Edition: March 2022

Orbit is an imprint of Hachette Book Group.
The Orbit name and logo are trademarks of Little, Brown Book Group Limited.

The publisher is not responsible for websites (or their content) that are not owned by the publisher.

The Hachette Speakers Bureau provides a wide range of authors for speaking events. To find out more, go to www.hachettespeakersbureau.com or call (866) 376-6591.

Library of Congress Cataloging-in-Publication Data
Names: Emmett, S. C., author.
Title: The bloody throne / S.C. Emmett.
Description: First Edition. | New York, NY : Orbit, 2022. | Series: Hostage of empire ; book 3
Identifiers: LCCN 2021033958 | ISBN 9780316453431 (trade paperback) |
    ISBN 9780316453448 (ebook) | ISBN 9780316453455
Subjects: GSAFD: Fantasy fiction.
Classification: LCC PS3619.A3984 B583 2022 | DDC 813/.6—dc23
LC record available at https://lccn.loc.gov/2021033958

ISBNs: 9780316453431 (trade paperback), 9780316453448 (ebook)

Printed in the United States of America

LSC-C

Printing 1, 2022

For Sarah Guan and Nivia Evans, with deepest gratitude

AUTHOR'S NOTE

The reader is presumed to have read Books One and Two of these adventures; certain matters will otherwise be somewhat opaque. Many terms, most notably in Khir, are difficult to translate, and much effort has been made to find the correct, if not the prettiest or simplest, overtones; footnotes have been discontinued due to great uncertainty over their utility. Any translation errors are of course the author's, and said author hopes for the reader's kind patience.

Now, let us return to the center of the world, great Zhaon-An...

Honor speaks loudly
But who listens?
Only fools, madmen, the truly great.
And all three suffer for it.

—Zhe Har, *The Book of Journeys*

ACCEDE WITH
GRACE

The dry time of summer was upon Zhaon. Dust lingered in every corner, curtained the roads, hung in the air as a golden haze. The fields stretched and shimmered under the sun's unforgiving stare like restive children under a maiden aunt's strictness, not yet willing to settle into sedate adulthood but too tired to protest.

North of Zhaon-An's smoky, bustling hive, the bright white stone of new imperial tombs glittered. The most recently filled shrines saw a steady stream of visitors from peasant to noble. Or at least, one of them did, for Garan Tamuron had held the blessing of Heaven and unified Zhaon.

His eldest son and heir's urn was also interred during the same ceremony three tendays ago, but few found it advisable to halt before Garan Takyeo's deep-carved name and the dates of his brief reign—less than a moon-cycle, hardly worth celebrating. After all, there was a new Emperor; the warlord of Garan had left his land well provided for in that respect.

It was considered unwise, as well as impolitic, to linger before the new Emperor's brotherly predecessor. After all, even the strictest filial mourning was done.

Still fewer visitors paused before Garan Takyeo's wife, the Khir princess resting so far from her ancestors. Yet her shade had the most faithful caller, for every day a slight noblewoman, at first in deep pale mourning but afterward with a single unbleached armband denoting an unwillingness to turn her grief loose, paused before Garan Tamuron's tomb to offer respects, paused for a longer while before Garan Takyeo's, and lingered long before the stone wall holding the urn of Ashan Mahara.

It was there, bareheaded under the glare, that Komor Yala bowed thrice with her hands together and settled to pray.

The man accompanying her, broad-shouldered in the black tunic Shan noblemen preferred, gave only the token offerings at the old Emperor's tomb, spent twice the time before the eldest son's, and bowed thrice with impeccable politeness before the grave-shrine of the Khir princess before retreating to the shade of a fringeleaf tree near the wall. His gaze, dark and hungry, rested upon Komor Yala, and after a short while he spoke a curt word to send the kaburei to hold a cup-shaped shelter of taut-stretched, oiled cloth over her lady. The sunbell was crimson, that shade of luck and wealth, a bright blood-clot against white stone.

Such an infringement upon her prayers did not discommode the noblewoman. In fact, she hardly seemed to notice it, and endured the sunbell's tiny, wobbling shade.

The nobleman—for such the quality of his cloth proclaimed him to be—waited with no sign of impatience, leaning against the fringeleaf's bole with his arms crossed. A glint of greenstone upon his left first finger denoted not just nobility but princely status, and only one son of Garan Tamuron would wear a Shan lord's somber costume with a hurai. Another glitter was a gold hoop in his left ear, a barbaric accoutrement most required to address him knew better than to mention. A leather-wrapped swordhilt protruded over his right shoulder, and his scarred face bore its usual sardonic expression, closed and distant. A faint sheen showed on his forehead, not quite sweat—for he was born to Zhaon's heat, and had endured Shan's as well for many a summer.

Finally, Komor Yala bowed thrice, her lips moving slightly, and retreated the prescribed number of steps from the august presence of her princess's shade without turning. The small broom she used to sweep the dimensions of a Khir *pailai* clean before lighting the incense to feed a shade's slight hunger was set neatly aside, and she turned to find Garan Takshin, Third Prince of Zhaon—for even if his now-eldest brother formally reordered the succession, Takshin was absent from its list and his title therefore static—regarding her as he often did, a line between his eyebrows and his mouth set as if puzzled by her mere existence.

Yala accepted the sunbell's stem from Anh. The heat was massive, a living thing; the wet oven of spring was bad enough, but this dust and the dry air threatening to steal the breath and turn the skin to a crack-glaze upon pottery were different only in kind, not degree. The afternoon storms of the summer rain-season had receded, occasional dry lightning crackling over distant mountains providing no relief.

The kaburei hurried ahead to the horses, visibly longing for relative coolness inside the thick walls and high ceilings of the palace compound. Yala, hobbled by decorum, laid the fingers of her free hand in the crook of Takshin's proffered elbow, and included him in the sunbell's shade as well as she could.

Such graciousness did not last, for he made a short, irritated sound and glanced sideways. "I will not wilt, little lure. Keep it for yourself." His scarred lip did not twist, though, and the words were sharp but not unkind.

"The sun hammers everything in Zhaon flat," she murmured.

A shadow approached from the opposite direction, drifting along the wide paved avenue with a deceptively lazy stride. His dun merchant's robe was of very fine quality and his boots even finer, though his topknot was caged merely in leather with a highly carved pin of fragrant ceduan. A flash of his glance showed pale grey like Yala's own, marking him as a Khir of a certain status.

The Zhaon held that a dark eye was a trustworthy one. In the North, the proverb was somewhat different.

Takshin slowed, which meant Yala must. Her gaze met the merchant's; she tilted her sunbell slightly. *Do not, please.*

Would he recognize the message? He either did not, or chose not to, for he swept them a deep, very formal bow. "My lord Third Prince, my lady Komor." His Zhaon was spiked with Khir's harsh consonants, but handled adroitly enough.

It would have been entirely Takshin's right to refuse notice, but he halted instead, and for once his tone was not overly cold. "Honorable Narikhi, is it? You are most unexpected."

"Hopefully not unwelcome, my lord prince." The Khir straightened, and he did not try to catch Yala's gaze. In any case, she did her best to appear utterly absorbed in the constitution of the paving-stones. Her cheeks were pale under their copper, but that could have been the heat.

"Not at all. I had little chance to thank you for your service to my Eldest Brother." A stray breath—far too languorous to be called a breeze—ruffled Takshin's topknot, caged in carved bone with an antique, dull silver pin. "I would have thought you eager to leave Zhaon-An." Many traders were milling about in frightened fashion, since northern Khir had closed their borders and word of a certain disaster befalling Zhaon's southron neighbor had begun to spread despite the Palace's best attempts to keep a lid upon the rai-pot.

"Ah, a man must stay where he is needed, or where he may make a living." The merchant's smile widened a trifle. A much brighter sheen of sweat clung to his brow; he was, after all, a northern creature. The summers of dagger-shaped Khir were torrid enough, but not to compare to Zhaon's. And their winters gave rise to the proverb *cold as a northerner.* "I have come today to make a few poor offerings."

"Half of the city has, of late. The other half are probably not far behind." Takshin regarded him levelly; many had quailed under the Third Prince's gaze. "You saved his life; do you come to propitiate his shade? Or to pray for the Crown Princess?"

If it was an insult to use Mahara's Zhaon title, it was a polite one, for naming the dead was unlucky and ill-mannered at once. The merchant Narikhi acknowledged as much with a gesture, spreading his hands, but his weight did not shift. He stood, indeed, in the manner of one who had more than a little martial training of the sort a mere merchant could not afford.

He was an enigma, then—but minor Khir lordlings were sometimes evicted from a family if there was not patrimony enough to feed them, and some few took to other occupations. This fellow could even be a byblow gotten upon a peasant girl in a moment of drunkenness or concupiscence, though his eyes spoke against such an estimation.

Yala's throat was dry, and not just from Zhaon's endless dust. It was a wonder the peasants had any soil to till, with so much of it hanging in the stale air. Her underlinen was uncomfortably damp; even sweating brought no relief.

"Both," the merchant replied. "Unless it is unwelcome. It seems to me Lady Komor is the only mourner for the Crown Princess."

Yala quelled another restless movement. Why was he doing this? She racked her brain and liver both for some polite way to send the Third Prince ahead, leaving her free to hiss a warning or, even better, utter a phrase of such manifest logic and soft power it would carry this man back to Khir.

It was far too dangerous for him here. She would never have thought Ashani Daoyan capable of this recklessness. If anyone discovered his true identity, he might well be closed in fetters and held in the Palace dungeons.

Having visited that place once, however briefly, she had no desire to return or to see her brother's childhood friend sent there.

Garan Takshin simply nodded, with the mannerly brusqueness of a nobleman speaking to another who had fallen upon hard times. "It speaks well of you, honorable sir. Please do not let us keep you, and should you need future aid, remember my name."

"How could I ever forget it?" The merchant bowed again, including Yala in the motion with easy grace. "I remain your humble servant, my lord prince, and the lady's as well." Mischief glittered in his pale gaze.

At least he was not wearing a pale mourning armband; that would have been entirely too much. Yala, numbly expecting disaster at any moment, suppressed the urge to bow in return. Takshin set off again, which meant she must glide at his side, her grey gaze properly lowered. There was no chance to address a mere merchant even if etiquette would have permitted, and in any case she was not entirely certain her voice would remain steady.

Did Daoyan watch her walk away under a sunbell's trembling shade? Takshin evidently thought her almost prostrate with the heat, for he moved at a much slower stride than usual, and when he glanced at her bowed head she was occupied in watching the paving again, thinking furiously.

"An interesting fellow," Takshin said, softly, and Yala made a soft, noncommittal noise.

There was no way he could guess. At least, she hoped not. Why had Dao not left as she begged him to? And coming to the tombs—was he mad, or simply stubborn?

By the time they reached the horses, her sorely tested equilibrium had returned. At least riding would create a breeze, even if they had to stay at a sedate pace for Anh to lead her mistress's palfrey. Takshin said nothing else beyond mere commonplaces, but she could not be certain.

The Third Prince, like Yala herself, did not speak of all he knew.

Still, who would credit the heir to the Great Rider of Khir masquerading as a merchant in the chief city of his land's greatest traditional enemy? Perhaps Ashani Daoyan only wished to visit his half-sister's tomb before he left.

Yet Yala did not believe it. It wasn't like Dao to admit defeat in anything, even when it would be better to retreat in order to strike twice as hard later, like the *yue* slicing clean air to gather strength.

The Third Prince swung into his saddle, and Yala let him lead the way. It was a relief to be out of his gaze save for the danger of an inadvisable word or gesture if relaxation made her unwary. The worries crowding her did not wait patiently while she visited the dead. No, they whispered in her ears, filled her head-meat, pressed behind her heart, and all but turned her liver pale.

She was to be married soon, for the filial mourning due Garan

Tamuron was done. And her future husband, the Third Prince of Zhaon, was altogether too intelligent—not to mention watchful— to evade if he decided to seriously question her upon the matter of a Khir merchant who was not acting at all as if he knew his station.

Yala wished she could gather her reins, but it was Anh's duty to lead her horse. Instead, she tried to look only wilting from heat instead of furiously untangling several mental threads at once. Her head was a jumbled sewing-basket, but one thing was clear.

It did not look as if Dao would accede to her plans or pleading with any grace. A sharp pressure behind Yala's eyes was not quite tears, but an onlooker would be forgiven for thinking her well advised to shed a few. Women were held to be made of water and cooler humors, anyway. She had to send Ashani Daoyan—using *Narikh*, his mother's clan-name, of all things, did he have no sense at all?—from Zhaon-An as soon as possible.

She watched her husband-to-be's broad back as he rode to clear the way for a lady, her veil turning the world to a hot, dust-laden blur, and tried to think of *how*.

FILIAL, SEVERE

The vermilion pillars of Zhaon's great throne-hall were a regimented forest, an army standing ready for a general's command. In winter great braziers would be lit to provide warmth; in the dry time of summer coils of healthful incense burned in conical holders placed at strictly regulated intervals, and palace servants in goldenrod cloth sallied through with quick apologetic footsteps to sweep any outside dust away through the great double doors. The massive stone floor with its deep bedrock roots was of unvarying temperature despite the weather, and a slight draft breathed from other chambers and hallways feeding into this giant space.

Nevertheless, even those born in this clime dabbed at their foreheads with linen squares, or swallowed near-boiling tea brought by yet more hurrying servants, to force the body to cool itself.

At the far end, the low carmine-upholstered bench meant to hold the nerve-heart and liver of Zhaon was vacant, for the Emperor had risen and advanced from the dais to meet his visitors. The eunuchs and scribes busily brushing edicts and policy updates for dispersal to the rest of the country's lords, scholars, magistrates, and other worthies made a series of quick movements, those on the benches closest to the august presence half-rising and bowing, the ministers—much closer to the throne, and therefore much more visible—bowing deeply, no few of them tucking fans into their sleeves to accomplish the movement with the requisite grace.

The new Emperor's visitors were, after all, royal personages in their own right. The former First Concubine Garan Daebo-a Luswone and her son Sixth Prince Garan Jin approached with all due and prescribed care. The First Concubine would have bowed low to Garan Kurin, once Second Prince and now Emperor of Zhaon, but he hurried forward, his scarlet and gold robe making a low sweet sound.

"Now, now," he said, quietly but firmly. The unbleached mourning-band upon his right arm bore three knots, a pale slash against crimson silk. "My gracious Third Mother, none of that."

Perhaps a ministerial ear tingled to hear such kindness in the Emperor's tone, and rapid calculations of relative power and influence were redone. It was still early in a new reign for true power or preference to show itself, but even the smallest trickle of pebbles might herald a stonefall, as those in the northern borderlands often muttered.

Luswone, her hair dressed in the high asymmetrical fashion of Daebo, sought to bow again. There was a trace of redness around her fine, lustrous dark eyes, and her lips did not hold the pale peach shine-paste she customarily wore. Her own dress was still full pale mourning, and there was no silverwork sheath over the smallest nail of her left hand. Fine lines had appeared at the corners of her eyes and mouth, where before there had been only rigid, pampered control.

The Emperor caught her wrists, keeping the woman from her second ceremonial obeisance. "Please," he said, courteously enough. "Walk with me, Third Mother. We shall speak."

"I do not know what to speak of," she replied, somewhat numbly. Her son, performing the bow due his now-eldest brother and sovereign, was unwonted pale and quite uncharacteristically silent. Garan Jin seemed to have aged as his mother did these past few weeks.

Of course, he was the only child remaining to her, his mother's prop in old age, and the lowest prince in succession. Still, he straightened, regarding Kurin with bloodshot eyes and a mouth drawn tight. His only pale accoutrement was an armband as well, though gossip said he had to be argued out of full mourning. He had ever been the more tranquil of Luswone's children, but what brother could be merry when his sister's head had been sent home without the rest of her?

And what mother, losing both her husband and her daughter in such short succession, could be forced out of unbleached cloth? Sympathy for the First Concubine was high at the moment. Even her new title—Third Mother to the Revered Emperor, a high rank indeed—would obviously bring little comfort. The Sixth Prince took his mother's elbow, providing more support, and did not quite look at his brother.

"You came to ask for something," Kurin prompted. The ministers exchanged glances at how filial he sounded; his uncle Binei Jinwon, Lord Yulehi and chief minister during the interregnum since it was his half of the year, did not smile fondly but instead watched with great attention. "I think I know what, too."

"It is small enough." Luswone's words halted; when she continued, she used the inflection of a dowager addressing a ruling Emperor, not a junior mother addressing a prince. "A small enough thing."

"Yes." The Emperor nodded, and he did not look to his ministers for agreement or direction. The funeral for the Queen of Shan—her reign had been as short as her eldest brother's, and just as dramatic—had left nothing to be desired in costliness or taste, despite whispers calling it somewhat inauspicious to have a whole cleansing pyre for what was, after all, merely a head. A life-size, jointed wooden frame had taken the place of the princess's bones, padding in the shape of a body wrapped solicitously in linen and then a robe of unbleached silk under a ceremonial crimson gown. "I have decided, Third Mother."

The flour-skinned barbarian who had carried First Princess Sabwone's head step by jolting step from Shan's burning capital was still in the dungeons, still awaiting the new Emperor's pleasure after three double hands of days. It was whispered that Zan Fein the head court eunuch had *not* put certain questions to the envoy from the Pale Horde; indeed, those who spoke of such things inevitably added the observation that refined techniques of information-gathering were surely wasted upon one of the Tabrak.

Besides, the Emperor was busy solidifying his rule, and it did not take great imagination or premonition to understand the Horde would be riding into Zhaon soon, if they had not already slept off the meal made by the sacking of Shan's capital.

"Decided?" Luswone blinked, as if reaching the great hall had taken all her strength and she was somewhat surprised to find a son here instead of Garan Tamuron. "Is that so?"

"Sabwone's urn will be placed in the new tombs near Father." Kurin's tone was low, confidential. The ministers, straining to hear, had to guess his decision from Sixth Prince Jin's sudden startled look, but very few had thought it likely the Emperor would deny such a thing. "Have no fear, Third Mother. It will be done."

Luswone swayed. Her son held her arm, but his chin rose, like a young stag scenting fire. And he finally spoke. "Eldest…" The wad of pounded rai in his throat bobbed. "Eldest Brother, we are grateful."

"She was my sister too, Jin." Kurin's mouth hardened, its beneficent smile turning masklike. "We are only waiting for the carvers. She will rest next to Father, and I will personally make the first offering."

The younger prince did not protest, though it was his duty and obligation to make said offering. He did glance past his imperial brother's shoulder at the knot of ministers in their court robes, watching avidly. Perhaps he was weighing the likelihood of protest from that quarter, but Kurin affected not to notice.

"Very…" Luswone paused. Her throat worked too, and her eyes welled. "Very kind of you, Secon—Your Majesty."

"*Kurin*, Third Mother. Before his mother, even the Emperor is only a son." It was a pretty aphorism, and a high honor. Luswone, her objective achieved, attempted to bow again with a stifled sob, but the Emperor caught her arms and prevented the maneuver.

"No more of that. Jin, return Third Mother to the Iejo. I shall send a physician; so much grief is not good for her."

"I am well enough," Luswone managed, and would have swayed again like an overburdened reed if not for their combined steadying.

"Come, Mother." Jin's voice had broken and was a man's huskiness instead of a boy's piping. "Lean on me. That's it."

The fetching scene—two sons and a grief-stricken mother—was worthy of a wall-hanging. The Third Mother and her remaining child did not halt to make their prescribed bows when leaving the Emperor's presence, but a mutter of gossip did not follow them after such an oversight.

All in all, the new Emperor was proving himself most solicitous of his grieving family. It struck at the heart of rumors that he had not always been so restrained. Or so clement.

"Your Majesty…" Binei Jinwon approached, his step very soft under dark, swaying ministerial robes. His mourning armband was unknotted, but no minister would dare to lay aside such an appurtenance while his ruler still wore one. "Is it wise to—" The sentence died in his throat as his nephew rounded upon him, pale under his copper and with his sleepy eyes glittering dangerously.

Some few among the remaining ministers were no doubt secretly pleased to see a son of Garan Tamuron halt Lord Yulehi in his tracks. Others reserved judgment, knowing the temper of the Emperor's birth-mother, now elevated to the status of first dowager queen. Binei Jinwon owed his position to that woman, and gossip painted her mad with grief for the loss of Garan Tamuron.

Or for some other, less traditionally wifely reason.

"Garan Daebo-a Sabwone's urn will be immured next to my father's, Lord Yulehi." The Emperor's tone was cold as he glided for the dais, effectively closing discussion. "Now, continue. The question of taxation in certain provinces."

The ministers hurried to approach the throne, one or two with a senior scribe in tow to make notes upon a small chest-desk held by a leather strap passed behind the nape, their slippered steps peculiarly soft in order to avoid splashing ink. Kurin mounted the steps, settled decisively upon the carmine bench, and beckoned Hailung Jedao, Lord Hanweo, closer.

It was not Lord Hanweo's half of the year for primacy, but he stepped forth anyway—the Emperor's summons could not be denied—and for the rest of morning court Binei Jinwon was all but ignored. A slight, angry flush mounted upon Lord Yulehi's throat, but he was forced to linger among those not called.

Filial in one direction, perhaps the Emperor was forced to be severe in another. The string-beads upon which power counted had fallen into a different configuration, and to some, it was high time.

More Curse Than Blessing

Zhaon's Northern Army was now a mere skeleton, but a well-trained one. Should it become necessary, the ranks would be thrown open again, swelling around the hard core of cadres into a mighty many-legged animal ready to march. Veterans released with a scrip for a certain minimum amount of arable land would be given a promotion should they return in the time of Zhaon's need, and be rewarded with yet more afterward—if they survived.

For now, the army was quiescent, its southron twin likewise emaciated and under the control of a trusted deputy. Even in slumber, head-meat and liver were necessary to a body, and for both armies those organs resided in the man beloved of the God of War, Garan Tamuron's soldier-son Zakkar Kai.

The soldiers were glad to have their father returned from the capital, and cheered him as he rode between their drawn-up ranks, shouts rising from dry throats under heavy golden sunshine. A double-ration of sohju was ordered, and if their general's face was forbidding under his horned parade helm, it was no more so than usual and expected. The ceremony of greeting was attended with all due solemnity, and ceremonial mourning for the Emperor—whether Garan Tamuron or his eldest son's short reign, who could tell—was announced finished. All the accessories of military grief were to be retired, and it was perhaps a measure of General Zakkar's grasp upon his men that no rumor of rebellion against a new regime, no matter how fleeting, had raced between the tents or fluttered across the drill grounds.

The line between obedient general and restive warlord was thin indeed; if any of Zakkar's junior generals or square leaders thought perhaps their master should sit upon the Throne of Five Winds, they were wise enough to keep it to themselves. The ancient keep of Tienzu echoed with their cheers, and its stone stairs, worn near the middle by near-constant foot traffic since the First Dynasty, rang with hurrying boots.

His broad-shouldered, moon-faced steward-adjutant Anlon met Kai at the door to the general's private quarters wearing a quite unwonted frown. News from Zhaon-An during the past few tendays had been spotty at best and Kai's departure hurried indeed, not to mention quite dramatic. Visibly relieved to have his master returned whole from what he considered a den of venomous things, the steward was still uneasy, as befitted his station.

Those discharging his duties were often called *mother hens*, levity found in their fussing married to a quite reasonable desire never to provoke the flapping fury of such a creature.

"My lord." Anlon bowed, relief and fresh worry creasing his brow. "Have you eaten? There is soldier-tea, and cakes. Come, let me take that."

In short order Kai was divested of helm and gauntlets, but he kept his dragon-hilted sword to hand. "'Tis good to see you too, Anlon. Have there been dispatches?" An army fought with weapons and marched upon its stomach, but the paper—pressed-rai or pounded rag—was how it thought, and how its pain was relayed upon nerve-paths to the head-meat.

"Near daily since your departure. I organized the papers in order of importance. Hurong Baihan is touring the northern bridges, and Sehon Doah—"

"Not now." Kai shook his head, lifting his arms so Anlon could unlace and pull stiffened leather shoulder-cups free. He would deal with dispatches later; it was enough to know they had arrived and there were no more stoppages in the flow of the army's rai-paper humors.

Since, of course, Kurin had won after all. Disgust he could not afford to show curdled in Kai's belly. At the moment, all he wanted was a bath and enough sohju to blind a man. He would only get the former; there was too much work to sink into his cups.

It was an unexpected mercy and a deadly grievance at once. "Letters?" The inquiry was sharp, the word cut short and crisp.

Anlon shook his greying head. "No, my lord." He did not add *Who in Zhaon-An would write to you now?* After all, Kanbina was gone, smoke from a pyre and free at last. And Yala…

Kai could not think upon her impending marriage.

Yet he thought of little else, attending to his duties with only half his head-meat and feeling a deadly burn of impatience behind his heart and liver both. "There will be a painting of my adoptive-mother from Zhaon-An, soon. There is a memorial tablet in my luggage; see that it is set in the shrine." He would offer to Kanbina daily, just as he did to the shades of his unremembered parents. Now all three were ash upon so many scorching winds.

"Yes, my lord." Anlon paused. "There are many gifts. From the men."

It was meant as a kindness, but all Kai felt was the burden of another duty upon his already sore shoulders. Anlon bent to the work of peeling away leather half-armor in earnest, and Kai brought himself back to the present with a jolt.

"Forgive me, old friend. I am of an ill temper today." It was something Yala, with her solicitousness, might have murmured to ease another's feelings. Kai denied the urge to squeeze his eyes shut, painting her face upon the inside of the lids. *I would go with you,* she had said. "How is your wound?"

"Nothing of it remains to speak of." Anlon grunted as he bent to separate the thigh-segments; he was lucky the assassin's knife had not punctured a bowel-channel. A lucky old soldier was, in many cases, better than an energetic young one. "You've lost weight. This isn't good." He clucked like a maiden auntie, solicitous of his general's health.

"At least I have it to lose." *Along with everything else.* Kai could not afford to wonder whether Heaven might have taken Anlon and spared Garan Takyeo from gut-rot had it suited their purposes better. Would he have traded one for the other, if given the chance? "I long for a bath hot enough to turn me into soup. How stands the army for provisions?"

"Summertime. Two large detachments at the first rai harvest, others helping with clearing. There was some grumbling, but not much." Anlon paused, knowing his master's moods well enough to risk a question or two of his own. "What of Zhaon-An, my lord? And the new Emperor?"

Kai was shaken with the sudden, uncharacteristic urge to kick something, anything. Even Anlon, who had been at his side during Kai's entire career as Zhaon's military architect and Tamuron's pet general. "Long may he reign," he muttered, and if his tone was more of a curse than a blessing, at least his adjutant would not gossip upon his lack of proper devotion.

Someone else might, though. There were ears in every corner, and no Tamuron to shield him from unfriendly mentions. It would please Kurin to put Kai in his place.

Zhaon's Head General would have preferred to serve Takyeo, but Kurin was also Garan Tamuron's son. And so far, while he was less kindly than Ah-Yeo would have been, he was capable enough at governance.

"Some expected the order to raise our banners." Anlon freed the shin-guards with quick snapping motions, and the padded tunic and trousers now revealed were dark with sweat, road-dust griming the damp creases. Most armor-sons called the process *peeling the beetle*, and the characters to express it could be filial or salacious according to the writer's intent. "It is no secret the Second Prin— ah, the Emperor—"

"Mind what you say, old friend." The general who had bled Khir to a standstill was too useful a tool for Kurin to lay aside just now, with Tabrak threatening and the Khir princess dead. At least the new Emperor recognized as much, even if there was little affection between him and a foundling raised to high station.

The First Queen had ensured as much; her hatred of any child not her own was perhaps natural enough to begin with but had been distilled over the years into a deep venom indeed. Still, he did not think she was more than indirectly responsible for recent events.

For one thing, Zakkar Kai had never found Tamuron's First Queen patient enough to achieve a true victory.

And it had all been arranged very neatly, indeed, the men chasing a lone messenger needing little inducement to give their patron's name when faced with Kai's wrath. They may have even believed what they said. Yet the idea of Fifth Prince Sensheo being forward-thinking, not to mention quick, enough to set a watch on the roads from Zhaon-An for a rider sent in Kai's direction was laughable.

And there was *still* the little matter of who had sent the last and very successful crop of assassins after Takyeo.

There was no shortage of suspects, and if Kai had been in the palace the attack might have been foiled. Who could tell?

The facts remained. Takyeo was gone, Kurin had reached the summit of his desires—and the First Queen, now a dowager, was no doubt beside herself with glee. The question of who had sent assassins after Kai himself was irrelevant at the moment, though hardly forgotten.

At least Takshin would keep Yala safe at court.

Kai suppressed a wince. There were far more important things to think about, with Khir menacing the northern borders, Tabrak riding through Shan, and Kurin—*Kurin*, of all people—upon Tamuron's battle-bought throne.

Yet Kai's heart ached like the stupid babu water-clock that it was, thump-thudding in his chest. Even his liver had gone pale upon seeing her, limp and bloodied as she was carried into this very Keep, gasping out her message over and over. *The Emperor is dead, the Crown Prince lies wounded, you are required, Zakkar Kai, you must come.*

It was either madness or an inspired choice to send *her*, and she had discharged her duty with a soldier's bravery indeed. Takyeo possessed the gift of inspiring loyalty in those of merit—or, he *had* possessed it—and Lady Komor had a habit of flinging herself into danger with only that greenmetal blade, too long for a dagger but far too short to be a proper sword, for protection.

If all northern women were of like mettle, no wonder Three Rivers had been such a hard-fought victory.

Takshin would prevent her from repeating such deeds, or at least so Kai hoped. He bit back a curse, and Anlon, his arms full of armor that would need cleaning, cast his master an inquiring glance. "My lord?"

"Nothing." Kai began peeling the quilted underlayers from his skin, sighing at the sudden coolness of moving air upon sweat. Of course a silk-wearing woman would prefer a prince to a stinking general who had bled her homeland white, no matter if the latter wore a prince's greenstone hurai by imperial decree.

Yet she had given him a priceless gift, some few words to hold close during battle or under the lash of inclement weather. *I would go with you. Wherever you willed, Zakkar Kai. My feelings have not changed.*

He could not even feel any anger at Takshin. Who, after all, would not want her? And Tamuron's third son had received little enough gentleness in life, packed off to Shan's Mad Queen as a hostage in his eighth summer; returning scarred and sharp-sarcastic, he was also unerringly faithful to his eldest brother and one of few men Kai wished never to cross blades with. He was better placed to keep her safe, and Kai had, after all, not told a single soul of his feelings for a Khir lady-in-waiting.

Not even her.

Had he said something, *anything*, Takyeo—with his usual attention to detail, even as he lay dying—might have brushed an entirely different marriage endorsement. But what then? A noblewoman could not follow an army, and the thought of Yala left alone in the Palace without a shield was enough to dry all Kai's humors to dust.

No, it was better thus, he told himself for the hundredth time, or perhaps the thousandth. It was better for her, better for Takshin, better for Zakkar Kai, who would have little time for a wife if Khir decided to become troublesome again, let alone if the Tabrak descended upon Zhaon once more as they had with some regularity since the Third Dynasty.

"My lord?" Anlon was uncharacteristically tentative, arranging the armor upon a cleaning stand. "The bath should be ready, I ordered it just as the ceremony was ending."

"Anticipating me again, old friend?" Kai sought a light tone, probably failing miserably. He was even sweating under the cursed hurai on his left first finger, its weight a reminder of the point a general balanced upon. There had seemed a chance of retirement even if Tamuron's ailment carried him away before his due time, with Takyeo upon the throne and Kai near at hand, vigilant against conspiracy and other dangers. "I hope our enemies will not find me so transparent."

"Have no fear." Anlon grinned, one of his canines fetchingly crooked. When his seamed face split like that, a glimpse of the boy he had been shone through. "Even those who eat with you find you a mystery."

"That could be a comment upon my manners, not my warplay." Kai stretched, his joints cracking in their accustomed manner after a long ride ending in parade or ceremony. He stalked for the inner door; the bath, drawn boiling, would be at the right temperature now.

"Well, you are with honest soldiers now, and not with *them*." His adjutant finished fastening the shin-guards on the stand and hurried in his wake, ready to attend to laces, heavy cotton cloth, and other bits of the carapace Kai was all too eager to shed. "There are some small discipline matters awaiting you."

"Stealing eggfowl again? Or menacing peasant daughters?" The joys of a soldier's life were few indeed; no wonder so many clung to them even in the face of punishment.

"Some few of both, one or two other matters. Tall Hurong sent a new armor-son, since the last one…well. I think this boy is a cousin of his."

"Mh. Very well." Kai paused before the low doorway to the inner quarters. The Keep was old, its plumbing creaky and ancient but still robust.

How long before the same was said of him? If he was lucky, he would die in the saddle. Maybe in his next life, he would be assigned a more peaceful place in the great hierarchy. He might even gain a glimpse of high cheekbones, pale Khir eyes, a feline grace, a light footstep, and a breath of jaelo upon a woman's blue-black hair. "Anlon? I am…grateful for you. It is good to be home."

"My lord." His steward bowed, coloring like a complimented maiden. "I should have gone to the city with you. It must have been dreadful."

Not in the way you might think. Kai decided no more should pass his lips, setting himself to the next task, and the next.

His innards might ache at it, his soul and liver might protest, but his duty was far from done. For all his faults, Kurin was the son of the man who had plucked Kai from obscurity and lingering starvation as a war orphan, and thus he commanded obedience. Did Tamuron see his general's faithfulness now, from his vantage point among Heaven's luminaries?

Kai suspected he would never know. He told himself not to think of Komor Yala again, and failed once more by the time he was sunk in an ancient, well-scrubbed stone tub of steaming water with a sigh.

Outward devotion to his duty was enough.

For now.

WISE AND HUMBLE

The hottest part of a summer afternoon folded over Zhaon-An. Most of those native to the country at the center of the world spent that time attempting a fitful nap or moving very slowly in whatever shade they could find; the broad stone avenues and crooked cobbled side-streets were a little less jammed. Nobody who could afford some shelter from the sun liked stepping outside it during the ox-hours, as they were called, for even oxen often refused to work under such conditions.

Through the glare and the dust, a single shadow moved with a measured step. What crowd there was parted before him, for a man in such fine cloth astir during this part of the day could only mean some important or unsavory business, and it was best not to question or to even notice such an event.

The Left Market was where certain items not quite legal or even very moral could be found for enough metal or barter; a slice near its northern edge was where a small contingent of Khir émigrés settled, taking advantage of thrifty lodgings. Traders and those who found it advisable not to return to the North clung together for fellow-feeling, if not for warmth, and those few crooked winding streets were alive with the smells of a strange land, spices used in different proportions; a tongue much different and sharper than Zhaon was used in the rooms and shops, not to mention the concomitant alleys and stables where horses were accorded far more space than those who owned them.

The man in dark Shan cloth entered a low stone building holding a tavern upon its first floor and found a bowing woman who gave directions in laborious Zhaon, tapping her index finger into her palm until he handed her an alloy sliver and accepted her thanks with a bare nod.

He mounted rickety wooden stairs to the upper common-room, and there he found his quarry. The merchant sat with his back to the wall, staring at a sweating sohju-jug. It was too hot for serious drinking, but it didn't look as if the grey-eyed man minded—or as if he wished to waste a sliver or two upon a container of chilled crushed fruit.

The merchant did not rise to greet his visitor, simply indicated the wooden bench placed at an angle to the table; that way, the guest could sit with his back to the wall as well.

A cautious man's politeness, perhaps. His tone held all the proper deference, though, and his smile was wide and welcoming. "Ah, Third Prince. You do me much honor, coming here."

"Do I?" Garan Takshin settled upon the bench without a sigh of relief, though a man in the dark cloth of a Shan noble was no doubt glad of any shade. His boots held traces of dust, but were of extremely high quality nonetheless. "Narikhi, is it? Honorable Narikhi."

"I am pleased and humbled that you remember my name." The merchant motioned for something appropriate to be brought his guest, and the prospect of earning a sliver or two spurred a sweating tavern-boy into motion.

"I see." The prince's scarred lip was often set in a disagreeable snarl, but now it was much relaxed. Almost thoughtful. Another thin scar clove his cheek, bisecting an eyebrow and vanishing into his hair; he was lucky to have retained the eye. "You seem a man who does not need much humility."

"It's safer, though." The merchant poured a healthy measure of sohju into a clean though somewhat misshapen earthen cup from the traditional stack of three upon the table, and now he bowed slightly, a nobleman serving an honored guest.

"Is it?" Takshin eyed the perspiring customers, none of whom seemed very interested in their drinks or the unglazed clay dishes of last year's paja nuts. Instead, they stared into whatever distance could be found, faces slack though their eyes gleamed with activity and thought. The humors turned inward under extreme heat or cold, burying resources deep like a peasant with a jar of alloy coinage to safeguard.

"Sometimes." The merchant filled his own cup, and a new wariness touched his grey Khir gaze. "The food here is terrible, but there is a restaurant not two doors down which—"

"No need." Takshin lifted his cup and touched it to his bottom lip with a short inhale, so his host could continue drinking at leisure. "I am not staying long."

"Then you must be upon urgent business indeed." But the Khir man did not seem hurried. In fact, he spaced his words like beads upon a kombin's knotted silken string, or drilled and stacked upon a counting-rack. "It is to my advantage to be of service. Especially so far from my homeland."

"*We are all guests upon the earth,*" the prince quoted, as the tavern-boy hurried back with a fresh jug of higher-grade sohju and a narrow-necked glazed jug of chilled crushed fruit.

"And you are a scholar, to know Cao Leong." The merchant nodded at the boy, tossing him a small tied-together trio of pierced copper coins. "Something for my guest to eat, from Banban's."

The boy bowed and hurried away again. One fed even a guest who had refused, in Khir as well as Zhaon.

To match this courtesy, the prince took his sohju in a single gulp as Shan dispatch riders often did. He did not shatter the cup upon the table or floor as some offended by the vintage or expressing deep appreciation in a festive manner might. "Your education is extensive."

The merchant's smile became distant, though no less cordial. "Too extensive for my station, some might say." Narikhi's callused fingers rested upon his cup, a pad of muscle upon his wrist bespeaking near-daily weapons practice.

Takshin's own hands were similar. "Knowledge is never wasted." The Third Prince eyed the door as well as the counter where the tavern's proprietor was nervously watching his august visitor. In fact, Garan Tamuron's third son seemed exquisitely aware of everything in the entire establishment except the merchant to his right. "And so I am seeking it."

"You came to discuss philosophy?" Narikhi did not ape surprise, his expression remaining curiously unmoved. "Or perhaps commerce?" Either, his tone suggested, was an equally pleasant subject upon a hot Zhaon afternoon.

The unscarred half of Takshin's mouth twitched upward; it was perhaps a wry smile. "I came to discuss Khir."

"I left that land some while ago; I am sadly behind on gossip." Narikhi moved languidly to pour for his guest and then himself, fulfilling a host's duty. "Though it flies through the air like the dust itself; consequently I have a wide selection of Zhaon-An wares, having been here some few fullmoons."

"I think I shall tell you a few items instead." The prince could have insulted his host by intimating he would do so for a price, but his tone remained distant, a mark of respect in its own right. "About the Crown Princess, perhaps."

"A sad tale, then?" The merchant made a peculiarly Khir sound, not quite an exhale nor a word, the tongue tapping the roof of the mouth several times to chop easily digestible pieces from the operation. "Sad tales are commonplace; happiness is expensive."

"True." Takshin apparently found this profound, for he nodded. The gold hoop in his left ear gleamed—a Khir ornament, and strange to see upon a southroner. "Do you know much of her passing?"

Narikhi shrugged, setting the more expensive sohju-jug down and spreading his hands to indicate the proper sadness at the event of his august countrywoman's demise. "Only what is reported upon every street-corner."

"I should think a Khir would be well-informed." Takshin paused, touching his cup with a fingertip; now that he had taken his first drink, the subtle motion politely freed his host from the duty of waiting for a guest's further consumption. "Especially since the manner of her death was singularly... northern."

"Was it?" The merchant did not seem to realize the Crown Princess could be a dangerous subject. Or he held Zhaon affairs of little consequence—which would be strange for a canny businessman, indeed. "We keep our women close, in Khir. We protect them."

"You must," Takshin observed, "for the Crown Princess was sent with a single lady-in-waiting." He raised his cup and downed its contents, again, in a single motion. Perhaps it was a compliment.

"Lady Komor, I presume." Having sensed where the true nature of his questioner's interest lay, the merchant did not set aside his attitude of calm helpfulness. "She is all things a Khir noblewoman should be; her family must long for her return. But why tell me this, Third Prince? I am merely a stranger, a humble merchant."

"A merchant who was to hand when an attempt was made upon my Eldest Brother." Takshin ticked off a few more strangenesses upon his fingers, like a trader's child learning to count. "A merchant who has made every effort to be of use to Lady Komor. A merchant who does not seem to have much in the way of wares to sell."

"Trade is difficult, since the borders are closed. Which is why I sought Lady Komor's patronage." Narikhi did not add that several of the tavern's morose drinkers were men much in his position, repaying the honor of directness with a reluctance to state the obvious.

The rumors from farther south were... disturbing. Shan was a much more heated source of gossip now than the poor northern Crown Princess's fate.

"She does seem well disposed toward you." The prince did not glower, but his Zhaon-dark glance was restless, and the merchant took it as a sign to refill his guest's cup.

This time, he used the more expensive vintage from the fresh jug for the prince, but poured himself the dregs of the old. It was the sort of economy a nobleman would never practice. "Other Khir merchants might be too afraid to bring their wares to the Palace.

Perhaps I am only foolhardy." His forehead gleamed, but it was indeed a very warm day.

"Perhaps you are more than you appear." The prince again touched his cup; would any at Zhaon's court be surprised by his scrupulous manners? He was not regarded as being overly concerned with such niceties—at least, not with aristocrats.

It could be that a merchant was too far beneath him for rudeness.

"Is not every man?" Narikhi's gentle expression had not changed, nor had his posture. "But I assure you, my lord Third Prince, I mean Lady Komor no harm at all." A direct statement, at last—a raid upon pickets in the manner of northern horse-lords. "I would be her friend, if allowed."

Takshin's smile, much more pronounced this time, made his scarred lip twitch disconcertingly. "You think she needs friends?"

"She is a Khir noblewoman trapped in Zhaon." Put that way, the wonder was that many more were not seeking the lady's perhaps-questionable influence—or, more likely, to take advantage of whatever anxiety said lady felt in her status. "It is every Khir nob—every Khir man's duty to provide assistance."

Now Garan Takshin's attention settled wholly upon his host. "And if I asked your fellow merchants, how many of them would assert such a thing?" He turned his sohju-cup a quarter, to absorb the luck and pleasure of conversation.

It could have been a compliment.

"If it were profitable?" Narikhi considered the question. "Quite a few." He downed his own measure, but only halfway.

"Ah." The single syllable was drawn out, a sound of comprehension. "So her patronage is profitable."

"Though not without certain dangers."

"For those who would take advantage, it is dangerous indeed. Lady Komor is not without Zhaon friends." The prince's tone could never be called *pleasant*, but it was, at least, indubitably civil, and the inference could be drawn that he numbered among the company of said lady's friends. "What do you know of riding, Honorable Narikhi?"

The merchant considered this fresh question, sensing Lady Komor was no longer a safe subject for two men in a breathlessly hot drinking-hole. "I am Khir." In other words, he was one of the horse-goddess's chosen.

Even a northern peasant was held to be among that divine being's favored ones; other men sat upon horses, but a Khir *rode*.

"I have heard of certain arrows used in the North." The prince took a decorous sip, because his host still had a half-measure, before putting his glazed but unpainted cup down with a small click. "*Ihenhua*. Horse-killers."

"Horses deserve a better fate." The merchant's mouth thinned slightly; even a man less than noble might well find this subject distasteful.

The Third Prince's unscarred eyebrow rose. "You would not happen to have any *ihenhua* lying about, would you?" How a man in such dark cloth did not sweat was a mystery; perhaps Shan's own torrid summers were far worse than his homeland's.

"My trade is not weapons, my lord Third Prince." The merchant paused, and his grey gaze locked with the prince's dark one. "Forgive me, that is the correct title, is it not? Zhaon's methods of address are complex; I do not wish to give offense."

Now Garan Takshin's smile was broad, though a steely glint lingered in his eyes. "I am of a singularly mild temper when dealing with merchants, Honorable Narikhi."

"*That is not your reputation.*" *And*, the merchant's tone suggested, *I sense you are laying a trap for a poor man far from his home.*

"So you have heard of me. How very droll." Takshin rubbed his hands together, glanced over the table at the drinking-hole's other occupants. So might a general study the ground before an engagement not serious enough to be called a battle, but nevertheless crucial to an overall victory. "Then you will no doubt take what I am about to say to heart."

"I am all attention, Third Prince." To prove it, the merchant pushed his cup aside and folded his hands upon the table's scarred, dingy wood.

"Lady Komor needs no false friends. And she is very well-guarded, so you may rest your Khir mind."

"Are you implying I am a false friend, or that I have designs upon a noblewoman's honor?" Now the merchant's smile matched the prince's, lacking only a scar to twist its edge. "Both would be deadly insults, were I not as I am."

"I should think us both above taking offense at the moment." Takshin's gaze glittered as fiercely as a Khir noble's for a moment. "Lady Komor is to be married soon, Honorable Narikhi. She is quite busy with preparations and will have no time for those seeking advantage."

"Married. What felicitations." The merchant made a slight movement, as if he would call for more sohju to celebrate the news. "I shall have to send a gift."

The prince allowed himself a single regretful noise—a very Zhaon sound, a slight not-quite word riding a soft pained exhale. "I do not think that would be wise."

"Must I be wise as well as humble?" All trace of humor had left the merchant's tone. Of course, had he been raised noble, this conversation could be seen as an affront, no matter how elegantly couched or reticently approached by one far above his reduced station.

Takshin nodded, a single brief dip of his chin. "I would recommend it."

Narikhi studied him for a long breathless moment. "I am, of course, very attentive to your advice."

One of the half-somnolent drinkers stirred, but only to pour for himself, since he had no host to perform the duty. Both prince and merchant cast a measuring glance in his direction, a pair of hunters briefly in accord.

"Good." The prince seemed about to speak further, shook his head slightly, and rose to leave.

"My lord Third Prince?" The merchant did not rise to bow his visitor to the door—of course, the lord was not waiting for the meal; one almost-insult matching another. "The earring you wear is quite curious. Is there a market for such things here, do you think?"

"I should hope not," Takshin said over his shoulder. He did not bother with any expression of parting regret, simply kept his back to the merchant and left the tavern, his stride lengthening. If the merchant followed him to the door or raced upstairs to a rented window, he could perhaps see the sword-straight black blot treading unhurried through the hammerglare of sunshine upon a Zhaon-An street, passing the tavern-boy bringing back a stack of round wooden containers, a meal the man who gave his name as Narikhi would now receive alone.

Ashani Daoyan did not move. Instead, he picked up his lumpy, misshapen cup.

He flung it to the floor. The sound of its breaking was lost in the mutter-rumble of Zhaon-An's streets. Even in this heat, even in winter's depths, the breathing of the great city never faded completely.

The proprietor, well used to patrons breaking small items in an excess of drunken glee or rage, took a second look at the grey-eyed man dressed like a merchant...and held his peace.

After all, the fellow had been drinking here before, and always paid his bill. It did not do to disturb a man hiding from his homeland.

A Sight One Should See

The Jonwa Palace, traditionally reserved for the Crown Prince of Zhaon, was a hive of well-regulated activity even during hot afternoons. "Lady Komor?" The voice from the doorway was soft, cultured, and heavily accented. Its owner was a solid-hipped woman in traditional Shan longshirt and trousers, both embroidered in a shade very close to the fabric. She wore looped braids in the fashion of that southron country, too, and her Zhaon held traces of its dialect despite being very correct. "There you are."

Yala set the bound book gently in its crate, folding a sheet of rai-paper to keep the cover pristine. The task of organizing a household's move from a palace was a new one, but not so bad when one had aid from servants well accustomed to such an operation. "I am almost done, Lady Kue," she answered. "Am I needed elsewhere?"

The former Crown Prince's housekeeper, her dark wooden hairpin dangling a single mellow silver bead, tucked her hands inside her sleeves. If they clutched at each other occasionally, none would blame her; a housekeeper without a master was a wife without a husband, as the proverb ran. And no doubt she found the new prince she was taking orders from somewhat of a trial, despite his familiarity with her native country. "The Third Prince has requested you in the large sitting-room. We have guests."

Guests? Their three tendays of deep mourning were but barely finished, and the work of removing Garan Takyeo's belongings from the Jonwa was immense. He had been planning to retreat to the countryside before the final, successful assassination attempt, so the preliminaries were well in hand, yet Yala's patience, not to mention her good temper, were beginning to fray under the assault of decisions that must be weighed, made, and deployed every waking hour she was not engaged at the white tombs. "I see," she said, though she did not see at all, and the other noblewoman in the room looked up from the small, expensive decorations she was carefully wrapping in rai-paper.

"Have no worries." Su Junha's eyes bore traces of pink; so did her nose. Her peach cotton dress bore an edging of roseate silk, and the pale mourning armband of bleached cotton on her left arm bore two knots, exquisitely performed and with their tails arranged just so. "I shall not retire until this is finished."

"A true battle cry." Yala straightened. Her back ached, and she was no closer to finding a solution to her most pressing problems than she had been this morning, or any other morning since she had discovered Daoyan was in Zhaon-An. "What manner of guests, Lady Kue?"

"Men." The Shan woman acknowledged the unsatisfactory nature of her reply, her head tilting and her mouth turning down wryly for a moment. "Foreign men, at that. They have just arrived at the Palace, met with the Emperor for some while, and now they are visiting us. Their eyes—forgive me, my lady, but their eyes are like yours. I believe they are Khir."

"Ah." Yala's heart leapt with hope, then crashed back into its seating with an unheard splash as implications blurred through her head-meat. Perhaps Dao had sent them—which was not, she admitted, very likely, given how long he had been in Zhaon-An. Yet that would mean she would need to arrange a few quiet moments for the purpose of convincing them to drag Ashani Zlorih's heir back to Khir.

Far more likely was that their provenance and mission lay

elsewhere, and she was faced with a different quandary altogether. Yala touched her sleeves and her ear-drops of twisted silver, ran her fingertips along her hairline, and shook her head slightly to make certain her hairpin's falling string of crystalline beads was not caught. "How many, Lady Kue?"

"Four, my lady, but only three came to visit." The Shan house-keeper's relief at a noblewoman's willingness to take over handling these guests was all but palpable. "They brought no servants; the last of their fellows is still at the Kaeje. Something diplomatic, I would guess."

Which was a relief—they could not be from Dao, unless he was performing a prank much larger than any they had ever attempted in the city under Khir's Great Keep. Once or twice they had accom-plished some mischief with her elder brother Baiyan's help, but a minor disturbance in noble society was far different from whisking a lady-in-waiting and a merchant from wary, guarded Zhaon-An.

Assuming, of course, that Yala would leave.

It was far more likely they were sent from Ashani Zlorih to inquire officially into the death of his daughter. And Yala, having failed to keep Mahara safe, might even find a stinging letter from her father waiting in their grasp.

"Do any of them wear devices, Lady Kue?" Propriety demanded she hurry to greet the guests, but any scrap of information she could gather beforehand would give her a weapon.

Now she was thinking like a general. What would Zakkar Kai say of this?

The thought managed to compress her much-abused heart, sending a jolt through her. She was losing her ability to absorb successive blows; keeping herself occupied with visits to Mahara's tomb and the business of moving the household managed to keep her from thinking upon the man she—

"One bears a ring with a crescent moon upon it, the second a very fine repeating-swallow pattern embroidered upon his cuffs." Lady Kue understood her putative mistress's lack of haste, though her expression plainly said she was very glad *she* was not required to decide what to do with these visitors. "The third…I am sorry, Lady Komor. I do not know."

"No need for sorrow upon that account, Lady Kue." Yala exhaled sharply, tucked her hands in her sleeves, and set out for the door with the decorous gliding pace of a noblewoman. "*Kienbah* tea, please, very hot. Whatever we have that is sweet and filling, since *kou bah* is not available. There are three blocks of fine sorrow-night incense in my quarters, Anh knows where; have her wrap them separately and bring them to the sitting-room. Tell Steward Keh to inquire especially at the stables for the care of their horses." The last was a small detail, but one appreciated by Khir noblemen. "The Third Prince is with them?"

"Indeed he is. And I think he is endeavoring to be charming." Lady Kue's eyebrows rose slightly, and her mouth twitched wryly. Her shoulders had eased, and the hem of her tunic did not tremble.

"Now there is a sight one should see." Su Junha selected a greenstone carving of a snow-pard, her fingers tenderly brushing the satiny finish. She held her sleeve aside as she contemplated the wooden crate it was to be packed in, giving thought to how best it could be nestled amid tangle-straw and other objects. "I almost long to greet these northerners myself."

"I should hold you to that." *But they would consider a Zhaon woman too forward.* Still, Yala could not banish a small smile. Lady Kue had been kind to Mahara; Su Junha and Hansei Liyue had chosen to stay even after her princess's death. Of course both were from somewhat poorer noble houses and princely shelter of any kind much sought-after, but they had proven themselves capable, docile, good-natured, and perhaps even that most reclusive and rare of qualities, actually trustworthy. "But then this room will never be finished."

"We are almost done." Lady Kue's usual sober mien returned, equanimity reestablished. She surveyed the library, its shelves sadly denuded. They had made quite a bit of progress, though she had been too busy to note it properly. "It may—pardon me, Lady Komor, but it may even be a relief to leave the Palace."

You need no pardon from me for that observation. "Indeed," she murmured, and passed the older woman with a grateful glance. She kept her pace to a decorous glide, her head down as if she were in the high, dim, cool halls of Hai Komori, about to greet her father's guests with quiet, retiring grace.

The sitting-room's doorway was a bright rectangle; she paused out of sight and listened intently.

"—glad of it." There was no mockery in Garan Takshin's tone, for once. Instead, he sounded merely affable, and very polite indeed. Very few would believe him capable of charm, but it seemed rather that he kept it in reserve until needed, like any weapon. "Though I cannot say we welcome such tidings; it will bring much grief."

"Human beings are born to grief." The sharp burrs of Khir rode behind laborious Zhaon, and Yala could not place the voice. She freed her hands to smooth her skirts and touch her ear-drops again. The Khir would see Takshin's *kyeogra*, and since Mahara would not be able to grant such a decoration their guess as to its provenance would be somewhat embarrassing.

How would they take the news of the impending marriage? If one of them could be persuaded to take a letter northward, she could plead for yet more time. It was ungrateful of her to hope that perhaps some miracle might occur during the wait, and Kai...

But that was useless. Her duty was clear; there was nothing to free her from its fetters. Yala pushed her shoulders back and ghosted forward quietly as a noble girl should. She appeared in the doorway, and surveyed the gathered men.

"Ah." Garan Takshin rose from his chair, and after a brief pause the three Khir did as well, their gazes taking in the quality of her deep-blue silk dress, modest at neckline and sleeves, and her hairpin—only dangling crystals, true, but otherwise of fine ceduan, its head filigreed with silver. "My lords, this is Komor Yala, the Crown Princess's companion." He used the word for a cherished noblewoman-friend instead of a mere lady-in-waiting, a small mark of honor.

She bowed, deeply, and waited in silence.

ILL NEWS

I t was a morning of petty annoyances building to an afternoon of flat-out indignities, but Garan Takshin was in a fine mood. Or at least, he had been before the Khir delegation presented itself in the great vermilion-pillared hall his eldest living brother now ruled from, and three of that group were directed to the Jonwa in search of his little lure.

Not only that, but they were bearing ill news.

Yala bowed, with that particular melting grace that was hers alone. It was good to see her out of deep mourning, if only because it meant other preparations could move forward. And the devouring, dazed sadness of the Crown Princess's death was no longer hanging upon her with its invisible, grasping veils.

The most senior of the Khir group—or the one who had enough knowledge of Zhaon to make himself understood—rose after Takshin did, with only a slight pause. Perhaps they did not honor silk-wearing women as Zhaon did, or perhaps there was another reason for hesitation. The foreign visitors performed their returning bows with some grace, though not nearly deep enough to suit him.

A volley of sharp-accented Khir from the man with the swallows upon his cuffs—Hazuni Ulo, a strange name—died away as the one with the great seal-ring carved with a crescent moon and stylized character bowed to Komor Yala in return. He spoke in clear, very accented and laborious Zhaon. "Lady Komor Yala, greetings. I was with your brother at Three Rivers; he fought well."

Yala's chin dipped modestly, the single bead hanging from her hairpin swinging in a graceful, restrained arc. "Lord Moruri Keiyan. You do me much honor." A bare murmur, as she hardly ever spoke to him; Takshin had to strain to hear it. "It is pleasant to see you again. I have heard Lord Hazuni's name; your companion is sadly beyond my knowledge. You are all most welcome here, though the household is somewhat disarranged at the moment. Please pardon us."

The third Khir rose slowly, his cheeks marked from childhood illness much as Mrong Banh the astrologer's. He was lean, and his left eyelid twitched as he regarded Yala. He said something in Khir, and Lord Moruri glanced sharply at him.

Yala straightened, tucking her hands in her sleeves, but she had gone quite pale. She regarded the Zhaon-speaker steadily, and Takshin had seen that look upon her sharp face before—clear grey eyes wide and limpid, mouth set in an accommodating smile, only a shadow of tension upon her slim shoulders giving any indication of her feelings.

It meant she had received ill news, and was bracing herself to bear it. Had the pockmark bastard spilled it without even giving her a greeting?

"Lord Namori Ekaian," Moruri said, with a short, mannerly gesture introducing the third Khir. "Forgive him, it has been quite a long journey, and he is of a sharp temper."

"Of course." Yala bowed again, a slight incline of her upper half. Her skirt quivered slightly. "I...I must ask. It is certain?"

"Very." Moruri eyed her. "Did you...my lady, forgive the question, but you did not know?"

Of course she did not, I told you as much. Takshin's temper woke, a sharp jab under his liver. "Lady Yala." He sought a quiet, reasonable tone, and to halt the conversation's flow for a moment. Such a pause would give her the means and space to collect herself. "Will you tell me what the noble northern lord has said to you? I have little facility with Khir."

Her grey gaze circled, touched his, slid away. Even more color had leached from her cheeks, and the dark circles under her eyes—sleeping in Zhaon's summer heat was difficult for those of cooler climes—were a taunt all their own. "My lord Third Prince," she said, softly, "Lord Namori asked why I am wearing a hairpin, and if I have no shame." She forestalled his response with another glance, this one lingering longer against his before flying to the open porch-door to one of the Jonwa's dry-gardens. "The closure of the borders is not the only reason why I have not heard from... from my father."

Ah, my little lure. Takshin forced himself to stand very still. If he half-turned to look at the pock-cheek Khir, he might do something foolish. "You have been very worried at the lack of letters; I know you have inquired daily." He fixed his gaze upon Moruri instead. "What has occurred?" As if he had not been told—but his tone was a warning.

It was the height of bad manners for guests to behave this way in Zhaon. They were northerners, though, and all Takshin had heard of that distant land was barbarous.

Except her. Yala's sleeves trembled too; an imploring silence was all he received from her quarter. Normally she would already be making some remark to smooth the incident, to forestall his ire—so soon, he had become accustomed to her working such wonders.

Even more miraculous that he did not begrudge the soothing. The silence stretched uncomfortably. He saw no need to break it; if the Khir men had any nobility at all, they would be acutely conscious of the insult they had given.

Moruri finally said something sharp in Khir; the pock-mark colored and rose, stiffly, giving a grudging half-bow in Yala's direction and muttering something that did not sound apologetic in the least. The scholars said Khir and her southron neighbor had shared the same tongue once, but such common parentage did not grant understanding to distant descendants.

It was, Takshin thought, quite the metaphor for current events. Even Shan was said to be an offshoot of that august ancestral language, though it was certainly easier to learn their dialect than to wrestle Khir to a Zhaon tongue.

"My lady Komor Yala, it is certain indeed." Moruri took up the burden of giving ill news in a language other than his native one; perhaps he had simply been arranging the words inside his head-meat. "Your father rides the Great Fields. Since the last day of the Festival of the Spring Ram." He did not return Takshin's steady glare, but his posture said he wanted to.

Yala's eyes widened. She did not stagger, but only because she was accustomed to overriding such movement, Takshin thought, like a rider well used to fractious mounts. "Then I am ill-dressed, and must beg leave to retire." She now did not look to him for succor or direction, and he did not like that at all. "Third Prince, please..."

"Go," he said, harshly. "I had thought to ask you to translate, but I shall stumble along with these men well enough."

"I may...I may return..." It was utterly unlike the careful, crisp woman he knew, and his heart and liver both ached. He longed to feed the third Khir a handful of steel, and *that* was unlike him.

Not the urge, but how close he was to actually committing the act. Still, these were her countrymen, and though Takshin had his little lure safely caged, he was more than ready to grant them some slight leeway to make themselves so forbidding she might find him a more palatable option indeed.

"Go," he repeated. "I shall send for you at dinner."

She bowed again, and her eyes were not swelling, they were simply translucent with gathering tears. He should have ached for her grief, and he did—under a faint, very ignoble sense of relief. There had been altogether too much mourning for her of late, but without her father's potential objection she was firmly in Garan Takshin's hands now. Unless one of these Khir bastards sought to change that.

Fortunately, he was well-supplied with plans in that eventuality. He watched as the last flicker of her dark blue dress faded from the doorway, and turned his attention fully to Moruri.

"Perhaps Lady Komor's fine manners have spoiled us." He took care to make the words flat and exceedingly colorless. "Is it considered noble to act thus, in Khir?"

"Lord Namori proffered an apology." Moruri clearly considered that sufficient, but his right hand had tensed. They carried no swords or other weapons into Zhaon's great palace complex, but Takshin wondered if one or more of them had a greenmetal blade like Yala's sharp, slender claw.

Or something similar.

"Did he." Takshin smiled, knowing the scar upon his lip would turn the expression into a sneer. "Now we are without a translator, my lord. Does it take three of you to deliver ill news to a lady?"

"We were to visit the tomb of the Great Rider's daughter, Third Prince." No wonder Moruri had been chosen for this; his Zhaon was merely adequate but he used every word cautiously, like a too-sharp blade. He was the most diplomatic of their group, by and so far. "We had a letter for our princess's husband. Our surprise at his passing—and our grief—is as deep as your own."

I doubt very much that is so. "I see." Takshin did not twitch as another movement in the door resolved into Takyeo's housekeeper Lady Kue, directing the setting of tea for the guests. There was a touch of Yala's attention upon the sweets offered, and the tea was *kienbah*, served much hotter than a Zhaon would like even in summer. The repast seemed to please even the pockmarked man, and Takshin set himself to the polite conversation his brother would have found so effortless with these foreigners.

If Takyeo's shade was lingering, he was probably relieved to be spared the effort, not to mention amused at his prickly younger brother's expense. It was unfair that he was gone and Kurin sitting upon the padded bench in the great vermilion-pillared hall, but Third Prince Garan Takshin had long ago stopped expecting such a thing as *fairness* to affect the world's working.

Yala did not reappear, which was probably for the best. Three blocks of wrapped incense were brought instead by her kaburei, whose leather-wrapped braids swung pertly as she bowed to present the gifts.

Takshin's smile held an edge, and no doubt the Khir lords were relieved to begin the laborious process of withdrawing from a visit that had definitely not gone as foreseen. Before they did, though, a triangular packet of rai- and pressed-paper was produced, tied with a scarlet ribbon, a familiar sharp crest—the flower and the setting sun—pressed deeply into the red wax seal.

"Letters that could not pass the border," Moruri murmured, and straightened from a bow that, while formal, did not extend quite far enough for Takshin's liking. "And some missives relating to... to the lady's father. Her clan will no doubt wish her return."

"No doubt," Takshin replied. *You will not have her.* "I will see she receives this. In the meantime, my lords, do not hesitate to present yourself should you need my assistance." A judicious pause. "You may find the new Emperor not nearly so moderate as the old."

With that, he left the sitting-room—a host should press his guests to stay, but they had been rude enough to deserve answering treatment. The remainder of their stay would not be comfortable. Khir had found Garan Tamuron a worthy adversary indeed, but also relatively mild in victory. Takyeo had only reigned for a week or two and had married their princess as well; Khir would have found him forgiving and moderate almost to a fault.

They would not find Kurin accommodating in any direction, or proportion. Takshin's elder brother had no pity for the weak; the fact that Zakkar Kai had bled Khir dry would irk the new Emperor but it would not go unremarked. Or unused.

No doubt Takyeo's shade would also be pleased Takshin didn't throw the bundle of papers meant for Yala into a handy fire, saving them all the trouble of dancing about the true state of affairs with polite words and their barbarous manners.

But his little lure would want this missive when she emerged from her rooms; it would pain her not to have her father's last brushstrokes and whatever news could be gleaned from her kin. So Takshin set his jaw and passed through the Jonwa halls like a shade himself, playing the game of avoiding contact or discovery. It was a reflex, and one he was glad of when he reached the little-used quarters he'd chosen when moving into his eldest brother's household.

He never liked to sleep where he could be found, but perhaps that would change. In the meantime, he had these Khir to outfox and his Yala to arrange a household for.

It would be a busy few moon-turns.

WISDOM AND AMBITION

E ven under house arrest, a prince had certain prerogatives. A nobleman feeling the pain of royal displeasure might move cautiously, waiting for a change in the weather, but Fifth Prince Garan Sensheo prided himself upon possessing a certain amount of royal stubbornness, not to mention being above the caution of the weak-livered.

After all, the new Emperor wasn't his lordly father. It was simply his elder brother Kurin, and even if they had their differences, Sensheo had helped put him upon the throne, had he not? A small amount of gratitude was to be expected, though of course Kurin couldn't be open about it.

Sensheo's house was alive with hurrying and confusion, servants running and the new arrivals—a band of traveling players his round, quaking steward Fah swore would amuse a prince—adding their own hubbub.

When another elder brother's visit was announced by his very same steward, Sensheo smiled and set aside the scroll he'd been pretending to read upon his massive black haga-wood desk. Haga was held to be an ill-luck material, which made its value much larger; he had outbid two other noblemen and a very rich merchant for this piece.

Just thinking of slipping the beast out from under all other buyers was enough to make him cheerful. What other pleasures did he have, really?

His housekeeper, Steward Fah's equally round but bitter-mouthed wife Ahwone—now there was a name with pretensions, though a pretty sound—bowed the guest in, and Sensheo's brother Garan Makar, in a sober scholar's robe embroidered with faintly contrasting thread at the cuffs, stepped into the Fifth Prince's study.

"You shouldn't be here." Sensheo took a certain amusement in stating the obvious, though not for the obvious reason. Visiting a disgraced relative was a duty that could hardly be avoided, unless their mother had forbidden it.

She probably wouldn't, though. And in a little while Second Queen Haesara—now the Second Mother of the Revered Emperor—would see just who was her cleverest child, indeed.

Makar's long nose was just as supercilious as ever. He couldn't grow even a smallbeard, yet he shaved every morning, and Sensheo thought it was probably because he wished it would encourage the production of a virile humor or two.

"Your household is very active." Makar did not scold him for impoliteness, for once. Instead, his brother tucked hands in sleeves and began to peruse the shelves as if this were *his* study, and Sensheo a guest. "Are you certain that's wise?"

"Oh, not only am I to be trammeled, but I should also be bored?" Sensheo tucked his own hands away, meeting rudeness with its like and refusing to rise from his seat. "Say what you want and leave, if you will play the disapproving maiden aunt. I have other matters to attend to."

"Those other matters would not be ones which would cause our mother grief, would they?" Makar sounded only mildly interested, and still did not bother to glance at his little brother. "Surely you must agree she has had enough."

"What is enough? I see no reason for her to be grieving." Sensheo brushed the desk's lacquered top with his buffed fingernails, enjoying its chill. Haga kept itself a few fractions below the warmth of the room it was placed in, like certain white quarried stone.

"Her husband is dead, Sensen. Our father, I might add." But Makar did not sound very scandalized.

Which only proved he was the hypocrite Sensheo always suspected. "Yes, well, *Father*." The syllables held sharp formality, treading upon the edge of ill-luck. One who had joined the ancestors was either held to be beyond caring about petty slights, or utterly determined to avenge them. Garan Tamuron had ignored most of his children while alive, except for his favorite from a long-dead spear-wife and maybe little Gamnae; why should he bother about his other sons now? "I'm sure he is untroubled about whatever *I* might do, too."

"You should not say such things." Makar examined a shelf full of tiny, exquisitely expensive carvings in greenstone, horn, bone, and ivory; they showed figures copulating in a variety of positions and attitudes from Cao Daolo's *Book of Middle Pleasures*. Sensheo had arranged them according to the chapters of that work, and someday would have a complete set.

The pursuit was more enjoyable than owning the whole collection would eventually be, but the goal was just achievable enough to hold his interest and provide a little excitement.

Of course it would have been nice to have his merit seen while Father was alive, but if a matter did not involve troop dispositions and clatter-banging at an opponent with a bright length of metal, Garan Tamuron had little use for it. Of course he'd been a mighty warlord, but Sensheo was of the opinion that while it might take parading around on horseback and killing to unify restive Zhaon's nobles and the provinces under their control, it took something entirely different to hold them.

Kurin agreed with him, of course. And Sensheo had known better than to broach the topic, even indirectly, with Takyeo. His judgment had been proven correct, but did anyone thank him? Of course not.

"What should I say, Elder Brother?" Sensheo drummed his

fingers on the desktop, one after another like galloping hooves. "I am, of course, eager for your wisdom."

"Now *there* is an untruth. What little wisdom I possess doesn't interest you." Makar leaned forward, examining a particularly intricate carving of a very athletic pose Cao Daolo swore was possible if both partners were trained as acrobats and also had flexible lyong saplings for bones. His nose wrinkled slightly. "I begin to see what does."

Sensheo gave a very unprincely snort. "As if you were not the one to show me that book." And as if Maki didn't visit a courtesan or two in the Theater District, as a prince was supposed to. Sensheo himself had two mistresses, though neither of them excited him much anymore. It was time for a new conquest, but he could not attend to that duty until he could publicly quit confinement. Sending a summons to a courtesan you had not seen before was a merchant's move. "Come to your point, Maki, or leave me in peace."

"Is there any peace to be found, these days?" Makar shook his head, turned on his heel, and settled his attention fully upon his younger brother. "I have told Mother you are obeying the Emperor's decree with all due decorum. Do not make a liar of me, Sensen."

"I haven't set foot outside my house since I was unjustly accused." It was laughable, really; had he thought someone would send a rider to bring Zakkar Kai to Takyeo's bedside, he would have done what he was blamed for. Not because he disliked Takyeo; his very eldest brother was a useful idiot indeed.

But anything that might inconvenience that commonborn brat Kai was exactly to Sensheo's tastes. It was ironic to be confined for an act he hadn't after all committed; still, the Fifth Prince—for Kurin hadn't had time or the traditional impetus to arrange the succession yet—decided it suited his purposes anyway.

When Kurin did have time free of mourning or other matters, or had the prospect of an heir, he would arrange the succession. And when that moment arrived, Sensheo was promised much.

Who knew? Kurin might even keep his end of the bargain, before the inevitable.

"Well enough." Makar's bland expression said he knew very well a prince did not have to step outside to cause a little mischief. "I come bearing news. Sabwone's urn is to be placed in the new tombs, next to Father. Kurin's made it official."

"The Emperor is gracious," Sensheo murmured. Poor Sabi. She would wander the many hells as a floating head with long hair, screaming while she searched fruitlessly for the rest of her body. Some shades could be fooled with a body of jointed wood, but their eldest sister was not of that temper; he suppressed a delicate shiver at the thought. "It's official, then? Tabrak?"

"The Pale Horde is riding. Yes." Makar's mouth turned down at the corners. A fresh burst of hurrying went through the hallway outside the study; a voice was raised somewhere in the depths of the house.

"Well, we have a fine army or two, and those stinking barbarians always come through like mehtuahghi and vanish anyway. A few peasants will moan, but the rest of us are safe enough." Sensheo tapped a finger against his lips. It would be very good, he decided, if Kurin sent Kai to face those screaming, dough-skinned, baby-eating monsters.

Then they would see who the God of War truly loved.

As pleasant a thought as that was, though, there were more important preparations to make and Sensheo wished to address them. "Shall I miss the interment, since I missed the pyre?"

"I asked Kurin as much." Makar's expression was not quite sour; he would not allow such an ill-bred arrangement. But Sensheo had grown up with his brother, and knew that particular, almost pained half-smile. "If you promise to behave yourself, you will be carried in his personal palanquin to view the ceremony."

"I see." Carted about in a wooden box, like a corpse or a woman. He would have to watch through a slatted window, breathing his own hot, trapped stink. "Of course he would make it as insulting as possible."

"It is the Emperor's will," Makar said, stiffly. He also cast an inadvertent glance at the door, like a wife afraid of servants' tingle-stretched ears. "Be careful, Sensen."

We both grew up with him, brother mine. Both Haesara's sons had seen Garan Kurin squat to shit, or sniveling when some childhood game went awry. "You call him *Kurin.*"

Maki's nose lifted, and though his hands were tucked decorously away his sleeve twitched. "A certain informality in the presence of my younger brother—"

"Oh, Maki, please." Was his elder brother, the one everyone thought such a *scholar*, truly so dim? Sensheo drummed his fingers for another round, the gallop of impatience. "You do realize you're the biggest threat to him now?"

"Of course not." Makar drifted away from the shelves, bearing down upon the desk and studying his younger brother closely. "I have no desire for the throne."

The Fifth Prince was hard put not to scoff. "Who's lying now?" A sathron was plucked somewhere in the house, a rill of quite serviceable music; soon the players would be practicing. If they did manage to ameliorate his boredom, he might even give them a royal imprimatur to display—and accept their very proper gratitude afterward, of course.

"If I were lying, do you not think Kurin would have arranged for me to be in my house like a long-ear in a hutch, waiting for the knife?" Makar made a *tch-tch* noise, very much like their mother or a maiden auntie when faced with a deliberately obtuse child. He halted a few steps from the desk, obviously attempting to use his height and a greater age to cow his younger sibling. "You have had the finest education modern times can provide, and yet you seem to avail yourself of none of its advantages."

"You think aping a scholar will save you?" It was Sensheo's turn to look disapproving, and he pursed his lips, flattening one hand on the desk surface. It reminded him of a knife game one could bet upon in certain taverns, a blade blurring between spread fingers, its tip touching wood with small satisfying sounds. The more times it touched without freeing blood, the more the performer earned. You could even bet upon odd or even strikes before the blade pierced flesh.

"I think Kurin is too wise to consider me a threat." Makar tilted his head slightly as the sathron playing resumed, another few moments of melody. "All my ambitions are reasonable enough."

"Meaning you are a coward." He had never said it quite so baldly before, but then again, Father had been alive, before.

The world had changed, and it seemed Sensheo was apparently the only one bothered to look past Kurin's ascension. Everyone else thought the game was finished.

It had barely begun, and a warm satisfied glow in the pit of his princely belly was the knowledge that he was well prepared indeed for its continuation. There was the tiny bottle with its soakwood stopper in his sleeve, the liquid inside making a soft sweet sound when he shook to make certain it was full. There were other small affairs as well, all moving with varying speeds to conclusions that would seem inevitable in retrospect.

Peasants and tradesmen might even breathe a sigh of relief when he achieved his goal. The common herd did not like uncertainty.

Maki regarded his younger brother for a few long, tense moments. Sensheo half expected him to take umbrage—when provoked, the Fourth Prince could be just as savage as Kurin, albeit far more patient in arranging vengeance—but instead, the scholar-prince merely smiled, a soft, reflective curve of his finely modeled lips.

"I am glad you think so." Makar turned upon his slippered heel and stalked for the doorway. "I thought to bring you good news, Sensheo, but I find you in a childish mood. Send me a letter when you are ready to behave as a prince should."

Oh, I shall send you more than that, my elder brother. Sensheo did not comment upon the rudeness of taking your leave in such a fashion, nor did he seek to smooth the folded fabric, as the saying went.

Instead, he listened, with a smile, to the hurrying of his household. The sathron halted; the players would not wish to show their skill too soon. He should enjoy himself now, he thought, before he was concerned with weightier matters.

And as he grinned, his hands plunged into his own sleeves, his fingertips caressing the bottle's cold smoothness.

A DELICATE TIME

The luxurious apartments in one of the smaller buildings of the palace complex—not one of the palaces proper, but a warren for nobles who had business with the court—were intended to be comfortable but instead only achieved stifling-hot, and those bred of northern mountains found it difficult to move, speak, or sleep in this swamp.

"You are a fool," Moruri Keiyan said, heavily. He was trying to decide whether the new ruler of Zhaon considered their diplomatic commission worse than useless, or if this treatment was a natural part of Zhaon protocol. Komor's daughter could have told them, or at least provided a hint, if Eka hadn't been so ready to squat over a mound to show who it belonged to. "That woman is our best source of information, and you insulted her not a water-clock's click upon meeting."

Namori Ekaian, his pocked cheeks now stain-flushed, said nothing. The Namori kept to the old ways, their women docile and retiring; besides, the rich southron food did not agree with him.

Though that did not stop him from taking what was offered. A warrior ate when he could.

"What has he done?" The quietest of their group, Shohuri Seiyan, scratched at his sweating neck as he dropped into a highly carved chair looking too spindly to bear a man's weight. The chair squeaked but held; he probably would not have been overly surprised if it hadn't. He looked sour, and weary unto death.

"Komor Yala did not know of her father's passing, of course. The border closed before the Great Rider could decide which cadet branch will bear Komori's prerogatives. Yet *this* fool—" Moruri, nephew to the man who had lately risen with dizzying speed to become the Great Rider's chief minister, was sore tempted to send a boot into Eka's shin. Even the table-edges here were carved, and all the hangings crowded with florid embroidery. How did the Zhaon stand it? "He insulted her as he would a common slattern."

"She was wearing a hairpin," Namori muttered, but his blush was as good as an apology. He was a distant cousin, so Keiyan could not be too harsh, but still. He shifted uneasily, staring at a sliding door to the outside, and his chair squeaked. "I begged her pardon, she should be glad of as much."

"Why are we nattering about a woman?" Hazuni Ulo shook his head, settling his swallow-crusted sleeves. "There is no sign of the Great Rider's son here; we were perhaps misled."

"Oh, he's here." Moruri was certain of very little, but he *felt* some things in his bones. His father said it was the horse-goddess whispering, as she did to all Khir before their birth; his mother, of course, held it was wit inherited from her family. Keiyan did not know which to believe, but it mattered naught. He had learned to trust that subtle speech, not least because it had saved his life during a hunt or two. "We tracked him to Dua-An, south was his direction. He would not leave this city without contacting Komori Dasho's daughter."

"Is she honorless, then?" Namori's clear grey gaze belied the muddiness inside his head-meat. Perhaps his frequent childhood fevers had cooked his liver; he was a doughty, dogged fighter and good in the saddle, but quick or deep thinking was not a quality he possessed.

Lord Namori was probably glad to have his son out of the Great Rider's city. It was a delicate time in Khir, and bumbling oafs were likely to mar not only their own chances, but their entire clans'.

Just look at what had happened to the Domari. One moment, they were poised to become the greatest of all, the next all their lands were forfeit and the Chief Minister deep in the Keep's bowels, enjoying the most violent of hospitalities. Only the most strenuous and careful of maneuvers had saved the Moruri from following their close cousins into the crevasse, and Keiyan intended to do his part to keep his family from the precipice.

It was a Khir nobleman's duty.

"Mind your tongue." Hazuni Ulo had reached the end of his considerable patience with Namori's thickheadedness, and his glower was almost fearsome. "I know the girl somewhat; she was the only noblewoman brave enough to accompany the Great Rider's daughter."

"Why send her here if she wasn't a whore?" But Namori rose, and stamped to the sliding door overlooking a tiny, very aesthetic water-garden; the palace complex was stuffed with them. All of Zhaon was recumbent, instead of standing proudly like terraced Khir with the deep valleys providing food and the high mountains providing safety.

"Because the Great Rider trusted Komori's rectitude," Moruri explained, patiently enough.

"He would not have sent a whore with his daughter, Eka. If you would be of use, check that garden for spies." Shohuri Seiyan settled himself more firmly in his chair. He rested his elbow upon the mirror-polished table—at least the surface was clean—in the attitude of profound thought he displayed in taverns and noble homes alike whenever something truly interested him. "We have other worries than a single noblewoman, my friends."

"Indeed we do, but should we return without the heir, it will go ill for us all," Moruri pointed out. He did not mind leading the chase for Seiyan; there was a benefit to laying a matter clearly in speech so it could be ridden down like a summerfat boar. "And our clans." He rose too, and ghosted to the door to the hallway, peering into its throat; the shadowed cavern was clear enough. Were the Zhaon so careless as to leave them in a room with no listening ears? Perhaps the new Emperor thought Khir so spent as to offer no threat, or perhaps he did not intend to let them leave Zhaon-An alive. "I tell you, the heir will not leave here without some contact with the Komor girl. And Eka called her shameless."

"She is a *woman*," Namori muttered, and stepped onto the porch, his slippers shushing over polished wood. He could not very well go for a walk, but at least he could be silent for a few moments.

Perhaps he might even learn something, though Keiyan doubted the feat would suddenly move within his power.

"What do we know of Garan's second son?" Shohuri preferred to focus upon the more immediate threat. "He welcomed us very prettily indeed."

Certainly there had been flowery speech from the son of Garan's first queen. There had even been gifts produced at the end of the interview—traditional bricks of golden tea sealed with the Emperor's own crest, very fine indeed for foreign dignitaries, as well as a costly piece of carved greenstone glowing with its own inner light upon soft padding in a filigreed case to be taken back to Khir's Great Rider. Either Garan Kurin had been warned of their coming—which was almost likely, they had ridden swiftly but not secretly—or such things were merely kept on hand as a matter of course, as princes of far Ch'han were said to do in case a representative of their potentate happened by.

Or both.

"I do not like him." Shohuri stretched his legs out and rubbed under his topknot; the filigreed silver pin holding it in its carven cage had slipped a fraction. Heat and dishevelment made men fractious, but he was merely, sullenly thoughtful. "This place is a midden. How do they *breathe* here?"

"Well, the Great Rider sent us to gather whatever can be gleaned from this particular shit-heap." Keiyan sought to bring the discussion back to its most productive course. Even his toes were sweating; at least these apartments had proper baths. "And need I remind you we will all be sent to the dungeons here should it please their blasted Emperor? We may need this girl's help; she has already survived the palace so far." Clearly Komor's daughter had enough sense to acquire a protector, though that scarred prince in his Shan costume could be considered more an ill spirit than a guardian.

"Her princess did not." But Shohuri shook his sleek head, still scrubbing under his topknot. It looked as if his head ached, and Keiyan's was well upon its way to doing likewise. "We shall be saddled with women upon our return, unless we leave her here."

"That may not be a problem," Hazuni commented. "Did you not hear the scarred one? He aims to marry her."

"No doubt she will be eager to escape such a betrothal." Moruri thought it very likely Komor Yala would have remained at home like the rest of the noble daughters had not her *damoi* become one of the honorable dead at Three Rivers. Baiyan, fierce in pride and strong in the saddle, was a great loss, and the only thing he had loved better than a good hunt was his sister, who bore very little breath of scandal before leaving Khir.

And all offers for Komor Yala's marriage had been turned aside by her father. Moruri's own mother had remarked upon that once, sniffing that the lord of Hai Komori valued a mere girlchild too highly. *It is his duty to remarry; when he has another daughter he will let this one go.*

The Komor girl would likely have a miserable time in a junior branch's household. They would fight over who to marry her off to, and the Great Rider might even be called to adjudicate in order to avoid internecine warfare. What would that austere ruler do with such a creature? Moruri did not know, but if Komor Yala was half the scholar she was reputed to be, she might well decide a prince of southroners was better than being a gamble-marker between junior branches of her clan now that the root had finally failed.

"No doubt." Hazuni's tone suggested he did not think Komor Yala would, indeed, wish to leave either. A few men, light and swift upon fine horses, could perhaps escape northward if they were canny, lucky, and armed. Carrying female deadweight, especially a fragile noblewoman and an honor-guarding chaperone, was not to be desired. "How best do we acquire this girl's aid, Moruri? You may leave the Emperor to me, I shall dance attendance and make many references to our paired misfortune. Or only so many as may be appropriate."

"He's probably glad his brother's dead. Not to mention his father," Shohuri said, heavily. Clearly he found the lack of filial feeling telling, but also wise. "And yet we cannot admit we are as well."

"The scarred one seems to think we will regret both passings. Do you think he..." Moruri glanced at the doorway. Traveling hunting-light meant no luxury; they would be forced to endure Zhaon servants soon, bustling in to bow, cook, clean, bow again, unlace, untie, arrange. Discussion would be curtailed; there must be *some* way to rein Eka's mouth.

Moruri Keiyan was simply too tired to think of it at the moment. He longed for boiling tea, and for his own bed as well.

"I think we are not here to answer such questions." Hazuni glanced at Shohuri. "I will have a word with Eka. You two are to find our prince, and I suggest you start with the Komor girl and Zhaon-An's Khir section. I shall keep the Emperor entertained and attempt to plumb that eunuch Zan Fein." His mouth tightened briefly, but he had more to say. "You seemed to smooth over the scarred one, Moruri. That was wise."

"He was packed off to Shan very young, I've heard." Shohuri shook his head. His topknot was even more disarranged now; no doubt he was too weary to attend it at the moment. "When they had their mad queen."

"What do they expect, being ruled by women?" Hazuni exhaled harshly. "I hear scurrying in the hall."

"Servants," Moruri agreed. It was downright pleasant to hear his efforts had been noticed, but he strangled the feeling promptly, as a nobleman ought. To rise above one's fellows was to take the risk of being cut down first when the scythe passed—or risk eventually shaming your clan. Neither outcome was acceptable. "At least the baths are supposed to be fine."

"How do they find them, in this maze?" Shohuri sagged farther into his chair, rubbing at his eyes with one hand.

"Through that doorway." Keiyan indicated the direction with a cupped hand; he gathered himself to rise and amble in that direction before they were accosted by a crowd of spying, thieving, superfluous southron servants. "They seem in good repair, too."

"Fine fortune." Shohuri made a languid gesture in lieu of a grateful bow. "Go bathe, I shall watch our little Eka." He used the word for a shepherd annoyed at a wandering beast, and Moruri had to hide a smile.

If he had to be far from home in a pit of venomous animals, he was, at least, in good company.

SURVIVE THIS

The day's excitement had worn upon Anh; the kaburei was asleep near her mistress's door as Yala ghosted over her, stepping high and carefully so as to wring no betraying squeak from the floorboards. Her skirt was heavy, and her hair was simply braided since she could not use a hairpin.

She would have preferred to dress otherwise, but at least she could take comfort in the fact that she had been in proper mourning for more than the requisite number of days allotted to the passing of a father, and that her usual morning devotions before the small ancestor-tablet brought from Khir sufficed, in her ignorance, to still fulfill her duty to him. At this point she was barred from full unbleached mourning lest it call her father's shade from his congress with the ancestors he had served so faithfully. Still, she would not wear a hairpin until she was married.

Komori Dasho had died while Mahara was still alive. It beggared belief. Dao must have left Khir before it happened, or he would have told her.

Wouldn't he? Which brought her to another question—how long had he been in Zhaon-An, waiting for a chance to contact her?

Or was that truly his business here?

The trouble, Yala thought as she glided through the Jonwa's halls, choosing deserted passages as far as possible, waiting until a guard nodded off or glanced away to ghost across certain intersections, was that she was well upon the road to suspecting everyone inside the palace complex or the teeming city. It had occurred to her that the question was not who would want her princess dead before she could give the Crown Prince of Zhaon an heir, but who would *not*.

And despite Yala's determination to find out who was responsible for the *ihenhua* pinning her princess's leg to a horse's side, mourning seclusion and court, not to mention usual, etiquette were all conspiring to keep her from hearing the gossip court ladies would drop and perhaps making a guess where the culprit truly lay.

Or what avenue would lead her to said culprit.

At least her daily visits to the tombs or walks through the gardens, mostly accompanied by Anh and a profoundly thoughtful, often silent Third Prince Takshin, had given her the wherewithal to find corners suitable for meetings like the one she was attempting now.

She would never have dared this in Khir. Even her midnight excursions to meet her brother for mischief had never left Hai Komori's comforting, confining enclosure; still, she was glad for every moment of Baiyan's teachings as she plunged into the baking-hot bath of a Zhaon night during the dry dust season. Autumn would bring a return of downpours, Lady Kue said, and the clinging, murderous humidity.

After that would come storms, and winter chill. Would she see them, or would she be returned to Khir?

Moving unseen outside was less difficult, for the night pressed close upon every surface, the moon was not full, and the torches or lamps carried by palace guards in their highly burnished armor— the Emperor's Golden, serving a new master now—made for more shadows than illumination.

The map she had sent bore enough markers for him to find his way, or so she hoped. She also hoped he would find it between the two thin pieces of rai-paper wrapping a brick of golden *zhe-udi* tea, a slightly too expensive gift for a useful merchant. Still, meeting him at the tombs gave her an excuse to send a marker of appreciation for offerings he would leave, albeit disguised as a stranger's, at his royal sister's tomb. She could merely imply she was grateful for anyone else leaving nourishment for her princess's shade, though it might be taken as faintly insulting.

The Zhaon were, after all, still her hosts. And she was a useless mouth, a lady-in-waiting with no princess to guard, to amuse, to pour tea for.

This particular overgrown water-garden had a hau tree leaning over what had once been a pond but was now merely a damp spot choked with rushes and weeds. She slipped between long thin dangling branches, suppressing a shiver—hau were held to be weeping trees, and hiding in one at night was a sure invitation to ill-luck.

With that done, Yala arranged her skirts. She could easily refold this dress and slip it back into the armoire; it was one of her old gowns from Khir and hung loosely upon her frame. She would never be plump-pretty as Mahara, and her face lacked the roundness of the Moon that made for beauty. Still, her lineage was ancient, her honor was unstained, and her *yue* was sharp.

Komori Dasho's shade would find little to chastise her for, had it lingered after his passing to watch his remaining child. At least she could find some comfort in *that* thought.

Yala closed her eyes, breathing in the night. There was a certain enjoyment in moving about freely after dark, but the pulse-pounding fear of discovery was unpleasant in the extreme.

Yala sensed him before she heard a slight scuff, boot against moss-choked stone pathway. There, riding a slight dust-smelling breeze that did nothing to cool sweating skin, was a faint acridity—leather, male sweat, a tang of horse, and the tiniest breath of sohju. Perhaps he had needed bolstering.

Heaven knew Yala might not have turned down a thimbleful of the drink. Her courage was failing at odd moments in the past few tendays, though it had not deserted her completely.

Not yet.

Her eyes flew open. She saw the indistinct shadow, and held her breath in case it was a different man. But no, he inhaled, and a faint whistle formed into an utterly familiar melody from a play popular the winter before she left Khir. It was from the third act in a staging of *The Tragedy of Seiwone*, involving a disguised prince, a court lady driven to suicide, and one of the Blood Years' most successful generals.

"*Ai*," she whispered, "cease, you will bring someone." The joy of Khir filled her mouth again, a proper language with the accents in all the right places. Her intonation was informal in the extreme, but it was perhaps forgivable.

Dao ghosted down the rest of the path, heading unerringly for her hiding place. He halted at the edge of the hau's skirts, like a courtier at the hem of a court lady, and a flash of white teeth showed her his smile. "There you are." He used the informal address as well, but he did not push past the hau's guarding fingers. "Your missive was unexpected, my lady. But most welcome."

"Unexpected as your appearance at the tombs. *Really*, Dao." *Did you know of my father's death?* Of course he could not have. The signet, safely tucked under her clothes upon a chain of fine silver, said as much; Komori Dasho had still been alive when he gave it to a prince intending to ride far from home.

And now her father's oblique comment in the letter sent with Daoyan about a soft landing for a falling leaf took on an altogether different cast. Had her father given indirect consent to a far different marriage-alliance? It would place her in a terrible position. And she had not thought to enquire if the envoys had brought a copy of her father's will.

There would be little provision in it for a daughter, but she could at least look upon the words he had spoken to a scribe and perhaps catch some echo of his voice.

"I had to see you." Dao made a sudden swift movement as if to catch her hands, reaching through the thin, whip-leaved, rustling branches.

"You must go home." Yala avoided him instinctively, stepping farther into deep shadow. The hau fingered her hair, draped over her shoulders. Her right hand, low and tense, was kept near her *yue*—if someone happened by, she would have to protect Dao from discovery. And herself. "Your father has sent—"

"He did not want me before." Of course he interrupted her, and of course his tone was full of low, fierce stubbornness. "He can live without me now."

"Daoyan." She tried a severe, quelling tone, wishing she was her father. He would set this to rights.

But Komori Dasho was gone. Her braid hung free, no hairpin thrust through to hold a coil. She would have to make do with unadorned bentpins. How long could she delay the marriage, pleading this new impediment? *I must mourn him somewhat, Takshin, even if I cannot wear unbleached cloth.*

Yet the longer she waited, the more dangerous it was. At least as a married woman she was explicitly safe. Or only saf*er*, unless the Third Prince suffered a sudden illness or assassination. What did Zhaon widows do?

Did she wish to learn?

"Come with me." Dao stilled, a hunter eyeing prey, knowing any sudden motion would force her to another withdrawal, perhaps more decided this time. Then, he uttered an absolute absurdity. "I will place thee upon my saddle, Yala."

"And rob me of my honor?" Yala attempted a light, jesting tone. He was her childhood friend, certainly. But he was also a man, and she was not the same girl who had left Khir as winter still held the mountains' throats, ice still upon the valley floors. "I thought better of you."

"Your honor would be in my keeping, then." Dao did not sound jesting, or even bitter. It was the most dangerous of his tones, the soft, flat finality she had only heard once or twice when the bastard son of the Great Rider had decided his forbearance of other nobles' insults needed a sharp reversal.

It was a fading, twisting path indeed, to refuse to take offense until he had to, then to strike so sharply, quickly, and invisibly others did not dare to push too far. He had learned etiquette and double meanings, piercing politeness and retiring refusal.

What else lurked under the surface of a man she had once known? Had she only thought she knew him? Some sages said you could never truly discern the liver or head-meat of another, let alone the heart. Now her memory was pitiless, serving up more than one verse or passage upon the subject.

"I *cannot*, Dao." Yala's voice broke. How did he not understand? She was nailed to this place until she had uncovered, beyond doubt, who had paid for her princess's death. "Not until I know."

Well, until she knew—and had performed her duty. It was the natural end to such determination, and Yala was only surprised she had not quite dared express it so clearly even to herself before this moment.

Was it cowardice, or was she becoming braver? She could not tell, and the confusion was made worse by Dao's new intransigence. He had been amiable enough indeed in Khir, with one or two exceptions.

"Then I stay as well." Dao turned aside slightly, glancing past the hau tree's bulk. "By the way, your husband-to-be visited me."

"What?" Her heart sank. Takshin was altogether too intelligent for comfort. He reminded her of her brother's fierceness, Dao of Baiyan's mercy. Between the two of them they could have made her *damoi*. "Dao, I had to. The Crown Prince uttered it as a dying wish, and brushed an endorsement as well. I could not refuse." Had she been hoping for a miraculously arriving letter bearing Komori Dasho's summons, or had she hoped Zakkar Kai would behave... dishonorably?

The questions were irrelevant at the moment, no matter how tormenting. More to the point, if Dao ever found out who she would have accepted without such an inducement as a kind prince's dying wish, what would he do? The thought of Zakkar Kai was a sharp jab against an unhealed bruise, her heart aching. The steady-thumping organ in her chest was a traitor, disobeying the dictates of liver and head-meat, as women were said to do unless watched and corrected.

It was, she suspected, too late for any correction to turn her from this course.

"Were you going to tell me?" Dao turned further, watching the path as if he sensed pursuit. "I could have sent a marriage-gift."

"There has not been time." Yala did not like where this conversation was riding, and her words quickened, tumbling over each other. "Besides, I am trapped in the Palace unless I go to the tombs, and we cannot meet in secret there."

"If you came with me now, we could be free of this city in a few hours." He did not sound merry, or joking, in the least. Rather, Ashani Daoyan sounded merely thoughtful, as if he had already laid his plans and only needed the slightest push to bring them to reality. He had sounded like this before he left for Three Rivers, too. "On two fast horses, beyond pursuit in a few hours more."

Yala's fingers ached. So did the rest of her. She let out a sharp breath. "My honor—"

"I do not care if that Zhaon pig has had you, Yala." Again, that soft, quiet, inflexible tone he had so rarely used before. He did not move, holding still as a hunter watching an unwary beast who had not quite left concealment enough to be chased. "I do not care if a hundred of them have. I will take you, we will *go*."

"And when we arrive at the Great Keep?" Of all the objections she could make—and they crowded her throat down to her liver, jostling for escape—this was the only one she could think to set free in the sticky hot darkness, hoping it would halt this madness. "What reception will an honorless saddle-bride gain? Why do you press me so?"

"Did you truly think it was your brother who held my affection, Yala?" Now he made a restless movement, sharply controlled halfway. It was a relief; perhaps he was willing to listen to reason. "I should have braved Hai Komori at night. Crept into your bedroom."

She was past being shocked, or so she had thought. Yala drew in a sharp breath. "If my father did not kill you, Baiyan would have. Please, Dao. You must go home. The Great Rider needs his son; Khir needs you too. Who is left?"

"I will not leave you." He said it as decisively as Ashani Zlorih had ever pronounced upon some matter or another; pointing out how much he sounded like his father would be unwise at the moment. "We could go to Anwei, Yala."

"There is trouble in Shan." And far worse, Yala knew. Takshin had told her of the pale-skinned, stinking envoy and his gift to the new Emperor, and she had not dared ask for many details. It was, after all, his sister. Instead, she had sought to comfort him, earning only a sharp glance and a soft but final remark closing the subject for her pains. "Your father…" She groped for another way to make him listen, to make him *see*. "There is a Khir delegation in the palace, Dao."

"Is there?" He kept watching the path, his profile sharpening as her gaze adapted to the darkness. Was he guarding her, alert for signs of discovery? Barring her retreat? Angry at her refusal?

Though her pupils were swelling, she could not see well enough to tell. "They arrived today." *And asked me if I was shameless, wearing a hairpin with my father dead.* "With their aid, I may arrange safe passage for you to—"

"You will not speak a word to them." Daoyan spoke harshly, each word cut short as if he could command her. As if she were still a docile, obedient Khir noblewoman.

Like Mahara.

"I cannot leave this place," Komor Yala repeated, steadily. "But you must." The words lodged sideways in her throat, Khir suddenly misbehaving because her tongue was so used to Zhaon's mush-mouth now. And, like a frightened horse, the truth bolted from her. "One of us must survive this."

The night swallowed her words. Fiddle-legs were droning in other gardens, a crackle in the underbrush to her right was probably some manner of night-rat ignoring their intrusion, and somewhere in the palace a gong was beaten, proclaiming another watch.

Daoyan was still for a long, breathless moment. "If they harm you—" He was not bothering to whisper, now.

"I am safe enough at the moment," she interrupted. *Safer than you, at least.* Now he was listening, and she sought the logic to make him accede. "But if Second Pr—ah, if the new Emperor finds out who is in his city, leaping his palace walls to confer with a foreign lady-in-waiting, it will not be pleasant, Dao. For *either* of us. If you ever cared for me, you will return to Khir and guard your life well." What else could she give him? He had said once before Baiyan had laughed at him for broaching the subject of a marriage-offer. Perhaps she was wishing the Great Rider's illegitimate son had formally made such an offer, and that her father had accepted? She would never have left Khir at Mahara's side, then. "It is... precious to me."

"Is it?" Almost flippant, as if they were jesting at a feast. There was a dark slim shape rising over his shoulder—a swordhilt. Were they caught, he might have to kill to escape.

"You know it is." Strangely, her voice broke in the middle of the phrase, and she had to halt to swallow dryly. "You are my trusted friend, Dao. As Hamori Baiyua was for Cao Zhien." She deliberately chose the phrase that held the least... troubling overtones, a soldier's word for a comrade.

"I should have offered for you twice." Dao made another restive movement, tossing his head as he had when he was younger and shaking away unpleasant thoughts. "Challenged your father. Something."

"Challenged my father?" The difficulty in speaking was now the rock in her throat. Thinking of Daoyan and Komori Dasho facing each other over bright blades threatened to unknot her knees and spill her to the ground. "I would have wept, Dao."

"May Heaven save us from that." His chin rose. Now, her fully dark-adapted eyes picked out the line of his jaw, the gleams of his eyes. He was in dark, close-fitting clothes, suitable for this excursion and well-worn. "Hist, someone comes."

"Go." *They must not find you here, not a single one of them.* She could explain her own presence and merely suffer gossip and some loss of reputation, but his was another matter. Her hands flew forward without her will, and he clasped them. "Do not tarry. I shall send to you for another meeting when I can."

His fingers were warm, a different heat than the humid

closeness. He squeezed, brutally hard, calluses from a nobleman's martial training scratching slightly. "If you keep—"

"*Go*, Dao." Yala freed herself from his grasp with a savage twist and faded into the shadows. The hau tree's branches surrounded her, and she did not hear Dao's exit. The sense of his presence merely faded, leached away upon a dust-scorching summer breeze.

Even the darkness brought no relief. And would she be trapped here for the rest of her days, sweltering in this cauldron of luxury and murder?

It was an uncomfortable thought.

The footsteps drew closer. Yala made herself a stone, her half-open eyes unblinking, and a stray gleam from somewhere fell across a young lithe form, a boy walking with his head down and his hands clasped, his shoulders quivering. There were other faint sounds, and she recognized both him and the small noises.

It was Sixth Prince Jin, and the hitching of his breath said he was weeping.

Yala's humors curdled within her. He was a merry boy, and had kept a secret or two admirably. But what his sister, married to the king of Shan, had suffered...oh, it was awful to even think of. These Tabrak were just as savage as their ancestors, coming like a plague of hungry insects to steal from peasant and noble alike before fading into the wastes. They rarely started in Shan, though, as far as Yala could remember. Normally, they cut through Zhaon to begin with, and turned north or south as an afterthought.

Reading of those things was certainly *not* for a young lady, no matter how much of a scholar she was reputed to be.

She waited until the youngest son of Garan Tamuron slowly climbed a flight of stone stairs carpeted with crunching, summer-dry moss and finally vanished into a crumbling gallery. This part of the palace complex was old, and apparently not as deserted at night as she had hoped.

Yala leaned against the hau tree, bark under her fingers and her breath coming quick and hard as if she'd just finished a game of *kaibok*. Her knees were distinctly soft, and she still had her return to the Jonwa to negotiate, as well as slipping past sleeping, faithful Anh.

She would go once she gathered herself. Her fingers tightened, and in the humming darkness, a strange thought occurred to her.

Perhaps Dao felt the loss of his royal sister so keenly he did not wish to speak upon it. But still, it was strange that he did not mention Mahara, even in passing, more often.

A First Strike

Clear, health-giving sohju brought no relief, and even changing into dark clothing and leaping the palace walls to drink among off-duty Golden guards palled. The world had turned off its course, tumbling like an acrobat at a festival, and there was no bowl to toss a sliver into and stop the whirling.

Even this overgrown garden, familiar from romps with Gamnae before her Red Ceremony meant she couldn't run and leap like a child anymore, looked strange tonight. They were the babies of the family, and he'd always thought they would be together forever like the great sage Aouan Taijeo and his sister, the nun Kinwone whose sathron playing was said to please the Awakened One himself.

But Gamnae was in the Kaeje with her mother, probably fast asleep at this hour. She was the sister of an Emperor now, and there was gossip swirling around about marrying her off.

Look how well that had turned out for his *other* sister. Garan Jin climbed a long flight of slippery stone, the moss clinging to each stair crackle-dry. The dust was already bad, and would only get worse. He disliked breathing it, but Sabi always liked the dry-sparks when the wind rose during summer drought.

He stopped between one stair and the next, his head full of fuzz from the sohju he'd managed to drink before the itching under his skin drove him from one of his favorite taverns. His chin almost touched his chest, and he was shaking like a horse run too hard.

Sabi.

The Iejo was full of mourning. His mother—once First Concubine to the Emperor, now Third Mother, even *that* had changed—had to be dosed with nightflower to sleep and the physicians all looked grave, consulting each other in the halls like nodding stilt-leg birds.

Jin hadn't seen the... the head, and he wondered if he should have tried to.

It was impossible to think of his sister *gone*. Why, here were the steps she'd once tried to push Sensheo down the summer Sensen broke every doll of hers and Gamnae's he could find, and down that colonnaded walkway was one of Sabi's favorite places when they were young, a small gazebo looking out on a much better cared-for water-garden. She used to play Hae Jinwone during the Blood Years, gazing from the tower as her brothers shouted and replayed the fifth Battle of Tienzu Keep before running out to spread her hands between them to halt the fighting, making horse-sounds to mimic the great lady's faithful steed Seopyeung, named for the westron wind.

Well, she'd been in a different tower, all the way south in Shan. Some barbarians had come, and Sabi had fallen like Hae Jinwone had not.

Jin shook his head, a restive toss. His loosened topknot flopped, but he didn't bother to tighten it. What was the point?

Mother weeping and dazed, Father dead, Takyeo—beloved, ever-patient Ah-Yeo—dead soon after, and now Sabwone. When would it stop?

How many times had he wished, with all a child's vengefulness, that his elder sister would simply vanish, putting an end to her pokes, her pinching, her prodding, her little games? She and Sensheo liked to torment, but still, she was Jin's *sister*.

Now he remembered Sabi bending with a sigh like a maiden auntie to set his shoes to rights when he was very young, or holding his hand tightly during ceremonies when the children of Garan Tamuron were arranged upon a dais to show their father's wealth in heirs. Or lying beside him on fragrant summer turf as stars glimmered into being through veils of indigo twilight, pointing out constellations Mrong Banh had taught her to look for. When she was in a fine mood, or when she wanted Jin to run a little errand, there was nobody sweeter.

Don't you hit my brother, she had hissed at Sensheo, times beyond counting. Of course *she* could pinch and tease, but she didn't let any of the older ones do too much. And she'd sobbed against his chest when news of her impending marriage came. *It's not fair, Jin! I won't go, I won't!*

He'd done nothing; what could he have done? His boots crushed more moss, he finally reached the head of the stairs and stood, head hanging again, his ribs heaving. Hot water slicked his cheeks.

Everything was wrong. Kai was gone north again—would he stand in the tower of Tienzu when news from the capital reached him, and think about Sabi? He'd grown up with them too, although she never let him forget he was a common foundling.

You shouldn't be mean, Jin had said more than once.

We are royal, she'd always reply. *It's not mean, it's simply what Heaven intends.*

Well, if Heaven intended to splatter his sister across paving stones and send her head back home tied to a barbarian's saddle, Jin thought Heaven perhaps wasn't worth all the bowing and propitiating everyone did. The thought was quite natural and so logical he couldn't find any blasphemy in it, though he knew it was there.

Now everyone was bowing to disdainful, dangerous Kurin. At least *he'd* liked Sabi; often, she seemed to be the Second Prince's favorite sibling.

Well, Kurin wasn't Second Prince anymore, and the implications made Jin's head spin. The horrible scene in the Jonwa, all his brothers gathered and shouting at each other while Takyeo lay dead, Kai miraculously arrived and Sensheo under arrest in his estate outside the palace walls—oh, that last part was a blessing, and how often had Jin wished Sensheo would just vanish too?

What if Heaven had heard Jin's most secret thoughts, and

answered? What if Heaven continued answering, punishing him for a blasphemy he could not help but think?

The way to the Iejo was so familiar he barely paid attention to his feet even while dodging the Golden guards and their swinging, fat-bellied lanterns as they performed the nightly patrols. They didn't seem to be doing a lot of good; someone had assassinated poor Ah-Yeo, who should have been sitting on the Throne of Five Winds and calling Second Concubine Luswone *Third Mother*.

Worst of all was the persistent thought that one of his very own brothers had handed over the ingots for that death. Oh, Sensheo liked to crush spiral-shells in the garden and Kurin played cruel jokes on junior eunuchs and hangers-on, Makar visibly considered Jin too stupid for any real conversation and Kai was forbidding when his face settled and he reached for that dragon-hilted sword Father had given him.

But to *kill* each other? Or even to try? When had they been capable of that, or had they been all along and Jin had been too stupid to see it? Of course there were assassins, there had been assassins all his life.

He simply hadn't thought his brothers would engage the walkers of the Shadowed Path for each other. Other families jealous of Garan Tamuron's success might, but for brothers to do so...it was not right.

A Heaven worthy of propitiation should not allow such things.

Booted heels ground against a cobbled walk as another pair of bright-armored guards approached, their lantern swinging and the sound of low conversation providing counterpoint to the footsteps. Jin's head jerked up and he melted into shadows pooled between two columns.

Before, he wouldn't have worried much about being caught. He was, after all, a prince. But it was part of the game, trying *not* to be caught, and who could tell what would happen with Kurin instead of Father in the great vermilion-pillared hall, sitting on the padded bench where all the power in Zhaon concentrated?

The guards passed, discussing one of the more popular shows

in the Theater District in low but earnest tones. Jin let out a pent breath as soon as they turned down the colonnaded walk, his top-knot flopping irritatingly again as he ghosted out of his cover and across the walkway.

It was only a short walk to his favorite way to enter the Iejo from here, and he moved as if in enemy territory, hearing Kai's voice far back in childhood memory.

Every step takes thought, Jinjin. Kai had shown him how to climb, patiently standing below short rough rock walls, ready to catch him. Takyeo sometimes helped, calling encouragement and wincing when Jin tumbled. And it was Takyeo who presented his youngest brother with his first sword. *Since you like bright metal so much.*

Sunk in thought, he almost didn't hear the slight scrape. Jin's chin jerked up, his night-adapted pupils flaring still further, and he was glad there were no lamps here. His head tilted back; he held his breath and scanned the Iejo's familiar bulk from this angle.

What is that? The sound came again, metal against something solid. Or perhaps a night-bird's scratching?

No, he realized. It was clawfoot grippers against tile, because something moved silhouetted against the roofline. If he'd been a few moments earlier or later, he'd have missed it; as it was, he stared for a few heartbeats, his jaw slack and his head-meat racing.

Why on earth would someone—someone other than him, of course—be on the *roof*?

Oh, Jin. Sabi's light, giggling voice came floating through his skull, like her shade was out searching for its body and had just stopped to say hello. *You know why.*

His body moved with thoughtless speed, the lightfoot blooming below his knees. You could run right up a wall if you practiced hard enough, a short-term disobedience of the law which caused things to plummet earthward. The technique was closely guarded, but a prince must know such things as a matter of course.

For a few moments all thought of Sabi, of Takyeo, of Father were blotted away, and he was only a clear gaze, a pumping heart, a liver full of excited buzzing, and limbs moving with almost preternatural speed. Weapons practice brought him to this place often, and it was a refuge. He could never explain it to his mother, or even his brothers except maybe Kai.

You have a gift, Jin. And for a great general, beloved of the God of War, to say so meant something indeed.

The inner clarity was the only place he felt any certainty, now. He skidded over roof-tiles, the lightfoot turning his step all but soundless, and might have crashed into the indigo-wrapped figure crouching at an edge over a shuttered attic window if Jin's body hadn't saved him once again with an instinctive flicker of his right leg, the left bending as the secret art drained away.

The impact jarred him to a halt, his right boot hard against the lumbar curve of a crouching figure, head muffled except for the eyes, hands and feet gloved with indigo material, braided rope soles providing some traction and cushioning with more twine diving between each toe to allow greater freedom of movement. Jin exhaled, and the next move—throwing himself back, an almost spine-cracking curve—didn't make sense until he heard the slight *whoosh* as a blackened blade cut sticky night air where his midsection had been a fraction of a moment earlier. His topknot-cage went flying, the pin making a forlorn pinging as it skittered across the sloping roof-tiles.

He's wrapped up like an acrobat. It was the second time he thought of festival performers that night, and Jin's body knew what to do again, his stomach tightening *hard* to pull him upright. His left hand flashed up and he pitched forward, smoothly continuing the motion. *Why is that?*

Now it was all speed; he was young and well-trained. The assassin—because it had to be a walker of the Shadowed Path—flipped his wrist, attempting to bring the short curved sword back, but Jin was well inside the arc of attack now, his clever left hand striking the wrist just at the nerve-juncture that would loosen the fingers. His right boot stamped, crunching on tile and causing a starring of breakage he would never suspect or see, and the strike with his left hand was robbed of strength by his left foot snapping out, a kick like the flicker of a stilt-leg bird's beak in muddy water.

He hadn't *meant* to, really. Jin's body knew what to do because he was half-drunk, very loose, and had been practicing play-combat almost since he could walk.

Kai and Takyeo hadn't said he was too young. Ah-Yeo had even presented his youngest brother with a small wooden practice sword when Jin was six summers high, and been promptly whacked across the shins with it while Jin crowed with delight.

A first strike, Kai had observed while Makar laughed fit to lose his throat. *And a good one too.*

You'll make a fine general, Jinjin. Takyeo, his eyes watering, wearing a rueful smile.

Oh but it was painful to hear his Eldest Brother's voice inside his skull. Jin's left foot hit the other fellow's knee, and the dry-stick crack of the strike was swallowed in a pained exhalation from the wrapped figure and an answering flicker of its left hand, heading upward for Jin's face, the heel of the palm meant to smash into a nose and drive the bone promontory into head-meat.

The sudden realization that he was in an actual *fight*, on a rooftop no less, with an assassin obviously intent on breaching his mother's part of the Iejo, crashed through him as he slapped the strike aside with a little more force than he intended. A dusty slither, a hard huffing exhale, and the assassin's rope-braided soles slipped.

Jin's own footing was somewhat precarious, but he was much farther from the edge. Tile cracked, the sound breaking the night's stillness, and at first he thought the assassin had vanished. His body, wiser than him again, threw itself into a crouch, weight pitched back, and caught its balance as there was a heavy crunch from below.

Jin found himself sweating, panting like a horse run too hard, salt water wrung from every inch of his skin and collecting in every fold. The roof-tiles, their cracked edges sharp, glared with fresh pale scarring. He caught his balance more surely and peered, huge-eyed, over the broken rim of the palace that had been his home for as long as he could remember, except for short summers at the Daebo estates before he was confirmed as last in succession for the Throne of Five Winds.

He did not know it, but he looked very young indeed in that moment.

A body lay folded like a bentpin over a half-wall between two walkways below, and the pale globes of swinging lanterns were approaching. Approaching guards couldn't help but see the corpse, even if they were engrossed in palace gossip or comparing various theater flowers, and for a moment Jin was afraid they would start beating gongs and looking all over the palace complex for him.

Why would one of the Shadowed Path be on his mother's roof?

The answer came quite naturally, as his heart pounded hard enough to explode like the flame-flowers for the new year, a wedding, or a victory celebration, a brief lovely glitter married to a massive noise. Even though the night was a hot mouth breathing over the entire complex, he was cold and slick as a fat bronzefish dragged from a rai-pond.

Second Concubine Kanbina's health had never been good, and gossip said she'd been poisoned years ago. Mother had a strange forbidding look when the story was mentioned, warning Jin to say nothing. Then there was a body on the steps of the First Queen's part of the Kaeje the morning after Takyeo's wedding, and the assassins attacking his eldest brother over and over until they finally managed to stab him in the gut, not to mention whoever had shot his pretty, brave foreign wife. Strange how Jin had known of those but never truly considered the implications until lately— they simply *were*, like his talent for weapon-play and the shape of his own teeth, or the fact that his second toe was longer than his first upon both feet.

The assassin had been coming for his mother. Or for him. And Jin had killed him, the same way he'd killed a treacherous Golden Guard in the market, with Komor Yala watching.

Lady Komor was brave too. *She* probably didn't feel like

throwing up after fending off an attacker. Jin, clinging to the edge of the roof like a child peeking into a basket, watched the lanterns bob ever closer, his muscles suddenly reminding him they had been pressed into unaccustomed use.

Real combat's different than practice, Jinjin. Even Kai had been afflicted with assassins more than once, for he was high in the confidence of Garan Tamuron.

But now Father was dead. Perhaps the world had always been this terrible, and Jin had merely been too stupid to know.

Jin's mouth closed with a snap, and he took stock. His hair was loose as if he was grieving or before dressing, and the entire palace complex lay under a strange deathly hush.

"Mother," he whispered, and before the lanterns could draw any closer he disappeared.

PRICE OF RULE

Dismissing the last of the servants had lately become the act he looked forward to most. In a windowless, practically buried Kaeje room Garan Kurin, Emperor of Zhaon, stretched himself upon his crimson-draped bed and exhaled thrice in the manner recommended by many sages as conducive to settling the humors for sleep. He closed his eyes and prepared for what would follow instead—at least half a watch's worth of deep thought, or what passed for it when there was too much to be done and not enough time to accomplish even a quarter of the list.

No wonder his father had fallen prey to a ravening illness; the business of rule was pure drudgery. Still, it was better than watching someone manifestly unfit bumble his way through.

He wondered if Garan Tamuron, safely ensconced in a celestial palace, realized as much now after the fact. Or if his first son, perhaps likewise situated, did.

Kurin scrubbed delicately at his scalp with his fingertips, a luxurious sensation sliding down his back though his hair was bound into a club at his nape. He preferred to sleep without clothing except in winter, when a clout was all he could tolerate; better to impersonate a hillock of blankets than be half-strangled with twisted clothing while attempting rest. Light prickles of sweat—usual during the drought time of summer—starred his back, his chest, gathered in hollows and creases. He had to resist the urge to light a taper and check his arms and legs for the thin angry rashes his father had sported.

He was young, and healthy, and had not after all committed any great sin.

At least his father had broken with tradition, not allowing even a close-servant in the royal bedchamber at night. A warlord's rest was snatched in bare handfuls, an Emperor gained even less; Garan Tamuron had determined it was better to sleep alone than trust even kaburei, eunuch, or wife while helpless in the shifting lands of slumber.

Perhaps Father had slept in the presence of his first, sainted spear-wife, but Kurin would not know. That woman had been safely dead when his own mother wed the warlord she expected to bring her to high station. Father had, of course, performed his part of the bargain, but First Queen Gamwone had found herself unsatisfied.

Sometimes Kurin wondered if anything would fill the gaping hole inside the woman who had borne him. Maybe his own birth had torn something from her humors—he could perhaps blame his siblings, but neither of them held his ambition. Takshin was a broken vessel, all sharp edges, and Gamnae was female.

He had to think of a suitable marriage for her soon. So many worries crowding his head-meat, each jostling to find a proper place and precedent.

There was gossip about his eldest brother's passing, of course. Some of it probably even touched near the truth, but nobody would believe Kurin innocent of the actual act. Merely being prepared for the inevitable was not culpability, of course, and it did not bother him overmuch.

No, what exercised him was exactly who had paid for the act. He did not like remaining ignorant of such a benefactor. His own plans, far more subtle, had not had time to come to fruition.

The list of suspects was dreadfully short, and even more unnervingly complete. In other words, he thought he already knew.

A susurration began in the hall outside his chamber door, and a heavy sigh worked its way from the pit of his belly as his eyes opened, staring unseeing at the ceiling. Was a few hours of dark unconsciousness too much to ask?

A lesser man might regret the steps taken to bring himself to the summit, or begin to chafe at his new position. Kurin merely sighed and waited, listening to the hushed voices. The sheer, almost transparent crimson cloth depending from a large iron hoop and swathing the royal bed to deny tiny insects a nighttime meal barely moved. It was a still night, and at least with the coils of healthful incense burning in each corner of this stone-walled, very warm room the many varieties of blood- or sweat-sucking insects were held at bay.

There were some things to like about his new position, indeed. Luxury was useful; it freed a man to concentrate upon other things.

More cloth moving, more hurried footsteps. Kurin heaved another deep sigh and rose from the healthfully firm bed, moving quietly and reaching for the small ceduan and silver box upon the dark ironwood nightstand. The imperial greenstone hurai, their silver sheathings still flesh-warm because he had, after all, just taken them off, slipped back onto his first fingers on each hand. In short order he shrugged into the yellow and green babu-patterned nightrobe from the stand set at a respectful distance, and just as he was knotting the sash, there was a soft scratching at the hall partition.

"Come in." It took more effort than he liked to make his tone thoughtful and unsurprised instead of irritable.

A tall shadow in a dark robe resolved into smooth-faced Zan Fein, the chief court eunuch, in one of his many rich dark traditional robes. His topknot was slightly askew and held in a cage of dark leather, the pin hastily thrust through; he was not accompanied by his usual reek of expensive umu scent. "Your Majesty."

"Fire, flood, or attack?" It was something his father might have said, and Kurin could perhaps be forgiven the very small smile he now wore.

"The last, I should think. A body has been found at the Iejo. Not a member of the royal family," Zan Fein hastened to add, finishing the deep bow required of those who entered the presence of Heaven's representative to Zhaon, no matter how immense their own standing. "A walker of the Shadowed Path, bearing some interesting trinkets."

The Iejo. Now why would it be there? Kurin suppressed a third sigh. The superstition that a trio of such actions would bring a catastrophe was unworthy of a modern ruler, but it was perhaps best to be safe. "Found, you say?"

"Thrown over a half-wall." Zan Fein's expression could best be described as *remote*. His triangular, beardless face was akin to a feline's, and the quiet with which he moved upon his raised jatajata sandals was likewise velvet-pawed. Now, however, he was in soft-soled, highly embroidered slippers. "Perhaps he slipped from the roof."

"A poor assassin indeed." Kurin rubbed at his left hurai thoughtfully with his thumb, a habitual movement. The only change was the silver clasping that great seal-ring and the carving upon it, his reign-name instead of the characters denoting a mere prince. "But why the Iejo?"

"I am sure *I* do not know." Zan Fein's hands disappeared into his sleeves. If he had been rudely shaken from his own attempt at slumber, it did not show overmuch. His dishevelment could even be the finish of a long day spent performing the functions of chief court eunuch. "But it is rather thought-provoking. Perhaps someone has a score to settle with the First Concubine."

Or her son. But Jin was far down the current line of succession, and not even Sensheo would be stupid enough to commit this act, especially while still under house arrest.

Which rather narrowed the list of suspects; others of even moderate intelligence would inevitably arrive at the same conclusion. A small, hot spot dilated deep in Kurin's belly, as if he had been stabbed and a gut-channel breached.

Like Takyeo. But Ah-Yeo would never have felt this surge of anger; he had been altogether too mild for rule. "Perhaps someone does," Kurin answered, carefully spacing the syllables in order to make it clear *he* had not authorized this attempt. "But whoever it is shall have to keep that score upon their counting-string. I will not have more assassins in the palace, Zan Fein. Double the watch and have the roofs searched—all of them, from the Kaeje to the outbuildings."

"Yes, Your Majesty. I shall question those who found the body most closely..." The end of the sentence did not lilt upward, but the question was plain.

"No," Kurin decided. "*I* shall question them. It will show that I am unwilling to let such things continue in this reign." He could also halt the interrogation before it reached a certain...point, if necessary.

"Or that..." Zan Fein's eyebrows raised slightly.

"Or that I sent the assassin myself and wish to cover my tracks, you mean?" The intimation did not bother the new Emperor; it was natural, and a chief eunuch who did not broach it, albeit with the proper reticence, would be all but useless. "I shall have the ministers awakened and brought to witness and add their own inquiries, so all may hear what transpires."

"In the morning?"

Perhaps his father would have delayed, but Kurin saw no need. "Of course not, Chief Court Eunuch. Immediately." He could almost smile at the thought of ministers shaken from their own couches or drawn from other amusements; it would provide a salutary reminder to one or two that their new ruler was not to be trifled with. "An attack upon my Third Mother or youngest brother is also an attack upon myself, and that cannot be borne by a filial son, can it."

"Of course not, Your Majesty." Zan Fein would never be so gauche as to express *approval*—that might imply that his disapproval of an Emperor's behavior had any weight. But still, it was pleasing to see a faint glow of satisfaction deep in the eunuch's sly, tranquil dark gaze.

"Besides, they have suffered enough." Kurin's tone turned meditative. "Send in the close-servants, and two secretaries." It would be well to send a small gift to Third Mother Luswone, too, in apology for the disturbance. And to make it utterly clear that he valued all his mothers, and would not brook more of this... behavior.

"Yes, Your Majesty." Zan Fein bowed again and withdrew. The entire palace complex would be alive with gossip by dawn, and Kurin was facing yet another sleepless night since his enthronement.

Such was the price of rule. He rubbed at his chin, yawned, and discovered he was still glad to pay it.

But not as glad as he had been at first.

QUITE
SERVICEABLE

S team hung over a deep shimmering pool, its sides of slick
white stone scrubbed during its draining every other day. The
Emperor's private bath, serving whoever held Zhaon's greatest city-
kernel, was being refilled, for a simple bath did not have the luxury
of mourning when one master had passed away.

Baths served the living; Heaven and the many hells were forced
to their own methods of cleanliness.

The Palace baths clung to the edge of the broad-backed river
protecting the vital liver of Zhaon-An, one of the deeper springs
sulfur-tinted but the rest sweet and clear, both healthful in their
own way. The springs fed the river and kept this section of the
city safe from attack even in high summer, the great girdling wall
attaching itself to the Palace's outcropping like skin stretched tight
over a beneficent tumor.

Within the great timbered galleries, pools were drained or filled
according to ancient schedule and rhythm, the numerous small
passages and warrens for the storage of herb and perfume, tincture
and paste, soap and cosmetic a society almost as old as Zhaon itself,
and one with its customs, its laws, its own mores.

A young woman in the uniform of the baths—goldenrod
cloth, braided hair coiled at the nape and a single scentwood pin

holding the mass, the wooden sandals and resin-dipped toes to keep her feet from rotting in ever-present moisture—hurried along the side of the great white pool. She reached her goal, the small door at its eastron end, and bowed to an older woman, supple as a reed.

"Your servant Dho Anha greets the representative of the Dowager Queen Mother," she said softly. The latter title, extremely ancient and honorific, was probably selected as the safest available, propitiating a vengeful goddess whose husband was no longer able to lay a heavy restraining hand upon her temper. "How may this handmaiden serve?"

It was not Garan Yulehi-a Gamwone who stood, straight as a stick and nearly as thin and dry, just inside the door. Instead, it was the great lady's chief servant Yona, her thin mouth a bitter line, who had arranged the toes of her bath-slippers at the very edge of permissible entry to the place where the most royal of bodies was uncovered and bathed. Yona's nose did not lift, and she gazed almost pityingly upon the girl.

Those in the baths might remark that Yona's sallowness was a sign of unbalanced humors, or that unrefined meat-husk oil should be added to her bath to return a simulacrum of soft roundness to her limbs. A paste of crushed redroot and astringent hau bark should be applied to her hair to provide luster, nia oil massaged between her fingers and toes as well as over her liver, and a physician consulted about her diet. But the First Queen—now First Mother of the Revered Emperor, a title busily being applied to new seals, hangings, and official correspondence—no doubt exerted herself for her cherished servants and their health precisely so far as she wished to.

The failing, then, must be in Yona herself. Or so the bath servants might imply, glancing at each other and tut-tutting quietly. Physicians were all very well, they held, but the ancient ways of dip, plunge, and various herbs or substances had their place too.

Garan Gamwone did not come to them very often, preferring

other—more modern—methods, not to mention her own very private bath in the depths of the Kaeje.

The fact that some of the servants of the great baths might be relieved at the absence of such a notoriously finicky royal body to minister to was quite beside the point, and never explicitly broached.

"The First Mother of the Emperor wishes to inquire of her son's bath." Yona's inflection was crisp but not overly formal. *We are but two servants*, it implied, *though I am necessarily of much higher status, I will not stand upon that hill to examine you.*

It was an unexpected graciousness, and Dho Anha's bow deepened. "The Emperor has expressed a preference for unjuo and citron. A very healthy choice; the physicians are all agreed."

"Is it the same bath as the Heaven-Ascended preferred?" The polite term for the former Emperor, now holding court among Heaven's luminaries, was still not quite proper for utterance here. One could never tell when ill-luck at the mention of death—or *ascension*, as it was called when the most august shade rose from its house to join shining, meritorious ancestors—would attach itself to water or a vulnerable naked body.

All such risk was to be avoided, and perhaps that was why Dho Anha straightened, though she kept her dark gaze properly upon the slick, dewy floor. "N-no, of course... It... it was otherwise."

"That is just as well." Yona paused. "Your hairpin is quite serviceable, treasured servant."

A dull flush crept into the girl's cheeks. She was a soft, cringing little thing; perhaps the late Emperor had found her shyness a piquant contrast to his other consorts. Gossip upon that point was rife, and even more pungent upon the marked preference the new Emperor—the First Mother's own eldest son—also displayed for this little slip of a servant, almost a kaburei.

Had not Garan Kurin, while still Second Prince, made a gift or two to this very bath servant? Oh, those with the right to attend the baths often gave small tokens to their favorite scrapers, cleansers, massagers, combers, or foot-washers, but two of such high station taking an interest in a single girl was a juicy morsel to chew over amid the bustle, the steam, the backbreaking work of filling the pools or cleaning the conveniences.

Implying that Dho Anha was not grateful for a gifted hairpin was not quite cruel. It could even be viewed as a subtle warning from a concerned fellow servant.

"It is a poor thing," the girl said desperately, "in keeping with my station. I would not like to lose a better one."

"You are most modest." Yona's mouth twitched. Had she not been known to be incapable of such a maneuver, it might almost be guessed she was attempting a beneficent smile. "Your devotion has been noticed, treasured servant. Especially by my mistress."

The girl's shoulders trembled. "I . . . am most grateful for a great lady's notice." If there was any sarcasm, it was well hidden. Most of the Palace's great mass of servants and underlings held that to come to Garan Gamwone's notice was a distinct danger, one to be avoided with all alacrity.

"Oh, don't look so taken aback." Yona's expression said she knew quite well how feared her august mistress was, but it softened almost immediately. "My queen has the highest standards, that is all. That which touches her son must be of a quality. To that end, she bade me give you this." Yona's thin right hand drew a small pot from her left sleeve. "It is some of the First Mother's own hand-oil, a small gift for a very capable handmaiden."

The girl visibly could not believe her good fortune, and bowed thrice in an embarrassing display of gratitude. Yona, still attempting a smile that could be construed as generous, finally placed the tiny blue ceramic container in the bath-girl's moist palms. "Now, now. You really must learn a little pride, Maiden Dho. You are a servant of the First Mother's peerless son, after all."

"Y-yes, my lady." The girl bobbed a few more times, her round face brimming with transparent relief. "I will use it faithfully, with prayers for the health of our revered Emperor and the First Mother."

"See that you do," Yona murmured, and glided away. She passed largely unremarked, having taken care to visit during the flurry of cleaning. Afterward, any who witnessed her in the baths thought she must have been in search of a remedy for the stomach pangs she was known to suffer.

If they thought otherwise, they knew to remain silent—at least for now. She was, after all, high in the First Mother's service, and had been for most of her life.

SEEKING EVIDENCE

To move a royal household was a considerable undertaking, and could not be decently finished while in full mourning. Still, after three tendays wrapped in unbleached cloth, wearing anything else felt odd. Anh had laced and buttoned Yala into a dark blue gown with a relatively high collar and long sleeves that morning; it was of Khir make and bore a pale armband with two knots upon the left sleeve.

Which meant the true chaos of moving could be under way, instead of simply the packing accomplished as part and parcel of grieving, and also that Komor Yala's marriage was approaching. Not like a hawk stooping upon prey, more in the manner of a wolf loping after a wounded, spring-legged curvehoof upon a grassy plain.

The end was assured, either way.

"How beautiful." Su Junha leaned over the neatly folded pile of scarlet silk, hardly daring to breathe upon such magnificence. "The embroidery... oh, my lady, look at the stitching there."

"Beautiful indeed," Yala concurred softly. Indeed it was, hair-fine golden thread worked in a pattern of komor flowers along hem and cuffs, the most auspicious characters for *Garan* in large upon the back, and the under-robes just as wonderfully decorated; her intended was spending ingots like water, and the seamstresses had been well remunerated for their busy efforts. "I can hardly believe it."

It was dishonorable of her to wish, even for a moment inside the secret chambers of her liver or head-meat, that there was a little less munificence—say, a general's, instead of a prince's. How far did outward obedience ameliorate inner rebellion, and could her father's shade see both? The copy of his will, patiently brushed from the original by a scribe, did not utter a wish for her marriage into a cadet branch of Hai Komori. Had he expected Daoyan to bring his daughter back upon a saddle, with the loss of honor that would entail? Or was it a signal that he had expected Mahara to arrange an advantageous match with a southroner, as a royal patroness should? Perhaps he had thought Yala's princess would send her home with a chaperone so she could be married to the Great Rider's only remaining heir.

It was impossible to tell. A few of his letters, turned back at the border, had been carried by the Khir lords; they held only commonplaces and their dates were not long after Ashani Daoyan must have left. The remainder of the papers were a miscellany from Hai Komori where she had spent her childhood, included only because nobody else wanted, had need of, or could tell what to do with them.

She could close her eyes and see the hall, from its smallest cramped attic-space to its deep stone-hollowed cellars, but the image would grant no comfort. She was to be married soon; she should have been properly grateful. Even *happy*.

"The headdress will be ready soon." Dreamy, moon-faced Hansei Liyue ran an approving fingertip over tissue-thin linen swathing the bridal dress. "I confess I am not sad to leave the Palace, my lady. There was a body found last night."

"*Shuh*." Su Junha made an *avert* motion with her left hand, brushing away ill-luck. Her sleeve swayed most fetchingly. "Not over the dress, Liyue."

"Of course." The other noble girl colored slightly and turned away, raising a violet cotton sleeve trimmed with a thin margin of plum silk to cover her mouth.

Yala simply shook her head slightly, missing the pleasant

swinging weight of a hairpin decoration. "It will be fumigated before it is worn; that should put paid to any ill-luck." Her equanimity was holding; that was most fortunate. Even if her heart ached inside its cage of ribs, even if she felt a strange floating sensation in her liver when she thought of the impending ceremony, she was outwardly the same serene lady-in-waiting she had been trained to be. "Let us put it away, though. There is much to be done."

"I heard from Lady Kue." Su Junha magnanimously consented to a change in subject, forgiveness in every syllable. Both she and Hansei Liyue had cause to be gratified; a princess was hardly the worst patroness, and their cleaving to Yala despite uncertainty showed a certain depth of character. "She says the Third Prince's house is most spacious, and the cleaning proceeds apace. The gardens will be lovely; there are yeoyan saplings being brought."

"Those are pleasant in spring." Yala had left Khir with Mahara just as those trees were showing hard maroon buds, before the blossoms truly began. Come their next blooming, what else would she have left behind?

"It has dark floors, and the ceilings are high. The baths have their own spring." Lady Hansei, eager to cover her gaffe, folded the linen carefully to hide the crimson gown from sight and injury. With its associated underlayers, the bridal dress would be heavy, and quite warm. Even after a tepid morning bath scented with jaelo, Yala's back and wrists prickled with sweat. Today promised to be as dry, dusty, and unsatisfying as the past few weeks, except without mourning to shield her from social obligations.

To be in the palace and yet absolutely unable to attend functions where she might hear some manner of gossip was maddening. She was no nearer to finding the source of the ingots that had paid for her princess's death, and she wondered if Heaven might be punishing her. Of course there was no shortage of transgressions deserving such ire, from her failure to protect Mahara to her wayward, honorless woman's heart clinging to her homeland's greatest enemy while a prince actively sought her hand. She should have been overjoyed at her impending marriage, like any well-bred noblewoman—was it not the summit of a noble girl's desires to make a good match? A *royal* match?

She even knew her prospective husband valued her. There was a whip-scar across his back to prove it.

A feline scratch upon the sitting-room's lintel, and as if her thoughts had summoned him, Garan Takshin strolled through the door, moving into bright mirrorlight that gilded his Shan black and brought a cheerful twinkle from the *kyeogra*-loop at his left ear. "There you are." His greeting, as usual, was sharp but not unkind, and the two girls, having largely lost their fear if not their caution of Garan Tamuron's spike-tempered son, hurried to bow in his direction.

Yala did not hurry, but she also did not tarry. It was strange to think that soon she would not have to perform this particular movement, at least not as deeply. "Third Prince," she answered, taking the burden of a reply so the junior ladies would not be pressed to. "Have you come for tea?" It was midmorning, a little early, but her daily visit to the tombs had been made in his company and thinking upon his refreshment was only polite.

"If I must." His mouth twitched; he did not smile often, but the subtle movements when he perhaps wished to were far more frequent now. "Honorable Keh and Lady Kue are occupied with the drays and porters; I bethought myself to see you are not bothered by such things."

Su Junha cast a mischievous look at Hansei Liyue, who hid a smile behind her sleeve and a polite cough. Both were roundly pleased. Yala could not blame them; a married patroness would be in a much better position to help them make their own matches, and she was a vigilant but not exacting chaperone.

"And escape the bother yourself, no doubt." Yala tucked her hands in her sleeves, grateful the bride's dress was out of sight in its carved scentwood box. "Lady Su, will you brave the hall to fetch some tea? And Lady Hansei, may I trouble you to take this to my kaburei? I hesitate to ask, but..."

"Certainly." With this further proof of forgiveness furnished, Liyue beamed. "You must have much to discuss." *I shall not hurry back*, her tone said, and Yala's cheeks were warm.

She had not meant to give the impression of a betrothed girl eager for her suitor's complete attention, but it could not be helped. "Most kind," she murmured, and let the girls hurry about their tasks with their parting bows. At least Junha waited until they were safely in the hall to giggle, and the sound—bright, careless, unaffected—was a spike through Yala's heart.

Mahara had laughed like that, once or twice. Had Yala? She could not remember, now.

"Alone at last." Takshin dropped into a chair at a nearby table, placing himself at an angle and a polite distance, so any hurrying servant in the hall could peer in and see how carefully he cherished her reputation.

They were not married yet, after all.

"And glad of it, though it will not last long." She set herself to organizing the other items upon the table, books and ephemera from the Crown Prince's library. Garan Takyeo had been most explicit that every scrap of his household's effects and servants was in Takshin's keeping, and the will, witnessed by both Garan Makar and Garan Kurin, was unassailable. Yala thought it quite likely the short-lived Emperor had not wanted to leave anything for an enemy to gloat over, and the pain in her heart sharpened once more.

Her princess's husband had been a rarity. She hoped his shade was not unsatisfied with her efforts.

"I thought to ask you a question or two," she hastened to add, for Takshin's full attention had indeed settled upon her, one eyebrow slightly raised and even his scarred lip relaxed.

"Of course, the gladness could not be simply for my merry company." His faint smile robbed the observation of any sting; he was merely determined to mock himself before the rest of the world could find an opportunity. At least she had learned that much of his temper. "What troubles you, little lure?"

"Must I be troubled?" Of course, troubling events followed each other like summer insects finding a fallen sweetbun, and had since Mahara's marriage. They robbed her of what sleep the heat did not thieve, and the shadows under her eyes proved as much. "Yet who could not be, after... well."

Just this morning, Lady Kue had brought word of another body found in the palace, tossed casually over a half-wall near the Iejo.

An assassin, the Shan woman said, and shivered upon mentioning such ill news. And it reminded her of Zakkar Kai too, for had he not dealt with the corpse of one who wished Yala's princess harm at summer's beginning? Only a fool would not see a parallel.

But Kai was to the north, in a keep Yala had very little memory of, for all she had ridden to and spent some confused hours within its confines.

"Indeed." Her husband-to-be did not tell her to put such things from her mind, as her *damoi* or Dao might have, or even her father. Instead, Takshin eyed her, and at least she knew enough by now to suffer it calmly. "Speak, then. I listen."

How honorless was she, indeed, to wish it was another man watching her so closely? "Have you heard anything, then?"

"I hear much, every day. A man cannot avoid it." His chin tipped slightly, though his gaze did not alter. "But you ask whether I know who paid for the Crown Princess's misfortune."

"You said you would not keep it from me, whatever you heard."

"Another woman would wish for a dress, or a brick of tea. You wish for heads to play your game of *kaibok* with." The unscarred half of his mouth curled into a smile, but no amusement lingered in his dark eyes. "I said I would bring you anything I found, little lure. That has not changed."

Yala's hands continued organizing the flatbooks and scrollcases upon the table without her direction. It was not quite a womanly occupation, even if that woman was said to be somewhat of a scholar. Her sewing basket would have been much better; she could have avoided his gaze for much longer if she had been sunk in its cheerful layers of floss, thread, bright needles, sample swatches, and other appurtenances. "It pains me," she said, finally. "To be left unknowing."

"Then we shall avoid it." Takshin's tone turned unaccountably gentle. Very few would believe him capable of such softness. "I would not have you pained, Yala."

Her honorless heart gave a strange, melting twitch. No wonder she was faithless; the organ could not decide between longing for Zakkar Kai's presence and turning liquid with something else when Garan Takshin said, plainly though not in so many words, that he . . .

Which was the more proper sensation? Of course, she should fix her affections severely and thoroughly upon her husband-to-be. It was expected of a Khir noblewoman, after all.

"Then you have heard naught?" she persisted. Gently and softly, laying the lure as if for a nervous hawk—oh, managing him was not quite a difficult task, now that she had agreed to what he desired.

Were all Zhaon men so easily pleased? Certainly her princess had seemed relieved at her own husband's soft temper. Khir husbands were more commanding, or so the proverbs of her homeland said.

Would she be able to fasten her affections more properly if Takshin was? Certainly he had little trouble ordering others about; perhaps after they were married he would become a tyrant. She risked a glance at him.

"Of course, or I would be telling you." Now there was a faint hint of irritation, his eyebrows drawing together. "I keep my promises. I will bring you their heads, sooner or later. There is simply some difficulty lately; changes in the Palace mean those who would ordinarily speak are waiting to see where the rain falls."

And now we are moving from the palace complex, which will make it even more difficult. Had the news of her father not reached her yet, Yala might well be weighing Daoyan's offer. She knew what she had to do, but oh, her heart and liver rebelled.

That was when the bolt of blinding clarity struck.

The terrible thought turned her hands motionless, and she stared at the table, unseeing. A tremor ran through her, crown to slippered sole, and she inhaled, attempting to muffle the noise once she realized it was a gasp.

Such sudden insights were the province of sages, or perhaps a shade was whispering frantically in her ear.

"Yala?" The chair creaked as Takshin all but leapt to his feet. "*Ai*, sit down. You are pale, I shall call for the tea to hurry."

"I am well enough," she lied, but lowered herself into the closest chair when he glowered. She settled her hands in her lap because they did not know quite how to behave, for once, and her palms had turned quite damp.

Takshin strode to the door, collared a passing servant, and snapped a brusque command. It gave her time to compose herself, and Yala was heartily glad of those few moments.

His return was swift and he examined her afresh. "What ails you? Do not lie, little lure."

"Impolite, to think I would," she murmured. "It is simply very warm, my lord. And...the delegation from Khir is a worry." Should she mention another assassin in the Palace? It would not be well-bred to refer to a newly discovered corpse.

"They could have broken the news to you with some gentleness." He used one foot to hook another chair closer to hers and settled at a polite distance, leaning forward enough to show how he longed to be less cautious. "I have half a mind to call that Namori fellow to account, for acting in such a fashion."

The prospect of such an encounter, possibly turning into a clash of blades, did not soothe her at all. "He was merely surprised." Yala's fingers, now well hidden in her sleeves, twisted against each other.

"You seek to smooth my temper." Takshin made a soft *tch-tch*, like a maiden auntie at a precocious child. "I wonder that I do not find it irritating."

"I do as well." How could she have been so blind, she wondered? "Much irritates you, Third Prince, and I fear I shall with much regularity."

Second Prince Garan Kurin was now the Emperor. Who had more cause to arrange for the Crown Prince's death than *he*, Yala wondered? And before he did so, like any tidy-minded person preparing for plowing or folding, perhaps he had thought to remove a foreign princess and the chance of an heir. She should have suspected him first, and once she proved or disproved such suspicion, she would have more pieces to arrange in their proper pattern, like a child's puzzle of carved, interlocking wooden pegs.

It was a neat solution, much as a perfectly performed one-finger embroidery knot. The use of horse-killer arrows could be a feint, attempting to throw any pursuit or detection from the scent. Gathering everyone who might profit or had a motivation was impossible, sorting them like thread-spools doubly so. She had been approaching the sentence from entirely the wrong word, as the translator Murong Haijung warned against when speaking upon Ch'han's poetry.

Perhaps, instead of seeking gossip, it was more efficient to focus upon the man with the most to gain and seek evidence. But *how*?

"I am sharp, true." Takshin used the term for an over-honed sword, and had she not been cold all through even in this terrible dusty summer baking, Yala might have admired the phrase. "But I could not bear to wound you, little lure. Soon you will understand as much."

There was little affection between Takshin and his mother's eldest son; Yala had seen as much for herself. And yet... what could even he do, against an Emperor enthroned? Even direct proof of the matter would avail Yala nothing, and she would be forced to a terrible choice.

The most appalling thing was not that she had not concentrated immediately upon the most fitting suspect—she was, after all, merely a woman, and even a scholarly one was not held to have much intelligence within her liver. It was that she felt the temptation, weak and honorless as she was, to leave Mahara's death unavenged. For if she did what she should when she acquired proof, no matter in which direction it lay—and assuming it was to be had—the Zhaon would take her to the dungeons again, and none of the Third Prince's sarcasm, sharp temper, or protection would save her.

The devouring smoke-veil of grief lifted fully from her shoulders *and* her vision, and if Yala had ever thought herself clever, she was roundly disabused of the notion now.

She had wasted enough time; further lambasting herself for stupidity would serve no purpose. The first question was, would Garan Kurin have dared to do this thing? She did not know enough of him, and she would have to ask her questions very carefully indeed.

"Yala." Takshin was not, after all, so enchanted by the prospect of marriage as to brook being ignored. "Shall I call your kaburei? You look..."

As if one of the honorable dead has brushed me with a fingertip, or as if I am half-dead of heat in this terrible place? Either is equally likely. "I am well enough," she repeated. "Merely somewhat overwhelmed. The past few moon-turns have been dreadfully interesting, and last night..."

"They found the body near the Iejo, but you should not think upon such things. I intend to bore you into somnolence before long." His hands, their calluses the product of sword-drill instead of peasant work, twitched upon his lap, as if he wished to reach for something but denied himself the movement. "All will be well, Komor Yala. Simply trust me; I will not let any ill befall you."

Had Garan Takyeo said as much to Mahara? The world was full of ill, and it fell in any direction it willed. Were she truly a scholar she could write a few couplets upon the theme, but others far more talented had done so long before.

"Yala." He leaned farther in her direction, and her gaze flew to his face like a startled bird, flushed by beaters and bolting for freedom before the hawk descended. "Do not look so. What is wrong? And do not tell me it is merely the heat."

"It was a passing thought, my lord. Nothing more." She sought composure, and years of training stood her in good stead. "You have hurried the tea; I think that shall set me right."

"Indeed it shall," he said darkly, as if he would hold the very tea leaves accountable if they did not. "Does it worry you so to marry me? I am not the gentlest of men, true, but—"

"It does not trouble me," she assured him, and hoped it was not an untruth. "Is it not any noblewoman's goal, a princely husband? I simply do not wish to place a foot wrong in this dance, that is all." *You cannot know how deeply I hope to be graceful in this particular footwork.*

And in whatever comes after. If she found the culprit, if she did what was required, would she have the courage to face what would inevitably follow?

It was a dreadful question, and one she had no answer for.

"No danger of that." Garan Takshin glanced at the doorway as one of the servants appeared with a tea-tray, biting her lip as she negotiated the corner on soft-padding feet and cast a fearful glance in his direction. "Do not move, I shall pour."

It was very solicitous of him, indeed. And yet she watched as he set about the task with as much grace as could be expected, wondering all the while.

How, under Heaven, was she to sort *this* tangle?

A Strange Effect

This Kaeje water-garden was only lately familiar; the Emperor's private preserve, it was a riot of lush green, crimson bellflowers, shimmering water, the regular thudding beats of babu water-clocks, the rustle of greenery under a scorching wind, tiny dots of blue, and a heady scent of jaelo from an overgrown gazebo gazing at its own reflection in a mirror-clear pond. Viewed from a covered porch, it provided a very aesthetic picture indeed.

Directly behind him was his father's sickroom; the furniture had been taken out and burned so no ill-luck would attach to the new reign. It was not worth the bother of changing shoes to walk in the garden. His ministers either lingered at a discreet distance upon mirror-polished wood or took small perambulations, their heads together as they conferred. Golden in bright armor stood at intervals, probably roasting inside their metal and leather casings.

"No sign of them yet," Zan Fein said softly, his draught of umu perfume somewhat ameliorated by open air. He balanced upon one of the wide covered stairs ascending to the porch, his jatajatas granting him a few fingerwidths' more height; sometimes even laborers wore the sandals with the wooden bars upon their soles to avoid deep muck. Highborn women used them to keep their hems free of mire, and the sway of their skirts—or a eunuch's robe—while walking with the particular mincing gait required was the subject of much allusion and theatrical punning. "Some cavalry scouts have crossed into Shan; we do not know if Suon Kiron survives."

"If he does not, Shan will need a new king." Kurin considered the notion. It would certainly irritate Takshin to be pressed into that service, though it would please their mother roundly. Perhaps he could even send Mother south for retirement in a balmier climate, turning her into his little brother's problem. "If Shan is brought closer to Zhaon, so much the better." His thumb caressed a large carved scentwood bead, tapping it against his hurai before he moved on to the next.

"No doubt." Zan Fein allowed as much, his fan opening. The serpent painted upon its side, in the style of Hua Luong's illustrations, twitched its shoulders. "Yet the Tabrak must retreat before we may even think of such things."

"They always have before." Now Kurin understood why Father had always carried kombin. Stroking prayer-beads was soothing even if one was a modern man and somewhat irreligious, and helped the head-meat remain systematic and nimble at once.

"They have never attacked Shan *first* before. Generally they come through the Westron Wastes and strike the fields north of Zhaon-An. And besieging Suon's capital..." Zan Fein's fan flicked. The serpent was a masterpiece of subtle scale-shading, a creature well known for its power and wisdom.

Irritation scraped under Kurin's liver, turning his skin into a mass of prickles. A few barbarians with mourning-colored skin were nothing, and he cared little for Shan's troubles as long as they did not become Zhaon's. But the filthy things had killed his sister— when questioned, their "envoy" only laughed and repeated *a pretty bird thought she could fly* in terribly accented, guttural tones.

Sabwone had always loved the story of Hae Jinwone during the Blood Years. It was entirely like her to throw herself from some battlements.

Where was Suon Kiron? If he was too weak to hold his country or keep Kurin's sister safe, perhaps Zhaon should take Shan under a protective wing once the Pale Horde had vanished again.

"And none of our agents have sent a word?" That was troubling. Kurin did not put it past the chief court eunuch to keep some tidbits to himself—a man was only as powerful as the secrets he kept.

Yet it would not be wise of chief court eunuch to keep such things from an Emperor. Not at *all*.

"No. Which is quite concerning as well." The fan moved lazily, Zan Fein's eyes half-lidded as usual while he contemplated some question of policy. His network of informers—some official, others definitely the opposite—was robust in the South. There were few traders averse to making even more profit by sending along information, whether they owed allegiance to one country or the other.

A susurration of activity along one of the garden paths drew Kurin's attention. *Ah.* "Little brother has appeared," he murmured, and counted off a few more kombin beads while layers of guards and ministerial protocol were navigated by a royal family member.

The arriving son of Garan Tamuron had not slept well last night, judging by the dark shadows under his eyes. He strode along a well-swept flagstone path from one of the Kaeje's smaller doors, halted at the foot of the stairs, and bowed—the salute of a younger brother to an elder. Then he caught himself, visibly, and added the depth and polish expected when the person you were saluting was the Emperor and not merely a family member.

"Good morning, Jin." Kurin hoped his greeting was warm enough; he beckoned Jin onto the porch. "Are you well? And Third Mother? I hope the unpleasantness last night did not cause her any upset."

"She slept through it." Jin had taken some care with dressing; his robe was almost sober enough to be one of Makar's and his topknot-cage bore no ornamentation. He straightened, casting a guilty glance at the chief eunuch, and did not take the invitation to ascend into shade. "Honorable Zan Fein."

"My lord Sixth Prince." Zan Fein's own bow was a marvel of accuracy, pausing just long enough to denote deep respect as well as kindliness, his fan closed and held well aside. "Your mother is in my daily prayers; if aught may soothe or comfort her from my household, it is already being wrapped."

The proverb quoted was kindness itself, and Kurin thought it quite possible the crafty fellow even meant it. The chief court eunuch had his own counting-frame for power, and yet another one for prestige.

The two were not nearly synonymous.

"You went over the walls again last night, my little longtail." Kurin would have liked to broach the subject gently, but he had much to accomplish today. The hem of his scarlet-and-gold robe moved slightly on a hot breeze, breath-moist from the water garden. "Really, that is not princely behavior."

Jin's chin set; he scowled like a much younger boy. Father had been too busy to pay much attention to his antics, but Kurin would have thought Second Concubine Luswone would have taught the boy some restraint or propriety.

Still, he was young.

"What else can I do?" the Sixth Prince burst out. "Sabi's gone, my mother is crying, and Ah-Yeo…" He halted; a deep flush worked up his neck, stained his cheeks, and died. A water-clock clip-clopped in the near distance, providing brief emphasis.

Kurin watched the expressions crossing his youngest brother's face. "Eldest Brother is gone," he said, overlooking the ill-luck of naming the dead even obliquely. Of course a sibling would grieve, and Jin had been in the sickroom with the gutsplit stink. It was rather a bad show to put on at the end, in Kurin's opinion, wanting all your brothers and remaining sister to see you suffer nobly without a thought for how it might turn their stomachs. Misguided virtue was worse than none at all. "So is Father. You've had much to bear, little brother. But honestly, you cannot leap the walls at night anymore. It isn't safe."

"Well, if I hadn't, I never would have…" Again the boy halted, and he tucked his hands in his sleeves. It was odd to see him out of practice-armor at this hour; he was usually at the drillyard with Golden and soldiers. They said he had a gift for weaponry, which would bear watching—but every royal family needed a general or two.

It would certainly be more to Kurin's taste than depending upon

Zakkar Kai's continued loyalty. Even if adopted, even if allowed to keep a princely hurai, there were reasons to be wary of foundlings.

"Never would have found the assassin on the roof." The kombin coiled neatly into his palm; Kurin reached into his capacious crimson sleeve with his free hand, bringing out a sadly abused topknot-cage instead. "You left this behind. Be more careful next time, or they will start sending better."

"They?" Jin's dark gaze, very much like his mother's, was nonetheless hot and direct as the First Concubine's would never be. "Who are *they*?"

Kurin could not remember hearing Garan Daebo-a Luswone ever speak above a well-bred murmur, or even deploying a sharp glance. "We are the sons of Garan Tamuron." The morning sunlight was very heavy, and very warm. Kurin studied his youngest brother, an unwelcome prickle at his lower back. Normally he did not sweat, but robes of state were a burden in more ways than one. "There are many who fear our family." He contented himself with that observation, proffering the topknot-cage upon his open palm. His other hand cupped the kombin, and he was annoyed at the tension in his own fingers. "You are old enough to know that other noble clans might think themselves fit for the throne."

Jin's mouth opened slightly. He studied Kurin in return, and the faint reddening of morning shaving upon his cheeks was unnecessary. Still, what boy did not long to be a man?

Finally, Garan Jin climbed three steps and took the battered leather topknot-cage with both hands as etiquette dictated, bowing as deeply as he ever had to Father. "The Emperor's kindness," he muttered, and if there was some childish sarcasm in the phrase, Kurin decided it was allowable in this instance.

But only this once.

"Jin." He tried for the paternal, kindly tone he had practiced so often lately. "It would grieve me, were you or Third Mother to suffer harm. Be more careful. Please."

It was, he dared say, even diplomatic of him, and no doubt Zan Fein was taking note.

"I will, Your Majesty." Jin must have been thinking of Sabi, because it was a perfect impression of their eldest sister's icy formality when she considered someone undeserving of any politesse and wished to be exquisitely clear it was deployed only because *she* was noble. No doubt the imitation was lent strength by the long Daebo nose both of them had gained from the First Concubine.

Still, it was downright uncanny, and a cool finger touched Kurin's nape. Even a man who did not believe in angry shades might well feel a qualm.

Yet there was nothing for Sabi to be angry with him over. Father had married her off, and Kurin could hardly be blamed for the Tabrak. He had been scrupulously filial, attending to her pyre and even ordering her head be given a jointed doll's body to carry into whatever heaven awaited a princess. Besides, even her shade must know she had been, so far as he could have one among his siblings, his favorite.

Beautiful, clawing, intelligent, merry—if only she had been a court lady, not his sister. Already his ministers were pressing him to show a preference among their daughters or nieces. He had no intention of accumulating wives or granting any noble clan the pride of that consideration just yet; giving any clan the chance of a pliable infant heir to profess some loyalty to would upset the current delicate balance.

Even the courtesans in the Theater District he had called upon as a prince had never been granted any sign of overweening favor; he had visited the most attractive or expensive precisely as much as was required of a man in his station and no more. Any who showed signs of swelling or ambition would have to be dealt with in one fashion or another.

He preferred his pleasures to be transitory for at least another winter or two, until he could prune certain noble branches of their heaviest fruit.

"See that you do," Kurin added, and made an affectionate brushing gesture, dismissing a younger sibling. "Comfort Third Mother, little brother. I do not wish her troubled."

"The Emperor speaks." Jin bowed again, and took the prescribed steps backward as if he were a courtier instead of a royal brother. Kurin waited for him to add a tremulous grin or even a longtail's scrunch-face, but neither came.

Instead, his youngest brother regarded him somberly, with a quite unwonted flatness to his dark gaze, before retreating from the royal presence with almost unprincely speed. The ministers parted before him, avid glances seeking to discern if the Sixth Prince had lost any royal favor. Daebo was not represented at court; though Luswone had kin among several minor clans, her own had made the mistake of refusing to submit to Garan Tamuron.

Submission had not been Sabwone's strong suit, either, though she had in the end accepted her marriage. Had Suon Kiron treated her well?

Zan Fein said nothing, his gaze turned across the garden as if lost in aesthetic appreciation of its balance between clipped, manicured green and the rioting flowers; his fan reopened and commenced lazy motion. A jaelo-scented breeze touched Kurin's cheeks.

He had many things to do today, yet he lingered upon the porch, kombin beads slipping through his fingers. Zan Fein still said nothing. Had Father ever been irritated by this man's silence?

"He is a boy," Kurin finally murmured. "I wonder that Third Mother did not teach him better manners."

"Grief has many a strange effect." The eunuch's fan did not halt its steady motion. A draught of umu scent reached Kurin, who could not now wrinkle his nose at it. Those positioned so far above all did not mention the stink of middens. "The Emperor's Third Mother is prostrate. The Second Mother refuses all visitors..."

And my own mother alternately rages and weeps; I cannot keep the gossip contained much longer. Kurin tucked the kombin away and produced his own fan, more to push away the umu scent than for any vestige of coolness. He half-turned, as if absorbing a fractionally different garden vista.

"And a certain bath-girl is sick with grief too." Zan Fein's words were hardly audible.

Kurin's fan did not halt. The quotation brushed upon its span was a scholarly exhortation to judicious patience, and he had selected it this morning with half a thought that the very quality it named would be called upon in great measure this afternoon.

In fact, the test had arrived sooner, as such tests often did.

"Dho Anha is ill?" Kurin did not lower his voice. If a courtier was hiding in the shrubbery, let them hear he knew the name of the bath-girl his father had shown such marked preference to in his last few moon-cycles of life. "It is a shame, she made my father's last days endurable. We shall send the best court physician to her aid."

"To a bath-girl's aid?" Zan Fein's eyebrow arched, but he was not remarking upon the impropriety of such a gesture.

No, the chief court eunuch was hinting, very delicately, that it would have to be a physician of surpassing renown if Kurin wished to avoid being seen as the author of the poor girl's misfortune. Of course, a prince would have no reason to ill-wish such a lowly creature.

But his mother...ah, Garan Yulehi-a Gamwone the First Mother of the Emperor, who gossip painted as the author of a certain concubine's miscarriage and barrenness, who had been named upon that concubine's deathbed where the words of the dying carried weight, whose own physician—rumored to know more than a little about the entire affair—had become inconvenient and died of a belly-gripe?

He had warned her to avoid such displays. A sour taste filled Kurin's mouth. He loved his mother as a filial son ought; he had also advised her, in the clearest possible terms, such behavior would not be tolerated. And over a silly bath-girl, too.

"She made my father's last days bearable," he repeated. "Send the *two* best court physicians to her, Zan Fein. And let us be about the rest of the morning's business. There is a visit I must make this afternoon."

"Yes, Your Majesty," the eunuch replied, inclining his top half as even the highest-ranked must when the Emperor gave a command.

SILLY GIRL

The stink was massive—roasting, ash, rot, middenheaps, dung and other detritus. A haze hung over the piercetowered capital of Shan, and the marks upon this wooded hill showed where another group of horsemen had used it recently, probably because it commanded such a fine view of Shan's liver and head-meat.

Tabrak's Pale Horde had melted into the northern hills not long before, possibly sensing his return with bloodriders and what other forces he had hurriedly gathered; a swathe of trampled devastation showed their passage much like the silvery trail of a greasebug or spiral-shell in a garden. From here, the breached gate could not be seen, but a gout of black smoke lifting from the palace hill showed even that hard kernel had been cracked.

And the king of Shan had not managed to meet the enemy at all. Oh, he had found their trail, but precious time had been lost since they were not behaving as they should.

Of course, they were barbarians. And yet.

The man upon the shuddering horse before his king had lost a great deal of weight, and was not smiling as was his usual wont. A smoke-stained bandage wrapped about his head, another around his right shoulder stained with old, crusted blood, and he stared at the hooves of the king's mount, too exhausted to blush with shame. His left arm was locked across his midsection, and it was quite

possible there was another wound there, not to mention the tatters
in the leather half-armor clinging to his muscled legs.

In short, Lord Buwon had nothing to be ashamed of, the shame
lay entirely elsewhere, and Suon Kiron wished one of his oldest
friends and bloodriders would cease hanging his head.

"She did not wait," Buwon repeated, heavily. "The moment the
gates were forced, she... my king, she..."

"She jumped." The exhausted woman upon a stubby-legged
pony at Buwon's side had hacked at her hair in an excess of grief,
or perhaps there had been some dishonor. Ragged tendrils of redblack brushed her thin shoulders. The soot clinging to her dress
did not hide the fact that it had been of high quality though sober
cloth and cut, and no hairpin clung to the mess of her shorn hair.
"I could not halt her. She... her dress tore, you see." She opened a
bruised hand, blisters showing where reins had cut cruelly into a
noblewoman's palm. A scrap of silk clung to the wounds, so dyed
with old blood and sweat the color could not be distinguished.
Great dark circles lingered under the woman's eyes, and her words
were tinted with the softness of Zhaon. "My lord... Great King..."
She swung between Zhaon and the Shan dialect, obviously at a loss
to decide how to address him.

Kiron remembered her name with a harsh mental effort. "Lady
Daebo Nijera." He hoped he sounded kind, but there was something sharp in his throat, like the crushed rocks pounded into
roadways by peasants during corvée labor. "No more need be said."

"It was not my lord Buwon's fault," she continued, as if she
had not heard him—or did not credit his words. Or as if she had
repeated her news so many times it had burned into her tongue,
as in certain stories of grief and lamentation. "It was *not*, the... *I*
failed, you see. I tried to catch her. If not for Lord Buwon..."

His mother would have ordered the woman's tongue ripped out
by the roots, perhaps. Or hot lead run down her throat. When the
Mad Queen wished for silence, not even the pinchnose rodents
dared squeak.

An uneasy susurration went through his assembled bloodriders.

Half the raiding party he had taken to find the Tabrak and convince them to leave his country alone was even now riding along the trail of devastation, moving in screen to find where the horde had gone. Messages were flying through Shan in every direction, provincial nobles called to bring their complements of riders and infantry.

If any dissembled, he might well turn his mother's savagery upon them. Was her shade watching this with glee? All manner of bloodshed had pleased his dam; he could not remember a time when a display of cruelty had not made her dark eyes sparkle and her fine teeth show behind thin lips.

The city, plundered and now abandoned by its conquerors, needed no battle to free it. The nobles who had fled before its investiture would come creeping back, and though wailing filled the smoky air, so did the sound of hammering, exhalations of effort, and the singsong chants of peasants and artisans working to repair what they could and traders finding something, anything to gather and barter amid the wreckage.

Shan was a vital beast, and though it could be damaged, to kill was another question entirely.

"The tunnels," Buwon said, hopelessly. "Most left, there were not enough to man the walls. I should have stayed, and died."

"Then I would have lost a bloodrider, and not known of the manner of my wife's..." For a moment, words failed Kiron; he fixed his gaze upon the palace keep's smoke-veiled bulk. *Silly girl.* He had called her *ekanha*, a well-bred but dangerous half-tamed creature; what beast, so named, would not lunge frantically to escape a trap? "Those who left will be taken to task." Once he had dealt with the Tabrak, and whatever barbarian beast rode at their head now. "Afterward." If they did not spill their blood in penance against the barbarians, that was.

"My lord?" Lord Suron, the eldest of his bloodriders, was at his right hand. He sounded uncharacteristically tentative—if he bothered to speak, it was usually with decision—and it was easy to guess why.

Suon Kiron supposed he perhaps looked very much like the Mad Queen in this moment, and it could hardly have been comfortable for even his closest bloodriders—those who ate at his table, rode at his side, and had the honor of guarding him as well as of sharing whatever within Shan's borders he chose to take or to give them.

It could be argued this was his own fault, leaving the city as he had. But the Tabrak had never acted thus before, not in any history he could remember. Even his mother, who spoke admiringly of their practices when she was in a fine mood, had never mentioned such an event. They *always* invaded Zhaon first; they did not come swiftly from the south, plunder, and pass northward.

He wished Takshin was here. Shin would have viewed the spectacle gravely, and he would have something to say that would quiet the noise within Kiron's skull, his head-meat buzzing as if the yellow and black spear-carrying soldiers of the insect world had decided to take up residence.

What manner of man—what kind of *king*—could not answer this deadly insult?

"Look to the lady." Lord Suron spoke again as Daebo Nijera, his now-dead queen's chief lady-in-waiting, swayed atop the pony. Suron and Ku Wuoru hurried to dismount and aid her, one at each arm guiding her for the camp being made behind Kiron and his bloodriders. The woman began to keen, grief finally breaking her shell of numb calm, and Lord Buwon's throat-stone moved as he swallowed dryly.

"She refused to leave," he husked. "She said a queen does not flee her city. My king, my lord, kill me. I have made my report, I beg you to order me executed. I do not deserve the honor of—"

"Nonsense," Kiron snapped. His mother would have ordered Buwon to suicide, probably in front of an audience of jeering, terrified peasants. "I need you too much to allow anything of the sort, Buwon Takhe. You are not permitted to die just yet. Follow Suron and Wuoru, have your wounds attended. I expect you fit to ride within a few days." He slapped his gauntlets against the half-armor of stiffened leather upon his right thigh; the sound was short and crisp, overriding any further protest.

Buwon bowed in the saddle and urged his lathered horse in the general direction of the camp. He looked ready to fall from its back at any moment, but at least he did not protest further. The Daebo woman's wailing receded, a thin sound pulled after her like a needle drawing thread through fabric.

The last time he saw his wife, she was not sewing but reading. *Do well in this*, he had told her.

And she had. A man could not ask more of a noble bride, even one who had insulted him deeply before the wedding day. He had thought her mettlesome but not very bright; now he was the one shamed. There was only one thing that would wash away the stain.

"My lord?" One of his bloodriders spoke, but Kiron did not recognize the voice through the roaring in his ears, through his head-meat, the buzzing settling in his liver. It was not mere anger, a familiar companion from childhood, but *rage*, the same feeling that had driven him into a dry well to bring another shattered boy from the depths.

Tying Garan Takshin to his back and climbing the well's throat had been easy enough, compared to this.

His bloodriders fell silent, not daring to discuss possibilities as they usually would. The sun reached its crest and began to fall, and still Suon Kiron sat upon his patient chestnut in uncertain shade, the gelding's tail flicking lazily as he lowered his head to tear at mouthfuls of summer-yellowing grass. There wasn't much; the Tabrak had probably watched the city for a few hours from here, and their own horses would be hungry.

Finally he stirred. "Silly girl," he murmured, and slapped his gauntlets against his leather-clad thigh once more. Still, he could not blame her. A husband was to keep his wife safe, and he had not. "But you did well," he amended.

They said his mother's madness had begun with such strange declarations, speaking to those not present, or malformed thoughts spilling from head-meat into free air. If he were subject to the same malady, Suon Kiron might almost welcome it. Was this what she had felt? By all accounts the king she had married was brutal—Suon Obon's preferred pastime was watching criminals flogged to death—and perhaps even a gentle noble girl could become cruel when yoked to such a beast.

Perhaps even a disdainful princess from luxurious Zhaon might have, in time.

But Suon Kiron was not here for what she might have become. He was required to answer what had been *done*—to her, to his city, and to the land he ruled.

"My lord?" It was Ku Wuoru, the lord of Toakmisho in the east of Shan, returned from his task and accepting the reins of his own mount from a fellow bloodrider. "What say you?"

"I say the Tabrak have made a mistake." His chin rose, and Kiron enunciated every word clearly. "We shall find them. In the meantime, the capital must be given aid and direction. There are many preparations to be made."

"Preparations." It was not quite a question, merely a repeating of the term to request further clarity, if Ku Wuoru's lord cared to give such.

"Shan will ride to war, my friends." Kiron gathered his own reins. "But first, we must repair this. Suron and Buwon will follow into the city when they can. Come."

HAND WIELDING
HER

H er mouth was drier than the Westron Wastes, a spot of molten pain burned steadily behind her breastbone. Both were familiar sensations, though the latter had grown more intense lately; her mistress's late, unlamented personal physician had even once condescended to examine her, poking at the spots where the invisible subtle body met Yona's physical flesh with an ivory-tipped pointer and prescribing a foul tonic that did absolutely nothing. Still, she had taken it faithfully. A superior's care, even when poisonous, was to be swallowed without complaint.

She made her obeisance carefully and waited, with her forehead almost touching the polished wooden floor, for whatever the new Emperor had to say. Her dark cotton dress was of the requisite quality, bearing only the faintest trace of cheerful blue embroidery at the cuffs; her mistress did not like servants to wear bright plumage. Even if she had better, there had been no time to change into it; when the greatest master of all called, there was barely even time to scrape at one's thinning hair to make sure any stray strands were tamped hurriedly down.

This most august being's request for her presence was ostensibly to discuss some care for the First Mother of Zhaon, and the pains taken to instruct or question Yona, as that great lady's most senior servant, either showed a great deal of filial feeling on Garan Kurin's part—or something else entirely.

"Oh, sit up," the Emperor said, irritably. "We are old friends, Yona. There is no need for this."

There was a need, and well she knew it. A superior could graciously wave aside an obeisance, but the whip or the sudo would descend with alacrity if a servant failed to attempt it first. She lingered for a fraction of a moment, to make her reluctance to rise above her station clear. She did not let her gaze mount past his crimson-and-gold-clad knees, but you could tell much by the angle of such limbs when their owner was taking his ease upon a padded chair.

He had fine hands, Gamwone's eldest son. They rested calmly upon his thighs, strong but sensitive, the nails buffed but not overly manicured, and there were calluses across the palm where a sword-hilt would rest. He was even stroking kombin beads as his father had been rumored to do; Yona had barely seen Garan Tamuron even when that master of all he surveyed visited his first wife to get heirs upon her and afterward during festivals or other occasions requiring the two of them to pretend they did not detest each other.

At least, Gamwone's feelings seemed to linger near detestation sometimes; all Yona had seen of Garan Tamuron was lofty inaccessibility.

Except once, after his second concubine had miscarried. Garan Tamuron had been wondrous wroth with his first queen, and if Gamwone knew Yona had witnessed that scene, her own food, drink, or hand-oil—if she were ever given leave for such luxury—would bear a subtle toxin soon enough. An exquisitely painful, absolutely fatal one.

Yona watched the carved scentwood kombin move as the beads rolled under fingertips before being set free—but only until the chain of knotted silk brought them back to the palm. Gamwone's son was somewhat of a known quantity, part of the household she had spent most of her life in, but power changed those it visited.

It stripped away any cringing and revealed what they truly were from the start.

Finally, the new Emperor spoke again. "We are old friends, are we not?"

"A very great honor to your humble handmaiden, Great Emperor of Zhaon." She could not speak very loudly, her throat was so parched. Even tea would not help, if he bothered to offer it to such a lowly creature. And sohju would simply make the live coal behind her breastbone dilate.

The new Emperor was probably very well aware of precisely how far he was honoring her. "You've served my mother well for years, Yona."

"As well as I can, Your Gracious Majesty." After all, what else was there to do? You either wielded the sudo for your mistress, or she wielded it upon you. There was no other choice.

The lord of all Zhaon, Heaven's most cherished representative to the center of the world, next saw fit to utter a banality. "She hasn't rewarded you for it."

"Service is its own reward," Yona intoned, as piously as she dared. Her knees ached, bones with a thin covering of skin pressed against unforgiving wooden floor, but the pain was so familiar—and so small next to the burning in her chest—it was all but ignored. "I have no complaints, oh Gracious Majesty."

"*My lord* will suffice, Yona. Otherwise I might think you mock me. You knew me as a boy, after all."

She had indeed; she had been scarcely older herself when she entered Gamwone's service. The rich were allowed much, and struggling against it was struggle against Heaven itself. "A peerless child, my lord."

"Debatable. You could continue uttering worthless praise, Yona, or you could look at me and speak for once."

Why would I wish to do that? Still, she raised her gaze to his chest. It was perhaps fine as such things were accounted, relatively broad, and of course the crimson cloth covering it was the best quality available. How many seamstresses had pricked their fingers with the golden embroidery? "What would you have of me, my lord?"

"That's better." He did not shift, but a servant didn't last long if she could not tell when a superior's gaze caught upon her, openly or otherwise. Peasant proverbs held that the eye's resting was a weight the crafty could turn to their advantage, in one way or another. "But not there yet. Look at me, Yona."

So she did.

Sleep-lidded and proud-nosed, he examined her much as he would a substandard horse offered by a poor provincial to a visiting noble. For all that, a hint of a smile lingered around his thin lips, and his well-trimmed smallbeard suited him. He did not favor his father much; the cruelty lingering in his pupils and around the corners of his lips was from another parent entirely.

"Dho Anha," he said, and Yona's entire body went cold. He had been cultivating the bath-girl for his own ends since the final days of his father's illness, and she had reported as much to her mistress.

But what could she do when a queen commanded? Oh, Gamwone was very careful, couching it in hint and allusion, but her servant understood what was to happen.

We must give her a gift, Yona.

"My lord?" she managed weakly, hoping against hope that some passing spirit or her own nimble head-meat would grant her something, anything else to say to escape this trap.

But who would take pity on *her*? She was a sudo in Garan Yulehi-a Gamwone's hands, and even Heaven itself knew as much. The celestial rulers handed out punishments aplenty for those who rebelled against their betters; obedience might leave you luckily, gratefully ignored.

"Don't pretend confusion, you're intelligent enough to have survived my mother for years." A shadow of irritation lay under his measured tone. "How was it delivered to the bath-girl? I don't care what it was, I'm merely curious about the method. I should think even the silliest cloudfur-headed girl would know better than to eat anything coming from the First Queen's hands."

First Queen, Garan Gamwone's old title, not *First Mother*. If it was a calculated slip, Yona could not discern the message behind it. "Hand-oil," she whispered. "Because…my lord, she said, your mother said…the hands which touch her son must be the finest." That part had been Yona's own invention, but if she was to be a weapon, didn't the blame rest with the arm wielding her?

Surely Heaven would take that into account. Or perhaps they would not, for they were all the same, those in power. Even the many hells were merely a mirror of the other realms, all lying against each other like folded linens in a cupboard.

"Ah. Clever, clever." The Emperor's left hand continued with the kombin while his right rose, stroked at his smallbeard twice, then returned to its home in his lap. "You've been wasted in that household. All these years."

"My lord…" She knew how a small animal in a peasant's trap felt, hearing the footsteps meaning she would soon be in the dinner pot.

It might even be a relief.

"Don't look so forlorn. You've served with much discretion, and you were far too young to have been a part of…" He trailed off, watching her narrowly. It was the only time he resembled his father instead, and that was probably all the mercy Yona could expect at this point. "Are you about to faint?"

"No, my lord." Though the noise inside her skull had reached a pitch that made such an outcome all but inevitable, she hung grimly to her wits, focusing upon the tip of his chin. The smallbeard was probably trimmed and sculpted daily, and she was glad to be spared *that* duty. Serving a male would be ever so much worse than what she endured.

The pain behind her breastbone was very bad now. When she arose before dawn, sometimes she heaved quietly in the privy before chivvying lazy slatterns toward the day's work, and the matter dredged up her throat carried traces of bright red more often now. A lucky, royal color, trapped inside her miserable self.

"You're rather pale." Of course he smiled now, the same small satisfied curve of lips his mother used when some tiny, helpless struggling thing pleased her. "I love my mother, Yona, and so do you. We must join forces, it seems."

What? She did not croak it by sheer force of will. Instead, she bowed again, grateful for the coolness of the floor against her palms, even if it bruised her skinny aching knees.

"Oh, cease." When she straightened reluctantly, the Emperor sighed. "You will attend me daily while my mother is at dinner. You will report to me what she does, what she orders you to do, and what she hints she would *like* done. You will make no move to obey her in certain areas unless I give permission."

"My lord . . ." She longed for a drink of water, though consuming anything made the pain worse. Though she ate barely enough to sustain life, and all as bland as possible, her belly was still slightly swollen as if she carried new life. She did not think it was so, for she had no time to engage in the activity that would spur such growth. And, after all, who would want the First Queen's old dry stick? Yes, she knew what they called her. Every single word. "My lord, she will be . . . angry."

"Whose anger would you prefer?" Garan Kurin asked, mildly. "Hers, or mine?"

A bright sharp flash of hatred revolved in the middle of Yona's head-meat, and she could not help but dart a glance at his face.

"Still . . ." Garan Kurin merely looked thoughtful, and interested. Still, when she did not respond he sighed, and stroked at his smallbeard again. Stiff hair rubbed at the silver-sheathed greenstone ring upon his right first finger. "I suppose you have a point. I shall make it clear to her you are not to be touched. Will that satisfy you?"

As if he did not know his mother had any number of ways to make her displeasure known—and if she was denied other victims, Gamwone would strike at anything nearby not likely to return the favor. Which would make Yona even more hated among the creeping, hurrying maids the court called *the First Queen's spiders*.

"I am satisfied to be of service, my lord," she heard herself say.

Perhaps one of her ancestors was taking pity upon her, though she did not think it likely.

Passing shades might speak through a poor servant's mouth in tales or plays, but in the real world, there was no pity to be found.

"You shouldn't be, Yona. Keep a strict watch on my mother, make certain what she plans reaches my ears, and I will settle a pension upon you." Garan Kurin moved slightly, settling himself in greater comfort upon his padded chair. "You may retire to the country and live quietly, knowing you have served Zhaon well."

"A pension?" She did not mean to repeat it, but it was somewhat shocking. Almost unheard of; though she was thrifty, she had not fattened in royal service as most servants did.

Gamwone had her ways of making certain her underlings received only, barely enough. Even planting in good soil could not make an empty pot grow, as the proverb said.

"You like the thought?" Gamwone's eldest son smiled, showing he knew full well she would. "I am the Emperor now, Yona. And my mother is not careful. We should keep her from committing any... indiscretion."

I wish you much luck in that endeavor, my lord. But such a thing could not be said. "I will do all I can," Yona promised, and bowed yet again, not quite knocking her forehead against the wood but certainly risking it. "Your humble handmaiden thanks thee, great and gracious Emperor of Zhaon."

"I'm sure you had other names for me, when we were children." Now he laughed, indulgent as his mother after some pain had been meted out to balance a perceived insult. "Run along back to my mother, Yona. Tell her what I've asked of you, if you like—but leave the pension out of it, shall we?"

Did he think her stupid? Well, every lord thought so of every underling, and they were mostly correct. Just not always. "Yes, my lord."

She made her obeisances and left, barely noticing the familiar Kaeje halls or the speculative glances of courtiers far above her station openly wondering why the First Mother's servant had been summoned. A dizzying prospect opened before her indeed, and the devouring pain between and underneath her withered breasts was so familiar as to be ignored as well.

She had not thought it possible she might survive Garan Yulehi-a Gamwone. But now, in the space of a few moments, she had not only the chance, but also the glimmerings of a plan.

According to Plan

I t was a fine thing to be the lord of a whole people. It was also a crushing, never-ending burden punctuated far too infrequently by the screams of battle to suit him.

The Horde liked open rolling grasslands best, though they could survive a trek across burning eastron wastes to the rich, damp lands of the clay people, those drudges whose function was to build like busy ants so their masters could take when the mood struck or necessity dictated.

The confinement of a forest was unpleasant, but not overwhelmingly so, especially when their lord said it was necessary. So they had plunged into the green depths, disliking but obedient since questioning the Horde's latest leader was not healthy, or wise.

Aro Ba Wistis tilted his head slightly, his hair—skull-shaved on either side, with sacred blue stonefat worked into the remainder to give a high, stiffened crest—striped with bright azure which ran down either side of his bearded face when the sweat of riding or battle rose, the sign of a warrior the Burning One favored above others. Traces of more blue paint lingered on his cheeks and hands. Indigo ink was forced under the skin of his fingers in the rune-scratch patterns of luck and battle-wisdom, twitching as he tapped at a knifehilt. The brace of daggers at his belt were of fine Bird make, with dappling in the bright metal and green stones sunk in their hilts; the matched set was all he had taken from the first city his Horde had ever pillaged.

The God's Arrow of Tabrak wished for some uninterrupted thought, but he could not even ride for the horizon as upon the grasslands of the Horde's traditional home. The dry heat and dust of the land beyond the forest's shade were no worse than the songs said were usual, but his plan required avoiding an open battle with the clay people just yet. They did not fight honorably, fearing loss of ground in a way the Horde never would—there was always more space to conquer in a different direction, after all.

Instead, the lord of the Pale Horde was in the hot still closeness of his personal round tent, passing a critical gaze over the piles of spoils from his stirrup-holders. They gave the best to their master, who rewarded them with a fraction in return, carefully chosen after every battle in which a man rode well. Pushed against the northern wall were a gaggle of prisoners, many young, some nubile, but none of them enticing in the least.

Not at the moment, though he would select a few in a little while, balancing the burden of more mouths to feed against the honor due his lieutenants' gifts. He needed a wife to perform some of these duties, but none of the jostling families within the Horde were worth strengthening to that degree yet.

"Who among the outriders has returned?" he asked, rubbing at his reddish beard. Tonight a temporarily favored scuni would oil and comb, and Aro might consent to a few beads braided into the mass. Perhaps the last Bird girl they had managed to catch on the edge of the waste, the one with the weak eyes—he liked her at the moment.

She fought only until the battle was lost, and submitted hatefully. *Just enough spice upon the meat*, as his father might have said.

"No word from Nunik yet." Short, meaty Etu was at his lord's right hand, his hair pulled back in a tail instead of crested. He wore the leather collar—they used to be made of metal, but that material was too precious to waste—and he was also literate. A warrior needed a scribe if he wished to amount to anything in the world, though Aro's father had beaten his son for once attempting, in secret, to learn the sorcery of letters.

Most usefully, Etu was from the fringe of the waste, and had known the clay people and their ways in childhood. He had been of very great use lately, especially in dealing with the ghost-eyed emissary from the northernmost clay people, those Aro liked best. The duo from Khir—emissary and the stirrup-holder to clean his boots and tend his horse—lingered near the door of the great pavilion, eyeing the spoils while clad in their strange half-womanly clothing, and if it disturbed them to see their fellows conquered and stripped so easily, they did not show it.

The clay people were not beautiful, though if one of their kings wished to offer a daughter the son of Wistis was more than prepared to accept and use that marriage to settle the Horde somewhat. It would be an elegant solution, but not one which had a chance of being employed, or so he privately thought.

"And Turik?" The envoy carrying a clay-bitch's head to the richer city to the north had been instructed to return, if possible. It had been Etu's idea, advanced diffidently and with proper respect for his master's temper. It would, he thought, unnerve the clay people and show them Aro was stronger than their own rulers.

"Too soon, perhaps." Etu did not need to say more. Plenty among the Horde envied his position at Aro's side; those possessed of more than common intelligence were said to pity him.

But not overmuch. If it was Aro's will that held the reins, it was Etu whose stringent arrangements made certain the horses were cared for and the riders fed—but the scun would have to be useful indeed for Aro's successor, whoever that might be, to keep in living service instead of opening his throat at the door of his dead lord's howe to serve in the next world.

"I like it not." But Aro let the matter rest, nodding in appreciation of a particularly fine pile, artistically arranged, from the Hastin family. Spoils were always organized thus, in grave-mounds; it was the prerogative of the living to pick and choose. Some of the rest would be given away during a mead-party, spread through the Horde to keep even the unlucky happy; another share would go to the Burning One himself in a vast immolation.

The piles were arranged in order of the stirrup-holder's rank; the closer to the seat made of broken, bronze-dipped arrows, the mightier the giver. Costly fabric, metalwork finer than the smiths of the Bird People the Horde had ridden against since time immemorial could produce, ceramic ware too heavy and fragile to carry for long but making a fine noise when sacrificed, leatherwork and lamps—the city had been rich indeed, and his riders' appetites were whetted. If all went well, they would spend the worst of winter inside one richer still.

It was almost enough to take the sting from the defeat upon the Blackwing Plain. The Bird People had bred like coneys in a fat year, like the insects that came when the Burning One was displeased; their settlements studded the open places to a far greater degree than they ever had before. A few of the walled hives could be plundered somewhat regularly, but the Great Grass Sea had changed; the Horde's advent was no longer seen as an inevitable cyclic disaster but as something which could—blasphemous as it sounded—be resisted.

The clay people were easier pickings, but still, the city they had just broken to gather supplies for the best prize had not fallen as quickly—or easily—as he liked. The narrow-eyed people's new bows, as well as the thunder-tubes on their wheeled carriages, were concerning; so too were a few of their new tactics.

The Bird People had forgotten their masters, and he did not have the numbers to teach them after the great sicknesses of the past eight summers, death grazing among the Horde like a hungry horse upon new verdure. Riding against the settled tribes of the Great Grass Sea in autumn before the great rains, when the granaries were full and the stock fattened, had ever been the Horde's way, but the Blackwing battle had changed things far more than any of his folk seemed able to comprehend.

Except him. Aro Ba Wistis saw the future, and it was grim

indeed. The Horde prized moving across the grass as the Burning One demanded, but unless that great and mighty fellow wished for his entire people to become scun themselves under the heel of the Bird People, they would have to settle in one place and multiply.

Put that way, the solution was obvious. But he knew better than to voice it to even his closest stirrup-holders, or to his most favored scun, just yet. Once he had performed a few more miracles to prove the Burning One's will, they would accept the change with gratitude or fear; he did not care which.

Aro half-turned and beckoned; the pale-eyed emissary with his stirrup-holder took note of the motion and both hastened to pick their way between the heaps of offerings, bowing when they came into range.

They bobbed up and down at the slightest provocation, like waterfowl on a disturbed pond. Still, they were useful, not least because sowing division among the settled peoples made them easier to fleece.

"Most favored of the Burning One." The pale-eyed emissary had grown somewhat more facile with the Horde's tongue, though he sang or chanted instead of speaking. His own language was much more tonal, a difficult one to master—not that the son of Wistis would.

Such work was for scun. Some distance was required; those the Horde ruled were inclined to grow restive if given the honor of a king speaking their nattering chatter.

"The city was full of marvelous things." Since he was temporarily pleased with them, he made his tone genial and hearty, using simple words a child could understand and pitching them a little more loudly than usual, to force his meaning across a river of incomprehension. "You shall each have a horse apiece from my own capture."

"Your graciousness overwhelms us." At least the grey-eyed man and his companion could ride like the Horde's own; the northerners treated four-legged cousins with the requisite respect, cementing themselves in Aro's opinion as the best of the clay people and those most likely to enforce his rule upon the others once he found the proper means of subjugating them. "But we are poor guests, to have nothing to offer in return."

"Ah, your help in taking that warren is gift enough." Aro waved a lordly hand. "But you have some business to put before me? Speak."

"Ah great king of the Horde, it pains us to even think of it." The emissary—Takari Daoyan, an odd name—bowed again. "But our homeland is soon to be at war with Zhaon, and we must go to aid our great father."

"What says my valued guest?" Aro turned to Etu in mock-astonishment, and did not miss the worried glance between emissary and stirrup-holder. "He wishes to be gone so soon?"

"His land will draw the forces of the greatest of the clay people from their center, Great Light." Etu's round brown face held no expression, as usual. "He is eager to be in battle against those he dislikes most, I am sure."

"A sentiment any man shares." Aro affected to think about this request, toeing a large ceramic thing—Etu said it was to hold soup, but why would such an article need notches in the rim—at the bottom of the Hastins' pile. "But it is too soon for such cherished guests to think of leaving. We shall speak further upon the matter tomorrow."

Takari bowed again. They never attacked directly, these creatures the Burning One had made clever and sedentary. True bravery was not to be found among them. "Of course we could not sadden such a gracious host. I fear we are useless guests, though."

"*Honored* guests," Etu murmured, at a glance from his master. "Come, you must choose fine mounts. Both of you, my lord would have it so."

"Make certain they choose the best there is to be had, Etu," Aro said mildly. "He is a good judge of four-legged cousins, my favored scun."

It would take the rest of the afternoon before they were finished with the selection, the guests insisting they could not possibly accept such wonderful animals and Etu insisting they must not insult their host. Clay people were treacherous; letting these two ride north through the lands of his next—and greatest—target was a risk he preferred not to take yet.

A long time ago, one of his grandfathers had held all three lands under a stirrup-heel, and wains of tribute had crossed the almost waterless waste west toward the Great Grass Sea. No doubt many of his riders thought the son of Wistis planned something similar.

The human spoils shrank as one as his gaze fell upon them, with that quality of collective movement the clay people excelled at. He might as well make his selections now; it would not matter what he kept or burned as long as he could take the greatest prize of all.

They called their great city *Zhaon-An*, but in the tongue of the Horde it was Zunnan, the golden wool-haired creature whose precious fur grew year after year, ready to shower whoever sheared it with riches. The northerners were rising, the southron land temporarily dealt with, and all was going according to plan.

Newcomers and
Old Friends

The vermilion-pillared hall was still the same, the padded bench where the fulcrum and focus of the civilized world sat in state had not changed, and the eunuchs at their ranked tables, brushing and sealing decisions into policy and edict, were familiar faces. The ministers were all reconfirmed in their rank and prerogatives, including Lord Yulehi, in whose half of the year disaster had struck.

Zhaon was a giant cart, and its wheels rolled more smoothly when there was a pair of ruts to fit into.

Even Mrong Banh's scrollcases were familiar, as well as the cushioned, leather-soled slippers he wore into the royal presence. Banh's dark but very fine scholar's robe was an old friend too, despite the unbleached cotton band knotted high upon his left arm.

Others might find it wise to put aside mourning, but he would not. After all, he had been with Garan Tamuron since almost the beginning.

The only other visible change in the hall was the man upon the padded bench, listening to Lord Yulehi with all the attention of a filial nephew and stroking the smallbeard he had taken to cultivating just before his elder brother's marriage. Silver gleamed, the most royal metal edging the double greenstone rings clasping his first fingers; his robe was crimson and gold as befitted one through whom Heaven's fortune flowed into Zhaon, and all in all, he was the very picture of a young Emperor.

And Banh, chief astrologer of Zhaon, was still called upon to serve. He stopped at every station required by custom to bow, though he had been the one to cast the new Emperor's horoscope many winters ago on the child's naming-day, when it was apparent Garan Tamuron's second son would survive the most perilous period of infancy.

"There he is, our most scholarly uncle." Kurin's smile was wide and beneficent; openly claiming Mrong Banh as a manner of kin was a piously filial move. "And bearing scrollcases, too. Come to give me lessons, Banh?"

"I should hope I have already discharged that duty well before now." Banh attempted a smile. It threatened to crack like pottery cooled too quickly; Tamuron's greeting would have been different. So would Garan Takyeo's. "Thankfully, all I must do is report the position of the stars."

"Heaven must be pleased with Zhaon," Lord Yulehi intoned, somewhat portentously.

"We shall see." The new Emperor made a brisk movement, his hand sweeping away something inconsequential. "I look forward to the amended taxation totals by evening, my lord uncle."

Dismissed in such a fashion, the uncle of the First Queen—First Mother of the Emperor, or Dowager First Queen, or, if one was exceeding formal and antiquated, First Consort of the Glorious One Departed to Heaven—bowed and retreated, casting the astrologer one indecipherable glance. If he expected Banh to ask for him to remain he was sadly mistaken, but it was more likely he was assessing the astrologer's usefulness in light of the imperial summons from his own nephew.

Banh also thought it quite likely Binei Jinwon, Lord Yulehi—despite his wealth and his reputation of penetrating intellect, not to mention subtle influence in every direction—was surprised by his nephew's taking the reins in his own well-manicured hands rather than letting an older, wiser minister move into what he considered his rightful place.

It was no doubt immensely frustrating for the grasping, squeezing, pretentious man who had done much to arrange the marriage of his clan-niece to a rising warlord. To be so near a goal and have a younger clan member, one you thought you controlled, make their lack of gratitude so plainly visible...it was a fitting punishment indeed, and perhaps Tamuron was amused, if he was watching from whatever celestial hall he had been installed in. Banh's own urge to smile grimly, with no true amusement, was well-nigh overwhelming.

He managed to cover it with a cough, pretending to fiddle with his scrollcases, the wide bands of leather serving them as a carrying case tightened with thoughtless habitual speed when he left the blue-tiled tower that had been his home for many a summer now.

It was disconcerting to realize just how immortal he'd assumed Garan Tamuron to be.

Garan Kurin watched his clan-uncle's reluctant departure, and his expression was one Banh had often seen upon him as a boy— thoughtful, just slightly cruel, and very certain he possessed the winning gambit in a complex but not terribly difficult game.

Children grew into adults, of course. It was the way of the world. But Banh wished it had not happened quite so quickly.

"He's rather upset at not being enthroned himself," Kurin remarked softly, and his gaze was bright and avid as it slid to the astrologer. It was the sort of thing Tamuron might have said, but in a much different tone, and missing his lord rose like hot bile behind Banh's breastbone. "I am sorry to call you out of mourning, Banh. But you're needed."

"When Zhaon calls, who cannot answer?" Banh waited for some indication of where Kurin—no, the *Emperor*—wished him. It would not be the first time he had spread out his charts while afoot, but Tamuron had rarely made him do so unless dire necessity was at hand.

For example, when a battle loomed, and the warlord wished

to know what currents among the stars might be harnessed or diverted to make victory a little more likely. *Merely another arrow in a general's quiver*, his lord had said once or twice, *but a useful one, Banh, especially with a truthful mouth.*

"Well said. Please, make yourself comfortable. My father had you sit there, did he not?" Kurin indicated the low scribe's table to his left, its highly carved front bearing a hunting scene. It was also painfully familiar, another old friend. It was from the ancestral manse of Garan itself, and Tamuron had remarked more than once upon its presence. *He should probably be repainted, but he's such a cheerful fellow.*

"Often." There was a knot in Banh's throat, and he had to swallow twice to clear it. "But you are Emperor now, and nobody should presume."

"Very true." Kurin folded his hands inside his sleeves, and his smile turned catlike. Indeed, the expression was very much like his mother's, and Banh had to stifle a flare of... was it disgust? He loved all Tamuron's children, suspecting he would have none of his own. "We are old friends, though. I should hope you would always speak your mind."

If it were your eldest brother sitting upon that bench, I would. It would be a foolish thing to say, but he was tempted.

Very tempted. "I shall do my best." Even the cushion behind the desk had not changed, its embroidery dingy but carefully, thoroughly done. For some reason it was the stitchery upon a simple pillow that made Banh's eyes prickle; it was one of the few items left from Tamuron's spear-wife Shiera. Her husband and son were both gone; Banh only hoped the lady herself was comfortably ensconced in one of Heaven's many halls. Possibly reunited with the man who had, for all his other queens and concubines, loved her first.

And, Banh thought, quite probably loved her the most.

"It's difficult, isn't it?" Kurin's gaze was not upon him, thankfully, though whether it was because he was allowing Banh a few moments to collect himself or because he was truly interested in the tables of eunuchs and ministers busily putting new seals upon the decrees was an open question. "I keep expecting to see him striding in, demanding to know why I'm in his seat."

What could Banh say? "*We see them oft, the shades; Who can tell what Heaven intends?*"

"Huar Guin's *Book of Tactics.*" Kurin nodded approvingly. "A fine quotation to start our session with. What does the night sky say, my old tutor? No doubt there have been one or two changes of late."

Oh, there have. "Newcomers, and yet more old friends." He loosened the cases from their leather belt, settled himself as usual, and spread out the first chart. "There is a new star in the northern sky, and several of the houses are in disarray."

"Oh, yes, portentous indeed. But please, my old teacher, do not take a wandering way to the heart of the lesson this time. What does it *mean*?" Kurin still gazed upon the eunuchs and scribes, his profile sharper than Garan Tamuron's and his topknot-cage glittering with golden filigree. "The stars are all very well, but we need certainties."

"And Heaven should strew them like stones upon the road? Even for emperors, the celestial lands do not perform like trained pets." The astrologer could not keep the sharpness from his tone. Kurin's tutors had ever found him bright enough, certainly, but sometimes even a loving uncle could think high station and a clinging mother might turn a child somewhat lazy.

"I see." Kurin's attention still apparently rested upon his scribes, busily turning his pronouncements and decisions into proclamation, directive, and decree. "So the stars cannot tell me when the assassin will strike, or where Khir will attack? Not to mention the Pale Horde, which my father was most exercised about?"

"Is that what you would ask of the stars, then? A schedule like a schoolboy's?" Banh clicked his tongue, an old disapproving noise. Kurin collected all the usual accomplishments, and had fulfilled princely requirements.

But the show, and not the substance, had ever filled his eyes and liver. He had set his sights on the throne, now he had it, and he wished for the stars to bow into his presence like a faithful steward bearing the day's appointments scribbled or neatly outlined upon a thin, temporary scroll.

"What use are the stars if they will not give details?" One of Kurin's eyebrows arched, and his mouth had tightened. He turned his gaze to the astrologer now, and there was no trace of the warmth a different child of Garan Tamuron's might bestow upon one of their father's oldest friends.

"The stars have many duties." Banh exhaled softly. It was only to be expected that grief—or other, darker feelings—would make a new ruler's temper sharp. Heaven knew it was turning his own to a sword sharp enough to please even Garan Jin, or Zakkar Kai. "To chart a nation's course, to provide warnings of great disruption, and to keep us from committing great wrongs."

"Ah." Kurin nodded as if he was a sage finding a hole in an interlocutor's argument. Well, power was headier than sohju, and it rested within him now. "So, the stars foretold the great disruption of my father's ascension?"

They did, and I was too blind to see. "The star in the North is likely your father's new mansion, oh Emperor of Zhaon."

For some reason, that made the young man frown. "*Kurin* will do, Banh, as usual."

"One may be invited to informality, but never presume it." Oh yes, Banh knew very well what he could presume, as a tavern-boy raised to greatness by a man who was now among Heaven's shining number.

"That sounds like my uncle talking." Kurin settled himself more firmly upon the Throne. Try as he might, Banh could not help but see the shadow of another man there—but not Garan Tamuron.

No, instead he saw his lord's eldest son, tall and broad-shouldered, with a bright gaze and a pained tightness to his mobile mouth. Takyeo would have already turned to the matters at hand after greeting Banh with much civility, and there would be none of the nebulous...what was it he was feeling?

He had helped to raise all Tamuron's children. It was not right that he should feel...afraid.

His head-meat, accustomed to pawing feline-light at questions even while the rest of him slept, ate, or performed other acts necessary to life, could not stop considering who had the most to gain from the relentless attacks upon Garan Takyeo and his new bride. Who had stood in the room with his eldest brother's swiftly cooling corpse and said, *This is where we discover who has won.*

Who, after all, had been the receptacle of Garan Yulehi-a Gamwone's soft, relentless, dripping poison for his entire life? The First Queen—or now, First Mother of the Revered Emperor—was now somewhat immured in her quarters. Her servants, those pale, large-eyed, skinny maids gossip called *the queen's spiders,* were in the process of being replaced with others just as creeping but whose loyalty lay with her son instead of her royal self, and though it was high time for such a development it should have been Takyeo commanding as much.

Even if Tamuron's eldest son and chosen heir might have been entirely too kind and filial to do so, he might have been prevailed upon. By Takshin, at least, if no one else—and it was chilling to think of what the First Queen could have done with a child of her second son's temper, if he had not been sent to Shan and marred by another queen.

The thought that perhaps Kurin was not responsible for Takyeo's death but had not moved to stop Garan Gamwone from doing something...drastic...was even more chilling, especially since Banh should have seen the danger more clearly. Not only that, but *Tamuron* should have seen it, and though thinking ill of your lord ascended to Heaven was a terrible thing, Banh was.

He absolutely was, and it pained him deeply. Mrong Banh cleared his throat. "I am not certain you mean that as a compliment, Kurin."

At least the new Emperor had the grace to look momentarily taken aback. "Merely an observation. What *can* the stars tell us?"

"There will be war before winter," Banh said, quietly. If this youth wished for predictions, he could make a few, either from the motions of Heaven or from solid peasant sense. "Famine looms, though the harvest will be fine. There is disease in the provinces, my lord." There had been since spring, and it was not retreating in the dry time as it usually did. "Heaven is angered."

Kurin freed a hand from his sleeve. His palm was full of carved scentwood beads—it was one of his father's kombin, certainly not his favorite. Those would have perished in flame, partly to provide an ascended Emperor with beloved articles and partly to keep illness from clinging to its surface and infecting a new reign.

"The Pale Horde will come north," he said, as thoughtfully as his father ever had. "It is not like them to begin so far south, nor so early in the year; it can only mean they are hungrier than usual. And they sent my sister's..." The words halted; his face hardened.

The bitterness in Banh's throat was just as thick. He had thought Sabwone's marriage a relief, that it would steady the Second Concubine's pretty, haughty daughter who had been such a winning if slightly spoiled child once. At least Tamuron had ascended before news of his eldest daughter's fate had reached Zhaon-An.

"Perhaps I should go to meet them," Kurin said. "What would come of such a decision, Banh?"

Glory in battle, like your father. Who would not have asked me whether he should ride or no, only the most advantageous day to set forth once he had decided to do so. It was unkind of Banh to judge a son so harshly. Who, after all, could compare with the man who had unified Zhaon? "Whatever Heaven wills, my lord Emperor. I can tell you the most auspicious day for such a journey, and can advise that you may wish to consult with a general or two."

"Meaning Kai." Kurin did not make a slightly ill-bred face as Fifth Prince Sensheo would have upon uttering the name. "Who will advise me with an eye to his own chances, no doubt."

"No." Mrong Banh would wish Kai was here to partake of this conversation, but that was a selfish wish indeed. The general was far safer where he was, though it no doubt galled him to depend on missives from the capital for news. "He will advise you with an eye to Zhaon's well-being."

"Perhaps he thinks they are one and the same." Kurin's gaze, uncomfortably sharp, was now avid as well.

Just like his mother's.

Banh had grown used to Tamuron estimating merit fairly. It was an uncommon quality, and of course Kurin had never truly liked Kai. He was not as hateful as Sensheo, but the new Emperor's antipathy was worrisome nonetheless. "You know better." It was all he could say.

"Do I?" Kurin examined his childhood tutor, and the gleam in his dark gaze was not quite new but certainly unpleasant. So was the faint color in his cheeks.

Zakkar Kai would not raise his banners and ride in the manner of his dead Emperor, who he had served to the end. Not unless it became…necessary, and Banh had comforted himself all during the tendays of full mourning with the thought that Kurin, bowed beneath the weight of his new status, might be amenable to learning a lesson or two from the men his father had trusted.

If it were necessary, Banh wondered, who would he choose? He hoped Heaven would not lay the quandary before him. "*A wise man only sees his true enemies.*"

"Huar Guin again." The new Emperor rubbed at the kombin's beads, but not as his father would have. "A very military choice for quotations, Banh."

There was nothing he could say if Kurin was determined to take offense. And there was very little he could do if the new Emperor was determined to see a threat where none existed. So Mrong Banh dropped his gaze to his charts, traced upon fine paper made of rags or pounded rai, and held his tongue. It was the silence of a peasant who knew very well which way the wind would comb the rai, as the proverb said, and it was his only means of chastising a former pupil of now almost celestial status.

The quiet stretched taut, a rope between a reluctant ox and the farmer seeking its strength in the field. What had Kurin

expected from a man who remembered him in a child's clout? Had
he thought Banh would mouth a merchant's fulsome praise or a
tavern-boy's obsequious falsity?

"Perhaps you'd best return to your tower, old friend." Kurin was
not now studying Banh; instead, his gaze turned a fair distance
down the vermilion-pillared hall, where a knot of rich-robed ministers had gathered, obviously waiting for the conference to be finished and weighing any change in the astrologer's status with avid
interest. "Consult the stars again, and we shall speak further later."

"As the Emperor commands." He rolled his charts quickly, not
caring if they wrinkled. Suddenly, he could not stand this glittering hall full of murmurs. He bowed, rose, bowed again, descended
the steps, bowed once more, and backed the few steps from the
royal presence as etiquette demanded. It was a ceremony he and
Tamuron had long ago dispensed with, but better safe than sorry.

Kurin had already beckoned the ministers forward. Perhaps the
new Emperor might even find himself a new astrologer.

Banh left the royal presence with a troubled heart, though his
expression was set and mild as ever. He was glad his upbringing
had granted him a peasant's stubborn habit of hiding true feelings.
It was no use misleading himself, even if he were young enough to
attempt such a thing.

He wished it were Garan Takyeo sitting upon that padded
bench.

Sooner or later Mrong Banh would fall from a royal patron's
favor, if he had not already, and his comfortable retirement would
be lost. His fate was too small for the stars to bother with a warning.
Zhaon's fate was another matter entirely, and already he mourned
for what the land Garan Tamuron had reunited would soon suffer.

He would retreat to his tower, certainly—but only to make such
arrangements as he reasonably could for his inevitable, poverty-
stricken old age. He could only hope to acquit himself with a fraction of the courage Garan Tamuron or his eldest son had shown
upon their deathbeds when it arrived.

Unbecoming in a
Noblewoman

Her braided, coiled hair was held in an unfamiliar fashion with only bentpins to secure it, and Komor Yala's dark blue dress was modest enough to satisfy even the most rigid of Khir etiquette. Anh had settled near the sitting-room door, glancing into the hall at intervals; her task was both to safeguard Yala's honor by watching what occurred and also to warn her lady of large-eared servants hurrying past.

Even the Jonwa was not safe, and well Yala knew it. She folded her hands inside her sleeves and bowed, a quick flicker-glance passing over the two Khir noblemen awaiting her with every evidence of patience, if not pleasure. "My lord Moruri, my lord Hazuni," she murmured. It was a relief to speak her native tongue again, even if Zhaon was slip-slurring, dragging at each word since she had spoken little else for such a long while. "Please, sit. Will you have tea? Though there is no *kou bah*. Forgive me, but the Zhaon cooks at this palace do not know how to prepare such a thing." One would have to send to the Khir section of the city to find some, and in this awful heat, by the time it arrived the pastry would be in sad shape indeed.

Dao, playing the clever merchant, had brought some to the Artisan's Home inside the palace complex. She had not even had the chance to taste it before disaster struck that day.

"Lady Komor." Moruri Keiyan bowed, perhaps a little more deeply than he should have, which forced the Hazuni son to do so as well. "Please accept my apology for the manner in which the news of your father was brought. Lord Namori would offer his apology directly, but he was called to attend Zhaon's Emperor with Lord Shohuri."

Shohuri. Ah, Father liked him. The thought of her father was a sewing-pin thrust through her heart, but Yala indicated the largest table, a gently steaming teapot placed upon a yeoyan-wood tray and a plate of Zhaon sweets standing sentinel nearby, ready for the guests. A pile of small gifts wrapped fetchingly in cheerful green babu-patterned silk stood upon another, smaller table nearby, awaiting the proper moment to be pressed upon her guests. "No apology is needed, Lord Moruri. I am grateful for Lord Namori's honesty. It is a rare quality, even among noblemen."

Even rarer was beginning a visit with an apology; even if Namori had consented to have one proffered on his behalf, it was a signal event.

Just what it denoted, though, she was not entirely certain. Yet.

"Indeed it is." Lord Hazuni, the swallows embroidered upon his sleeves dipping as he moved, waited until she and Moruri were seated to settle himself. "You have naught to fear, Lady Komor. By all accounts you have left nothing undone, before the princess's... misfortune, and after. Felicitations upon your upcoming wedding, by the way."

"My lord Hazuni does me much honor." She fastened her gaze upon the teapot, and poured as carefully as if she were still at Hai Komori under her father's searching grey gaze. "The former Emperor brushed the endorsement upon his deathbed." Unspoken was the fact that a noblewoman could not have argued with such an offer unless her father had banned the match, and her cheeks were warm. Her blush was not shame, Yala reminded herself sternly, but modesty.

Her humors were in a riot this morning. She longed to scream, to shout, to *make* these two listen—but the visit had to proceed at its own pace, waiting for the prey to be flushed before she could loose her hawk.

"So we are told." Moruri lifted his cup and breathed in the steam, with a small nod to show polite appreciation. In Khir, it could be served at boiling instead of merely near it, and swallowed in a gulp at the proper moment. "And now I must beg your pardon for bringing our visit to business so quickly. It is not mannerly of me, but we may only have a short while to speak privately."

"Indeed," she said softly, holding her sleeve aside to finish pouring into Lord Hazuni's cup. "I was about to beg your pardon for the very same thing, Lord Moruri."

A few moments of silence and a searching look exchanged between her guests could mean surprise or relief; she could not quite tell yet. If Takshin arrived, despite having escorted the other two Khir lords to his elder brother's royal presence, she would have to think quickly—and speak with even more speed.

"In Khir, a woman does not speak of politics." Lord Hazuni lifted his own cup, fine Gurai slipware painted with a particularly aesthetic character for *health*. "However, we are in Zhaon, and you have been uniquely placed to observe this new Emperor. I must ask you to set aside any maidenly reserve and speak plainly. Were your father alive, I would no doubt carry a missive from him granting permission."

"No doubt." The girl who had left her homeland at Mahara's side would have almost-quailed at daring to speak of such matters before two Khir noblemen. But since then, she had faced assassins, treachery, and much worse; she was no longer that Komor Yala.

It was strange that she could bear the same name, the same face, the same dresses, and yet be utterly changed in the secret chambers of her liver and head-meat.

"You are in very great danger," she continued, speaking low and quickly. At any moment Takshin might return; Lady Su or Lady Hansei might arrive to share a hostess's duty and not so incidentally gape at the foreigners. "I do not know yet who paid for my princess's misfortune, and until I do I cannot leave this warren.

There is more at stake here than you may know, my lords. I cannot tell with any certainty what the new Emperor intends since mourning and other duties have kept me trammeled here instead of listening to what I may learn." She poured a half-measure into her own cup, as a Khir woman must do when drinking with men not of her clan.

They exchanged another look. "Is there aught else you may tell us?" Moruri, brusque but not insulted by her directness, was wearing what he probably thought to be an encouraging expression.

Yala considered him through the steam rising from her tea. She barely touched her lips to the ceramic rim, freeing her guests of any duty to their hostess's comfort. She said nothing. Demure quiet was a weapon now, to be wielded like the *yue*.

"What my lord Moruri means," Hazuni said hastily, "is that our mission was to present condolences to the Crown Prince. We arrive to find him Emperor *and* ascended to Heaven, and of course the danger in presenting ourselves to his brother is immense. But we also have a second mission." He paused, glancing again at his leader like the second upon a hunt, gauging whether the chase could begin. "Ashani Daoyan is missing."

Yala set her cup down. "Forgive my bluntness, my lords, but there are those in Khir no doubt overjoyed at the fact."

She gazed fully upon them as a Khir noblewoman would be ashamed to do, alert to any small, flickering expressions. Hazuni looked shocked, Moruri slightly pained but then grudgingly admiring. Or so she thought, and a lifetime of observing other fleeting changes upon noble faces stood Yala in good stead now.

Mahara was not the only one who had suffered assassination attempts. Komori Baiyan's expression had oft been a thundercloud when there was one upon his friend Dao, and Yala had never dared ask her brother about them directly, simply glad they seemed always to fail. Nor had Ashani Daoyan ever alluded to them in her presence—what nobleman would, before a Khir lady?—but the fact, like a rock in a swift stream, was impossible to ignore.

And now she wondered what else Daoyan had never told her,

what slights he had borne she never witnessed. If these nobles wished him some ill, she would misdirect them.

"The Great Rider is not among them," Moruri said, diplomatically enough. "Nor am I, nor any of my fellow lords, Lady Komor."

The chase had begun. Yala could not stand in her stirrups, nor could she cry aloud at a well-aimed bolt. She was forced to study her teacup, turning it a quarter for luck and returning her hands to her lap, demurely clasped. Professions of loyalty were all very well, but she needed more if she was to do what she intended.

And her gaze did not flicker. She quelled the urge to drop it to her lap with her hands, as a Khir noblewoman should.

"We lost his trail at Dua-An," Hazuni said quietly. "He almost certainly went south from there. And, Komor Yala, he would not pass through this place without attempting…" He did not quite blush or look disgusted, but he did cough slightly, forced to utter something indelicate before her. "Forgive me. But your *damoi* was his friend, and the son of the Great Rider seemed to prefer the company of Hai Komori above all others."

"Illegitimate son," she murmured, much as Dao might have. No—he would say it with a bright, unsettling smile, forcing his interlocutors to address his charge or flee before it.

"He was legitimized before you left Khir, Lady Komor." Still, Hazuni's tone was respectful. Another Khir lord might hiss an imprecation at her daring, especially if he sought to remove a stain left upon a clan by a woman's honorlessness. "You are seeking to protect him, as you protected the Great Rider's daughter."

The allusion to her failure threatened to stain Yala's cheeks even more deeply with red humors, but she held grimly to her silence and self-control. The partitions to the garden-porch were drawn tight, conserving any cool air that could be found and denying dust entrance to this room; she wished they were open, if only so she could look outside and gather herself. Instead, she studied both lords of her homeland with quite unbecoming directness.

Oh, Dao. Forgive me, I am doing what I must.

"My lady Komor." Moruri Keiyan finally spoke. "I swear to

you, by the great goddess herself and the honor of my family, by the shades of my ancestors and my hope for strong sons, Ashani Daoyan has nothing to fear from me or those in my company. We are charged by the Great Rider to return his last remaining son to Khir, and I would not fail in my duty."

It was the strongest, most binding oath a nobleman of Khir could swear, and its breaking would anger the goddess of horse and hunt. Even the most irreligious would hesitate to utter it as a lie; besides, if they meant Dao harm, Yala had a way of ensuring she could at least protect Mahara's royal brother during any meeting she could arrange.

After all, her *yue* had already tasted a man's blood. And if she fell defending Dao from yet another attempt, it might expunge the shame of having failed her princess.

Perhaps they read the decision upon her face, for Moruri leaned slightly toward her; Hazuni lifted his teacup, turning his gaze to the door. Yala glanced at Anh, who had never given any indication of knowing the Khir language; her kaburei regarded her with wide, anxious dark eyes and shook her head slightly. There was nobody in the Jonwa hall outside this small sitting-room.

It was the very room she had received the news of Mahara's death in. Now she hoped to save her princess's brother.

"My lords," she said softly, "there are new tombs to the north of the city, white as mourning itself. You have paid your respects there already. I must beg you to listen well and do exactly as I bid, though it is not fit for even a noblewoman to command lords such as yourself."

Moruri nodded. "Consider us your attentive students, Lady Komor." He paused, and his grey Khir gaze, clear and honest, locked with hers. "Your father would be proud of your service to Hai Ashani."

Yala could, at least, be glad Komori Dasho was not alive to witness this. "I thank you for your kindness in saying so, Lord Moruri. Now, listen closely. At dusk three days from now I shall go to the tombs, and you shall as well."

Quietly, quickly, Komor Yala laid out her plan.

Whichever Will Suit

The barbarians had damaged much, but theirs was a child's tantrum for the sheer pleasure of breakage and wrack. Perhaps Nijera's princess—her queen, of however short a duration the title—could have waited, could have escaped at the last moment as the doors of Shan's ancestral palace gave under the onslaught and the filthy rai-pale beasts cavorted through the halls tearing at hangings, breaking crockery, splintering furniture, and destroying whatever they did not wish to carry away as plunder.

Or perhaps not. A girl stubborn enough to slit her wrists in a palanquin could probably not be dissuaded from a grand gesture while screaming barbarians ready for rape and murder swarmed up palace stairs. Daebo Nijera, safe again among civilized people and a strong cortege of well-armed lords, now had to face the knowledge that she had fled instead of attempting to force herself through the same aperture her cousin's brattish child had utilized for an honorable death.

And for what? A young royal life gone, so many other lives broken or gone as well, the careful work of many hands smashed or ripped or simply defaced—just sheer, idiot waste.

Hiding in sewer-tunnels and among peasant huts while the barbarians went about their work had been a terrifying penance, but now that she and Buwon had reached safety she was entirely certain she deserved something far worse. The Shan lord had been scrupulously respectful of her person, and had snatched the knife from her hands as she finished shearing her hair and attempted to turn it upon her own throat.

None of that, he had hissed, in their dialect. *You are needed, Lady Nijera, and I will have you remember as much.*

At the time she had thought she was merely called upon to give a witness's account of his queen's last moments before the king of Shan gave them both leave to commit an honorable suicide. At least, the stunned witless noise inside her head had grasped that notion, and she had set about making herself as useful as possible in the meantime.

The selfish, grasping thing within her, the one which clung to life as all creatures did, had even been miserably grateful for the reprieve.

Now the palace of Shan hummed with activity, cleaning and reordering, but Nijera sent the kaburei and maid ordered to attend her away as kindly as possible. Her entire body ached, and this tiny room, while familiar enough—adjacent to her royal charge's quarters so that even at night the sound of movement or a servant's hurrying would alert her to Sabwone's needs—also bore signs of the Pale Horde's dirt.

It would be fitting to clean it with her own hands, but there were larger considerations. After the frantic escape—Lord Buwon dragging her from the casement, the slippery splashing through the palace's hidden tunnel-exits reeking of sewage they habitually carried into other even more malodorous tunnels, then an unsteady galloping upon wild-eyed, hard-caught horses through a bloody sunset in the direction the round, grim-faced Shan lord thought most likely to bring them to some aid before taking shelter in the smoking ruin of a peasant hut—it was strange to sit upon a torn cushion in the fashion of a noblewoman, staring at her unfamiliar, rein-blistered hands, her skin crawling with the need for a hot bath.

A luxury she did not deserve.

Hadn't this been such a pretty room? Certainly nicer than her closet at the great ancestral keep near Duhau-An where she had spent her days attempting to make herself serviceable enough the servants would not gaze pityingly upon a poor, cast-aside cousin. This room was big enough for a bed instead of a pallet, a wardrobe with shelves and cubbyholes behind a painted door, and a tiny writing-table that had been chopped to splinters. At least soft mirrorlight could burnish the polished wooden floor, bright and comforting; even in the time they had squatted here, the beasts had not been able to reach the great lenses bringing light into the heart of stone structures.

They had broken into the wardrobe and dragged out every dress and shift, though, even and probably especially the pretty ones which did not need much darning or alteration, gifts from Garan Daebo-a Luswone. A gesture of thanks for the careful care Nijera had promised to take with the First Concubine's daughter.

A soft step and a mannerly throat-clearing jerked her head up, like a tired horse scenting fire.

For a moment she could not quite put a name to the lean, beak-nosed figure in Shan nobleman's black at the doorway. He was still in his riding-boots, disdaining the cleanliness of slippers indoors— well, who could blame him, with what the pale barbarians had smeared upon the floors? Even the lowest beggar in Zhaon, Shan, Anwei, or Khir knew not to squat in a hallway to unload their bowels.

A great bright flash of pointless hate burned behind Nijera's breastbone and passed away, probably into her liver to poison her humors. It was not meet for a noblewoman to feel such things, but she could not help herself.

Tall, proud-nosed Lord Suron Haon examined her, and she wondered if he bore some message or simply wished to view the wreckage for himself. The pad of pounded rai in his throat moved as he swallowed, his gaze finally catching hers. "You are alive," he said, in laborious Zhaon. The burring of the Shan dialect under the words was not quite unpleasant.

Nijera set her chin. "Sadly, yes."

Oh, it was all useless; she was fated to suffer, but it took very little effort to twist scraps of cotton together to make a rope. Then she would only have to find a beam strong enough to bear her weight. It was an unexpected relief to have an end in sight.

His expression changed slightly, but she was not required to watch it. She dropped her gaze to her brutalized hands again. They looked like a peasant girl's; perhaps she would have been happier as such a creature.

"I should not have left you."

What, under Heaven, could she say to *that*? She had thought, before he left, that they...understood each other. Certainly she had cherished a silly hope or two unfitting in a poor relation, even one raised to the position of chief lady-in-waiting to a queen. "You had no choice, Lord Suron." In other words, she released him from any obligation, however unspoken.

I shall return, he had said before he left, standing in the door of Sabwone's quarters with his head bent toward hers, the mere fact of his presence burning in her middle like strong sweet tea. *And if our queen does not behave, I shall take the matter to our lord king. Fear nothing.*

Suron took a step into the room. The floor creaked slightly; his boot-toe ground smashed porcelain—the remains of a jar of nia oil, once painted with a character for *patience*.

It had been carried step by step, li by li, from her ancestral home. Now it was merely shards.

"Lady Nijera." Why did he have to sound so...so soft, so uncertain, and use her personal name as well? There was no need to remind her she had failed in her duty.

She knew as much. If he would simply say what he had come to and leave, she could set about finding enough scraps to twist into a rope. "Lord Suron Haon." She took refuge in formality and lifted her hands slightly, ashamed of their disrepair but unable to help the movement. "There is no need to speak."

"Is there not?" Of course a nobleman would wish to fulfill a duty promptly, however painful. She could even admire it in him.

"I do not wish you to feel...beholden." A furious heat mounted her cheeks. She knew she was sallow, round enough for beauty but lacking the grace that would bring it, and a bearer of ill-luck besides. What other explanation was there for such tragedy to follow her faltering footsteps?

There had not even been the chance to gather the princess's body. How could Nijera face her ancestors to offer incense or anything else, how could she face the First Concubine, let alone the Emperor of Zhaon? Of course that august being would not deign to take any notice of her, nor would the already-disappointed shades of her clan, and yet Nijera's heart quaked within her ribs at the thought.

"Beholden?" Suron repeated the word, as if he did not know what the Zhaon meant.

She was far too exhausted to translate it into her imperfect Shan. "My lord, I am...I feel somewhat ill." There. He would be able to withdraw now, understanding she had no desire to hold him to whatever he might have promised. Or perhaps he had only been amusing himself with pretty implications, as noblemen at court were wont to do.

"Where are your maids?" His tone approached *thunderous*. "I shall take the sudo to them myself."

"I sent them..." She made another gesture, her throat aching. If he stayed much longer she would begin to sob like a harried child, and that was not proper. "I sent them away, my lord." Her tongue would not handle the burring of Shan; still, she did her best to make her Zhaon clear and soft.

"Silly." He took another step, toeing a broken comb aside— but gently, with the delicacy of a paw-flicking feline. "Have you changed your mind then, Nijera?"

Daebo Nijera stared at her knees, covered with the remains of a dirty, horse-smelling dress. How many days had she worn it? She could not remember. "I..." Her throat was dry as the wastes the barbarians had ridden over. Why would they spend all that effort merely to smash what their betters had built and vanish afresh? Had they no shame?

She was shameless too, for she was still alive.

"I must tell you, it matters little if you have." Lord Suron took another slow deliberate step, avoiding the rags of a pretty peach cotton dress edged with pale yellow silk—one she had sewn herself from scraps and leavings in the keep near Duhau-An. It looked as if a barbarian had wiped himself with it after defecating, or used it to clean something filthy-crusted by another's foul habits. Bile whipped the back of her throat. "You are here, and will not leave."

Not alive, no. Nijera nodded, to show she understood. "Yes, my lord. I shall not leave."

"Good." Suron Haon continued his slow, inexorable approach. "My estate suffered little from the depredations, being somewhat small; you will be carried there in a bridal palanquin as soon as we may arrange for proper cloth and attendants. I have already spoken to my lord king. He thinks it a fine idea."

What? "It is unkind," she managed. "To jest with me so, my lord Suron, is *unkind.*" The tears spilled free; she could not contain them. She should not have expected better of a southron man, for all Shan was Zhaon's younger sister.

"It is not the most auspicious of beginnings, I grant." He carefully mixed a Shan word or two in with Zhaon, but very simple ones, as if speaking to a child. His tone, in fact, was one Nijera remembered using herself on the poor princess, and her shame intensified. "But it is what we have."

"I did not stop her," Nijera whispered. The scrap of silk was still in her left palm, burning through the dirt, the blisters, the throbbing that still felt the horse's shudder-gallop beneath her. She had spent at least one night—she could not remember, for their escape from the barbarians was taking on a nightmarish, slippery quality inside her head-meat—unchaperoned with Lord Buwon, never mind that dodging the victory-drunk barbarians left no time for... anything else, and she was unmarriageable anyway, too old and too poor and under the cloud of her father's fall from ministerial grace.

"I find it difficult to believe you could have," the Shan lord observed, finally halting just at the edge of the space propriety demanded between a nobleman and a lady. "She was a queen, and a thoroughgoing brat."

It was useless to bristle, but she had to make some manner of answer. "It is not meet to speak so." Nijera had been so certain Sabwone would grow past her…difficulties, and into queenly behavior. Her chin rose; she gazed steadily at him.

"I have had enough of avoiding the truth, my lady Nijera. I had to do so for years under my lord king's *mother*." His lip curled slightly, and it was perhaps a great honor that she saw his true feelings so clearly. Or—more likely—she was not judged a threat, for she was well acquainted with what people of high rank let slip when they knew you would not be believed. "Speak quickly, will you deny me?"

"I…" What could she say? "My lord Suron Haon, I am a poor cousin of a great clan, and I have failed in my duty."

"Nevertheless." He was pitiless, gazing down at her, his dark gaze utterly piercing. "You will marry me."

After the past few days, she had not thought she would ever feel shocked again, but somehow, the single sentence managed.

"Do you ask, or command?" It was an echo of their first true conversation, held just outside Zhaon-An upon a gasping-hot summer evening, Nijera aching all over from a day's worth of unaccustomed riding and further trouble settling Sabwone in the best room an inn could provide, finally retreating from the princess's presence to find the beak-nosed man wearing Shan black lingering in the hallway.

The memory was curve-edged as one of the barbarians' hook-blades, meant for sweeping a fellow rider from his saddle. She liked most of the Shan lords much better than their Zhaon counterparts, finding them direct but not cruel.

At least, not *very* cruel, despite the rumors of their Mad Queen's proclivities. *Take care*, the First Concubine had murmured. *They called the king's mother mad, and if the son follows her temper, you shall have to defend my daughter.*

Would Luswone understand that Nijera had tried? It seemed

impossible that she would ever face the First Concubine again, let alone speak to her. Surely it was cowardly, unfitting of even a poor Daebo cousin, to feel a certain relief at the thought.

"Both, my lady." Suron Haon took another cautious, considered half-step, intruding upon propriety cautiously, as if he feared *her* temper. Who ever had? "Whichever will suit."

"And do you think we will?" She squeezed both fists as a noblewoman should not, an unladylike tension, driving broken fingernails into her palms. A true noblewoman should be indolent, but what woman in her position could be? She itched all over under her filthy dress, and longed for a bath. "Suit, that is?"

"Better than your princess suited my king."

"She is—was your queen, too." Nijera regarded him steadily, her neck craned at a most unbecoming angle. Tears welling in her eyes turned him into a stretching, distorting spirit, perhaps come to drag her unworthy self into a hell. Which one, though? She had not *meant* to fail.

Daebo Nijera had meant to do her duty to the very end, but what remained when your young royal charge scrambled through a slit in stone walls and took flight, her pretty babu-patterned dress fluttering like a bird's, and a lord grabbed one's arm in a bruising grip, hissing *hist, they come; you shall not be dishonored here, my lady*?

"Yes." Then Lord Suron Haon uttered an absurdity. "Forgive me; I spoke rashly. You oft tempt me to such measures."

Had she ever been asked for forgiveness before? Nijera could not remember. "I do not mean to." Perhaps she had been misformed in her poor mother's womb. Heaven allowed such things, and often she thought perhaps that meant the celestial world was just as cruel as the middle, or the many hells beneath.

But she was a woman. What did she know? It was a matter for sages to argue upon, not her.

"I know, Daebo Nijera." The burr-buzz of Shan under her name sharpened the last syllable, the tongue vibrating behind the upper teeth. Sometimes, upon her pallet at night while traveling south to bring her princess to this land of pierced towers singing as the wind passed through, she thought of how he said her name and tried to discern why it did not irritate her to have such a mispronunciation. "Should I ask instead of commanding? I do not think you will deny me."

You are more correct than you know. "Perhaps I should," she whispered. "My princess—my queen. I was to look after her, Suron Haon. I was to protect her, I was to help her when she conceived an heir and keep her from mischief in a foreign court."

"The Tabrak are not your error, my lady, nor your concern." He folded down, an easy, fluid movement, and crouched easily as if reading a beast's tracks upon a hunt. It meant her neck did not ache as she regarded him, but it also meant he would see her disrepair and perhaps change his mind, or laugh and say *what a jest, and you believed it.* "We ride against them soon."

"Soon?" It was a whisper; the conversation was turning this way and that like a child's rai-paper kite upon a windy festival day, and she was too exhausted to follow the dancing.

Suron gazed steadily at her, and his expression was somber indeed. His boots creaked slightly as he shifted; the room's ruin had all but vanished. "As soon as we find them."

"Then I marry you, and you leave?" *Do not be stupid, Nijera.* She braced herself for laughter, or for a cold gaze and being informed she had misunderstood. It was doubly difficult to think with the warmth of his living flesh so close, a brazier upon a winter's night.

"Not right away." He shrugged, easily, his hands dangling loose as his forearms were braced upon his thighs. Any passing servant could look in, and her ruin would be complete. "But I shall return."

"Men do not return." She knew as much, from Zhaon's wars, from her own father's opening of his veins after disgrace, from every story she had ever heard around corners while she fetched, carried, sewed, served, made herself as useful as possible to apologize for her shameful survival.

"Then you will be a widow, with my estate to support you. In Shan, such creatures are not treated badly." Suron Haon tensed, though his expression—set, focused, his gaze moving over her dirty face—did not alter. "I will not brook refusal, for you would do so merely for honor's sake. Accede, and let me call the servants to attend you."

If he would not brook refusal, what did her consent matter? But Nijera did not have the heart to withhold it. If it was a failing upon her part, it was nothing new. "If you are not shamed by—"

"Do not." Now he was abrupt, sensing he had what he wished— well, he was a man. "It is agreed, and it will be so."

The tears would not halt. Nijera buried her face in her filthy hands and sobbed, and it was a lord of Shan who stroked her dress's torn shoulder, uttering soothing words. Her heart ached, though she should have been happy beyond measure at finally receiving an offer of marriage, especially from a man who was not objectionable at all and whose touch was so gentle—but oh, it came at such a cost.

Such a horrible, hideous cost.

CERTAIN CHANGES

A country bumpkin, visiting a relative lucky enough to have secured employment in Zhaon-An, might have been forgiven for thinking life in the city, let alone the great glittering palace complex, had not changed overmuch if at all. An Emperor had ascended, true—but a son of his line sat upon the Throne of Five Winds, meaning all was right under Heaven's great vault. There were still queens in the Kaeje, though they were dowager, and a concubine in the Iejo. If the Jonwa held no Crown Prince, well, it had been empty before and that would change in due time. An astrologer lived in the blue-tiled Old Tower, eunuchs hurried about upon jatajatas with their dark robes swaying, and the same ministers who had attended the ascended Emperor gathered around the new one to provide a ruler with the steady counsel of elders. The Golden in their bright armor stood at their appointed places, trained in the same manner and paved courtyards they had for the many years of Garan Tamuron's reign—and further back during the First, Second, and Third Dynasties when Zhaon had been likewise unified—and held to the same watch schedules.

The bumpkin's relative would smile fondly or bitterly, taking their cousin's arm. Were they highly educated—an aristocrat or successful merchant, a well-read courtesan or a scholar who had achieved some sinecure with the re-instituted imperial examinations the warlord from Garan had rescued from old tradition—they might murmur an allusion from the Hundreds. Others not quite so lofty, from middling merchants or successful artists and artisans to those with less legal but still highly profitable skills, might hum a tune from a successful play in the Theater District or deliver a quotation from a popular novel.

The mass underneath, from tradesman to petty merchant, theater flower to acrobat, water-seller to gutter-cleaner, might sniff and snap a proverb of pithy peasant wisdom, though peasants who worked the farmlands outside the city's encroaching arms—for like every clotting of human habitations left to itself in a modicum of peace, Zhaon-An grew beyond its ancient defensive walls along paved roads and beaten-dirt pathways, fringed by the ever-present fields necessary for its sustenance—had little time for such questions, and would put their visitor to work helping with pruning, weeding, or preliminary harvest.

In any case, the meaning, from classical allusion to expletive-laced folk saying, remained the same.

It isn't what it used to be. Yet the transition to a new reign was always a nervous time, and, well, Garan Tamuron had possessed sons aplenty to assure there would be a representative of Heaven's blessing upon the immemorial throne.

Inside the palace complex, the Second and Third Mothers of the Revered Emperor still gathered their ladies in pavilions, while courtiers, ministers, and eunuchs passed by or halted to exchange a few witty words. They sat together at many a table, the two mothers, and their concord—always pleasing, always apparent—now appeared total. Yet the place of primacy in each pavilion was left neglected, no longer dusted or arranged with embroidered cushions against the chance that a certain first-among-equals might be inclined to make an appearance. Garan Yulehi-a Gamwone was still ensconced in the luxurious Kaeje apartments that had been her home since Tamuron's taking of the city, with every corner padded and most walls double-hung with tapestries; but instead of leaving rarely, she did not leave them at all.

It was still Lord Yulehi's half of the year, but he was not followed down every hall by a chain of courtiers, nor was his attention solicited for matters minor, major, or profitable. The clan-uncle of the new Emperor attended to the ceremonial functions of chief minister, but it was Lord Hanweo who Garan Kurin tasked with those items most useful.

Or, some might say, most apt to accrue true power.

The remaining ministers and courtiers who could claim friendship with or the patronage of Lord Yulehi observed a respectful distance, but were always glad to accommodate Lord Hanweo and his clients. Who, to their credit, did not openly enjoy the event, for Lord Hanweo, as he always had during his half of the year, did not consider such enjoyment well-bred. Second Mother Garan Hanweo-a Haesara, his clan-niece, did not turn her shoulder to ladies who had sought the First Queen's favor; in any case, those were few indeed, and had been for some time.

The Golden still occupied their posts, but there were new leaders of many a shield-square. Their triumvirate of captains had been appointed by the ascended Emperor, and were apparently more than satisfied with his second-eldest son, though sometimes it was whispered that Lord Yulehi had paid signal attention to two of their number in the uncertain time of Garan Tamuron's illness.

And there was a surfeit of princes still. The Third Prince in his Shan black was just as sharp and ill-tempered as ever, but he was removing to an estate outside the city walls, and he appeared to be the next of the sons of Garan allowed to marry. Of course he could not ever take the Throne, being adopted to Shan many years ago ... but there were disturbing rumors from that southron neighbor he did not care to speak upon.

Fourth Prince Makar had preferred his estate in the Noble District even before his father's ascension, and he punctually visited his mother as he always had. He held discussions and concourse with scholars as usual during sedate teas, dinners, and evenings, and if he petitioned the new Emperor for a marriage endorsement he had done so privately. No few court ladies would have repaid his interest with lowered eyelids and subtle smiles, but without the Emperor's favor—or the Emperor's marriage and an heir produced—nothing could be arranged.

Fifth Prince Sensheo had been under house arrest after some unpleasantness, but what kind was never quite alluded to. Still, since attaining his majority he had shown no interest in anything other than racing, gambling, and short dalliances with very popular courtesans forced into retirement soon after his attentions to them faded. And the Sixth Prince was a boy yet, still living with Third Mother as he had all his life.

It was unfortunate about the First Princess, of course, but speaking of such things was impolite at best. Gossip held the Emperor would ride out to war like his father and punish the barbarians if they dared to come northward, not merely for Zhaon but for a beloved sister. And there was, after all, Second Princess Gamnae, not quite ready for a marriage alliance but certainly, soon…

Courtiers arrived to seek a post or preferment, nobles to be confirmed in their ancestral holdings and to perhaps make an alliance or gain a patron closer to the font of power. Yet those who had kin already highly placed to greet them were given fresh advice about who to cultivate or avoid, advice that would have been unthinkable a few moon-turnings ago.

The servants still hurried to and fro, yet there were new faces among their number. Some were merely replacements for those honorably retired with whatever spoils a career spent close to the good luck flowing from wealth and power could grant, pensions or sinecures. There were familiar faces still, of course—Yona for one, who had served the First Mother almost all her life—but their habits had subtly changed, in one way or another.

And, in a hut secluded from the royal baths, a certain bath-girl who had offered signal service to the ascended Emperor breathed her tortuous last. Of course no illness could be allowed near the pools and steam-rooms, the places where the bodies of royalty or nobility were washed, scraped, cleansed, massaged, or otherwise tended to.

It simply wasn't safe.

Servants sickened even in the most benign and Heaven-blessed of reigns, and perhaps her malady had come from grief, or even from proximity to the ascended Emperor's final ailment. A surprising number of palace inhabitants, though, commented quietly upon the death of an insignificant bath-girl. The news reached even into the Kaeje, where, it was implied—oh, certainly never stated explicitly, that would be ill-bred or outright dangerous— that the First Mother of the Revered Emperor was informed of the event by the new Emperor himself during a tense family dinner. Second Princess Gamnae was not present, being invited to the Second Mother's apartments more and more often.

And accepting the invitations with the new Emperor's blessing, it was said.

It was also said very quietly, with half-smiles or significantly raised eyebrows, that the First Mother had noticed the faces among her servants changing, one by one. That she had noticed the gifts arriving at punctual intervals according to the complex calendar of court life had changed ever so subtly. Not in quality, of course, but in kind. And even those who might have been desperate or foolish enough to seek her patronage before suddenly found other avenues for advancement, other risks to take.

She was First Mother of the Revered Emperor of Zhaon, first among equals. Not only that, but her second son was to be married soon to a woman who, if foreign, wore silk.

But she had not yet been visited by her prospective daughter-in-law.

Garan Yulehi-a Gamwone, the feared First Queen of Zhaon, lingered in her silken, padded prison. And if she raged, if she flung small items or pinched the hands that helped her dress, if she hissed imprecations or made hints that before that would have sent certain underlings scurrying, none could tell.

None of her servants *dared* tell. They knew their true master, and his grasp was absolute. Like any loving son, though, he protected his mother.

At least that had not changed.

For now.

WOLF'S PAW

D usk gathered bruise-purple at the close of yet another hot Zhaon day. He did not feel the discomfort, either of sweat or of short breath in the oppressiveness. Instead, Ashani Daoyan felt like the heat-lightning striking distant mountains, or leaping from pregnant-bellied clouds who had decided, after all, not to drop their cargo of rain.

Not yet.

He had not expected another meeting so soon. Perhaps something had occurred to change Yala's mind. He was, after all, her oldest friend, and with her father gone, who did she have to cling to? Certainly no one in Zhaon.

Or so he hoped. There were disturbing signs, like that scar-faced Zhaon prince calling her *little lure*, with all his hints and attempting to force her into a marriage so far beneath her worth.

It would be a fine prank to subtract her from that grasp.

He was cogitating upon the best way to do so—would it be worth the trouble to leave a small note after the fact, to let that prince know he'd been outplayed?—when a tingle went across his nerves. The question of just where to secrete himself in the new, bone-white tomb complex just north of the city's walls was a difficult one, and he thought he'd done rather well.

Especially since the lady had arrived with company.

Komor Yala walked upon empty white paving, her head down

and that constant kaburei at her shoulder. The girl with the leather-wrapped braids was attempting to look in every direction at once, as if she suspected Daoyan had brought an army to spirit her precious lady away. Of course he could handle such a slight problem; the peasant girl might even be left alive to attend her mistress's needs during the journey if Dao was in a giving mood.

For this particular lady, who could be otherwise? He hopped lithely from the top of the unused tomb-wall, glad for the dusk. There were rumors he didn't like swirling through the Khir quarter where his countrymen accreted, refugees and merchants—not to mention a few noble sons—come to make their fortunes in a land less strict than their own.

He could play any of those parts, and more, but he would be glad to leave this stinking, filthy, luxurious city behind. Daoyan had decided south to Anwei, despite the troubling rumors of barbarians the color of polished rai, would be best. Eluding pursuit in that direction would be a child's game, even if he had a reluctant Khir noblewoman to shepherd.

She would not remain reluctant for long. Every fresh li between them and Khir would be a liberation.

He followed the women at a distance, keeping a line of decorative just-planted shrubbery between him and his quarry. Attendants housed in shacks clinging to the outer wall of the complex scurried forth before dawn and a decent interval after sundown to water the forlorn things, attempting to keep them alive until the rains of autumn. They also beat gongs to warn any august spirits of their advent, which was all to the better.

Yala moved with such grace, though there was slight stiffness as she made her bows at the old Emperor's tomb, lingered slightly longer before the freshly carved characters on the carved stone slab sealing Garan's firstborn son's urn into the wall, then proceeded to her obvious goal: a princess's death-marker. Still, if she was consenting to leave with him, he could afford to let her say goodbye.

The kaburei kept craning her neck, peering into the shadows. She carried an unlit lamp, but a bobbing luminescent rai-paper globe and a single female servant were faint protection for a noble-woman after dusk. The Zhaon did not protect their women as they should. Soon Yala would not stir a step without Ashani Daoyan's explicit permission, and though he did not intend to be too exact-ing, he would also be cautious.

It was eerie here as the shadows gathered and the sun was a dying crimson ember in the west. He had thought of braving that sand sea full of spiny succulents, but not with such precious cargo. Anwei would do, despite the rumors. Swinging wide to avoid the barbarians would even add piquancy to the journey.

The Tabrak were welcome to their latest meal. They could eat the North too, for all Dao cared. Imagining his father dealing with such visitors almost made him smile.

He approached cautiously, his ears prickling with alertness. Small sounds told of others visiting—perhaps the attendants, per-haps those who wished to beg intercession from one newly ascended to Heaven's many-chambered palaces—if that was, indeed, where Garan Tamuron had gone.

Dao had his doubts.

The kaburei started and let out a thin little cry when she noticed his presence; Yala turned her head and caught sight of him. She was somber, his beautiful girl, especially in indigo silk with the pale slash of mourning upon her sleeve. Her hair was dressed low in a nest of complicated braids, but no hairpin's shivering decora-tion swung with the motion as she faced him.

That was the only wrongness; he paused between one step and the next. "My lady," he said, softly, in Khir. "I did not mean to startle you."

The kaburei took a single step sideways, meaning to thrust her-self between her mistress and any danger; for that, he could forgive her much. If she understood the northern language she made no sign.

"Ashani Daoyan." Yala bowed, the deep obeisance due the acknowledged son and heir of the Great Rider. There was a telltale stiffness at the very end of the motion—was she in pain? Had one of the filthy Zhaon dared to lay hands upon her? Or perhaps an ambitious assassin, since she refused to stay cloistered as a noble girl should? "You honor a humble handmaiden."

"Very formal." Dao tensed, his head cocking. "And you are not alone, my lady Komor."

"No." Her eyes, the silver of a noble's gaze more precious than ingots of gold or copper, were wide, though her pupils were swelling in the fast-falling gloom. Upon her tongue Khir was a song, a sathron's melody after the mush-mouth dissonance of Zhaon. "Forgive me. You must forgive me, Dao."

"Of course." *What would I not forgive thee, my love?* How he had longed to quote Khao Cao to her, despite that fellow's sometimes illbred behavior. It was the only poetry that could even begin to approach doing her justice. "What is it you are supposed to have done?"

"The Khir delegation." Her hands were folded inside her sleeves, but he caught a betraying quiver in indigo silk. "They brought news, and..." Her throat worked, but she lifted her chin, her eyes glimmering with heavy salt water. "My father. He is..."

Apparently she could not make herself say it.

"I am grieved to hear it, though he knew it would not be long." Daoyan longed to push the kaburei aside, to draw Yala into his arms for the first time and comfort her. "He wished for you to land safely, did he not? The last falling blossom of Hai Komori; I will keep you safe." It was even a promising couplet, the rhyme staggered as in some of Khao's finer work.

"I cannot be safe." The sadness in the syllables was too much to be borne; Komor Yala's gaze dropped. No doubt she would feel the burden of shame at surviving an august parent's loss more than most. "Not until I know."

Ah. So she was still determined to dig in the middenheap of Ashan Mahara's death. There were good reasons not to let her. "Let it be enough that you have not shared her fate. I will free you, especially of that *prince*."

"My captivity is endurable, Dao. I must avenge my princess. You should understand as much." Did she seek to shame him?

He could have pointed out that Mahara had never even been allowed to meet him, or that he had not cared overmuch until she had stolen his Yala to attend her in this terrible, dangerous land. Of course, if she had not, Ashani Daoyan might never have traveled and found the world to be far less straitened than a bastard son of the Great Rider could have dreamed.

He could consider his royal half-sister the giver of a gift, perhaps. The merchant he had impersonated on the way south from their homeland would have called the balance even.

"I weary of this." He heard other stealthy movement around them, but it was not close enough to cause him much concern. Not yet. "We must be gone, I have horses waiting, I will even bring the kaburei if it pleases you."

"I must know who paid for the death of my princess," Yala said, steadily. The hem of her dress moved slightly, a betraying tremble. "That needs no forgiveness. But this does, Dao. You must understand, your father needs you. Khir needs you."

So, she thought to teach him about duty? He could even forgive that, Dao supposed. "He can go on without me." After all, Ashani Zlorih had done quite well without his bastard son for many a summer, and many a winter besides. "So can Khir; by Heaven, I owe them *nothing*."

"He is your father. You must return to him." Of course she would say it with that air of quiet earnestness. One owed one's parents everything, or so a noble girl was raised to believe. If Daoyan had been a son acknowledged from the beginning no doubt he would feel the same, and step into his role with little to no grumbling.

But he was an embarrassment, a stain upon his mother's clan, as they had spared no effort to remind him over and over again. Even here, assassins seeking to blot him from the earth's face had appeared—and she expected him to return to the viper's nest he had already survived once?

"I will go nowhere for that man's pleasure, Yala." So this Khir delegation had visited, and perhaps filled her head with dutiful nonsense. Daoyan took a single step forward, his shoulders settling.

If the kaburei made any deterring movement he would strike her down, and though Yala should not see such things, he was past the edge of his patience. "Come with me. Now."

"Daoyan..." Was her hesitation merely well-bred? Of course no noble girl could act as if she *wished* to be placed upon a saddle.

"I will take thee south." How often had he longed to use the most intimate of inflections in Khir, speaking to her? How often had he, inside the secret chambers of his liver and head-meat, addressed her thus? "We will see Anwei, and maybe even far N'hon. They will not follow us there."

"You are my very dear friend." Her own inflection was painfully formal, as one warrior to another; there was an echo of her *damoi* Baiyan lingering behind the words. Was his shade watching, perhaps? "I cannot, Dao. My honor—"

"Were you not listening?" Dao glanced at the tomb-slab hovering ghostly over her shoulder, his royal half-sister probably roundly amused at this turn of events. Amused—and possibly it was her shade making Yala so stubborn, for reasons of her own. Heaven knew that if Mahara truly cared for the Komor girl, she should not have brought Yala hence. "I do not care if a hundred of these Zhaon pigs have had you. I will take you, we will *go*." He took another step, and though he was much taller and noble besides, the Zhaon kaburei didn't move. Instead, she gazed at him with her great dark cow-eyes, her leather-wrapped braids dangling over her shoulders and her entire posture expressing mute intransigence. Perhaps she truly did not understand what was being said. "And if you do not wish this filthy kaburei to lose her life you will set her aside, and tell her not to stare at a nobleman so."

"Anh has served me well, my lord prince." Now Yala's tone turned chill, as if he were the merchant he had such amusement impersonating. "If you must strike, let it be at me, not at a servant performing her duty." Her hands dropped, the sleeves falling gracefully to hide all but her fingertips, and he wondered if she had her maiden's blade.

If she did... "Yala—"

"And I must do my duty no less than she," Yala continued, slightly louder than was necessary. Her voice did not quite ring from the stones, and he wondered at its volume. "My lord prince Ashani Daoyan, son of the Great Rider, you must return to Khir. If I ever mattered to you, you will go."

If you ever... Words failed him, even inside his head-meat, and his temper—well-reined always, after a lifetime of petty insults from those who thought his mother's honorless passion made him less than noble—all but broke.

A single armored footstep, a Khir riding-boot making itself known, was all the warning he received or needed. Daoyan froze. They approached from a few different directions, and suddenly Yala's pleading for forgiveness made a mad manner of sense. "The delegation," he said, flatly. "No doubt they questioned you harshly."

"They did not have to." Her chin rose, and that grey gaze rested upon him clear and sure. No quarter asked, of course—Komor Yala looked, at the moment, just like her elder brother lost at Three Rivers. Dao had not seen Komori Baiyan's death, but he often wished he had been able to save the man.

His only friend, other than Yala. And now she not only balked him, but had brought the hounds to circle the stag. If it was a hunt, he had been caught by a well-thrown lure indeed.

Little lure, the Zhaon prince called her. Well, he had reason.

"It is him," someone else said in Khir, a nobleman's accent. "My lord Ashani Daoyan, one addresses you—Moruri Keiyan, your father's servant. We have come to accompany you northward."

Dao's eyes half-closed. He stood in the hot damp dusk, his hands turning to fists at his sides. Of course Ashani Zlorih would send the eldest Moruri boy to fetch him; the clan had provided most of the guards for Narikh Arasoe while she and her infant son tarried in a mountain keep so many winters ago. Their loyalty, even to a Great Rider who demanded the safety of his honorless concubine and bastard son, was assured—especially if by protecting said bastard they could thumb the eye of the Narikhi and the Domari at once. "Ah, Keiyan. How are you liking Zhaon?"

"It is a wasteful land." The tall, bright-eyed shadow that was Moruri paused at Yala's shoulder. He spoke in Zhaon now, the language of the land that was about to rob Daoyan of even *more* of his hopes after cruelly dangling them within reach. "You should go, my lady Komor. It grows dark."

"Indeed it does." She was very tense, her right hand held very low, though she touched the kaburei's arm with her left, a soft, forgiving pressure. Now she too spoke in Zhaon. "Anh, go to my princess's threshold and light your lamp. Lord Moruri, your letters?"

"Here." Moruri handed over a packet of paper, which Yala stowed in her sleeve as if she were well used to such an operation. "I mislike leaving you here, Lady Komor. Will you not accompany us? Your honor will be safe; you may even bring your kaburei."

A single shake of her head, no swinging hairpin-decoration to mark the movement. "I must stay, both to discover who killed my princess and to muddy your trail. Though there is not much I can promise upon that last account once I present your regrets to the new Emperor."

"And...the Third Prince?" Moruri paid no more attention to Ashani Daoyan than to a feral curltail writhing upon a well-cast javelin. "Will he at least..."

"I have already visited the dungeons of Zhaon-An's palace once," she said, steadily. Her gaze did not leave Daoyan's, and if there was a message in that stubborn, despairing look, he did not wish to decipher it. If he moved, even so much as a muscle, he would draw his sword and might not stop until they were all dead save her. Even the kaburei. "If I am sent thence again, they still will not hear of our prince's presence here. I shall think of many other tales to tell them should they put me energetically to the question."

His temper broke. Daoyan would have surged forward, but there was a hand upon his shoulder and a familiar *tch-tch* tongue-cluck, like a maiden auntie with a fractious child. "*Ai*, my prince." It was Hazuni Ulo, another who had bestirred himself sometimes to graciously notice the Great Rider's bastard son. "Komor

serves, as Hazuni and Moruri do. Come, we have a good horse for
you, and a letter from your father. The Great Rider longs to see his
son again."

"He did not wish it when I was in Khir." Daoyan's belly was
a mass of serpents, churning. Of *course* Yala had done what she
thought her duty. He could not even find much anger at the
thought, merely weary astonishment that he had not foreseen as
much. Had his father ever been similarly vexed with Narikh Arasoe? But that lady had been soft and retiring, not stubborn in any
way except one. "Yala. Come with me—with *us*." He could endure
a return to Khir if she consented. And now she did not even have to
worry for her precious honor. "Please."

"You will curse me for disobedience," she answered softly. Her
dress melded with twilight, as if she were an ancestral shade. "But
this I must do, Dao. My... my father would agree."

"He sent you to this place to die, Yala. Do you not understand as
much?" He longed to say more, to curse Komori Dasho instead of
her—but she would take it ill.

He was well and truly caught. And just a few moments ago he
was contemplating closing a pretty gilded cage-door upon her.

Now her left hand rose, a graceful movement, wiping at her
cheek. "*Left in the trap the wolf's paw...*" The quotation in soft
Khir broke; she turned away so sharply her skirt flared, her steps
quickening as she followed the kaburei. The servant moved muti-
nously slowly, casting glances over her shoulder every few steps,
and when she saw her mistress tacking uncertainly over the white
stone, her golden lamp bobbed as she hurried back to take her lady's
arm and draw her away, murmuring fiercely in Zhaon.

Yala had *turned her back* upon him.

"Zhe Har," Daoyan said, and heard his own stunned disbelief.
The Archer was held, by readers of the Hundreds, to be either a
madman or a sage beyond compare. "*The wolf's own paw, The
hunter will not find his prey.*"

It was a pretty sentiment. It could mean that she expected to die
here, covering the trail of a prince as he was dragged home. It could

even mean that she thought Daoyan blind with hunt-madness, a weakness proper and fitting in a nobleman or prince, a spell only broken when the prey was irretrievably lost.

Did she think him merely lustful, as his father had apparently once been?

"Poetic." Another Khir, this one behind and to his left, ready for whatever a madman might attempt, cleared his throat as if he might spit, but did not. It would not be meet, before the august dead. "I hate this place. Let us away."

"Yala." Ashani Daoyan's throat was too dry for a scream. He sounded, in fact, rather as if he had been struck in the gut with a mailed fist. "Komor Yala."

She stopped, her head down, her slim shoulders curved. But she did not turn, and Hazuni Ulo's hand tightened upon Daoyan's shoulder.

"Do not make it more difficult for her," he said softly. "She is a noblewoman."

"And the sons of Khir will leave her here?" If he could shame them into not leaving her to Zhaon's mercy—what would they do if he attacked them now?

And she had already visited the dungeons once? Yala had not told him of such an event. He would have repaid the Zhaon roundly for that disgrace, had he but known.

"We do not like it, but she is right. It is necessary." Moruri made a gesture, and Hazuni's hand tensed. "Come."

"Yala," Daoyan repeated, loudly now. "Komor Yala, *hear me*."

She did not move. The kaburei cast an agonized, fearful glance over her shoulder.

"I will return for you," he said, desperately. "Do you hear me? If Khir wishes to cage me thus, I shall wait for my father's death and bring the sons of every clan worthy of the name—"

The third man hissed. "We are at a *pailai*," he objected, low and fierce. "Do not say such things."

He could have killed all three of them, of course. Later, he knew he should have, especially when he found they had brought no

guards or servants, just the four nobles—including Shohuri Seiyan, whose clan prided itself on unblinking fealty to the Ashani—
to pry him away from what someone had, after all, known was the
only trap capable of bringing a son of the Great Rider down.

Now he knew beyond a doubt his half-sister's shade was laughing. Perhaps she, with the vision of the vengeful dead, even knew
his great sin—but that was ridiculous, it was no sin to take the
knife from an inexpert butcher and strike an animal surely.

It was even a lesser cruelty, to spare the beast pain.

Ashani Daoyan let himself be hurried away, chivvied by noblemen relieved their clans would not suffer a penalty for failure.
The Great Rider had been most explicit in his orders, and he had
chosen swordsmen likely to give even his son trouble if escape was
attempted.

Komor Yala did not bid them farewell. She stood at her princess's tomb, her kaburei's lamp a false golden moon each time
Ashani Daoyan could steal a glance over his shoulder, and was lost
to sight when they turned a corner.

A Pair of
Reasons

Oh, my princess. Yala's throat ached with unshed tears. She bowed apologetically at the carved stone slab bearing Mahara's name, the movement halted near the end by a relatively healed but still tender wound from a heavy-headed crossbow bolt. *Forgive me, but it was necessary. And now your brother will be safe as your father would wish.* Hopefully her princess would hear, and understand.

Anh fussed with the lantern, the pole occupying her hands so she could not do as she wished and fuss at her mistress instead. At least she could claim much innocence; she did not know Khir. "Oh, my lady." She glanced quickly at Yala, gauging her lady's willingness to be gently scolded. "So dangerous. We should go, and quickly. Perhaps we might even reach the Palace without—"

"I have come to visit, Anh. I must not leave without greeting my hostess." The proverb was different in Zhaon but it still carried her meaning, like a pot of strange shape catching roof-leaks during an autumn rainstorm. The most complex part of her duty was performed—Dao was safely in the hands of the Great Rider's representatives, probably fuming at Yala's betrayal.

He could fume all he liked, so long as he was safely alive in Khir to do so. She could not worry for his journey; four Khir noblemen chosen for their martial skill as well as loyalty were a heavy insurance, and besides, she could do nothing to aid them now except stay quietly to her normal routine, never mind that a dusk instead of morning visit was an extraordinary occurrence.

An occurrence that would beg for an answer or two once the delegation's absence was noticed. She was not looking forward to carrying the farewell letters into a royal presence. However, managing to return to the Palace this evening without incident was a complex matter too, and much closer; the stories were explicit about what an unprotected noblewoman could expect upon any road after the sun fell.

I have my yue. *I am not worried.* Except she was. She would have to defend both herself and Anh from mistreatment. At least her dress was so dark it was difficult to tell the quality of the cloth, but the fine black mare would draw attention, as well as a lone woman with only a single servant—perhaps they would mistake her for a widow, or for something else.

She could do nothing about it at the moment, so she turned to her prayers. The ostensible reason for her tardiness was unavoidable duties this morning "helping" Lady Kue arrange for leaving the Jonwa, not to mention the afternoon's invitation to tea with Lady Gonwa—a sign that the change in Yala's position from the Crown Princess's forlorn leftover lady-in-waiting to the intended of a Zhaon prince who, though adopted out to Shan and held to be the least pleasant of Garan Tamuron's sons, was still *royal* and therefore nothing to be sniffed at—was duly noted, and duly noticed by the court itself. If the invitations continued she could conceivably hear enough gossip to achieve her main purpose, and then...

It was no use. Her thoughts would not settle to tranquil prayer *or* much-needed planning. "Forgive me," she murmured once more, in Khir. "I shall be better tomorrow, my princess. But for tonight..." At least Daoyan was safe, even if he would never forgive her.

She swept the dimensions of a *pailai* with the small broom

tucked in a handy carven niche; the Crown Prince had done his best to ensure his wife would rest with those supplies and appurtenances her native land employed for the care of ancestors. Yala made her obeisances instead of spending her accustomed time in more prayer; the day's dry dust-heat pressed through gathering darkness like stones upon a sinner in the Hell of Many Weights.

She had only done what she must. And yet she felt obliquely shamed.

Anh was relieved to be upon their way at last, but also full of fresh worry. "The lantern will help," she said for the third time as she hurried at her lady's side, almost skipping with impatience. "If anyone attempts to...I shall *hit* them, with the lantern." She glanced at her mistress, unnerved by Yala's silence. "Maybe it will set them on fire?"

"Perhaps." Yala's head lifted. She put out her left hand, her right dropping to linger close to her *yue*'s hidden hilt, and halted her kaburei.

Another horse stood companionably close to the black mare from the Crown Prince's stables—those beasts, too fine for merchants, would go to his brothers; this particular one had been set aside in his will for Garan Takshin. She had sought permission for the mare's use that very afternoon, in fact, and had been hard-pressed to arrange this trip quietly enough to avoid the Third Prince's notice.

The other horse was a matching black gelding from the stall next door; she recognized him almost immediately. And from a bar of deep shadow under an ancient, gnarl-trunked yeoyan tree, left in place as the tombs were built for its luck and obvious antiquity, a single golden gleam alerted her to his rider.

"Third Prince," she greeted, equably enough. Anh let out a squeak.

"Lady Spyling." Takshin stepped from the deeper darkness like an unpropitiated shade. The gleam was the *kyeogra* in his left ear; his expression could not be discerned. "Should I be surprised to find you here?"

"I had a visit to perform." Yala cursed the slight quaver in her voice, but it could merely be deep surprise at his sudden advent. "Surely you would not grudge me such duties, even after..."

She could not make herself say *after we are married,* not with Dao's words ringing in her ears. *I will return for you.*

Yala hoped he would be dissuaded from such a course. She could even pray as much, though Heaven might not take much heed of a noblewoman forced to such exigencies as she had been lately.

"Not ever." Takshin's approach was all but silent except for his voice. It was merely his habit to move thus, she knew, and yet it was unsettling. "I am merely taken aback to see you upon such an errand at this hour. I would have accompanied you."

"I thought you busy with the Khir lords." It slipped naturally from her tongue; she preferred euphemism, misdirection, or a carefully misleading truth to an actual lie, but even most sages of the Hundreds realized sometimes it was unavoidable. She wished the lantern was not quite so bright, though it trembled in Anh's hands as if she were dancing; hopefully, what could be seen of Yala's expression was opaque. "I did not wish to disturb such merriment."

"You mean have that pocked one insult you again?" A slight gleam of teeth was his smile, probably no more than a pained grimace bearing little amusement. "Don't fear it, I suspect they have found what they came for and are long gone."

He knows. A wet tendril of dread slid down her back, but caught in this heat, even terror could not offer relief. "Gone?" She almost winced; she should not sound so shocked.

"Why else would they keep their horses at stables in the Khir quarter instead of at the Palace?" Takshin's tone was soft, almost excessively neutral. "And why else would they come to this place at this hour, if not to pay their respects before leaving? I do wonder about one thing, though."

"Takshin..." Her lips refused to work quite properly. If she could only see his expression, she could perhaps guess at what would extricate her from this.

"They could certainly offer to escort you north; you are a fine enough rider. And your faithful kaburei would accompany you as chaperone." He didn't move, but Yala sensed coiled readiness in him. At any other moment, it would have been comforting.

Now? Her right hand was numb, tense and ready. The *yue* would not flash free to harm him, she thought. No, it would plunge into her own throat to halt her tongue from spilling every secret she possessed in a vain attempt to avoid being sent to the dungeons again or possibly, shamefully, tied to a whipping-post.

Garan Takshin would not save her twice. Would he?

"Yala?" he prompted. "Did they offer to take you home?"

What a strange word. It could mean the high dark halls of Hai Komori, Khir as a whole, the palace complex of Zhaon-An, her room in the Jonwa that would not be hers much longer—so many places called *home*, at one moment or another. It was enough to make even a sage dizzy with conflicting feelings, head-meat and heart full of different humors and the liver seeking vainly to force the two to pull a chariot.

"They offered," she managed. He knew she had just lied to him about the reason for her visit to the tombs, of course, and was perhaps giving her enough rope to tie herself irrevocably to the post. "Yes."

"Well? Why do you stay?" Now there was a shadow of irritation. Was he playing with her, a granary feline with a pinchnose mouse? He sounded as if he cared nothing for the answer, but she knew better than to think so.

Garan Takshin did not sound so disdainful of things he cared little for.

She was a coward, so she chose the reason he would be flattered to hear first. "You are to be my husband," she said, quietly. "It would not be right. And I still must discover who paid for... paid for a shameful act."

It was not a lie, she told herself firmly. She could no more disobey Garan Takyeo's dying wish for her to marry his brother than she could lay aside whatever vengeance she might possibly wreak upon whoever paid for Mahara's death. It was shameful to hope whatever Takshin felt for her would blind him to a treacherous involvement in the escape of Khir's only living prince—and she devoutly hoped he had no idea who Daoyan was, other than a Khir merchant with some few ideas above his station.

The evening breeze pressed dusty, sweat-wringing fingers against her cheek; she longed for a tepid bath, for crushed fruit, for a sudden plunge into an icy pool. Her knees trembled. The day had been an agony, wondering if Dao would receive her note, if his finely tuned instincts would sense somewhat amiss, if Shohuri was one of the nobles for whom Dao's very existence was a sordid little blot, and enduring any other free-floating anxiety her hair could catch while keeping her outer appearance as serene as possible.

Now there was no relief, either, from the terrible muscle-loosening fear that Takshin *was* simply playing with her, that he had planned to catch Ashani Daoyan as coldly and thoroughly as he'd arranged his and Yala's own exit from Zhaon-An's walls when she rode for Zakkar Kai.

She had a healthy respect for his ability to strike where needed, now.

The silence was full of the rustle of evening skybreath and insect calls, a faint faraway ribbon of cart wheels from the Road. You could not hear the city, but you could sense it like the heat of a large, dozing creature nearby.

When Garan Takshin spoke, it was a soft, meditative sentence. "A pair of reasons, I suppose."

"I..." The pressure behind her eyes, her heart, her tongue mounted; it was the urge to babble like a child caught in mischief. "I had to render such aid as I was capable of. They are from Khir, Takshin."

"Hm?" The shadow before her moved, shaking his head as if interrupted from deep, unpleasant thought. "Oh, that. I don't blame them, I'd rather leave than deal with Kurin too. I suppose they gave you letters full of flowery apology and a tissue-thin pretext."

"Y-yes." They were in her sleeve even now, suddenly heavy,

burning, guilty weights instead of expensive brushed, folded, and sealed paper.

"At least that. I'll take them to Kurin in the morning."

What? "What?" She did not mean to sound so stunned. But approaching Zhaon's new Emperor, even with so patent a cause as letters from foreign dignitaries called away in highly irregular fashion, was an unpleasant and dangerous duty at best; she had not even turned her head-meat to the problem of how to do so yet. It was an unexpected relief that he would.

Or did he mean he would take them from a corpse or a shivering wreck once he had finished dealing with an errant woman?

"It's safer," Takshin said, patiently, and took the last step of his slow approach, looking down at her through quivering lampglow. "Did it not occur to you I would keep you safe, Yala? We are at a dismal start to married life, if so."

"Ah." The relief was almost as bad as the fear. It poured through her and she swayed, her shoulder bumping Anh's. "I had not thought so far ahead, my lord."

"That is very unlike you indeed. But you have suffered much of late." He offered his arm, and she had to politely take it even though they were only a few steps from the horses. "Come, into the saddle. I should have suspected, and brought a palanquin."

"Not from the tombs." It wasn't difficult to sound somewhat shocked. "It would bring ill-luck."

"Is that what they say in Khir?" He stopped at the black mare's side, a pretty bit of courtesy either genuine or ironic; she could not tell which. "You're trembling."

There was no shame in such quivering, Yala told herself. She was, after all, only a woman. "It has been an extremely warm day."

"And you have not fully recovered from . . ." He exhaled sharply. "Nobody would ever guess who rode for Kai, but still, you should not strain yourself so."

The wound upon her back, healing nicely even though it itched, gave a twinge. "You are very solicitous, my lord Third Prince." At least her arms and legs were equal to the task of mounting; she felt much better once a-horse. The mare was placid, one ear flicking as she sensed Yala's unease. A more skittish mount might have responded with a sidle. "I thought you would be angry, instead."

"I considered it," he said thoughtfully, and Anh edged to her usual spot near the mare's head with many a glance at Yala, as if willing strength in her mistress's direction. The round golden lantern bobbed, casting fitful shadows over his sharp, scar-seamed face. "As far as anyone knows, I accompanied you tonight. The *entire* time, understood?" A sharp glance at Anh, who squeaked again and nodded while the lantern danced. The mare flicked her ear once more, moderately displeased.

Yala gathered her reins, her knees clamping so the horse knew her rider was well aware of this new development and did not consider it cause for concern. "Of course, my lord."

"Still so formal." A familiar, sharp amusement under the words. He was just the same as ever. If it was a trap it was a long-drawn one. "I do not like you out with only a kaburei at this hour, Yala."

The rebuke did not sting nearly as much as it could. She bowed her head, as if her father was expressing measured displeasure. The familiarity was even comforting, now that she was almost certain he did not suspect her betrayal. "Yes, Takshin," she murmured. Daoyan was as safe as possible, returning to Khir unremarked by this most perceptive of Garan Tamuron's sons. Her largest worry was completely relieved.

Perhaps that was why she was suddenly so sweat-wrung and exhausted.

Takshin mounted and they set off, the lamp bobbing in Anh's hand as she walked sedately before her mistress's horse. Normally she would precede the nobleman too, but Takshin told her curtly to stay where she was, for he needed his dark-vision. They rode in the gloaming, and it took a long while for Komor Yala's hands to stop shaking.

FORMS OBSERVED

Apparently Garan Sensheo was fully forgiven, for a Red Letter had arrived at his estate just this morning, bearing the Emperor's invitation. He was to return to the palace and pay a visit to his mother, which was welcome news to the Fifth Prince of Zhaon, even if he did have to ride in a palanquin like a woman.

Once he paid his respects he could go where he pleased, but the forms must be observed.

So it was he climbed the familiar steps leading to Garan Hanweo-a Haesara's quarters in the Kaeje, the door still bearing banners of pale cloth as if a dowager queen mourned both her husband and a son that was none of hers. Of course she had two fine sons still living, did Garan Tamuron's second queen, and it could be that her mourning was flagrant enough to be apologetic for that great good fortune, propitiating a jealous Heaven.

He was expected, of course. Servants hurried to bring his usual house slippers, his preferred fan while visiting, and the news that his mother and elder brother were enjoying the view from the large verandah, looking onto his mother's tiny, exquisitely half-wild personal garden.

It irked him that Makar would intrude on the visit, but Sensheo was in such a fine mood it hardly mattered. His plans could now move forward.

Well, at least the important ones.

He brushed aside a few bowing servants—but kindly, with a remote smile, never let it be said that the Fifth Prince was anything less than gracious while visiting his royal dam. The thick archer's thumb-ring of carved horn upon his thumb was a familiar weight, and he ran a fingertip over its carving as he strode with measured haste through halls as familiar as his own estate.

Kurin had tried to make Sensheo's princely retreat outside the palace complex into a trap. It was one more thing to hold him to account for.

"Ah." His mother, her resin-dipped fingertips glowing bright amber, was in plain, unembroidered silk dyed the very faintest of pinks, edged with unbleached silk. A band of similarly unbleached silk was sewn into her left sleeve, a broad slash of mourning. A simple, undecorated hairpin kept her nest of braids low upon her nape; it was strange to see her without a glittering fall of crystals or precious stones from that accoutrement. No ear-drops, no necklace, a simple greenstone bangle clasping a wrist still slim as a girl's, his mother looked up from the act of pouring a steady stream of jaelo tea and smiled warmly. "And here he is now. Come, we have all your favorites."

"So I see." He cast an appreciative glance over the table and nodded to Makar, whose dark scholar's robes, as usual, were of the finest quality. Makar's sleeve bore an armband as well, with knots in its tucked tail like a whipped dog. Of course a good son followed his mother's gentle urging—and Sensheo's close-servant this morning had produced an armband to knot around the sleeve of his princely blue robe, though the Fifth Prince had glowered at the man for presuming to suggest instead of merely bringing forth what was commanded. "Elder Brother. How like you to invite yourself."

Perhaps he had not quite forgiven Makar for that little display in his own foyer a few visits ago. *Stay in your house, little brother. Leave the arrangements to me, and I will see you freed soon enough.*

It was a good thing none of the servants had witnessed that.

"He did not, *I* invited him, and how rude you are." Haesara made a soft, disapproving noise, offering her cool, firm, scented cheek for a kiss. Her bath favored twigs of clarifying jusso and measured scoops of red crushflower, that most royal of flowers; her skin barely needed the lightest dusting of zhu powder to provide a pleasing matte glow. She set the square iron teapot—held to be healthful, though of a very martial metal—aside, and beamed at him. "Sit there, my darling boy. It is good to see you."

"My apologies, Mother. Did you worry very much?" There was no shame in playing the boy at her table, and a great deal of utility.

Makar's teacup was the same heavy Eunai-An ware he had favored growing up, too; he would stubbornly refuse to drink from any others when a child. Apparently their mother wished to accentuate the past.

Either that, or she found Maki just as insufferable as Sensheo did nowadays.

"To be a mother is to worry, my son. Makar, will you have some aiju? It is very fresh." She selected slices of the musky fruit, laying them upon his elder brother's favorite blue-patterned plate; for Sensheo she chose pearlfruit and even poured for him, his own favorite teacup from many years ago with its diamond-patterned blue glaze. "And for you. The weather is very fine, though the dust will be bad this year, I am told."

She wished to speak of the *weather*? Sensheo restrained the dual urge to scoff and to point out he had not liked pearlfruit for many winters. Still, he had loved them as a child, and there was sweet rai as well. "Everyone complains of the dust when it is dry, and the rain when it is not. How lucky Zhaon is, to have a second sun." The glaze on his cup reminded him of a tiny bottle with a soakwood stopper, nestling in his sleeve like the treasure it was.

And Kurin didn't suspect a thing.

Makar sighed. He would not miss the subtle play on words, implying a shoddy replacement for a quality item. "Must you? Mother has been worried, you know. It's taken far more effort than I like to spend, convincing Kurin you are ready to behave."

"*Kurin*, he says." Sensheo affected mild shock, rather like that old biddy Lady Gonwa. He did not reach for his tea, since Mother had not yet touched hers. "Not *beloved Emperor of Zhaon*?"

Haesara sighed, her gaze turning to the garden's green blur under a flood of heavy yellow sunshine. This year the blue star-flowers were in riotous profusion, and the rai from the Knee-High Festival was quite tall, swelling with hard buds next to the tiny, gem-bright pond. Soon the fields would be utterly dry, and the dust everyone bemoaned would suck away the humidity leading to rai-rot and the black fungus. "Sensheo," she said, quietly. "Please."

"What? I am merely being cautious, Mother. Are those Nanh's dumplings?" His mother's cook was a treasure, and knew it. "How lovely."

"You may not have one, if you persist in being rude." His mother still did not look directly at him, a line appearing between her eyebrows. Normally, such an expression was quickly banished; like all noblewomen of a certain age, the lady of Hanweo allowed very little to crease her face. The decorations graven by wisdom were marks of high honor, true—but a queen had to remain ready for her husband.

A dowager was under no such stricture, but Sensheo could not tell if his mother was relieved or not. Certainly she had always attended to her ceremonial and protocol duties as Garan Tamuron's second wife with all appropriateness and no little degree of taste, but now she was freed of those, as well. No doubt the First Queen—now the First Dowager Mother of the Emperor—wished to wrest those duties away, since some of them might prove remunerative with her son upon the throne.

Kurin's mother was a common tradesman's brat, and every noble chafed at bowing and scraping to her get even if the whelp had an admixture of Garan in his veins—or so the Fifth Prince sensed. Takyeo had been a spear-bride's son, but he was indubitably first and the custom of the hall made of spears and placing two under one shield was an ancient one. Far more ancient than a family genealogy purchased and scribbled upon goatskin rolls instead of carved into stone stele, as Hanweo, Daebo, and ancient, lost Wurei.

Now that Ah-Yeo was safely dead, Sensheo could even admit Eldest Brother had been somewhat of a paragon. But, regrettably, too weak.

It could even be argued that Kurin had done the realm a service; if he hadn't tried to lay the blame at Sensheo's door, it could almost be *admired*. "Then I shall be polite." Sensheo summoned a sunny smile. "I am a little out of practice, Mother, locked up in my house and nobody coming to visit."

Garan Hanweo-a Haesara did not reply, contenting herself with lifting her teacup so her sons could begin.

"Your captivity was endurable," Makar noted—not quite sourly, but certainly with an elder sibling's patent patience. "Considering."

"As if you do not know it was all a fiction." Sensheo shrugged. "And everyone else knows it, too."

"Unlikely." Makar lifted his cup, inhaling tea-fragrance. "In any case, *he* is on the throne now."

"And that means both my sons must be careful." Mother was apparently finished with the mannerly refusal to speak of business before a certain amount of tea had been consumed. "What he has taken, he must suspect another might well help himself to. It would be unwise were any preparations made."

"Without proper camouflage, you mean." Sensheo disliked stating the obvious, but his family seemed determined to force it upon him today. Even the garden was not soothing.

"I mean *at all*." She fixed him with a direct, pinning stare, one that might have made him quail were he still six summers high. An edge of color crept into her cheeks below the zhu powder, her humors rising as they so rarely did. "You must not let Kurin fix another such stain to your sleeve, Sensheo. He is dangerous."

Only if he suspects what I'm doing. "Why not look at Makar while you say such things?" Summer breeze full of fragrance, if not any coolth, brushed across the laden table and fingered Sensheo's robe. "He is the one they call the scholar, and is next in succession."

Haesara glanced at her eldest son, one of those maddening looks of silent accord they were prone to. Sensheo was always left out, maybe because he took more after Father. After all, the two of them were content merely to bemoan their lot, where *he* actually performed a deed or two to push aside disaster.

He had not done badly so far. Nobody seriously believed Sensheo had anything to do with Takyeo's death, after all.

"Kurin knows better than to fear me." Makar set his teacup down, not even glancing at his dish. "I have given him every reason not to, in fact. You, on the other hand—"

"And what about Kai?" Sensheo burst out. If they were to speak of these things, very well, but they should speak of them all, not just the parts Mother and Maki wished to bludgeon him with. "A warlord with a hurai, he and Takshin have always been allies."

"But neither of them have been here," Haesara said, in that gentle tone he disliked so much. It was not meet or fit to admit you disliked your own mother, but she persisted in speaking as if he were still a child, and one prone to tantrums as well. "The general was always in the field, and the Third Prince in Shan. *That woman's* son will strike closer to home first. Especially since he needs Zakkar Kai against Khir, and the Third Prince to smooth Shan's wrinkled dress."

"Oh, Shan." Sensheo waved an airy hand, wishing he could take a dumpling and be done with this. Maybe the breakfast invitation had been a ploy, and Makar was in league with the new Emperor against his own younger brother. It would be entirely like both of them to ally against a younger sibling; had they not done so all Sensheo's life? "Their king is probably dead, since those barbarians sent Sabi's head. Maybe Kurin will go out to chastise them." And if he did, well.

Certain things could be arranged upon a confused battlefield, could they not?

Makar looked pained. Mother's teacup hovered near her mouth before being lowered to the table with a precise, tiny click. She did not quite glance at the partition behind Sensheo, but her gaze fixed itself slightly over his shoulder and he knew she wanted to.

There were ears everywhere, in the Kaeje. Many of them

belonged to the First Queen, ever jealous of her prerogatives. It didn't matter—Sensheo had a plan for her, too. A *true* son of Garan would sit upon the Throne of Five Winds, and Sensheo intended to give the nobles of Zhaon one to rally behind.

Already there were encouraging signs.

It was Makar who spoke instead, severely as befit an elder, even one with only a few summers' more worth of breathing. "You do not seem to be grieving for our sister."

"Well, I have." He shook his head. Sabi was royal, of course, but she was only a concubine's child, and besides, it wasn't Sensheo's fault her husband had let the Tabrak do...whatever they'd done to her. It could even be said, were one being absolutely truthful as most in Zhaon never bothered to be, that Sabwone's fate was a payment for all her little malicious games and sly pinches. "And for Father, and for Ah-Yeo. But we are still alive, Makar, and I'd like us to remain so."

"Then you will cease your intriguing?" Makar did not touch his eating-sticks, but he lifted his teacup again and sipped, his eyebrows rising a little in a polite compliment to his mother's impeccable taste. When he set it down, though, he had shifted to the attack. "I weary of tidying up after your little blunders, Sensheo. If you were adept as you think yourself, we should have no trouble at all."

Sensheo could barely believe his ears. "There's nothing to tidy up, Makar." It was not quite true, of course; he suspected Makar knew nothing and was simply dragging bait through a rai-pond, like a peasant so hungry he wanted a bronzefish for dinner. "You're the one Kurin will go after next. You should ready yourself for that instead of insulting me."

"Enough." The word was unwonted sharp; Mother did not ever raise her voice, but she was perilously close. "Do you not understand why the new Emperor allowed you to break your house arrest by attending your sister's pyre?" She used the ancient term for a warlord's retainer ordered to immure himself, and a fresh flush mounted her powdered cheeks. "It is a warning, Sensheo. If you continue to intrigue against Kurin, he will not simply overlook it.

He will kill all three of us just as he removed your Eldest Brother, and *that woman* will be very pleased."

A shocked, stinging silence descended. Makar rose, his knee almost striking the table, and flowed silently to the partition; his hand flashed out and the door slid open a few inches.

The hall outside was empty. The garden rustled under a hot morning wind, drenching all three of them with fragrant breath.

"Are there spies in your household, Mother?" Sensheo shook his head. "Perhaps your steward should be more vigilant."

"Cease your noise." She pinned him with a fierce, direct look, and for the first time Garan Sensheo began to feel slightly uneasy. "You are my son, Sensheo. Hanweo depends upon us. Makar performs his duty to the clan and his family while you strut about preening like an eyebird and fouling the garden. You will do *nothing* more, do you understand me? No more impresarios, no more attempts upon Zakkar Kai, nothing to give Kurin any reason to doubt your discretion."

"Do you not see? He will attempt to kill us all, whether I protect us or not!" The sudden, violent desire to sweep the table clear of dishes, dumplings, sweet rai, broth tureen, and fruit plates, not to mention the teacups and the square iron teapot, turned his palms damp and made his fingers tingle, especially the one bearing his own hurai.

He was a *prince*, yet even his mother kept treating him as a child.

Makar did not turn from the door. "You protect nothing, Sensheo. That is my task. All you must do is keep from cluttering the path while I perform it."

And Mother calls me *a preening eyebird.* The injustice, as usual, threatened to block Sensheo's throat. "If I leave it to you, we'll all die. You do *nothing*, Makar."

"On the contrary." Haesara folded her hands in her sleeves, perhaps because a noblewoman should not make fists at the breakfast-table. "Not only does your brother clean up your fumbling attempts, but he has guided the clan for several years and kept *that woman* from doing me much mischief. You have not seen it because unlike you, he is discreet and capable."

Never in his life had his mother spoken to Sensheo so coldly. He tucked his thumb with the archer's ring inside his palm and squeezed, carved horn biting at his flesh. "Perhaps you wish he was your only son, then."

The garden turned utterly quiet, a tangled green spy listening breathlessly to its betters.

"Of course not." Haesara's gaze bored into him, dark and hot as he could never remember seeing before. "I bore you after a day and a half of labor, Sensheo. I have two sons, I love them both, and you must listen to your mother and your elder brother. What do you think I have suffered, trapped here while you are in seclusion, wondering if the next letter to arrive would bear *shih*?" The well-bred referral to "eight" instead of "death" upon an imperial proclamation was the hiss of an adder no longer needing to lie hidden. "Do you have any idea what that is like, my son?"

Now he did indeed feel six summers high again, and chastised as well. "I only want to save us." It wasn't even half a mistruth, he did want to save his mother and brother—if they would let him. "And the clan."

But most of all, he wanted them to *look* at him, and recognize that though he might have been born near the tail of Father's puissance, it only meant he had time and refinement to truly surpass.

It irked a man to see his elders were not necessarily his betters, indeed.

"Then will you halt?" His mother freed one of her cool, scented, beautiful hands, and reached to lay it upon his. The touch would have been a balm, had he still been the child they thought him. "For me? I would not ask it, my beloved son, if I did not deem it wise. Will you not listen to your mother?"

His irritation had to be muzzled, shoved under a table like an unsightly limb. "Of course, Mother. For you, I will do anything." He even smiled, and managed to thank her very prettily for the dumplings she now heaped upon his plate. Even Makar, when he returned to the table, was polite instead of dismissive.

But Garan Sensheo was not misled. They thought him too

young, too weak, too hasty. Just let them survive without him, though.

That thought sustained him through the entire light meal, through the mannerly familial goodbyes, through his promise to visit his mother again on the morrow for more tea. And once he was finished enduring the visit, he was free to go where he willed.

There was much to be done.

Usual Formality

Their father had probably used this small Kaeje sitting-room relatively often for private conference; it was only a short distance from the Great Hall and the two Golden at the door were far enough away to avoid eavesdropping, unless they had ears from a sage's tale. It held a scarred, round, antique table of heavy nut-tree wood that would probably have pleased Tamuron, and the chairs were simply functional instead of padded to over-elegance. Upon the table, a packet of letters had been unfolded, their northern authors vanished last night.

The sitting-room was also breathlessly hot, of course, but in winter it might almost be cozy. A faint sheen clung to the new Emperor's forehead, despite the early hour—perhaps only a function of the heaviness of his robe.

"Gone?" Kurin was probably not pretending a certain measure of astonishment, but something in the lift of his elder brother's eyebrows pointed to the emotion being mostly genuine.

Or so Takshin thought. "I suppose they collected what they came for." The Third Prince was, for once, in something approaching a sunny mood. Who could not be, when someone had decided a man was worth staying for? Yala was safely in the Jonwa, preparing for her advent to the princely house in Zhaon-An's Noble District he had never thought to use.

"To come so far south, and then to leave so quickly…" Zan

Fein's fan moved in its usual lazy pattern, the stilt-legged bird upon its side performing an enthusiastic, knotted pose, beak up and long flexible neck contorted while its wings bent impossibly back. If it was a metaphor or comment, it was an exceedingly oblique one, which matched the chief eunuch's reputation perfectly. "I wonder that they did not take more with them than a few meals and a report of Zhaon's new Emperor."

As long as they had left behind the most important article, Takshin did not much care. Still, he watched Kurin's expression, for the entire matter bothered him somewhat.

And if his elder brother wished to vent his displeasure upon a Khir, it would not be Takshin's bride.

"How interesting." His elder brother had a fan too, although it was painted very simply with a very antique, arcane character for *patience*, one which resembled two players hunched over a chessboard. "The lady-in-waiting—Komor, is it?"

As if he did not know her name. Takshin shrugged. "Safe at home this morn, and somewhat glad to avoid translation duties." A man spoke for his wife, and it mattered little whether she had been dragged to his door in a palanquin yet or not.

He was almost in a fever of impatience waiting for the event, but mourning, politeness, and removing those Takyeo had left in his care from the palace's maw took priority.

"Ah, I see." Kurin, of course, would not be deterred from causing pain or inconvenience so easily. "Mother is eager for her prospective daughter-in-law to visit."

"I'm sure she is." Takshin had no intention of letting his mother close to anything approaching satisfying prey; besides, Yala had endured enough. "However, I have forbidden it."

You may only push me so far, his tone said, and well Kurin would know it. Balking his elder brother's attempts to mar or break another sibling's toy was not a feat he had performed often, being many li away to the south for plenty of their childhoods.

But he had done it often enough. And successfully, too, which no doubt rankled.

"The Khir do not prize their women." Zan Fein attempted to bring the conversation to the clearly more pressing matter. A delegation leaving without bows, especially in the current unsettled time, was either a grievous insult or a dark promise. "But perhaps they left because there is nothing to say, with the former Crown Princess gone." Of course the chief court eunuch had always been one to intimate rather than speak directly; Takshin wondered what he would have said to Father in this instance.

"Perhaps." With their princess dead, a delegation's remit suddenly collapsing was a reasonable assumption. And yet they had to have left Khir after the news of Ashan Mahara's fate arrived, which meant it was absolutely incorrect—unless they had decided Kurin was not worth staying for, or that Takyeo's death had changed the chessboard beyond repair or further play. "They came with no servants, no train of tribute, and very few gifts."

"Sent to retrieve an item of great value, perhaps? That lady-in-waiting might have been holding it for them." Kurin studied Takshin's expression, his faint smile familiar from childhood. He was not quite ready to strike, that smile said—but soon.

So Takshin allowed his own lips to curve, just slightly. *You may strike if you wish, Rinrin, and I shall return the favor.* "Careful, Elder Brother. You might start quoting Khao Cao next." A eunuch obsessed with a warlord's wife was not the most appetizing comparison, even if Khao was part of the Hundreds.

"A pair of scholarly princes." Zan Fein's fan did not cease its steady motion, and a stray breath of his umu scent reached Takshin. It was not the most winning perfume, and Heaven alone knew why the chief court eunuch bathed himself in it—but who knew what such creatures smelled, their noses possibly altered by the operation making them what they were? "Perhaps they did visit Zhaon-An to retrieve something, as Third Prince Takshin points out." *Come now, lads,* his tone implied, an avuncular almost-reproof. *Do not play about when there is work to be done.*

"Or to leave something behind." Kurin's retreat promised trouble later, but at least both Emperor and brother could be content that the threat of their mother extending an invitation Yala could not refuse balanced Takshin's semi-insult of mentioning a general who had flagrantly desired another man's wife. "I wonder, little brother and Honorable Zan, whether the author of our late Eldest Brother's misfortune might be found to the north instead of... elsewhere."

Ah. There it is. It was as good an explanation as any, and it would rather neatly deal with some lingering court suspicions of Kurin's part in Takyeo's death. Takshin swallowed a sudden sour taste. "Do you think so?" He allowed his own smile to widen just a trifle.

"You did tell Mother you would hold her responsible." Kurin stroked at his smallbeard. Was he growing it to irritate Mother, since it aped Father's facial hair? "Perhaps you should reconsider?"

"You have concrete proof of someone's guilt, then?" Takshin parried. He did not intend to reconsider a single promise he had made; it was why he was so reluctant to give them in the first place. "I would ask that you share it. He was my brother too." *And I liked him far better than you.*

In other words, he would not actively pursue Garan Yulehi-a Gamwone as long as Kurin left Yala alone. Takyeo was safely ensconced in Heaven now; he would care little what Takshin did, or did not, to avenge him. And Kurin did not need to know Takshin's suspicions of a certain Khir merchant, who was altogether too familiar with Komor Yala and had been present during the last attempt upon Takyeo's life, too.

That fellow was interesting, and Takshin had already sent a Golden—one of Takyeo's few clients who was not averse to Takshin as a patron—to bring him to the palace.

If, that was, Honorable Narikhi was still in residence. Considering higher-ranked countrymen had fled, Takshin did not think it likely. Narikhi's gaze had been very like those of the delegations', and his manners strikingly similar.

His cultivation of a foreign lady-in-waiting must have had some intended end. Yala, with her strict honor, would likely never suspect the fellow had attempted to use her.

"Sadly, our efforts to investigate have come to naught." Kurin indicated Zan Fein with a cupped hand, to avoid the impoliteness of pointing even though an Emperor was, in many cases, above politeness. Or so everyone believed. "Unless you have something, Honorable Zan Fein?"

"No more than the last time we spoke upon the matter." The eunuch's fan still did not alter its steady motion. "The possibility exists of more than one author of the previous Emperor's misfortune. Chasing each distracts us from the problems now at hand. Does it matter so much who, in the end, succeeded—especially when Tabrak is arriving and Khir is restive? Perhaps our Khir guests were merely sent to make certain the princess's tomb is well cared for. Khir is notoriously traditional."

It suited Takshin to let the matter seemingly drop there. He said nothing.

"And while they travel they may view the roads and whatever measures Kai has taken to the north." Kurin did not wrinkle his nose at the mention of Zakkar Kai, which was worrying. If he considered the general a problem already solved Takshin would have to move to insulate a man he, after all, rather liked. "Perhaps a short sharp lesson might teach them some manners."

Certainly Takshin liked Kai better than the brother he shared a mother with, as well. He had long ago decided to shelve any guilt at his own apparent failure of filial feeling. "You intend to ride to battle then?" He gave his teacup a quarter-turn, to absorb luck and the presumed pleasure of conversation, but mostly to punctuate the question. "Father would be very proud."

"Khir is of less moment than the Tabrak." The new Emperor's visage turned stony, and his gaze lifted in unconscious imitation of Father, kombin in his palm and weighty matters filling his head-meat. Or at least, so Takshin seemed to remember; being sent from home at a young age to endure Shan and the Mad Queen seemed now more a gift than a hardship, even with his scars twitching.

It was almost pleasant to balk his elder brother, and to witness Kurin learning that the throne he considered himself best suited for was more burden than pleasure. But even that witness held a bitter edge, for it should be Takyeo sitting upon that padded bench, making decisions Takshin could carry out with a minimum of fuss or second thoughts.

Ah-Yeo's kindness would have needed a sharp shield not overly concerned with niceties, rather as Yala's fragile determination to commit honorable acts did.

All the same, the rai-pale barbarians clustering like metuahghi had sent Sabwone's head. Which worried him, though if Kiron was dead too, he would know, would he not? Some strange internal spinning would cease, and he would be certain as he had been once or twice, bandit-hunting with his battle-brother, that something had happened and the time to strike was at hand.

Sabwone, for all her clawing and pinching and nasty tricks, was still his sister. She had written dutiful letters each month while he was in Shan, full of weightless gossip. He had dismissed them until he realized they were all she had to give, and furthermore given without thought of debt or recompense. The letters had never faltered, arriving like a babu water-clock steadily chopping a day or night into equal fragments, even in the darkest times under the Mad Queen.

He owed the Tabrak for Sabi, but doubted he would ever get a chance to administer the debt. The sooner he could marry Yala and possibly take her elsewhere, the better. But there was much to be done beforehand.

Including satisfying his curiosity upon one or two points, like the Khir merchant and who, precisely, had paid for the last and most successful group of assassins sent after his Eldest Brother. The prime suspect was, of course, sitting across the table, staring at a tapestry of a battle in the Blood Years as if he expected a screaming horde to appear at any moment while his thumb stroked a silver-chased hurai upon his royal finger.

It wasn't like Kurin to move directly when someone else could be induced to. Whether that someone else was Sensheo—highly unlikely—or another remained to be seen.

"The Southron Army is awakening." Zan Fein took the change of subject with, perhaps, a certain amount of relief. "Which only leaves the question of who will command it."

Takshin held his peace. Plenty, in Zhaon or Shan, committed the mistake of thinking his particular silence meant an absence of activity in his ears or head-meat.

"Kai will recommend a general. Or Jin may finally leave the nursery." Kurin's mouth tightened; he really did look very much like Father, wearing that expression. It probably drove Mother to fury. "Or perhaps I should ride against the barbarians, to teach them a lesson before we turn to Khir."

Takshin could have murmured *Father would approve of that, also.* It would tip Kurin into intransigence. Instead, he pursed his lips slightly and turned his gaze to a hanging upon the opposite wall, of a summer garden in the style of the Second Dynasty. "Between the pot and the millstone," he muttered, as if either Khir or Tabrak mattered to him.

"First we shall cook, then polish more rai." Kurin clearly considered that enough discussion. "Do reconsider having your wife-to-be visit Mother, Shin. It would do her good."

Their mother was ever happiest with something defenseless to savage. "I'm sure it would, Rinrin." Takshin was not in the succession and did not need to address Kurin with more than his usual formality. Especially if the new Emperor wanted to trade childhood nicknames. "If you mention my betrothed again, I may think you truly enamored." One insult to match the other, and he had the pleasure of seeing dull crushflowers bloom in Kurin's cheeks.

"Have a little more politesse, little brother." If the new Emperor wished Takshin to quail, he should look less like a spoiled brat denied a favored toy. Well, he had ever been Mother's favorite, her shining hope. "Our positions have changed."

Not so much. "I should address you as the Glorious Ruler of Zhaon?" The ancient honorific dripped with sarcasm; Takshin took a perverse pleasure in drawing out the syllables and drawling further ancient honorifics. "He who carries the Five Winds in a bag, he whom Heaven has adorned? Perhaps I shall wear my fingers to bone brushing titles upon rai-paper for you to hang in your entryway."

"Or perhaps I should send you south to bar Tabrak from Zhaon." No doubt Kurin considered it a threat couched in a silken reminder.

I am not yours to command. He could, after all, take Yala and be gone southward in a trice. But his purposes required Kurin thinking he had bargained and bought Takshin's support, so he nodded. "Giving me an army is a bold move, Elder Brother. One might think you wish me removed before my marriage."

"One might." Since he could not menace Takshin in the way he used to during childhood, Kurin made a short, irritable gesture at the opened letters from the fled delegation, their brushwork sharp as Khir's mountains. "I would thank you for bringing these, but you are in a terrible mood this morning."

Takshin summoned a lopsided, unamused grimace that could pass for a smile if an observer did not know him well. "Delivering ill news always puts me in one. Shall I take my leave then, oh Reflection of Heaven's Mirror?" He wished Kiron was here, or that Takyeo had survived. He might as well wish for Sabwone to be returned to life, her head reunited with her body and her mischief ready to claim another victim.

Wishes were no good when confronted with the world's cruelty. He had learned as much in the bottom of one of the palace wells of Shan.

"Do. But have a care, Shin." Balked as he so rarely was, Kurin could not deny himself another threat. "I have told Mother she must behave, and as long as she does…"

"A loving son. She must be *ever* so happy with you." Takshin rose, made the briefest of required bows, and noted Zan Fein's immobility. No doubt the chief court eunuch and Kurin would natter on about the Khir letters, and while he did not trust the umu-scented fellow overmuch, at least Zan Fein was not…hasty.

And he would know better than to recommend a move that would force Garan Suon-ei Takshin to unbrotherly action.

Takshin had much to think upon, and as he left the Kaeje yet more arrived.

The Golden sent to find a Khir merchant fell into step beside his new patron in one of the palace complex's many gardens and reported the Honorable Narikhi missing, though it was too soon to tell if he was truly vanished or simply about some business he wished unremarked. The fellow had purchased two very fine horses, stabled in the Khir quarter, and ordered them saddled and ready late last night, though he had not returned to take them hence.

FELICITOUS

So much to do, especially today. *A busy kaburei is a happy creature*, the proverb ran, but sometimes Anh thought it was merely the lack of time to exercise one's head-meat while the rest of the body fetched, arranged, hurried, and planned that led to a sullen exhaustion masquerading as serenity. All the same, she was not in the hot fields, backsore and sun-dazed, the prey of fatigue, heat, or passing male things.

And soon her lady would be married, to a prince no less. Which meant Anh's own status was rising correspondingly, enough that other kaburei were viewing her with awe and Lady Hansei's close-maid was not so distant—indeed, Nah Aen was almost friendly now. Not entirely, of course; the distance between them was too great.

But almost.

And today was the busiest day of all, for her lady was to be carried out of the Jonwa and to a prince's door in a bridal palanquin that very afternoon. Anh hurried through a dry-garden full of rocks and spiny succulents as well as broad-leaved uebyeua which would have to be burlap-wrapped in winter, their feet piled with rocks to drain away root-rotting moisture. She barely noticed her surroundings, instead being occupied with counting upon her fingers to make certain she remembered everything that must be done.

A shadow fell across the path and she automatically stepped aside, for the hem of a silken orange robe fluttered in her periphery vision and *that* meant a superior being was deigning to approach upon this dusty paved walk. There was no shadow of a sunbell, so it was not a lady; Anh bowed deeply, waiting for whoever it was to pass.

"There she is, the pretty girl." A drawling nobleman's accent broke the low humming of fiddle-leg insects, already active in the drowsing heat of a droughtsummer morning.

Anh's head-meat froze between counting one task and the next. She dared to let her gaze run swiftly upward, halting at a pair of well-manicured hands, one bearing an archer's thumb-ring of carven horn. That, and the male voice, could only mean one thing. "My...my lord?"

"I've been away." Garan Sensheo sounded amused. He had addressed her once before, and Anh's stomach turned into a ball of writhing snakes as if she'd eaten eggs instead of a substantial ball of polished rai and healthful, vinegary greens this morning. "Did you miss me?"

How was she supposed to answer such a question? "Glorious Fifth Prince..." Anh ran out of words, and sweat that had nothing to do with the heat gathered behind her knees, in the bends of her elbows, at the curve of her lower back.

"Your lady is about to be my sister-in-law." The prince's hands vanished into his sleeves, and he addressed her lightly, almost as he would a court lady. "Felicitous, is it not?"

"Y-yes, Glorious Fifth Prince." What else could she say? It was felicitous indeed, and good fortune flowed downhill from such an event. Even to *her*, since Anh tended to the closest and most personal of details. She hoped a close-maid would not be brought into her lady's service to push her aside.

"Perhaps she'll manumit you after the wedding," the Fifth Prince observed.

And now there was absolutely nothing to say, so Anh was silent, trapped in a deep bow and staring at the garden walk, her cheeks flaming. There was only one possible reason for such a prince to address her, and Anh had heard enough palace gossip since being brought to the kitchens as a junior scrubber when she was only eight summers high to guess what it was.

Fifth Prince Garan Sensheo wished to do Anh's mistress some mischief. At least that made her duty clear; Anh, despite being a mere kaburei, was to protect her mistress as Lady Yala had protected the princess.

Had Anh's lady been with the Crown Princess, the kaburei suspected no assassin would have been successful. But arrows... it made Anh's head hurt. Sometimes her mistress slipped from the room at night, but not for an assignation like another court lady might. Instead, she practiced with that greenmetal blade, and Anh's heart was near to bursting with pride at the thought of such a noble, secret skill kept under her lady's dresses.

Of course her lady never spoke of it, but she did not have to. Anh's own creeping in her lady's nighttime footsteps was part of her duties, as was pretending sleep when necessary.

And keeping certain other matters locked within the deepest recesses of her liver, like her lady meeting several pale-eyed Khir lords near the poor Crown Princess's tomb.

"Would you like that?" The prince now sounded cajoling, and Anh's skin chilled. A peasant girl knew very well what such a man's kindness truly meant.

"I serve my lady, Glorious Fifth Prince," Anh managed through numb lips, hoping the bare statement of fact would give nothing else away.

"Only one kaburei for such a lady, though. My brother Takshin should give her a few more. Aren't you afraid of losing your place?"

Was he possessed of the ability to read others' head-meat? No, it was impossible; it was simply something any servant might fear. Anh made an inarticulate noise, not daring to express assent or its opposite. Either was equally dangerous.

The prince's hem fluttered as he took a step toward her. "Perhaps I can help such a pretty girl. Would you like that?"

Oh, Heaven help me. Anh could not even move; any retreat would be an insult, an approach would imply acceptance of… something.

"Ah! Sensen, there you are." A light male tenor, also lilting with a nobleman's accent, was accompanied by the sound of boot-steps. "Maki told me you were out taking a walk this morning. I want to ask you about that bow from Ch'han you were talking about—"

"Jin. What a pleasant surprise." The Fifth Prince's tone shouted it was anything but and he turned away, a sharp movement.

Which meant Anh could cast a swift glance at her deliverer.

Sixth Prince Garan Jin, in the leather half-armor he favored for morning practice, scratched cheerfully under his rumpled topknot, thankfully taking no more notice of her than he would of a wall-hanging. A sword was at his belt, too; since he was returning from the drillyard his face gleamed with sweat and the half-armor bore a few dusty impressions from strikes with weighted wooden blades. He looked very young, more like a boy costumed in an elder brother's clothes; and though he smiled, there were dark shadows under his eyes.

Anh took all of this in swiftly and stepped even farther to the side, her toes tracing the very edge of the paved stone walk. The Sixth Prince had been with the Crown Princess and Anh's lady that terrible day in the Yaol, the Great Market; he was very brave. He peppered his elder with questions about a certain style of bow while Anh made her escape with all the seemliness and speed she could muster.

Being addressed by a prince once was unsettling enough. Now she had to wonder what grudge the fifth son of Heaven-ascended Garan Tamuron bore her lady.

Her head-meat was all a-jumble, and her liver shivered within her. What could a mere kaburei do against a prince? Should she tell someone?

The traditional punishment for a servant carrying tales was the tongue torn out by the roots; the Hell of Chattering was full of laundry vats containing boiling oil for the torment of those who accused their betters of things which could not be proven. Besides, what proof did she have beyond nebulous dread and deep unease?

It was a quandary, and one she had no time to think upon while there was so much to do before sunset. Her lady was even now being prepared for the palanquin, and Anh's next stop was the palace laundries.

She set upon her way, sorely grieved, knowing she would not be able to sleep tonight as even the seamstresses who had provided the wedding finery, exhausted and with sohju as a reward, would.

SCARLET AND GOLD

At least the marriage of a prince to a mere noblewoman did not require a public procession through the streets of Zhaon-An as the sun sank in the furious crimson-gold west, or a feast attended by the entire court. Mrong Banh had decreed an auspicious date closest to the end of mourning for two emperors, and if it fit nicely with the vacating and sealing of the Jonwa, it was perhaps merely a comment upon an astrologer's skill—and a royal bridegroom's male impatience.

A friendless foreign lady-in-waiting might have had to depend upon a servant to comb her hair for the nuptials, but Lady Gonwa, chief among court women and held to be the final judge and arbiter of matters of taste in the female side of court life, sent several ili of her famous heaven tea—blended by that redoubtable lady's very own hand—wrapped in thin, very expensive crimson rai-tissue and a very pretty note volunteering her own hands and a fine scentwood comb for such a duty. Yala had no present to send in return with an acceptance, but when Su Junha mentioned as much to Garan Takshin, a greenstone hairpin with a broad, exquisitely carved head appeared, and a lyong-wood box to carefully nestle it, wrapped in fine black satin, within as well.

The new Emperor, as befit an elder brother who approved of his junior sibling's choice, sent ribboned ear-drops of thin beaten gold, fluttering like the leaves of white-bark namyeo trees. Etiquette in this particular case required a ceremonial letter of thanks brushed by both bride and groom, and if Yala's hand threatened to tremble as she wrote the ritual phrases and the expected wishes for Garan Kurin's continued robust health, it could be attributed to maidenly modesty. Other gifts required finely calibrated responses, but she was saved the dubious pleasure of replying to the First Mother's present, for none arrived from that quarter.

The court took notice, of course. Still, Garan Suon-ei Takshin had been adopted by the queen of Shan, and perhaps the First Mother thought a gift would be...indelicate. Those possessed of charitable humors murmured as much, often with their fan held in the particular half-open manner denoting a pretty utterance which was not believed but must be given breath.

Those with no such humors said nothing at all, merely exchanged significant looks. One or two, including Lady Aoan Mau—a particular favorite of Second Mother Garan Hanweo-a Haesara—was rumored to have remarked softly that a bride whose mother-in-law had already passed from the living was generally held to be a fortunate creature. It could have been a bare statement of fact, for the Mad Queen had sent Garan Tamuron's third son home scarred and reticent, but the added fillip of savage delight at further proof of First Mother Garan Gamwone's crassness could not go unnoticed.

It could even be thought that perhaps the foreign lady-in-waiting would feel a certain relief at being able to forego traditional visits to Gamwone's part of the Kaeje, unless her husband was very particular. And it did not seem that he would be.

No, in fact, Komor Yala—despite the gossip that she carried a green claw like a feline demon, despite the scandal of the whipping-post—was largely regarded as a retiring, graceful, and largely inoffensive lady partly to be pitied for being so far from her home *and* for catching the eye of the least mild-tempered of the old Emperor's sons, and partly to be admired for the quiet with which she bore both burdens.

So it was that Komor Yala was dressed in scarlet and gold, veiled from head to foot, and solicitously helped to the bridal palanquin with its reddish wood and brightly polished beaten-brass adornments inspected and judged worthy by Lady Gonwa, who moved slowly with her cane in one hand and her other arm bearing the Khir maiden's light fingertips. Everything outside the veil was a reddish blur, and it was stifling; of course a bride's steps must be hesitant. Several women performed the traditional lament at a daughter leaving the house, led by Lady Kue—once Garan Takyeo's housekeeper, now taken into Garan Takshin's service, as had been most of the household of that ill-fated Emperor who had not even reigned for a moon-cycle.

At least with the Third Prince adopted by Shan there was no question of impropriety in the transfer of furniture and other items. Who else could the dying son of a spear-wife and a warlord have left his dependents to, after all?

"Courage, child," Lady Gonwa murmured as she helped Yala into the palanquin, aided by Mrong Banh. The musicians struck up an exceedingly traditional racket, the discordant noise to drive any passing vengeful spirit or ill-luck away. "It is only a short distance, after all."

Yala could not make herself heard through the veil or over the noise, so she nodded gratefully, her headdress shivering with more thin beaten-gold leaves. Su Junha and Hansei Liyue had helped her practice, so she knew exactly what would transpire—Fourth Prince Makar and Sixth Prince Jin would ride upon either side of the palanquin, both performing a duty for a beloved, even if adopted-out and prickly, brother.

She did press the good dame Gonwa's hand with her own resin-painted fingertips, though, seeking to convey her thanks once more without scratching with the filigreed gold sheath over her smallest nail, growing back nicely since her wasted, frantic ride to fetch a general to a dying brother-emperor's bedside. The court lady nodded, squinting slightly as she straightened, and Mrong Banh closed the palanquin's door with a decisive motion. Lady Kue's voice was a

silver string, singing the Zhaon lament though she might have preferred one in her native dialect; the other women followed suit in
bright sad harmony, including the seamstresses looking forward to
their shared jars of colorless sohju approved by their lord for a task
well performed and sweet celebratory honey-thick kouri besides,
for their luck and blessings went through the needles and into the
bridal gown's exquisite stitchery. It was the only gown a woman
was not allowed to put a single stitch of her own upon, and the
richer the embroidery, the better the luck brought to the marriage.

The palanquin lifted, and Yala's eyes burned with tears. It
should have been Mahara leading her to the wooden box. It should
have been Mahara combing her hair, or making borderline-ribald
jokes as a married woman could during such a ceremony, or lighting the health-giving, spirit-warding incense coil under the gown
that morning, Mahara telling her in hushed tones what a girl going
to the marriage bed should know. Lady Gonwa was held to be kind
but distant as befit such an arbiter of taste; Yala had wondered why
the dame had taken it upon herself to show such signal graciousness to a foreign lady-in-waiting—but Mrong Banh had thanked
Lady Gonwa especially, and seeing the stout, redoubtable noblewoman beam at the astrologer like a flattered girl was both amusing and heartening at once.

The Jonwa receded behind her. There were no slats to open, and
the confinement was close and unwelcome. She had to shut her
eyes and remind herself there was, indeed, enough air inside the
palanquin. She would not suffocate, despite stories from the Second Dynasty of Zhehao Anwone's plaintive singing while being
carried to a cruel warlord drawing the maiden's soul forth.

Her *yue*, warm metal indistinguishable from skin, rested against
her thigh. She had wondered briefly, before Garan Takyeo's death,
what it would be like to have her honor in Zakkar Kai's keeping.

Now it would rest in Garan Takshin's. She had not seen him for
three days, a tradition Zhaon and Khir shared. Even letters could
not pass between them, all necessary messages—there were not
many—passing through Lady Kue and Lady Gonwa.

She knew what happened in a marital bed, of course—one could hardly avoid the knowledge, especially if one's clan bred horses or other livestock. But to contemplate it happening to her own body, her own *self*...

Yala lifted her hand in the swaying, close dimness. The only light came from tiny carved holes patterned around the roofline, but it was enough to see her fingers vibrating far more than the conveyance's movement called for.

How much more fearful had her princess been? *She* had suffered this with admirable grace and obedience, that most central of noble female qualities. Had Mahara's heart beat so thinly in her throat, had her palms been so soaked, had she yearned to push the door open and flee in the soft slippers, tearing heavy decorations and cloth away with great horrified sounds?

Was Komori Dasho's shade watching this with disapproval? With some other emotion? He had wanted her to land gently; no doubt he had been hoping Daoyan could work some miracle and somehow free her. If Mahara had been alive...

But she was not. Yala's princess was gone, riding the Great Fields, and Yala was alone.

Heart pounding, throat dry, fighting the urge to move moment by moment, the bride found her lips moving silently. And why, of all things, should she be repeating the Moon Maiden's reply to Zhe Har's hero?

I must go, my sleeve is caught.

It was a terrible sin to be thinking of another man upon her very wedding day, but Komor Yala wished she were being carried elsewhere, and it was useless to deny it. Just as useless as fleeing would be, or bemoaning her fate, or even drawing her *yue* and loosing her humors in a deeper scarlet tide against the palanquin's walls, if she truly loved Zakkar Kai enough to perform such a deed.

She was utterly, completely helpless. Perhaps she had been all along.

Soup and War

Aman ideally became a general by the efforts of his sword alone, but the reward was endless stacks of rai- and pressed-rag paper, the processing of which required long hours after drill, inspection, parade, and the issuing of daily or monthly orders. Even viewing the stacks of orders, dispatches, and other ephemera in a stone keep's relative comfort instead of a tent was only a minor improvement. At least his scouts were well-trained and it was still nominally peacetime; missing dispatches were not yet holes through which a vanguard could drive.

Since Takyeo's death every missive had arrived like the sound of a babu water-clock, at all the expected intervals. That was not a comfort, for their contents were often a thin rai-paper screen of supposition from commanders whose temperaments or fears led them to huddle in an outpost rather than putting their surroundings under the hooves of a good fast horse and bringing back news.

For all that, there were disturbing signs, and his nape tingled more often than not while reading. It was rather like waiting for a rai-pot to boil. While watched, it would only absorb the heat and store it in humors like a seething underling; once you glanced away it would foam into life and spill half your meager dinner into the flames. The keep's mirrorlights were full of a ruddy sunset fading into twilight, and he wondered what Yala was doing at the moment. Probably brushing a last few characters upon a letter before her kaburei appeared to help her dress for dinner, or performing some other task with quiet, peaceful thoroughness, her clear grey gaze thoughtful and her mouth—

"My lord?" Anlon appeared at the door, bearing a tray. "You have had nothing but soldier-tea since midday."

Kai's own humors were seething like a watched rai-pot as well. The last letter from Yala carefully mentioned nothing but commonplaces, and nothing about her impending marriage at all. He knew it was to save his feelings; he had lost a battle largely through inaction and it irked him. Waiting until Garan Tamuron's temper improved, while at the time no doubt the proper tactical response, had been a strategic blunder.

It was enough to make Kai wonder if he'd deliberately held his hand, not wishing to leave a wife in the palace viper-pit or risk her in an army camp. Yala was, for all her bravery, a noblewoman. You did not take such creatures upon a campaign even if there were stories of noble wives in the First and Third Dynasties following their warlord husbands.

These were modern times, and while a soldier might bring a woman along, a general—especially one wearing a hurai—was a different beast.

"Don't tell me you have eaten either, Anlon." Kai neatened the pile of dispatches with a single habitual movement and motioned his faithful servant in. Anlon was moving with a little less alacrity lately; the wound from the last assassination attempt was healing quite nicely but he was still no young soldier. "I would know it a lie. We are busier than ants preparing for rain."

"And yet nothing seems to happen. Such is a soldier's life." The greying man settled the tray upon a triangular folding table, another familiar underling pressed into unvarying service. "I know that look. Another letter?"

"With nothing of import, at least." At least Kai could pretend to be worried by the change in Emperors instead of brooding over a graceful sleeve, a pair of pale eyes, or a certain lady's way of speaking with sharp Khir consonants in prettily arranged

Zhaon. "Things seem rather quiet, except for troubling news from the south." Yala had alluded to something not quite right in her husband-to-be's adopted land, but whatever the news was, Kurin had not thought to add a précis in his latest directive, as Tamuron would have.

A man fought better when he knew exactly what was behind him. Takshin's own letters gave Kai some idea of what was happening but the man was busy fending off Kurin's ill temper in various directions, Makar's were brief but could be used to infer much, just not in the directions Kai needed. Sensheo, of course, did not bother—which was probably a blessing. Jin's were a delight, full of weapons-trivia, Gamnae's similarly delightful but not very useful.

He wished Takyeo were still alive, but that was useless too.

"At least that." Even Anlon did not suspect Kai's...affections. Or if he did, he kept the knowledge loyally confined to his own liver. "Come, eat. Cook has made floating-flower soup for dinner, to tempt you."

"Floating *flower*?" It was a weak attempt at humor; still, the pun upon what a child could leave in a bathtub if not properly taught to excrete elsewhere would delight any soldier. Kai made a theatrical grimace, perilously close to a child's upon tasting something awful. "It sounds rather bitter, my son."

Anlon's laugh was just as merry as it had been when he was half his current age. "*Ai*, my lord, it is good to hear you at last. You have been horse-faced since you returned."

"With good reason." Kai scratched under his topknot; it was disheveled, since he had settled at his desk just after afternoon drill, not bothering with another tepid wash. Why, when he sought to impress no one? "I shall take a bath, then inspect the outer pickets this evening. They have not seen me in some days, it will do them good." Riding would also grant him a measure of peace, or so he hoped.

Lying abed and thinking about his own failures was not restful in the slightest.

Anlon's gnarled hands moved with habitual speed, readying a

light repast for consumption. "A fine idea, but first, eat." He would bring something more substantial after the picket-ride; he must have suspected Kai would be driven to recheck the defensive screen.

It did not irk him to be anticipated in this matter. Anlon was, after all, not an enemy. "Only if you do. I see two bowls, do not be shy."

"Cook insisted." Anlon shrugged, but his pleasure was clear. "I said I would keep you company, since both Tall and Short Hurong are away."

"Ah, the cooks always know best." His marshals were just as uneasy as he was, which was not quite cheerful news but at least meant Kai's instincts were not as disarranged as his humors. "Come, come. Pass me the eating-sticks, I suddenly remember how hungry I am."

It was good to eat with a fellow soldier, paying only the most cursory attention to manners. To gulp tea without restraint, and ignoring his table-mate while gazing at a worrisome dispatch from Sehon Doah, stationed northward, was not rude at all. Anlon, for his part, set to with a will and much splashing. Soup was too watery to fuel a man's humors for long, but there was also rai and fine skinfruit from surrounding orchards. Care had to be taken not to despoil the last too badly, and ordinary soldiers were supposed to pay for what they ate or receive a flogging.

That, at least, was the goal. Still, the army was restless. Well they might be, for Kai's nape would not cease its tingling, and that meant battle was near no matter how unlikely the prospect seemed at the surface.

There were proverbs about the speed with which a soldier could make anything even remotely comestible disappear, and for good reason. No sooner had Kai finished his first bowl of clear broth with swimming, fan-trailing dumplings than hurrying bootsteps filled the hallway outside; his hand leapt for the well-wrapped hilt of his sword—the dragon's eye peering between leather laces, a baleful glare—and Anlon stiffened, half-rising.

Neither of them had forgotten the last attempt upon Kai's life.

The hurrying was a dispatch rider, covered with dust and bearing a pouch sadly the worse for wear. "My lord!" he gasped, and he had not been halted by the guards because of the medallion he presented, the character for *urgent* in bright crimson over General Sehon Doah's name. "News from General Sehon! To the north, my lord! To the north at Bomor-An!"

Kai's stomach settled with a jolt, and his almost-dry bowl hit the desktop, eating-sticks clattering into its wide-astonished mouth. *Ah. So that is what they are thinking.* The configuration of his forces rose inside his head-meat. "Anlon, maps from here to the bridge over the Tehua. You, come in. What's your name?"

"Kurong Bai, my lord general Zakkar Kai! Dispatch from Bomor-An!" The round-faced fellow was pale, and a glaring bandage was wrapped about his head. It was difficult to see, he was coated so thickly in yellow road-dust. He kept shouting as if he were at drill, every syllable crisp with the particular cadence that meant *army*. "The Khir have attacked! They came at us out of the fog!" His hands worked at the bag-strap, freeing it with a practiced jerk against the buckle.

Steady, my fine fellow. "Give him some tea too, Anlon." Kai found himself around the desk, his scabbarded sword in his left hand, subtracting the bag from the poor fellow. "My soldier-son, come, sit. You have done your duty."

Afterward, he wondered if his words had carried ill-luck, for Kurong Bai's knees gave and he almost went down. This close, his leather half-armor was terribly battered. It seemed he had escaped more than just a few li of heavy riding.

He left the soldier to Anlon's care; his steward half-carried the man to a handy chair and bellowed for a physician before hurrying to the map-cabinet. The call for medical aid was taken up outside the door; Kai broke the seal upon the first dispatch pouch, scattering the contents across his desk among the dishes.

The Khir had made the first move, after all. A little too far to the west, as if they meant to skirt the wastes...or as if they meant to turn his flank. *They will not fall for Three Rivers again*, he had told

Tamuron—and he was right. The solution was easy enough, but as he read—blessing whoever had packed the dispatch bag neatly from the bottom instead of hodgepodge, so he had a half-moon's worth of news in proper order and could see the situation develop—the tingling upon his nape halted and his stomach clenched.

It was not merely battle. The list of standards noted by scouts conversant with Khir writing was long and troubling, and he recognized no few of the devices. Border lords were expected, but there were the other powerful clans—Hazuni, Narikhi, Domari, no doubt Yala would recognize the names.

No, this was not simply battle, or a raid to test Zhaon's readiness just after an accession to the Throne of Five Winds.

It was, in fact, war.

COMPLETE, UNEXPECTED, SWEET

The last wedding feast he attended had been full of merriment and dark undercurrents, all of Garan Tamuron's sons gathered at a table and pretending, in their various ways, a measure of familial harmony. Some, including Takshin himself, had no doubt believed the pretense, and that was bitter to think upon.

These nuptials were much more sober, though the traditional toasts were made and there was a full complement of guests. Even Mrong Banh, after performing the duty of walking alongside the bridal palanquin, made no less than six salutations, and drank deep at each one. Jin and Makar also did their best, after delivering Yala safely to her intended's door.

She was with her kaburei and the Su and Hansei girls now, being prepared. Was she frightened? Anticipating? Simply resigned?

He longed for this to be over, but there must be nothing left undone. He wished Takyeo were here, smiling broadly and keeping the peace; he wished Kai were drinking and making soldier's jokes that skirted the edge of decency; he wished his mother's clan-uncle had not sent an overly ostentatious gift, perhaps to make up for Garan Gamwone's ill-wishing.

If Lord Yulehi thought to ingratiate himself with Mother by doing a disfavored son's bride a disservice, Takshin had a response ready. Worse, of course, would be Binei Jinwon thinking Garan Takshin could be induced to forgiveness of a lifetime of slights and petty insults by a single red-wrapped box. Even before being sent to Shan, he'd disliked the man.

Even the lack of mourning armbands, set aside so as not to bring ill-luck to such a felicitous ceremony, did not bring him the cheer it might have. He simply wished this part of the matter over.

At least Makar had brought several of his clients and Mrong Banh was telling amusing tales, while a few of the Golden beholden to Takyeo—and now Takshin—to some degree or another struck up a drinking-song approaching the edge of ribaldry but nevertheless enthusiastically full of good wishes. Sensheo, who could hardly have been left out of the festivities, was in a bright orange robe with his topknot just slightly askew as he tossed another cup of colorless sohju far back, matching a square-captain with wide shoulders and a hard soldier's gut who had a reputation for being able to hold a prodigious amount of that healthful drink without sliding into somnolence *or* ill-advised japing.

The Fifth Prince managed to refrain from making any mannerless jests, at least so far. It was near miraculous, and Takshin did not miss the pointed glances Makar sent his brother when there seemed a prospect of liquor loosening an ill-wishing tongue.

Near the end of the banquet, there were crashing cymbals and beaten gongs, and every man present leapt to his feet. It was not quite unheard-of for an Emperor to visit a wedding party, but Kurin was, after all, his elder brother, and dressed soberly in a dark robe and stiffened leather topknot-cage besides. Musicians followed in his train, and if it was a gift it had a sting in the tail, for the new Emperor was making a point of blessing this marriage.

Which meant he wanted something. Or their mother did, and Kurin saw no reason to deny her. The Emperor settled in the place of highest honor near the bridegroom, and his presence made the well-wishing even more frantic.

Still, the traditional drinking, witticisms, and other foolery
had to be endured, and Garan Suon-ei Takshin did. When the
cry of *hist, hist, listen* came, he was more than ready for the gongs
announcing the end of first watch to sound. The guests rose as one,
loudly wishing him much happiness, and it was Makar, Jin, and
Mrong Banh who accompanied him through the half-familiar
halls of the house he had never thought to occupy, settled upon
him as a prince of Zhaon by the distant father who had, after all,
sent him to die in Shan.

That Tamuron could not have known the depth of the Mad
Queen's insanity—despite the fact that she was known to be the
mad queen—was, to a young Takshin enduring her rages and
the shame of visiting Zhaon as a weak, scarred shadow, utterly
irrelevant.

And unforgivable. Like so much else.

"Takshin." Makar was at his elbow, the hall's floor moving
slightly under his slippers, by the way he was gently weaving. "Are
you steady?"

"Steady enough." Jin hiccuped, blinking against sohju fumes.
"He's always... and anyway, I drank most of his."

"A truly brotherly feat." Mrong Banh's hazy smile, the product
of no few cups itself, faded a whit. "But you are unwonted silent,
Takshin."

"When was he ever a chatterbox?" Makar might have meant the
question ironically, but Jin performed a stagger-step as if dancing.

"Before he went away, I'm told." Their youngest brother immediately sobered—at least, outwardly. Not much but time would
clear the sohju from his head-meat, at this point. "*Ai*, Shin, a bad
jest. Forgive me."

They thought him so complicated, his family, when the truth was
otherwise. Treated with a modicum of respect, or even just left alone,
Takshin was content to likewise leave them to their own devices. But
Shan had taught him, above all else, to protect what he could.

And to repay what he could, as well.

"*Ai*, Jin, stop worrying. 'Tis amusing enough." This was the last thing to endure before he could be alone with his goal. But Kurin's appearance, though held to be a high and signal honor, was worrisome. So were the dispatches from the south; few merchants were crossing the border from Shan, and Kiron had sent no word at all—of course, if he was fighting off those who had taken his queen's head, he would be too busy to send a note or two. The North was deeply troubling as well; Khir had done nothing more than reoccupy the border posts and some few bridges, but Kai's dispatches—bare, soldierly, well-written, and giving no purchase to any accusation of undutifulness—contained reports from scouts of cavalry sighted along two of the valleys traditionally used for invasion. The general's letters were likewise pessimistic, and hinted that the new Emperor was not sending enough information for the proper disposal of forces. "And I should be forgiving, today of all days."

"Tonight of all nights," Makar corrected sententiously, but a burp caught by the backs of his fingers ruined the effect. He had drained no few of Takshin's cups as well, to leave a bridegroom capable of his later duty instead of unmanned by sohju's fiery touch. "I shall have to write a poem for this, Shin. Never did I envision you with a Khir girl."

"You thought me too ugly to marry, Maki." There was even a certain amount of satisfaction to be had in speaking truth among the thicket of mannerly speech grown high and rank at court. "Admit it."

The Fourth Prince's smile was a marvel of gently beaming goodwill, such as he had not displayed since childhood—or if he had, his elder brother had not seen it. "Apparently a particular lady does not think so."

She was not given a chance to refuse. The bitterness was familiar, and Takshin swallowed it.

He would not let this particular victory be hollow. "Perhaps Khir eyes see what others do not." The hallway was not rocking underfoot; he was not very drunk.

Was he?

"Lady Komor is very brave. Why, once she even—" Jin clapped a hand over his mouth, sensing an indiscretion a moment before Takshin could gather the wherewithal to glare at him.

"She must be, to overcome Shin's temper." Makar appeared not to notice, concentrating very visibly upon setting his blue-slippered feet in proper order. "Never did I think you would be the first of us married, either."

"I wasn't." Takshin's throat was suddenly full. He had welcomed the end of deep mourning more than was quite proper, and the fact that his eldest brother of all people would have forgiven him was a knife in his guts.

Except the knife had been in Takyeo's guts, hadn't it.

"*Tcha.*" Mrong Banh made a short, sharp noise, and his left hand leapt in a gesture to avert ill-luck. "Not tonight, my sons. Tonight is for celebration."

He must be very drunk indeed, to address us thus. The cursed unforgiving clarity he had suffered almost all his life descended upon Takshin in double measure, and he found himself all but coldly sober, treading down a hall toward a door festooned with red ribbons. Behind it, Yala would be alone, perhaps hearing their approach.

"Far enough," he said, and freed his arm from Jin's grasp with a determined yank. "That is quite far enough, all of you. Good night."

"*May all be harmonious,*" Makar quoted. Of course he would have a scholarly reference ready. The Fourth Prince drew himself up, blinking like a nightbird. His topknot tilted slightly to the left, and the slight dishevelment suited him. "Come, Jin. There is still drinking to do tonight."

"But...we have to, right to the threshold. To avoid ill-luck." Jin blinked furiously too, probably trying to rid himself of the sohju-veil. It was a losing battle.

"*Right to the threshold, Ma Nui my love...*" Banh crooned suddenly, startling them all. He had quite a fine tenor, for all he rarely let it loose. "What? You don't remember that song?"

"I think it was before our time," Makar said gravely, and Jin broke into clear young unaffected laughter.

Takshin shook them away and strode for the door. He opened it carefully, so as not to show the bride to any jealous gaze, and slipped through as the merriment did. It was a good omen, he hoped, and his breath caught in his throat.

Komor Yala—now Garan Komor-a Yala—sat upon the edge of the bed, her hands clasped in her lap. She wore a simple linen shift, her hair unbound in a blue-black river down her back, and her wide grey eyes were lustrous, perhaps with tears. She cradled that strange greenmetal blade—no hilt-wrapping, just crosshatching upon the tang, too long for a knife and too short for a sword—and the exotic idea that she would turn it against him swam though his head-meat once, then drifted away.

He would welcome the wound, he realized, leaning against the door to make certain it was closed and latched. From her hands, what would he not receive with a faintly shameful gratitude? In a moment he would turn the lock and use the bar, if only for her defense. It could not be to hinder her escape, could it?

Finally, Garan Takshin had won something. The victory was complete, unexpected, and sweet enough to rid him of any lingering bitterness as well as the last ghost of sohju and the unremitting, sullen fury that had been his companion since he endured his first night in Shan's central palace, a child trapped far from home.

Yala studied him, her chin up, but there was a betraying tremor in her shoulders. She lifted the blade, slightly, upon both palms. He knew how sharp it was, having held it in his own.

"This is my honor," she said, softly. "It is now yours, my husband." The rhythm of Khir lingered behind her words.

Takshin's throat was dry as the Westron Wastes. All else—Tabrak, Khir, his elder brother upon a bloodstained throne, the many vengeances he owed both for Takyeo's sake and his own—vanished.

"Is there a reply?" he managed, his tongue not quite wishing to obey. "In Khir?"

She nodded, solemnly. Once before he had seen her hair unbound, but not like this. "If you wish me to lay it aside, you take it from me. If you...if you think I may need to use it, or if you think me less weak than a woman usually is, you..." Her throat moved as she swallowed. "You tell me to keep it close, and unstained, as my father did before I left Khir."

He tried to imagine having a daughter, or letting such a bird fly south to a cruel foreign land, and utterly failed. "Then keep it close." He sounded curiously husky, even to himself. "But not so close as to stab me, I would ask."

"Oh." She lowered the metal to her lap again, and for a moment looked very young, lost and forlorn. "Of course not. You are my *husband*."

Now I am. "Yes." There was an obstruction in his throat. He sounded, in fact, as if he were being strangled. "I am." *Except for one small thing.* He longed to tell her he would not force her, that he would wait until she was ready, as the Third Emperor in the tale of Jehnao Har and the Courtesan of Shadows. He longed to be that man—and if he had not been sent to Shan, would he have been?

It was an unanswerable question. So, instead, Garan Takshin locked the door, settled the bar in its brackets, and turned to his new wife.

WHAT YOU WISHED FOR

When he was merely Second Prince of Zhaon, it had often pleased Garan Kurin to perform morning drill upon the wide white stone plain where many Golden—and Zakkar Kai, when he was in Zhaon-An—daily practiced the civilized arts of sword, shield, pike, and other means of separating an opponent from his liver and life.

His royal father had been wont to spar with ordinary soldiers while he was still warlord, but had discontinued the practice after enthronement since even a loyal Golden bound to execute every imperial order was not likely to give their best effort when success *or* failure could mean a trip to the dungeons or worse, some mischance damaging Heaven's representative to Zhaon. Still, a royal brother was not an ordinary soldier, so the new Emperor had eschewed the practice of weapons-forms in his private Kaeje salle this morning under a sun hanging like a ripe fruit in the dust-hazed sky.

"You are in fine temper." Kurin grinned, a flash of teeth visible in the shadow cast by his helm's nose-guard as he tested the heft of a blunted wooden practice sword. "The celebration seems to have done you some ill."

"A little too much sohju." Fourth Prince Makar was a regular visitor to the drillyard, when not practicing privately with the best tutors of the warlike arts. If he suffered any trepidation at the sight of his elder brother, it was well hidden. "But when drinking to a brother's health, it cannot be helped." He leaned forward, testing the heft of his own sword, and the line between his brows, as well as the set of his mouth, did not change.

"Ah, yes." Kurin frowned slightly, tugging at a gauntlet-lace on his practice armor. Still, he waved away the armor-son he had selected from the attending Golden, a rawboned youth who turned pale at the honor—not to mention the peril—of such a duty. "Imagine, our Takshin all grown up and married. Your turn is coming, Makar."

"Is it?" The Fourth Prince sounded only mildly interested in such a momentous announcement. His practice armor was plain but very serviceable, and the weighted wooden blade he carried was dark ironwood, its hilt carved with much skill into the head of a snarling, immortal everbird, stylized flames running down the blade. It had been a gift from a certain lady, one he had asked to wait just a little longer. "One would think my mother would tell me."

"One would." The crimson feathers cresting Kurin's helm waved proudly as he nodded. "How is our Second Mother?"

Was that his next move? It wasn't likely, so Makar tilted his upper half in a subtle bow, thanking his brother for even false solicitousness. "In good health, for which we daily thank Heaven. Are you certain you wish to do this, Your Majesty?"

There was little hope Kurin would halt. His elder brother was in a mood Makar recognized from childhood, and if he was not given what he wanted—or balked by a greater authority—he would strike at someone perhaps a little less prepared to handle his ire than the Fourth Prince.

"If you plead a sour head, I will let you withdraw." Kurin had his gauntlets settled to his satisfaction now, and half-turned to glance at the way the shadows lay, possibly calculating the time. No doubt there were council meetings to attend and ministerial questions to answer, though none could begin until he appeared. "But it's been a while since we played together, Maki."

"Indeed it has." Makar took care not to glance at the crowded terraces upon either side of the drillground, brightly clad court ladies in the colonnaded shade, dark-robed eunuchs with their hats nodding cloth crushflower-balls at the end of stiff wrapped-wire arcs to denote rank, ministers either soberly or flashily clad, and other courtiers or noble hopefuls. Some still wore mourning-bands upon their left arms.

Others did not.

Some affected to critique the display of martial prowess, others—mostly those court ladies with daughters to place among the Palace garden, as the saying went—compared matrimonial aspects in elliptical discussion laden with references to popular novels or the Theater District's current choral offerings. Others discussed intrigue in similarly camouflaged terms, or busied themselves with recondite scholarly arguments. Some even conducted a manner of business despite the traditional prohibition upon such things.

Even noblemen needed to eat. *That* was no proverb, but Makar often thought it should be.

Emperor and prince bowed, Kurin only slightly to honor a younger brother, Makar deeply as was due an Emperor but without the finishing obeisance that would intrude upon his own royalty, and the first few exchanges were somewhat tentative. The preliminaries over, the armor-sons waiting at the sidelines to dart in and retighten any loosened laces, Makar and his now-eldest living brother circled. Their boots creaked slightly as they warmed to the morning's work, sunshine beating at their padded helms, leather half-armor ready to turn aside a halfhearted blow or two.

The sounds of drill were familiar—ringing metal, thumping weighted wood, creak of leather, exhalation of effort, curses quickly swallowed and exhortations from square-captains or onlookers bouncing from hot white paving.

It took very little to gain the measure of a man you had known since your own birth; perhaps the soreness in Makar's head and stiffness in his liver from last night's overindulgence accounted for his loginess. He took the first hit, high on the outside of his left shoulder, and the murmur of approval from the onlookers was almost inaudible.

Almost.

"I have a question." Kurin feinted to the side, retiring a half-step when the invitation was declined.

Makar chose to circle a few more steps before moving in, his blade sweeping laterally and batted aside with ease. "A question or a command?" The exchange gave him a moment to breathe, and also showed a small hesitation in Kurin's overhand strike.

"My uncle tells me I should reorder the succession." A bright dart of sunshine glittered from the Emperor's helm. He gave ground before Makar's flurry, but not easily, and both of them were breathing quickly by the time the rhythm faltered and they broke apart.

The Fourth Prince moved easily to the center of their combat-space, performing the retreat with no hint of an opening. "That is traditional only after the first full year of a reign."

Kurin's shoulder lifted in a shrug, dropped. His blade did not quiver. "Since there are so many heirs, he says."

"No doubt your uncle is wise." Another flurry, wood cracking against wood, each move distinct and crisp. Another smattering of applause ran through the terraces. Boots stamped or scuffed along stone, sweat trapped under leather soaking into cloth, salt-moisture greasing his forehead—this exertion was necessary and had to be performed with grace, but Garan Makar did not like it overmuch.

Despite the luxury of princely existence, there was little to actually *like* within its confines.

"Wise or frightened." The shape of Kurin's chin, left free of the helm's shadow, meant he was either smiling or teeth-bare grimacing.

"What has he to fear?" Makar's point was plain; Lord Yulehi was the uncle of the new Emperor and, at least formally, the chief minister for this half of the year. It was all but impossible to lever him from his position—unless, of course, his nephew took an active dislike to him.

Which Makar thought very possible indeed. He moved in, testing Kurin's defenses, lulling his elder into rhythm.

"We are living in unsettled times, my brother. Tabrak somewhere to the south, Khir growing restive, our father and an heir suddenly gone in their prime—the old men are muttering." Kurin responded just as Makar knew he would—side-downsweep, step back, another parry, two short jabbing strikes.

"Old men always mutter." Makar parried, then was forced to turn lightly upon the forefoot as Kurin circled further. Engaging just enough to keep his opponent occupied, drawing them into a pattern, subtly preparing them to make a mistake—it took more effort upon the practice-ground, but it was paradoxically easier and much more direct than his usual games. "It is their nature."

"You are next in succession." Kurin set to work in earnest, and for a short while neither of them spoke, too busy with feint, cut, shoulder-strike, kick, and the closely guarded secret of the light-foot blooming from toe to hip, the subtle body called upon to aid the physical move in ways mere peasants or tradesmen could not dream of.

When they separated again, Makar's temper had been thoroughly roused. He disliked this display; it could only mean his now-eldest brother had decided to provoke some manner of mistake upon Makar's part. "Alas, I shall refuse the honor."

"When Zhaon calls, you must answer."

"I did answer." Makar slapped aside a questing blow with the flat of his blade—a showy move, and the tightening around Kurin's mouth, visible even in helm-shade, said he knew as much.

Yes, the Emperor wished his brother to make a mistake. Makar's plans were not quite ready yet, but he knew his own limitations—or at least, he hoped he did. He could scheme forever and still be outdone if he did not take action at some point, and this was as good as any.

Kurin's sword described a full circle, testing its balance before the bout quickened once more, the hilt settling firmly back into his palm. "You would disobey your emperor?"

"I would tell my brother I have no interest in being his successor." The Fourth Prince had little hope his elder would accept such a statement.

And he was right, it appeared, for Kurin darted forward, more dancing than attacking, clearly certain he had the upper hand. "Whether you are interested or not—"

Makar struck.

The rhythm of blow and counterblow was shattered; he drove past Kurin, the weighted blade connecting solidly, almost horizontal across his brother's belly. Were it sharp metal, the Emperor's guts would be laid open, especially if Makar took the half-step sideways and used the twisting to drag the blade through stiffened leather and flesh beneath. It was a textbook move, only possible because Kurin had been concentrating upon conversation instead of combat.

The observers were silent. To cheer, applaud, or otherwise expostulate might imply delight in the Emperor's misfortune, or worse. Many of the Golden, busy with their own drills or practice bouts, did not notice the outcome of the fight; those who did froze, caught between the urge to save their superior the embarrassment of remarking upon a minor defeat and the duty of the Emperor's guard to meet any danger to him with bared blade.

Of course the Emperor's brother was a prince, and very filial, so no danger was possible...and yet.

Makar did not continue with the natural succession of blows to make certain a gutsplit enemy did not strike before dying. Instead, he stood, almost cheek to cheek with Kurin, a statue like Two-Face the god of doorways and eunuchs. He breathed deeply, staring half-focused at the bright blur of the drillyard and the sheer wall broken by wide, turning flights of stairs, guarded by snarling, freshly gilded statues of fantastical beasts somewhere between dragons and striped pards.

"I am your brother," Garan Makar said softly. If Kurin now felt his grasp upon power firm enough to perform this sort of idiocy, it was time for the Fourth Prince to do a little provoking of his own. "Not your kaburei. You have what you wished for." It took a physical effort not to add *now leave the rest of us in peace*.

But he was fairly certain his brother would hear the words anyway. If he knew Kurin well, the Emperor also knew *him*. You could not escape being known, but you could be a little less than predictable.

In that direction lay whatever safety Makar could gain for his mother, his clan, and even his foolish little brother.

Kurin struggled to draw breath. This close, he could be examined under the helm-shadow. The blow, all the more severe for being unanticipated, also dyed his cheeks with the most royal of crushflowers, and sweat gleamed upon his proud nose. He said nothing, but his lips pulled back from his teeth, and in that moment he looked very like Father—if Garan Tamuron had ever shown rage instead of a sober, controlled mien.

Makar could not remember such an occasion, but he was sure it had occurred once or twice. Perhaps Kai could describe it, if asked.

He stepped smartly away without finishing the strike, a light shuffle that kept him balanced at every point. It was a move Kai would have recognized; Makar wondered if it were time to bring the general into some of his more subtle and thoroughly hidden plans.

Kurin stood stock-still as his younger brother saluted, the traditional gesture of concession. It was a very filial movement, refraining from pressing an advantage, and the onlookers would no doubt be remarking to each other—with glances and vague facial expressions, instead of aloud—that Garan Makar had, after all, much more restraint than his other brothers.

Perhaps one or two of them would even grasp the true message. *Here is one who does not wish the throne.*

The fact that several would think him weak did not bother him; nor did the companion consideration that some would think him a much better fit for the seat of power than the First Queen's first-born with his strong whiff of familial murder. Whether Kurin had or had not engaged the assassins who had finally managed to kill Takyeo—oh, very carefully, indeed—did not matter. The affair simply *looked* bad; legitimacy was fragile ice upon a thawing pond even at the best of times.

And Garan Makar found he was, after all, angry. Perhaps it was the sohju lingering in his humors, perhaps it was Takshin's wedding reminding him of his Eldest Brother's, which was not, after all, so very long ago.

The feeling was so new he handed the weighted blade back to the Golden serving as his armor-son this morning, and did not stay to engage in another friendly bout with a soldier or two as he perhaps should have.

And the new Emperor did not either, but stalked from the wide white expanse of stone with a forbidding expression, as his court hurried in his wake.

LADIES' COURT

S he was not a queen or crown princess, so the customary three days of bridal seclusion common in both Khir and Zhaon were sufficient. Still, Yala might have wished for more. Not only was the heat a punishing, dragging weight even during the hours supposedly set aside for rest, but a new husband was often properly enthusiastic about his... duties.

And now she was married. Lady Kue's bows upon entering her presence were correspondingly deeper, the steward Keh hurrying to both prove himself to a new master and be of use to a new mistress with flutters of his pudgy hands and just as many half-mumbled confidential asides; Su Junha and Hansei Liyue properly changed their address and accents in Zhaon but otherwise behaved just as usual, which was a deep relief all its own.

Much stranger was the sudden freedom. So much more was possible for a prince's bride than for a lone, unmarried foreign lady. For example, entering the palace complex on horseback to visit Lady Gonwa, her retinue not so much chaperones as necessary to carry the required gifts to thank those who had deigned to notice her nuptials. There was even a small, exquisitely fragrant block of toubanh incense, held to be healthful especially by devotees of the Awakened One, wrapped with much care and addressed to the First Mother of the Revered Emperor, to be handed over in a Kaeje hall by a palace servant well used to these sorts of duties.

Garan Yulehi-a Gamwone was, after all, Yala's new mother-in-law. Even if the First Queen had not sent a wedding-gift, Yala was determined to give the woman nothing to complain of.

Takshin had not addressed the matter beyond formally forbidding his new wife to visit his mother. The refusal was witnessed by Lady Kue and no less a personage than Zan Fein himself, which Yala thought was quite intentional upon her new husband's part. He did very little without a reason; so, as Yala rode through between the great vermilion pillars of the entrance reserved for nobility, she did not have to brace herself for such an unpleasant meeting.

Zan Fein's visit to Takshin's estate had been to instruct a Khir bride upon the proper etiquette and precedence required for her new station; Mahara's own instruction in such arcana had been codified in a long missive from the chief court eunuch and studied during the journey south. It was slight comfort that Yala knew or guessed most of the thornier rules from reading that earlier collection of pressed-rag paper with the careful flowing brushstrokes of a ministerial hand.

The Jonwa was sealed, its great, heavy, dark front doors atop their steps bearing a red blot and a proclamation in the Emperor's own hand. If Garan Takyeo's shade walked there, it did so alone; an entire cortege of exorcists from the most highly regarded temples had paced with bowl, gong, salt, rai, and burning incense through the small palace's halls once Takshin had moved his eldest brother's household—now his own—outside the complex's walls. Once the new Emperor codified the succession in his own hand, his then-named successor would break the seal and move in.

But not, Yala thought, without another round of exorcists. It was apparently held to be ill-luck for a new Emperor to order the succession right away; even Garan Tamuron had waited until his first-born was to be married to perform such a bureaucratic necessity.

So, while she rode between the great crimson-painted pillars, she immediately turned aside and did not allow her fine black mare to set a single hoof upon the great processional way leading past the Jonwa to the Kaeje's main entrance. Her mount could be left at the smaller of the princely stables, and her retinue was already dispersing to carry several gifts to their recipients. Su Junha and Hansei Liyue could not accompany her upon this first visit, but ever-faithful Anh was in Yala's wake, clutching at the pommel of a small but exquisitely caparisoned pony and looking extremely ill at ease even though a minor princess's kaburei was sometimes allowed the privilege of a small mount.

The pony was another gift from Takshin. He took his bride-groom duties seriously, though Yala could have wished...

No, that was a thought unworthy of a wife. A certain amount of trepidation at entering a new role was healthy, she told herself again, and did not allow a Golden Guard to help her from the saddle.

In some small ways, she would remain Khir.

"*Ai*," Anh said, rubbing at her lower back after being helped from her own saddle by a stable-hand. "I know it is proper, my lady, but walking is less painful."

"Not while hunting, my Anh." The jest could mean she was seeking matrimonial prospects for the noble girls in her care, that she wished to secure some victory of social standing, or—closer to the truth—she was now prepared to begin laying her lures to find a certain malefactor within the palace walls. Yala could not help but smile, though the expression felt not quite natural and she quickly sobered. "You have the packages?"

"Of course. The Silver Pavilion is in the Iejo." Anh no doubt knew her mistress was aware of the location, but perhaps she was nervous too.

Even the water-gardens were breathless and oppressive in this heat, ponds shimmering and babu water-clocks thunking away reg-ularly. The dry-gardens shimmered with heat, succulents luxuriat-ing under a layer of thin golden dust. Yala's pace, sedate as befitted a new bride, still caused sweat to gather under her dress, and even the three strands of bright crystals depending from her hairpin— now that she had a husband, she could wear one again—were hot when they brushed against her neck. At least she had a bright crimson sunbell to mute the force of the day's yellow eye; falling into one of the garden-pools like an overwhelmed jewelwing might provide some transitory relief but would be a very bad omen.

The Silver Pavilion was full of court ladies in vivid gowns, servants hurrying to fetch this or that small article required by conversation or etiquette, a smattering of dark-robed eunuch scribes at the edges ready to brush and seal letters for the indolent. Her arrival was noticed with a polite but very restrained fuss.

Lady Gonwa rose from a bright yellow cushion at a low hauwood table, its legs carved with watery dragons twining in sinuous support. "Ah, this brightens our day. We have been waiting for you—oh, how beautiful." The redoubtable dame motioned to her cousin, Gonwa Eulin, who came forward very prettily in blue cotton and a hairpin dangling filigree-dipped chatterbird feathers to accept the well-wrapped gift due her aunt. "You are so kind, my dear." She took Yala's arm, drawing her along—next would come the promenade through the different ranks of court ladies, setting the tone for further interactions. It was dull, tedious work requiring deep attention to tone, posture, and poise in order to stay alert to hidden undercurrents and catch subtle signals.

It was also utterly familiar, and a great relief. This was a game all Khir noble girls trained from birth for.

Like hunting.

Anh settled upon a thin, unembroidered cushion near the pavilion's entrance, alert for any signal that her lady would need her to fetch an item. Lady Gonwa had not taken up her cane, so she leaned heavily upon Yala's arm. Their first stop was a low circular part of the pavilion well-stocked with rich cushions and only a few small tables, all probably arranged every morning by sweating servants with anxious care. For central to the space was Garan Haesara, the old Emperor's second queen, and the dilemma of how to greet such an august personage in the current situation was solved by the dowager's visible brightening as Yala approached.

"How lovely!" Haesara said, and beckoned them closer. "It is our new daughter. You must address me as *mother-in-law*." The term she used was the most affectionate honorific for a husband's mother in Zhaon instead of Zan Fein's suggestion of *Second Dowager Mother to the Revered Emperor*, and Yala did not know yet whether to be relieved or doubly cautious. "Look, my dear. Here she is."

"Ah. Yes." Next to her, and in matching silk of the palest possible pink edged with a strip of unbleached mourning, was Garan Luswone, the First Concubine. Now she was the Third Mother of the Revered Emperor, or so Zan Fein had cautioned Yala. Her nose was slightly pink and her eyes red-rimmed, but her hair was dressed most fetchingly in a high asymmetric style and her fingertips were dipped with fragrant resin. "Our Takshin's new bride. You must call me *mother-in-law* as well—it will be quite confusing, but we shall bear it."

Unexpected high favor could be a trap all its own; Gonwa Eulin hurried forward to take her familial elder's other arm so Yala could perform the bow due to such august personages with the deepest possible reverence. A daughter-in-law's required greeting, according to etiquette, was thankfully quite clear. "You grant a humble stranger much honor, Mothers of Zhaon."

"Charming, isn't she?" Haesara beckoned again, this time a shade peremptorily. "Do sit with us a short while, daughter. And you, Lady Gonwa—your arrival is fortunate, we were just about to enjoy some of your incomparable heaven tea."

That placed the affair upon an altogether different footing. The dowager queen was honoring not just Yala but her patroness; she would not make such a point of it if she were at least not mildly well-disposed toward the new addition to the family.

The mystery was partly solved when the ladies settled, Gonwa Eulin pouring for all as befit the most junior member of the table. It was Third Mother Luswone who indicated a small filigreed plate of pounded-rai cakes and pressed one upon Yala, with a tremulous smile. "You must be as a daughter to both of us," she murmured. "We know you were very kind to Fourth Mother."

The other ladies of the court would merely see a mark of preferment toward a foreign bride, but the quiet aside solved the mystery
of such favor. *Fourth Mother* could only mean Kai's adoptive-
mother, and Yala's visits in that direction could not have gone
unremarked.

"I wish to please my new husband's family," Yala parried, a filial response indeed. So much had happened, the tranquil hours
spent with Garan Kanbina seemed to belong to another life, as the
Awakened One said all were prone to before they acquired enough
merit to step directly into Heaven.

"Quite right, quite right." Haesara lifted her teacup, which
meant the rest of them could as well. "We find you very pleasing,
my dear, and long to continue doing so." Her gaze lifted, and settled pointedly upon an empty table of dark, wax-rubbed eir-wood,
surrounded by likewise empty though expensively embroidered
cushions. It was a shame it was unoccupied, for the location was
the best and would receive a pleasant breeze from the largest garden of those ringing the Pavilion. Still, the cushions were scattered
in quite unaesthetic disarray, and the table's top was not polished
but held a sheen of summer dust. "It's a pity others could not be
here to welcome you."

It was rather elegant—she could mean Garan Kanbina, recently
ascended to Heaven to prepare a place for her lordly husband, who
had after all followed her quickly. But it was not very likely, for the
only woman of the court who could possibly have occupied that
dark table with her retinue and clients was the First Queen.

"There has been much...upset, in the court of Zhaon." Yala
ducked her head, letting her hairpin's string of crystals swing sadly.
"In truth my good fortune seems rather impolite."

Luswone gazed at her steadily, thoughts moving in her very fine
dark eyes. Her mouth turned down a fraction, and her ribboned
ear-drops trembled. This close, the fragility of grief was apparent.
Yala longed to say something kind, but she could not presume
upon a woman who had lost a child, never mind if that child was
an adult princess who had, after all, made an advantageous match

beforehand. The sum of all noble girls' desires, even if it bore a bitter fruit, had been attained.

Haesara lifted the fingertips of her left hand to her mouth, palm out, unsuccessfully hiding a smile. "Well spoken indeed, daughter. Lady Gonwa, what a treasure you have brought us."

"It is your third son who has brought the treasure." But Lady Gonwa inclined the upper half of her body fractionally, accepting the compliment with pleasure. "I inquired after the First Dowager Queen's health this morning; sadly, I did not receive a reply." She did not glance significantly at Yala, who gathered herself for a declaration of intent.

"How very sad indeed." She lifted the cake Luswone had pressed upon her to her lips, touching it elegantly but not daring to nibble yet, for such would be uncouth. "I was honored to meet that great lady of Zhaon once before, however glancingly." She had listened while the woman insulted Mahara, in fact, and Haesara had been there as well. "Is she ... often ill?"

Now the queen, the concubine, and the chief court lady could guess that rumors of the Third Prince's disdain for his mother were quite well-founded, and that Yala was relieved to be spared subjecting herself to the woman. If they were in league against Gamwone, Yala had plainly made her feelings known, but also left them a graceful retreat if they did not choose such an ally.

It seemed the First Mother had precious few ready to raise their banners in her defense at this table, which could be helpful to Yala's own purposes. She let the cake linger at her lips and let her eyebrows rise, mimicking culinary appreciation.

"Is an eyebird ever lonely?" One of Haesara's shoulders lifted a fraction, dropped. "I see we may speak plainly to you, daughter."

For the moment. Yala laid the cake upon the plate Luswone had readied for her, a fine piece of Gurai slipware with triangles stamped into its rim. "I must listen to my mother-in-law as I obey my husband. It is only proper."

"My daughter..." Third Mother Luswone pursed her lips, avoiding the ill-luck mention of a shade's proper name. "She was quite taken with the First Queen."

First Queen, not *First Mother*. Indeed Gamwone had no friends here, but Yala was still cautious. She settled herself in an attitude of attentiveness, letting her eyelashes veil her non-Zhaon gaze as her hands, properly hidden by her sleeves, arranged themselves in her lap.

"She was young, my dear." If Haesara was not kind, she certainly gave a wonderful impression of it. "How is Jin? Will you be sending him to Daebo until the autumn?"

"It might be wise, but..." Luswone's sigh trembled like the rest of her. The asymmetric hairstyle quite suited her; some of her ladies followed suit but not with the same charm. "I do not like to be without him. I cannot decide, Haesara. It was all so sudden."

"More tea?" Lady Gonwa was somewhat anxious. "Eulin, dear, fetch my sewing basket, I have a mind to ask Princess Yala's opinion upon a shade or two. You are always so modestly attired, princess."

It was strange to hear herself referred to by such a title. "Khir fashions are very different," Yala murmured. "I must ask you to tell me, if I look ridiculous."

It was the right thing to say, for most of the tension at the table fled. An approaching rustle was a court lady with almost-disheveled hair held low upon her nape with a single plain hairpin, her summery blue dress belted very low. The effect was like an illustration scroll of a Fourth Dynasty concubine, helped along by the woman's high forehead and wide, catlike eyes. This was Lady Aoan, held to have impeccable taste as well. "Forgive me, my queen," she inquired sweetly. "But Lady Suek and I are arguing, and it must be settled."

Perhaps she was merely curious about the new arrival. Yala regarded her with bright interest, letting the court lady look her fill.

"What would I not forgive you, Lady Aoan?" Haesara brightened with what appeared to be genuine pleasure. "Princess Yala, do meet one of my particular favorites, Lady Aoan Mau. She is a fine sathron player."

"Nothing like Fourth Mother Garan Kanbina, certainly." Lady Aoan bowed very prettily indeed, and the avid light in her dark eyes was familiar. She had been charged with bringing word of the queen and concubine's true feelings to the others, and had a ready pretext for doing so. "I practice and practice, though. My princess, perhaps you may settle the matter."

"I am not certain I will be of any help," Yala parried. The noblewoman was old to be still unmarried, but the reasons could be various.

"Let us hear the question." Haesara folded her hands in her lap as well, tilting her head so her hairpin decorations moved as they should. "Proceed."

"Lady Suek thinks we should play the Song of the Drums from Ao Xi's latest epic. *I* think we should play Flowers of the Stream from Ni Jiqua's play, even though it is old. Does our new princess visit the theater often?"

Ah. So Yala's theater visit with Garan Gamnae had been remarked upon, and Lady Aoan anxious to remind her benefactress of the fact in case the First Queen was likely to find an ally or spy in her new daughter-in-law. Yala freed a hand, treating herself to a single sip of Lady Gonwa's tea while she appeared to give the question deep thought. The jaelo in the tea was overpowering today; it was a good thing she liked the small, highly fragrant flowers. In any case, it would be highly impolite to speak before the Second Mother had given her opinion.

"Did not Sixth Prince Jin go with you?" Haesara addressed Yala. In other words, she did not think it likely Gamnae's attention to Yala had been solely at the First Queen's behest, and invited Yala to answer.

So Yala nodded. "He accompanied his sister the Second Princess, very attentively. It was a pleasant evening indeed."

"A love song then, to cool the afternoon. And to honor the love of a prince." Queen Haesara's laugh was clear and bright; Lady Aoan's rose to meet it, and Yala smiled. Lady Gonwa beamed— apparently, this was a good sign; only Third Mother Luswone did not share the merriment. Instead, she stared into her own cup, apparently lost in thought.

"Mother-in-law?" Yala said it as tentatively and honorifically as she could. "My husband did ask me to invite Sixth Prince Jin to his house for dinner, if it would suit the Sixth Prince to come. Our household is unsettled just at the moment, but my husband is quite fond of his youngest brother and longs to see him again."

Luswone—what a pretty name, and had she not been grieving, she would have been just as much an illustration as Lady Aoan, a matron instead of a maiden—gave her a startled look. "So," she said softly. "Will he protect my son?"

Haesara glanced sharply at her. Lady Aoan made a half-embarrassed sound masquerading as a laugh. "A love song it is, then." She bowed to her patroness and fluttered away.

A sharp sudden chill went through Yala, despite the heat of the day. If even the First Concubine was this worried for her child, everyone at this table suspected the current Emperor of a hand in Garan Takyeo's misfortune. And, quite possibly, in that of Mahara's, since they were paying such signal attention to a foreign lady-in-waiting but newly married to a prince who made his disdain of court etiquette plain.

Had Yala been able to attend such gatherings of the court women before now, she might have been able to lay a few plans, and perhaps warn Takyeo. But her princess's husband must have known his next-eldest brother desired the throne. He was not—or had not been, she reminded herself, he was irretrievably gone though his shade was no doubt watching with some interest—stupid, after all.

Why had he not moved to avenge Mahara's death? He *had* to have known something. Perhaps the new Emperor was blameless in the matter of a Khir princess, but—

"My husband is very fond indeed of his brother Sixth Prince Jin," Yala said, firmly. She set her teacup down with a decided click, yet another signal. "The Sixth Prince is *always* welcome in our home."

There. She had committed herself to defending Jin, in whatever fashion she could. She did not think Takshin would mind much. Especially not when Luswone pressed her hand, the royal concubine's lower lip trembling for just a moment before she mastered her humors.

"Music in the afternoon is quite appropriate," Third Mother said, brightly. The contrast between her tone and expression might have been piquant in a play, but it made Yala's chest ache. She did not know yet what a mother suffered, though if Takshin continued his nightly attentions, she might soon.

Surely Yala was a good enough wife to wish for such an advent. It was what she had been raised for, and yet her treacherous heart ached.

She had other matters to attend to at the moment, and they crowded her close. She could hope Kai was safe, surrounded by soldiers and away from court intrigues. Perhaps she could even move to shield him in some oblique fashion.

"Indeed." Haesara essayed a beneficent smile, and her approval, though quite properly masked by manners, was evident. "My daughter, you must visit my part of the Kaeje soon. Did you embroider your cuffs? May I see the stitchwork? It is very fine."

In other words, Yala was counted among this hunting party instead of the First Mother's. It made her way smoother, and her task much easier. If one of those present had made arrangements for a Crown Princess's death, she would sooner or later find out.

If the culprit lay in another direction, she would also find out. Confirmation of her suspicions would bring terrible decisions of its own, but she had left the bailey with her hawk to wrist, and was now riding to flush prey.

In her own fashion.

Komor Yala, now a princess of Zhaon, smiled and ducked her head again, freeing her sleeve for her new mother-in-law's examination. Her hawks had struck true more than once, in Khir.

"My mother-in-law is very kind to compliment my poor work," she murmured. "I struggled with the thread."

A Faithful
Servant

He saw the kaburei belonging to the Khir-flower Takshin was so enamored with again, but his plans for that girl could wait. Sensheo stayed where he was, and eventually, many *thump-thocks* of a babu water-clock later, his patience was rewarded. His true quarry came hurrying into sight, her mouth a drawn-down line and her dark dress not nearly of the quality necessary for a royal servant. It was almost painful to see such parsimoniousness.

In any case, the thin woman hurried past, her gaze fixed assiduously upon the stone path, and if he hadn't deliberately drawn aside into the damp shadow of a yeoyan with its leaves crisping at the edge despite painstaking nightly dousing, he might almost have been piqued that a servant could fail to register his presence.

"Hello, Yona," he said softly, and his hand shot out, closing around her bony upper arm. He drew her aside, and her startled resistance was quelled as soon as the fact of his silk robe—dark blue, just the thing for staying motionless in whatever shade could be found upon a morning in Zhaon's dry season—registered. Even his topknot-cage and its pin were varnished to a matching hue, and he drew her aside into an overgrown arbor. An onlooker might think he was witnessing the beginning of a tryst, but as the proverb said, nobody bothered with a dry well.

Garan Gamwone's chief servant went limp as a rabbit in a hawk's claws, only the flaring of her ribs with harsh deep breathing showing she was, indeed, alive and conscious rather than fainting from heat or shock.

Yona was not a noblewoman; one of those creatures accosted thus would perhaps actually lose consciousness. Plays and novels were full of such vapid creatures. Eventually he would have to marry one—he would certainly not, if his plans went well, even need an imperial endorsement—but he could safely leave that event in his mother's hands.

Perhaps she'd be so busy with her precious Makar's flirtation with her favorite Aoan she would put off matrimony for her disappointing younger son. But soon, *soon* he would show her his mettle.

He would show them all.

"Glorious Fifth Prince Garan Sensheo." Yona's voice was a dry croak; maybe she had no moisture left in her liver. "Your handmaiden... *ulp*..." The ritual greeting cut off with a short, pained sound, though he had not shaken her very hard at all.

"Hush, Yona." Why, even a kitten would ignore his grasp. He was being gentle. "I'm a friend, you know. *Your* friend."

"My lord..." She was sallow as ever; her face had thinned still further. Old before her time, like all the other spiders the First Queen selected for her halls. "I have no friends, Glorious Fifth Prince."

"That's sad, but wouldn't you like one?" He could be more abrupt instead of cajoling, but it was very necessary she *participate*, and Sensheo longed to shake her again in order to gain acquiescence.

Her pale tongue darted out to touch her colorless lower lip, vanished. "I am but a lowly—"

"I know you perform certain duties for the First Queen, Yona." Oh, he had very little patience for the tissue of pleasant lies beginning each conversation, and anyway, one did not bother with such graces for servants. "You are a sheath upon her smallest nail, are you not?"

"I... I serve my mistress the First Mother of the Revered Emperor." The old stick had some strength in her liver, it appeared.

Another might have thought her quivering the result of fear instead of suppressed rage, but Sensheo knew a kindred spirit when he scented one.

"I know you do." And he had long thought this particular spirit would be useful, at the proper time. He suspected just how well she served, indeed. A faint hot breeze rustled the garden; he checked over her shoulder, making certain no others were likely to come upon this conversation. "But she doesn't treat you well, does she."

"My mistress the First Mother of..." Yona darted him a small, calculating look. Even her gown did nothing for her, the shade turning her sallowness more pronounced. For all that, a small bump lingered under her waistband, shocking upon such a skinny frame. Well, if even Takshin could find a paramour, anyone could. "No," the servant finally whispered. "She does not."

"And she's asked you to do more and more lately, hasn't she? First Mother has been busy indeed." The title for the first among your father's wives could hold a great deal of affection, Sensheo supposed, if he did not pronounce it so venomously. "You visited the baths lately."

Yona was already an unappetizing hue, but any remaining color fled her thin, planed cheeks. This close, and actually looking at her instead of simply glancing and cataloguing *a servant, one of the First Queen's*, Sensheo could see she appeared downright ill.

Who in her position wouldn't, though?

"Everyone visits the baths." But Yona's dark eyes still held that fierce, hateful, calculating shine. She did not move to tuck her hands politely in her sleeves, merely letting them hang like dead things at her sides.

Sensheo knew that light in a servant's gaze. He had seen it, once or twice, in a round, polished brazen mirror. "Be at peace, my handmaiden. You did well; even I was hard-pressed to discover just who had visited that particular bath-girl. First Mother could not brook Father having a little rest, for whatever reason I care not. But *you*, Yona. You are ill-used. Wouldn't you like an annuity? A small stipend, perhaps a cottage of your own? You are past marrying, I should think, but who knows?"

Yona almost staggered as he let go of her arm. He restrained himself from rubbing his hand against his robe; the feel of wasted muscle over thin bone smacked of ill-luck. Perhaps the summer plague in the provinces would reach Zhaon-An; that would put a black stroke against Kurin's new reign.

Of course various sicknesses raged with every turn in seasons, especially among the peasants. It was inevitable, like the dry time or the breaking of drought itself. But there were murmurs in the lower parts of the city, which meant the provinces would be infected with them in due time.

Excellent for Sensheo's plans, indeed.

The servant smoothed her plain, serviceable dress, rubbed her dry hands with their prominent tendons together nervously. "What would you have of me?" she finally said, softly, in the most honorific inflection possible.

He was not fooled. She had not capitulated, she was merely waiting for some indication of what he wished her to do—and more importantly, what he would pay.

"I'd like to be your friend, Yona." It beggared belief that she was only a winter or two older than Kurin. Work wore away at the physical body, just as it did at the less-visible subtle one. At least his own labors gained a decent amount of recompense and the promise of more to come. "We can help each other. We have both been wronged."

She glanced nervously past his shoulder, but he heard nobody approaching and did not bother to look. She could escape through the close-clutching vines if his attention faltered, and he did not wish that.

Not yet.

"Wronged?" Her thinning eyebrows rose in patent surprise, and she hurriedly dropped her gaze to his chest. There was no hairpin decoration swinging to accentuate the motion, and indeed she looked much like a pinchnose mouse from this angle. "I am too lowly to be wronged, Glorious Fifth Prince."

"If all felt as you did, none would strive for any betterment."

Which might or might not be a blessing, Sensheo thought; the sages of the Hundreds disagreed upon the matter according to their own standing and comfort. "Merit would go unanswered—and you do have merit, Yona. You've served faithfully, and been ill-used for it. I offer a remedy, and it does not require much of your effort at all."

The woman was silent for a long moment, weighing the likelihood of a trap.

Sensheo forged ahead much as his own father had forded the Jujei River early in his career, beginning the expansion of Garan at the expense of neighbors. "How long do you think it will be before First Mother finds a fresh sheath for her small nail? Father did nothing to restrain her, the new Emperor will do even less. You have changed a great deal of bedding, Yona; what you know is invaluable. I ask only for a few small things, then you may retire with an annuity from a grateful patron. Imagine, you will only have to pour tea for yourself in the morning."

"Some small things are valuable," she allowed, the last half of a proverb about aged servants and removable boot-heels. "Others are merely dangerous."

"True." He reached for her right wrist, trapping it easily even as she sought to retreat. He pressed the copper half-ingot into her palm—more wages than Gamwone had seen fit to give her in a long time, he was certain. The First Queen was a daughter of merchants after all, without any noble liberality. "If she does nothing, consider this merely a mark of my respect for such a faithful servant. If she hints at . . . certain measures, Yona, you may confide in me. Not only that, but should you fear for your safety, my household is ready to receive such a paragon of faithfulness."

That gained her attention, and another swift calculating glance taking in the set of his mouth and shoulders. She did not quite dare to stare into his face, a servant's habitual reticence difficult to break. A tendril of her hair, losing its redblack and fading into grey, had worked loose and drooped dispirited along her thin cheek. "Why would you do such a thing?"

Why do you think, servant? "You are a small thing, Yona. But valuable, in certain hands."

"Your hands, Glorious Fifth Prince?" In other words, she wished a statement of intent.

"None better." It did no harm to give what could be subtracted later. "And should you simply tire of bowing and running your feet to the bone for such mistress…well, you know how to sweep a room, do you not?"

Her chin rose, slowly, and there was a fire far back in Yona's dead, dry eyes. Now she studied him with quite unbecoming closeness for a mere servant, but he suffered it; wearing a faint smile as a mask. It was an expression he had perfected before that bronze mirror, especially after Father's illness reached a certain point and the shape of a world without the restraining hand of a parental god became clearer and clearer within Sensheo's head-meat.

"I have been taught how to clean almost anything," she said, softly. A hot wind touched their shelter, brushed the hem of his robe, caressed her greying hair. "And should the Glorious Fifth Prince have need of my poor skills, I am ready to serve."

Well, that was easier than expected. Sensheo's smile broadened, became natural. "You are possessed of much merit indeed, Yona. We shall suit each other very well."

"I must be about my work, Glorious Fifth Prince." She dropped her gaze again, and her thin shoulders had drawn up. Really, she looked positively unhealthy; the First Queen would be happy to be rid of an ill-luck sight. That she hadn't removed Yona meant that the woman was more than mildly useful, and Sensheo had his own uses for such a tool.

Afterward, of course, it would be easy to set it aside. So he let her brush past him, half-turning to listen to her hurrying footsteps upon the stone path. There was little chance of a passerby here; still, prudence was not merely Makar's preserve.

There was much else to do, but he allowed himself a lingering moment of satisfaction.

Things were going very well.

Names and
Schemes

A soft, sticky summer night enfolded the forest. Cooking
fires had burned to embers, and the dough-skinned Tabrak
were sleeping off their nightly gorging. They did not seem able to
moderate their appetites in any degree, and in the center of their
camp a great bonfire still burned, various bits of loot consigned to
the flames to please their filthy, burning god. They broke tureens
and cups to feed that ireful spirit, but tonight's display—in honor
of their jealous, nasty god—was meant to be some manner of
celebration.

Their cursed, blue-painted lord even cut a horse's throat and
sprayed the blood into flames, and the carcass was burnt in the
reeking as well. Hui had almost lost whatever remained in his middle of their heavy, inelegant cuisine; his companion had looked
rather pale as well, witnessing that blasphemy.

The feast that followed, with its open-air displays of martial
prowess, might have been entertaining except for the similarly open
displays of copulation. The Tabrak mounted their rai-pale slatterns
almost at will, it seemed, and proper marriage among them looked
all but unknown.

When the two Khir were finally allowed to retire to the tent
given their use—a round felted affair, very much like an inelegantly

constructed campaign tent in the borderlands and lacking entirely civilized appurtenances such as mirrorlights—Takari Daoyan made a full circuit of its interior, listening intently for signs that a spy had been posted outside the thick cloth wall. Finally he turned to his shield-husband, pale grey eyes gleaming in the smoky dimness. "Tonight," he said, flatly. "I do not like this."

"Nor do I." Hui's own gaze was muddy; in Khir he was considered baseborn. A noble youth had felt a passing fancy for a merchant's daughter; the resultant issue was raised to hunt and use a sword, but never to entertain ideas above his station.

Outside the borders of their mountainous land, though, Hui was a different proposition entirely, and sometimes he wondered if Dao would have ever returned his affections if not for the battlefield, the mud and death and stink, blood slipping hot through his fingers and the cries of the Zhaon pressing through a thinning, greasy fog as they stripped the dead.

That was an unhelpful thought, so he simply stationed himself near the flap, peering out at the seething anthill that was the Pale Horde at rest. No wonder the old books were full of imprecations upon these barbarians. Next to them, even the Zhaon looked utterly civilized.

At least the southroners drank tea, and bathed just as frequently as his own people. Or did Hui have a people now, considering what he was planning?

Takari Daoyan, having satisfied himself there were no listeners, turned to the task of preparing the saddlebags. They could not take much, and in any case it would be a pleasure to leave behind most of the graceless, ill-chosen gifts from the Horde's leader—there was no way to call him a king, or Great Rider as the leader of Khir was addressed, though this barbarian was very adept in the saddle. One might almost have liked him upon that last point, if he were not so utterly filthy. One could certainly not call him Emperor either, as the Zhaon styled the greatest warlords who managed to weld the rich, fractious bits of their land into one unit.

Even *lord* was too fine a word for Aro Ba Wistis. He had three names but used them in improper order, like a goatskin roll with a merchant's bloodline scratched upon it.

Hui watched, a lone sentry peering between folds of cloth. Firelight flashed, moans and cries rang through the forest's quiet, and the barbarians set a few pickets but no orderly watch like a Khir army would have. Even hill-bandits took more care than this.

"You've sighed twice," Dao said quietly. "Do it again, and I might think of ill-luck."

"He will not expect us to go south." It was good to speak Khir again, instead of the Horde's stupid, atonal tongue. He was far more adroit at the latter than Dao, but his husband was the one others treated with. Some even thought nobility made Dao soft, but underestimating a son of Takari was not a mistake a foe wished to make, especially if he glimpsed the well-worn hilt of Daoyan's ancient family sword.

Underestimating Hui was inevitable, though, and the pair had used it to their advantage more than once upon this trip. The Great Rider had possibly wished to punish the Takari in some oblique fashion, or to rob their allies the Khitani of support. It was most likely the latter; the Chief Minister was a Domari, and positioned to become much more if the line of Ashani failed.

Hui thought it likely that if he intended to return to Khir, it would be a land under a new Great Rider.

"Nobody would expect us to go south. Shan is confused, we shall make Anwei with little difficulty." Dao sank back upon his haunches, and in the smoky firelight—these tents were not well ventilated either—he looked half wraithlike. Maybe it was the fire's breath that so poisoned the liver and head-meat of these stinking, pale child-animals.

He could not even hate them, Hui decided, rubbing his fingertips over the plain leather-wrapped hilt of his own serviceable but hardly antique saber. Any more than he could hate his father for dishonoring a girl who had believed a nobleman's lies, or the merchant's daughter who had believed a nobleman's word, or the family who had kept Hui since he was after all a boy-child but cast his mother into the streets of the city under the Great Rider's keep to starve or earn her living as an honorless drab.

What else could a Khir family do, when tradition and rectitude demanded?

And he could not hate the Tabrak any more than he could hate the Zhaon, who were after all simply obeying their nature. All under Heaven obeyed such dictates, and he was no different.

"That's the third sigh." Daoyan unfolded from the saddlebags and paced to the tent flap. He slid his arms around Hui's waist, and his familiar warmth was a balm even in the sultry, breathless heat trapped between trees and undergrowth. His chin rested upon Hui's shoulder, his stubble scratching pleasantly. "You're thinking about the past."

There was no reason to deny it. "You could return to Khir, you know." *Though I will not. At least, not willingly.*

And what did it say of his own commitment to a shield-husband, that he would not return to Khir even for the only love he would have under Heaven? Hui knew enough of himself to also know, rather depressingly, that he was ruined for other affairs now.

"Ah, he just wed me, and now he longs to be rid of me." Dao's amusement turned the words into a song. "I feel rather like a woman."

Hui banished a very slight smile. *"A shield is more constant than death."*

"Don't quote Murong Cao to me, I hated him." Dao rubbed his chin against his husband's shoulder again, thoughtfully. "You would have done much better with my tutors."

It was kind of him to say so. "I'm serious, Dao."

"So am I." The heir of Takari sighed as well, his breath flavored with the barbarians' strange liquor, fermented mare's milk with similarly fermented honey. At least the barbarians knew to leave hives largely unmolested, and indeed reverenced the keepers of those who harvested such gold even during their attacks upon cities and towns. It was the only mark of civilization they seemed to possess. "I have been thinking."

"Now a disaster is truly upon us." Hui could not help but groan. "Another one of your schemes?"

"You'll like this one. I stole some very fine sohju from their loot-piles; we will pour out a measure when we leave here."

So he was determined to accompany Hui. It was a comfort, but Hui forced his mouth not to curl into a smile, and further forced himself to stillness. He could be misunderstanding; Heaven had witnessed many an embarrassment in his young life before he learned to school his expression into one proper to a bastard son. "An offering for the road?"

"No, my dour companion. We will change our names." Dao nuzzled at the side of his neck, a warm spot sweet as kouri. "I will be Cao Zhien, you will be Hamori Baiyua."

Hui's shoulders sagged. He rubbed at his face, telling himself it was only the smoke, and Dao exhaled softly, his own tension slackening for a few moments.

"Or," he continued finally, "you may be Takari Hui, and I will be Takari Dao, and we shall sell our services to lords who do not deserve such fine defense. Or you may choose a name, I care not."

"I should name you for Murong Cao's faithful steed."

"*Ai*, my love calls me a donkey." The joke was only partly sala-cious; Dao laughed softly and shivers slid like silk down Hui's spine. "Come help me pack."

"Dao." Hui caught his husband's wrists, unwilling to relinquish the closeness just yet. "I would not...if you chose to return to Khir, I would not hold it against you. Your clan—"

"As far as they know, I am dead. They will miss the sword, but should we leave our host, who is to say whether we survived the fall of Shan's capital or not? We will be *free*, Hui. Is not that a thing to long for?"

It was, and yet Hui could not halt the objections, like a maiden denying a suitor she did, after all, desperately want. "I do not wish you to regret it."

"I regret I did not meet you sooner, that is all." Dao rocked back upon his heels, drawing Hui away from the tent flap. "Come. The earlier we are rid of these barbarians, the better."

"You only wish to enjoy yourself upon a saddle instead of a pile of skins." He let himself be drawn, for the suspicious prickling in his eyes had turned to a deep loosening behind his heart. His liver, still cautious, had not quite properly seated itself.

Dao laughed; he was of a much merrier temper than his husband. "Not to mention a proper bed, once we reach a place these beasts have not fouled. And is there anything wrong with that, I ask?"

Well, tomorrow Dao could change his mind, and Hui would accept the pain then. For now, he seemed sure, and it was enough. "No," he answered, and let himself be coaxed farther into the smoke-haze to finish their preparations. "Nothing wrong at all."

MIDMORNING
MEAL

Early upon a fine bright summer morning, the Second Mother's part of the Kaeje was full of well-ordered bustle. Haesara was at a low, exquisitely carved desk of hau-tree wood, traditional for writing letters in the hope that a hau's graceful fluidity would be imparted to a writer's brush. Her hair was piled high upon her head and her morning-robe was slightly disheveled, but neither mattered to her eldest son, who was consuming a very fine cup or two of smoky eong tea while he read a treatise upon certain mechanical innovations in harnessing the power of streams and other flowing water. Eong was far too strong for a morning drink, but he preferred it to cut the dust in the dry season, so his mother made certain to have it to hand on those frequent occasions her eldest visited for breakfast.

By long-standing habit, neither of them spoke. The quality of their silence was such that it provided all the commonplace polite observations others might have made on a fine morning—the weather, the night's rest, if one had eaten recently. The first midmorning meal, light as both preferred, would be brought in a short while and neither would speak, again, until it was halfway consumed.

Then the day could begin.

Makar poured himself a fresh ration, not needing to glance at table, pot, or cup to perform such a familiar operation. The cargo of hot, fragrant liquid was arrested halfway to his mouth and he cocked his head, his topknot-cage of stiffened leather incised with the character for *abundance* well secured by a pin of darkened bone. He would change his dark scholar's robe for something more fitting later in the day while attending a council meeting with the new Emperor and chief ministers, but at the moment he wore what pleased him.

Raised voices, hurrying feet. Makar set the treatise aside, watching his mother's steady writing, the brush held just so, her profile one of serene concentration. It was pleasant to see her working without a care, and he hoped it would continue until the partition opened.

When it did, revealing the long horse-face of his mother's faithful steward Nehu, he was ready.

"My lord Fourth Prince." Nehu was upon his knees, the traditional posture from which a servant delivered bad news. It was strange to see him so; he was very conscious of his high position in comparison to other household dependents. "There is a letter from the peerless Emperor of Zhaon. The Golden bringing it—"

So soon? Well, he had lost his temper the other day on the training ground; it was too much to hope for that Kurin would see that another son of Garan Tamuron might have a right to a measure of his own pride. "I see. Mother, will you pardon me for a moment? This needs attending."

His mother had half-turned upon her cushion. A fat ink-drop depended from the tip of her brush, and she paled with alarming rapidity, the color draining from her beautiful coppery cheeks, only needing the lightest dusting of zhu to achieve the most pleasing effect.

She lifted her chin slightly. "Bring the Golden to us, Nehu. I would hear what the lord Emperor intends for my son."

Nehu, knowing finality when he heard it in his mistress's voice despite her son's ruling of the Hanweo clan, bowed again and pulled the partition shut. There was more hurrying, and excited murmurs.

"I would spare you this," Makar said quietly.

"I shall be spared nothing." She remembered her brush and laid it aside, frowning at an unsightly blot upon what had no doubt been a well-constructed letter. "Is it Sensheo, do you think?"

"I may have embarrassed Kurin the other day." He took care to make his hand steady upon the cup, his tone even and unconcerned. "You have little need to worry, Mother. I have made arrangements for your safety."

"What good are they, if my son is not safe?" She set to arranging the paper, inkstone, and brush to rights, stacked neatly or set aside so her entire attention could be given to another task. Her quality of serene precision had been his early guide, and he was grateful for it now, too, though she was still very pale.

"He cannot afford to kill me just yet." A humorless smile touched Makar's rather thin lips. He did not bear the round face that was a mark of handsomeness, and his nose was too large—but he was certainly striking, or so his mother had often told him. "And if it is some mischief of Sensheo's . . ." He did not complete the sentence; she would not agree that perhaps his little brother might need a salutary, if fatal, lesson upon his own lack of discretion and talent.

A mother loved all her children, filial or otherwise. A brother could do no less than care for his junior so far as fate would allow. "Hush," she said, a quite unnecessary precaution, for he could hear the steps in the hall.

The partition opened, and Nehu bowed the Golden in. Bright-armored but bootless, the man had taken some time to remove his footwear—which boded well. But the missive in his hands was bright scarlet, borne before him with reverence as an Emperor's official wishes should always be.

For a moment Makar's humors turned cool and loose, pooling in his belly. The physical body was a timid beast when lashed by worry; a sage was supposed to master such irrelevancies by living fully *now*. The Awakened One had many lessons upon the matter, but Makar preferred Hurong Dhun and his observation that fear was quite natural, and the attempt not to feel it caused more irritation than simply noting its effects as if they belonged to some other person's baggage.

He rose as custom demanded, performing a deep bow to the letter clutched and held aloft—the poor soldier's arms must be aching by now. All the same, Garan Makar could not forego a minor show of pride.

Again. "What beneficence," he observed. "My brother the Emperor has sent a missive. What does Heaven intend?"

Haesara, as a dowager queen, did not need to rise, but she arranged herself in an attitude of profound reverence while Makar bowed again, broke the seal ceremonially, and deliberately did not dismiss the Golden. Let his show of obedience be spread and gossiped about, it would only advance his cause.

And it seemed Garan Makar would have a cause, sooner rather than later.

Kurin's brushwork was fine indeed, though not as strong as his father's, and not as vigorously clear as some of the scholars among Makar's clients. The Fourth Prince scanned the letter twice, his head-meat working furiously but his outer self composed, an eyebrow rising slightly as the chessboard took on a different configuration inside his skull.

Oh, my elder brother. You think yourself very clever indeed.

It was a command to take the generalship of Zhaon's Southron Army, to meet the Tabrak in battle, and to destroy them.

Which was not quite what Makar had hoped. But it could be turned to advantage indeed. "The Emperor speaks," he intoned. "And his brother obeys. Pray tarry for a while and accept a cup of tea, my Golden friend, while I brush a reply."

His mother did not make a sound. What it cost her to wait to find out, Makar did not like to think—but he hoped she trusted him enough to keep her peace. Sensheo would not have, of course.

But Sensheo was not here, and Makar was, in very unbrotherly fashion, glad of that fact.

*   *   *

She could not eat much in this terrible heat, but Yala did enjoy midmorning tea. There was double-strained broth with walanir greens floating upon its broad yellow back, too, and that was most agreeable. Best of all, her new husband was largely taciturn until he had finished his own morning repast, which suited her own preferences perfectly. Of course, had he been a morning singer, as the proverb went, she would have accommodated with conversation.

But it was...pleasant, to pour his tea and attend to her own while watching the small gemlike garden of this new house, just beginning to recover from a certain measure of neglect, blink sleepily under thick golden sunlight. The pond had been attended to, and a new babu water-clock chopped equal fragments of time with indefatigable punctiliousness.

Takshin selected a piece of aiju, offering it balanced upon his eating-sticks with a quick, delicate motion; she shook her head. The musky melons were not her favorite, though sometimes after an evening meal they were pleasant enough. He nodded, understanding, and returned to his own breakfast.

Yala took another sip of tea, her smallest finger held just so. "I have invited Sixth Prince Jin to dinner," she said softly, watching for any hint of irritation.

Takshin simply nodded again, staring at the garden. The *kyeogra* in his left ear gleamed, bright and burnished; a wind whispered through yeoyan saplings in broad ceramic pots, arranged to give pleasant lacy shade. Sometimes, when he relaxed into thoughtfulness, there was an intimation of what he would have looked like without the scars.

"Third Mother is still grieving," she prompted, and that gained her a single dark glance, his brow furrowing.

"Over Sabi? She always was a brat." But the shadow that crossed his face was pained instead of displeased, and he exhaled sharply, setting his eating-sticks aside. "I am not able to bring those barbarians to account for her just yet. I worry for Kiron, too."

The king of Shan. Of course, Takshin felt much affection for his adoptive-brother. As much as Kai felt for his adoptive-mother—though Yala should not be thinking of Zhaon's great general. So she schooled her expression and took another sip. Plain golden tea from Arun-An to the north, a blessing upon such a hot morning. The dust crawled into one's nose, dried one's mouth, and quite possibly settled in one's joints too. "I believe her worries lie in a different direction."

"And well they might," Takshin muttered. "Don't worry, little lure. Kurin is easily managed, and has other affairs which need tending at the moment. Or is it *that woman* she fears?"

Well, at least he was not unaware, nor did he chide her for discussing something close to politics at breakfast. Still, it was thought-provoking, especially the fact that he rarely said *my mother*. Only *that woman*, and his scarred lip twisted each time. "There are many dangers at court."

"I see they have already made you a shield. Or have you been prodding about, trying to discover who ordered a princess's fate?" His lip twisted again, but not with ill humor. All his attention had settled upon her now. Some would no doubt quail under such a weight, but Yala was beginning to believe she had his measure, now. "I would not trouble you with such matters at breakfast, Lady Spyling."

"Nor would I trouble you, my husband." She settled her teacup, holding her sleeve—pale yellow silk, a very fine morning-robe—well aside. "It seems the way of Zhaon wives to be troublesome, though."

"I look forward to it." The slight curve to the unscarred half of his mouth was true amusement. "Who else has requested your patronage, little lure?"

"None as of yet." Yala was faintly surprised he would ask so directly, but then again, such seemed his nature. "Second Mother has shown me every kindness, Lady Gonwa as well. It will make matters easier."

"Hm." He glanced at his eating-sticks as if he could not remember laying them aside, their tips upon a small fish-shaped dish meant expressly for such a duty, and reached for his teacup without needing to glance at where it rested. "Your merchant friend Narikh. What do you know of him?"

Her heart lunged inside her ribs, and she was glad she was not engaged upon the act of swallowing tea. "He was the son of a nobleman," she said, carefully. "And he rendered much aid during the Crown Prince...the Emperor's..." For a moment she could not remember the proper address.

Takshin saved her the trouble in a very husbandly way, forging ahead. "The merchant is gone now, but he left traces. Yala, have you considered..." He paused, and she was for a single vertiginous instant certain the Khir emissaries and Daoyan had been caught. "Have you considered," he began again, "that there may have been those in the North who did not wish your princess to live?"

Had she heard him correctly? Yala's hand twitched; her fingertips wanted to rise and touch her mouth. She denied the movement. "But my princess brought peace," she managed, blankly. "And none would dare..." After all, Mahara was the daughter of the Great Rider. It would be akin to blasphemy for a Khir to even attempt such a thing.

"Your friend Narikh had at least three bolt-holes in the Khir quarter. Probably more, though there is little use in looking for them now. None who met him believed him a mere merchant and more than one noted his martial skill, though he sought to hide it. He made no transactions save the buying of a few baubles, no doubt to pique your interest. And he was seen with at least two impresarios—you are familiar with the term?" When she shook her head, he continued. "It means a theater-manager, but it also means those who arrange for certain walkers of the Shadowed Path to find rich clients who cannot risk their reputations, and vice versa. Your friend Narikh was very busy among them."

He kept mispronouncing the clan name of Ashani Daoyan's mother, which was quite natural for a Zhaon, but she could not find the strength to correct him. How close was he to guessing Daoyan's true name? And yet, *impresarios*. The word took on an ominous cast.

Did she truly believe Dao had come all the way from Khir just for a single noblewoman? Was he attempting to save his sister, hunting from behind, and thus had to spend time among such theater-managers? Why would he not tell Yala as much, then, after Mahara's misfortune?

Her fingers were cold. So were her toes, which was odd. It was such a warm morning.

"He was not the only one." Takshin was eyeing her rather closely. "While I do not know who exactly bought my Eldest Brother's death, I am fairly certain your princess was prey for a Northern hunter, little lure."

It cannot be so. "You... there is no doubt?" She sounded breathless even to herself.

"Not much, I am afraid. I suspected *that woman* of the deed in order to avoid an heir, but I think it unlikely she would plan so far ahead. She merely lashes out at the closest helpless thing, rather like the Mad Queen." One of his broad shoulders twitched. Now Yala knew all that lay under the black Shan tunics he always wore, and the map of scars across his muscled torso was enough to make her ashamed she had not, in the secret chambers of her liver, wished to marry him.

No wonder he was bitter. He had suffered much, including a whip-scar gained from protecting Yala herself, and such treatment made for an acrid stew indeed. The only wonder was that he was not actively cruel.

"So." Takshin regarded her steadily. Was there pity in his dark gaze? It did not seem possible. "The two impresarios Narikhi was seen with are currently guests of the Night Watch captain in the Khir quarter, as a personal favor to me, and being put energetically to the question. Sooner or later they will mention if the merchant was part of the plot, but one thing is clear: A Khir noble paid for the death. Possibly upon Zlorih's orders, though I cannot be sure of that part."

"But... her father. He is her *father.*" Everything within Yala revolted at the thought. The Great Rider was a terrifying figure; Mahara had confided he was sometimes given to banging upon the table at dinner when displeased, too. The very thought of that august man's anger had certainly made young Yala quail, and there was no shame in such trepidation since even a minister or head of a clan might well feel it too. "To do such a thing..."

"Perhaps they wish another war. Perhaps an heir to both countries was not to be desired on that side of the border, either. Khir has no wish to be ruled by Zhaon." His expression changed, and Yala realized her own face must be speaking rather loudly at the moment. "I am sorry, little lure. It is unwelcome news, no matter who is to blame. And I am rather glad the fellow is gone, for it is probable you were his next target."

Ridiculous. Dao would never... She could not even complete a thought, the news was so unexpected. "You are certain?" she persisted.

"I am certain of little under Heaven, Yala. But in this particular matter..." He halted, and his expression softened as he regarded her. Precious few would believe him capable of this much tenderness, and she was surprised each time by its advent. "I am sorry."

Her silence did not anger him; Takshin seemed to understand she required some short while to absorb this news. He returned to his breakfast, and she to her tea. Yala stared into her cup, the amber liquid innocent and fragrant, and sought to *think*.

The girl who left Khir at Mahara's side would have considered it a pack of Zhaon lies. But... it made a certain amount of sense. The jostling for position among the noblewomen of the Great Rider's keep and the city nestling under it was fierce, for all it was never admitted that they considered politics during their intrigues instead of simple marriage-ambition. But their fathers, brothers, husbands? Which of those—the Great Rider's ministers, other noble families with less rectitude than Komori Dasho's, the many allied clans or those seeking to buy some manner of nobility— would have sent ingots, silver and copper both, south to pay for a princess's death?

Perhaps she should have returned to Khir with Daoyan after all. She had been so sure it was a Zhaon in the palace's warren who had paid for the deed. The sudden reverse left a bitterness in her mouth, and she wondered if a general ever felt this way when a battle turned.

Ashani Daoyan had left Khir before knowing of his sister's death. He had brought her father's ring, and the emissaries said her father had been struck down very close to that time. It was hideous to think ill of her childhood friend, even more hideous to wonder what other missives he might have been carrying for Khir trapped as she was in Zhaon-An's busy guts.

Or if one or more among the noble Khir emissaries had been in the city before their "official" arrival, and had brought a few ingots along to pay for a royal death.

Her appetite was gone, but she was still under her husband's gaze. So Yala consumed broth and her tea, with small ladylike sips, and blinked furiously against the hot prickling in her eyes.

Every wall was double-hung with tapestries, and every corner rounded in the First Dowager Mother of Zhaon's usual breakfast room. This morning her eldest son was not present; the business of rule did not permit leisurely rising. More unusual was her daughter's absence, but Gamnae was visiting Third Mother Luswone in the hopes that she might ease some of that lady's grief. The Emperor had suggested the move with a friendly letter to his younger sister, who took it—quite rightly—as a command, and hastened to obey.

Her relief at the event was not visible—the child had enough self-control for that—but it was guessed at all the same by every servant in this part of the Kaeje. Adept at sensing the slightest shift in household currents, the remaining spiders of Queen Gamwone—those thin-fingered, big-eyed, skinny girls she seemed to prefer, their flesh pared down to bone despite their position supposedly and traditionally admitting enough scrapings and leavings to feed a detachment of soldiers several times over—exchanged somber looks as they hurried about their tasks, and if their silence was not quite as fearful or complete as it had been, it was at least sufficient.

The new servants, despite their lack of pejorative title, were just as quiet.

Even Yona, feared almost as much as her mistress, moved a little more slowly than usual. Lately she had eaten nothing but polished rai, that staple of health and life, but it did not seem to be doing much good. Any sauce, salt, or additive for her bowl, however timidly offered, was brusquely refused. Perhaps she had made a vow to one of Heaven's governors or the Awakened One; in any case, everyone in the First Mother's household knew to leave well enough alone.

There were no alliances among these servants, old or new, except the most temporary. To think otherwise was to court disaster—and the sudo, for Gamwone had a very fine collection of those instruments hanging in a polished wooden cupboard.

It was Yona who supervised the setting of the table to her mistress's liking, with the tureens of broth both meat and vegetable, the sweet rai, the greens with the piquant sauce customary in the Yulehi family's ancient lands, the sliced fruit arranged in pleasing patterns, the pot of haurang tea, the sweating, covered clay jar of crushed fruit. All the parts of a royal breakfast were in place, along with the dishes least likely to garner a stern reprimand from the mistress as being aesthetically displeasing.

Gamwone's refined sensibilities changed from day to day; what was pleasant one morn was unbearable the next. It could have been a mark of noble sensitivity.

If it was attributed otherwise, at least no servant had the foolhardiness to mention as much openly.

Yona shooed the maids forth with her usual alacrity, though, and turned back to the table, perhaps to right some small angle between a plate and eating-sticks held ready upon a small fish-shaped stand, perhaps to check that the tea was properly hot, or perhaps to arrange the rai-paper squares for couth dabbing at fingers or lips between courses or sips.

As she did, she glanced at the partition—not even a shadow. She had a few moments before her mistress came shuffling down the hall in heavily embroidered morning slippers.

What was most likely? There was one thing Garan Yulehi-a

Gamwone never failed to take at her first meal, were it available—the toothsome, musky, sugary aiju, square slices presented in a chessboard pattern upon their own whisper-thin Ihengua porcelain plate.

Yona's bony yellowing hand dove into her sleeve. She produced a small blue ceramic bottle with a sliver of soakwood as a stopper, and took care to hold it well away while sliding the sliver out. Her heart beat high and thin in her chest; she glanced again at the partition.

No shadow, no footstep. Activity elsewhere in the household was a distant rhythm of footstep, soft voices, moving cloth; she scattered a minuscule quantity of white powder from the bottle's pursed lips with finger-taps on the bottle's neck like a sathron player producing counterpoint. It took skill and patience to land each tiny puff upon a square of aiju, where the dry crystals vanished into the melon's pallor, soaking into its damp humors.

The sliver returned to the bottle's mouth, and blue-enameled ceramic slipped into a pocket in her sleeve holding other small, necessary items for the day's work. She lingered a little longer to make certain the column of rai-paper squares upon the table was twisted to make it an architectural folly-tower, its sides spiraling, and folded the top one in half as manners demanded.

Then she hurried to the partition, checking the empty hall outside one more time. There was motion drawing closer; her sharp ears caught the familiar drag at the end of each step as her mistress's morning-robe swept the spotless floor behind her.

Many a spider had learned to dread hall-washing duty if even a single smear were found upon the First Queen of Zhaon's hem.

Yona was in her proper attitude just inside the partition as First Mother of the Revered Emperor Garan Gamwone appeared, her round, beautiful, indolent face lightly dusted with zhu and her cheerful orange morning-robe embroidered with chevrons in a slightly darker shade at hems and cuff. The stitchery was Second Princess Gamnae's work, and perhaps the mistress wore it since her daughter was unable to attend the meal. In any case, it suited her, though her high-piled hair, perpetually stiff with lacquer, was slightly disarranged. Perhaps a close-maid had been slapped away from the task of morning twisting and thrusting a plain hairpin through, or perhaps Gamwone's tender scalp could not bear such pressure this morning.

Yona bowed deeply. Her mistress did not see—who, after all, takes much notice of a familiar chair, a bench, a hanging one passes daily in a hall? Gamwone settled at the table, and when Yona hurried forward upon her knees to pour the tea, she was waved peremptorily away. The first lady of the Kaeje wished to breakfast without help.

Her most favored, faithful servant retreated to the other side of the partition and pulled it closed, her ears pricked for any tiny aggrieved sigh or expostulation from inside. Such slight sounds would be a gong summoning her to duty, and long practice had given her antennae as sensitive as a granary feline's whiskers as it crouched motionless before a wall-hole.

The giver of the tiny blue bottle—bought from a shop tucked under an apothecary's sign in the Left Market and well paid for his many services—assured her it would not take effect at once, and Grandfather never lied.

Yona composed herself, as she had so often in her life, to wait. The morning's usual retching, attended to in a tiny, out of the way water-closet before dawn, held more bright blood than usual, and she could barely even eat plain rai.

Nevertheless, she wore a very small, very faint smile.

Burdens of Rule

I t did not give him much pleasure to be sending one of his broth-ers to war. But it did not pain him overmuch, either, and Garan Kurin could not let that show. Etiquette demanded a ponderous gravity in solemn leave-taking, even if one's heart and liver sat very easily within.

The vermilion-pillared hall was alive with witnesses, from the square-captains of the Golden who would serve as Makar's personal bodyguards to the court ladies sorry to see him go, the eunuchs freed from endless brushing and the daily petty intrigue by a high ceremonial event, the ministers greater and lesser—most of them confirmed in their positions, for continuity was a way to calm the restive beast of public opinion—and, inevitably, more royal family.

Second Mother Haesara, exquisite in rosy silk with a character for *abundance* embroidered at hem and cuffs, was at the head of her train of court ladies. Lady Aoan Mau, skirting the edge of dishevel-ment, did not quite droop with sadness, but her gaze held the Fourth Prince's several times during the formalities.

Perhaps the rumors about a certain partiality were true. In any case, the formal leave-taking of Garan Tamuron's second queen and her eldest son was exceedingly aesthetic, and Makar made a soft observation for his mother's ears alone that was no doubt scholarly, for she gave him a pained glance but smiled nonetheless.

The Third Prince, in his customary black Shan attire, gave his next-youngest brother a lopsided smile and no doubt a few stinging words of advice. Nothing Takshin said was without an edge; Kurin wondered how the Khir lady at his side stood such a husband. She was thin for a new bride, but there had been much upset in that lady's recent past, and she had eschewed the indigo Kurin had seen her in a few times for a bright, pleasing babu-green gown prettily worked with hau characters at the sleeves. Her hairpin held a small, irregular stone wrapped with crimson thread at the top and dangled a string of bright green crystals; her ear-drops, held close with green ribbons, were shivering, ruddy metal with small green stones glittering at piquant points. For her first court ceremonial as a player instead of a spectator, she did well enough, clasping her brother-in-law's hands and quoting from the Hundreds in a soft but very clear voice with the spike-scars of Khir consonants behind each word.

Garan Gamnae stood next to Haesara, glancing nervously at her now-eldest brother upon the Throne. The First Mother of the Revered Emperor was not in attendance, so Second Mother and the daughter stepped in to fill her role; Gamwone was not feeling well.

Or so his mother said, and since she had not risen from her bed in two days save to make her way to bath or soil-pan with Yona's solicitous assistance, Kurin let it rest. At least she had ceased her ill-considered intriguing.

Or become far more adept at it in a very short while. He supposed the latter was just barely possible, and was alert for any indication that it had become the case.

Even Fifth Prince Sensheo—in bright orange silk despite having just shed house arrest and mourning both—behaved impeccably, bowing to his elder brother and wishing him both victory and a safe return in ornate, ceremonial Zhaon.

Mrong Banh, who had found the most auspicious day for a farewell, clasped Makar's hands and nodded several times, his dark eyes very bright. He had kept himself in the Old Tower sheathed with blue tile for days, like a courtesan silly enough to think she was being cast aside. It was no matter; Kurin had already brought the old man explicitly back into favor, though Banh should have expected some gentle questions. He was only an astrologer who had once been a tavern-boy, not a sage.

Next to Banh stood Sixth Prince Jin, deep shadows under his eyes that had no business upon a boy his age. He bowed to Makar and bid him farewell in a somewhat choked voice.

The height of the ceremony was the solemn blessing, Emperor to general, elder brother to younger. Makar took the seal of military authority and their father's priceless, ancient sword of Garan. "Use it well," Kurin intoned, and wondered if any present saw past the high honor to the insult.

Father would have wanted Kai or Takyeo to carry it, but the more everyone focused on Makar instead of an upstart general who could not be stripped of a hurai just yet, the better. Makar would be painfully aware the gift was meant to spur him to great achievement. Now was the time to show he was not just a scholar but a warlord like his father, and Kurin could not wait for the inevitable.

Tabrak galloped over all in its way except strong-walled cities, but the Southron Army would bleed them before they reached Zhaon-An. Besides, an Emperor could not very well sit and wait for the Horde, especially when they had sent Sabi's head in a box.

It was unpleasant to think of Sabwone. Of course, it was only natural he should have an ill dream—or two—haunted by her headless shade, his humors strained by the burdens of rule.

"Avenge our sister," he added.

"My lord Emperor." Makar's bow was not perfunctory in the least, the sword of Garan held high upon both his palms. A ripple ran through the court, probably admiration for the scroll-illustration they made. Later, of course, it might be a point of high tragedy.

Kurin could affect high grief for his beloved brother at the proper time; if Maki survived, there were other plans in place. But for now, the Emperor simply performed his ceremonial duties, and his gaze rested once or twice, speculatively, upon his Second Mother's second son instead of her first.

Sensheo, busy accepting muted congratulations for his release and condolences upon his brother's departure, did not notice.

WELL PLEASED

Riding through a scorch-hot Zhaon summer was unpleasant, even with the thickening copses along their route to provide shade and relief. The company was likewise not to his taste; Ashani Daoyan was well-practiced in not letting his disdain show, but his fellow nobles would not cease their yammering and his temper had thinned with each step from Zhaon-An.

"It is not so bad," Moruri repeated. "She will be well cared for even among the Zhaon, and you may marry a princess instead."

Daoyan, his knees tight to his horse's sides and his hands aching for swordhilt or bow, did not reply. His face might be set to the North but his heart and liver were full of rebellion, and yet he rode. There was no point in doing anything else.

"Is he still sulking?" Namori Ekaian leaned in his saddle, grinning hugely. The pockmark fellow was very pleased by his prince's discomfiture, and sometimes Dao amused himself with planning how to kill the fellow without suspicion.

Each hoof-fall led him farther away. Let it, then. Let Yala find out how the Zhaon treated their wives, and when he returned to that stinking midden of a city he would burn it to the ground and spit that mocking, scarred fellow like a haunch for roasting. *Then* she would see.

"Leave him be." Hazuni Ulo's leather half-armor was stamped with swallow designs, both beautiful and functional. The man inside it was paradoxically as prosaic as possible, though his clear grey gaze moved over hill, valley, field, and woods with a hunter's watchfulness. He had announced that morning they were not being pursued, and the others accorded him the honor of being believed without question or jest.

Which meant he was far more dangerous than he appeared. Maybe he should be dealt with first.

The last member of the quartet—a shield-square, but they obeyed one of their own instead of the man they pretended to honor—was lean dark Shohuri; words could not be pried easily out of him. Still, he did not mock, and kneed his horse closer to Dao's. That meant Namori had to fall back to take another position in their scout-pattern; it also meant the clodlike, ill-favored lord could not jape. Shohuri cast Dao an indecipherable glance, and of them all, his quiet gaze was most like Yala's.

He was trying not to think about her. He should have dragged her from that filthy palace by her hair, slung her over his saddle, and been done with it. He would never make the same mistake again.

Zhaon passed away underneath them. It might have been a pleasant ride in a hunting-party with hawks at the wrist or a summer-fat feral curltail to track. Even a game of *kaibok* in one of the fields would have been a relief, but instead they were ghosts moving northward, avoiding towns and villages, eschewing the main road during daylight and reserving their mounts' strength carefully. And even that might have been acceptable if a certain noblewoman had consented to leave the morass, the great Zhaon city like a giant hornbeast sinking in a bottomless mudhole.

At least her father could not stand in Dao's way, though it was faint comfort now. If he could have just pried her free of Zhaon-An...

They followed the edge of a thick wood, staying to the shade both for camouflage and coolth. The hills would start to rise soon; they were traveling swift and light, but far to the west, using the broken ground in the foothills to cover their approach to Khir. The bridges and fords were probably still held by Zhaon detachments, and in the borderlands there was a chance of being halted, then questioned—if not outright recognized by those they had fought before and during Three Rivers.

Hazuni's horse, a fine bay, shook her mane as she trotted, her step slowing for a fraction of a babu water-clock's ticking. Her rider reined her immediately, his head upflung like a widehorn shagcoat hearing a hunting horn, and Daoyan smelled it too.

Smoke.

They halted, four Khir lords and a mutinous royal scion. Their mounts, well-trained and used to sudden stops, barely flicked an ear.

"No villages close," Moruri said quietly. "At least, not when we passed this way before." The land here was richer than the foothills, of course, but the war had probably drained this province, those who survived retreating to more fortified locations like rodents fleeing a burning barn.

"Perhaps a clearing party." Hazuni scanned the far hills shimmering under heat, and his cheek twitched like a feline's whiskers. "But I like it not. My neck is itching."

"You and your neck." Namori's grumble was merely for appearance's sake. There was a slight sound—he was unlimbering his bow, and the rest of them fell silent, listening intently.

It was, Daoyan had to admit, rather comforting to be in the midst of a hunting party once again. The running raids leading up to Three Rivers had been full of this tense, dangerous quiet, though no Khir had realized Zakkar Kai was drawing them, subtly and carefully, into a trap.

Even a hated enemy could be grudgingly admired for his skill and dedication. Yala had never mentioned the general, even in passing. Of course a Khir noblewoman would consider the author of her country's defeat a creature not fit for conversation.

"Let us move." Moruri kneed his chestnut forward. "But soft, and protect the prince." At least he did not add the latter with an ironic or mocking twist to the words.

If one of them wished to remove Daoyan from the living, there was no lack of opportunity. Had the Great Rider counted upon as much? Ashani Zlorih could still father a child or two; he was, after all, not yet dead. It was entirely like the man to wish Dao returned, though; some men would spend twice the cost of even a cheap, hated possession to bring it back into their grasping just for the pleasure of breaking it themselves.

What was owned by such a man could never be allowed free, only cast away once completely marred. The pleasure of such complete possession must be intense to them, Dao thought, and sometimes wondered if he bore a similar flaw in his temperament.

The Khir kept to the edges of the wood, and the smell of smoke faded. Still, Hazuni's unease visibly intensified. Perhaps, like Yala, the horse-goddess had whispered in his infant ear some secret or another, granting him the hunting-sense. Some men had it, their humors delicately sensitive to any subtle shift in the world's great flow.

They halted again at a clear, summer-shrunken streamlet, dismounting to fill waterskins and letting the horses drink. The banks were a confusion of prints both horse and human, and Dao recognized some of the boot-shapes. They were distinctive indeed.

Zhaon army scouts. But why would an army be *here*? Gossip in the capital only said Zakkar Kai had gone north, and he would no doubt stay closer to the main valley-entrance to Khir's mountain-locked central heartland, both to keep control of the major river crossings and to bottleneck any invasion.

"This is unsettling," Moruri observed. "Shohuri?"

Whatever the quiet man would have said was lost, for Namori Ekaian's bow spoke instead, the string's snap loud in the dusty hush of a Zhaon summerdrought afternoon. "*Go!*" the pockmarked man snapped, and drew to his ear again. "Protect him, and go!"

Dao's sword was half out of its sheath; Shohuri's hand landed upon his, forcing bright metal back into its dark home. He pushed Dao toward the horses with a bruising shove that respected neither royalty nor nobility in the face of sudden danger. Hazuni was already behind a screen of foliage, his own bow humming. Arrows flew, and it was a raid again—Daoyan in the saddle before he realized it, his sword rasping free and the beast under him, well-trained, understanding his intention in a single moment. The black gelding wheeled as Dao's knees clamped home, and when he applied his heels the horse shot forward. Arrows pocked down, and he had a moment of thinking how ironic it would be if an *ihenhua* was buried in his own body, just as in his royal half-sister's.

"*To Ashani!*" Moruri Keiyan bellowed, the traditional cry, and hooves pounded behind him.

Ashani Daoyan expected to ride down a dismounted Zhaon patrol and maybe win a chance at escape once they had whittled or distracted his companions. Instead, he flashed past a Zhaon picket creeping forward to investigate a party of horsemen at a nearby streamlet and crested a slight rise at a gallop, meaning to curve back and drive the fools toward his fellow hunters. The trees receded, and he found himself galloping toward a rather large Zhaon army detachment sheltering in a handy summer-dry ravine, only the faintest smoke above their tents because Zakkar Kai, the great general, had ordered only one cooking-brazier lit for every five squares to ameliorate the risk of a drought-fire on dried grass and yeozhur scrub. The wind, a false friend, had veered to mask the scent of burning and also carried nose-news of the Khir to the Zhaon horses, less disciplined than Khir mounts but just as perceptive.

It was too late to halt or change his course, so Ashani Daoyan did the only thing he could.

He attacked.

The soldiers of Zhaon were well pleased, for that afternoon they had two bound Khir captives—evidently noblemen, and of some martial skill besides—to show their visiting general.

SISTERS

"Everyone is leaving." Garan Gamnae, Second Princess of Zhaon, tucked her pretty plump hands inside her sleeves despite the heat. "I am glad you will stay, at least."

"A poor substitute for your brothers, indeed, but it is kind of you to say so." Lady—no, now she was *Princess*—Yala smiled, the string of bright colorless crystals hanging from her hairpin swaying as she chose her steps with care. The jatajatas Zhaon women and eunuchs wore to keep their hems from the mud and also reserve their humors from being pulled into the earth required a certain amount of looseness in the ankle, not to mention forethought ere the foot was placed, and she professed to be unused to them.

Though the day had not achieved its full scorching yet, Gamnae's throat was already dry and her modest linen shift uncomfortably damp in places. But she could not invite her brother's new wife to the Kaeje for a visit without risking her mother demanding to see a daughter-in-law and also could not leave the Palace without a chaperone, plus a palanquin and guards. It was far easier for them to meet in a garden at a time arranged by graceful allusions in the letters they exchanged near-daily. It was pleasant to look forward to Yala's missives; each brushstroke was elegant but not ornate and she never made Gamnae feel silly or stupid.

At least Zhaon's Second Princess could be sure her own dress was very becoming, blue with slightly darker thread contrasting at the hem, a forest of branches reaching up in strictly stylized patterns to match the geometric figures at her cuffs. With Sabwone gone, she didn't feel much like dressing up. A touch of red crushflower juice to her lips and a light dusting of zhu powder was all her round face needed, and she wore only one bracelet today, of silver-sheathed greenstone. It was pleasant to think she could share in some of the new princess's restrained grace, instead of attempting to rival Sabwone's beauty. "Have you heard from Kai?"

"A letter arrived yesterday." Princess Yala glanced at her, those pale eyes bright but distant in the shade of a jaelo-covered trellis. They paused, to absorb both the smell and the green-glimmering garden vista. "His health remains secure, and he says the orchards there are very heavy with fruit. Perhaps he will send some."

"That would be nice. He's always thoughtful; he sent Kanbina— I mean, Fourth Mother..." Gamnae sighed, her sleeves moving slightly as her hands switched places inside their cover. "So much keeps changing. It's like being on a boat."

"I am not overly fond of boats." Yala glanced at bright dresses in another part of the garden; Gonwa Eulin, free of her elder's eagle eye for the moment, was promenading with Su Junha. The two leaned very close, conferring upon what was no doubt a question of great import.

"Nor am I," Gamnae agreed hastily. "They rock so, and one cannot keep one's humors from slipping about. My mother says..." She glanced at her companion, gauging Yala's reaction to a mention of Mother, and continued upon receiving merely an encouraging, inquisitive look. "She says I am silly to fear them, since I only ever go on small ones during summers in Yulehi. I wish I were there instead of the Palace, it is a little cooler."

Of course, the new princess had a well-bred quotation ready. "*In summer I think it unlikely I shall ever be cool again, in the autumn I dislike the rain, in winter I will never be warm, but spring, ah, spring!*" Yala turned her head to gaze at Lady Aoan Mau settled in the shade of a spreading thorn-nut tree with a collection of court ladies; two black blots were eunuchs busily brushing upon portable desks for those too indolent or important to perform such a duty themselves. Perhaps a poetry competition, maybe a novel-pastiche being written in tiny sips; maybe Lady Aoan was simply attending to correspondence outdoors. A bright white gazebo rose upon the other side of a clear, shimmering pond lensed with padflowers, their white cups and great green leaves providing reflection and contrast at once. From that hovering illustration, a sathron's plucking rose in bright ribbons, with the distinctive ringing at the note-ends that meant Second Queen Haesara—no, Second Mother, Gamnae reminded herself—was playing.

Second Mother was much sought after among the ladies since Gamnae's own mother had taken to her bed. Which was a worry all its own, but not one that could be alluded to at the moment. The visit was still young.

"I like Zhe Har," Gamnae agreed. "Do you think the Tabrak will come?"

Of course, with the First Queen abed—laid flat by an excess of joy at her son's ascension to the throne or by illness, Gamnae certainly could not begin to tell—there was much to worry a dutiful daughter. Even if she was a terrible, unfilial child for thinking maybe this was one of Mother's tantrums, like the awful headaches she claimed whenever things weren't going her way.

Sabwone had tried that trick once or twice, too. Poor Sabi. Gamnae wanted to make the *avert* sign to brush aside ill-luck, but it would have been rude to her companion.

With unspoken accord, they moved from the overgrown trellis to a covered walkway, its sides left open between pillars to catch any stray breeze. In winter it was miserable and little-used, but in summer any shade was welcome.

"If they do, the Fourth Prince will certainly give them something to think about." Princess Yala's mouth drew down at the corners, and though she was very quiet, her worry was almost visible. It matched Gamnae's own, perhaps. Of course Kurin would send Makar away; gossip said the Fourth Prince had won a sparring match in front of the Golden. It wasn't like him, of course—Maki was usually wiser.

Maybe he'd *wanted* to be sent away. Though it might be disloyal, Gamnae could admit it certainly seemed…well, safer. "My uncle says that the Southron Army is weak, since Kai has all the best units. Makar doesn't seem worried, but then he never does." Gamnae stole another glance at her. "Forgive me for asking, but what does Takshin say?" *And why did you marry him? Of course, you get to be outside the Palace. Lucky.*

Takyeo upon his deathbed had made Gamnae promise to consider any marriage carefully indeed, but the thought of escaping the tension now in every corner of the Kaeje was powerfully attractive.

Their jatas made slow, soft companionable noises upon the paved walk. "Not much." But Yala's gaze met hers for a moment, and she seemed to realize Gamnae needed more. "He remarked that the Fourth Prince will soon be putting his scholarship into practice."

"It's only a matter of time," the Second Princess muttered darkly, but whatever else she would have said was lost in the banging of gongs and the cry *The Emperor approaches!*

Glittering in burnished golden armor, the Emperor's personal guard moved along a garden path. In their wake, a cortege of brightly robed ministers clustered a figure in bright scarlet, his sleeves with only token touches of gold thread and his topknot-cage of dyed-crimson leather.

Gamnae halted, which meant Yala must too. *Maybe he won't see us.* Of course Gamnae hoped for as much, and of course that hope was forlorn, like wishing for rai during a famine. The Emperor viewed the garden, a minister leaning close to mutter in his ear, and the royal gaze fell upon his remaining sister—and her companion.

Kurin set off decisively down the path that would bring him to the pair, Golden sweeping before him and the ministers falling back. Gamnae's throat turned dry as the Westron Wastes at his approach, but she could not even give Yala a warning glance.

It would not be wise.

"There is my sister." Kurin held out his hands, relieving her of the obligation to bow to her elder brother; she was forced to clasp them, knowing her palms were unbecomingly damp from hiding in her sleeves. "How was Mother this morning, Gamnae? I will visit her as soon as I might."

"She is..." Gamnae glanced at Yala, who could not politely retreat. The new sister-in-law did the next best thing, though, looking across the garden with every evidence of curiosity about what amusement other groups were engaged upon. "Her stomach pains her so she can hardly eat. She calls for you." Her voice dropped still further. "Or for... for Father."

Father was safely ascended to one of Heaven's many mansions, and hopefully would not answer such a summons. Gamnae had quite enough to worry about with the persistent idea that Sabi's shade—long hair flowing, her body missing or replaced by a jointed wooden doll's—would invade her waking as well as the other ill dreams she was suffering more and more frequently now.

Yala drifted a step to her right, as if entranced by the vision Lady Aoan and her companions made. Gamnae's sweating fingers were cold despite the heat, and she wondered what Kurin wanted now.

And how he would set about getting it.

"It must be difficult for you. I'm glad you were able to slip away to take a turn in the garden." It would sound like a gentle remonstrance to anyone else, but Gamnae's skin roughened. Maybe only Jin would understand why she had the frantic desire to find somewhere, anywhere else to be.

"The morning physician said she needed rest." Gamnae rather liked Honorable Nuahan; her mother's old physician Tian Ha looked like a grinning skull most days. There was unsettling gossip about Honorable Tian—he had suffered some summer grippe or another, though one would think a physician would know how to keep such things at bay. Still, misfortune landed where it willed.

And the way other court ladies glanced meaningfully at each other when his sickness was alluded to was puzzling as well. Gamnae did not like to think upon it; the suppositions filling her head were deeply unfilial.

As well as terrifying.

"Well, physicians are always at noblewomen to rest." At least Kurin released his sister's hands without a final brutal squeeze. "Perhaps our new sister-in-law could allow Honorable Kihon Jiao to visit the Kaeje?"

Now Yala could not pretend graceful deafness. She turned to the Emperor, bowing with exactly the correct degree of respect and consciousness of her own position at once. "I must ask my husband, Your Majesty," she murmured.

"Khir women do nothing without a husband's consent." Kurin's smile was wide and beneficent, but Gamnae's stomach shuddered within her and she wished again, uselessly, that she could warn Yala. "Do you think Zhaon men should train their wives to follow your example?"

His sister-in-law regarded him with an accommodating smile. *In a foreign land, a visitor must cut his meat differently.* The allusion, part of a treatise upon travel and the sacred duties of hospitality, was from Cao Lung's *Green Book*, not usually read by women. But then, she was held to be very scholarly.

"And do you cut yours with a green claw?" Kurin turned slightly, regarding Yala with bright interest. For a moment Gamnae did not understand.

Then she did. Father had sent Lady Yala to the dungeons for bearing an unsanctioned weapon within the Palace; Gamnae's own uncle had sealed the order for a flogging to be administered early in the day. If not for Takshin, Yala might not even be *alive*; the shame of a whip-bite alone would kill a noblewoman.

Was that why she had married him? Gamnae had no way of asking. Not politely, anyway.

"Why, no." Yala's eyes widened, a creditable impression of shock, and her Khir accent, sometimes almost erased when she spoke to Gamnae, had thickened considerably. "Do they do so in Zhaon? I thought a husband performed that duty with a table-knife, here."

Gamnae's mouth threatened to drop wide enough to catch a shimmerwing insect. Kurin could now make a jest unsuitable for his younger, unmarried sister's ears if he wished to pursue the matter, or he could make a very ill-bred and more direct enquiry about that greenmetal blade. If he truly thought Yala was carrying a weapon, the Golden must be called to take it from her, and Takshin would take that very ill indeed.

A Khir woman had neatly outmaneuvered an Emperor, with nothing but a few words.

"Well said, sister-in-law." Kurin used the most respectful term for the relationship, accenting it lightly and almost affectionately near the end. "I see Takshin, as usual, has hidden a treasure just under our noses."

"The Emperor compliments his handmaiden." It was not quite right of Yala to address him so, giving herself such a subordinate title. Yet it was exactly the mistake a foreign noblewoman would make, and sharp Khir consonants prickled through each word. "I shall report his wishes faithfully to my husband."

Gamnae knew perfectly well that Takshin would send the shabby physician who had attended Takyeo, or not, as it pleased him, and she suspected Yala did too.

"And will you be visiting your mother-in-law?" Kurin, being balked once, was not yet ready to let go of his prey. "She would so dearly love to see her second son's new wife."

"I long to visit all my new mothers." Yala seemed to droop, a slight graceful movement though her jatas were firmly planted. Her mouth drew down too, and her sleeves moved slightly, a veritable scroll-illustration of deep regret. "My husband tells me First Mother is very unwell, though, and her physician will not allow small annoyances such as myself. I plead to be able to bring her some silk when she recovers; he has not yet given his consent."

Again, she neatly parried the implicit scolding for her neglect of an important social duty. Gamnae's jaw remained loose; *nobody* denied Kurin something he wanted like this. A woman could not very well do what her husband forbade, especially one from Khir where they sometimes fettered their wives with iron at night, either as punishment or to keep them from wandering like cloudfur.

Or so Gamnae had heard. She could not very well ask, could

she? The list of things she could not say was growing considerably long, and the idea that they might burst free at some inopportune moment gave her an unsteady feeling in her belly, her humors sloshing.

Women were held to be made of water anyway; she could wish for her liver to hold more courage, but it was like wishing for rain. Heaven granted as it pleased, and Gamnae was developing the opinion that importuning the celestial realm was almost a waste of time.

Like Mother, or Kurin, or even Father while he was alive, Heaven never listened.

"Ah, Takshin. He does as he pleases." Kurin shook his head, tut-tutting rather fondly. But his eyes had narrowed, and he studied the new princess very much as Sensheo would a small bug he wished to mount upon a sewing pin filched from his mother's basket. "I hope you shall moderate his temper, sister-in-law."

"A rather large task," Yala murmured. Her grey gaze locked with his, and Gamnae suddenly realized they had not looked away from each other since Kurin had addressed her. It was rather like seeing a sparring match upon the practice-ground, soldiers circling, not quite engaged yet but testing each other's defenses. "I shall do all I may."

"I believe you." Kurin's smile was a thin coat of winter ice upon a deep puddle, one that would turn a horse's hoof and send a rider expecting easy passage headlong. He turned his shoulders slightly, addressing Gamnae though he still held Garan Yala's gaze. "Little sister, do not leave Mother alone too long with only a physician nearby."

Gamnae's entire body prickled, as if wrapped in a damp woolen blanket. She did not recognize the feeling. "Yona is there," she said, and heard the sharp edge to her tone. "Mother prefers her, anyway."

"Nevertheless. I wish you a pleasant walk, my sisters." Kurin inclined his head, turning away to rejoin his Golden. Gamnae gave the bow due an elder brother ascended to the Throne; Yala's obeisance was deeper, of course, and performed very gracefully.

When the new princess straightened, there was a flash of feeling upon her sharp, piquant features—she lacked the roundness necessary for beauty, though she would hopefully gain marriage-weight soon—and Gamnae realized what the prickling under her own dress was, for it was reflected upon the other woman's face.

That was more frightening than Kurin, frankly, for Garan Gamnae did not like being angry. She never had. "Be careful," she whispered, very softly indeed. She *liked* Yala, and Kurin always had to spoil anything nice.

"Yes, Second Princess," her new sister replied, her grey gaze very direct and locked with Gamnae's for a moment before sliding politely away to look at the gazebo again. "Always."

Hammer and Anvil

"Two Khir?" The greatest general of Zhaon, despite a punishing day spent a-saddle to personally visit some carefully chosen troops, was not overly cold, but his tone was brusque. Dust clung to his half-armor, but his muddy gaze was sharp indeed. He wore little in the way of ostentation, but a greenstone hurai circled the first finger of his left hand, and that single detail was enough to make any intelligent soldier quail. "Lost merchants? Stray cloud-fur? Speak plainly, soldier."

To waste a great patron's time was not a flogging offense, but Zakkar Kai's mien did not bode well.

Still, Dahua Jin—newly promoted to junior general, and moving his men stealthily through this part of the borderlands to arrive in the ordered position in five days or so, Heaven willing—knew, deep in his bones, that their visitors were something important. Questioning that deep instinct had always led to ill fortune, and though his patron was visibly saddle-dusty and quite probably annoyed, he still accepted the proffered cup of soldier's tea with a grateful nod.

"Armed and armored, my lord general." Dahua accepted another mismatched wooden cup slopping with sweet hot strength from his lean silent adjutant Hua Dhu, grateful of the tent's shade even as it trapped the day's heat in fabric folds. A column of mirror-light provided illumination, and the foldable table for dispatches and other business was arranged precisely where it should be, as was every other article in the camp or he would order the soldier responsible chastised. "Five of them initially; we kept two alive to answer questions. For your visit, they are held in the Rack." The soldier's word for the tent or blockhouse where offenders waited for military penance or absolution was a double pun, both on the word for a locked armory and a certain instrument used by magistrates and town watches to extract truth or confession from a malefactor. "They have no answer for questions, and if you'll forgive me, they just don't *feel* right."

"Did you weigh their balls or their swords?" the marshal Tall Hurong Baihan interjected, clearly annoyed at the waste of time on what should be a routine inspection. That he was with General Zakkar was confirmation that Khir had decided to be troublesome again, and Dahua Jin was certain there would be action soon. "Just kill the spies and be done with it."

"Why would they be spying here?" Zakkar Kai shook his head, and Dahua was glad to hear his own vague but inarguable discomfort articulated so clearly. Some men had the gift of naming even the nebulous; of course Zhaon's great general would as well. "Unless they have outguessed me, and if they have *that* is something I very much need to know. Did they give you names, these two?"

"Not yet. We did not question them fully, my lord general Zakkar, since I knew you would be visiting." Fortunately, Dahua was able to give the answer in a crisp, though respectful, military bark.

"And you suspected I would wish to view—and hear for myself. Excellent decision, Junior General Dahua." Zakkar Kai glanced at Tall Hurong, who bolted his soldier's tea as if he did not care what temperature it was. In the army, a man learned to drink even if it burned the throat and eat even if the stomach rebelled; you simply did not know when another opportunity would arise.

The same principle applied to seeking other nourishment, but

Zakkar Kai frowned on more than the minimum of that particular sport.

"We will not make Jihau-An by sunset." The other marshal—Short Hurong, another luminary of the Northern Army Dahua had not expected to see upon this routine visit—accepted his own scorching cup of soldier's tea from the adjutant, whose visible admiration for a man with a leather throat, as the saying went—impervious to boiling water and winter ice both—would no doubt soothe some small irritation. "We might as well."

"I am curious, Tai. We would not have anyway; it always takes twice as long as you think." The ending of an old jest beloved of every Zhaon soldier was pleasing indeed; the great general had not forgotten what it was like to be in the rank and file. "What else troubles you, Dahua Jin? I know that look upon your face."

It was both heartening and disconcerting to think that Zakkar Kai did, but the junior general was past being amazed at his patron's perspicacity. "Not much. The pay-bags arrived; the soldiers are very pleased with the new Emperor's beneficence." Especially since the half-ingots could be sent to families bracing for harvest's activity and winter's hunger. Garan Tamuron had died early enough in summer that the ascension of one of his sons dispensed largesse at just the right time for many a soldier, and they blessed the old warlord for his last act of care. They were in good hands with their Heaven-favored general; Khir would be swiftly trounced.

Any other troubling rumors were a problem for wiser heads than theirs, though no soldier ever passed by an opportunity to complain. One could even call sour remarks an army's mistress, since sleep or food was longed for as a wife.

Zakkar Kai inspected the shield-squares drawn up outside their tents, stopping every now and again to point out a particular soldier. Most of his comments were strict but fair, and a few of those under Dahua Jin merited a word from the great man. He never seemed to forget a soldier's face, did Zakkar Kai, and even though there were dark circles under his keen, muddy eyes his carriage was erect and his booted step firm and sure. It did the men who carried swords good to feel their lives would not be wasted, though they might be called upon to give them; by the time they reached the Rack, Dahua was more than pleased with the day.

Of course, it could turn to shit in a heartbeat; the army had taught him that much. But still, it was pleasant to see some of the changes he'd instituted in this particular segment of the many-legged fighting creature responsible for Zhaon's defense met with such illustrious approval. The great general even once said, *That's a fine idea, Anlon, make a note of it for the entire army*, and his own grey-haired adjutant—famous for saving Zakkar Kai's life more than once, a subordinate of merit—nodded, his face expressionless.

The two Khir were chained to a deep-driven staple, not to mention ankle-hobbled together. One, with swallows worked into the stamped leather of his half-armor, stared fiercely and fixedly at the door with his strange, mourning-colored eyes. The other, somewhat the worse for wear since he would not stop struggling, sagged against his partner's back, looking at a tent-wall as if it was the most important piece of cloth in the history of any realm.

Dahua had some knowledge of Khir; it was more difficult to learn than the Shan dialect, but one couldn't very well question a spy or menace a northern peasant effectively without a few of their native words. Of course the great general had more of the tongue, and a few sharp, consonant-laden exchanges with the swallow-armored fellow later, Zakkar Kai glided forward, his boots very quiet. He circled the two prisoners, examined the staple that kept them in the tent, but did not go close and test the chains.

It was best not to taunt a caged beast too closely.

Zakkar Kai had asked their names; the swallow-decorated fellow spoke for both of them. Dahua caught a few mentions of bridges, rivers—and when the general shifted back to proper Zhaon outside the Rack in the blazing afternoon, he wore a faint frown. The sun beat down, but all the same, Dahua was glad to be out of that tent. Even with mirrorlight it was an unpleasant place, especially with the wooden implements and benches to hold a body in place for chastisement or worse standing sentinel, shrouded with heavy, travel-stained cloth.

"I know Khir are fond of hunting, but these fellows are far afield indeed." Zakkar Kai's eyebrows had drawn together. "And that one with the bruised face claims to speak no Zhaon. Very puzzling."

"Flog them both until they sing." Hurong Baihan shrugged. The other Hurong did not venture an opinion, merely gazed upon the remainder of the camp with his brows drawn together.

"My lord?" The iron-haired adjutant met his general's gaze. "We have something far finer than we know, I suspect. The swallows mean Hazuni, and theirs is a highly placed clan. Yet that man does not allow the other to speak, even if he would."

"As if he fears what he would say." Zakkar Kai nodded. "Exactly. This is good work, Dahua, especially keeping them in one piece. Send them under heavy guard to my camp at Zhehau-An, and make certain you choose steady soldiers for the task. I want them both alive and in good condition when they arrive, no matter what."

Dahua bowed. "It shall be done." Who could he trust with such a cargo? Many under his command were immediately ruled out; the Northern Army was full of those who had long memories and deep grudges against the horse-lords who thought it fine indeed to run down southron peasants in the borderlands, not to mention extract tribute from them with little mercy or care for what shape such payments took. He was about to make another suggestion when a rising mutter of interest and exclamation sounded from the camp.

It was yet another visitor, a dust-coated dispatch rider who brightened visibly upon seeing Zakkar Kai, though his gait held the stagger of one who still felt the horse's gallop in his own legs. "News for the great general, my lord!" he shouted, producing a sealed message bag. "Sehon Doah sends greetings, he has received reinforcement and thanks you for it. The Khir are at Navah-An, and have taken the tower at Cheku."

Cheku? But that's . . . Dahua tensed, watching the head general's face, which immediately split into a wide, very white smile. The beloved of Zhaon's God of War even elbowed Hurong Tai, not hard enough to bruise but still staggering the round, oft-smiling fellow.

"*Ai*, I owe you an ingot, do not poke me, my lord." Short Hurong was not smiling now, but he also did not look particularly displeased. "Haven't I always paid?" He also did not look overly saddened by losing whatever wager the two of them had made, and Tall Hurong upon Zakkar Kai's other side snorted a laugh.

"I have stopped counting the debt, Tai." Zakkar Kai sobered as his iron-haired adjutant accepted the dispatch bag. "In any case, sooner or later I will misjudge and you will gain it all back."

"On that day the sky will be dark indeed, my lord." Short Hurong sucked at his teeth for a moment, thinking. "Jihau-An will have to wait."

"Not for you. Take some cavalry from Dahua here and tell Sehon Doah 'tis time to move northeast. We shall catch them between hammer and anvil if we hurry, or starve them if we are slow." Zakkar Kai beckoned Dahua's adjutant, who pinkened at the cheeks like a peasant girl and hurried forward. "Come, listen. My lads, you have done well here; the Khir have no idea. Now there is a night march. Strike for just south of Cheku; arrive as fast as you may but with strength enough to fight. You shall be a second hammer if my first breaks."

"My lord?" General Zakkar's adjutant indicated the Rack.

"No change in their disposition, Anlon, though I thank you for the reminder." Zakkar Kai reached for his riding gloves, thrust through his belt. "It almost makes me wonder ... never mind." He brushed the thought away with a single impatient gesture. "Well done, my soldier-sons. Now is time for haste."

Dahua Jin hurried away, barking orders; the entire camp, already in a state of suppressed excitement, became a poked anthill roiling in every direction. Within a short while Zakkar Kai was gone with his cavalry guard and Short Hurong departed in a different direction, and the only problem remaining was who to send the cursed prisoners with. Had the great general not been visiting, the two of them might have been simply tortured until they gave up whatever could be gleaned of the enemy's dispositions; it was, it seemed, a very lucky day for them.

Dahua Jin hoped their luck would not continue, but if Zakkar Kai had something planned for their uninvited guests, it was bound to be more unpleasant than anything a mere junior general could produce.

He did not envy the Khir. Not during the journey, not during their arrival at the main camp, and certainly not when Zakkar Kai had more time to devote to them.

No. He did not envy them one whit.

MEDICINE

In his mother's house there was no need for the Golden or eunuchs shouting *the Emperor approaches*, and the liberating silence was the only pleasant part of visiting. This was his least favorite part of the day. Which said something, Garan Kurin thought, about the burdens of rule and of filial obedience. He tucked his hands in his sleeves, sending a swift glance out of the alcove and down the hallway.

They were unobserved, though certainly not for long. Even the servants he had placed here would creep to peer around corners, rather as peasants paid slivers to gawk at a curious foreign animal held in a tent by traveling players.

His sister, casting him many a frightened look, was only a small annoyance, as usual. "She had polished rai and greens," Gamnae said. "But tea upsets her stomach, she says. She refused the medicine and threw a comb at the physician."

Oh, by Heaven... Had Father ever prayed for patience as Kurin was tempted to? Heaven might even answer an emperor, though history was full of instances to the contrary. It was blasphemous to think that perhaps the celestial realm had its own affairs and did not trouble with the Middle World—or, maybe, did not exist at all.

Still, everyone assumed it did, and some wisdom was best left unquestioned—at least by peasants, merchants, and artisans. A nobleman was afforded some leeway, though he must be careful not to disturb the sentiments of those beneath him *too* much.

"How did the honorable physician respond?" he asked, very mildly, and wished Gamnae would not cringe so. It rather gave one the urge to poke or kick, and that was unbecoming in an Emperor.

It was a mercy Sabwone was no longer here. Neither she nor Sensheo could abide weak tea, as the saying went, and she would torment Gamnae with unrelenting passion.

A sharp unpleasant thrill ran down Kurin's back at the thought of his other sister. Hopefully Maki would drain the Tabrak enough they would be a spent force by the time they reached Zhaon-An, if such was indeed their goal. Perhaps they were even now riding back across the Wastes to their far, legendary home, and he would be forced to other, less covert moves in the game.

"He bowed and withdrew." Gamnae's shrug was arrested halfway, and she hurried to add more to the sentence. "What else could he do? Kurin, he said..." His sister's fair round face was creased most unbecomingly with worry. Perhaps she had gained all the filial feeling Takshin and Kurin himself had left behind in their mother's womb.

And Takshin, keeping that shabby little physician to himself. Well, let him. As long as Shin was useful, he could be allowed a certain amount of intransigence.

"Well?" Kurin prompted.

Gamnae glanced to either side, as if the hall would grow bleeding ears from every inch like the Hell of Lying In-Laws. She was not painting herself or doubling pretty accoutrements lately, attempting to rival Sabi's beauty. Restraint suited her. "He said it appeared not a natural illness."

Is that so. Mother had no shortage of enemies. Still, matters were very delicate right now, and another royal death would be an exceedingly bad omen. Especially with the plague in the provinces making the peasants mutter, as if they did not suffer the same thing every summer. "Well, Mother adores exorcists. Did the physician recommend one?"

Gamnae stared at him, wide-eyed, and he realized she was not so stupid as to think he was serious, nor to think he had not perceived her meaning. Hadn't he often cautioned Sabwone that their smallest sister was not unintelligent, simply uninterested in making a fuss?

So Kurin indicated a small, hardly used sitting-room, and when the partition was closed he turned to face her. "What precisely did the physician say?"

"It was *how* he said it, Eldest Brother." She was pale in the dimness, her yellow dinner gown a floating cloth like a gesekai come to harry a faithless suitor. "And before you tell me I am imagining it—"

"You are not." Kurin's head-meat, exercised by a day of balancing ministers against each other and brushing characters again and again upon—not to mention sealing—proclamations, policy decisions, summons to the imperial presence, directives to the Northern Army and to the Southron . . . it was endless, and he wondered if sometimes Father had wanted to burn all the paper and start anew.

Swinging a sword atop a plunging horse must be less draining than this.

"Kurin . . ." Gamnae's breath seemed to have failed her. She stared at him, her large, very fine dark eyes wide. "What have you done?"

What? Oh, by Heaven, you will regret that, sister mine. "You think I . . . she is our *mother,* Gamnae." Never mind that he had contemplated certain actions if Gamwone did not cease her meddling; he had always considered Gamnae, at least, willing to think the best of him.

Even if she was wrong.

"I know." Where had the brat learned this quiet, declarative tone? Even the way she regarded him was uncomfortably direct, and startlingly adult. "But there will be questions."

"Not the right ones."

She fell silent. He longed to pinch her, perhaps, or find a more fitting punishment. "You are my beloved sister," he said, persuasively enough. "Any of *them* may say as they please. But you, Gamnae?" It was not quite what he had meant to express, and his irritation mounted.

"Oh, I know I may not say anything, and I will not." She shook her head, her hairpin's bright dangle swinging. "She calls for you, Kurin. Over and over, for her favorite."

And that is my fault too, I gather. "It is not as pleasant as you might suppose, holding that title." Still, it must irk his sister that she was set aside so routinely. Kurin grasped for patience, and found some lurking within his liver.

A sliver, at least, and it would have to do.

"And all the others?" She sought to go past him, her left hand lifting and the plain, uncarved hurai upon the first finger glinting.

As if she expected him to strike her. A brother might do such a thing as a child, but a nobleman had other ways of gaining compliance—and an Emperor did, as well.

"Listen to me." He grabbed her left arm, but did not let his fingers bite. "You are upset with me because Eldest Brother is dead and I must make difficult decisions. I am your brother, Gamnae."

"So was Takyeo." She clapped her right hand over her mouth, her eyebrows rising, the picture of a child caught saying a naughty word.

"Don't call him back, now." There was a certain satisfaction in tweaking her superstition, especially if she was determined to be such a dolt. "Which physician?"

Gamnae shook her head, her left arm caught and her right hand against her mouth, not the backs of the fingers as if she was a court lady affecting astonishment or hiding a smile.

He shook her—not very hard, just enough to focus her humors upon the question asked. "Which *one*, Gamnae?"

"Honorable Yung Yeo." Her voice was muffled. "He comes in the afternoons. The one...the one Mother wanted to..."

To replace Tian Ha. Well, that's a pity. Had it been a physician sent, for example, by Second or Third Mother, he could easily arrange either silence or speaking as it suited him. "Honorable

Yung," he murmured. "Very well. You will have dinner in your rooms tonight, Gamnae, and think well upon what you would accuse your Eldest Brother of." He could not use the familial title accorded Takyeo, of course, but he was eldest in his own way, and due a little respect. After all, he had been first through their mother's gate, and though sometimes an unfilial action had to be taken, Gamnae certainly had no reason to perform it nor aptitude to do so correctly.

His were thankless tasks, but she could at least pretend a little graciousness in his direction. Kurin gave her one final shake, ignoring her gasp and the bobbling of her head like a melon upon a spindly stem. "Do you understand?" Her surrender was assured, he only wished for it to be official. "Say you understand, little sister."

"I . . . I understand."

He let go of her, patting at the sleeve he had wrinkled. Soft, heavy silk, a royal luxury; she had no idea what deeds kept it upon her back. He would have to marry her off soon, but where? Possibly Khir, though the horse-lords there would tie her to a kitchen stove. What a shuddering, cringing thing she was.

He was glad to have been born a man.

Kurin forgot Gamnae as soon as he stepped back into the hallway proper, smoothing his own sleeves and making certain his topknot-cage was in place. This part of the Kaeje was so familiar as to be completely ignored as he strode through the corridors, barely noticing Yona bowing as she withdrew into an alcove, probably on her way to terrorize some of the other maids. Of all his worries, she was the least—perhaps she would moan and throw herself upon her mistress's pyre, just like Hua Dinha's faithful dog.

Assuming, of course, that Mother was actually ill, and not simply furious that her eldest son was not dancing attendance upon her every whim.

In short order his presence caused commotion in the hall leading to Gamwone's sleeping chamber, and he heard his presence announced by one of her remaining little spiders—the frail-fingered, big-eyed girl who had often brought his tea upon princely mornings before he ascended to his rightful place. He allowed her to remain because she had been his creature from the start; Kurin had also applied some pressure to his mother's steward and now owned him as well.

Beyond the partition, it smelled of tangy medicinal herbs and a faint odor of burning ice-resin; the whitish globules kept moths from woolen cloth but were also held to clear foul air. A table had been carried in, and was now loaded with medical paraphernalia; her beauty bench sat neglected, its brazen mirror shrouded so it did not draw away any invisible, healthful humor or magnify an unhealthy one.

"Out," he said, and the spiders scattered. "Well, Mother, how are…" The sentence trailed off as he stepped into the circle of lampglow, a halu lamp burning faithfully upon her nightstand, the thin fabric swathing to keep bloodneedle insects from her nightly rest pulled carefully away.

His mother lay under a light counterpane, her long black hair—innocent of any winter just yet—a river over the stiff rectangular bolsters she preferred. A blue slipware cup and a wooden flask of sharp-smelling jikao tonic—good for the nerves and available from any apothecary, though the painted characters on the outside of the flask shouted it had come from the Artisan's Home and was consequently thrice the price of such an article acquired elsewhere—stood to attention in the lampglow as well, soldiers ready for battle inside an ailing human body.

Gamwone's cheeks had sunk alarmingly in the past few days. Her breathing was a shallow rasp, and scarcely seemed to lift the light embroidered counterpane, Gamnae's careful stitches tangling the characters for *Yulehi* with those for *peaceful sleep*. It had been a New Moon Festival gift from his sister four winters ago, and he remembered how hard she had worked on it despite Sabwone's teasing that a dress was better.

His mother's skin was mottled, and her hand, with the silver filigree sheath over its smallest nail, trembled upon the counterpane's folded top. Kurin glanced at the partition, his ears pricked for even the faintest noise of breathing, a pulse, any sign that he was being observed.

None was apparent, but he crossed the room again and glanced into the hall. Closing the partition would be a sign there was something to hide, so he left it half open and retraced his steps to the bedside. His hand dove into his sleeve, and he had a moment's qualm.

Do not.

It had been a long while since he had hesitated, or been unsure of the next step to take. He eyed the flask of tonic, examined his mother's sleeping face again.

There were tiny glimmers under her thick black eyelashes. She was beautiful, still. As a boy he had peered around the edge of a screen, watching her dabbing nia oil and patting zhu on her face; it had seemed, then, that his mother was Heaven's greatest consort, the one whose infrequent dictates not even the emperor of the celestial realms could disobey.

Garan Gamwone's lips were chapped now, and as he watched her feet moved at the end of the bed, a pair of hillocks contorting under a grassy carapace. Her eyelids fluttered, and her other hand must have been resting upon her illness-swollen belly. It twitched, moving atop a parody of early pregnancy, and Kurin's humors were indeed disarranged, for he felt cold fingers brush his back again.

When one of Yona's little household spies crept to the partition, she was treated to the sight of the Emperor of all Zhaon holding his ailing mother's shoulders and a blue cup of tonic to her lips. "Drink your medicine, Mother," Garan Kurin said very softly, and though it was a filial scene indeed, the maid's throat was dry and well-banked hatred burned in her protruding eyes.

Her mistress, only half conscious, drank without complaint.

A USEFUL CRIME

I t was a hot, pleasant morning, though there was a smudge of dark cloud to the north. Such a thing was not uncommon in late summer, and heralded a return of the rains and the swampy chill of autumn. The first harvest had passed, the second crop of rai planted in those places peasants knew would be sheltered from the plunging temperatures of almost-winter in a few moon-cycles, and Garan Jin rode with his chin almost touching his chest, sunk in profound thought.

His companion, a lady upon a black mare, rode with similar quiet. Garan Komor-a Yala accorded the Sixth Prince silence during this morning ritual, and he appreciated the gift. Of course, the lady was not known for chatter, but an observer might have thought them wholly unrelated, for all their converse.

At length, however, the bone-white tombs came into view, and Jin shook off the uncomfortable pressure building inside his head-meat, glancing at his charge. Even a married noblewoman should not travel outside the city walls alone, and he now remembered the duty of conversation as well as protection his presence implied.

"I'm very rude again," he said, tentatively. Today the kaburei who usually held Yala's reins was left at Takshin's house, helping bring some order to the last bits of unpacking. "But you never take me to task, sister-in-law."

"What good would come of that?" Yala laughed, a soft restful sound; he could see why Takshin liked her so much. *"A querulous in-law is a curse upon a household."*

"I know that is a quotation, but I can't tell from who." He shook his head, an unwilling smile blooming. Any enjoyment seemed wrong, especially with his mother so...upset.

The world had changed out of all recognition. And he was so weary.

"Now, if it were a weapon..." A light, amused lilt lay under Yala's words, and it wasn't unpleasant in the least.

If it were a weapon, he would certainly know more. "You sound like Mother."

"A high compliment, Sixth Prince Jin." She bent slightly in the saddle, a shadow of a bow in his direction. Their horses had fallen entirely into companionable step; they sounded like one person riding down the road.

"If you do not call me *brother* I shall be quite put out." At least he could try to be more polite, now that he realized he hadn't spoken since before the gate in the palace complex's wall. "Gamnae calls me a smelly longtail, though I don't recommend that."

"I would never." The new princess outright laughed at the notion, as she hardly ever did; her black mare's ears flicked at the pleasant sound. "She wrote to me this morning; she says First Mother is doing a little better."

Jin wanted to remark that he didn't give a single swelling muah-gua if the First Queen was doing better, but that was rude, not to mention unfilial. His neck itched, but he did not scratch—a small penance. "That's good." His tone turned neutral, and Yala glanced at him.

"She also mentioned the theater," she continued. "And she has done so twice. Do you think it would be acceptable to invite her? A daytime farce, not an evening one."

It was a capital idea, and one Jin should have broached himself. "Just the thing to take her mind from...well, from everything. But let me brush the invitation." He didn't want to think about what the First Queen might make Gamnae suffer if *Yala* did so.

As much as the woman disliked all other wives and children—that was perhaps only normal for a senior wife, all the books said so— she would reserve a special ire for Takshin's new bride, especially since Yala had been a lady-in-waiting to the Crown Princess.

Anything given to Takyeo drove the First Queen into a fury. It had been a fact of life for so long Jin had thought it quite normal. Surely it was a tiny bit unfilial to compare patient, mild Ah-Yeo to the scary, coldly beautiful woman who stared hatefully at other wives' children during public rituals.

Father had married her because of Yulehi, but it had occurred to Jin lately that perhaps, just perhaps it might have been a mistake. It was quite a foreign notion—that the remote, sometimes benevolent but always terrifying god of his childhood could do anything so mortal as commit an error. Still, it had to be possible.

Because Father, after all, was dead. *Ascended* was a pretty way to put it, and Jin supposed it was even possible that Heaven existed and Garan Tamuron was ensconced comfortably in a mansion there.

It was far more believable to think of his Eldest Brother there, though he didn't know why he felt so. And there was no one to ask. Even Mrong Banh was distracted lately.

"That was indeed why I mentioned it." Yala's hands rested prettily upon the reins; married life suited her, and she had even gained some weight. Of course, how anyone could eat with Takshin glaring at them all day was beyond Jin, but she did not seem to mind much.

It was one thing to have a brother. It was quite another to have *married* brothers, and he found himself studying Takshin closely, wondering what he'd done to attract such a lady's notice. He also studied Su Junha, who always bowed and murmured *Sixth Prince Jin, how is your health* with a merry twinkle in her solemn dark gaze upon meeting him.

He did not know quite how to answer, despite etiquette providing all the fine words a prince could ever want. Instead he always mumbled something silly and retreated, hoping the heat in his cheeks wasn't a blush like an embarrassed maiden's. "Will you bring your ladies? It might seem...well, if there was a large group, Gamnae might..." He meant to say his sister could escape gossip if more ladies came along, but suddenly could not think of a way to do so gracefully.

"I thought Su Junha might wish to come along." Yala considered the question gravely, and gave a slight shake of her head, her hair-pin swinging. Her veil was tucked aside; it must be dreadfully hard to breathe underneath it, though it would filter the dust somewhat. "Lady Hansei, though, would much prefer a book."

That was no secret, and there seemed no hidden message in the observation.

They reached the tombs, and Jin remembered not to hurry to her horse this time. Khir noblewomen preferred to alight without aid, and such preferences were a lady's prerogative.

Once she was safely aground she consented to take his arm, as usual, and they set off for Father's tomb. The new princess walked with her head down, watching her steps; her bright green dress and veil bore a light coating of yellow road-dust, as did his sober dark blue robe.

"Have you heard anything?" Princess Yala finally murmured.

"Not much," he had to admit. "All the gossip is of First Mother's illness. And your marriage. Some say she is livid at her son marry-ing...well, you know."

"Indeed I do." Yala's fingers weighed scarcely anything in the crook of his elbow. "What say the Golden?"

This was his favorite part of these visits. It was exciting to gather little snippets of gossip and half-heard asides, to decipher mean-ingful looks. Kurin might be angry, but what could he do, put Jin under house arrest in the Iejo for doing something even Father had winked at?

Besides, a court lady would hear different things than Jin might. And it pleased him to be of use to her.

"They like Eldest Brother a great deal," he was forced to admit, and it irked him to call Kurin by a word that could possibly refer to

Takyeo if one did not know better. "He has added to their stipend by at least a third. They say not even Father was this liberal. But do you recall, that day in the market..."

A delicate shudder paused her steady steps for a moment, and the new princess glanced at him. Her sharp features were blurred by the fine veil lowered in deference to the august ancestors, but there was a flash of paleness, her gaze with that clear ghostly quality of Khir. "It would be hard to forget."

"Yes, well." At least he didn't have to describe it afresh; she had, after all, been present. The feel of a sword sinking into another man's flesh was enough to unseat one's liver, but he supposed being a nobleman entailed such things. "Kai and Takshin questioned the rest of that Golden's square. Obviously they weren't involved. But they were arrested two days ago."

"How very odd," Yala said softly, though her tone said she did not find it odd but instead troubling.

And so did he.

"None will speak of the reason. But I wonder." Jin found himself patting her fingers with his free hand as if he were walking with Gamnae, attempting to express protection and fondness at once.

"And now it is my turn." Yala did not seem to mind the touch, but her fingers tensed upon his arm. "I overheard Third Mother speaking to Lady Gonwa—a quotation from Ihen Jiao. *My son sleeps elsewhere.*"

Jin strained his memory. "I admit I do not know the work," he admitted.

And as usual, his new sister-in-law did not make him feel silly or stupid for not recognizing an allusion to the Hundreds. Instead, like Mrong Banh, she simply gave the information quietly, somewhat as if reciting her own lessons before an unforgiving tutor. "He was a Third Dynasty minister. His son escaped an attempt upon his life by the simple expedient of being with his mistress one night, instead of where he was supposed to be. Lady Gonwa replied with Tien Zhu. *Heaven guards the innocent.*"

Jin thought it over. His mother needed no more worries. Just that morn she had been staring at the breakfast table as if witless-adrift, and he thought it likely she was momentarily perplexed at why Sabwone's place was not set. Of course Sabi had been gone a long while before her...misfortune, but the shock had probably unfixed some of Mother's humors.

He had to admit his own were none too steady, either. "Do you think it does?"

"Hm?" Yala's sound of inquiry was thoughtful, not pressing or dismissive.

"Heaven." The question had long been circling his head-meat, Jin realized. "Do you think the celestial ones guard innocents?"

"They are said to, in tales." The slight pause before her reply as well as the spacing between her words said she had not seen such a thing with her own eyes, and she paused long enough for the full meaning to sink in before continuing. "I am also told very few nobles or ministers have left the Palace complex for provincial estates this year, though it is the time to do so."

The sun beat down, gathering strength to lay everything in Zhaon flat during the afternoon. Jin made a short noise of assent, very much like Takshin. What would be happening if Ah-Yeo wasn't dead? Every time he halted to pray before his eldest brother's carving in the bone-white wall, he found himself speechless mentally as well as physically.

Worst of all was the nagging notion that he should have seen something, suspected something, *done* something. "I tried to suggest Mother go to Hanweo. She began to cry." It was not quite right to speak thus about one's parent, but who else could he tell? Kurin was busy with what he'd always wanted, Kai was gone, Takshin forbiddingly distant even with Yala's intercession, Maki riding south to deal with barbarians—Kurin was probably hoping he'd fail or fall to an arrow—and one should never show Sensheo a weakness if it could be helped. And Gamnae? She had her own worries, tending to the First Queen.

First *Mother*. Perhaps she was even satisfied with the title, now.

"The countryside may be dangerous too." Yala's steps slowed

further. They were approaching Father's tomb, paying their respects there first as tradition demanded. "It might be best to leave a candle in your bedroom and sleep elsewhere, Sixth Prince Jin."

"It has to be one of my brothers." It was an agonizing relief to admit it openly, when he had barely dared think such a thing before. They could scarcely be overheard here—and besides, he knew just how well Yala could keep a secret. Jin halted, and looked down at her. How strange this was, that a foreign lady could be the repository of such confidence. "But nobody cares about me, I am practically out of the succession."

"I do not know." Yala's brow was troubled, and damp as well, the veil sticking in thin folds. Northerners did not take well to heat trapped in the lowland bowl-plains. "It might be well for your mother to leave a candle burning in her stead as well."

Of course, Yala was a foreign wife; she could not be quite as direct as a prince. Jin's mouth had gone dry as the dust, and he suddenly understood, youth though he was, why a man might want sohju to blot out unpleasant thoughts instead of for the pleasant disarrangement of the senses. "But my mother..." Who would want to harm *her*?

Well, put that way, the answer was obvious.

"I am told there is a certain Zhaon term for a theater-manager. Its characters bear another meaning; I am told anyone with sufficient coin may engage certain services. Such a client must be very useful not only for merchants, but for nobles as well. Even for royalty." Yala lifted her head and gazed at him, steadily. A hot breeze tugged at the edges of her veil, and though it screened her features he saw the worry stamped plainly there, as it must be upon his own face. Did she speak to Takshin like this? "I have little proof, Sixth Prince. All I have are suppositions and half-heard words."

"I know." And that was the point of hiring impresarios, of course. The world had become a thin bright rai-paper screen over a deep well of things almost too nasty to be thought, let alone given voice. Just a few moon-turns ago, he had known of such things as assassins and impresarios, but had not fully understood them.

Now...well, Gamnae called it growing up, but Jin wasn't so sure. It was more like the miracle of Gauhua the Fan-Sage, blindness disappearing and the cosmos revealed all at once. "Do you think... I should not say such things. But do you think that perhaps First Mother's illness is not quite natural?"

"If it is not, and that can be proved by a physician, the Emperor may have to blame someone." Yala regarded him steadily. "It would be a very useful crime to accuse another mother or her children of."

They examined each other for a short while, the new princess and the Sixth Prince of Zhaon. When they set off for the tombs again, neither spoke beyond commonplaces.

There was nothing else to say.

VENOMOUS TAIL

It was a mark of Zakkar Kai's thoroughness that the Southron Army, while not quite to its northern twin's standard, was nevertheless in good order, its marshals and junior generals reporting to a newly arrived prince with every evidence of cautious respect. A swift dispatch from Zhaon's greatest general had arrived just before Makar, with another private missive folded into its sheaf; the junior generals were exhorted to do their utmost for Zhaon and for Garan Makar, who would not spend their lives needlessly and who expected the filial obedience due any general from his soldier-sons.

By the date brushed upon its top right corner, Kai had heard of this appointment nearly a moon-turn ago, which meant Kurin had been planning it well before Takshin's wedding.

He could almost admire Kurin's forethought. Almost.

The rider must have been sent the moment Kai received confirmation, and ridden to almost-foundering along Zhaon's stone-paved arteries. Covered with dust and half-dead of heat, the fellow was carried away.

A short passage from the dispatch was read to the troops assembled in shield-square formations by cohort leaders, and finally Makar was bowed into a hastily erected commander's tent, his dark but well-crafted leather half-armor removed by a tongue-tied youth from Hanweo who would serve Garan Makar as armor-son now, and a lean man with a scar tracing his jaw as an adjutant.

The scarred man, Tiang Huo, was of the same efficient stripe as Kai's shadow Anlon, and was visibly relieved that the prince sent to the army was not a preening eyebird but of a more thoughtful cast. Makar also lost no time in asking the man's opinion upon one or two points, since it was one of Kai's adages that while a soldier was relieved to have reasonable orders to follow, he also relished the chance to give his opinion without flinching.

It was a balance akin to playing chess against a canny opponent, or navigating a court's murkier depths.

Tiang would be the one taking news of the new commander's habits and faults to the rest of the army; Makar hoped an old soldier would find nothing of deep concern in either. It was no use attempting to act as if he was an experienced general instead of an encumbrance quite possibly sent only to die in battle and remove one of Kurin's potential rivals from the Middle World.

Finally, Garan Makar was left alone with his thoughts and the sound of an army camp settling itself for bed, the gongs of watch and picket rung and the mutter of male conversation underscored with the smoke of cooking-braziers and halu lamps, those wonderful contraptions which would extinguish themselves upon tipping. He settled at the camp table piled high with dispatches awaiting attention, reports from patrols brushed in military jargon. It was too early to expect a letter from anyone at home; he hoped Mother could rein in Sensheo while he was gone. He had left no few precautions in place as a hedge about the Second Dowager Queen of Zhaon, but it irked him to be absent while she was in a snake-pit.

At least he did not have to fear a gift with a venomous tail when he broke the seal on Kai's private letter. It began with wishing long life and health upon the Emperor, as it should, and inquired after Makar's health in perfunctory fashion. There was no congratulation for his advancement to command of half Zhaon's armies, which told him Kai understood very well this was not meant to be an honor.

In the meat of the missive his adoptive-brother's tone was brusque but no character was wasted; there were a few bits of useful advice about the generals of the Southron Army—who could be trusted, who was beholden to another prince in some fashion, and who would give counsel clean of any ulterior motive during battle.

The next-to-last lines bore a small blotch as if Kai had paused, the brush held suspended while he thought—probably at a table very much like this one, cunningly designed to fold flat and be carried upon a lumbering army-cart.

Do not doubt yourself, Makar. That is poison in battle. This is no different than the assassin in Hanweo when you were eight winters high; you will do well.

It was...comforting, to hear one so beloved of the God of War had such faith in his abilities.

Still, he might have preferred a letter from his mother, or from a certain lady whose dress was never belted too tightly. What were they doing now? He closed his eyes, thinking of the palace complex as dusk rose velvet-purple in every corner. If there was actual homesickness, it centered more upon his own house in the Noble District, and his own familiar bed.

The last lines were even more hurried, though Kai's brushwork did not suffer overmuch, and a chill traced down Makar's back as he read them. So, Khir was not quite as supine as Kurin supposed, and Kai was perfectly aware the new Emperor might not listen to an adopted brother's warning upon that point. Kai was also perfectly aware Kurin would not be overly saddened if his father's foundling fell in battle, though it would be a bother finding another of his ability to hold off even a weakened northern dagger-country.

The message was plain. *We are both superfluous; take care, Maki.* At least Kai did not attempt to sweeten the ball of bitter medicine.

Makar rose and surveyed the tent's appurtenances, pacing with his hands clasped behind his back as he often did while deep in thought in his own study. He was exhausted, worried for his mother, and worried to a lesser degree for his bumbling younger brother. Yet even the weariness from a day spent in the saddle and then enduring a ceremonial military welcome felt...clean. Certainly cleaner than a few other things a prince had to endure.

According to Kai, all that remained was to do his duty. Makar found himself hoping the great general of Zhaon was correct.

A tenday later, the morn rose bright and hot, the beginning of autumn fog disappearing in a haze. The dust had not broken yet, but perhaps it would soon. Accustomed to rising early when he wished to study some particularly engaging topic, Garan Makar could perhaps be forgiven for thinking he was adjusting to army life far better than one or two of his brothers might, though days in the saddle visiting outlying detachments, while bracing, also drove weariness deep into his bones.

Nevertheless, he was cautiously hopeful, and taking his morning meals outside his tent not only displayed him to the army but strengthened his appetite.

That particular morning, however, a screening picket sent a message racing back to the army's nerve-center, and a runner skidded to a stop before Garan Makar's tent during breakfast, his sides heaving and high color in his cheeks when he halted before the open-air table.

"Smoke," the young soldier gasped, after bobbing hurried bows to a prince and his marshals, his eyes wide as his no doubt equally excited horse's. "Above the forest to the southwest. Too much for clearing parties."

Makar closed his own eyes for a moment, calling up the maps he had spent many a previous evening studying under fitful lamplight. *Ah, yes, I see. A canny decision indeed.* "Interesting," he murmured, and turned to the marshals Binwon Ko and Dohon Sek, sharing his table with much courtesy even if their appetites seemed blunted.

"Perhaps the forest is alight from some other source." Broadshouldered Marshal Binwon often sat with his hands laced over a small, respectable peasant's paunch. Now, however, his greying eyebrows slightly raised and his mouth pursed as he laid his eatingsticks down. His manners were rough but not entirely absent, and Makar found he rather liked them.

"It will not hurt to see," slim fiery Marshal Dohon remarked, with a quick glance to the prince to see how he would take this suggestion. Makar was already upon his feet, pushing aside the tent-flap and moving for his armor-stand. His cuirass was already laced into place, but the shoulders and greaves, not to mention gauntlets, were needed.

Tiang Huo, busy with brushing orders for the day, looked up from another table, a cup of strong sweet soldier's tea halfway to his mouth; the armor-son, busily consuming a rai-ball as he polished bits of metal or leather, hurried to his feet and popped the rest of his breakfast wholesale into his cheek so he could chew as he worked.

The marshals followed him inside, and it was perhaps a mark of respect that they waited for orders instead of setting about in a babble of speculation. "Cavalry upon the wings," Makar said. "Ready the infantry and light the touchsticks for the cannon. If all goes well we may draw them out of the trees."

Tiang Huo leapt to his feet and strode for his own armor-stand, not bothering to ask a question. He began to buckle what he could; Makar's armor-son would attend to him as soon as the prince was fully encased, if Tiang's was about on other business. Still, the greying adjutant's gaze strayed often to his new lord, waiting for commands.

"What, the peasants?" Binwon Ko's laugh was sharp but not dismissive. "My lord, it could well be—"

"It could be," Makar agreed. "It will do no harm to see how the army responds, and I am unused to commanding such a large beast. *A rider must practice before he becomes skilled.*" He doubted any of them would know the quotation, and found he did not mind in the least.

"Forest-fighting is difficult," Dohon Sek noted, but thoughtfully, working his hands into the gloves that had been thrust through his belt.

"I have no doubt." Makar strangled a flare of impatience. Could they not *see*? Yet he took care to use a tone very close to one he'd heard Kai employ more than once, brisk but not rude, direct but not quite over-commanding. "Then we will use the cannon to set the forest alight and drive them forth. The Horde moves as a whole, the books say—warriors, wives, and kaburei."

"Like flushing coneys in long grass." Binwon Ko slapped his small, hard leather-armored paunch, rising as well. "Where is your armor-son? Come, Sek my friend, it is a good day. Soldier-tea and a battle, even if only against peasants—"

"Firing the woods—it is the dry season. It may spread." Dohon Sek, despite his youth and his appearance of restlessness, was far more cautious. Still, he did not speak as a worried maiden aunt, but merely thought aloud, obviously used to his elder's decisiveness. Obviously Kai had chosen these two with a great deal of thought; one was a hare ready for gallop and the other a tortoise holding to a steady pace.

Let it spread, if it must. Makar's heart settled into a high hard rhythm; Tiang Huo's gangly armor-son, his wrists protruding from his sleeves as he burst through the tent-flap with half a pounded-rai cake hanging upon his lips, scrambled toward the stand to do his duty.

But the question of the forest was rendered moot by a clashing, crashing din, a yell from many throats, and the sound of hooves.

Makar stiffened. *Ah. Of course.* Barbarians, by definition, did not let battle wait for breakfast.

"What in the seven hells is that?" Binwon Ko, however, had turned somewhat pale, for he knew very well.

"Tabrak," Garan Makar answered, grimly. The battle was upon them, whether they willed or no.

How to Rule

The new Emperor's midday meal was frugal, as had been his habit for several years now. Today, Kurin was settled at a low table upon a newly familiar porch overlooking the Kaeje garden Father had been able to see from his sickbed; there was motion among the deep green and bright red flowers as birds and insects flickered through the heat. A few touches of white showed, jaelo blossoms past their time but still vigorous because the vine-roots were carefully watered. During the dry time it took much work to keep the gemlike gardens in their proper order; in winter those who bent their backs to that labor would be much occupied with firewood and keeping warm instead.

An invitation to dine with one's brother was supposed to be a pleasant affair. At least Sensheo bowed his way properly into the occasion, and waited until the meal was halfway finished before beginning what he no doubt thought was a well-camouflaged raid.

Kurin's head ached, but no amount of physician's tonics would aid it. "You have no proof, Sensheo."

"I don't need his brushwork to know what he'll do." The Fifth Prince, his bright yellow robe far too cheerful for such a dusty day, laid his eating-sticks aside to pour another measure of tea for them both. Did he think himself very clever, bringing such concocted fables to his elder brother? Gossip was not enough to remove Zha-on's head general from his perch.

Not so long as Kai was useful, and the moment he was not Kurin had plans well laid. So the Emperor of Zhaon found himself in the rather strange position of defending a foundling brat raised by his father to his own brother, and while he might later think it amusing, at the moment his temper was severely frayed. "You have always hated him."

It was not even pleasant to speak an undeniable truth at the moment. Especially since Mother was fading so quickly. It would be very damaging were any whisper of suspicion about her condition to escape, but Kurin knew it was only a matter of time.

"Oh, I don't deny he's useful." Sensheo made a small gesture, brushing aside Kai's usefulness. "But does it do any harm to look to what will happen once Khir is subject to us and Tabrak is smashed? If Kai wins both battles—"

"Do you doubt Makar's ability then?" The Emperor suppressed a sigh. The angle of Sensheo's argument was faintly ridiculous in and of itself, but then again, this brother was never one to look for a deeper logic when the one he wanted would do. "He is generally held to be a peerless scholar." He sipped smoky siao, just the thing for cutting the dust settling in every crevice during the drought season, even painting the inside of one's nose.

"Maki is more comfortable sitting behind a chessboard, Kurin. And this Aro fellow has already plundered Shan." Sensheo shrugged. "I will mourn Makar when it is time, not before. I do not wish to mourn you as well, and find my own head upon a chopping-block once Kai decides to follow Father's example."

"Ah. That, at least, I can believe." Kurin eyed his brother, a slight smile playing under his smallbeard. A fine meal was being ruined for no real reason, although it was always better to know what silly caprice Sensheo would indulge in next. Maki had probably taken all his mother's quality of discretion through the womb-gate, leaving nothing for his brother. "No doubt you have some sort of plan."

"Must I? You could solve the problem easily enough." Sensheo even said it airily, as if removing a general beloved by the God of War when your land was threatened both north and south was a minor matter. Why had he decided *now* was the proper moment for this particular intrigue? "But it must be at the right time."

"Do you counsel me as a brother, or as a minister? I have a plague of the latter." In fact, Zhaon's emperor was beginning to think he had a plague of both. Kurin's irritation mounted another notch. Mother's breathing was shallow and harsh, and the tonics were not helping. As the ruler of the center of the world, he did not have a prince's freedom to descend into Zhaon-An and find a certain shop in the Left Market where a blind man sat upon a stool and dispensed useful articles—and information, if he were asked in the right manner. "And once Kai is..."

"He must be dealt with." Sensheo lifted his cup, delicately, and made a show of appreciating the aroma. Bright blur-wing birds zipped through the garden; they were tiny and beautiful, but also vicious. One hovered near the porch, sword-beak and tiny body motionless as he hung in midair, then bolted away, clearly deciding there was nothing approaching its usual fare near the much larger creatures sitting so ponderously. "But in the proper way, at the proper time."

Thinking of the Yuin reminded Kurin of a small bottle with a soakwood stopper taken from Sensheo's sleeve during a game of Ch'han kujiu, and the effects of the liquid within. It was just as well he had tested it, and now he was faced with the prospect that Sensheo had not merely acquired the wrong article but had substituted one thing for another, like a Ch'han sage performing the everflower trick in the Hundreds.

It would be far more cunning than he had surmised his little brother capable of, but the artifice would only work once. Let Sensheo think he had not tested it, let this particular brother think, in fact, what he willed. "And your only reward will be the satisfaction of seeing him disgraced?" Kurin shook his head. Perhaps Sensheo did truly think himself this clever.

It boggled the head-meat, indeed.

Sensheo's lips pursed slightly as he lowered his cup. "Disgrace is not enough."

"Are you so certain?" *By Heaven*, Kurin realized, a faint chill brushing his spine. *He truly hates Kai. It is not just envy, he is consumed.*

"Would it have stopped Father?" Sensheo looked away, over the garden's riot. The Golden guarding the Emperor were too far away to hear this discussion, at least; a few in their eye-watering armor patrolled the bright green, others stood at either end of the long porch. Still others were just inside, ready to respond to any call or clash. Had Father ever felt hemmed in by the constant watch?

He began to think Jin was wiser than most, leaping the palace walls at night.

"What would Father think of this, I wonder?" The Emperor decided his appetite had fled. The body of Zhaon was scrutinized near daily, as was everything it shed—even bowel-leavings. Perhaps Father's health had failed under the incessant poking, prodding, and scrutiny.

"He would think his true heir did not shy from making difficult decisions." Sensheo inclined his head, his right forefinger caressing the horn thumb-ring. He was only a middling archer, but he liked the decoration enough to wear it near-daily. "I suspect I am wearying you with my warnings. How is First Mother today?"

"Well enough." Kurin did not say that perhaps the only thing keeping her alive had been her hatred of her husband. But as he studied his excitable little brother, he decided it was time for a subtle reminder. "One of her physicians mentioned a curious thing."

Sensheo's eyebrows lifted. "Oh?"

"He said her illness did not appear quite natural." Kurin's smile did not alter. Nor did he pick up his eating-sticks again, or reach for his tea.

His little brother paused. "That is indeed odd. Perhaps that shabby fellow Takshin and Kai set such store by could be called to give an opinion?" His tone was helpful, though somewhat distant. Of course, Gamwone had never paid him much attention. Perhaps it was a blessing. "He tried mightily to save Eldest Brother."

"Indeed he did." And now Takshin was keeping Kihon Jiao all

to himself, perhaps suspecting Kurin would seek to pin blame upon a lower-ranking sleeve. Kurin could not quite tell if his bolt had hit home, but if Sensheo were wise, he would heed the reminder—and might even suffer a pang or two of conscience, a thing he seemed to lack. Perhaps his humors were unbalanced, or perhaps the Second Queen's second son had a greater ambition than disposing of a hated childhood enemy. "But Takshin seems as enamored of the fellow as he is of his new wife."

"Perhaps that is what broke First Mother's heart," Sensheo offered, somewhat diplomatically. His topknot-cage glistened with bright smoky light reflected from the garden's depths. "Her son, already given to Shan, decides to marry a Khir demon with a green claw."

Now *that* was too far, and Kurin's irritation turned sharp. "Princess Yala is very scholarly, and very modest besides," he said severely. The Khir girl was not worth spending any time upon; let Takshin play with his new toy. It might even smooth his brother's temper some fraction. "Gamnae is quite taken with her. So are Second and Third Mother. In fact, all the court ladies seem to enjoy her company."

"Women are foolish sometimes." The Fifth Prince's smile turned paternal. "But the new princess has not yet visited our First Mother."

"How can she, with Mother so ill?" Kurin restrained the urge to tut-tut like a maiden aunt, wishing his chair had a back to lean against for a moment. The heat was draining, for all he had suffered it every year since birth, and the padded bench that had been his father's usual lunchtime perch was almost as uncomfortable as the throne itself. "Are you a eunuch, to worry so deeply over what the court ladies do? Come now, Sensheo. I might almost think you ready to attempt mischief with Takshin's new bride. He would not take that kindly indeed."

Which might be a rather elegant solution, if it could be achieved. It would at least be amusing to see the short work Shin would make of Sensen.

"*A man newly married is a dangerous thing.*" The quotation, always delivered in the archaic form and from the anonymous part of the Hundreds, was usually attributed to a traveling Ch'han sage. Most scholars agreed that section was a fictional repository of several collected peasant sayings. Why Sensheo had retained a particular saying instead of a thousand other more useful ones was a mystery. "I am rather surprised you let him leave the Palace, too."

"Careful, Sensen." It was a perverse pleasure to use the nickname, since he suspected Sensheo hated it. "It sounds rather as if you wish to tell an Emperor how he should rule."

His younger sibling took the opportunity to smile like a feline with a small dead thing between its front paws. "A minister should not fear to speak truth."

If you were capable of truth, I might think you speaking it once or twice a year. And for all his scheming, Sensheo was not a minister yet. "Very true." Kurin played with the idea of giving him some sinecure or flowery title, merely for the pleasure of stripping it away later. "But unless you have something pleasant to say, little brother, cease. Speak of the theater, speak of courtesans, speak of painting or even of buildings. But halt your petty intriguing."

He did not mean to sound quite so sharp, but the afternoon loomed full of council meetings and two northern provinces were applying for relief of taxes. Granting such relief would leave a hole in the realm's finances, and Kurin had not quite decided whether that was acceptable in the first year of a reign intended to be long and glorious.

Sensheo bent slightly in a mannerly approximation of a bow, setting his teacup down for the last time. "Since I have displeased you, Elder Brother, I beg leave to retire."

"Do." Kurin watched the Fifth Prince's eyes turn cold. If his brother would not take a hint, an emperor might well be forced to other methods.

He could not even enjoy a few moments' worth of peace, because a palace servant hurried to the partition, passing Sensheo with a deep and reverent bow, with the news that the Ministers of the Left and Right Feet requested audience with their ruler upon a rather urgent matter.

Probably dealing with the question of certain noble prerogatives Kurin had not decided whether to reaffirm yet, also having to do with waiving taxes. It was unbecoming of nobles to be so concerned for their ingots.

His head-meat returned to the most pressing problem. Mother's symptoms could be natural, yes. But they were also consonant with what a blind man in the Yuin had assured him was possible with a certain powdery substance sprinkled into an obstruction's food. Kurin had not directly purchased the insurance, keeping the knowledge of its existence in reserve since such a thing was useful and of course Sensheo would not be discreet when he went to retrieve it as a favor to his second-eldest brother.

And anyone else sent to retrieve it would be even *less* trustworthy. Yet perhaps someone else had asked the same question of a certain Grandfather. Who would dare—and who would have access? Every one of Mother's servants was now Kurin's creature, in one way or another.

The appearance of scandal was worse than actual crime, in some cases. Yet now Garan Kurin, Emperor of Zhaon, wondered if both had been committed.

A GOOD WIFE

It was quietly, calmly familiar to take the reins of a household again; once or twice, Yala caught herself thinking of Hai Komori's high dark halls as she attended to some task that could just as easily have been the purview of a noble widower's eldest daughter in Khir. It was very nearly the summit of a noble girl's desires to have a household of her own, and with both an experienced steward and housekeeper, Garan Takshin's estate in Zhaon-An's Noble District ran like the fabled water-clock of the Brimming Sage.

It was a blessing, for there was a stack of correspondence to answer daily, sorted by precedence and placed in a small rectangular brass dish upon a writing-desk in a pleasant sitting-room looking out over a central garden, where a constant hum of clipping, pruning, watering, tying, and digging was taming an overgrown wilderness. Even the pillars at the front gate were smoothed, with Garan Takshin's name and rank re-carved upon them. The Third Prince's Zhaon estates were small but well-managed jewels indeed, and apparently the King of Shan had settled no few similarly exquisite ones upon his adoptive-brother. Hai Komori had been modest but not threadbare; Zhaon was... different, and Takshin was apparently determined to show his new wife she had no poverty to fear.

After all, etiquette demanded a certain show from a prince,

especially a married one. Fortunately Lady Kue and Steward Keh were well aware of what was required, so Yala could concentrate upon her letters, her visits, and the household accounts when the moon was half-full waxing or waning—not to mention the complicated business of daily dresses and shepherding two young ladies through court life, possibly finding them good matches as a patroness must.

Laying snares was a peasant's method; a noble rode to hunt. Still, Yala was finding both necessary for her purposes. Not many would be so indelicate as to refer to her princess's misfortune directly, but by subtle hints and keeping her ears sharp she was quietly building a picture of the court's gossip-currents. Any small sliver of information might fit next to another, providing illumination; there were disturbing intimations upon the First Mother's usual methods of striking at those she considered enemies.

And also upon her son's. Even Lady Gonwa referred to certain past matters with the eyebrow-lift or sharply accented circumlocution that was as good as a shout from a hunting-band which had flushed proper prey, and since Yala was considered under the protection and in the good graces of Second and Third Mother as well, it was inevitable that soon she would catch *something*.

Letters were part and parcel of such hunting; she had begun to think of days free of visits and tea-gossip as akin to those spent preparing one's horse and visiting the mews to train a hawk.

The top letter in today's pile was from the Palace, and she sighed involuntarily as she saw the brushwork upon its outer jacket. It was Gamnae's careful writing and the particular fillip she gave the cross-strokes, but the pleasure of receiving a missive from the Second Princess was drained by the fact that she was writing upon another's behalf.

"Pretty as a scroll-illustration." Takshin stepped from the shadow near the doorway, and Yala's heart gave a pounding start. "But why does she sigh?" The two sentences made quite a pleasing couplet, accents falling and rising in the proper places and the final word adding an affectionate lilt.

"Oh, nothing much." She would never have believed him capable of poetry upon their first meeting. Yala did not need to rise and bow, though it was a difficult habit to break. "Simply a letter from the First Dowager Mother, my husband."

"Let me open it." He paced across the sitting-room catfoot, sparing not a glance for the pretty tables, the embroidered cushions, or the hangings Lady Kue had thought might suit. It could have been a stable, for all the attention he paid; at least his wife could commend the Shan lady's work. "The wax might be poisoned."

Yala made a soft sound near the back of her palate, the way Zhaon matrons were wont to. "You should not say such things," she murmured. A Khir wife would rarely if ever chide a husband; it seemed a Zhaon one was expected to. Gamnae said there were even whole farces dedicated to such things between acts of tragedy at the theater. The prospect of seeing a few was pleasant.

"Why not? 'Tis true enough." He subtracted the letter from her hand with a quick flicker, and his scarred face settled into watchfulness as he broke the seal with a decisive crackle, scanning the contents. "And she makes Gamnae brush it. Typical."

Was her duty to soothe his ire, or simply to obey his whim? Yala half-turned upon her chair, settling the sleeves of her pale peach morning-gown and gazing at the man she had married. "She is by all accounts very ill."

"Good." He shrugged; his black Shan tunic was the same as ever, and so were his scars. An onlooker might think nothing else had changed.

"Takshin." Yala risked a soft remonstrance. A breeze, far too warm but pleasant enough when it touched a damp brow, tiptoed through a slatted partition to the central garden. It carried a faint tang of moisture from the pond in the central garden, and the smell of cut babu; the neglect of this estate had very nearly been remedied.

"Ah, there she is, scolding me as a wife should." His tone was absent, though, and he did not glance at her. Not only was his temper sharp-polished as ever, but he carried his sword as well, and she could not tell if it were merely custom for a prince to do so outside the Palace or if there was another, darker reason. "Where is a lamp? I shall burn this."

Yala suppressed a flare of quite uncharacteristic irritation. "She is your *mother*, Takshin. Would you wish your son to treat me so?" It was her duty to provide an heir, and though it was too soon to tell, sometimes she hoped she would quickly. It was the final achievement a noble girl was supposed to reach, a duty paid not just to her husband's family but to her own ancestors. Even her father's shade might well be pleased that she had fulfilled every expectation.

Perhaps then she could...what? What was left with Mahara gone, the country of Yala's birth at war with her husband's, and Zakkar Kai absent as well?

Her weak, treacherous heart gave a pang, as it rarely did in Takshin's presence. He was unfailingly gentle, for all his stubbornness and habit of avoiding pleasantries. Even the nightly attentions, merely endurable at first, had grown much easier to bear though a little shocking, and she wished her princess was still alive to tell her if the Crown Prince had treated *her* so gently.

"Do you send our future son into the den of a rabid animal to be broken when he reaches but eight winters high, I might consider it fair." He crumpled the letter in his fist, and Yala could not help but glance to the doorway to see if any passing servant would bear witness.

Of course their household was loyal and a prince could act largely as he pleased, but treating a letter from the mother of the Emperor so could carry dire consequences. And Garan Kurin was not his father, who had left Takshin largely to his own devices.

She had never dreamed, upon leaving Khir, that she would come to wish for anything other than Garan Tamuron's misfortune. Though the hated enemy of her land was gone, his second-eldest son filled her with deep misgiving.

Even if her husband was correct and the author of Mahara's death was not Zhaon at all.

How, under Heaven, could she hope to avenge her princess from this position? The chessboard had changed in the flicker of an eyelash—oh, *chess*, how Yala hated that game. Her *damoi* Baiyan had too, for all he played well enough.

You must hate what you fight, he had sometimes remarked. Their father was a very good player too, but she could not imagine Komori Dasho being so ill-bred as to truly hate anything.

Missing her father and brother was suddenly a pressure in her throat and behind her heartbeat. Her humors were in outright rebellion this morning.

"Takshin." She rose from the heavy but gracefully carved chair of dark je-yong wood, arranging her skirts with habitual speed and tucking her hands in her sleeves despite the heat. "She is your mother, and it is quite possible she is ascending to Heaven soon. Everyone thinks so."

"Perhaps." Her husband's scarred lip twitched, and she wondered—as she often did—if this was the moment his changeable temper would snap and the sharp edge whistle in her direction. He did not move or glance as she approached, but that was no indication. "She has been threatening it for a long while. I think it unlikely that is where she is bound, but nobody asks my opinion."

"Perhaps because they fear what you will say." Her throat was very dry indeed; there was a fine cup of jaelo tea upon the desk to be sipped while she attended to a duty she rather liked, but she suspected it would cool quite a bit by the time she could return to either.

For some reason, that seemed to ease his ire. His mouth relaxed and he left off his glowering to study her without the usual line between his eyebrows. "I value you, Yala. I will not place you in harm's way." Today his scars were pale; when she traced the one vanishing under his hair, in the confines of their shared bed, he often half-closed his eyes and leaned into the touch.

"And I am very grateful for that, indeed." How could such a small movement confuse her so? "Your elder brother mentioned that I have not visited her yet."

"Kurin?" The news brought fresh wariness to his dark gaze, and

Takshin's shoulders stiffened slightly. His topknot-cage today was of carved bone with a similar pin, a wedding-gift from Sixth Prince Jin. "When?"

"A few days ago at the Palace. I was in the gardens with Gamnae, and he—"

Her husband's scarred lip twitched. "Perhaps he needs a lesson in leaving my toys alone." His hand tightened around the letter, the wax seal fragmenting even further with small sounds like tiny bones breaking. "I taught him once or twice when we were younger."

"Takshin." Perhaps it would be wise to retake Gamnae's missive. She freed a hand from the sleeve of what had become her favorite morning-dress, the peach silk with an undertone of red instead of blue to save her complexion from sallowness and the cut Zhaon instead of Khir-modest. "The letter was sent to me, after all. I must give some manner of reply."

"There is no need, I will do so." He cast about, as if looking for a brazier, and Yala swallowed another pinprick of irritation, holding her hand politely cupped.

"That might make it worse," she pointed out, mildly enough.

"Worse than what?" Now he scowled, not precisely in her direction but at some point over her shoulder. "Do you think I'll allow any of them to harm you?"

"There is the household to think of as well, my husband." It was like arguing with Baiyan in one of his more obdurate moods, or with Dao. What would have happened if she had allowed him to place her upon his saddle? If she had known of Takshin's suspicions of Khir involvement in Mahara's death... "And whether you will or no, First Mother still bore you, and—"

"And I must let her mar the one..." Takshin shook his head, his teeth bared for a moment as a wolf might lift its lip at hunters. The *kyeogra* gave a sharp, flickering gleam. "No, Yala. I will brush an answer to this, and you will be troubled no further."

"What can she do to me, my husband?" Yala folded her hands in her sleeves again, since he would not give the letter back. He had not stalked away in one of his black humors, though, which meant he was still willing to listen. "Some small embarrassment, perhaps, or—"

"Don't forget it was my uncle who almost had you flogged." His shrug was almost feline, and his expression had smoothed with astonishing swiftness. She had discovered such a change meant he had made a decision and no amount of patient reasoning would affect it, though he would endure a remonstrance or two further. "You think there is a single thing *that woman* will not stoop to? The Emperor is ascended to Heaven; her reins have been cut. It is not some petty scandal I fear but much worse, and you will not be subjected to either."

"She is sending for everyone, I think." Yala stepped closer, hoping to at least soothe his temper so the next member of the household to require something of their lord would not receive a sharp reply. "Second Mother mentioned an invitation in passing to Lady Gonwa, and Su Junha heard that Sixth Prince Jin was invited to dinner in the Kaeje."

"Looking for fresh meat, no doubt," Takshin muttered, his eyebrows drawing together. "She may reap the rai she planted, and no more. The only time you may visit *that woman* is when she is upon her pyre, Yala. And perhaps not even then; I do not put it past her to rise with the smoke and do some mischief."

Yala could not help it; her left hand flashed into the *avert* motion to guard against ill-luck and she glanced again at the hallway. Still no sign of a servant, but that was a mercy of short duration. "Takshin, please."

"Ah." He noticed the direction of her gaze and nodded brusquely, though a small bitter smile now curved his scarred lip. "If a tattling tongue goes elsewhere, I shall cut it out soon enough. Do not *worry*, little lure." His free hand twitched, then lifted, and he smoothed his fingertips along her silk-clad shoulder, a brief, restrained caress. "I will do her the honor of answering this invitation, and there shall be no more to bother you."

It was useless to argue further, and a good wife should not

anyway. So Yala bowed her head, accepting the pronouncement—but there was one small detail she must mention. "It is very difficult for the Second Princess," she murmured. "The Sixth Prince has invited her to the theater for an afternoon farce, I would ask leave to—"

"Of course, and I shall likely go with you." He touched her shoulder again, very lightly; he rarely let her finish asking permission for a venture before granting it. No Khir husband would be so liberal; she supposed she was lucky. "There is another worry lingering in your liver, I can sense it. Well?"

"The same as always," she admitted. "My poor princess, and her misfortune. If there was some manner of concrete proof..." She let the sentence trail away. Her husband hunting in what might be the wrong direction was not irksome, but it was not helpful, either.

Her best hope was probably Sixth Prince Jin.

"Then I would have already brought it to you." The gentle tone he reserved solely for her was yet another surprise, one she would not quite become accustomed to for a long while. "But my *nahuagua*—do you know the word? It is Shan, for what a wolf-hunter feels in his bones. It has never led me astray, little lure, and it tells me someone in the North paid for your princess's misfortune. I would have liked to question that Narikh fellow, but he is gone, and will not return."

In that, Garan Takshin was more right than he knew. Still, the injustice of blaming Daoyan rankled, all the more intense for being inexpressible. "Then I have failed her twice."

"You would have perhaps preferred that horse-killer take your own life? Commendable, Yala. But I would not have it so. Not then, and not now." Both hands dropped, one holding its cargo of paper, ink, and wax, still creaking with the strength of his grasp; the *kyeogra's* gleam turned mellow and secretive. He was a scroll-illustration himself, or perhaps only married eyes would see him thus. "I will be gone until dinner. Send a rider to the Palace should you have need of me."

Her afternoon would be her own, then, since today was free of visits. "Yes, husband."

Her agreement must have pleased him, for he leaned closer, much in the manner of a potted plant in a window. "Say it again."

"Yes, husband." Was she blushing? The brazier-warmth in her cheeks was not quite from Zhaon's summer dust-wending toward autumn.

His lopsided grin was almost a boy's, but the heat in his gaze was not childish at all. He even pressed his lips to her cheek, a hint of the clarifying junho twigs in his morning bath enfolding her, before swinging away and leaving Yala to her letters with a soft but decided step.

It was not so bad, being married. But still Garan Komor-a Yala's treacherous heart hurt, and for quite which of many reasons she could not discern.

COMFORTING LIES

The Old Tower, blue tiles sheathing its outer walls glimmering like a garden pond, had been Mrong Banh's home for a long while now. Any place an astrologer nested gained its share of ephemera, but a sea of cunningly constructed machines of twisted paper and babu splinters no longer hung from the ceiling of its largest central room. The bookshelves still stood in their accepted places, but there were certain holes between their inhabitants. The astrologer's long table, where all of Garan Tamuron's children had gathered at one time or another for lectures, to pass a few hours with scrolls, asking for advice or seeking comfort—oh, there were memories in every corner.

Takyeo, a solemn boy already feeling the weight of his father's expectations. Kurin, ever ready to run a small errand for his mother; Takshin before he left for Shan, prickly and ready to fling himself into any scrap to right a perceived wrong—and after, sullen and silent but often willing to be coaxed into some pursuit or another. Makar's precocity, Sensheo's indolence good-natured at first, Sabwone's chatter, Jin's bright cheerfulness, Gamnae serious and sweet-tempered from the moment her first tooth appeared.

Those children were now lost inside adults, like under-robes in storage with their bright outer shells. When had that happened?

Mrong Banh settled the brass sextant carefully in its nest of packing-paper, glancing up as a shadow fell across the table. Jin would not cease his pacing, Tamuron's youngest son looking very much like his sire as he performed a sharp military turn at each end of the table.

"You do not *truly* mean to go, do you?"

It was the second time he'd asked. His topknot was fractionally askew and his eyes bore dark circles, shocking in one so young. Today his robe was as dark as those Makar favored, with only a token embroidery of an ornate character for *patience* at its cuffs, and a sword rode his back—another change, for though a prince had the privilege to bear weaponry inside the Palace complex, Jin had rarely availed himself of one unless he was bound for the drillyard.

And this weapon, a gift from Zakkar Kai upon Jin's last birthday, was exceedingly functional instead of aesthetic.

"Perhaps not until spring." It was not quite a lie, Banh told himself, and his eyes were only smarting because of dust and bright mirrorlight. The clouds lingering over far mountains grew darker each afternoon, their bellies stitched with dry lightning, yet no rain fell even at night. The entire world was parched, mud dried to crack-glaze in corners, peasants eyeing both the sky and the levels in river-fed irrigation canals anxiously. The first harvest was well under way in most places; it promised to be a good one. The second, for those fortunate enough to have the water, was still some time away. Much would depend upon when the summer drought broke. In some places, there were already sheaves laid alongside roads or in sheds to dry. "I am simply rearranging a few things, Jin. There is no need to worry."

"But I do worry." Jin halted, turned on a slippered heel, and glared at his favorite tutor. "Everything is changing, and you cannot leave too."

"I do not have plans to leave just yet." Preparations were not quite plans, after all. Banh could tell himself he was merely suffering a natural impulse to clean and reorder his domestic world after a vast upset, and that he might well wake tomorrow or the next day, sweating as a man did after a fever and finding grief still piercing but manageable. "Besides, it was rather crowded in here, you must admit. When the old passes, there is room for the new."

"Is that a quotation? I hate quotations." Jin folded his arms over a broadening chest. When had he become taller than Banh? The change had happened so gradually, a padfoot predator like the snow-pard Takyeo had taken for his device sneaking, inch by cushioned inch, toward prey.

Was this what old age felt like, the sting in an ailing chest when the name of a dead child floated through one's head-meat? Oh, Takyeo was Garan Tamuron's son, the great warlord's pride, but he was also Mrong Banh's, and so was Sabwone. So were they all. There was a word for an uncle who could have no children of his own and consequently spoiled those of his relatives.

There had always seemed time enough for everything and anything, while his lord was alive.

"It is not a quotation." He covered the sextant with a faded, folded scrap of cloth, a remnant of an old army banner. "But I could find one, and ask you to brush it twenty times—"

"*Ai*, not that." Jin's face scrunched like a longtail's, and at least he stopped pacing, instead glowering in Banh's direction. "Is it because of Kurin? Did he do something to you?"

He couldn't help it; Mrong Banh glanced at the partition to the hall and staircase, alert to any shadow that would mean a visitor. The stairs creaked under the slightest step, but that was no indication; an inadvisable word could fly to an unfriendly ear even when you were certain the lord at the center of Zhaon would look upon any of your utterances kindly.

The son was not the father, and Mrong Banh had overlooked Kurin just as he had missed Jin's growing into manhood *and* the danger to Tamuron's eldest child.

The worst thought was that the great warlord, the man Mrong Banh would have cheerfully followed through any of the multiple hells, had not seen the danger either—or neglected to prepare for it, letting his first queen mar both her sons. It was not meet to speak ill of the dead, and he was certain he should not even think it, and yet...

"Banh?" Jin's fingers dug into his upper arms, causing divots in his sleeves. "Did he? If he did, I swear—"

"Hush." The proper tone was firm but kind, an elder's admonishment while he settled the sleeve of his almost-threadbare brown house robe. When had he become old? That was another creeping sneakthief occasion. "The Emperor has done no wrong, Jin. I am merely cleaning, and have no wife or servant to do it for me."

"Well, maybe you should marry." Jin was not quite mollified, but he did cease regarding Banh so closely. "Mother says it makes a man."

"Playing matchmaker, Sixth Prince?" An unwilling smile tugged at the astrologer's mouth; he cast a glance over the table, attempting to decide what to pack next. "You are not an old woman yet, do not hurry."

Before this summer, Jin would have found the jest hilarious. Now he merely gave a tight, worried grin far older than his years. Normally he took after his mother, with the Daebo nose and a pointed chin; now, however, he looked like Tamuron, and a fresh sewing-pin slipped through Banh's heart.

"In any case, I would not leave you," Banh continued, realizing it afresh. Days of rearranging, nights spent gazing skyward, and two of the terrible headaches that robbed him of strength and vision both led him inexorably to the same place. "Or any of my other students," he added hastily.

It was not right to have favorites among your children, but he was not their father. Not even an uncle, as Kurin seemed bent upon reminding him. Just an astrologer, a tool for those in higher positions—which had not bothered him when the hand holding him to his work was so manifestly meritorious.

"Good." Jin's relief was transparent. "Because I came to ask your advice."

Now there was a relief—Mrong Banh was not quite useless yet. "Upon what matter, Sixth Prince?"

The youth made another longtail's face, scrunching his cheeks and sticking his tongue out. "So formal. Kai said before he left that I should ask you things I fear to ask others."

"Did he?" It was obliquely warming. The general—younger than Banh, but never seeming so—would not have given such advice lightly.

Especially not with Kurin upon the throne.

"Of course. Not that he needed to, Father said the same thing before he..." Jin paused, his throat working for a moment, and picked up the remains of an attempt at a gliding machine Banh had constructed laboriously out of rai-paper and small brush-cleaning sticks. "There was an assassin outside our house lately, you know. Mother is very upset."

"As well she should be." The trouble with watching the heavens was that his was an imperfect eye. He could have, *should* have predicted more. Returning to gaze upon his charts and measurements, Banh could now see the stars not precisely warning of the fate of Jin's sister, but giving subtle indications he should have heeded. Still, Tamuron needed the alliance with Shan, and Kurin—if he were wise—would aid Zhaon's southron little sibling, if only to keep Tabrak from riding north to inflict more damage upon the land under his care.

Takyeo would have already sent the Southron Army to find Suon Kiron, though maybe not with Makar at its head. And that was another worry, Kurin had obviously planned to remove Maki from Zhaon-An before now; even an emperor did not simply change generals upon a whim. Had he been merely waiting for some pretext or another?

Any possible end requiring such a pretext was troubling.

"I've been thinking and thinking." Jin's voice dropped, and he glanced at the door as Banh had merely a few moments before. "And I think it's *her*."

Banh had a sinking sensation he knew who the youngest Garan prince meant. And, furthermore, he could not give a comforting lie. "She is very ill, Jin." In fact, Banh understood Garan Yulehi-a

Gamwone was dying, as some women did after their husbands left for Heaven, following faithfully from affection or spleen. "Why would she do such a thing?"

"Because she hated Eldest Brother, and now he's...well, she hated his new wife too. And she tried to have Princess Yala flogged—oh, it was Lord Yulehi, I know, but he always does what she says, and so does Kurin. And then there was the affair of Sabi's gloves that one summer, and when Fourth Mother was dying they say she..." Jin trailed off, searching Banh's expression. "Why didn't Father stop her, Banh? He could have, couldn't he?"

How could he possibly explain? "Your father was wise, Jin. He needed the Yulehi, and she...I should not say such things to you."

"There is nobody else to say them." Jin folded his hands in his sleeves, again looking uncomfortably like Tamuron. But Banh's lord had never appeared this uncertain. "I can't even sleep in my bed. I guard my mother's door at night, too."

He was far too young for such a worry. And yet, a prince must learn such things quickly and thoroughly. Even Makar had killed his first assassin at eight summers high—and the culprit paying the ingots for that attempt had never been found.

If the source of that money had been uncovered, could even Tamuron have moved against it? Banh was aware he had let the silence grow between them for far too long while his head-meat worked. "Perhaps your mother should return to Daebo," he hedged. "And stay there this winter."

"Except then there will be nobody protecting the clan at court, the assassins might not stop, and if war comes she is safer here." Jin even *sounded* like his father now, impatient because he had already exercised his head-meat about a certain problem and could not see a better remedy.

Tamuron had learned in war that sometimes there was no remedy to be found. Now Jin was learning, and it was a bitter lesson indeed.

Better that he absorb it now, Banh admitted. But a fresh needle pierced his laboring heart. "The heavens are in some disarray," he admitted. At least the boy wasn't asking *Why didn't the stars warn about my sister, Banh?*

Was he a coward to feel grateful for that tiny mercy?

"So you can't leave at all, Banh. I need you. So does Takshin, and Makar, even though he's gone. And I think Kurin sent him away hoping he'd get killed." Jin's cheeks paled swiftly. Saying it aloud must cost him dear. "Before this summer I would never have thought it. Is this what growing up means, Banh? Gamnae thinks so, and I think she's right but I don't like it. I don't like it at all."

"Nobody does." It wasn't a quotation from a sage or a scholar's observation; it was the bitter knowledge of a tavern-boy who had been plucked from obscurity, placed upon a summit past his ambition, and thought merit would protect him even when a patron ascended to Heaven. Now, wearier and wiser, he must witness the young committing follies.

And apparently little Gamnae was worried, too. At least she had the sense to speak to her youngest brother; the two of them had ever been allies.

"If something happens to Makar, that leaves Sensheo." Jin's sleeves trembled slightly as if his hands wrung at each other. "And me."

"And Kai," Banh said, heavily. Garan Tamuron was Heaven-blessed in battle and in heirs, but that blessing had turned rancid. More war, more misery for the peasants trapped between mill-stones, a rising tide of blood—and it had happened so quickly, as if a foreign princess was the stone at the top of an arch, its removal provoking swift collapse.

"Takshin's no danger," Jin continued, "but I worry for him. Because I don't think it was just First Mother, Banh. I think there were others. But even if it was *her*, I don't think Kurin minded one bit."

"You really should not say such things," Banh murmured. "Not where anyone else can hear you, at least."

"I *know* that, Banh. What do I *do* about it?"

There is nothing you can do, child. Another bitter physician's tonic to be swallowed. They were in Heaven's hands now, and the grasp of the celestials did not care for the fragility of those in the Middle World.

Nor did those from the many hells, feared and propitiated in equal measure. Banh had never been overly religious, but as a man aged, there was no help for it. "If I knew what to do, I would do it," he admitted. "Perhaps that is why I am cleaning. It helps arrange my head-meat."

"You really won't go?" Jin's eyebrows up, his brow wrinkled, there was no echo of mother or father in the boy's face now. He was once again the child Banh had taught to hold a brush, the boy whose facility with weapons would only be troubling later.

Later had arrived.

"No," Banh said, heavily. "I am merely cleaning, Jin. If you will pester me so, you should help."

"Oh, certainly." Jin's hands reappeared and he seized the model glider. "May I have this one? It should fly a long way from the top of a wall."

There was nothing wrong with his heart or his liver, Banh decided. It was merely old age, creeping up hand in hand with time to devour a man in tiny, daily bites. "Put it by the door, then. I shall have to make new ones."

HANDS APLENTY

The wind died; dust lay in every corner, and Garan Takshin's black Shan cloth had a patina even a close-servant's brushing could not efface after the relatively short ride to the Palace. He was so occupied in brooding over his mother's attempts to sink her claws into Yala he almost missed the glances exchanged between eunuchs or courtiers and junior ministers as he strode through the complex, the fans held to cover tittering mouths or bright avid gazes. The Mad Queen of Shan would have indicated one or two as she passed through her own palace, whether for flogging or to be given a few ingots and sent home to the provinces a decision left to chance or whatever unbalanced humor was crowding her head-meat or liver at the moment. Coming to her notice was almost as dangerous as being ignored, and he was sourly amused to find he almost longed for her shade to stalk through these halls, pointing her fan or a raising a cupped hand to single out a whispering fool.

After dealing with *her*, Kurin was a small bronzefish indeed.

He glanced at the Old Tower's bright blue bulk, wishing he was here to visit Mrong Banh. The astrologer was a pleasant enough companion, and there were still certain items hidden among his books and charts. Yala mentioned the court gossip that Banh was cleaning his quarters, perhaps preparatory to retreating to the countryside.

Takshin certainly hoped not. But if he did, the astrologer would need a guard and a household, and that was an exercise for his head-meat as well until he realized he had a wife now, and at least the household half of such matters could be left in her capable hands. He chose the shortest route to the Kaeje, cutting through three gardens and the Night-Flower Pavilion where the first full moon after the winter solstice was celebrated, and he was so occupied his hand leapt to a swordhilt almost before the subliminal rasp of awareness warned him he was being eyed with intent, not just apprehension.

The other man was lean and tall in travel-stained Shan black, and his face was so familiar Garan Takshin was in the piercetowered palace above Shan's capital again for a moment. His heart thumped, settled into a high pounding, and he forced his fingers away from the leather-wrapped hilt with its ruby peeking through the lacing. "Ah, Sunjosi." It was good to see one of the bloodriders again; he offered his right hand for the warriors' clasp and furthermore gave the lean sunburnt Shan lord a clout upon his opposite shoulder to express his joy at seeing the other fellow again. "He's alive, then."

"Of course. We went a-raiding to meet them; they have never come so far south before." Sunjosi shrugged; there were great shadows under his dark eyes and his cheeks held a growth of new beard. And, blessedly, he did not waste time with a dance of greetings and empty compliments, knowing Takshin's hatred of such things all too well. "He is wroth, my lord. He valued his wife."

"Did he?" Well, it was only natural, though he could not see Kiron feeling a fraction of what Takshin did for his own. "What man could not answer this, after all." It felt good to speak in Shan dialect again, and doubly good to know Kiron was alive.

Not that he had truly doubted... and yet, the relief was deep. The wolf-sense was still with him, and that was a comforting thing.

"I come from speaking with your brother." Sunjosi's expression was remote, but with the slight lifting of his lip that denoted an unpleasant duty carried out as well as could be expected. A garden-breeze swirled about both of them, and Takshin was glad there were no unfriendly ears within range. Not that many at the court bothered to learn Shan, indeed. "Many pretty words he gives, but no help. Tabrak is riding north, though the roads were clear enough for my journey with a half-dozen riders. We do not know what route the barbarians take."

It was unpleasant news indeed. "They have never done this before that I can recall." Takshin blinked against bright dusty sunlight, indicating a shaded portico. "Do not stand in the sun, my friend."

"I thank you for the thought, but I am weary near to death." Sunjosi shook his dark head, and each word carried a slight edge of sheer exhaustion. "You will gain more from me after some soldier-tea and a bath, my lord Garan, though I shall go with you to your brother's presence, should you require it."

"Leave him to me; Kiron shall have all the aid I can muster. My house is open to you and your guard, of course."

"I just heard of your marriage." Sunjosi's eyebrow twitched, but the rest of his face remained granite. A trellis of nodding crimson trumpet-flowers behind his dusty black turned the Shan lord into an ink-blot upon heavily decorated fabric. "Felicitations, or...?"

"You shall meet her soon, and yes, felicitations." There was no need for merriment, but a smile attempted to tug at his lips. Yala would appreciate Shan, and there would certainly be much less in the way of distraction or danger there. "I shall send word for my household to expect you and your riders, and also to the palace gates to provide a guide."

"That eases my mind." Sunjosi's shrug was a marvel of fluid expression, full of resignation and the careful cognizance that anyone passing by in a garden could hear their converse. "I will be a bad guest, bearing no gifts and longing only for a bed." He had survived the Mad Queen too; taken twice to the dungeons and released when she changed her mind about his potential usefulness. Neither occasion had much altered his demeanor, which bespoke a will of iron or flint under his deceptively placid exterior.

Now we are released from chains, he had muttered to Takshin before her pyre, his lips barely moving.

"*Ai*, a bloodrider need bring nothing to my house but his blade, Sunjosi." The ritual of welcome to one of the King of Shan's most favored noble warriors rolled off his tongue as if they were far and safely south. "Off with you now, and many thanks for waylaying me."

"It was fortunate, my lord, not intentional." But the Shan lord's face eased, and his farewell bow held all the relief such a motion was capable of. "Ride well."

"And you." Takshin set off again, aware of speculative glances from a brace of eunuchs upon another garden path. Zan Fein might have done him the courtesy of sending a message, but if Sunjosi had just arrived...

The Kaeje enfolded him, the vermilion-pillared hall swallowed him whole, and Takshin performed merely the barest of perfunctory observances as he passed through its throat. To the right, past the dais, were the council chambers, and the Golden Guard at the door was not one of his clients. The insouciant look the creature gave him might not have been borne at another time, but between Yala and Sunjosi, his temper was somewhat mellowed.

After a fashion.

"There he is." Kurin looked up as his younger brother appeared. Lord Hanweo, his broad face glistening and his smallbeard neatly trimmed, sat at the Emperor's right; Zan Fein rose to bow to a new princely visitor. Lord Nahjin, Minister of the Left Foot, and Lord Tansin, Minister of the Right Feather, were there as well, the latter looking sour and the former entirely too pleased with this turn of events.

Makar should have been present, and Kai. He hoped they were looking after themselves as well as possible; he had all he could drink in his tea-cup at the moment. The business of greeting was performed with the same perfunctory attention he gave his bows upon approaching the royal presence, and he had hardly settled before a cup of hot smoky eong poured by Zan Fein than Kurin gave the chess match away.

"You just missed one of our Shan friends," the Emperor said,

weighing his now ever-present kombin in his right hand. Even Father
had not dressed in crimson silk every day, but Kurin of course would
wear nothing less. "Apparently the King of Shan is alive."

"I saw Sunjosi in the gardens, yes." Takshin took great pleasure
in the news *not* being a surprise, thanking Zan Fein with a nod.
"What aid do you intend to send our younger sibling Shan?"

"The Tabrak are riding north; they may decide to turn back
and plunder Shan again." Lord Hanweo scratched under his smallbeard. Apparently he was the courser leading this tiny council-
within-a-council in the direction Kurin desired—their uncle would
have taken much pleasure in the game, but he was still being obliquely
punished. Mother, Takshin thought sourly, would approve. "Either
way, we cannot send the Southron Army. It is a shield over the heart
of Zhaon, just as the Northern is."

"Any news from Kai?" Takshin took a grim pleasure in seeing Kurin's mouth tighten. A Third Prince should not bark such
questions before an Emperor, but by Heaven, how he hated the
petty lies, the bragging, the transparent angling for position or
preferment.

"No dispatches for two days." Kurin's left hand rose to touch
his own smallbeard; if he meant to look like Father, it was a dismal failure. He looked, instead, a little like Lord Hanweo, who was
studying Takshin with the faintly nose-wrinkled expression of an
elder forced to deal with impetuous youth.

Takshin almost wished Lord Yulehi was here to see the resem-
blance. It would irk him to no end.

"Perhaps you should confirm the roads out of town are not
blocked by Golden no longer on duty, or by mercenaries." Takshin
lifted his teacup, met Zan Fein's worried gaze. "I seem to remember missing dispatches not so long ago."

The pained silence following his observation was satisfying in
the extreme. Takshin turned his gaze to his brother, knowing full
well Kurin would attempt to extract a price for the embarrassment.

Finally, Zan Fein undertook to break the quiet. "Rather than
sending aid to Shan, it appears Shan might be in a position to

render aid to her elder sister." He used the most remote, honorific word possible to describe a female sibling, aware of the possible indelicacy of reminding the court of Sabwone's fate. "If Shan moves north, we may catch the horde between a spoon and the side of a tureen, and do them some damage."

"Break the dumpling into the soup." Takshin considered the notion. Kurin's aim was now depressingly, absolutely clear. "You mean to send me to Shan, then, to pressure Kiron. He'll ride after them with or without me."

"Then you might restrain any excesses Shan soldiers might be likely to commit north of the border." Lord Hanweo could not contain himself, apparently.

"Why, Lord Hanweo." Takshin's expression of mock-astonishment was belied by his slow, even drawl. He set his cup down and settled more deeply into his chair, eyeing the Second Mother's uncle sidelong. "Surely that is no way to speak of my adoptive-kin."

"If the Emperor commands, even his brothers must go," Lord Tansin intoned, sententious as usual. So that was why Kurin wanted him here; he usually followed Lord Hanweo. And Haesara's clan-uncle, conscious that it was not his half of the year and that Kurin could very easily reinstate his own kin at the ministerial apex, would be anxious to keep his new Emperor placated.

"Oh, I'll go." Takshin eyed Kurin narrowly, setting his cup down with a slight click to punctuate his acceptance. "And I shall be taking my wife with me."

Kurin's faint smile now bespoke pleasure that Takshin had joined battle so directly. "Surely she'd be more comfortable here in Zhaon-An."

You want Mother's claws in her, because you cannot stand to see another happy with a toy. He might well be forced to leave her behind, but he wanted to warn every man present who a certain Khir lady belonged to. Zhaon had sent him to die once and been disappointed; if he returned and found Yala menaced in any fashion, he had no compunction about revenging the slight. "A wife follows her husband."

Kurin tapped his tongue to the roof of his mouth, tut-tutting like a maiden aunt. "My lord ministers, I will speak to my brother and Zan Fein more fully upon this matter. Council will resume after the midday meal; until then, I wish you good health."

"May the Emperor live ten thousand years," Lord Tansin intoned, and hefted himself afoot. Lord Nahjin, lean and restless, withdrew with alacrity and a troubled brow. Lord Hanweo, with many a weighing glance at Takshin, lingered as if he expected Kurin to change his mind—or had been coached to expect it—but finally was forced to politely withdraw as well.

That left Zan Fein, Takshin, and the Emperor, who fixed his little brother with an indulgent look, his fingers beginning busy work with scentwood beads. "I know you are newly married, Shin, but Zhaon has need of you."

"Zhaon sacrificed me when I was eight summers high, Kurin." Takshin settled himself more comfortably in his chair. If even Father could not budge him—and Garan Tamuron had tried once or twice—*Kurin* certainly could not. Takshin had promised Sunjosi whatever aid he could deliver; now it was a matter of extracting a more-than-fair price for whatever Kurin desired. "I am no longer yours to move upon a chessboard."

"Tabrak is a menace to us all." Zan Fein attempted to smooth the wrinkled fabric. He kept his hands tucked inside his sleeves; in the council room's breathless stillness, a fan would send umu perfume in every direction with sickening intensity. "Your new bride is safer if—"

"If I leave her here for my lady mother to worry at?" There was great satisfaction in saying it aloud. Others would pretend and mouth pretty lies; he was Garan Gamwone's second son and might speak as they could or would not. "No. My wife goes with me, Honorable Zan Fein."

"Come now, Takshin." Kurin's air of patent reason was merely for the eunuch's benefit. "She *will* be more comfortable here."

"Did you not hear me? I said no." Takshin eyed his teacup, turned it a quarter to absorb the conversation. It was a maneuver performed more and more often lately.

"I will make certain Mother does not issue another invitation." *Really, Takshin*, Kurin's tone said, and the balked gleam in his dark gaze promised trouble later unless he was well and thoroughly dealt with *now*. "She is dying, Shin. A visit is a little enough thing to ask—"

Takshin pushed himself upright, his chair's legs scraping against wooden flooring, and had the dubious pleasure of seeing his elder brother stiffen slightly.

Takshin, after all, carried a sword even in the presence of the Emperor. Being regarded as unpredictable had definite advantages. "You mean to take me from Zhaon-An while you commit more mischief, and hopefully bleed Shan against Tabrak. Then you will be after me to force Kiron to some kind of accommodation. I do not mind the attempt, Rinrin. I *do* mind being treated as if I possess less head-meat than a repeating bird."

"Then do me the favor of acting calmly, for once." Kurin halted his playing with kombin and tucked his hands in his sleeves. He had barely touched his own tea, which was not like him. Perhaps he suspected something untoward in its depths. "You have the wife you wanted, the endorsement was signed, was it not? You will only be away a short while, and I give you my word as Emperor and brother she shall be well cared for."

Takshin eyed him, his head cocked. Of course Kurin would pressure him with the endorsement; had there been any trouble with Takyeo's, Kurin's could be produced. He had wanted a double surety, and knew a cost would be extracted later.

It was not like Garan Kurin to spend an advantage so soon in the game, or so flagrantly. He lowered himself into his chair again, not quite caring that he had handed his now-eldest brother a weapon—letting him *or* Garan Gamwone know you cared for something was an invitation for them to break, bend, or mar it.

He was past wondering if he possessed the same urge. It was one tool among many in service of his desire to be left alone in his own little corner of the world. "Your hospitality had best be flawless," he muttered. "You know how *she* is, Kurin. In this one small matter, I will have not just your word but a surety."

After all, the gossip that their clan was merely a merchant-bought approximation of an old and princely but defunct family's genealogy might even bear a certain truth. He would drive whatever bargain he must in this matter. Carrying Yala into what might become a battlefield overrun with screaming flour-pale barbarians was hardly an appetizing thought, for all Sunjosi had told him the roads were clear.

She would not complain, but his wife had suffered enough.

"By Heaven, it is just a wife." Kurin clearly considered such creatures superfluous at best, never mind that he had been born of a spouse and was expected to take one to provide an heir, unless he planned upon living forever. Perhaps he did, or perhaps he intended to marry some pale nonentity with no other purpose than to squeeze out pups. "Mother cannot bestir herself from bed, do you think she will ride the night-wind to your house?"

I would not put it past her. "She has hands aplenty to serve her purposes." And to make it exquisitely clear that Takshin was aware of his mother's efforts to banish whoever she took a dislike to from the living, he continued. "Rather like an Emperor."

"I am well aware." At least his elder brother had the grace to admit it, and furthermore, to look as if he found their mother's behavior distasteful indeed. *That* was a change; perhaps the business of rule was altering him in some small ways. "Come now, Shin. This is childish. You are needed."

No. I am useful, there is a difference. Takshin turned his cup a quarter again. "Not quite. Kiron will ride for them anyway; he could not do otherwise." At least if Takshin was sent, he could press for some manner of reinforcement. A prince traveled with a guard, after all. "And you haven't mentioned our sister yet. Surely vengeance for her fate is our duty." What he meant, of course, was that it was Kurin's—if a king could not afford to let the matter rest, how much less could an Emperor?

And if Garan Kurin made a habit of sending his brothers to die, it might secure his power but it would damage his legitimacy. In more ways than one.

Kurin forgot his pose of lofty imperial calm, and outright scowled. "If I thought the mention would do anything other than drive you to fresh intransigence, I would undertake it."

A palpable hit; Takshin stretched his legs under the table as a petty provincial would at a banquet without low perches and cushions. "Very well." His left thumb caressed the hurai upon his first finger, the characters carved sharply enough to bite. "What else would you have of me, Kurin? Speak quickly, for if you mean to send me I shall take whatever troops seem fit, the better to travel light and swift as the Horde itself."

"The better to return to your bride in haste." The Emperor's features smoothed but he did not smile, perhaps sensing mockery might yet turn his adopted-out brother's temper fully. "I mean it, Shin. I will keep Mother from your precious princess. I will not have to for long—are you so certain you will not visit her? She calls for you."

Zan Fein stared across the table, all but withdrawing his humors into secret caves. He scarcely even seemed to breathe; had he performed that trick when Father was engaged upon sensitive discussions?

It was, Takshin thought, very likely.

"I called for her, too, when I was sent to Shan. This was the answer." Takshin lifted his right hand, touched the scar along his cheek, vanishing under his hair. Just last night Yala had traced it, her fingertips robbing the mark of its power to ache afresh. A prince could sometimes afford to speak the truth, and he hoped Kurin would hear its bitter ring in his brother's voice. "*That woman* bore me, and she cast me away. I do not stay where I am unwanted, brother mine. Now, tell me what you would tell Suon Kiron, and fetch a scribe. Letters must be written if this is to be done properly."

He was already planning how to guard Yala while he was away—and how to escape Kurin's clutches with her once the entire affair with Tabrak was brought to a conclusion.

Whether said conclusion was good or ill for the Emperor of Zhaon remained to be seen.

HELD THE HORN
SPOON

The First Queen of Zhaon, the First Mother to a revered Emperor, was trapped in her bed like a leg-shattered oxen in a mudhole, as her hated husband was before his death. A potion of nightflower and omyei coursed through her, a forgiving warmth doing little to blunt the deep hole of tearing pain in her middle. A hot stone lived inside her belly, occasionally swelling up through her rib cage to claw at her throat with bile-whips.

Yona was bending over her, the old hag's eyes large in her yellowing face, their pupils holding tiny images of Gamwone's own raddled countenance. The First Queen was first among equals, they said, but she knew well enough that she had no peers. She, who always took such care with her lacquered hair and plump, soft beauty, also knew her hair was unbound, streaming over the rectangular bolsters she usually preferred but were now stones pressed against her aching flesh. Her face was lined with pain, her lips chalky, and the smallest nail upon her left hand, normally daubed with resin and slipped into a scrolled-silver sheath, was broken when the fits came upon her and she thrashed, crying out like an animal in labor.

"First Queen." Yona's dry voice, soft and inflectionless, rasped against her tender ears. "It is your tonic, First Queen, only that."

"Get *away*!" Gamwone summoned enough strength to slap feebly at Yona's hands. The deep horn spoon went flying, clattering against the partition, and Gamwone giggled, a high childish sound. For a moment she was in her father's house again, a girl looking forward to a bright noble life, having no idea what lurked around the angle of Time's corridor.

Yona sighed, a weary sound, and shuffled to the partition. Halfway there she had to stop and sink to her knees despite the obvious pain the operation caused her; a clatter of gongs drifted to Gamwone's throbbing ears.

It could only mean one thing.

The Emperor! The Emperor approaches!

Oh, hadn't Tamuron been fine indeed, young and strong in the saddle? She would have done anything for him, had he only loved her—but it was useless, there was only room in the man's heart for his dead spear-wife, some peasant trash with pretensions to minor nobility. It was not enough for Tamuron to grieve, he had to insult his *proper* wife and his true heir...

Time shivered, dilating and constricting around her. Yona closed the partition soundlessly, then, summoned by a peremptory wave, hurried to attend their imperial visitor.

A strange face hovered over Gamwone's, and she gasped before she recognized her own eldest son, filling out handsomely now and wearing a smallbeard that quite suited him. "Mother," he said, firmly. "That is enough. The physician left strict orders for your tonic."

Oh, the tonic. "Kurin," she moaned, the name slurring as if she had taken far too much sohju. "Kurin...it is not well...it is not right..."

"She does not recognize me sometimes," Yona murmured, pouring out another measure from the small blue-glazed bottle standing expectant at Gamwone's bedside. "Refuses the tonic. She flung a pillow at Honorable—"

"I do not *care*, Yona. You are dismissed." He barely glanced at his mother's oldest servant; a bright dart of hatred, well-banked, showed in the woman's glance before she hurried away, pausing only to bow deeply before closing the partition again with thoughtless exactitude.

"Bitch," Gamwone hissed. "Someone...Kurin, my darling... someone has..." The truth swelled in her throat like Reng Shua's great toad; the owner of the Hell of Many Waters kept the creature to ride upon over the wave-drenched heads of its perpetually drowning inhabitants.

"Yes," her darling son said softly, and poured out a full measure from the small blue tonic-bottle. "You must take your medicine, Mother."

Someone has fucking poisoned me, you idiot. A moment of great and terrible lucidity descended upon the foremost queen in the Middle World, Garan Tamuron's first wife, the woman who had provided him with sons, sacrificed one of those sons to diplomacy to a Shan flush with trade money from Anwei, and even given the Emperor a daughter before settling into years of being slighted, dishonored, disgraced, and set upon a pedestal she must defend alone. There was no reason for her to think of the many hells, or the acts she had been forced—yes, *forced*—to, even if she found some small enjoyment in them.

Those who said they did not glory in their enemies' demise were lying worse than she ever had.

"Kurin," she gasped. His arm was behind her shoulders; he lifted her as if she weighed nothing. The flesh was melting from her bones. This illness would rob her of beauty jealously guarded by oils, unguents, cosmetics, and baths; she would be a withered stick like Yona soon. "Kurin, someone...someone has..." Her tongue was too thick for her mouth; her skin was slippery and burning. Her bedroom, the nest she fought to preserve, to keep safe and quiet and cushioned, was now a trap.

"Yes, yes. Here." He was not listening. Men never did. Not when they sold you to a warlord, not when you married and lay under them, not when all you wanted was a fraction of the affection they lavished upon a peasant girl's illegitimate get or a stupid, cringing bath-girl.

Maybe it was the bath-girl who had done it—but no, Yona had

said that loose end was tucked away, as unsightly threads must be. She had to save Kurin from the wiles of those grasping bitches.

All of them.

He held the tonic-spoon to her mouth. "Drink your medicine, Mother." His eyes were thoughtful, his gaze far away. He was thinking of other things while pouring this brew down her throat, his hands impersonal and almost casual, and for a moment the most horrifying idea possible floated through her head-meat.

You must behave, Mother. Leave the intrigues to me.

Oh, she could—if he would use them properly. But no, Gamwone had to suffer, to struggle, to strive. Nothing was ever done correctly unless she did it herself.

And where were her other children? Her second son, her useless daughter? The other queen and concubine, though knowing their duty and summoned by letters far more polite than they deserved, did not come either. They did not even bother to reply to the gracious missives honoring their stupid little selves.

Friends would have served a First Queen better, Haesara had sneered—oh, she would take care of *that* haughty bitch, just as soon as she recovered.

Gamwone dutifully swallowed, though her throat was afire and tears brimmed in her burning, aching eyes. Some deep-buried part of her was speaking, quietly but with great authority.

You know what was done, Yulehi Gamwone. As if she were a child again, her mother dead in labor. Young Gamwone, scolded by nurses and ladies who shrank and bowed when her father appeared, but hissed and pinched their unruly young charge when authority was absent—oh yes, she knew how underlings behaved. You had to be strong, or they would steal what they could.

The First Queen choked, stiffening in her son's arms. Half the dose of useless, ill-tasting medicine sprayed across his robe and her shift, soaking into bedclothes. The maids wouldn't like that; the lazy things acted like changing their superiors' linens was an imposition instead of work they should be grateful to perform under Heaven's beneficent, careless gaze.

"Look at this," Kurin said quietly. "A double dose now, Mother. It won't take long."

The terrible idea circled her head-meat again. It lodged deep, no matter how she twisted and turned, sweating in a thin linen shift under grasping blankets like the tentacles of things brought from the sea by Anwei's great ships, or from the tiny townships clinging to the eastron coast. The nasty, writhing things packed in salt water for trips inland, with their strange gelatinous flesh—they were hateful and fascinating at once, like certain tinctures and pastes used to free a queen from her rivals, from those who would take away her sons and her position.

"Kurin," a mother moaned, but he spared her barely a glance, pouring out another measure from that damn blue bottle like a garden-pond's hateful, unblinking eye.

Blood, spreading upon sheets. And the concubine from Wurei screaming upon her deathbed, attempting to unseat Gamwone as they all had failed to do for years uncounted.

Nobody had unseated the First Queen. But now she was undone.

"M-my son," she croaked. "Someone has done this. Someone has *done this to me*."

"No doubt," he answered, softly, and raised her shoulders again. "Yona will sit with you tonight, Mother. There are matters afoot I must answer."

What could be more important than his own mother's suffering? The terrible idea would not leave her be, it wracked her afresh.

Kurin waited until the spasm passed, then poured the contents of the horn spoon into her unresisting mouth. "There." His tone was not quite grim, a weary parent attending an often-hypochondriac child. "Now for another dose. You must take it, Mother. Nothing must be left undone."

It cannot be. He wouldn't. He was her precious, shining eldest, her greatest hope, the infant boy she had pushed out with so much agony to cement her position—and found nothing would, because her husband didn't love her.

Nobody loved her. Not even her daughter, hiding in her rooms to avoid a mother's unpretty illness. Or worse, drinking tea and dining with her mother's enemies.

"Thieves," she croaked. "All of you. You have stolen me, and what do I have to show for it all?" Her voice, stronger now, rose almost to a shriek. "*They have poisoned me! Poisoned your mother, Kurin! Kill them! Kill them all!*"

"Oh, by *Heaven*." Her darling boy sounded, of all things, irritated. "Drink."

It gurgled in her throat, slid past burning inner tissues, and though she knew it was poison, Gamwone finally drank.

What else was there to do, when your child held the horn spoon?

She lapsed into grey semiconsciousness, barely cognizant of his settling the sheet against her chest. "Rest," he said, softly enough she almost forgave him, as a mother always did. He was her only true love, though it was just as unsatisfactory as all the others.

Garan Kurin had, for once, spoken more truly to his brother than he knew.

It would not, indeed, be long.

No Doubt Ending

Upon a field some distance from the ancient river-city of Cheku, pandemonium reigned.

The cacophony was usual, so Zakkar Kai ignored it, his knees clamping hard to a horse's heaving, lathered sides. His last mount had foundered with a heavy arrow through its right eye; catching this Khir beast with its flowing saddle was battle-luck indeed, and he was past caring that the stirrups were a little too long.

Everything now depended upon pressing the advantage. He had grasped what appeared to be half a Khir army; if his own, unwieldy beast that it was, could simply finish off this thrashing animal quickly enough he could turn his attention to the other half, which *must* be somewhere close.

Normally he would be upon the hill to the east, sending runners and riders carrying the head-meat's commands to the developing battle-body, but a fresh group of Khir nobles on horseback had driven against the left wing and a charge was necessary to restore the faltering line. Tamuron never asked of his men what he was unwilling to do himself, and Zakkar Kai followed suit. Besides, the leader of the fresh battalion had been struck down by another horse-killer arrow—the Khir were using them with abandon, since their usual bows were too light for the disparity between their forces and Zhaon's might—and both his marshals were busy with their own parts of the battle.

He had to find his third marshal too, but Sehon Doah probably had troubles of his own at the moment.

"*Zhaon!*" Kai yelled, smoke-scraped throats around him taking up the hoarse-croaking cry. The cohorts re-formed as Khir cavalry curved away, the conscript mass following the horselords' charge at full run over rocky but largely flat ground. Cannons boomed behind him, and holes torn in the Khir infantry ranks were slow to close.

A few soldiers nearby recognized him, and another cheer shook the smoke-laden air pierced with screams of equine and human wounded. The soldiers still upright shouted the name of the God of War, whether to gather his protection or to mark his appearance on a battlefield, and he had never told Tamuron that sometimes he indeed felt possessed by that most martial of Heaven's inhabitants, a hair-stiffening, bloodcurdling, terrifying thrill running through all his humors in the midst of carnage.

His horse, well-trained as all Khir mounts, obeyed the pressure of knee and weight-shift, barely shying as they trotted for the oncoming mass, threading between blocks of Zhaon who took up the chant, swords out and shields braced, moving forward to meet the shock of contact with Khir conscripts as the pikes and javelins in the heart of each square bristled. Though his mount's reins were cut, Kai rose in the too-long stirrups, his own sword a blood-dripping bar and the dragon upon its hilt adding its own silent scream.

The two armies met once more, wrestlers with their heels slipping in blood and ordure. The crash was felt in heart and eyes and breath, Zhaon shields locked together as a unit and the pikes flickering, madmen straining bruised arms and using dry throats as trumpets. A horse-killer arrow flickered past, and the bright thought of Komor Yala in a sitting-room, a string of crystals dangling from her hairpin as she brushed a letter, flashed through Zakkar Kai and away.

He had no time to think of what she would feel, were she witnessing this slaughter of her countrymen. The Khir line broke; trumpets and gongs pierced the din with bright brass stitchery, passing information through a heavy tapestry of noise. The right flank was holding steady, the center moving forward; here upon the left, though, the actual crisis of the battle had been reached.

So his battle-sense told him, and that singing awareness had not once failed Zhaon's head general.

Zhaon cannons boomed again, the Khir horse surged forward as the opposite cavalry re-formed behind the conscripts. They had comparatively little artillery—the harvest of Khir munitions after Three Rivers had been vast—but they were readying another charge, and the instinct of many similar fights told Kai this was the last gasp of an exhausted swimmer before the waves closed over his head.

"*Forward!*" he screamed, waving his sword; more arrows rained down. What cannon Khir had was brought from Ch'han and not as advanced as Zhaon's, and furthermore happened to be just barely outranged, for Artillery Lieutenant Tanh Yaoyeo had a genius for the dispositions of his metal children and their fiery eggs. Zhaon also had mighty city-crossbows, each serviced by a three-man team and humming; their cloud of bolts rained down behind the front of the Khir line, a morass of corpses gathering new freshets of blood every few moments.

The Zhaon squares forged ahead, step by step, the shield-wall threatening to crumble in a few places before the turning maneuver—a fresh man coming forward to replace one exhausted by the shock, the transfer behind a shield relentlessly drilled day in and out upon every army's central camp-square—gathered strength. New force flowed into the left flank, the reserve battalion making itself felt, and even though his horse foundered under him, the hanging armor at its chest studded with Khir bolts, he knew the battle was won.

The poor beast went down with a high, womanish scream, and Kai was flung. His armor took most of the shock, but he still sprawled dizzy and momentarily helpless as a child, his entire body a loosened sathron-string.

Kanbina might need a new set of strings, and another gift, he thought, forgetting his adoptive-mother was dead.

Yanked to his feet by a passing pikeman who vanished into the swirling smoke a moment later, Kai shook the mazement from his skull, found his sword still in his hand even though his helm had been knocked free, and the thought of turning into an anonymous corpse upon this blood-sodden piece of northern Zhaon filled him with crystalline rage like burning sohju.

The Khir cavalry made one last charge. Pikes rushed to brace the shield-wall, a forest of bristling, and a collective cry rose from attackers and defenders both.

Kai gripped the dragon hilt and strode forward, calling to his soldier-sons. Without the great horned helm he was all but anonymous, though his armor would speak of officer status. The pikes knew their business, though. The Khir charge was shattered, and the Battle of Khefu-An—named for the closest village, civilians huddling in their houses and praying for neither victory nor defeat but for deliverance from a plague of soldiers in either event—would not be finished yet for some hours.

But the ending was not in doubt, and all that remained was tending to the living, granting mercy to those too wounded to be saved, and picking the corpse of half a Khir army.

When Zakkar Kai returned to the main camp through a haze of smoke turning the descending sun into a child's red ball hanging in the sky, he was greeted by a victory-roar, a pile of dispatches, Anlon's visible relief, and the news that the other half of the Khir army had been sighted by a flying column of Sehon Doah's cavalry some distance to the west in the valley of Huawei.

Not only that, but one of his captives—to save the other from further torment—had spoken, confirming his name was Hazuni Ulo. The other was a Lord Narikhi, and that name bothered Zakkar Kai slightly, some half-buried memory lingering just out of reach.

No matter, he had time to coax it from its rodent-hole. It was a good day, and once again he had survived a battle. But all Kai wanted was sohju, paper, and a brush.

BLEEDING THE HORDE

I t was the third day of battle, and the fire was a living thing. It roared between the tree-trunks, eating like a hungry peasant at a piled-high festival table. Barbarians were ghostly figures through the smoke, screaming with their bright hookblades high; they crashed into Zhaon shield-squares, surrounding them like starch-thickened milk flowing around dense cakes of pounded rai before oozing away. Discipline and pikes told, but the junior generals were worried, and the smoke was felling many a slowly retreating soldier.

Bleeding a Horde was a messy business.

Greying, soot-covered Tiang Huo drew to his ear; the arrow flew free with a twang lost in the confusion. A shadow toppled from a plunging, indistinct horse-shape. *"Back!"* the adjutant cried, and Garan Makar struck down another fur-wrapped, stinking Tabrak, the barbarian's sweating dough-pale skin streaked with melting blue clay. The lightfoot bloomed below his knees; Makar leapt, the leather-wrapped hilt of his father's sword shearing a neck. Arterial spray splashed, a high crimson jet, and the point had just missed the cervical spine by luck instead of design.

The assassin he had killed at eight summers high had beshat himself upon dying, too, but this reek was multiplied, added to smoke and a brassy odor that seemed purely death itself. The thought that little Jin might soon smell this massive, terrible rot was unhelpful, but kept tiptoeing through Makar's head-meat at strange times.

For all Jin's love of weaponry, he did not think his youngest brother would like a battle much.

A hard knot of soldiers surrounded their prince, but it was Tiang Huo who commanded them and Makar had enough sense to stay out of the way. It was difficult to breathe through the dampened cloth wrapped around each man's nose and mouth—which, paradoxically, did not block the stench—and the roaring of the fire was like the breathing of some giant scaled beasts he had read of in the core of mountains, rising to belch molten rock at hapless villages below.

Had the shield-wall not broken upon the second day, they might well have driven the Horde back into the flames. But Aro Ba Wistis was flagrant with his riders' lives. Those Tabrak fighting upon foot caught whatever maddened steed they could and became screaming things straight from the Hell of Smoking Mirrors, and though the Southron Army was mighty it could not hold the entire treeline.

Still, they were giving a good account of themselves, and bleeding the Horde. Whether or not the beast could be drained to death remained to be seen.

"My lord prince." Tiang was at his side. "We must bring you to safety."

Makar listened to the gongs and trumpets, the noise floating eerily through the smoke. A fighting retreat was the most difficult of maneuvers; Binwon Ko was heavily engaged upon the right and Dohon Sek the left; the center was a morass of confusion now that the wind had veered and was sending a column of firebreath directly across the battlefield. When night fell the exhausted combatants, clinging to each other, were lit by the glare of burning trees; the battle became knifework in the dark, and the lack of sleep was telling upon both Tabrak and Zhaon.

"My *lord*!" Tiang plucked at his sleeve. Makar blinked, hot salt water welling in his eyes, a momentary cleansing leaving streaks upon smoke-blackened cheeks. "We must—"

A high ululating cry, a ringing sound, and a shaggy horseman melded out of the smoke. Two soldiers went sprawling, Tiang drew, but the arrow did not have a chance to find a home. Makar, his head-meat strangely empty, found his swordhilt near his cheek, the high-guard for use against a mounted attacker, and the light-foot clasped his weary muscles again. His boots flickered; he was airborne for a single heavy, stomach-clenching moment. The lunging effort ended when he hit trampled, smoking grass. The rider, a mass of fur and blue-coated high-crested hair, toppled with a sound like sacks of rai tossed into a cart; the horse reared, striking out in the only way it could.

In a trice two soldiers caught its reins, and Makar was dragged upright by a third. The squat man with a broad round peasant's face wiped at his brow with the back of one sweating hand and nodded sharply, an ungrudging salute to a fellow soldier, and a spark of justifiable pride touched the Fourth Prince's thumping heart.

"Tiang!" He coughed, rackingly, and lifted the dampened cloth over the lower half of his face before spitting upon the corpse to clear his mouth. "Ride for Marshal Binwon and tell him we need reinforcement, if any is to be had."

"But, my lord—"

"I shall do well enough here!" Makar yelled over the din as another knot of screaming horsemen engaged the square to their immediate right. The battle line was changing into a bewildered jumble. "Use the trumpets, the gongs are confusing. Go. *Go!*"

It was the only logical choice; the last he had heard, Binwon had a small reserve. Dohon had nothing, and Makar was not far behind.

Tiang Huo must have concurred, for he was a-saddle in a heartbeat and Makar turned back to the direction most of the barbarians seemed to be coming from. Perhaps the wind—a friend as fickle as favor at court—would veer again; in any case, he and his fellows had retreated enough for the moment.

"Come, my soldier-sons." He produced a creditable imitation of a shouting Zakkar Kai, right down to clapping the shoulder of a nearby indistinct Zhaon-armored shape on his left. "We are to hold this ground."

A clanging clatter, metal against metal, swallowed the last of the words. Makar lifted his sword again, barely noticing the wound upon his left shoulder sending a hot stream of blood down his arm, and a shield-square of Zhaon soldiers closed around him once more.

HEAR ME

Apparently even a Zhaon summer must come to an end, and intimations of its closing had begun to accumulate. There were whispers of rain over the far mountains; every night, lightning flickered and the sky spoke over Zhaon-An. No droplet fell onto the smoke-choked city, though the sunsets were lakes of blood. The mornings were bright and hot, though not quite like standing before an oven.

Sixth Prince Jin was announced at the house of Third Prince Garan Takshin, and Yala, touching her hairpin to make certain it was at the correct angle, gave her primrose-silk sleeves a quick tug as well. Su Junha, gliding beside her, was occupied with the same motions, very usual for a noblewoman with an honored guest to greet; her new dress of green cotton edged with exactly the correct shade of plum silk suited her very well. Hansei Liyue, tucking a small pamphlet upon new methods of housekeeping into her green babu-patterned sleeve for later reading, trailed behind them, hurriedly performing her own last-moment adjustments.

"Sixth Prince." Yala swept into the larger of the two sitting-rooms, stepping aside so her charges could arrange themselves beside her, and performed her bow. "You brighten our home."

"I am visiting the sun itself, how could it not be bright?" The quotation rolled easily from his tongue, accompanied by a swift smile, but he sobered immediately after making his own bow. Jin had

grown taller this summer, she realized, and his face had changed somewhat, leaner and more mature. His gaze strayed to Su Junha, whose eyes were properly downcast, and his brow wrinkled quite uncharacteristically. "I come from the Old Tower; Mrong Banh sends his greetings and a ream of very fine paper. Will you let me have a sheet or two?"

"Of a certainty, you must take half. Lady Hansei, please arrange for tea." Yala tucked her hands into her sleeves, unease filling her chest. "I regret my husband is not—"

"He left for Shan this morning, didn't he?" Jin stepped toward the chair she indicated and halted, his worry plainly visible.

He had taken to scholar-sober dark robes lately and he had grown, but he was still very young. A single summer had wreaked many a change upon them all.

"Yes, just at dawn." It was difficult to keep her expression neutral. Takshin had been in a bleak mood indeed during his leave-taking, holding her hands so tightly her bones almost creaked while his noble Shan friend—Lord Sunjosi, very mannerly indeed, and apologizing several times for not bringing a wedding-gift—stood behind him. The buzz-burring of the Shan dialect was somewhat unpleasant, but Sunjosi spoke good Zhaon, and he promised to take every care with her husband and return him in good order.

There were a half-dozen Shan riders as well; Lady Kue had remarked wryly that their depredations upon the larder were quite the reminder of her native country. Yala had not been required to bid them farewell, at least. Smiling at Sunjosi's attempted jests had fair cracked her cheeks, but the man was attempting to help.

Far more painful was Takshin's grasp during the leave-taking. In defiance of public behavior he had rested his forehead against hers and spoke so low and fierce she almost thought him angry at her instead of merely irritated at the world in general.

Do not visit the Palace more than necessary. Avoid Kurin if you can. If need be, Mrong Banh will help you—and remember, little lure, you are mine, *and I will return.*

"Early, of course. My eldest brother thinks he can..." Jin looked to Su Junha again as the Hansei girl hurried into the hall to supervise the fetching of said tea. "I am being a very bad guest, and the visit has barely begun. Forgive me. Mother sends her regards as well, and her thanks for the Daebo tea. She says it is like drinking in her childhood home again."

"Ah." Yala knew the Third Mother's intended allusion, even filtered through another's report. She too had been reading Zhe Har much, of late. "It was a tiny gift indeed, but I thought she might enjoy the taste. Come, sit, and do not trouble yourself. Here, guests speak as they like. Tell me, how is the Second Princess?"

"I haven't seen Gamnae today. They say First Mother is very poorly indeed." Jun waited until Yala and Su Junha had settled themselves, the tall girl's dress giving her an air of stateliness beyond her years, especially when her face, in repose, took on the cast of a thoughtful scroll-illustration. "Lady Su, it is pleasant to see you."

"Sixth Prince honors a humble handmaiden," the girl murmured, but her smile was quick and her blush very fetching indeed. "Is your mother indeed well?"

"Well enough." Jin caught himself, and there was an edge of flush upon his cheeks too. He had taken to shaving daily, it seemed, though he had little need of it. "Yes, quite well, and I shall tell her you inquired."

"Have you eaten?" Yala inquired, solicitously. "Lady Su, please, some refreshment for our guest, and for ourselves. It was a very early morning."

Su Junha rose, bowed, and glided away, but not very quickly. Of course she would guess her princess and the young prince might have matters to discuss other ears should not catch—and what she and Hansei Liyue did not hear, they could not be forced to speak upon.

"I am sorry." Jin's words came quick and low as soon as the noble girl had fluttered through the doorway. "I came as soon as I could. Is it very bad? What can I do?"

He thought to help, and Yala's heart suffered one of the strange pangs it had been giving her lately. A measure of peace in a household must have disarranged her usually iron grasp upon her own humors, or she was suffering aftershocks from the summer's events. "Nothing _can_ be done. The Emperor has sent my husband to Shan." Yala settled her aching hands politely in her lap. Through the sitting-room's open partition to the balcony, a breeze from the central garden even held a hint of fresh coolness, welcome indeed. "I am more worried for you. How is your mother, truly?"

"I fear for her." Jin glanced at the doorway; at court such precautions were becoming more and more common. Even Lady Gonwa occasionally halted to gaze at some quarter where unfriendly ears might be lurking, before continuing whatever confidence she had a mind to share in a hushed tone. "Riders from the Southron Army arrived just after dawn watch. The roads are still clear, but they were a sorry pair of fellows, all bandaged."

"So there has been some battle." Yala's humors shrank within her. And Takshin was riding south.

"Of course Maki is very scholarly. And not so bad with a sword." But Jin searched her face, anxiously. "I thought you would want to know the roads seem to be clear. But of course there were men sent from Shan, so they will take care of Takshin. You mustn't worry."

There was little else to do _but_ brood upon what could happen. Yala summoned the same pained, gentle smile she had employed upon the Shan lord and his guards, as well as some few Golden. Takshin and Sunjosi had mentioned Kurin's refusal to send proper Zhaon reinforcements to Suon Kiron after all, pleading the need to keep the capital city covered and using the bravery of Shan riders as an edged compliment. Both had halted when she entered the room slightly before a servant carrying tea, but the gleam in Takshin's dark gaze said he knew very well she had heard, and he had sought to reassure her the night before his departure.

A small group, light and swift—her husband going south, and Ashani Daoyan north. There was no news from Zakkar Kai; his letters, usually punctual, had not arrived for a good ten days.

It was a mercy she was settled in a chair. Her legs did not quite seem resigned to their usual task of carrying her. "I will worry nonetheless," she said softly. It was a relief to admit as much. "How is the mood at the Palace?"

"Uncertain." Jin's newly broadened shoulders hunched. "Sensheo is much in evidence, speaking to the ministers, soothing the eunuchs. The Emperor attends First Mother. There are disturbing rumors."

You mean more *disturbing ones.* "No doubt." Yala listened intently, alert to any whisper in the passageway. "You are not sleeping, brother-in-law. Your eyes are bruised."

"*A candle does my sleeping for me.*" There was no childishness in his tone, nor in his mien. The youngest son of Garan Tamuron had not laid aside his sword while entering his elder brother's house, either. "Have you heard from Kai?"

"Not for days," she admitted. "Have you?"

"No. He usually sends Banh letters too, but… nothing." Jin settled his folded hands on the polished table, watching her closely. His topknot-cage was one she had seen before, of dark stiffened leather with an antique silver pin. It must have been a gift, and a comfort. "It must be difficult for you, not knowing what happens in the North."

Nobody else alluded to the fact directly. It was another relief to have it spoken, and Yala's breath caught in her throat. "What should I wish for?" she heard herself say. "The victory of my… of my husband's people, or my own? A wife belongs to her husband's house, and yet…"

"I wish Eldest Brother were still…" Jin glanced guiltily at the door again. "Forgive me. I come to visit and speak unguarded."

"Where else can you, if not here?" Yala composed herself. "Soft, though; I hear tea approaching."

He took the hint with alacrity. When Hansei Liyue re-entered, Lady Kue glided behind her carrying the teapot upon a tray of painted glass. Several junior maids laden with cups, plates, and other appurtenances followed, and by that time Jin was deep in a cavalcade of light gossip upon the current fashion for songbirds in osier cages sweeping the Ladies' Court.

"—Lady Aoan's did not like the heat, and she says it is gone. Then Lady Gonwa asked her if she left the cage door open and my mother laughed. It was pleasant to hear, but Lady Aoan did not reply. She seems saddened, of late, and Second Mother keeps asking her to play the sathron but she has an excuse each time."

"How very sad," Yala commented, and waited for the tea to be arranged. There was some gossip that Second Mother's favorite and eldest son had an understanding of sorts; Yala had seen no proof, but Lady Gonwa certainly seemed to think there was truth to that particular rumor.

Now she was grateful Zakkar Kai had been so . . . circumspect, as well.

Su Junha returned too, and in her wake were plates of pounded-rai dainties and delicacies appropriate for a midmorning social visit. She colored slightly again when Jin brightened at her arrival, and Yala was hard put not to smile.

They had reached the third cup, Hansei Liyue arguing politely with the prince about the value of reading light novels for women, when hurrying feet sounded in the corridor and Yala half-rose, her right hand dropping to her side, close to her *yue*'s hidden hilt.

But it was only Lady Kue, who bowed deeply upon entering. "Princess, there is a letter for you, arrived by military courier."

It could only mean Kai. "Pardon me, my lord Sixth Prince," Yala murmured, and did not miss Jin's stiffness, nor his own hand tensing upon the table with the effort to keep from a hilt.

So he too thought it was likely the Emperor—or the Fifth Prince—would send a barbed gift to Takshin's house while its lord was absent. It was small comfort that his suspicions paralleled her own.

For neither of them, after all, could do very much about anything at all.

The letter was travel-stained; the lean, dust-covered courier at least appeared uninjured. "Victory in the North," he said with a wide grin, and Yala's humors were cold and loose within her indeed.

It was some consolation his dispatch-bag was over half full. Had he any message for the Emperor he would have passed the Noble Quarter and visited the Palace first; Kai must have sent a separate courier with *those* letters. It made sense for him to weight a second one with any personal missives, for a courier so laden could halt at whatever house was first upon his way.

Returning to the sitting-room might mean reading the letter aloud to her ladies and her princely visitor; instead, she charged Lady Kue with taking the courier to the kitchens for a meal and plenty of sohju. "If you return this way you will spend tonight as our guest, I hope," she said, and the soldier brightened much as Jin did when Su Junha appeared. "I may brush a reply much sooner, though, if you are under strict orders to hasten."

"No, my lady Princess." He bobbed into his fourth bow, clearly overwhelmed at being addressed directly by a royal personage. "My saddle-brother had the official letters; I am to meet him outside of town in two days or return to the army as I may. My lord General Zakkar gave me a message for Third Prince Takshin, too, but 'tis written upon air."

"My husband has gone to Shan," Yala said, steadily enough, and paused. When the fellow did not hasten to deliver whatever Kai would say to Takshin, she spoke again. "Go, then, Honorable...?"

"Hui Banh, my lady Princess." His fifth bow exhibited no little saddle-weariness; he was bobbing like a toy boat upon fountain waves.

"Honorable Hui, Lady Kue shall show you to the kitchen. I will brush a reply as soon as possible. You have traveled far, and I thank you for your care."

A sixth bow in her direction, and he bowed yet again to Lady Kue as well, whose mouth was twitching with repressed merriment. She led him away; Yala set off, her step decided and her head high, and a well-traveled, dusty letter tucked into her sleeve.

Takshin's study was upon the second level; the books had hardly been unpacked. She crossed to the balcony partition overlooking the garden, sparing a glance for the heavy dark desk with its shining-clean surface, the brushes lined neatly upon their rack, the inkstone in its case, the water-dish dry as Zhaon's late summer.

The seal was very simple; she broke it with a crisp sound. Her hands were trembling.

My lady Moon,

I have returned from battle near Khefu-An full of strange thoughts, and so I take my brush to hand. Tomorrow we face another Khir army. By the time you read this the matter will be decided.

My will is brushed and witnessed. Everything that survives me is yours. Should your husband ask, it is merely a kindness repaid—use exactly those words, he will understand.

There was a single line, blotted out. The paper shook because her hand quivered. Her husband was riding south at risk of Tabrak's horde; why did her traitorous heart seek to turn north and fly?

The closing was simple.

I should have spoken; I am weary of my own silence. Hear me, if not in this life, then in the next.

He had signed his name, but the *Zakkar* was slightly changed from his usual characters. It could have been a jest, or the kind of change a man's signature underwent over the course of a lifetime. But Yala knew it was neither.

Instead of *Zakkar*, it was *Zhehar*. Neither were proper names in Zhaon. The first was acceptable, though, for a foundling taken up by a warlord who became Emperor.

The second was...otherwise.

"*I must go,*" Yala whispered, leaning against the partition. She gazed unseeing across the central garden's green tangle. There were workers among the potted yeoyan saplings and babu, watering, snipping, brushing the pathways clear, tying and arranging thin jaelo vines upon trellises. Her husband wished his bride to have comfort and solace in the heart of their house. *"My sleeve is caught."*

The sob caught between her teeth shook her entire body. The letter crumpled in her fist, the wax seal breaking; how like Garan Takshin she was, after all.

She was married. Her red time was late; it could simply be the disturbance to her humors in changing residences, or it could be an heir, that once-faraway summit of a noble girl's ambitions. Not only that, but her husband *valued* her.

And she not only betrayed him by concealing Ashani Daoyan and sending him North, but in the secret chambers of her heart and head-meat—perhaps all the way into her liver, that seat of judgment and courage—as well. She was betraying even the young brother-in-law who sat conversing with her ladies at the moment, probably worrying about what news the courier had brought.

The paroxysm passed. She sucked in a deep dust-freighted breath, and crimson-purple hatred of Zhaon filled her for a single dizzying moment. She hated this country, she hated this city, she hated the palace that had stolen and murdered her princess—and yet, if her husband was correct, perhaps the Great Rider of Khir had sent his daughter to die, and arranged the event as well.

Yala had utterly failed at everything she had been raised to accomplish, and she could not even be a proper wife. By all rights she should draw her *yue* and plunge it into her own throat, expunging her guilt.

It occurred to her then, quite naturally, that if her red time appeared, freeing her of the suspicion of new life gathering in her belly, there was truly no reason not to.

A RIDER

A thunderous twilight descended well before sunset, clouds streaming from the north and west. Along with the deep unsettling beating of Heaven's gongs in the halls of celestial palaces came a breathless hush over most of Zhaon-An. Those in the streets glanced frequently at the sky, horses sidling nervously, oxen grumbling in protest; even stray dogs slunk, tail-tucked like mourning knots.

An exhausted, smoke-stained, bandaged rider limped through the great city's South Gate, his mount's head hanging whenever a cluster of carts forced a pause. He wore leather half-armor, sadly battered, but he was waved through the press once a gate-guard in his red-feathered helmet glanced at the sealed packet he bore. The guard's eyes widened appreciably, but the rider paid little attention, kneeing his mount into a bone-jolting imitation of a weary trot.

The soldier's goal was the Palace complex, and by the time he reached it the thunder had become nearly continuous over fields where peasants worked frantically to move harvested rai to drying sheds instead of spread under swiftly thickening clouds. Sudden unnatural darkness splashed against city and town walls, filtering through the apertures in sharply pitched roofs meant for bringing mirrorlight to shadowed interiors.

The Golden at the Palace gates glanced at the packet's seal and waved the soldier through much as the city gate-guards had, exchanging significant looks. The horse took three steps inside the massive timbered gate and halted, its head very low indeed, but it was the rider who crumpled, falling from the saddle and hitting stone paving with a hideous crack.

The horse was hastened to the stables, shuddering and foam-spattered, the rider to the Golden infirmary. The missive, however, was carried from hand to hand up the great chain of court life—Golden to Golden, then to junior eunuch, to senior eunuch, from senior eunuch to Zan Fein, and from Zan Fein to the Emperor himself at a pace that honorable quasi-minister rarely employed. The chief court eunuch's jatajatas tapped frantically instead of landing feline-soft, and in short order he presented the packet to Garan Kurin upon both hands with a deep bow.

The horse survived; the rider, his duty discharged, sank into a slumbrous three-day fever, attended by Palace physicians eager for him to wake and share what news he could of the Southron Army—for that was the insignia upon his sleeve.

By the time he did achieve a manner of consciousness, though, the peerless Emperor of Zhaon had learned of the fate of the junior of Zhaon's two great armies—and its commander, Garan Makar, both considered lost in a four-day battle at the edge of the great Nenzhua forest, said to be inhabited by tengrahu and other mythical creatures, hard upon the Shan border.

So, too, had Garan Hanweo-a Haesara, Second Mother to the Emperor, and she uttered a piercing scream when a perspiring but otherwise impassive Zan Fein told her the news and her uncle Lord Hanweo—not in his half-year of prominence but still an important personage—presented her with her husband's sword, the blade but recently given to her eldest son. The cry, terrible enough in itself, was swallowed by increasing thunder and a restless spatter of warm, almost oily drops of rain striking thick street-dust without easing it.

The clouds did not burst; the dust remained, so did the peculiar stormlight as the sun choked to death upon a crimson bed. Garan Makar's mother collapsed, and her second son was sent for. It was

Garan Sensheo who held his sobbing mother in her grief, and if he was pale and grim it was entirely appropriate.

And yet, sometimes, a servant or two thought they saw a very small, very slight, very satisfied smile upon the younger brother's lips. Still, they said nothing, for to set your mouth upon that particular prince's actions was a dangerous occupation lately—and who cared for the gossip of underlings, anyway?

Nobody of any note, indeed.

A LENGTH OF SILK

M any of the unmarried noblewomen of the court resided within the households of their nominal royal patrons; others, however, chose or were forced to live in the small buildings painted the color of bright, sacred greenstone adjoining the Silver and Bronze Pavilions. Though minute, each apartment was furnished as exquisitely as its owner's taste, stipend, or patrons would allow; the smallest building was the most remote, and likewise the most exclusive despite the distance from its low, heavy ironwood threshold to the center of court life.

It was generally agreed that the most tastefully decorated—indeed, almost gemlike—apartment belonged to a certain lady with loose-belted dresses and the high favor of Second Mother to the Revered Emperor Garan Haesara. Upon the third day after a rider had brought news of great misfortune to her patroness's eldest son, the lady living there arose, breakfasted as usual with a cup of Lady Gonwa's heaven tea, and spent time in her tiny sitting-room brushing many a letter in her inimitable style, a halu lamp nearby since a pall of overcast smothered Zhaon-An. No rain yet fell; it was weather the poets and sages called *kuhleu* after an archaic word for the space under a rai-pot's lid. The wind flirted uneasily, raising spinning dust-spirits along roads both paved and hard-packed; exorcists went from house to house, drinking ceremonial thimbles of sohju, beating gongs, and affixing paper charms to lintels, not to mention over cradles and hearths.

The Emperor had the prerogative of ordering cannon at the city walls to fire empty shouts skyward, in order to possibly provoke the downpour. Yet he refrained; it was often held best to let Heaven order the weather as it would.

Or perhaps his own grief was too immense to risk incurring Heaven's notice. He had, after all, sent his younger brother south to die.

Lady Aoan Mau swept her wet brush across the inkstone and paused, looking from the small, restrained hau-wood desk to the door of her bedroom, curtained with a fall of subtly patterned, green, heavily beaded cotton. The Aoan family, while noble, had only middling-deep coffers, and much of what was considered her distinctive style was a nod to that fact.

Besides, she enjoyed beauty. What noblewoman didn't?

"My lady?" Her close-servant—her only servant, but she did not need more—Kho Khawone pushed aside the partition from the common hallway, bowing herself through and bringing a tea-tray of filigreed yeoyan wood. The tray—and the set upon it, square iron teapot and whisper thin blue-glazed cups painted with a character for *serenity*—had been a princely gift, and a fresh needle pierced Aoan Mau's chest. "Tea. You must take some; it is sweetened and has citron."

Harsh fermented oulian would have been more appropriate, or smoky eong. But the lady nodded, taking care to make the gesture languid and graceful. Much was expected of one in her position, and much had almost been achieved.

Almost. *Wait for me*, he had said, looking away because it was his habit, like hers, to hide what he felt as much as possible.

"Bring it in, then." She indicated the precise spot upon the table where the pot and cup should rest; Khawone knew her preferences and did not need more. "There are letters; you may take the ones already written."

"Of course." Khawone eyed her mistress somewhat nervously after the cup was set in its proper place. "My lady…"

By Heaven and the Many Hells, get out. But a noblewoman

should never act so; it was not meet to use the sudo of your voice upon a subordinate who was, after all, simply worried. "All is well, little rai-ball." The affectionate shortening of Khawone's name was rarely indulged in, but Mau was feeling savage indeed and so should take especial care to be kind. "I am almost finished."

"Yes, my lady." Khawone bowed and withdrew, shutting the partition very softly, as if upon an invalid.

Oh, Mau had suspected it would come to this as soon as news reached her of the Emperor's decree. And his carefully brushed letter of farewell, consigning his mother to her especial care should aught befall him—she had almost believed his message one of a deeper farewell until the postscript.

A jeweled earring rests within silk; I keep it close to my heart.

An allusion to another farewell in the Hundreds, one only temporary. In other words, his feelings had not changed. The old Emperor had denied him permission to marry until his eldest brother produced an heir; Aoan was an old family and very respectable, and thus a son from their alliance could be a rallying point for...certain influences. A filial son and loyal noblewoman had bowed their heads and accepted fate.

Even Garan Tamuron's ascension to Heaven had not been too concerning, since his eldest son prized his most scholarly brother and would no doubt give an endorsement at the proper time.

But Garan Takyeo was ascended to Heaven as well, and all her hopes were ashes.

Mau finished the last letter and sealed it before rinsing her brushes and settling at an angle to the table, drinking sweetened tea with citron—almost soldier-tea, but lacking the strength of that rough beverage—while she studied the hanging upon the opposite wall. Two bronzefish in a winter pond, drawn by the space between suggestive brushstrokes rather than outlined, curved protectively around each other. It was a gift from Garan Haesara last year, and the note accompanying it hinted the Second Queen was not averse to her favorite and her eldest son making an alliance despite her lord husband's refusal to grant an endorsement.

It was Haesara she would miss the most, Mau thought, holding her sleeve at the proper angle as she sipped. There was nobody to see, but life was a display for Heaven as well as those around you, and if a certain shade lingered as they were said to do before the pyre set them free, he might be watching.

It was the Second Queen who had shown a gangly girl from a far province signal favor, gathering her into court life during the years of Garan Tamuron's solidifying power, and Mau had done her best to be worthy of the attention. It was Haesara who had sent small useful presents each naming-day, who had also smoothed over the affair of the taxes upon Father's manse, and who had comforted her when Mother died and Mau was trapped in the capital by the last battles against the final rival warlord unwilling to bow to an Emperor. The Second Queen had not only performed as a patroness should, but she had done so quietly and politely, without expecting the distasteful over-obeisance the First Queen exacted from her temporarily favored ones.

Mau shut her eyes, a ghost of sweetness lingering upon her tongue and turning by degrees into citron-spurred dryness. The small green building creaked and breathed around her, other unmarried women going about their business—dressing, drinking tea, writing letters, gossiping, sewing, preparing to visit one another, whispering behind fans, all making a soft song familiar as her own breath.

Her patroness's grief was so much deeper than her own; she was contemplating a selfish act. And yet Aoan Mau's heart and liver were in accord, and her head-meat as well.

It was only a question of *when*. Her letters were finished now, all matters arranged tidily. Despite the opulence of court life, a noblewoman within the Palace complex could not be said to own much. A teapot or two; some robes reworked or, if you were fortunate, new; jewelry rented from the Artisan's Home or gifted by a patron who wished for more than a piece was worth from those considered both attractive and impecunious...

"Not very much at all," Aoan Mau murmured, and was surprised by her own voice.

She set the cup down carefully. Her eyelids drifted up; she studied the tiny sitting-room and its embroidered cushions with each stitch achingly familiar, the small cabinet for brushes, paper, her sewing basket, and other genteel sundries. Though the green hanging cloth covered her bedroom, she knew every inch of the dark wardrobe, the sathron-case in the corner, the narrow maiden's bed—she had not even given herself to the one she loved as so many others would.

All their restraint, all their careful refusal to glance at each other in public, all their feeling held in check, all turned to smoke upon a barbarian wind.

She rose, swiftly and gracefully, and pushed aside the green hanging. Upon her wardrobe's lowest shelf, tucked in the back, was a neatly hemmed length of crimson silk she had thought to use for her wedding headdress. It smelled of the ceduan oil used to keep moths away, and she turned it over in her long hands, each fingertip dipped in noble resin. It was a trifle too long for what she intended, but everything that did not fit could be cut down, remade, reworked, or used for another purpose.

Mau had often bemoaned her own unwomanly height, but it was a gift she had not needed until this moment. She knew exactly how to twist the silk—what noble girl did not? And now the low ceiling of her bedroom was a blessing instead of an insult to ignore, and so were the age-blackened, exposed beams.

Silence fell in the small green building. Tea was consumed, fans were whispered behind, needles pricked fabric and resin-dipped fingers.

Overhead, the ruthless sky rumbled but still gave no rain.

A Loose
Windowsill

The blue-sheathed Old Tower was more and more a refuge these days; Jin even sometimes napped in one of the upper rooms, though he did not like to leave his mother alone more than absolutely necessary. This chamber at the top of the north stairs, small with a high plastered ceiling, held a well-used army cot and a table; the latticed window had mended wooden shutters and a trimmed lamp stood upon the sill. There was a small dent in the cot's rectangular head-bolster; Jin thought it likely more than one of his brothers had sought refuge here.

The mystery was solved when he braced a knee upon the windowsill to pull the shutters aside—this high room was perfect for testing a few of the flying models Banh was always building, including those he had little use for now and had given permission for Jin to set free. They would either plummet into a water-garden, if they did not work well, or perhaps make it to the Palace's curtain-wall if the wind was good and the model well-built.

The sill wobbled strangely under his weight, so Jin lowered himself gingerly to the floor and tested its base. There was a trick to lifting it; the same distinct, instinctive sense which told him how to use a new weapon exerted a certain pressure upon his fingertips and the wooden covering slab lifted easily.

Inside were some packets wrapped in oiled or waxed paper, tied with string. A scrap of indigo silk, very much the color Princess Yala favored, was wrapped around a small ceramic figure of a lucky feline, its paw lifted and its grin secretive. There were a few other items—a Shan-style eating knife with a rusted blade, a red child's ball Jin vaguely remembered seeing before but not precisely where, a tiny empty scent-bottle with a broken, fluted top, a scentwood hairpin with a broken string of crimson beads he thought had once been Sabwone's.

Jin closed the sill, his heart in his throat. He glanced over his shoulder—the door was half-open, the hall beyond quiet. Subtle sounds filled the stairway: the sough of a breeze against the tower's sides, Mrong Banh dropping something far below and swallowing a curse unfit for children's ears as if he knew Jin could hear him, or as if Jin were still a child.

He did not feel like a child anymore, Garan Jin decided, and he had not for some time. He turned back to the window. His heart still lodged behind the pad of pounded rai visible in a man's throat the Shan called a stone instead, and he applied the deft pressure that would re-lift the sill.

The top packet was securely wrapped; he untied the string holding it closed. It was a complicated knot, but it too yielded its secret the way any weapon did and he was fairly certain he could retie it in proper order. The heavy waxed rai-paper folded aside, and a sheaf of other papers—some stained, others half-burnt, the remainder as pristine as could be expected—offered themselves for inspection.

They were a heterogenous collection, some of rai-paper and others of pounded rag. Some made little sense; they looked like bills of lading or merchant ledger-sheets. One looked like a listing of household accounts, but the characters were strange. After a few moments of deep thought, he decided the writing was probably Khir. Then, in the middle, brushed upon very fine heavy paper suitable for such a thing, was a marriage endorsement.

Jin's cheeks turned hot, but he was committed to this act, so he read it. His jaw loosened, and he gasped as if punched hard in the middle, a blow he had not seen approaching.

Of course the handwriting was familiar. But why would Kurin have...

The groom's name was there, in solid brushstrokes; the bride's name was blank. He touched a trembling, callused fingertip to the date, and hot bile whipped the back of his throat.

It was the day before Takyeo's death. And Takyeo had given Takshin an endorsement, too; had his third-eldest brother just been planning, or was there some darker reason? For Kurin never did anything without a reason, nor did Takshin himself.

"Oh, Shin," Garan Jin whispered. His humors turned hot, flushing him from crown to sole. Then they chilled, withdrawing and leaving greasy sweat upon him, before flooding back to scald him again. "What did you do?"

Did Yala know? Should he...

Jin took a closer look at the other papers. The ledger sheet in Khir bothered him for some reason he could not quite define, and its date was odd too—about a full moon before Crown Princess Mahara's... misfortune.

"Jin!" Mrong Banh's voice drifted up the stairs. "I found another model you may test. Come have some tea."

"In a moment," Jin heard himself call. He even sounded normal, despite the crack running through the last syllable, a hated reminder of childhood still lingering in a man's voice. Soon it would deepen truly, a river running between the banks it would follow for the rest of his life.

A faint thundery breeze rattled the shutters. The peasants were worried the rain would come too early and rot the rai, the court was worried both about Khir and Tabrak, Kurin was probably worried about his own hateful, ailing mother and Sensheo about his graceful, kindly one—there was no shortage of anxiety floating through the Palace or the land itself.

Of course he should rewrap the package and put it back under the sill. He knew that—but had not Princess Yala said they were to share gossip, and keep each other safe? And she would know what the ledger sheet in Khir meant, even though its edges were fringed with burns. It looked very much as if it had rested in the middle of a sheaf tossed carelessly, or quite deliberately, into a brazier yet somehow survived.

When Takshin came home from Shan he would know someone had found this trove. He might even question Banh and guess it was Jin. Kurin was cruel, yes, but Takshin was *unpredictable*. What would he do?

Yet…did not Yala need to know? She was determined to find out who had sent the assassins after the Crown Princess, who had been pretty and kind, and did not treat him as a child. In fact, that terrible day in the Yaol, Garan Mahara had placed herself under his protection just as if he were older, and his liver still swelled to think of it.

There was also the secret of just who had ridden to alert Zakkar Kai to Takyeo's condition, kept locked safe in Jin's liver and head-meat. It had been Yala who enjoined his silence, as forthright and soft as if he and not Takshin had been responsible for taking her through the city gates. She *deserved* to know whatever these papers could tell her, did she not?

She was his friend. Sensheo said princes didn't have friends, only brothers and clients; Takshin seemed to do perfectly well without anyone, though he had married. Takyeo, though…

What would his Eldest Brother say? Or poor Makar, sent to die because he had touched Kurin's stupid pride? Oh, Jin had heard much of the sparring match between the Emperor and the Fourth Prince. Even his own companions among the Golden were treating him differently these days, not wishing to offend the man now upon the Throne of Five Winds.

That stung, though he did not care to admit it. Jin had been certain his facility with weapons and his habit of standing rounds of sohju had gained him some goodwill, at least.

Jin's hands folded the packet's covering neatly; he retied the knot. Then, carefully, he seated the sill again, and tucked the slim collection of papers inside his robe. The other papers could rest there until he knew whether this particular trove held anything of use. He would have to move carefully to make certain the packet didn't crackle, and maybe even turn down Banh's offer of midafternoon tea.

Just as he was mentally rehearsing his polite refusal, though, a distant, muffled, hollow noise shivered the air. For a moment he thought it was Heaven itself warning him against a transgression, and his broad shoulders hunched. He was much taller than he had been at the beginning of summer, but in that moment, halted in the doorway at the top of the Old Tower's northern staircase, he felt very small indeed.

But it was only the thunder, grown very close. The Tower shivered slightly, vibrating like an unplucked sathron-string next to a just-tapped one.

Mother never played the sathron anymore.

"Jin?" Banh sounded anxious now, and his voice echoed; he was upon the stairs.

"Lightning," Jin said, and his leather-soled slippers slid slightly against dusty stone. He kept one hand lightly upon the wall as he descended. "Very close, too. Perhaps even in the eastron fields before Kihua." That village was upon the way to Hanweo; he had passed through it often enough.

"Come, have some tea. It smells like rain, but who can tell?" Banh's wrinkled forehead smoothed as Jin came into sight. "I found another model you may fling from the battlements. I should have cleaned this pile many summers ago."

Jin's smile felt unnatural, his face too tight. "You need a wife, Banh."

"Ah, my young prince, I appreciate the offer, but I do not think we should suit." Banh's eyebrows wiggled like caterpillars, and laughter surprised them both. "*Ai*, it is an old man's jest; I said much the same to Kai the last time we ate together."

There was another worry. What would Kai say of this? "Do you think he's all right?"

"I hope so." But Banh sobered, the familiar look of an adult unwilling to give a child a worrying thought. "Come, the tea will grow cool."

"A tragedy," Jin agreed somberly, and made a longtail's face, scrunching his cheeks and sticking out his tongue. At least it made Banh smile once more, and pushed aside any questions.

Gamnae said they were both growing up. If this was what it felt like—a paper packet heavy against his skip-galloping heart, sweat and the consciousness of possibly doing a great but unavoidable wrong gathering in the hollows of his arms, knees, and lower back—he thought it a very poor occurrence indeed.

ONLY A SKIRMISH

Only a skirmish, after all," Anlon said, eyeing the smoking wasteland of yet another battlefield under a flood of almost directionless yellow-green afternoon stormlight. A white bandage glared at his shoulder; the Northern Army's main camp lay behind them. The Khir had driven almost past the pickets, but Sehon Doah had arrived in time, and the hammer-anvil had worked better than it had any right to. A long string of prisoners shuffled to the large depression beaten in yellow grass where they would spend the night under guard; those without fine armor might even be allowed to slip away northward once the bloodlust of the victorious was sated.

Moans and cries rose amid the cannonsmoke; the army physicians' battle had just begun. Any peasants living nearby would bring lanterns for corpse-picking tonight; the character for that particular word was a bulbous rai-paper lamp over a broken body. Kai might let them do their work unmolested, if not for the risk that they would strip not just Khir but wounded Zhaon soldiers.

He ached all over, and his left arm did not quite wish to obey him. His great horned helm, tucked in the crook of that elbow, was more of a support than a carried item, and he took the sohju-jug his armor-son carried with profound relief, washing his mouth and spitting to clear the stench and dust. Anlon stiffened slightly; he had not forgotten the boy from Wurei and the last attempt upon his master's life.

No assassins had troubled Kai since leaving Zhaon-An last, only this somewhat cleaner battle. The absence of walkers of the Shadowed Path was thought-provoking, and when he thought they might merely be employed elsewhere in his absence from the capital a great dull wave of anger and disgust passed through him.

Kurin still had not written, other than to require Kai to turn over the Southron Army to Makar. It was beneath a son of Garan Tamuron to act in this fashion.

Cleaner was not the word for this battlefield, he thought, with the reek of split bowel and brassy death hanging in the air, but it was the only one Kai could find. He coughed, handed the jug to Anlon, and half-turned as Hurong Baihan approached, his sharp Daebo features pale with weariness under a heavy coating of grime and spattered blood.

"Everyone who can be spared is combing the field." Tall Hurong accepted the jug after Anlon had quenched battle-thirst, tossing a huge mouthful far back, then rinsing his mouth for luck much as Kai had. "The losses are less than I feared, but I am uneasy."

"As am I." Kai squinted through the veils of dust and smoke, calculating the time until sunset. Hurong Tai and Sehon Doah would be attending to their troops, Short Hurong coordinating the physicians' efforts as well and Sehon gathering all the cavalry reports to make a full accounting this evening. "None of the banners for this lot are from the great houses, and there was too much infantry. Where are the other lords? I mislike it, Tall Hurong."

Had Yala received his letter yet? He was amazed to have survived once again, almost undamaged. A man's mind sought anything other than the horror of battle once the killing stopped; all he felt was weary surprise that whatever presentiment had whispered in his ear to brush his will before this fight had been a false exorcist.

Or it could have spoken truth, for his bones told him the battle was not yet finished, despite the incontrovertible evidence spread before him.

"Where could these lords be?" Hurong Baihan closed his eyes, his head-meat most likely occupied with viewing the same map

Kai could see clearly against the smoke. "They swung very far west, perhaps meaning to take the Inhua valley... We were fortunate to catch them."

"Indeed." Dried blood crackled under Kai's fingertips; he touched the shallow slice upon his cheek. It was not as deep as Takshin's scars, but enough to ache a little now. He couldn't even remember how he gained it. "I want patrols from here to Cheku. And south, too. Did we capture any of their generals, or—"

"I came to tell you as much." Tall Hurong did not brighten; he was too weary even for good news. "Difficult to catch a horse-lord alive, but they did not have time to set fire to their papers. A detachment is searching their commander's tent."

"Now *that* is good news." Cautious hope warred with the knowledge that war gave with one hand only to take with the other, and all was uncertain even after peace was declared. At least two small-ish Khir armies would not rampage into the central bowl of Zhaon, spreading suffering in their wake.

Writing to Kurin about this victory might even be pleasant, once Kai actually had time to do so. And yet, if he were honest with himself...

"Indeed. Shall we put our other prisoners with this lot?" Tall Hurong would not ordinarily ask such a question, but Zakkar Kai had been very clear that he wished the two Khir foolish enough to charge Zhaon pickets some while ago left relatively unmolested.

There were musicians at this feast, but the tune was halting and Kai wanted to find the instrument responsible. It could turn out to be nothing, a false standard dipping over a chaotic field—but he did not think it would. "No," he said, the word heavy as his armor. "Break out the sohju, but only half a victory-ration. I must know where the bulk of their cavalry is, and quickly."

"My lord." The lanky marshal saluted, and took his leave.

Anlon exhaled harshly. "Some soldier-tea for us both," the adju-tant said. "I won't hear a single argument, my lord; you look weary indeed."

"My thanks," Kai replied sourly, but the corners of his mouth twitched. Anlon clapped him on the shoulder and set about the task of finding said tea; more runners and dispatches arrived along with lean, saddle-dirty Sehon Doah.

"I like this not," was the latter's greeting as they clasped hands, foregoing a bow. "Something is wrong, my lord general, and I don't mind saying as much."

"In that, Doah, we are in agreement. How stand our ranks?"

"Less casualties than feared. We shall not have to throw replacements in half-trained; Short Hurong set the squares to selecting from the armor-sons. Everyone is ready for their sohju, and the rapine."

It was little enough repayment for the work they had done today, yet Kai would not loose their leash just yet. "I want guards set and the pickets alert. They did not have nearly enough cavalry."

"Already done, my lord." Another salute, and Doah returned to his own work. Marshals, junior generals, square leaders, even a sutler or two needed a word; like a physician's, a head general's work was not finished when the battle was done but just beginning.

And *still* Zakkar Kai's nerves refused to settle, even when Anlon reappeared with two large mugs of soldier-tea and a grim expression showing he was feeling his aches.

The tent-flap to the Rack was pushed aside; Zakkar Kai strode into the place of punishment with Anlon at his shoulder and his three highest marshals in tow.

Their Khir prisoners were both slightly worse for wear; the swallows-painted fellow bore no few bruises, and had given not the slightest indication of caring. But it was the other Kai studied, one hand to his sword's snarling hilt, and he found the young proud-nosed man's clear grey gaze a reminder of Komor Yala's.

What would she think of the choice now facing him? His task was to win Zhaon's wars, not cushion the feelings of another man's wife. He could not afford to brood in that direction, unless it was to hope Takshin was guarding her well.

The papers within the unfired Khir command tent had offered a solution to the mystery before him, one Kai knew, as soon as it was spoken, to be right indeed.

"Hazuni Ulo," he said, politely enough. "You have performed honorable service to your king, and have my admiration. And you, my lord Ashani Daoyan, Crown Prince of Khir, have also performed well, as befits such a noble son." He did not miss the troubled glance Hazuni cast in his prince's direction; said prince tensed, and had clearly been working at the bindings upon his wrists. Fresh blood welled under the iron cuffs, and perhaps he was determined enough to do himself some injury while slipping free. "We have little time to bring our two countries to peace, and I will have your aid."

Propitiating
Enough

A heavy, haze-oppressive lid lay upon Zhaon-An, smoke refusing to rise as it should and gathering in corners under a sky that was a featureless yellow-green dome. Coughing filled the lower quarters of the city, and each instance was viewed askance as a possible indicator of provincial plague breaking past the walls.

Many nobles had not retreated to their provinces as they generally did during summer's dry time; even the young had not been sent to slightly more congenial climes. War looming, whispers of illness in outlying areas, and the unsettled beginning of a new reign meant those whose interests required it stayed at court. Yet those who could slipped from the Palace complex to their homes in the Noble Quarter, invitations and letters flying from house to house as gossip intensified.

Be that as it may, all who had even the slightest reason were in attendance for yet another pair of royal pyres.

The new Emperor had carried a spitting, resinous everflame torch for the consuming of his eldest brother's body; now he performed the same duty for his mother's. Again the flame did not falter, and a slight rustle of relief might have made its way through the assembled crowd—no less than the well-disguised ripple through the entire court when news of Garan Gamwone's final breath had been verified by a single mournful note from the Great Bell. Mrong Banh had cast the horoscope and found an auspicious date for this ceremony, and if it was perhaps quicker than was quite decent, it could be because Heaven understood corpses spoiled in dry heat as well as wet.

Or, as some remarked to those they trusted, softly and behind a fan so their lips could not be read by a sharp-eyed eunuch or other spy, the astrologer might think there was a chance the First Mother might perform one of the tricks angry female shades were prone to, and move to forestall the cleansing flame so she could wreak yet more havoc.

Still, the body of Garan Tamuron's first wife had been examined by Zan Fein and his eunuchs as well as a contingent of physicians including the formerly quite shabby Kihon Jiao, appearing from his new patron's house in a similarly new robe. All agreed there was no sign of... anything untoward, and yet there was a sudden dearth of physicians to be found in the Palace just after the honorables had made their public report to the Emperor and his ministers.

Many tongues wagged, but the general consensus was that perhaps the First Queen had, after all, grieved for her royal spouse, and lived only long enough to see her son enthroned before taking herself to Heaven—or whatever awaited her—as a faithful wife should.

The fact that the astrologer Mrong Banh remained at the Great Bell, watching as its shadow made indistinct by the stormlight approached the chalked line that would denote the proper time for the ceremony to begin and did not hasten to the pyre as he had for some other funerals, was perhaps a sign of tasteful restraint in one who knew he had lost his greatest patron at court.

The second royal pyre was empty, and far more problematic. The Emperor, his mourning garb brought out of its ceduan-scented resting place once more, approached it, and the gifts nestled amid stacked, oil-drenched wood lacked nothing in costliness or taste. Whispers raced among the mourners at a certain distance from the first-lit blaze; those closer, though, did not have the luxury of even exchanging significant looks.

Garan Komor-a Yala stood at Garan Gamnae's side, holding her sister-in-law's arm as the girl had held hers during a different ceremony. Many speculative gazes rested upon the Khir lady, but her form was veiled even in this oppressive thunder-gathering weather, and she patted Gamnae's plump hand several times. Her husband had been sent upon some mission or another, probably southward into the jaws of barbarians, and the lady no doubt knew how precarious her position was without his presence.

The Second and Third Mothers of the Revered Emperor also stood very close, First Concubine Luswone's face much thinner than it had been. The shock of losing children could bring two matrons closer; Luswone steadied Second Queen Haesara when the latter's knees threatened to give.

The Fifth and Sixth Princes bracketed their respective dams. Fifth Prince Sensheo held Second Queen Haesara's arm as she swayed, watched the lighting of his elder brother's empty pyre without expression as the everflame torch sputtered and almost died in his now-eldest brother's hand. Sixth Prince Jin, glancing nervously between his own mother's expression and the pyre, was thinner too, and many admiring glances were cast upon Garan Tamuron's youngest son.

It took four tries before Garan Makar's oil-drenched pyre would light; it could be blamed upon the soft, smoke-choked breeze or the fact that the Fourth Prince's body was not present, his shade reluctant to be wafted to Heaven. Or perhaps it had already left; the Nenzhua forest was burning as it sometimes did during exceptionally dry years, and that was a princely pyre indeed.

It was better to think of that than of the Pale Horde outraging yet another royal body. The filthy barbarian with skin like polished rai who had brought the Queen of Shan's head to her newly enthroned brother had been dragged from the deepest recesses of the dungeons and executed just that morning, rolled into matting and beaten with threshing-sticks until he breathed his last.

If it was a traditional offering to the Fourth Prince's shade, it did not seem to be propitiating enough.

Finally the oil-drenched wood caught, and the Emperor retreated, step by august step, from the twin pyres. The Second Princess's cheeks gleamed with tears, though her expression did not change.

There was other gossip, of course—the Second Queen's great favorite, Aoan Mau, had been found hanging from a ceiling-beam in the green house, and her own pyre upon the ceremonial grounds just outside the city walls lacked nothing either, for Garan Haesara had given orders and sent many a gift to placate her shade. The most likely explanation was some dishonor, but the Second Queen had remarked to Lady Gonwa that had fate decreed, she would have welcomed Lady Aoan as a daughter-in-law.

This was a toothsome saying indeed, reported from court lady to court lady with speed rivaling that of the fire burning upon the tinder-dry borders. There were already reports of songs in the Theater District, lover's laments between a prince and a lady who let all other admirers languish, waiting for permission to wed her lord. The choruses usually made reference to Heaven's justice in uniting them after cruel separation; none quite dared mention the source of said separation yet, but all gazes resting upon the new Emperor's broad shoulders were speculative indeed.

After all, he had let one of his brothers wed, no matter that gossip insisted the necessary imperial endorsement had been signed by Garan Takyeo as he lay dying.

The Second Princess turned her head slightly to murmur to her companion, who nodded and took a firmer grasp upon the girl's arm. Princess Yala's veil fluttered in the hot, smoke-freighted breeze, and if she squeezed the girl's hand, her knuckles whitening, it was no doubt to provide a salutary bite, a sting to keep a grieving woman upright.

A eunuch hurried forward to take the everflame torch; Emperor Garan Kurin's face was terribly set and all but bloodless. He returned to his ceremonial place and bowed thrice to his mother's pyre, then once to his younger brother's; the court hurried to follow suit. None could leave while the Emperor stood in grief, and he watched the flames crawl through his mother's prepared body, the smoke settling in thick greasy veils instead of rising.

The Fourth Prince's pyre sputtered, and the Second Mother to the Revered Emperor made a low noise which gathered strength as it vibrated through her veiled body. She swayed even further; Third Mother Luswone echoed the restrained wail, grief too large to be contained even by matrons so tightly hemmed by etiquette and expectation. Thunder muttered, Heaven itself answering a mother's inarticulate prayer, and droplets spattered the wide white stone plain that had seen altogether too many royal pyres this summer.

Zan Fein, standing in an attitude of profound thought in his proper place, glanced at the sky. Another brushing of raindrops hissed against the paving, each one giving rise to a tiny spire of disturbed dust.

Garan Gamnae moaned and faltered, her knees giving; Princess Yala held her upright, casting a quick glance at the Emperor. He did not notice his sister's collapse; the new princess's attendants Su and Hansei hurried forward instead, as well as Lady Gonwa, her cane tapping authoritatively.

A vivid, deathly flash lit the funeral grounds, and Heaven's gongs spoke a moment later. Thunder shivered all of Zhaon-An from the buildings in their stony beds to the people seeking shelter or motionless in shock, hoping the celestial battle would pass them by.

The Emperor stayed for a long while, though his sister was half-carried from the sight of her mother's pyre to the Kaeje. His Second and Third Mothers' wails increased in intensity—perhaps mourning a first among equals, or perhaps two matrons who had endured childbirth's battle and the long siege of raising tiny dependents to adulthood making the only protest they could in the presence of an Emperor.

It was an open question, and when the cloudburst drenched the still-burning pyres, scattering charcoal and half-consumed wood as well as perhaps an iota or two of an earthly body, it was held to be a distinctly bad omen.

Though not, of course, in the Emperor's hearing.

A Pard of Folded Paper

How was I to know he was a pard made of folded paper?"
Garan Kurin longed to fix his uncle with a quelling stare,
but was trapped in a wet mourning robe. The trembling close-
servant responsible for stripping sodden cloth fussed with knotted lacings, and the Emperor of all Zhaon was also caught in the
position of wishing to administer a ringing smack to a cringing
peasant as well as rip pale silk from his own back like a jewelwing
escaping its cocoon. "Not only that, but I should have Mrong Banh
flogged. What kind of astrologer can't predict the rain?"

"Quite right upon both counts," Lord Yulehi said, soothingly,
on the other side of a screen painted with the sinuous, flowing
forms of the most royal beast of all, despite the fact that none in
Kurin's memory had ever claimed to lay their own eyes upon a
dragon. The man's satisfaction at being called to attend his imperial nephew was visible enough to be obscene; had he no discretion at all? "But gently, my illustrious nephew. The astrologer has
powerful patrons, and was your childhood tutor besides. A trip to
the dungeons might do him much good, but it will further unsettle
the court. We must be cautious."

*We, old man? You think yourself upon the Throne indeed; oh,
Mother had your measure.* And now his mother was gone, weeping

with pain as blood and sputum bubbled in her throat. Few physicians were left in the palace; most had discovered urgent business outside the complex.

Not only that, but Kurin had certain thoughts of a tiny bottle he had sent Sensheo to collect from the Yuin, and Sensheo's unwillingness to let the bauble out of his sleeve. Kurin had insisted, and had the wit to test what he gained from that contest—but had he been mistaken?

It would be galling indeed to be outplayed by *Sensheo*, of all people. But not even he would dare to strike at a queen, let alone the *First* Queen.

Would he?

"Your Majesty?" There was a faint creak as Lord Yulehi shifted behind his own screen; a pair of his close-servants had brought a fresh robe and accoutrements from his estate in the Noble Quarter. The servants were both familiar faces, and now Kurin had to think of what to do about Mother's remaining little spiders and the maids he had placed in her part of the Kaeje recently. Distributing them among other households might be useful—but it would be too overt. Giving them each a dowry and wishing them well was by far the better option, yet it irked him to see such already thoroughly trained material go to waste.

He must also think about Mother's steward. Some of the attendants would have to stay to keep a watch upon Gamnae, too, who had taken to her bed like a heroine in a silly novel.

There was little other sound except for the rain striking the Kaeje, a fresh breeze pouring through the half-open partition to yet another garden. The dripping mourning robe finally gave up its clasp upon Kurin's body; the cowering close-servant began chafing at Zhaon's royal limbs with a dry cloth. Even Kurin's topknot was draggled.

"Your Gracious Majesty?" Now Lord Yulehi sounded somewhat alarmed.

By Heaven and the Five Winds, let me think, you bag of wind. "What, uncle?" He took care to make the words as patient as possible, but an edge crept in.

"The mood of the court is quite unsettled. Perhaps an exorcism might be—"

"Oh, certainly." *Mother loved her exorcists; perhaps it is a family trait.* "That will make the Emperor seem strong, will it not? Have you other ideas, uncle mine?" Sarcasm was hardly princely; Kurin did not miss the close-servant's nervous glance. The boy, a Zhaon-An native of the artisan class, was wide-faced, slinking like a whipped cur, and usually far more deft than this, but perhaps the rain-chill was making his thick fingers clumsy.

At least he could not gossip, being struck mute by a childhood fever. Kurin could not even worry about his uncle's dependents at the moment.

"Your Majesty is undoubtedly correct," Lord Yulehi answered, sourly.

Kurin should have had a cortege of young noblemen to perform some of these duties, but war had taken many of them and few clans wished to send their sons to Garan Tamuron's true heir just yet. Besides, Father had—perhaps wisely—not insisted upon such creatures brought into closeness to the font of power and legitimacy. Instead, Tamuron had trusted the care of his body to bath-girls and petty servants.

It had not gained him anything, as far as Kurin could see. Nor had it gained any of those lowly creatures power or preferment. Even the bath-girl Father favored in his last years of life had fallen prey to jealousy.

Now Kurin must think of how to arrange the matter of Yona, too. A prized servant knowing too much of her mistress's affairs was a dangerous creature indeed. Still, she looked more ill than ever, sallow and cringing just like this close-servant, who almost dropped the drying-cloth when Kurin made an irritable movement.

In short order he was closed in a fresh dry mourning-robe and seated upon a low padded stool his father had often used while another close-servant fussed with his topknot. His uncle skirted the edge of the other screen, tugging at his sleeves, and not only did he sound sour, but his mouth was drawn tight instead of in its usual accommodating smile.

If it were Takyeo sitting in Kurin's position, would Binei Jinwon look so disapproving? Ah-Yeo would probably treat the man courteously, and even listen to his bleating.

More servants bustled into the small room, the heart of Zhaon's power crowding full of those tending to his needs. Kurin's hands were chafed into dry warmth and oiled afresh, a pair of favored slippers produced, a topknot-cage of pale shell chosen, and still Lord Yulehi lingered, watching.

"That will be all, uncle." Kurin restrained the urge to make a dismissive motion. "Unless there is business to conduct."

"Grief makes your tongue sharp, my illustrious nephew."

I am sharp in more ways than one. "I will grieve Mother all my life, uncle." That much was true—if only Gamwone had simply confined herself to her role once her eldest son had performed his duty, he would have made certain she wanted for nothing. He had *warned* her not to meddle, over and over again—but not only had she removed the bath-girl, but there was the little matter of assassins sent for Luswone, and the constant petty slights to Haesara, too.

Yona had faithfully reported each one.

He must attend to that dry stick soon, but in the kindest, quickest way possible. She had served her purpose, and Mother would need an attendant in whatever mansion Heaven saw fit to appoint Garan Tamuron's first queen.

"There is much uncertainty." Lord Yulehi had apparently decided to press further.

Kurin, his hand clasped by a trembling bath-girl attending to buffing the royal nails, fixed him with a distant stare. "Fear not, uncle. Zhaon is strong, and will weather this squall. We will be in Council this afternoon, once I have had tea. Notify your fellow ministers personally; I wish all present."

It was a deliberately calculated insult; one did not send a head minister during his half of the year to collect his fellows like a tutor trapping young nobles at a gaming-den. It was no matter, the man would swallow it, grateful for a signal that Lord Hanweo's ascendancy might be short-lived. Kurin's uncle flushed, but he also performed his bow, uttered a formulaic farewell, and disappeared, which was what Kurin desired.

If only he could shove the rest of them from the room, bar the door, and have a few uninterrupted moments of peace. There were kaburei attempting to hold vast oiled covers upon poles over the still-burning pyres; the rain was a solid silvery curtain past the porch where Father had often paced, counting his kombin.

A flicker of motion was simply falling water instead of Takyeo's shade imitating their father, and Kurin squeezed his eyes shut briefly, taking what privacy he could find as hands pampered his flesh, combed his hair, worked hopefully unadulterated oil between his fingers, and tugged at his mourning robe.

He should not be seeing such things, but lately, there was motion in his peripheral vision anywhere in the Palace he went. And now that Mother was gone...

Kurin dispelled that thought with a shudder, and the close-servants, not to mention the two bath-girls, froze. He gave the short, irritable command for them to continue, and found himself thinking perhaps he should have let Takyeo take this burden after all.

At least, for a short while. But what was done could not be *undone*, and he was Zhaon's ruler now.

"Where is my kombin?" he said, and there was a scurry as underlings sought to find it.

Heaven
Displeased

The first rain of autumn had arrived with a theater-flower's sense of the dramatic, and the Fifth Prince of Zhaon, for one, thought it a fine jest. Of course he could not say as much, but the amusement was a warm glow inside his chest, warring uneasily with the unpleasant fact that his elder brother was irretrievably gone.

No matter how many times one wished for the advent of a certain absence, it was still a shock. Even a peasant with a rotten tooth yanked from his maw still tongued the hole, relieved of pain but also missing something that had, after all, been with him since birth, lingering under the gums.

Pale mourning was uncomfortable, and he was spending far too long in it lately. Jatajatas to keep his feet from the wet were also a minor annoyance to his aching ankles, and so was his heavily oiled rainbell dripping silver strings of downpour before he set it aside upon the slice of Kaeje porch reserved for such items during the damp season. One other rainbell lay there, its throat open to the wind and its handle-strap around a handy protrusion; it belonged to the man regarding him with a sour expression and a fresh mourning-robe nonetheless daubed with drops near the hem.

"Chief Minister." Sensheo bowed a trifle more deeply than

Lord Yulehi's rank demanded, but it cost him nothing to give the fellow a little thrill. "May I offer my profound condolences once again."

"You are kind to do so, Fifth Prince, especially amid your own grief." Lord Yulehi's bow was likewise calibrated to express profound respect. There was a gleam far back in his dark gaze, of course; with the First Queen gone he rested solely for support upon his regal nephew's whim. He had clients, of course—Yulehi was a rich province indeed, and he had not hesitated to fill his clan's coffers and dispense some largesse where necessary—but there was no shortage of other noble clans ready to see him brought down a measuring-mark or two, and also to rob the new Emperor of some fraction of family support.

"My brother was a peerless scholar," Sensheo allowed. It was no trouble at all to feign some small sadness. "I fear the shock will overturn my mother; he was her favorite."

"I am surprised," Lord Yulehi observed, his gaze shifting over Sensheo's shoulder. Waiting for other ministers, perhaps, and weighing how expensive the Fifth Prince's support was likely to be. "But mothers are partial, are they not? They cannot see any flaws in their beloved children."

"Oh, *they see what they wish to find,*" Sensheo quoted, though he was sure a man with more than a few cupfuls of merchant blood mixed with whatever nobility a cadet branch of the current Yulehi could claim had not the requisite education to place the allusion. Still, if he did, it would be a pleasing enough compliment. "A man must love his mother anyway, Lord Yulehi. So the sages say." The rain intensified, slapping long-thirsty earth. The peasants would be alternately cursing the downpour and thanking Heaven for it; they were confused creatures at best.

"Ah, you are scholarly too." The Chief Minister's tone was cautious, but not overly so, and had he been against any sort of alliance at all he might have scolded even a prince for a slightly unfilial remark. "We must be glad of what has been spared to us, under Heaven."

In other words, there were sons of Garan still alive. Sensheo nodded as if the observation was profound. "Indeed we must."

Side by side upon the porch for some few moments, the prince and Chief Minister watched a solid wall of rain shimmer like the sides of muscular fish in a fast-moving mountain stream. Lightning flashed, and the attendant gongs of the celestial kingdom reverberated over Zhaon's heart.

"The physicians said what was necessary," the Chief Minister said, finally, his voice barely audible over falling water and clattering sky-pans. The dust would return; this was simply a raised banner for autumn's storms, not the entire army. "That Kihon fellow was reluctant, but ingots won the rest."

"Something should be done about that shabby fellow," Sensheo agreed. A hot burst of satisfaction filled him, from liver to heart. Kurin's uncle had made the first move. "But not yet; it will look very bad."

"How could it look worse?" Lord Yulehi, for all he was a merchant aping his betters, had a point. "Four attempts to light your brother's pyre, and my nephew's grieving has robbed him of filial feeling for his remaining kin."

It was his mother; do you expect him to like you better? But Sensheo made a soft sound of agreement, as if he were an ancient uncle too, or as if he considered Makar a small price to pay for Kurin's continued reign, considering. "We must protect him from himself."

"Yes." Lord Yulehi was silent for a long while, and Sensheo forced himself to *wait*.

Hadn't Makar always said that was his largest flaw, the inability to sit still? Maki should be proud; he'd irritated Kurin and been sent to his death, all his fine accomplishments rotting under the Horde's filthy barbarian hooves.

It was very sad, of course. It also meant a junior brother had a chance to prove his worth to an ailing mother, and wouldn't she be glad she had him soon?

"Are you sleeping well, Fifth Prince?" the minister asked, all sudden solicitousness.

Sensheo's opposite thumb caressed the archer's ring of heavy horn. "The weather is quite unsettled," he allowed. There would never be an appropriate—or wise—time to tell anyone of his dreams, a twisted, fire-blackened shade rising under a cavalcade of hoofbeats and pointing an accusing finger at a little brother.

Are you happy now, Sensen?

"Zhaon is suffering much," the Chief Minister murmured in return. "The reports of illness in the provinces have not abated, either...do you think, perhaps, that Heaven is displeased?"

Another wave of fierce, hot joy bloomed in Sensheo's middle. It was almost the same feeling as when a sought-after courtesan surrendered—the most pleasant part of a pursuit, indeed. Far better than even the languor afterward, and certainly nicer than tidying up once she became importunate or a new star appeared in the Theater District's firmament.

Garan Sensheo had decided long ago it was not quite so much having what one wanted as hunting it that mattered. Now was the moment for a thoughtful pause, so he produced a fan from his sleeve, opened it with a flick, and set it to work moving slowly back and forth, pushing a cargo of damp-laden air to his face. No sweat would evaporate while the rain was this warm, but come evening there might be a breath or two of cooler air to be found somewhere.

"I do not know what to think," he finally allowed, in his imitation of Makar's most cautious tone. "But it certainly seems so, does it not? I am quite worried, Chief Minister." His inflection was as honorific as possible, given their respective stations.

"As am I, Fifth Prince." The Yulehi uncle could not be any more painfully obsequious. "You are right; we must save my nephew from himself."

A rancid laugh rose in Sensheo's throat; he longed to ask just how Lord Yulehi thought such a feat could be accomplished. Instead, he let his fan speak, halting for just a moment as he turned his chin and met the older man's gaze. Much could be accomplished with the eyes alone—even courtesans knew as much, and Sensheo decided he would visit his current favorite very soon.

Victories should be celebrated, and though his dreams were increasingly bad of late, they were merely a product of uncertain times. Nightmares would dissipate once he reached a certain summit, he was sure.

It was yet another reason to continue the climb.

SACRIFICE

In the dialect of his youth the Tabrak were oft called *metu-ghi*, the insects periodically filling sky and earth with their hunger before falling in chitinous droves to be plowed into denuded fields, their greed killing them en masse as farmers with torches could not hope to. The soil afterward was held to be richer for their corpses, though few survived to reap a harvest from it.

"No doubt they ran north, carrying our numbers and dispositions with them." Etu rubbed at his chin; his tunic and leggings were ash-stained and his left forearm bore a nasty burn wrapped with grease and a stained bandage. "At least we are free of their empty gestures."

Aro Ba Wistis surveyed the Horde spread below this prominent hilltop; this part of what the Horde called *the clay peoples' country* lay under a thin veil of smoke from the burning to the south. Only a portion of the forest's vastness was aflame; even the Horde could not destroy such a massive beast.

Besides, they were wary among its columns and underbrush. No few reported glimpsing strange things in its depths, though any shade was welcome in summer heat.

The wind had shifted, blowing the scent of smoke back along Tabrak's trail; Etu's master seemed almost pettily glad the two northern envoys had disappeared without a trace. Perhaps one or two of his stirrup-holders had feared their lord was close to being seduced by the pair, or did not like the way the grey-eyed lordling bowed.

Etu could have told the stirrup-holders not to fear, but it suited his purposes to let them mutter at the son of Wistis's policies.

It suited them very well indeed.

Four days of running battle, surrounding an army amid the choking breath of the Burning One's attention, and while there had been losses—Jardik, Nalu Ba Sentsov, a whole coffle of Bird People scun perishing where they had been chained—the Horde was still terrible and strong. Now they were moving again, slow day-jogs north as they stripped the countryside of anything edible or valuable. The farmsteads here were scattered but each easily taken, and their stacks of dry straw holding the tiny starch-berries they lived upon made wonderful offerings when set alight. Their wailing helped the sacrifice reach the Burning One's ears, and if the god of the Horde was not fully propitiated, he certainly gave every indication of being at least halfway there.

He had almost forgotten the starch-berries were named *rai*. The bright sword of hate in Etu's vitals was polished afresh each day, as it had been since his childhood. Even the weight of the collar upon his throat gave it fuel.

The Horde's burning god was pleased with any holocaust as long as the flame was bright, and Etu was preparing a sacrifice of his own.

"Let them," Aro Ba Wistis said, leaning forward to stroke his great bay stallion's neck. The beast with a white blaze upon his face and two white hocks was canny, war-trained, and ill-tempered; the Horde's leader often remarked it was a joy to ride such a cousin. "They will be brought under our spurs in due time."

Etu was silent for a long moment. He was allowed a mount when it suited his master, despite no scun being worthy of such a gift; were he to jog behind Aro's horse he might be breathless or worse when the leader of the Horde needed counsel. The rawbone nag he straddled was at the very edge of permissibility for one wearing the collar. He ran a fingertip underneath the leather's edge, glancing at the soot blackening his hand when pulled away. His mouth tightened. What he would not give for a bath, and some food that wasn't smoke-charred—but ever since he had been taken from his family he was scun, and the Horde's language and ways crept into his skin and bone and breath. "My lord intends to take Zunnan before winter."

It was an easy guess, and Etu had prepared the ground for such a desire for many summers. It did not take much. A feeding of a cruel lord's pride here, a subtle balking of his purposes there, proving what the son of Wistis thought was loyalty with information gleaned from other scun, setting these pale bastards at each other further down in the ranks…yes, he had worked assiduously. Even their homeland had aided him. The Great Grass Sea had slowly grown too crowded for the Horde over the last few generations.

Of course, left to their own devices, they could perhaps eke out a living among the Bird People for a long while.

Too long. Etu was not young anymore, and his plans were so close to fruition he could almost taste the finished dish.

"I do." Aro glanced north; the haze was so bad any rain could not be seen. As long as the ground remained somewhat firm the king of Tabrak was sanguine; the army they had just demolished had died relatively hard for a collection of sedentary scun as far as he was concerned. Was he thinking one of the clay people guessed his intent and sought to delay him? Or that perhaps the two northern envoys had warned their fellows in some fashion?

It mattered little. Etu hoped the Khir envoys were well on their way, safe from the depredations of this collection of violent, vile barbarians.

"Zunnan's walls are much thicker than the others. And they have the new thunder-tubes." Etu's tone was speculative, not cringing, he had many summers and winters to perfect it. He studied Aro's profile thoughtfully, outwardly as a scun must seek to anticipate a lord's desire but with a much different inward feeling. "Tikris's scun are ill with the swellings; he does not leave his tent. Some of the First Horse are sacrificing fowl; Niko's wife bears the red marks. He is wroth. The Second Horse demanded more fodder of the Third; Aejir told Hanus to bring his blade should he covet more of a free man and brother."

"They are children." Aro shook his head; a whiff of ripe long-unwashed scent rose from his furred tunic. The Horde did not bathe; sweat crack-glazed the blue streaking his face, and his high-crested hair was stiff at the roots but wore into softness farther up. A long battle made for wilting of both horse and limb, but they had still indisputably won. "We must take Zunnan; the survival of the Horde depends upon it. So we will."

If you take it, you may well choke upon it. "Yes, my lord." Etu returned to scanning what could be seen of the smoke-drifting horizon. The bleeding of this collection of howling, stinking bastards was proceeding apace. Convincing his master to begin from the south was succeeding better than he had ever dreamed; Aro thought he was wiser than all his forefathers. Certainly he was far more arrogant than even that collection of dirty horsefuckers. "The Fifth Horse was shattered. Shall they join the Fourth?"

"No. We will hold gauntlets for the scun after travel for seven days. Those who survive will ride; those who do not, will not eat." It was a time-honored tradition in the Horde, a way for the scun to lift themselves to freedom—but only if their masters did not object at the chance.

Some, like Etu himself, were too valuable to be allowed a horse and hookblade. He did not even bother to think of winning his freedom that way.

He longed to remove the collar, but even more than that, he longed for *vengeance*, and he would take it upon this whole menagerie.

But for now the man they called *Etu* was a faithful scun, and acting the part was disturbingly easy, as it had been for many a summer. "No new horses." He turned to the next item needing his lord's attention. Oh, it was fairly easy to set out a meal this lordly barbarian would eat; even shit would stir the Horde's appetite if prepared in the right fashion. "Oxen, though. They may pull carts of tribute and spoil." He already knew the son of Wistis would not like the idea.

"No. We travel lightly, and will take the best of the clay people's nags. For the rest of the livestock, sacrifice what will please the Burning One, and turn the others loose. If the clay people are chasing their oxen they are not hiding to take unwary riders." His tone suggested that if one of his followers was unwary, he was a liability, and should be pruned. There was no room for weakness among the Tabrak.

Etu nodded, concealing his glee. It had become almost comically easy to predict his master's decisions. Of course, the longer the Horde lingered in these lands, the further all possibilities would narrow.

Now came seeding more dissension—laying an egg between two snakes, as his mother used to say. "Jasov Ba Jasov wishes to send you his middle daughter." She was considered a winning child among the barbarians, despite stinking like all the rest of them and with her hair like dried yellow grass stacked in greasy braids upon a head too large and a neck too scrawny for such a burden.

"He may keep her. I must not be weighed down."

Etu's face was a placid mask, but a savage delight bit at his vitals next to the hate-sword. He could not remember his mother's face, but he remembered some few of her sayings in a dialect that now did not exist, for the Horde had erased their small settlement at the edge of the waste so many years ago. "My lord, he may challenge you."

Aro stiffened, and the bay lifted his head, sensing his rider's tension. "Do you think so?"

"He has Aejir's support, and Niko and Krilov of the First Horse's as well. They have given each other many mares these past moons." Etu was very careful not to let disdain creep into the words. These barbarians killed each other over any slight; they had no shame or true honor. Not that he was any better—he had worn the collar for many years before a plan had occurred to him, simple and devastating, upon the night the Horde celebrated the ascension of a son of Wistis to the first stirrup.

Feeding that child carefully—nurturing pride, aiding his pettiness, abetting his rise—had produced *this*. Etu had not been sure Aro would listen to the plan, but in the end, the barbarian had considered it his own idea.

And that was almost, *almost* the best revenge of all.

"Should he be dealt with?" Aro's gaze was uncomfortably piercing, but it was focused on the northern horizon as if he could see Zunnan shimmering there, that fabled city of riches.

Etu knew his master did not really wish a reply; he was simply thinking aloud as one could do before a mute beast or a scun. To Aro Ba Wistis, Etu was simply a *thing*, possessing slightly less importance than the cousins he rode into battle or gifted his stirrup-holders to keep his primacy and position.

But even an ox could crush its tormentor, if it was patient enough. If it waited for the proper moment.

The king of the Horde finished his ruminations and gathered his reins. "What else, my faithful Etu? I should give you a mate; you would make many fine scun scribes for me."

Loathing filled him to the brim, but Etu ducked his head as if pleased, his chin touching the filthy leathern collar. Applied when wet, it shrank to a choking fit, and some scun even decorated theirs, as if it were not a deep, killing shame to wear such a thing. "My lord is kind to a scun," he said softly, and hoped the hatred was not leaking from his eyes. The Tabrak had a word for mutinous possessions; it was close to their term for disembowelment, which was the penalty for rising against a mounted man.

"Nonsense, you deserve it. I shall think upon the matter more." The son of Wistis kneed the bay into a walk down the rocky hill, and the stallion's tail flicked. "Come, we shall rejoin the Horde."

And Etu—whose name as a child had been Turong Lai, and would be again once he finished the task he had set himself—persuaded his nag to follow at a slow walk, tasting his own bitter fury.

But not for long.

BLOOD BOILS
WITHIN ME

The sky's tears fell in silver strings all afternoon; Yala had rarely been so happy to hear rain. There was even a breath or two of cool breeze as the sun sank, a presage of autumn. Dinner was a very quiet affair, Su Junha and Hansei Liyue discussing several novels and which plays they were likely to attend at the theater once the Second Princess's mourning was done. There were other court ladies eager to place their daughters, nieces, or cousins in a princely household, but the dance of doing so was hemmed by much etiquette and many indirect compliments.

Far more worrying was the attempt to spread the First Mother's household servants among the surviving princes' dependents. Both Steward Keh and Lady Kue gave the notion short shrift, the former muttering something about *little spiders* and Lady Kue shaking her head, her Shan-style braids looped over her ears swinging slightly. *I would rather take in a collection of venomous rodents*, that lady said, with quite uncharacteristic vehemence.

Yala was content to follow their advice, but parrying a direct gift from the Emperor, should he choose to force the matter, was a troubling prospect.

The conversation at the dinner table did not touch upon the royal pyres, though Su Junha inquired whether her patroness thought the Sixth Prince would welcome a letter of condolence, perhaps with a quotation from the *Green Book*, which held much upon the subject of mourning.

Garan Takyeo had been reading that text before his misfortune; Yala's short thoughtful pause was taken as a gentle caution, and Junha looked rather chastened before her patroness remarked that it seemed a very kindly idea, so long as the quotation was chosen with care. Junha then very prettily asked for her patroness to suggest one, and the resultant conversation, with Liyuc's ardent help, finished the meal nicely indeed.

The evening round of letters flew between houses in the Noble Quarter, and Yala's preferred place for answering them was the library, still smelling faintly of dust but now full of the good green fragrance of rain. Several of the scrollcases and spines upon the dark wooden shelves were familiar from the Jonwa; the young, dying Emperor had been most specific that not even a scrap of paper was to be left in the palace for his enemies, and Takshin had scrupulously carried out his wishes.

There was much to admire in her husband, Yala told herself again as she drew her wet brush over the inkstone. Kai's missive was anonymous ash in a brazier, even its wax seal charred into invisibility. She considered the half-finished letter, thinking over her next few character choices; Lady Gonwa's subtle offer of her young cousin Eulin for placement within Yala's household must not be accepted quickly nor absolutely refused.

After all, Eulin had attended the Crown Princess well enough, but Yala had not forgotten how her elder reclaimed the girl after Mahara's pyre. Still, it was a matron's duty to keep younger kin from dangerous alliances, much as it was a patroness's, and Yala could not afford to displease Lady Gonwa.

She was not required to bow immediately, though.

The flame in the glass lamp upon her desk wavered slightly; she glanced at the sliding door to the verandah, the garden beyond finishing its soaked, murmuring descent into twilight. She set her brush aside and stood, as if temporarily weary of writing; her right hand dropped to her side, her fingers tingling.

"Hist," a familiar voice said in the gloom outside. There was a small creak as he shifted upon the verandah's wooden floor. "'Tis only me, my lady; do not call out, I should not be here."

That is a severe understatement. "Sixth Prince." She glanced at the hall partition, firmly shut and on the other side of the room as well; then she glided for the porch. Her shadow distorted over bookshelves and a very fine Anwei woven rug; her heart pounded in her wrists and behind her knees. "How, under Heaven—"

"Kurin doesn't like me leaping the palace walls, but I don't care. Besides, Father let me." Jin's lean shadow detached from a deeper pool of gloom to her right; the gleam of his eyes and teeth were the only things giving him away. Not only had he left the palace, but he had somehow penetrated his elder brother's house with apparently little trouble. It was good that he was an ally; he would make a difficult foe indeed. "I can't drink with the Golden anymore, though."

"I am sorry you must forego that pleasure, but your visit is a pleasant surprise." She refrained from pointing out not drinking with palace soldiers was probably a blessing, tucking her shaking hands into her sleeves. Her *yue* could remain in its sheath; she had even been thinking of practicing tonight, once the rest of the household was safely abed. "But you would not come merely to say hello and leave like Dhao Kailung. What has happened?"

"Nothing. Well, nothing *new*." Still, the youngest prince sounded uncertain. "May we speak, Princess Yala?"

"I hardly think anyone can hear us." She leaned against the sliding door, bracing her shoulder against heavy dark wood. "You have chosen your time well, but when the next watch is called my kaburei will come to put me to bed or bring some jaelo tea."

"We have some few moments, then." His shoulders hunched uneasily; he was not in pale mourning, which said his errand was urgent indeed. "I do not know quite what to say. You may be angry with me."

"Tell me what has happened, and we shall see." The oppressive heat was returning under cover of darkness, and if Jin could reach the inner courtyard of her own home, what could halt a follower of the Shadowed Path from doing the same? At least Takshin had left her *yue* in her hands; it was another reason to fix her traitorous heart more firmly upon her husband.

Tossing in her bed at night, though, Yala could not help herself from thinking upon something, some*one* else entirely.

"I wasn't looking for them," Jin said hurriedly, the words tumbling excitedly over each other. "I wasn't spying or sneaking, I swear. I was in Banh's tower and there was a windowsill—"

Yala held up a hand. "Quietly, Prince Jin. Please."

"I found papers," he continued, in a heated but thankfully much more sedate whisper. "I don't know what they mean and you might hate me for it, but...here." And he proffered a packet of waxed paper, the string holding it tied in a complex knot. "I think they're Takshin's."

Ah. "He lived in the Old Tower before the Crown Prince...ah, before your eldest brother asked him to move into the Jonwa." It stood to reason her husband would leave some things he prized there. "But, Sixth Prince—"

"One of them is from Kurin." Jin almost spat the words, audibly relieved to share a heavy burden. "And, sister-in-law, it concerns *you.*"

Yala's breath caught. "Concerns me?" Her heart, wiser than her head-meat, continued its frantic throb; she could feel her pulse even in her underarms. Sweat greased her all over, but that was nothing new, here in Zhaon. "In what manner?"

"You should...look, the knot is easy to untie. There are ledger-notes too, written in Khir. I cannot read them but you..." Jin all but hopped from foot to foot. "I do not know if I have done well, sister-in-law. I have nobody to ask except perhaps Gamnae, and she is abed with grief."

Or something close to it. Yala weighed the packet. "Will you come in? You may listen at the hall door so we are not surprised."

"I'm wearing *shoes.*" He sounded scandalized, and she did not mean to laugh but could not help herself, catching the sound upon the back of her fingers as she carried her burden to the desk. The knot was indeed complex but not overly so, and she folded the bundle's outside layers back.

Jin stepped inside despite being shod. He ghosted across the library, moving as cautious as a granary feline and casting many a glance at Yala, whose hands had grown very cold despite summer's reasserting its dusty primacy outside.

She suspected it would be even more difficult to sleep tonight than usual.

Zhe Har wrote that the world could change in the blink of an eye, between one character in a letter and the next, even in the space between two breaths or heart-thumps. It changed as she scanned the marriage endorsement from Garan Kurin to Garan Suon-ei Takshin, dated some few days before their eldest brother's death.

Yala did not gasp, nor did she stagger. She laid the heavy, expensive paper aside, and eyed the remainders. Zhe Har was twice proved correct, and at the second blow she did sway, her head-meat refusing to credit what her eyes reported, like a general disbelieving a courier's report.

No. It cannot be.

"Princess? Sister?" Jin's whisper turned quite alarmed.

Yala returned to herself, sweat-drenched, her hands flat upon the desktop and the brushes in their rack swaying gently as her trembling communicated itself through wood, paper, inkstone, and the lamp's wavering flame. *No. Please, no.*

It was no use. She could not un-see. It flashed through her like the afternoon's lightning, and the thunder afterward was slow in coming.

Takshin was thorough, and he could not have expected his eldest brother to live. He had prepared his trap, and she had been lured—oh, very well indeed. She could even forgive him that, for he...he *valued* her.

But it was the notes in Khir which stole her breath, because she recognized the hand upon them.

How could she not?

"My lady?" Jin was at her shoulder instead of the door. "Sit. You are pale, I shall...shall I call for tea? Or—"

"No," Yala managed, through numb lips. *Calling for tea, when you are not supposed to be here? Really, you are so very young.* "I am merely...it is a shock."

"I am sorry." And he was, transparently so, his eyes wide and almost luminous, his bottom lip trembling before his mouth firmed. "I did not think it would—listen, I shall return them."

For the love of Heaven, simply give me a moment to think. Her irritation crested; a lifetime's worth of training in throttling that particular humor stood her in good stead. Yala shook her head, her hairpin's bead-string swinging, and a bright thin blade turned in her chest. Her heart was pierced, all the more painfully because the wound was invisible.

How could he? How could *he*, of all the men in Zhaon, Shan, Khir itself, do this? And then Takshin, keeping it from her when he *swore*...

"Yala?" Jin touched her elbow, and the urge to draw her *yue* and strike sent another fierce shiver through her.

"Let me *think*," she hissed, and realized she had spoken in Khir. She swallowed sour rage, attempted to calm her breathing, and repeated it in Zhaon, clear and low. "Let me think, Jin. Please. I must, for this is very dangerous."

"Then I found something useful." He gazed anxiously at her profile. "At last."

"How could he?" Yala could not halt the words, Khir rubbing through Zhaon, both languages bitter upon her tongue. "How *could* he?"

"Takshin means well." The young prince scratched at his cheek; he was sweating too, and his eyes were a frightened feline's. "But the papers in Khir—I did not think he knew how to write in that tongue?"

"They are not his," she said, and the realization was an icy bath amid summer's muggy broil. "The endorsement is...well, no doubt he has an explanation." *But not one I would care to hear, if I were honest. Still, I am his wife now.*

Garan Takshin was owed her loyalty. Yet he had told her their marriage was one of Garan Takyeo's deathbed arrangements.

In the end, her marriage was a private matter. The sheets in Khir were otherwise.

The hand upon them was utterly familiar and damning; she read again, to make certain there could be no doubt. It had rained that terrible day in Zhaon-An's Great Market, too, and Sixth Prince Jin had been there. Was Heaven itself taking pity upon a wayward woman who had failed to protect her princess, her best of friends, by showing her the truth once she could no longer perform her duty of striking at her princess's murderer?

For Ashani Daoyan, Mahara's half-brother, was riding north, safe with four Khir lords. And it was his particular handwriting upon the papers, a hand she knew as well as her own—how many letters had they written each other, before and after her departure? She had a bundle of his missives sent from Khir, carefully wrapped and hidden among her dresses—she had to find a better place. Or burn them.

My lady Komor Yala, you have been gone for thirteen days, and my blood boils within me.

Now Yala knew what boiling truly was.

When they had sought to kidnap her princess and taken Yala instead, they spoke of bringing her to one they called *the Big Man.* Who else could it be? There, black ink upon ledger paper, were the accounts. Silver and copper ingots paid, a contract for the removal of a thorn—except the Khir characters used held darker double meanings. Yala had heard rumors of such things even in Hai Komori's high dark halls, though a noblewoman of Khir was not supposed to know politics even existed outside the narrow confines of making a good marriage. Let alone assassins.

In Zhaon, they discussed such things openly over tea. And now the puzzle made sense. The blindfold was taken from her; like Zhe Har the Archer, she could see which bolts had pierced the target.

Ihenhua, bought in the market and signed for with a careless set of characters, *nah-ha-ri-khi*.

His mother's clan-name. Had he smiled while he brushed it? A grand jest, indeed. And Garan Takshin had the answer to all her questions before him; could he truly not read Khir?

What did he know? What did he merely *suspect*?

It did not matter, after all.

Oh, Daoyan. No. Please, let it not be true.

"Takshin always has a reason," Jin said, tentatively. "You have gone quite pale. What is it, sister? Tell me."

Think, Yala. You must think.

"You must return these," she said, heavily. Her head-meat was working now, but fitfully, like a shivering, much-beaten horse. "Take them back, place them exactly where they were hidden. I must ask you to swear—to *swear* to me, Sixth Prince Garan Jin, that you will say nothing of this to anyone. Ever."

"I told nobody of seeing you and Shin when you rode for Kai." His young face was grave. "Is it very bad? Is it about…the princess? Your princess?"

"Indeed it is. Sixth Prince, please. Swear to me you will say nothing of this, ever, to anyone. Not to the Second Princess, not to your mother, not to my husband." *Husband*, how bitter the word was. She hated its sound in Zhaon. "Please. I will ask you for nothing else so long as I live, but *please*. I beg of you, swear this to me."

"You needn't beg." He drew himself up, all gangly grace and seriousness, then performed a very courtly bow indeed. "I shall tell no one, ever. You may rely upon me, sister. I know how to keep a secret."

So do I. Yala essayed a fragile, trembling smile. "You must go. Do not run about at night; stay with your mother. She needs you."

"But I found something, didn't I? Tell me, what else can I do?" He caught her sleeve between two fingers, heavy unbleached silk to mourn her mother-in-law wrinkling; she would not have to wear it much longer. "There must be something."

"You must care for yourself, Sixth Prince, and for your mother."

Yala's hands took to straightening the papers with no direction from the rest of her. She could not tie the string in its former fashion without some thought, but she could perform an embroidery-knot, and she did quickly. "Court is very dangerous right now."

His gaze met hers, and Garan Komor-a Yala hoped her fear was not as plainly visible as his.

"Takshin will return," Jin said, finally. "Won't he?"

"He might." A good wife would pray for his return, but Yala's head felt too light for her neck, and her entire body was cold despite the promise of baking later. Summer's back was not yet broken; the afternoon rain was merely a promise. A distant noise startled both of them; her hip struck the desk and the brushes swayed again. So did the lamp-flame; they called these lamps *halu*, a strange word. "There is the watch-gong. You must go. A thousand thanks for this, Garan Jin; I am your handmaiden until my death."

"Do not say such things." He let go of her sleeve reluctantly, gathering up the packet. It made a slight forlorn rustle, like the skirt of a fleeing woman. "If anything happens, sister, come to me. I will protect you."

He sounded as if he thought protection possible. Yala tried another smile. "You are the best of your brothers," she murmured. *If you only knew how much I mean that.* "Go, so I do not worry for you."

He cast two long looks over his shoulder, but finally vanished into the garden's full, wet darkness. Not even damp footprints remained upon the library floor; he was utterly gone. Yala listened, but heard no sound of him clambering walls or running across rooftops. Gossip said any weapon he held revealed its secrets to him in a whisper, and she hoped it was true.

She suspected he would need that skill before long; Garan Kurin did not have too many brothers left.

It was faint comfort that Takshin's "wolf-sense" had been correct—unless that were a lie he had told to cover his certainty. Zhaon had not killed her princess after all. The blame lay elsewhere, and Yala had sent the assassin to safety. There was nothing she could do after all, and she stood amid the ashes of her honor and all her hopes for a long while before a tentative brushing in the hallway broke her reverie.

It was faithful Anh, coming to put her mistress to bed like an errant child, and Yala had to arrange both her sleeves and her expression. The first was easy.

The last? Not so much.

CHILD'S PLAY

None would think it strange that she left the Palace; Yona often did so upon some personal errand or another for her mistress. The bundle upon her back was a little odd, for the Palace laundry could easily handle whatever a servant might wear. Still, she was a familiar face, and so all but invisible; also, her patroness was gone, and it was unlikely any other household in the complex would take the dry stick Garan Gamwone had used as both sudo and carpet-beater.

The Second Princess would now move to Garan Haesara's household in the Kaeje, as was proper and fitting for an unmarried girl; the Emperor had not called for Yona to present herself after her last report upon his mother's illness. Of course that august being had little time for a single servant, but Yona was fully aware that she was a loose thread, and it would be somewhat injurious to his reign were her silence not assured. The two of them had grown up in the same household; she knew buying her quiet was not nearly as effective as guaranteeing it by other methods.

Zhaon-An swallowed her and the hot, constant coal burning behind her breastbone. She still could not eat much beyond polished rai, the blander the better, and even that was difficult. No physician had a cure; perhaps her humors were unbalanced, or perhaps living under the weight of servitude had malformed her inner organs.

It didn't matter. She had served, her beautiful, hateful mistress was dead, and Yona was...free? Was that the word?

It did not seem so. Exchanging one yoke for another was the best she could hope for.

Dusk turned into a steaming dark night, stinking puddles gathered in the gutters alongside paved streets. She knew her route, keeping her gaze downcast as she threaded through an indifferent crowd. A noblewoman, or even a merchant's wife or daughter in bright clothing, might have been accosted. One more elderly drab, though, passed invisibly, working her way toward the fringes of the Yuin.

Of all the slices of the greatest city of the Middle World, the Left Market was the best place to hide.

Though Yona had been thrifty all her life, she had never managed to accumulate enough to cushion her old age; Garan Gamwone had never believed in liberality unless it was to show other nobles her own status. Now, though, her most trusted servant was promised a pension.

That it was payment for being held in reserve like a chess-piece by another prince did not overly trouble her. In any case, Yona thought as her worn jatajatas—hardly deserving the name, their slats were ground down by many years of hurrying over paving, cobblestone, or wooden way upon her mistress's behalf—made their soft authoritative sounds amid the crowd, many of whom were wearing similar footwear to keep their hems free of moisture. Some lucky few even carried oiled rainbells, though there was little chance of another downpour until the next afternoon and perhaps not even then.

The dry time of Zhaon was a dust-snake with a strong spine; it would not be broken all at once. Sometimes even an ox-hoof required two blows in order to be effective.

Sellers in street carts chanted their wares, their voices falling into evening babble as the last bits of business were conducted, artisans hurrying home after a long day's work or lounging on the doorsteps of their shops and smoking long-barrelled pipes as they watched the world pass by, children fractious before dinner darting here, there, and everywhere or wrapped and wailing upon their mother's backs; the crowd held palanquin bearers, too, shouting in unison as they carried their cargo of noblewoman or lord too indolent to ride. Sesahma and other oils bubbled, wafting the smell of cooking along the thoroughfare; Yona's nose twitched even as her chest was burning. The bright blood in her sputum each morning no longer worried her; she had adapted to worse.

Still, her arms and legs were leaden by the time she hurried through a malodorous, crooked alley; her new patron's directions had been clear and explicit. There was the sign of the hare under a half-sun, swinging upon leather hinges over an inn-door; she counted three more doors and turned right.

Just as she had been told, a tenement was squeezed between a blacksmith's shop and a rollicking teahouse, the latter's slatted windows all flung wide to take advantage of any cool breath the afternoon's downpour could provide. The smell of cooked meat, fried rai, simmering vegetables, and a breath of sohju made her mouth water afresh, though any morsel of such things would tear her innards to shreds. Even her stool was blackened, and daily straining in the privy was one more indignity.

The tenement's door-woman, tugging at her tunic-sleeves, peered at the small wooden chit Yona produced, nodding her iron-grey head and settling back upon her stool.

The stairs were lit only by mirrorlight dependent upon the absent sun, navigated more by touch than sight; the close fug of almost-poverty swallowed her and her bundle whole. He wanted to meet her away from prying eyes, of course; still, this could be an illustration of what she risked if she displeased him.

Or if she allowed certain secrets to slip from their home in her head-meat before their proper time.

Yona slipped into a long hallway lit by a flickering halu lamp, cunningly designed to keep this entire tinderbox from catching alight if it tipped from its single-nail perch upon the thin lathe-and-plaster wall. There was a door with the correct character painted upon it, matching the chit; Yona let out a soft sigh and tested the latch.

It gave easily; she leaned against the hall wall for a moment, her breath coming harshly. At least in the Palace all the stairwells were lit—but that simply meant the shitstains were easier to see. Even if she ended her days in a ramshackle building such as this, or a hut upon the edge of the city's farm-fields, at least she would clean no night-pots but her own ever again.

Yona stepped into the room, shifting her bundle upon her thin back. The small space held a pallet in one corner, the edge of a terracotta pot visible under its sagging side, and a rickety table with a single candle guttering in a brass holder. Fitful light played over the bare walls; it looked like a bolt-hole, and she was glad of it.

Although tinier than a Palace closet, the room was nevertheless too large for the candle's gleam, and deep shadow lingered in its corners. Yona swept the thin wooden door closed, and some soft intrinsic sense—maybe that of a hunted animal, maybe only that of a creature used to others breathing nearby—warned her a bare moment before the man melded out of the dark in the angle hidden by the door's opening.

A muscular forearm snaked about her throat; she was lifted from her feet. Her bundle, mashed against her attacker's chest, bent Yona's spine in a backward curve, and her rib cage was full of hot molten agony. She kicked and clawed, but he braced himself against the door and tightened his grip, increment by increment.

One jatajata flew free, skittering across the ill-swept floor and vanishing under the cot. Her fingernails attempted to dig bloody furrows in a silk-covered arm, and one splintered as she scratched wildly.

It did not take very long. The First Queen's stick to beat carpets with sagged, a sharp stink rising as sphincters loosened for the last time. Tiny creaking sounds from her throat were muffled by silk, and her attacker let out a short, satisfied sigh as her struggles finally ceased.

"Poor thing," Garan Sensheo whispered, before hauling her

stinking, surprisingly heavy corpse to the cot. He laid her out, almost prettily, his nose wrinkling at the deathsmell. This place had an unguarded exit upon the roof; child's play for a man trained to combat and in the subtle skill of the lightfoot since he could walk.

He stood for a moment by the cot's side, gazing at her slack, swelling, discolored face, her tongue poking between her lips, her wide, staring, accusatory eyes.

His father always said a man should look upon what he had done. Sensheo did, and his small smile implied he found it acceptable indeed.

Before he left, he paused by the table, and carefully tipped the candle's holder. The proper arrangement against dry wood, liquid wax spilling free, was easily accomplished, and a few moments later the room was empty except for the strengthening flicker of a hungry flame.

It was always best to be thorough, and in the first part of a new reign, all disasters were considered omens.

NEATLY
OUTMANEUVERED

"Half the Yuin is gutted," the Emperor said, quietly but crisply, and such was his mien that the entire vermilion-pillared Great Hall heard every syllable. "What was the source of the blaze?"

"Your great and gracious Majesty, we do not know." Lord Yulehi was pale, and he was—despite his age and honorable position—upon his knees on hard stone. His court hat was slightly askew, and his robe gave every indication of being hastily donned. Even his slippers were mismatched; outside, the gongs had just beat the midnight watch.

Those well-informed among the court knew he had perhaps been in the Theater District instead of his estate in the Noble Quarter; just which bed he had been dragged from was not yet common knowledge.

But it would be soon.

Smoke lifted in a great column over Zhaon-An, underlit by hellish flickering orange and red. Bucket-snakes and the wheeled water-carriers heaved liquid cargo from nearby streams at their summer lows, the river girdling the Alwan and public baths outside the city's northern wall—shared with the Palace complex's back—sloping into a mere green-tinged fen during summer instead of its spring or autumn torrent and so, not very useful. City Guard and Night

Watch had been shaken from their usual routines and pressed into service; word had reached the Palace of this new disaster as the blaze raced through close-packed leaning wooden buildings, their stone foundations relatively safe but everything above not so lucky at all.

Even roof-tiles were exploding from the buildings bordering the Left Market; the afternoon's rain, while welcome, had not erased the dust's moisture-sucking dryness in attics, teahouse or inn or sohju-hole walls, or in the spaces of tall crowded tenements where petty artisans, cooks, street-sellers, porters, day laborers, and the like retreated at dusk.

There was some question whether or not the fire could be contained at all.

"You do not know?" Garan Kurin stroked at his smallbeard, meditatively. Zan Fein had arrived, passing through the stations of obeisance catfoot-quiet; he was not disheveled in the slightest, but a fresh application of umu scent hung in invisible scarves over his passage. "Ah, Honorable Zan Fein, a welcome sight. Come closer, and tell me, who has responsibility for the arrangements against the danger of fire in Zhaon-An?"

"Your gracious Majesty." Zan Fein finished the last of his approach-bows, each one impeccable. "It is the Chief Minister's responsibility."

"Quite a lucrative one too." The Emperor frowned slightly; everyone present knew the punishing fire tax levied upon the masses of Zhaon-An was a highly sought-after source of ministerial revenue. "Well, uncle? Is the blaze contained? The city is restless; this is not a happy circumstance."

"My illustrious nephew, there has..." Lord Yulehi's countenance was unwonted pale, and shining with great drops of clear sweat. His topknot was sadly disarranged, too, the pin thrust through its cage only halfway. "It is the dry time, and all conceivable measures have been taken to keep any spark from—"

"Clearly." The Emperor's tone could not be kinder, but his uncle paled further, if such a thing were possible. "Where is Minister Lord Hanweo?"

"I passed him near the Blue Pavilion, Your Majesty." Zan Fein produced a fan; its side was painted with a character for *balanced humors*—something the sons of Two-Face were held to uniquely possess. "He goes to oversee the battle against the fire; his entire household and every client he can find are called upon to help."

A susurration went through the court. The Second Mother's uncle was not even of the Emperor's clan, and it seemed he had neatly outmaneuvered Lord Yulehi once more. Zhaon-An, fickle in many ways, would remember who appeared first to aid its poor against the hungry flames. Every minister was required to attend the Emperor during a disaster of this magnitude, yet all knew Lord Hanweo would not be disgraced for his absence. Several among the scribes, eunuchs, courtiers, and other ministers were aware of a final shift in the humor-balance of the inmost court.

No doubt Lord Yulehi was, too.

"At least that." The Emperor gestured, as if he were the clan elder and the man upon his knees not an uncle. Of course, Garan Kurin was Emperor, but he had until now at least made an effort at the appearance of filial obedience. "Uncle, perhaps you should aid Lord Hanweo; please, go and follow that worthy minister's every direction. I await news that the fire has been vanquished."

Another soft commotion near the door to the Great Hall was Sixth Prince Jin, just as hastily buttoned and rumpled as Lord Yulehi, rubbing at his eyes as he hurried through the crowd. In his wake glided Fifth Prince Sensheo—perhaps also come from the Theater District, but his topknot was perfectly aligned and his mourning armband precisely knotted.

"Eldest Brother," Jin cried as soon as he was within range, as Lord Yulehi bowed from his knees and began to rise. "I hear of fire; how may I help?"

If being hailed so informally displeased the Emperor, he made no sign. "Stay a while, little brother. And you, Sensheo; Lord Yulehi goes to your uncle Hanweo. Perhaps you could accompany him, so he does not become lost? The city is in a ferment."

Zan Fein's fan paused. Jin's eyebrows shot up. The insult was breathtaking, but Lord Yulehi did not seem to notice. He merely performed his farewell obeisances and hurried from the great hall; Fifth Prince Sensheo's bow was deeply respectful before he turned to follow suit.

"Let us hope Heaven will aid the Fifth Prince and Lord Hanweo." Kurin beckoned the Ministers of the Feet forward; upon them would rest some manner of finding taxation revenues to cover whatever could be done to rebuild once the flames were quenched. "Come, my friends, we must discuss how to ease the suffering of Zhaon-An."

Upon the way to the Yuin, Fifth Prince Sensheo and Lord Yulehi discussed much.

No Good Either

Riding south always robbed him of anything approaching a good mood, not that Garan Takshin was usually possessed of one unless he was in the company of a certain grey-eyed northern lady. At least he had been able to select the handful of Golden Kurin had so *kindly* offered for accompaniment, though he would have much preferred to bring either an army to Kiron's aid or no Zhaon that could possibly be his elder brother's spy.

Sunjosi and the half-dozen Shan with him cast many a baleful look at the Golden, as if they suspected somewhat; it was a relief to have a fellow bloodrider at his side. They made good time, and the border approached as it always had.

The great stone road unreeled under horse-hooves; there were fresh horses meant for royal couriers at all the usual stages though he would have preferred also to be riding the large grey Tooth. That particular horse, bred for the use of prince and Golden, loitered safely in Takshin's estate stable, since he had carried Yala with such signal speed and what safety could be managed not so long ago.

Takshin's stomach still churned to think about that ride and her return. In the saddle from dawn until well after dusk over and over again, he had little to do but brood. The days blurred together as travel toward Shan had always done when he was a child, each step bringing him closer to the Mad Queen and her disorienting mixture of flagrant tenderness with violent punishment.

A tenday after leaving Zhaon-An, Toh Danh, the leader of the Golden shield-square at least ostensibly glad to be journeying with a prince, gazed around him with much interest instead of the numbed apathy of fatigue. He was from this part of Zhaon, to judge by his accent, and it was also he who sighted the first mass of refugees.

They streamed along the Road, a tide of misery mostly clothed in Zhaon cotton. Yet there was a heavy leavening of the black of traditional Shan men, along with the bright trousers and buttoned tunics of their peasant women. Many pushed barrows or dragged handcarts, and their faces were lined and pinched. Children wailed or simply clutched at the nearest adult, whether or not it was their kin. Eggfowl clucked in osier cages, oxen lowed, carts were piled high with household possessions.

Toh attempted to question a few as they passed, but most simply shook their heads despite his bright armor and obvious authority. Even Takshin and Sunjosi, addressing one or two in the Shan dialect, gained no information but wailing.

They had seen the Horde. Clearly, Tabrak was unsatisfied with its first meal and was riding north; they had never, in all the histories Takshin read, behaved thus.

Still, Zhaon-An's walls were strong, and he had planned for Yala's escape should it be necessary—Steward Keh could be trusted, Lady Kue as well. And Takshin *had* to know how Kiron fared.

But it burned in his gut worse than returning to the Mad Queen ever had.

Finally the shield-captain managed to halt a merchant upon a fine chestnut thoroughbred with rolling eyes, a high-strung beast scenting fear and obviously beyond his means.

"To the west, that's what everyone says. Maybe they have gone home," the merchant said, casting nervous glances over his shoulder as if a crowd of rai-pale barbarians might crest a nearby hill at any moment. "The capital is retaken, the king of Shan is hunting *them*—but who wishes to return now?"

Sunjosi, straight-backed in his saddle, glared at the merchant; he evidently suspected the chestnut had been liberated from a previous owner in not quite legal fashion, and any mention of Kiron before one of his bloodriders required the proper deference.

"The king?" Takshin leaned upon his saddle-horn, pinning the man with a fixed stare. Perhaps he would be taken for a Shan himself. "He is alive?"

"Oh yes; he was hunting *them*, but *they*...my lord, south is no good, north is no good either, what are we to do?" The merchant all but gabbled, his fear just as stinking-raw as his horse's. It was a wonder the animal hadn't thrown him yet. "Are you bound for Anwei?"

"I am bound for the capital, if that is where Suon Kiron is." Takshin caught Sunjosi's gaze and shook his head slightly; he was hard put not to scowl, but the round, blue-robed merchant was already skittish enough. "What other news, Honorable?" His inflection was not overly familiar, but then again, how many Zhaon with greenstone hurai would know the Shan dialect and inquire after the king, especially with a nobleman in black present and respectfully silent while he did so?

Still, not every peasant in Shan knew his face, and a good thing, too. Did they, it would probably keep their rai from cooking.

"They say the new queen went mad and flung herself from the battlements to avoid dishonor. Or that she turned into a bird and flew north, crying for her father." The merchant cast another nervous glance hindward, more worried about barbarians than Sunjosi's renewed tension and quelling glare. "Is it true? The great Garan has ascended to Heaven, and the God of War fights in the North?"

A well-informed man. "Both are true," Takshin said grimly, and nodded to the shield-captain, who produced a slice of copper ingot to recompense the merchant for his trouble. A few of the shuffling peasants nearby noticed this largesse, their faces brightening, but Takshin straightened, his horse already weary and the next post some li away. "You would do well to return home, Honorable. Tabrak will be crushed."

"Oh, aye," the merchant replied, bitterly. "'Tis what was said last time they rode, too. One cannot crush the metahghi." In the dialect, the word for the rapacious insects descending upon crops like Heaven's judgment was much sharper than in Zhaon.

Takshin decided teaching the man a lesson in respecting his betters was not the finest use of his time, and simply kneed his grey forward.

"Frightened beasts," Sunjosi muttered, and the Third Prince agreed.

The next post-stop had its full complement of horses, but they were not the large greys; the Golden rarely came this far south. Still, remounted and cantering along, they made good time until the oncoming traffic thickened again, and a group of Shan riders coming north had decided to travel on the southbound side of the road, no doubt because the other was choked and spreading into ditches and fields.

Toh hailed them with rough words, but Takshin kneed his bay mare into a gallop, for he knew the round figure in the lead and could barely believe his luck. "Buwon!" he cried, and let out the piercing whistle of one bloodrider greeting another. Sunjosi cursed, with the disbelieving pleasure of a man finding a friend in a theater-crowd; his horse matched Takshin's stride for stride.

It was indeed Lord Buwon, somewhat thinner than usual, and very grave. Marks of sleeplessness carved themselves into his broad face, but he brightened appreciably upon seeing Takshin.

"What luck," he called across a river of bent peasant heads. A dog barked; one of the larger Shan contingent's mounts stamped uneasily as they halted. "Sunjosi, well met indeed! I think of you, and you appear like a sage, Shin."

"Or a nightmare." Relief took the place of ill feeling deep in Takshin's belly. If more of Kiron's fellow bloodriders were here, there was little to fear. "How fares my battle-brother?"

That was how he learned for certain Kiron was alive, mourning his wife—and had called for Shan's banners to raise, sending Buwon north to spread the word in the borderlands and then cross the border and curve west to pick up Tabrak's trail, could it be found.

The king of Shan was hunting the Horde, and Takshin thought it high time indeed.

BATTLE OF FIVE

*F*or Khir! For Khir! Ashaniiiiiiiiii!"
The cannons boomed. Ashani Zlorih, the Great Rider of his people, clamped his knees against his black battle-steed's sides and cut down a stray Zhaon soldier, his throat scorching with a battle-yell. Veils of acrid smoke poured over the rocky field; where were his other armies?

It did not matter. What mattered was the battle before him, and the young sons of Khir houses upon their blooded steeds, their own high hunting-cries piercing the clashing of metal, the thunder of hooves, the cannons punctuating the din with their own painful bursts, horses screaming as injury or death found them, the infantry swearing or making rough ratcheting sounds of pained effort—yes, it was familiar; Zlorih had won more than one battle, and they all sounded like this.

It was even better than hunting, and far more direct than the constant balancing of ministers, jealous noble clans, and other considerations filling the Great Keep. Zlorih's mount, a massive black charger with his brazen shoes changed to clawed war-feet just that morn, bucked frantically, but not to remove his rider; instead, with a prey animal's exquisite sensitivity, he knew he was being crowded and consequently struck at a tormentor.

Another rider might well have fallen, but Zlorih was *Khir*, and that meant he stuck to his saddle like a thornburr in rough cotton.

There was a jolt, a sound like an overripe aiju melon dropped upon hot paving, and High-Arch—named for the proud carriage of his neck and head—let out a ringing neigh as his hooves dropped. He bunched like a child's string-toy and shot forward, understanding only that he must flee.

Zlorih let him, for High-Arch's head was aimed directly at a knot of Zhaon banners, and the melee at its foot held a familiar, wide-horned helm bobbing as an unhorsed general laid about him with a singing, dragon-hilted sword. It was pure chance to catch a commander so near strips of cloth holding a cohort's or division's honor aloft; the men surrounding him, taking heart from his presence, were driven slightly apart as a squad of Khir cavalry, noblemen with sabers, splashed against their front.

The man they called God of War—or simply beloved of that most martial of Heaven's inhabitants—was instead a fiend from one of the many hells, and Zlorih knew as much. Zakkar Kai surged forward, perhaps shouting something in their mush-mouth language, for those around him moved likewise, and two of the Khir cavalry were unhorsed by pikes.

You idiots. Battle-rage smoked red inside Ashani Zlorih's skull. It was the same fury from a hundred other hunts, whether for feral curltail, mountain pards, or the shaggy ursines with bright patches on their chests where the goddess of the moon had once struck their lord, denying a marriage all of Heaven was opposed to. It was the same as many battles, whether bandit-hunting when he was heir to the throne of Khir or later, taking the field against Ch'han's faraway but still acute rapaciousness or Garan Tamuron to the south.

He had outlived that foul warlord, but *this* man was the true danger. He always had been. Zhaon had taken much from the king of Khir, and it seemed likely they would take all that remained as well.

But if he could strike down this one of Hell's scions, he would die content.

Zlorih's sword, tied to his wrist with a hank of scarlet silk—Narikh Arasoe's stitchery faded and torn upon its edge, but worn during every battle since he had taken the scrap from her hands and kissed her on one glorious warm summer day in the fields outside Khir's great city—whistled as High-Arch galloped. More Khir, seeing their king flash past, cheered and pressed onward, though the Zhaon army was threatening to swamp them as a mudslide upon a rain-weakened hill surrounded any structure unlucky enough to be in its path.

Where were his other two armies? Slipping to the west was supposed to grant them an advantage; Three Rivers had taught Khir much. But somehow, Zakkar Kai was *here*, and there were no dispatches from the others, no time to send scouts to possibly bring them or track along Zakkar's trail. If he could hold them here, the rest of Khir would fall upon Zhaon's back like the ravening *kesaicha* wyrms carved into *shinkesai* falling upon stray cattle in the western foothills fading into the waterless waste.

Each hoof-fall was a jolt through Zlorih's entire body. He could still ride, and he had made his rule safe—but for how long? His sons were dead, his daughter—oh, how that ached within him, even if only a girl-child she had been bright and willing, and now he regretted his harshness in raising her correctly—sacrificed for Khir's honor not just once but twice, and Arasoe's son, the hope of his old age, the only piece remaining of the woman he still loved more than even the people Heaven had entrusted to him, was gone as well, leaving only a well-brushed letter.

I have business to attend to, Father.

"*For Khir!*" Ashani Zlorih heard himself bellowing, and the heat in his chest, the grasping fist high up in the left side of his rib cage, was pure hatred.

A man in battle had no time for anything other than hate. To kill required bright clarity; High-Arch caracoled and threw out his hind hooves again, catching a pikeman crosswise and flinging the Zhaon into a knot of his fellows. Zlorih laughed, dropping the reins and standing in his stirrups, the horse a sudden extension of his own body, finishing the strike and wheeling again.

The Zhaon cohort parted, Khir infantry—those who could not

afford a horse, useless in battle unless it was to weigh the enemy
down while the cavalry charged—scrambling after them as they
realized what was about to happen. The horned helm turned and
Zakkar Kai, seen through a tide of streaming smoke, recognized
the richly caparisoned rider bearing down upon him.

The general's sword, fouled with blood and other matter,
described a single shimmering circle, preparing for this next
engagement, filth splattering free of shining steel. High-Arch
neighed defiance and bolted forward, his rider standing tall.

Calm descended upon the ruler of Khir. If he could strike down
this ill spirit, it would do much to break Zhaon's will, even if Zlorih's own army foundered in the attempt. His grasp upon the hilt
turned light and loving, the edge of Arasoe's red silk snapping in
the wind of his passing, the Zhaon banners trembling as their bearers moved aside, mouths opening and shouts rising as they realized
what was about to happen too.

The rest of the battle went away. There was only the horse under
him, haunches bunching as he hopped a pair of soldier-bodies knotted together in death, Zlorih's sword cleaving stinking air, and Arasoe's wide grey gaze meeting his as she showed him the embroidery.

A son, Great Rider. Or so I pray.

Where was the boy now? His face was like his mother's; each
time Zlorih glimpsed the product of his union with a woman all of
Khir called honorless his heart and liver both clenched within him.
Daoyan had gone south, perhaps to rescue his sister—oh, he was a
noble child, as if any product of *hers* could be any less.

Zakkar Kai pushed aside a scurrying pikeman and loped forward a few paces, assuring his attacker of clear ground. The sword
held in high-guard flashed, smoke-filtered sunlight turned bloody
and the cannon-flashes sparking off its length.

How many other sons of Khir had died upon that blade? Had
it drunk the blood of Zlorih's legitimate sons, his long-ago wife
dead in the battle of bringing Mahara into the world? Why would
Heaven give a man so much only to rob him of it in his fading
years?

Because Heaven is cruel. All is cruelty, and I must match it.

High-Arch understood what was required now. The horse's head lifted proudly, and he called upon his last reserves of strength. It was time for the final cry, the one reverberating in a Great Rider's heart since he had received the news of his only beloved's death.

"Arasoooooooooe!"

Ashani Zlorih the ruler of Khir rode down upon Zakkar Kai, who stood stock-still, his face shadowed by the high-horned helm. Closer, closer, and the shock of the clash rippled up and down the lines of struggling, dying soldiers, shrieking horses, banners wildly waving, gongs and trumpets attempting to pierce the chaos with direction and order, and cannonfire ripping great holes in the milling, screaming Khir conscripts. The noble cavalry, suddenly aware their Great Rider was engaged with the leader of Zhaon's armies, gathered like raindrops running down a sheet of tiled wall, and surged toward their ruler.

It was ever after called the Battle of Five, since the two parts of Zhaon's Northern Army not only caught two separate smaller Khir armies hammer-and-anvil, but also pursued a night march and surprised the third segment.

The Northern Army was pushed almost beyond endurance by the demands of its head general, whose muddy, exhaustion-ringed gaze seemed to burn even the simple soldiers who whisper-cheered him as he rode along their marching ranks before morning showed the last Khir camp below them upon a rocky plain. Yet they trusted Zakkar Kai, and the cavalry-heavy Khir, led by their aging king, had no choice but to stand fast.

Much was written of the battle, of Zakkar Kai's relentlessness, of the final duel between the God of War and the Great Rider—of the seven passes, of a giant black horse foundering and his rider leaping from the saddle, of the bladework and lightfoot the two foes used...

...and of how Zakkar Kai removed his great horned helm and knelt by the body of his defeated foe, seemingly lost to the world while his exhausted army let forth a great bellow and the Khir nobles performed charge after charge to reach their Great Rider's side, each one broken by the re-formed cohorts under leather-lunged captains who knew their business and did not need a general's commands to meet such a threat.

A TURNED DISH

At least they had unchained him. Not only that, but a camp-bath had been provided as well as meals brought by the general's own adjutant, an iron-haired peasant soldier whose dark, crafty gaze roved over every surface as if seeking small valuables to steal.

Hazuni Ulo had been taken from the tent, though, and that gentleman's last look had been eloquent of suffering. Daoyan expected him beheaded in short order, especially since the chaotic noise of a battle had raged all day to the east. Being dragged along in a tumbril during the night march was an insult all its own, but letting a pair of Khir noblemen ride at night was a recipe for escape—and the Zhaon knew as much.

Ashani Daoyan did not touch his dinner, but he took a long draft from the small sohju-jug. They did not ration the drink for officers; he could have sotted himself, but he took only enough to relax his taut-strung nerves. There was little in this prison-tent that could serve as a weapon; at least he was clean. He and Ulo had spent the day stretching and testing stiffened muscles; irons bit at wrist and ankle, cutting off the free circulation of humors and inducing a weakness no man could suffer to remain once removed.

It was therefore no surprise when the tent-flap billowed and a pair of Zhaon soldiers entered, exchanging a somber look as they noted Daoyan standing by the knee-high folding table loaded with covered dishes, his hands loose and ready. What *was* startling was that they were not alone.

Behind them, Ulo reappeared, but the Hazuni heir's face was grey and his gaze somewhat unfocused.

At least you are still alive, my friend. Dao said nothing, the sohju drying in his mouth and fresh tension spilling through his aching limbs. The tent's mirrorlight sank low and bloody as the sun died, and the entire camp reeked of cannonsmoke.

In Ulo's wake a grim specter walked, striped with blood and fouler matter, a colorless fume of bloodlust and violence clinging to battered but very fine armor. His topknot was askew, some of his hair fallen to his shoulders, and he was covered in dried effluvia and sweat but lithe, lean Zakkar Kai did not seem to care. His adjutant trailed him with a gangly armor-son, and so did another figure Dao had never expected to see again.

Narikhi Keiyeo, head of his honorless mother's clan, was in full armor as well, and just as filthy-disheveled as the Zhaon general. His almost triangular face was the very essence of what Khir called *mountain bones*, every plane sharply edged and his nose a high beak.

The adjutant carried another sohju-jug and the armor-son a stack of cups; they crossed to the table, the adjutant shaking his elderly head as he noticed the covers upon the dinner-dishes had not even been lifted, and in short order the untouched food was whisked away and the cups filled. Zakkar Kai made a quick, graceful motion, offering refreshment to his "guests"—and how it must have galled Lord Narikhi to accept direction or a mannerly drink from Khir's largest foe, especially while standing in the presence of a bastard grandson.

"You are alive," Narikhi greeted Daoyan coldly, in Khir. "I suppose there is that, at least."

Considering how many times this particular man had either nodded while others sent assassins to expunge Ashani Daoyan from the living or paid an impresario himself to take care of the deed, it was a fine jest. On any other day Dao would have laughed. "I am sorry to disappoint you, Grandfather."

"Please." Hazuni lifted his hands, a placating motion as he spoke in Khir as well. They were a sorry group of nobles indeed, all disheveled as peasants after planting. Camp-baths did nothing to truly clean a man. "This is a bleak day, but all is not yet lost for Khir. My lord Ashani Daoyan..." The pad of pounded rai at Ulo's throat moved as he swallowed, hard. "Your father has ascended to Heaven. You are the Great Rider of Khir, and Head General Zakkar is offering terms for the last Khir army's surrender."

Very well. "Do those terms include my head?" He even managed to inquire calmly, while his gaze settled upon the adjutant. The fellow bore a shortsword and two daggers; it would be somewhat easy to take at least one from him. Then, armed and at bay, he could show his honorless mother's father what the daughter of their clan had wrought.

"Only incidentally." Zakkar Kai's voice was rough with smoke and battle. He coughed, turning his head aside in mannerly fashion, before accepting a cup of sohju from his chief adjutant. He saluted them all, fingertips of his free hand at the bottom of the rough glazed terracotta, and took a long drink.

He had apparently been practicing his Khir. It made sense; a man had to understand what he fought if he expected to survive.

"Well, then." Daoyan selected a filled cup, lifted it, and tossed the contents far back. Another outrageous violation of etiquette, but if his father...

It was impossible, though. Ashani Zlorih was eternal, or so Dao found out he had always believed until this moment. The armorson scurried forward to refill, and Dao barely let him do so before pouring the brimming cup out as a relative would do upon hearing of the death of a clan-head.

"Grief makes a man do strange things." Hazuni Ulo's unease was visible; of course, what nobleman expecting a swift beheading would be completely comfortable with perhaps-dishonorable survival? Living ready for death left a mark.

The sages all said so, when they weren't arguing over the nature of enlightenment, the various events of history, or the faithlessness of women.

What would Yala think of this? At least she had not been taken prisoner with him.

"It falls to you to negotiate peace." Zakkar Kai fixed Dao with a bloodshot glare, nodding as his own cup was refilled. His Khir was rough and slurring, Zhaon dragging at the syllables and turning any attempt at poetry into a sad jest. "Though perhaps you may not wish to, in which case you shall remain my guest while I return Lord Narikhi to the army and proceed with their utter destruction."

"This field is bloody enough." Lord Narikhi merely touched his chapped lips to the rim of his cup, though battle was thirsty work. He would not unbend enough to take even a single sip from a foundling warlord, his stiff posture shouted. "And this whelp, sitting at his ease in a tent while his betters—"

"*Enough*, my lord." Hazuni Ulo's tone was, for once, sharp. "I have explained to you how Ashani Daoyan came to be here. Vengeance upon Zhaon for their murder of his sister is a noble duty, and one he took upon himself." Ulo did not look to Dao while uttering this astonishing assertion, which was probably for the best; the new Great Rider might well lose his wits with laughter.

Had Yala told them that was what he had arrived in Zhaon-An for? Of course, the lady would not be able to compass his true purpose.

Such a tender heart she had. All he asked was a sliver of its ingot.

"Is that what you thought to do?" Zakkar Kai shook his head; he salted his mother tongue into Khir with some facility. "I am not altogether certain that death may be laid upon Zhaon's steps, but no doubt you expect as much from me. Well, my lord Ashani Daoyan, king of Khir?" The title was of course given in Zhaon, since *Great Rider* seemed beyond the ability of the southrons to understand. "This fellow tells me your father had a compact with Tabrak. You will, of course, disavow it, and stand ready to aid Zhaon against the Horde."

"I will?" Daoyan watched Ulo take a hearty draught from his own cup. The swallows upon the Hazuni heir's cuffs were looking sadly the worse for wear, and his dusty boots crushed the hurriedly arranged carpets flooring this tent.

"Little whelp." Narikhi Keiyeo was turning crimson. If the battle had not killed him, this might loosen some vital connection and let his humors explode. "You will do what you must, to ensure Khir survives."

The adjutant bustled about, lighting halu lamps as blood-drenched sunset mirrorlight faded. Daoyan regarded his grandfather steadily.

No doubt you think you will be a chief minister, and use me as a stick to beat carpets with until you may install a rider of your own choosing. Finally, when Dao was certain he had made the point that he was not disposed to receive orders from the head of Narikhi, he spoke. "You sent Cousin Bai to visit me in Zhaon, Grandfather. He was not a pleasant guest."

Lord Narikhi's choler drained; he glanced nervously at Hazuni Ulo, who took another hurried drink, his gaze fastened across the tent. Zakkar Kai half-turned away, his adjutant, now finished with lamp-lighting, murmuring in his ear.

Yet Dao would never make the mistake of thinking this man unaware of his surroundings.

"Tabrak rides north," Grandfather finally muttered. "As much was certain when the barbarian envoy came to our Great Rider. Once we fight at Zhaon's side, we will be left unmolested, the border returned to before Three Rivers—"

"I did not agree to that," Zakkar Kai said, mildly enough. "But perhaps the new king may offer some concession to make it worthwhile."

It was amusing to see Grandfather, the severe, unapproachable terror of Daoyan's childhood, forced to swallow a bitter pill by a man who had once been a foundling.

"As in marrying a Zhaon princess?" Dao did not have to say *which* princess; perhaps he could yet wrest Yala from that scarred, mocking fellow. "Do you have any you think would suit?"

"The Emperor must be consulted upon that point." Zakkar

Kai's expression did not change, and his deep-set eyes were those of a wolf who had downed the hunter chasing him, and was preparing to feast upon a man's entrails. "What would Khir ask of Zhaon, Ashani Daoyan? You must admit our hospitality has been warmer than you had any right to expect."

For a moment Dao was certain Zakkar knew more than he should, and a spear of ice passed through him. He studied his sohju-cup's black interior as a last ruddy gleam descended from the tent's mirrors. Trembling lamplight replaced it, fitful illumination nevertheless enough to read by.

When he spoke, it was quiet, meditative. "Do you remember what you told me upon my naming-day, Grandfather?"

A charged silence fell. Hazuni Ulo glanced from Lord Narikhi to the dead Great Rider's son, but wisely held his tongue. So did Zakkar Kai, whose adjutant sent the armor-son scurrying—no doubt for paper and brush so the surrender could be made official.

"I remember." Fierce and unbending, Narikhi Keiyeo glowered. "I will not lie and say I did not mean it, *Ashani*. Yet Khir must endure, and whatever sacrifices I must make—"

"I'm so glad you said that." Daoyan's tone cut across the gathering storm. It was highly rude to interrupt an elder; he saw Ulo's cheeks pinken a little. The young man looked miserable; he was about to be even more so. "Sacrifice will be called for indeed. My lord general, here are *my* terms." He waited a breath in case Zakkar wished to object to a conquered party exercising such arrogance, but the general simply regarded him, waiting. His air of self-possession was very like Yala's; had she passed words with him?

Of course not; she would be too wise to speak to Khir's greatest enemy, even if she would be forced to marry one of them. Perhaps the wedding was accomplished by now. Even mourning could not dissuade a prince when he wanted something, and that scarred ill-spirit in Shan black had made his desires clear.

"The borders may stay as they were after Three Rivers for ten summers," Dao said, giving each word particular weight. Slow speech gave him time to think, to test each response. "I will gather those of Khir's sons among the prisoners and today's army who may still fight; you will return their weapons and armor, and we shall ride south to Zhaon-An. You may have me ride with your army to ensure my own army's compliance within the borders of Zhaon; no doubt we shall find other hostages among the nobles assembled here. There shall be no tribute, though Khir will pass all Anwei trade through Zhaon's customs on the way south and ask only half the traditional abatement for the same ten years. I shall take you as a battle-brother, and shall take a noblewoman raised to princess for a wife—your Emperor cannot cavil at that, Zhaon has wanted to marry Khir since the Second Dynasty." And he would ask for a specific princess indeed; the scarred one would learn what it was to lose a wife like his eldest brother. "There is one small matter, though, upon which all the rest hinges upon."

"My lord—" Ulo began, anxiously. No doubt he thought Dao about to ask for Yala's return, but why show his hunt so clearly? Dao cut him off with a short gesture he had seen the Great Rider make once or twice, a peremptory silencing.

And it *worked*. Hazuni Ulo subsided.

"If it is a small matter, I shall be glad to settle it for you." Zakkar Kai took another draught of sohju. His hand rested upon the wrapped head of his ancient sword, and the way he stood was echoed in Daoyan's own posture.

It would be interesting, Daoyan thought, to duel this man.

"My grandfather is a melon-span too tall," Daoyan said, relishing each single word. "You will relieve him of that extra height this evening, and accept me as battle-brother."

"By Heaven." Ulo sounded as if he had been struck in the gut with a mailed fist, and Dao should know, for such a love-tap had been part of Zhaon's recent hospitality. "He is your *grandfather*."

Do you think that makes a difference? Still, Hazuni and his friends had kept Daoyan alive, and now, in another breathtaking turn, an illegitimate son had what he wanted—a Khir army, and a road south.

Lord Narikhi did not move. It was exquisite, seeing him realize just how thoroughly the great dish at the center of a feast-table could be turned.

As the saying went.

"No doubt the Narikhi wish to settle one of their own under the Great Calendar once I am disposed of, probably upon a battlefield with one of my grandfather's daggers in my back." It wasn't necessary to explain himself, but Ashani Daoyan did, so Hazuni Ulo could later report his words to other nobles who might be deterred from any...unwise acts. "How often have you tried to kill me, clan-head? Did it never strike you that I might one day be able to respond?" Daoyan lifted his sohju-cup, and turned his attention to Zakkar Kai once more. "What say you, Head General of Zhaon?"

Zakkar Kai wore a very slight smile. He also viewed Daoyan rather as a man might a speaking animal in the age of sages, with a slight quizzical lift of his eyebrows. "And you avoid any ill-luck from the death of your grandfather, pinning it neatly upon my sleeve."

"*Friends may help each other*," Dao quoted. Khao Cao had longed for another man's wife, and the Khir present would hear the bitter jest in the allusion without knowing it did not refer to his own mother.

Let them think what they willed.

"*Lost in a rainstorm, one may share a cave with any man.*" Zakkar Kai's returning quotation was Zhe Har; an odd choice, but perhaps the man had pretensions at scholarship. His muddy gaze—perhaps there was some nobility in his blood after all—turned to Lord Narikhi, who bore it admirably, though the pounded rai in Grandfather's throat flickered. "I regret to accept this offer in your presence, my lord; I will have paper and brush brought for your last reflections."

The general's adjutant stiffened; the soldiers at the door, perhaps unable to understand more than a few words in Khir, saw as much and tensed as well, stray dogs scenting blood.

"You would do this," Lord Narikhi said, but to Daoyan. "To your own *clan*."

"Oh, Grandfather, I was never Narikhi." *Except for a few moon-turns in Zhaon-An. They passed wonderfully, if you must know, but ended before I gained all I sought.* He would not make the mistake of waiting ever again. "Did you not tell me as much, over and over? I am Ashani, and you may share a pyre with my father tonight." He took a fresh swallow of sohju, enjoying the bite. "I presume my father's body has not been savaged, and the fire is being prepared?"

"Naturally." Zakkar Kai bent to set his cup down upon the low table, and despite his armor the motion was fluid, though somewhat slow. "Will you come with me and attend to other details, Ashani Daoyan?"

"Certainly. Lord Hazuni, you are required as well." Dao beckoned, another movement he had seen his father perform. Zlorih had rarely spoken to him, but young Dao had copied his gestures before a brazen mirror, wondering if it would help.

Even a toy could prepare a child to become a man.

"Very well," Lord Narikhi said, colorlessly. "But I will not die for *you*, bastard Ashani. I die for Khir."

As long as you enter Heaven, Grandfather, I care not. But he could not say it. Leaping to take advantage of a sudden change was merely one more way to survive, and Zakkar Kai might learn to rue the day he offered his bargain.

So Dao contented himself with a slight bow, his face a frozen mask as he set his own cup upon the table with a small click. "Goodbye, Grandfather."

"You may leave me a dagger and I will attend to myself, Head General." The old man had some hunrao; that was certain.

"It would be poor hospitality," Zakkar Kai said politely, well aware that executing the old man as a defeated foe had to be done properly, in plain sight, or not at all. "I would not think to trouble a guest so."

And with that the Head General of Zhaon stalked from the tent. Ashani Daoyan followed, and so did Hazuni Ulo.

* * *

There were two great pyres and many smaller ones upon the battlefield that night; the defeated Khir could not even slip into the darkness, for they were ringed by Zhaon's Northern Army. And between the two largest fires, the son of Ashani Zlorih and his only love watched the consumption of a pair of old bodies, mixed smoke rising to Heaven and his grey eyes clear and thoughtful.

FIRST HARVEST

The days wore on, hot and dry. No more downpours had occurred, though the overcast intensified each afternoon and streamed away overnight.

Huge colored lanterns like swollen, glowing melons swung upon poles, and Yala could not help a small admiring sound at the sight of the great processional way inside the Palace lit with their bobbing glow. Fireflowers exploded in the overcast night sky, and one could imagine the tinge of smoke to each breath was the residue of such transitory blooms instead of the wrack of the Yuin. The blaze in the Left Market was defeated and the moon hung ripe in twilight sky; Emperor Garan Kurin had decreed the first great harvest festival would commence.

Mrong Banh, restored to royal favor, had chosen the most auspicious hour for the tolling of the Great Bell, and at its sounding the procession to the formal banquet could also begin.

"Pretty, isn't it?" Garan Gamnae's peach dress, brocaded in slightly contrasting thread, suited her very well since her hairpin only dangled a single string of gold leaves and her ear-drops were likewise restrained. In Zhaon, even a royal mother was only mourned for two tendays; this was the Second Princess's return to full court life. In any case, not even an armband could be worn at this festival, for fear of insulting the celestial beings who guarded and guided the rai's growth. "I used to be frightened of the fireflowers."

The sounds were alarming, and they reminded Yala of her princess's wedding, or the Knee-High Festival spent with Garan Kanbina. She patted Gamnae's hand upon her arm, glancing at their feet to make certain the hem of her own festival dress—a slightly deeper peach, and trimmed with blushing thread in a character for *abundance* tangling against itself at hem and cuffs—hung properly. The gilded jatajatas were a torment to walk in, but she would exchange them for the court slippers in a perfumed bag hanging from her belt when they reached the threshold of the Great Hall.

Before them, the two remaining mothers of the Emperor held the cortege to a slow, graceful pace. Second Mother Haesara was in pale pinkish silk, not quite mourning-color and curiously restrained in ornamentation. Third Mother Luswone was in the same shade, though cut from a different bolt; it was a sign the two mothers were thoroughly in accord, as the two princesses had taken care to be.

The Mothers' common cause was said to be grief, but Yala thought it quite possible the truth was...otherwise. Lady Mau's misfortune hung almost as heavily upon the Second Mother as the loss of her eldest son; she had not called for sathron music since the day of the discovery, and those attending her wisely refrained from suggesting that amusement.

The Fifth and Sixth Princes strolled shoulder to shoulder, though Garan Jin was unwonted somber and in the dark brown he had lately taken to wearing. Whether it was a nod to Garan Makar's misfortune or his scarred, absent brother in perpetual Shan black was an open question.

Garan Sensheo was in black silk, three different characters for *good fortune* gold-embroidered in repeating patterns at cuffs, hem, neckline. The broken tower of Clan Hanweo had been worked upon his back in that same golden thread. His topknot-cage was not gold, however; it was just as dark and sober as his little brother's.

More might have been gauche. He wore his hurai, of course, but also wore the archer's thumb-ring of carved horn; still, his hands were tucked in his sleeves as he observed a stately pace.

More fireflowers showered noise and bright light over the Palace complex. The massive doors to the banquet hall were open, dark-robed eunuchs with their hats sporting tiny tassels upon stiffened wire arcs bowing as court luminaries passed. Court ladies and ministers followed Yala and Gamnae at a discreet distance, observing the same stately step-pause-step pace.

Lord Yulehi was temporarily disgraced—the affair of fire readiness, Yala understood, though she also thought it likely the Emperor wished his own position secure from a prying ministerial relative whose nominal headship of their clan meant certain benefits could be wrung free of royal incomes. It was an understandable move, though hardly a discreet one, and Yala wondered what the maternal uncle had done to provoke it.

Or perhaps the court was meant to wonder. Certainly the ladies, including Lady Gonwa, had much else to occupy their busy tongues with.

The Emperor was upon the high dais, tall and lean in scarlet with gold and black embroidery describing the noblest of creatures upon his chest; the Golden ranged along the walls in bright armor. At least Yala knew the protocol and etiquette; the dowagers took the dais to the Emperor's right. Gamnae led Yala to a small table upon a half-moon second dais lower than the princes' upon the Emperor's left. Kurin smiled beneficently, his gaze moving from one member of his family to the next; if Takshin were here, he and Yala would have their own table upon the second dais with his brothers, and Gamnae would be the queen of her own third dais with high-ranking court ladies toasting her between every course.

Upon the several raised round platforms for royalty, the tables were low and hung with scarlet. The rest of the banqueting court spread away in the cone-shaped hall, tables arranged by size and precedence placed in rigid order. Servants in palace goldenrod and festival black to match good bountiful earth bustled about, their gazes downcast and their shoulders rounded; the first-fruit celebratory sohju, thin and raw, was even now being poured into women's thimbles and the men's small teacups.

Mrong Banh attended at the princes' table; Jin brightened considerably upon seeing him. Sensheo's greeting was a nod, but upon such an occasion it was a high honor indeed. Zan Fein, surrounded by those among his eunuchs who showed marked promise, eyed the high ministerial table across the way, where Lord Hanweo was in the most honored seat despite it not being his half of the year. Lord Yulehi did not appear to mind, taking a lower-ranked seat; the rest of the ministers were apparently Garan Tamuron's, and confirmed in their prerogatives by his son. Ministers of Foot, of Fan, of Eye—the great organs of the state, all obedient to the head-meat and liver resting within the Emperor's august self.

A great brazen gong ringed with deep-stamped characters for *harvest* and *plenty* shivered the air as it was struck, and the First Harvest Feast began. Gamnae had recommended a very light late luncheon, since the banquet would be interminable and each dish had to be sampled—but not *finished*; the more leavings for the beggars already clustering the Palace's main gate, the more bountiful the harvest would eventually be.

The first-fruits sohju was acrid, but Yala downed her thimbleful at the proper moment anyway. Banquets in Khir were different, the women behind a screen and confined to safe topics such as marriage or hunting, the men discussing politics, war, and other subjects unfit for female ears at their half-moon tables.

In other words, they were always deadly boring affairs except for the chance of some mischief to be worked with the aid of her brother or Daoyan. If Takshin were home, perhaps he would have refused to attend this one. She could not quite decide if it would be a relief.

"I hate these," Gamnae whispered behind her dress-cuff, leaning close as possible while their thimbles were refilled with better sohju. "I always feel sleepy the next day, and my stomach rolls so."

"They are very long in Khir, too." Yala tried not to smile. Of course harmony between the Second Princess and the new sister-in-law was a pleasing picture; the thorny question of who should pour the sohju was solved by neither woman touching the jug and servants hurrying to do so whenever a lack was likely. When tea came, the solution proposed by Zan Fein was adopted—the junior in age pouring first, then the princess-by-marriage instead of birth for the next round, and so they would alternate.

Just-harvested fruit, the rai from the first drying, summerfat meat in sauces, a traditional dish of acidic early nahm to cleanse the palate, more dishes brought with clockwork regularity as toasts were called from table to table. The princes saluted the Emperor, then the dowagers; the ministers followed suit before toasting the princesses. The dowagers and princesses next drank to the health of the Emperor, and of course, during each salute the rest of the assembled court had to follow suit.

There was an art to simulating a deep draft of sohju; Yala suspected it would be much utilized that evening. The gong rang again, drums beginning to throb. Acrobats filed past the assembled court, many upon stilts. The spirits of good harvest were all there, from the green-clad maidens whose tiny stamping feet granted strength to the damp shaggy wind that caused the stalks to stretch, the stout and completely wrapped representations of good black earth to the child-acrobats dressed as bronzefish darting around the rai's flooded knees. The god of sickle and the goddess of flail danced in marriage, a deep swelling harvest-song accompanying; the choir was dressed as moisture-loving hau trees and swayed as they sang.

More musicians poured into the hall, the Golden eyeing each moving body warily; more acrobats crowded the great central sunken floor. A whirlwind of color and stamping, music swelling, sweat glistening upon powdered foreheads—Yala quite enjoyed the show, though Gamnae glanced anxiously at the princes' table more than once.

More courses came as dances from every province spilled into the hall and out again, bearing luck and strength from the Emperor's presence through the palace complex and out the great crimson-pillared imperial gate, passing between cheering throngs under another fusillade of fireflowers. The parade would wind through the city, stamping upon thrown flowers both fresh and made of bright rai-paper; each troupe would gather alloy slivers tossed to the bronzefish-costumed children along its route.

Yala selected a succulent bit of fat-crispy, heavily salted curltail, laying it in Gamnae's dish; the Second Princess thanked her with a smile. But the girl's gaze wandered to the princes' table again, and Yala was hard pressed not to glance until after a decent interval had passed.

Prince Jin and Mrong Banh leaned together, conversing with what was to all appearances great enjoyment. Fifth Prince Sensheo, on the other hand, studied the Emperor upon his dais. Gamnae's unease was almost palpable, though Sensheo simply looked intent. He kept turning his teacup a quarter for luck; his mouth was too tight for a smile, though the corners of his lips definitely tilted up.

"Second Princess?" Yala's tongue burned; for a moment she had almost said *my princess*, as if this was Khir and Mahara was next to her.

"Forgive me." Gamnae glanced at the tables arranged for the court ladies, where Lady Gonwa was being saluted by Lady Hankeo, who was much in fashion now since her room was next to what had been Lady Mau's in the green house. The shock to her nerves had been extreme, and everyone wished to hear her tell the tale of the hue and cry when Lady Aoan's close-servant had begun to wail. "I am distracted."

The servant was not celebrated, though every exorcist summoned to cleanse the space attended to the girl as well. Yala thought it quite likely the Second Mother had arranged another placement for such a faithful dependent, though. It would not be like Haesara to overlook such a small gesture to her departed favorite.

"What is it?" Yala ducked her head and smiled as Lord Hanweo saluted the princesses' table, Gamnae very prettily doing the same as her ear-drops swung upon ribbons close to her ears. No doubt the Second Mother had communicated her approval of a new daughter-in-law to her uncle; the signal was welcome and would not go unnoticed in any quarter. Takshin might well find himself besieged by potential clients upon his return.

She could not think of that event with any equanimity, so Yala did her best not to.

"I shouldn't—" Gamnae had to lean away as servants cleared the lightly sampled course, hurrying away to spread the largesse elsewhere. A slightly sweeter set of dishes followed, which meant the banquet was only a third of the way upon its journey.

The music quieted; the acrobats streamed away. The second wave would appear after the barrels of five-year sohju were poured from. The relative quiet was a balm, and Yala shifted upon her embroidered cushions. Much would be made of the harmony between the women of the royal family, surely.

The entire hall quieted. Now was the traditional time for the Emperor's toasts, to show his approval.

Garan Kurin lifted his silver-sheathed greenstone sohju cup, and distant drums throbbed under clear, carrying words. "Heaven blesses Zhaon," he intoned.

Yala, well coached by Zan Fein and the dowagers, murmured the ritual response in unison with Gamnae. "*Heaven blesses Zhaon.*" Was her father watching, frowning as she drank to the health of Khir's enemy?

What was Kai doing at this moment? It was past twilight; perhaps the soldiers were celebrating First Harvest in their own way, or among the peasants. No further letters had reached her, though Jin hinted he was sending regular missives north with royal couriers as a prince could, brushed with Mrong Banh's aid—not that the Sixth Prince needed his penmanship corrected, but the astrologer knew what to leave unsaid, in case the letters were opened and their contents reported.

Or so Yala hoped.

Had Takshin reached Shan yet? The roads were supposed to be clear, but there were disturbing rumors in the markets, Lady Kue said.

She lowered her cup, her hands cradling it and each other just so. The Second Mother also shot a dark glance to the princes' table, where Jin drank with every appearance of enjoyment, Mrong Banh copied him, and the Fifth Prince took a long draught.

"Zhaon salutes Heaven," Kurin intoned.

"*Zhaon salutes Heaven*," the court replied in unison.

"May the Five Winds blow."

"*May the Five Winds blow*." The phrase dissolved into a cheer; the Emperor saluted Heaven again and drank.

An antique black and white sohju-jug in the florid fat-bellied shape of the First Dynasty was brought, he sniffed ceremonially at its mouth and accepted a tray with two much smaller greenstone cups, the sacred material glowing in bright lamplight. Candle-flames bent under a collective exhalation; the Emperor rose.

"Now he salutes his mothers." Gamnae's voice caught, and she had paled. "Yala..."

"What is it?" she murmured. Something was wrong; her fellow princess's tension was infectious. "Tell me."

Kurin descended from the dais, with a stately step. His robe was resplendent indeed; his topknot-cage of hammered gold gleamed sharply, its pin bearing a bright winking ruby. He settled, bending with fluid authority, at the dowagers' table, pouring for both his remaining and esteemed mothers.

Second Mother Haesara, her resin-dipped fingers graceful, accepted her cup; so did Third Mother Luswone, her hair dressed high in the asymmetrical fashion of Daebo and the silver sheath over her left smallest nail gleaming. They lifted the greenstone containers slightly, their heads dipping—even an Emperor bowed before his mothers, but they were bound to respect his commands in return.

Garan Hanweo-a Haesara, as the senior mother, lifted her cup first; the rim touched her lips before she paused, perhaps because there was so much more to consume during the night. Third Mother Luswone followed a breath behind, and she swallowed first.

"*Hold!*" The cry pierced distant drumming, a nail puncturing a paper lantern's shade. "*Hold, Mother! Do not drink!*"

"Oh, no," Gamnae whispered.

Ever after, there was disagreement of just who had spoken. The cry was high and wild, and seemed to come from the shadows; some even gossiped that a brazen mouth-trumpet of the kind used for shouted military commands upon the Golden drillyard was found in a little-used gallery along one side of the great banquet hall, where Second Dynasty royal concubines had watched the great feasts.

Had Yala not been following the Second Princess's gaze, she might not have seen Garan Sensheo twitch just before the first word.

HOLD, MOTHER

A moment of absolute silence followed the cry; it repeated.

"Hold, Mother! Do not drink!"

Garan Sensheo unfolded from his seat, his knee striking the princes' table. Dishes danced, a sohju-jug swayed, and Mrong Banh caught sight of a bright steel gleam. The astrologer, who had accompanied Garan Tamuron through many a battle, reacted with quite martial speed, throwing himself over Garan Jin, who let out a short blurt of surprise as he sprawled.

The metallic gleam was a princely sword, and Sensheo cleared the table in a leap. *"Mother!"* he cried, and his voice was different than the high sweet clarion, which repeated its wailing a third time.

"Hold, Mother! Do not drink!"

Second Mother Haesara had just enough time to glance up, startled, as her remaining son hurtled across the banquet hall. Third Mother Luswone froze, her eyes widening, and the liquid she had just swallowed *burned*.

Garan Kurin, Emperor of Zhaon, looked up to discern whence the high sweet metallic voice floated. He had paled, but he remained upon his cushion, his right hand still loosely clasping the antique black and white jug upon the polished wooden table.

The new Khir princess's right hand flashed into her lap; she stiffened but did not rise because the Second Princess grasped her arm, fingers sinking in as if Garan Gamnae sought to drag herself from a deep nightmare using that grip.

The Golden, beginning to react to a drawn weapon in the banquet hall, reached for their own weapons; spearmen dropped instinctively into the first guard, their shortened indoor lances held at the proper parade-ground angle, crimson tassels swinging. The swordsmen drew, more metal hissing from sheaths, but the rank of the attacker made them hesitate for a single, critical moment.

Two things happened at once, then.

The Third Mother of the Revered Emperor choked, adulterated sohju dribbling down her zhu-powdered chin; her back arched and her eyes squeezed shut, tears leaking between her lids. It *hurt*, much more than such a drink should. She swayed, and a short shocked cry from Second Mother Haesara was lost in Luswone's gurgling, choking rasp; the Second Mother's cup fell from her nerveless hand.

And Garan Sensheo, with the sword given him by his great warlord father upon the day he reached full adulthood and received his first hurai, struck down his elder brother. The blade bit deep at the juncture between shoulder and neck, sinking like a peasant's axe into seasoned wood.

Blood sprayed. The Emperor made a low noise, akin to a tired ox finally struck by the butcher's mallet.

"*Do not drink!*" Garan Sensheo cried, and his next strike shattered the black and white jug—an ill omen, to be sure. Third Mother Luswone fell backward, her skirts awry and her hands turned into claws, her nail-sheath scratching her burning throat.

Garan Jin, struggling free of Mrong Banh's stunned clutches, screamed.

A Star
Displeased

The richest land of the clay people was a great bowl, collecting offerings for the Burning One. This particular town—Etu said its name meant *sweet-fruit tree*, or something similar—cooked merrily, and the din of battle had given way to the screams of plunder. The land to the south was better suited to riding, of course, but the season had shifted. Rolling the air in his mouth while his great bay steed cantered, the leader of the Horde decided autumn was upon their heels, but not quite yet fast enough to catch the Horde. Drying bundles of the clay people's starch-flower grain were easy to set alight along the roads and in sheds; even many men of the clay people cried at the sight.

Before they were cut down by hookblade, that was.

Allowing his riders to sharpen their lust for blood, plunder, or rape was an exercise in balance, like archery from the back of a galloping horse. The Horde did not follow the weak; a leader must provide battle and loot but also rein excess lest success strip the land of everything necessary to sustain their wandering life. Consequently, Aro Ba Wistis was allowing even the uncollared scun—those of free status who only lacked a horse—a share of spoils to whet their appetites.

When they took Zunnan, the resultant orgy of destruction would need to be brought swiftly to heel. He gorged them now to feed moderately later.

The clay people had some manner of militia with red tassels tied to their spiked helms and wicked pikes; the riders around Aro let out a bloodcurdling cry as they descended upon a knot of those unfortunates.

Did they think to halt the Horde with a paltry single block of spears?

At Aro's right rode Jasov Ba Jasov, tall and proud in the saddle since the leader had consented to look at his middle daughter. Catching the matrimonial eye of the great warrior had many benefits, and Aro had invited him to ride closest—which meant he would take his pick of the spoils second only to the Burning One's favorite. No little of that spoil-share would be immolated to bring the girl closer to Aro's notice.

Or so Jasov no doubt thought.

Aro Ba Wistis's throat swelled with the cry of Tabrak, the high serrated scream of a predator descending upon helpless meat. The leader of the pikemen cried aloud, too, and the clay people braced themselves before they were borne under, horses shrieking and the stink of cut bowel and fearshit rising in a brassy wave.

Every battle meant casualties. Aro's hookblade flashed, a throat-cut gurgle was lost under the melee, and as the Tabrak rode over the pike square, numbers and weight telling even as horses were impaled and mounted men died, Jasov was borne from the saddle, falling to hoof-ploughed, bloodsoaked earth as a star who had displeased the Burning One was flung from the heavens.

Later, when the spoils were counted and Etu the scun-scribe made his endless marks upon tally-rolls of scraped hide, the keening from Jasov's tent rose with the smoke of burned offerings, and Aro Ba Wistis did not even glance at the middle daughter, though her wide sky-blue eyes were fixed upon him and her mourning-disheveled hair lay against her bare dough-pale shoulders.

Even the Tabrak mourned their fallen.

Though not for very long. Zunnan was a few weeks' wandering ride away, and the wain of collared scun and plunder stretched far, weighing the Horde down.

HAPPY CHANCE
INDEED

S ending the Golden away just past the border was a blessing;
Shan riders closed about Garan Suon-ei Takshin like a warm
blanket as they thundered south.

The first night they only rested between sunset and moonrise;
Buwon beckoned Takshin aside and attempted to apologize for
his royal sister's misfortune. Perhaps he expected anger, or a cutting word, but the battle-brother of Shan's king merely shook his
head, remarking that a queen would certainly choose death over
dishonor.

There was nothing for Buwon to say after that, but he did give
his old friend several long, somewhat piercing looks, as if he suspected Takshin of saving his ire for Kiron.

As if upon a hunting-raid, Shan riders traveled light and swift,
parallel to the trade-roads or striking across country as their path-
finders sensed the knots in the stream of refugees. The flood was
slowing, since the Tabrak seemed to be keeping to westward as
they moved steadily north; perhaps he *should* have brought Yala
with him.

Some sages had foreknowledge; mere men—even princes—did
not. And he had not reached Kiron yet.

Crossing the border was anticlimactic; still, Takshin paused at the highest point of the bridge over the Enshuan that the Shan named *Golyeon*, glancing over his shoulder at Zhaon. The river, summer-low and chuckling over rocks, was not quite an old friend. Sabwone had been carried over this bridge in a palanquin; what he would not give to have his own wife beside him, in the saddle of the large, ugly grey who had carried her with such signal speed and wit before.

The pierced towers of Shan rose around him, familiar as his own fingers; Buwon and his fellow riders did not speak much. All strength was conserved for speed, the horses checked at every stop for injury or exhaustion, day folding into night with the peculiar rapidity the Shan called *hunter's mind*.

As a child, the trip away from Shan's capital was tortuously slow, his time in Zhaon over too soon, and the return accomplished too speedily. Now irritation rasped under his breast-bone, and his thoughts were with Zhaon-An's walls. They were strong, and she had that dappled greenmetal blade. Takyeo's dependents and Mrong Banh would look after her—yet everything in Takshin wished to wheel his horse and retrace his steps north like one of the Shan hunting-god's bolts flying for its home in the heart of a giant hell-beast.

The day they reached the capital a pall of autumn mist lay over the towers, and the work to repair Tabrak's tantrum was well under way. The first harvest was accomplished, the festival missed while they rode, and so it was Garan Takshin returned to the palace he knew much better than Zhaon's, his weary horse head-hanging and travel-dust thick upon all his garments.

"*There* he is." Kiron's relief shone from wide dark eyes above a proud nose and a generous mouth; he hurried forward past bowing, brown-clad ministers and a few eunuchs in brightly trimmed high court robes. Some familiar faces were missing; Takshin took in those present with a single burning glance. The high vaulted ceiling of the throne-hall was familiar too, full of remembered whispers and the lump of a boy's heart in his throat while the woman he was to call *Mother* pinned him with an excruciating stare. "Now we may begin the hunt, my lords; our wolf has returned."

"Battle-brother." Takshin clasped the king of Shan's right forearm, the salute between warriors. Shan's throne was a padded bench too, set under a replica of the tallest pierced tower ever built in the mists of time before Heaven reordered the world, the building said to be blessed by both Heaven and the Awakened One and lifted bodily into the sky in order to preserve its excellence. "Sunjosi reached me in good time. I was already flying home like an arrow; Buwon chanced across us upon the road."

"Happy chance indeed," Lord Buwon commented. "My king, I thought this enough of a gift to turn homeward to bring; I will return to the road as soon as fresh horses are—"

"You will not," Kiron said, and his tone became stern. "You are not given leave to lay aside your life, Lord Buwon. The blame for my queen's misfortune rests with me, and I shall purge it by riding north in pursuit of Tabrak. We lacked only my battle-brother; now he is returned, and we may fly."

The words were crisp and clear. No few ministers blanched, casting wary glances at Takshin.

He could have laughed, did the bitterness in his throat permit anything other than a sharp unamused bark. "He's been arguing the entire way." He strove for the correct tone—not light, not laughing, but not severe either. "It is Tabrak who shall feel my wrath over my sister's misfortune, Lord Buwon. Not you, and not my battle-brother."

A susurration slid through the crowded hall; more nobles, not to mention highly placed onlookers, were arriving. Ill news traveled swift, and his arrival was often held to be such.

Or maybe some of them actually thought a scarred wolf at their king's side was a powerful ally. No doubt Yala would have murmured such an observation, blunting his temper's sharpest edge.

I should have brought her. But there was another familiar face, mostly nose, and Lord Suron stepped between the two ministers of interior taxation—both in Shan black but with bright topknot-cages, one blue, one yellow—to bow, a trifle more deeply than his usual wont. "Garan Suon-ei Takshin," he said, also more formally than usual, and for a moment Takshin was almost certain Suron meant to challenge him for some mad reason. "I greet you."

The trouble with being in this great hall again was the memories rising like angry shades to choke him. At least the fading tang of smoke from burnt orchards made him think of pyres, as if the Mad Queen was safely in one of the many hells and he could breathe again.

"Felicitations, Lord Suron." Takshin offered his hand for the same warrior's clasp he shared with Kiron. "We have both had nuptials recently; how does the married life suit you so far?"

Deep relief warred with Suron's habit of keeping his expression carefully neutral; he had survived the Mad Queen's displeasure more than once by not showing a whit of emotion. Still, his mouth softened slightly and his eyes spoke before he coughed slightly.

Takshin's greeting made it clear a prince of Zhaon adopted to Shan would not hold Suron Daebo-a Nijera—though of course, in Shan her clan name would be treated differently than in Zhaon—responsible for Sabwone's fate.

Yala would be proud of this. Or so he thought, and as Suron clasped his forearm, Takshin tried a facsimile of a smile, knowing it would twist his scarred lip.

"It seems to have done *you* some good," Suron replied, and his own smile, rare as an unwary split-horn gazelle in the Westron Wastes, surfaced for a brief moment as well.

"Married?" Kiron shook his head. Here in the hall, the cynosure of many gazes both noble and servant, he was playing the king, and it suited him well. Everyone present now knew Takshin's position was well-nigh unassailable—many might even think Zhaon had sent its son to aid against Tabrak, and that more aid was forthcoming. While they were mistaken, all would agree it could only mean war. "You may tell me as we ride, Shin. I have not been idle, Shan is rising. We will fall upon the Pale Horde like the wolves we are."

And rescue Zhaon, who may even be grateful if Kurin has to risk his own skin leading the defense of the capital. No doubt Kiron would press for trade concessions; Anwei could only be reached by ship or through Shan, and trade with that great entrepôt spread wealth northward along the roads, collecting in Zhaon's bowl.

Only the trimmings reached Khir, but even that was more than enough. Or it would be, if the northerners were not so stubborn. Even his Yala had a streak of steel running through her liver, though it was well-camouflaged indeed.

"Good." It was Takshin's role to play the bloodthirsty spirit at a king's side, and sometimes he even enjoyed it. "When does the hunt begin?"

Rule Itself

The Kaeje was alive with hurrying feet, commands, and the ferment of gossip. Outside, the city celebrated First Harvest, the parade going forth as planned but the performers displaying their art before the Kaeje steps instead of in the banquet hall. The throbbing of fireflowers had not abated, and their crackles and booms through the thick stone walls made more than one courtier flinch.

"Swift, and caustic." Kihon Jiao's medicine-stained fingertips rubbed under his topknot, disarranging it even further. His festival garb—dark and modest, but of very high quality—was a distinct change from his usual shabby physician's robe, and he must have feared the worst when messengers and a cortege of Golden from the palace complex arrived at Garan Takshin's estate to request his presence with all speed. A hastily brushed entreaty from Princess Yala had no doubt eased some of his worry, and he glanced often at the grey-eyed lady who embraced a pale, trembling Second Princess, speaking softly to her almost as a mother might. This hallway adjacent to the Second Mother's apartments was full of bustle; beyond the partition, the Third Mother of a slain Emperor was no longer making that terrible gurgling sound, being dosed with omyei and nightflower as antidotes and other medicines were administered. The Second Mother was at her bedside, watching the gathered physicians intently. "Without the substance itself I cannot be sure, but she did not drink much."

"Not very much indeed." Mrong Banh, likewise rumpled, looked steadily over the physician's shoulder. Garan Sensheo, surrounded by ministers, still held the gore-stained sword he had struck his brother down with. "I cannot... But what do you think it was?"

The physician's shrug was arrested halfway, and he shook his head. "There are a few poisons I can think of. Mostly very expensive. There was much burning of the mouth, but..."

Gamnae let out a tiny, smothered moan. "It is too awful," she whispered against Yala's shoulder. "But Sensen... *Sensheo*..."

"Perhaps the Second Princess should be taken to her chambers?" Banh's own voice was none too steady.

Eunuchs clustered the partition; they parted to reveal Garan Jin, pale and wearing an expression of blank distraction.

"Jin," Gamnae called, and broke from Yala's arms. She flew to her youngest brother, and his mouth worked for a moment, as if tasting something very bitter indeed.

"I must return to my work." Physician Kihon cast another glance at Princess Yala, who nodded. A single tendril of dark hair fell from her braids; she brushed it from her face with no change of expression.

"I shall not return home until you are released, Honorable Kihon," she said quietly, and Mrong Banh's eyebrows shot up almost to his hairline.

It would, after all, be very easy to blame a physician for any ill turn in the Third Mother's condition. Especially a physician who had attended Garan Takyeo in his final extremity—and had that happened earlier this summer?

It seemed a lifetime ago.

"Princess." Honorable Kihon bowed, a movement of surprising polish despite the usual state of his clothing, and made no further ado, brushing past Garan Luswone's son and Garan Gamwone's daughter. The two royal children made a very filial picture of grief, and Banh's right hand pressed high upon the left side of his chest, attempting to rub away a deeply internal pang.

"I am aware of what was found." Zan Fein, his round face set and pale, made a short, peremptory gesture. Despite that, his tone was low and reasonable. "But who spoke *through* it?"

"No footprints, Honorable Zan." Lihaon Baikan, the most senior of the triumvirate leading the Palace Golden, regarded Garan Sensheo narrowly. "It is not even clear the trumpet was used; the rooms there are full of old furniture. The dust was quite disturbed; there have been servants in and out for at least ten days preparing for the festival."

"Quite a puzzle." Garan Sensheo's gaze was fixed somewhere across the hall. Spots of dried blood dewed his cheek. His thumb-ring and hurai bore crimson splatters, as did his robes. "Where is Lord Yulehi?"

"He cannot be found." Hailung Jedao, Lord Hanweo, was just as round and imposing as ever, his own festival garb not much marred. "Yet why would he perform such a feat so publicly? I cannot understand—"

"I do not accuse him." Sensheo's shoulders rounded; he appeared not to notice he still carried his sword. "I simply wonder at his absence, though Kur—" He hunched still further, swallowing the rest of the name. The shade of a murderous, murdered Emperor could, after all, still be present. "My elder brother…" Again he halted.

"The First Queen, taken so ill. And now this," Lord Tansin intoned. "And the attempts upon the previous Emperor, when he was Crown Prince."

"The situation is bad enough." Zan Fein's tone did not alter, but his gaze had sharpened. "Gossip will not help it."

"Lord Tansin merely says what the rest of us are thinking," Hailung Jedao observed, mildly. But his hands wrung at each other briefly inside his sleeves, making the fabric swell and distort. "The city—and the peasants—must be told something, let us think upon that."

Garan Sensheo shook his head, a toss like a nervous horse. "The servant who brought the jug to table? Has anyone—"

"Vanished as well." Zan Fein produced a fan from his sleeve, opened it with meditative slowness instead of its usual snap. Its edge was dabbed with gold leaf, and a character for *abundance* in honor of the harvest showed upon its broad side. "The jug stood open next to the Emperor for half the banquet, though, waiting for its turn and being passed by servants and Golden."

"I should not have shattered it," Sensheo said, mournfully. "But... Third Mother..."

"How did you know?" The Minister of the Lower Feather, Daebo Luashuo Tualih, rested an avuncular hand upon the Fifth Prince's shoulder. He was a gleaming man, well-oiled, and he evidently thought it wise to appear very supportive of Sensheo at this juncture.

"I... I suspected. I have had many misgivings." Sensheo seemed to realize he still held the sword, and lifted it slightly as Lord Hanweo withdrew a half-step, his eyes widening. "Then it seemed a voice was crying to me."

"Just as in a novel." Zan Fein turned his attention to the Sixth Prince and Second Princess, holding each other near the door like children during a thunderstorm. "Arrangements must be made. And another enthronement."

Perhaps those assembled had not thought so far ahead, or were surprised to hear the matter stated so clearly. Garan Sensheo, in particular, seemed stunned, and a ripple passed through the crowd of ministers. The last two of the Golden triumvirate were at the other end of the hall, holding back a tide of curious servants and other nobles.

"What?" Sensheo offered the sword's hilt to Lihaon Baikan; the stocky man in his bright armor held his hands up, denying the touch of metal that had killed an Emperor he was sworn to protect. "You must take this, I cannot hold it. Something must be done."

"Oh, indeed," Lord Daebo said, in the hush that followed. Garan Jin's voice was a bare whisper as he stroked Gamnae's hair; behind them, the new princess hovered, her quiet grey gaze moving from one man to the next. "You are next in succession, Glorious Fifth Prince Garan Sensheo."

"But..." Sensheo's mouth opened further, closed. "But I cannot, Lord Daebo."

"Tabrak approaches, there is battle in the North." Zan Fein's fan twitched, and began to work lazily. "A son of Garan Tamuron is needed."

Nobody observed that the Emperor had possessed a wealth of heirs, now whittled to two—and one adopted to Shan, sent across the path of the Horde by a brother who may have just committed an unthinkable sin and been immediately punished.

Garan Takshin could not inherit the Throne of Five Winds, after all, and Zakkar Kai was merely adopted by a concubine.

"Perhaps it should be Jin." Garan Sensheo lifted the bloody sword again, slightly. It was a familiar pose, a hero holding a painted prop, but then again he did spend much of his time in the Theater District. What else could fill the time of a prince so low in the succession? "After all, I—"

"—struck in defense of your mother," Lord Hanweo supplied. He was very pale. "Your brother has ascended to Heaven, and Zhaon needs you."

Zan Fein's fan did not halt, but his gaze settled upon Princess Yala's. There was a terrible depth to those dark Zhaon eyes, but she might be forgiven for thinking he did not precisely see her. Instead, some vision rose before the chief court eunuch, and it was perhaps a good thing every other eye was upon Garan Sensheo.

For the chief court eunuch looked, for a brief moment, almost afraid. And the sentiment was echoed upon a Khir woman's face for that heartbeat.

Princess Yala glided to Gamnae and Jin. "Come," she said softly, with the sharp edges of Khir lingering behind her Zhaon. "Some tea, and a quiet place to sit. That would be best, would it not?"

Garan Jin, hollow-eyed, stared at the new princess over his sister's head, as if he could not quite place the face or voice addressing him. "M-my mother."

"Honorable Kihon says she will live." Princess Yala touched Gamnae's shoulder, a brief, sisterly brush. "I will stay here; you must attend to Gamnae and change your robe, then return. Honorable Mrong, perhaps you…" She did not quite falter when she realized she was the only one speaking, but she did drop her pale gaze and brush at that stray tendril of blue-black hair again.

"Very filial." Lord Hanweo's tone carried nothing but warm approval; he could hardly sound otherwise at this moment. "Sixth Prince, you must be strong now, for your sister and your mother."

Jin did not even glance at the minister. Instead, he freed himself gently from Gamnae, and bowed deeply in Yala's direction. "I shall leave Mother to your care for a brief while," he said, and there was a steely glint to his dark eyes. "Thank you, Elder Sister." The term was almost painfully honorific.

Gamnae managed a somewhat shorter but very creditable bow too, and was drawn away. Mrong Banh followed, an anxious fatherhen trailing two chicks, with many a glance over his shoulder and his hands scrubbing at each other openly instead of hiding in his sleeves. The new princess kept her gaze downcast, and glided for the partition; Zan Fein's fan began to move a little more intently.

"The enthronement must proceed swiftly," he said, a clan-head turning to business now that the children were abed.

"Indeed," Lord Hanweo agreed, and pinned the most senior of the Golden with his most jovial, bright, and paralyzing stare. His clan-niece had escaped something terrible, his greatest rival had vanished, and though Garan Kurin had shown him much preferment, it could not stand in the way of arranging the realm. "The official proclamation must be given some thought, too. And you, nephew, must be made ready."

"Uncle…" Sensheo shook his head, his mouth twitching once. Surely it was simply a product of shock, not the flicker of a pleased smile. "Is there no other way? My elder brother has a pyre, but perhaps there is some hope…"

"Do not protest overmuch," Lord Tansin murmured. "Some might take it as an invitation, Glorious Fifth Prince."

"But not your clan, eh, Tansin?" Lord Hanweo reached for the swordhilt, ready to risk pollution by touching a weapon that had struck down an Emperor; Sensheo surrendered it without demur. "There is much to do. We must be about it; Zhaon will not rule itself."

"Nor should it." Garan Sensheo's shoulders firmed. He drew himself up, still in the attitude of a public actor, and those assembled perhaps watched with some admiration. "But first, my...my brother's body must be cared for, Zan Fein. There must be exorcists, and every proper, ah, proper step must be taken."

"And Lord Yulehi must be found," Zan Fein added. "I believe we may leave that to you, Honorable Lihaon."

"It is my duty," the elder Golden said, perhaps a trifle sourly. Still, it was not entirely a loathsome duty, for all present knew how in Garan Tamuron's reign Lord Yulehi had argued against his raising to the post his seniority had granted, and all because his family were distant Daebo cousins. Garan Kurin had shown Lihaon favor, but now...

Well, the situation had changed.

Indeed, Garan Kurin's clan-uncle had few friends among ministers *or* Golden at the moment, especially now that Garan Tamuron's second son had ascended to Heaven. And in such a fashion, too.

Nobody needed to remark aloud that Binei Jinwon, Lord Yulehi, could not be far behind his illustrious nephew.

A Bloodstained Throne

The fireflowers were still roiling the sky over Zhaon-An, but the bulk of the Kaeje muffled their explosions. In the spacious, elegant chambers of Zhaon's only remaining queen, restrained hangings occupied their usual spaces, furniture with clean uncluttered lines was arranged in aesthetically pleasing groups, and every surface was polished-glowing in muted colors.

Servants fussed over her endlessly—bundling her into an evening robe, fetching tea, dabbing her with nia oil, offering sweets and a sedative draught she waved aside even when two physicians recommended it. Neither worthy fellow was the shabby physician Garan Takyeo and Garan Takshin had placed so much faith in; Honorable Kihon had declared Third Mother Luswone unlikely to ascend to Heaven that night and escorted the new princess upon her return to her husband's estate in the Noble District.

Garan Hanweo-a Haesara, Second Dowager Queen of Zhaon and Second Mother to one Emperor, dismissed her servants softly but firmly. Behind the screen cordoning her beauty-table with its regimented ranks of bottles, jars, unguents, powders, and cosmetics, her remaining son—hurriedly stripped and rubbed free of gore, then helped into a princely robe a mother kept against an adult child's infrequent overnight visits—dismissed the physicians with many thanks for their care, and when the door closed behind the last honorable visitor Haesara was shaken with the urge to sweep every implement and jar from the beauty-table and onto the floor, then upend the heavy wooden thing to crush their scattering if her strength would allow.

The urge was deeply uncharacteristic; aesthetic restraint was a noblewoman's duty and even more a queen's. But oh, how she longed to smash, to destroy.

"Mother?" Sensheo was at the screen, his shadow swelling as he leaned toward its edge, as if he were six summers high and peeping at her nighttime routine again. He had been a winning child for so long—sometimes spoiled, but what cherished boy was not? "Are you well? I realize it was shocking, but..."

Her hair, loosely braided for bed, swung as she turned upon her knees, staring at the screen. "My child." Quiet and grave, the title fell from numb lips. She had almost drunk from the cup, hesitating only because she disliked the swimming too much sohju provoked inside her skull. "What have you done?"

He paused while his shadow moved again. "Did you not hear the voice, Mother? I saved you."

"Straight from *The Adventures of Prince Jen-ji.*" Of course courtiers would pretend to be unaware, and so would many ministers—but it was a shoddy play indeed. Still, the peasants would believe wholeheartedly in strange voices, Heaven taking an interest in the doings of the imperial court and sending a guardian spirit to whisper through a brazen trumpet. "You could have chosen a less common tale."

The silence before his reply was loud to a mother's ears, though perhaps to none other. Sensheo did not do what Makar would—move silently for the hall partition to make certain no unfriendly ears were pressed to it. Instead, he settled at the very edge of the screen between them, his shadow misshapen as the lamp upon her nightstand cast its steady glow.

"Jen-ji had a mother too," he said, finally. "She praised his cleverness, if I recall aright."

She had not expected him to be quite so direct. There was a deep tearing pain in her rib cage as if she had quaffed whatever was in the ancient jug; poor Luswone's mouth was a bloody pulp-mass, and the physicians were worried about her voice as well. Was there deeper damage trickling down her throat, nestling in her internal organs?

"Your own brother," Haesara whispered. Her hands were cold, and her feet too, despite the still-breathless heat of a Zhaon summer. "And Luswone. She has been my friend, Sensheo, when *that woman* would have destroyed us both."

"Well, *that woman* is gone now." An airy statement of fact, one shadow-hand lifting—oh, it was a copy of a gesture his father had performed more than once, and a bright dart of hatred shot through Haesara from crown to heels.

She would never have allowed herself to name it while Garan Tamuron was alive. She had done her duty, she had even poured his tea. But the warlord she had married and given sons to for the good of her clan was safely ascended now—or was he watching this?

Who could tell? And if Tamuron knew she hated him, he had at least appreciated that she kept the fact silently locked within her own head-meat. Not like his First Queen, that grasping bitch.

"Sensheo." She sounded about to scold him for stealing Kanbina's plums, but it was only because she could not gain enough breath to raise her voice. Of course such a thing would bring servants at a run, but at the moment, she was hard-pressed to care. *"What have you done?"*

"Your eldest son knew he was being sent to his death," Sensheo said, calmly enough. Soon they would come to bring him to the ancient windowless room in the bowels of the Kaeje, to prepare him for enthronement. The Golden would pound their spear-butts against the paving in shifts, the ancient ceremonies would move forward. Maybe the peasants would even celebrate; her clan-uncle certainly would. The oily man was no doubt beside himself with restrained glee. "And he went anyway—not very intelligent of him,

Mother. No doubt the former Emperor had a soldier ready to snip a loose piece of thread in one manner or another. Did you not guess it, when his sword returned without him? He was not here to protect you, Mother. *I* have done so, and you chide me."

"You..." Oh, *now* it was clear. One of Sensheo's intrigues had finally borne fruit, and Makar had not been here to halt him or ameliorate the consequences.

Her beloved eldest, so bright and so rare, was gone. She had attended the pyre and worn her mourning, but it had not seemed possible she would never see him again. Surely it was some manner of mistake, surely it was one of his long, subtle games, always a step ahead of others, always with an ultimate goal in mind. Surely he would return, step out of the shadows like another prince in another tale, one a little more refined than this...this *murder*.

Her husband had welded Zhaon together with murder upon a scale both grand and small. None stood in the way of Garan Tamuron's desires. And even Makar, at eight summers high, had defended his mother and baby brother against assassins.

"I will be Emperor of Zhaon," Sensheo said, quite calmly. "Nobody will ever harm us again, Mother. It is done. I do not expect you to thank me; you never have."

"I am your mother," she reminded him. She sounded, even to herself, as if she had been struck. At least Tamuron had never done so. "And Luswone..." *Heaven forgive me, for I carried this child, and look at what he has done.*

"She is only a concubine." Airily, as if he did not know what he owed to another mother in his father's household—one who had protected his own dam more than once, and been repaid as far as Haesara could. Allies were not merely for warlords and generals. "Jin is no problem, but if he becomes one, we shall see."

"He is your *brother*." *What did I give birth to?* Chills ran down Haesara's back, Luswone's agonized choking still filling her ears. She would never forget that sound—and her own *son* had...how had he managed it? Should she ask? "And Luswone's son. You will not touch him, or I will—"

"What, Mother? What will you do?" He did not even sound angry, merely thoughtful. "I know I am not Ma—" He halted, aware that naming the dead was ill-luck in the extreme. "I am not your eldest, but you could at least act as if you love me."

"How can you say such a thing to me? I labored a day—"

"—and a half to bear me, yes. You have told me, my dearest one, and I am running short of ways to make you proud. Another mother might think her son as Emperor, with the help of Heaven itself, was something to take some comfort in." He exhaled sharply; there was motion in the corridor now, footsteps and quiet voices. They were coming to collect her youngest son and place him upon a bloodstained throne, replacing a similarly bloody child—for who could deny that Garan Kurin had arranged his eldest brother's death?

And she had half suspected him of an even deadlier sin, feeding the woman who bore him some tincture or powder to keep her from meddling in his reign. Very little attributed to the once-Second Prince, then Emperor of Zhaon, would have surprised her.

But now, she wondered. The most successful venom-bearing creature was the one who stayed still and quiet long enough to strike.

"Was it indeed Heaven who helped you?" Her lips tingled, not wanting to quite work properly. What would stop her second son from deciding *she* was an impediment? A man who would kill his brother like a theater star striking down a demon-clad fellow actor upon the stage, with no more thought than brushing away a fly hovering over a meat dish—what else would such a man do?

And she had borne him, fed him, raised him. Her only remaining prop for old age, and if anyone else even *suspected* what he had done, the blame would lie with her.

Perhaps it already did.

"Of course it was, did you not hear? *Mother, do not drink.*" He mimicked the soft, eerie tone. "Fear not, all who might say otherwise are safely silenced. And I saved you, as Makar once did. Because you are my mother." A note of anxiety had crept into her second son's quiet, reasonable tone. "Surely you must see as much."

Oh, now there was *much* she saw. A sage had struck her upon the forehead with paired fingers and now she was no longer blind—but what mother was not when it came to her precious, beloved sons?

"You must be careful," she heard herself say. "You must take no step without consulting me, Sensheo. This is dangerous, and many will seek to topple you."

"Oh, I know." Did he even sound amused? The noise in the corridor was growing ever closer. "But you will not rule through me. All you must do is play your sathron and sew your pretty dresses, Mother. Your son is the Emperor now. You will want for nothing."

His shadow changed shape; he had risen, and was calmly arranging his robe.

GRANDFATHER
AND LITTLE TWO

F ireflowers were not blooming as frequently; the rumble
of drums and skirling of flutes from the parade winding
through Zhaon-An's greatest central artery was audible between
the booming and crackling. The most highly anticipated part of
the festival, at least for the children, was the great rain-dragon,
its mouth grinning wide and its mane shaking. It shuffled upon
many feet, dancers underneath its cloth carapace stamping in the
traditional pattern and dewed with each other's sweat. Little ones
screamed and pointed, festival bladders were broken with showers
of glitter or torn red rai-paper, adults cheered and applauded until
their hands hurt. The great feast funded by the merchants of both
Great and Left Markets was brought to the East Gate for the beggars; even its leavings were munificent in the extreme.

The rain-dragon wound its way to the South Gate, breaking
into individual segments as it passed through, peasants and those
who crowded into the shacks pressed against Zhaon-An's walls, not
to mention those who worked the great estates of nobles, surging
forward to touch the costume and perhaps gain a fragment of its
luck. Tiny bundles of black powder, lacking a bright flash but making a satisfying noise, crunched and snapped underfoot; sparklers
cast garish shadows.

Near the smoking ruins of the Yuin, the celebration was more muted. Still, many hands had been at the work of clearing and rebuilding, and the Emperor Garan Kurin had decreed relief for the poorest among them.

A man in a laborer's trousers and shortened tunic pushed through the crowd gathered to see the performers parading through the Left Market, bringing the harvest's luck. The great dragon's route avoided the scorching, but it varied every year, after all, and had been planned long in advance.

The man, his topknot caged in plain leather pierced with a wooden pin, moved fluidly through the fringes of the gathering, barely glancing at acrobats and dancers. A sound of collective wonder left the crowds' throats as another barrage of fireflowers filled the sky.

The risk of combustion, so close to another great fire, was negligible. Or so they seemed to think.

The man found a certain door in a rickety, charred building and knocked in a particular manner. Though it seemed unlikely even the most vigorous hammering could be heard through the festival din, the smoke-blackened door swung open just enough to permit a single entry, then closed with an unheard snap.

He nodded to the grandson on duty that night, the boy's ear flattened from pressing against wood, and passed down a long corridor, turning aside and scratching at the jamb of a wide low room where several women were busily sewing by lamplight, taxing their eyesight in order to finish the morrow's costumes. In the morn the festival would spill out of the city and into the fields again. "How goes it, Ah-li?"

The girl so addressed tossed her head, her cheeks slicked with the tears of concentration welling from her fine dark eyes. "Well enough, and where were *you*? I had to sup alone."

"I'll make it up to you." He vanished into the darkness, and the girl smiled before bending back to her work, her shoulders suddenly loosening.

Up a flight of creaking stairs, shedding his tunic as he went and revealing close-fitting indigo cloth, the assassin—for the fluidity with which he moved denoted a walker of the Shadowed Path, as did the dark wrappings under his laborer's disguise—hummed a tune currently popular in the Theater District. Tonight's job would mean ingots, and enough of them meant he could afford a wife.

He sobered and straightened as he knocked upon another door, this one bearing a painted character holding the particular meaning of a theater-manager; it was the impresario's little joke.

"Come in," Grandfather said, irritably. He disliked the noise, but festivals meant profit. The child thieves and finer pickpockets were having a lovely evening; so too were some of the highly skilled in the young man's profession.

The young man entered, bowing deeply to his elder. "Grandfather, here I am."

"Who speaks? Ah, Little Two, come in." The rotund man sitting at a massive mahu-wood desk bore no grey in his hair; he was busy brushing within a giant rope-bound ledger. A halu lamp upon the desktop cast just enough light to aid him. "There is tea; you must drink."

"Thank you, Grandfather." The assassin glided in, wary of the sawed-through places in the flooring, avoiding the traps with unconscious ease. He poured from the cooling pot set at the corner of the desk, refilling the impresario's small slipware cup first.

It was heavy sweet laborer's tea, almost strong enough for soldiers. Just the thing after a night spent breathing dust and contorted atop furniture, waiting for the signal to breathe his lines into a brazen trumpet before scrambling across rooftops once the task was finished. He drank quietly, studiously avoiding looking at the ledger's pages. The circle of lamplight was warm gold; the room was otherwise bare and its only window heavily barred.

Finally, the impresario sighed and rinsed his brush, settling it in a cheap scribe's rack. "Is it done?"

"Done, and done well." The traditional reply, meaning none had seen him about his work and the loose end—a haughty Palace servant in goldenrod, waiting at the appointed place for her payment after effecting the assassin's entry into a heavily guarded complex—had been addressed.

"Ah." The impresario gave a slight nod. His brush continued, unhurried. "Tell me, Little Two, how long have you been with me?"

"Since I was six summers high, Grandfather." A shadow of unease crossed the young man's round face, rubbed with blacksmith's soot. This part of the task could not be hurried—indeed, a walker of the Path learned never to hurry if it could be helped.

"You do quite well, young man."

The young man's unease sharpened. There was generally no pleasing his elder; it was usual, for praise might well make a youth impulsive. "Thank you, Grandfather."

The impresario rinsed his brush and set it carefully in a rack to dry. He reached for a drawer on his side of the desk; the assassin did not stiffen, though his grasp upon the teacup shifted.

Just slightly. Just enough.

A small heavy bundle wrapped in broadcloth was heaved onto the desk with a grunt. "Here it is," the older man said. "But there is ill news for you, Little Two."

"The Path holds nothing but," the assassin murmured, dutifully. Proverbs became what they were because they carried a cargo of truth upon their backs, like bent old men under loads of firewood.

"True, true." Grandfather nodded, running his tongue over his top teeth in the familiar fashion that meant he was not quite finished speaking and a junior would be well to observe respectful silence. "Well, the lord paying for this particular task wished the worker of Heaven's wonders to be silenced forever."

More fireflowers boomed outside; the crowd's noise was a surf-roar blunted by the building's weight. The assassin said nothing, studying his teacup. One did not look directly at a threat; peripheral vision alerted you much more quickly to an attack's direction.

"Did you see Ah-li?" the impresario asked, quietly.

What did it matter? But the young man nodded. "I did."

"Do you...forgive an old man, Little Two, but do you still wish to marry her?"

"Of course." He could hope that the payment for the night's work would go to her, at least, if he was to be removed as a loose thread upon a garment's edge. Lacking a fraction for Grandfather's trouble, of course, but that was the way of the world.

"Well." The elder rubbed his palms together, calluses stropping with a whisper. "You have two choices, then. You shall take the fee for a job well done, take Ah-li from Zhaon-An tonight, and never return. There is enough for a farm, or a stake for a caravan-guard, or several other jobs. Ah-li is thrifty; she will use it well. Or, should you wish to remain...well, it will not be as pleasant."

It was even, as such things went, relatively fair, or so the young assassin thought. "What would Grandfather have me do?" Sweat dripped, a single cool fingertip, down the channel of his spine. He should have known the payment was far too much for such a simple task.

And yet, when your grandfather asked, a junior paid what was owed. Even Ah-li, who could have been sent to the Theater District to work as a flower once their affection for each other was discovered.

"Oh, Little Two." The impresario sighed, and finished chafing his hands. Now he stretched every finger in turn, keeping them supple. Brushwork required much dexterity, and so did his many other tasks. "You are a fine grandson, and I should be sorry to lose you. Those high and mighty may kill their kin, but we are different."

"Yes, Grandfather." The assassin had suspected the night's work would bear ill consequences, but what else could he do? The man he called Grandfather had fed him, clothed him, made certain he was trained—brutally, yes, but the Path did not forgive weakness.

Much like life itself.

"*Ai*, listen to me go on." The older man cleared his throat once, twice, shook his dexterous paws, reached for his cup, and took a large swallow to cleanse his mouth. "Well, don't just stand there, boy. Take the ingots, drag Ah-li from her sewing, and the two of you must leave Zhaon-An tonight. Kurrah at the stable on the

Street of Blue Feathers has a long-eared temperbeast for you. Mind you go safely, and get Ah-li some dinner; she was worried for you tonight."

Relief wrung sweat from a man worse than harsh effort did. The young man ducked his head, shyly; the smile made him even younger. "Yes, Grandfather."

"Well, go." The elder made an irritated gesture, tapped his cup upon the table once to prove it was empty, and set it aside before reaching for his brush. "You stink of fire, and of rich assholes. Get thee gone, small thing. Do not return."

"Yes, Grandfather." The assassin drained his cup, setting it in the dirty stack; there had been many coming to see the impresario tonight. He took the ingots with a bow; the weight was comforting and thrilling at once. He bowed again, retreated to the door, and paused.

The impresario seemed to have forgotten his presence, but Little Two—all walkers of the Path bore such names, since plenty did not survive the training—turned again, drew himself up, and bowed very deeply, the highest mark of respect possible without dropping to his knees. He held his position for quite a few moments before straightening, and his eyes glimmered.

He hurried out the door and down the creaking stairs. The impresario laid his dry brush aside again, rubbing at his burning eyes.

"Children," he muttered thickly. "Always a torment."

He returned to his work, pausing only to whisper a small prayer to Heaven to watch over the two young ones sent from the city of their birth. Neither of them had ever been beyond the walls before, but remaining would be far too dangerous. All in their hive would miss Ah-li's cheerful singing, and her skill with the needle; he would miss Little Two's quiet competence. But there were others, and the next crop of children was growing nicely, just like the rai.

It was a fine Harvest, even if he had to dab at his damp cheeks with his sleeve so the next visitor would not see any suspicious gleam.

TRANSLATOR I MAY TRUST

The news burst over Zhaon-An like an afternoon thunderclap; the streets, still scattered with crimson bits of rai-paper and spent straw sparkler-tips, were full of rushing whispers instead of the usual babble. The enthronement of Garan Sensheo proceeded apace. Though somewhat hurried, nothing was left undone—the three refusals upon the Kaeje steps, the Golden drumming their spear-butts through the watches of the night, some of them head-sore from too much festival sohju but holding grimly to their duty. The royal family—their ranks sadly thinned, though no courtier, minister, lady, or eunuch dared observe as much—gathered afterward to perform their ceremonial obeisance to their new head, who accepted their bows and small gifts with a slight, stiff, satisfied smile.

None were allowed to wear mourning. The passing of an unfil-ial tyrant did not permit it.

Hard upon the heels of the celebration of a new Emperor upon the Throne of Five Winds arrived dispatches from the North; Zak-kar Kai had won a great victory.

The king of Khir was dead.

Garan Komor-a Yala heard the news at the Silver Pavilion with Second Mother Haesara, and little perceptible emotion passed over the Khir woman's face, though she did gaze at her hands in her lap for a few moments, dark lashes veiling her gaze. Haesara patted her arm, kindly enough; perched upon an embroidered cushion upon the new princess's other side, Garan Gamnae, her eyes ringed with sleeplessness, shifted slightly so her hip touched Yala's. It was a subtle movement, though remarked by no few of the court ladies with meaningful glances.

To her credit, though, the new princess attended the victory celebration that afternoon. After all, her husband's family was her own.

The next morn a proclamation, artfully arranged by Zan Fein, was read by Lord Hanweo—now formally Chief Minister—in a ringing, resonant tone as the court assembled in the glittering, crimson-pillared great hall. Afterward, a collection of sober-robed Khir merchants were brought from the quarter of Zhaon-An northerners traditionally settled in, most dark-eyed as Zhaon but some few muddy-gazed, and two with clear grey eyes that marked true nobility in the North.

"Where is my new sister?" Garan Sensheo said, and beckoned at the smaller dais where his elder brother's wife stood at his mother's side. "Come, attend me."

Princess Garan Yala moved forward, performing the ritual bows at the proper places. She glanced at Zan Fein upon the last; the chief court eunuch in his accustomed place next to the Chief Minister's was impassive, but his fan flicked once. The illustration upon its ridged face was a branch of yeoyan blossoms—perhaps a sign of renewal, perhaps a comment upon the fragility of high position.

"Your Gracious Majesty." Yala straightened. "How might this handmaiden serve?"

A rustle ran through the court. Perhaps the princess's grasp of Zhaon was slightly imperfect, or her grasp of etiquette, for the double honor of the address was a trifle much.

"Closer, my sister. You must call me *brother*." The word for a slightly elder male sibling could even be affectionate; his smile widened. He did not wear the archer's thumb-ring of carven horn now;

the double hurai upon his first fingers, carved with the name of his reign, were heavy enough. "Come, stand here." He indicated a spot to his left, where Mrong Banh had once been wont to stand during the ceremonials of Garan Tamuron's court.

The astrologer—and Garan Jin—were in the Iejo, hovering over Third Mother Luswone. That great lady was still abed after what was being referred to as *the unfortunate harvest.*

The term held several layers of meaning, not least a miscarriage or a field of rotting rai. Much was made of the new Emperor's delicacy in allowing his youngest brother to be absent from this celebration.

The Emperor beckoned, a lazy motion. "Bring the traitors forward. Now, sister, you speak Zhaon well."

The Khir merchants, most slightly disheveled though two were in robes of sumptuously bright cotton, grouped together like frightened cloudfur. The Golden behind them moved forward, and though their pikes were not lowered, they were still an effective prod.

"I have tried to study Zhaon, to please my husband and his family." The princess's tone was low and clear. Her accent was called *piquant* by some of the court ladies; one or two of the courtiers said it was *charming*, but not very loudly since her scarred husband was well known to have a ferocious temper.

And they had not heard news of *his* death. Not yet.

"Indeed." The Emperor studied his sister-in-law, his hands resting upon his thighs as his father had been often wont to sit. "I have need of a translator I may trust, my sister. Here are your countrymen. Ask them if they have heard the news."

"I beg forgiveness, I do not understand." She did not look puzzled, but neither did she immediately turn to the merchants. "Which news, Emperor of Zhaon?" Her tone was neutral, perhaps excessively so.

"Heaven preserve us." Sensheo's smile widened. He did not play with kombin like his elder brother; some courtiers had been heard to intimate that perhaps the former emperor had felt much need of prayer to still his conscience. "Do you not know?"

"I do not wish any misunderstanding, illustrious brother." The princess's hands were tucked quite properly in her sleeves. Her hem did not tremble, though she was pale—well, no doubt she was worried for her absent husband. "There have been many events of late; I would not wish to refer to the wrong one."

A susurration slipped through the court. Whether it was admiration for her bravery or approbation for her precision was an open question. Lord Hanweo's fan was out too, its paper side painted with an abstract pattern of chevrons. Perhaps he felt any other design might be...misconstrued.

"Very well." The new Emperor's expression remained fixed, and his gaze was very bright. His slipper-toes, heavily embroidered, peered from under his crimson hem. Seamstresses were working diligently, it was rumored, to provide him with an imperial wardrobe. His elder brother's clothes, heaped upon a great burning pile to rid the palace of ill-luck, were still smouldering. "I shall be very clear. Ask them if they mourn the loss of their king."

"There is no word for *king* in Khir, illustrious brother." His sister-in-law was evidently very anxious to please the new ruler; she was rumored to be somewhat of a scholar, and those creatures always endeavored for accuracy. "I shall have to say Great Rider instead."

Sensheo's right thumb rubbed against a silver-chased hurai. "Then do so."

The princess addressed the merchants in the sharply musical language of the northerners. One of them, as grey-eyed as she, was elected leader by a collection of subtle glances passed between them. He stepped slightly forward and bowed, dividing the honor of the obeisance between Emperor and princess. His reply, though given in a different language, was pitched to carry; he had spoken to crowds before.

Finally, the princess returned to Zhaon, and bowed deeply before straightening to address the Emperor. "They say Zhaon is to be congratulated, and may the Emperor reign a thousand thousand years. Such is the wish for rulers in the North, my illustrious brother."

"Very prettily put." Zhaon's newest emperor nodded, his hands carefully cupped about each other in his lap as if he were a statue of the Enlightened One. "Very prettily put indeed. Ask them how they feel about Zakkar Kai."

The princess's hesitation was slight, but noticeable. "Please forgive me, illustrious brother. I do not understand." Her sleeves did not change shape; she was not clutching at her hands within them. It was rumored she bore a greenstone claw like some manner of Northern demon, but surely a woman in her delicate position would not bring such a thing before the Emperor.

The consequences would be extreme. Heaven itself had spoken in warning to Garan Sensheo, had it not? Surely whatever celestial inhabitant had done so would be watching this favored son of Garan Tamuron closely.

"You do not need to." The Emperor's gaze flickered to Zan Fein, who studied a point above the princess's head as if it contained an interesting passage he wished to decode. So did Lord Hanweo; most of the ministers were assiduously looking elsewhere. There was no trace of avidity upon their features. Second Mother Haesara, though, gazed steadily at her son, and her mouth was a tight thin line.

The princess made a subtle movement, a graceful, wilting motion. She looked very small next to the Throne and its richly caparisoned inhabitant. "I would not like to anger the Emperor of Zhaon with a poor translation."

"I think you are uniquely fitted to this task. Now *ask*." A hint of command crept into the final word.

Another volley of sharp, liquid Khir passed between the two northerners. Finally, with another deep bow, the princess spoke in Zhaon. Her voice, while low and accented with sharp consonants, was very clear. "They feel the Emperor of Zhaon is mighty indeed to command one so beloved of the God of War. Heaven smiles upon Zhaon." The princess was very pale now.

She was, after all, only a woman.

"Really. Well, most commendable." Sensheo inclined his royal head. His topknot-cage's golden pin flashed. "Now, dear sister, ask which of their number conspires against Zhaon."

More Khir. A more definite murmur slipped through the court; the princess's back was straight as an antique sword and her hands clasped demurely in her sleeves. Her slipper-tips peered from beneath her hem; she did not shift uneasily.

She performed another deep bow before she addressed the ruler of Zhaon. A few courtiers glanced at each other—really, it was faintly unsettling to see a poor foreign woman forced to this. "They reply that none conspire against Zhaon the mighty, Emperor of Zhaon. Should one of their number do so, they would kill him themselves, for they are bound by the laws of Zhaon."

"Well, then." The Emperor seemed pleased by this, or aware that his actions began to tread the edge of pettiness. "That is a great comfort, sister. Please, return to my mother; I believe she requires you."

The princess bowed, and glided down the steps. The merchants, wary, did not relax, simply watched their countrywoman to see if she would glance in their direction.

She did not. She fixed her gaze upon the Second Mother, who still studied her illustrious son.

"Wait." The Emperor lifted one hurai-clad finger. "My sister, please, return."

Dutifully, she bowed and did so.

"Do me the very great favor, my sister, of asking them how I may be sure."

The entire court hushed. Deep in the bowels of a dry-dust afternoon, a rumble of thunder walked; the autumn rains were drawing very close.

Now the princess appeared perplexed. "Sure, my illustrious brother?"

"Ask them," Garan Sensheo clarified, "how I may be certain they do not conspire against Zhaon himself."

The princess paused, then spoke in Khir again. The leader of the merchants replied, a short sharp declarative sentence.

Garan Yala performed another of those deep, possibly uncomfortable bows. More fans appeared among the courtiers, opening and beginning languid work. "My illustrious brother, their leader says they do not conspire against Zhaon at all."

"But that is not what I asked." Patent surprise filled the Emperor's tone, and his eyebrows raised. "Are you certain you translated correctly?"

"To the best of my ability, Emperor of Zhaon." Princess Yala's tone remained utterly honorific. Was she aware of any danger? Perhaps she was not—but in any case, she was behaving quite correctly indeed. It was almost, *almost* an insult to treat a silk-wearing woman as a common translator, no matter how honorable such a function was when performed by eunuch, scribe, or scholar. "Shall I ask again?"

"No, I have heard quite enough. Return to my mother, sister, and I thank you for your pains."

This time he did not call her back. The leader of the merchants spoke in accented Zhaon as she passed before them. "We do not conspire," he declared. "We came to Zhaon to—"

"Silence," the Emperor barked, and the Golden behind the merchants tensed, pike-tips dipping slightly. "Take them outside the city walls and behead them. I will have no treachery in Zhaon, there has been quite enough of it already."

The princess's steady step faltered as she mounted the dais occupied by royal women, the briefest of pauses; Garan Haesara beckoned her almost peremptorily.

"Unclean one," the Khir merchant shouted. "Do you think anyone here does not know you, son of a bloodthirsty dog? You wash your hands in the blood of your brother and dare to accuse *us*?"

"Come here," Haesara whispered fiercely, and drew her daughter-in-law to her side. Garan Gamnae, deathly pale as well, turned her shoulder and stepped subtly before Yala, her round chin quivering but her shoulders rigid.

Zan Fein's fan snapped shut. Golden hurried forward, bright armor glittering as they laid hands upon the unfortunate merchants.

Their leader still shouted in accented Zhaon, heaping abuse upon the conqueror of his country; the spectacle was enough that in the ensuing hubbub, the foreign lady-in-waiting, now a princess, was almost forgotten.

But those who knew the subtle ways of Zhaon's court knew she would not be completely, and not for long.

WOMEN ALWAYS DO

That night, while dry thunder cavorted over Zhaon-An and a wet warm wind brushed the roof tiles, Garan Yala slipped from her bed, a sleeveless linen shift fluttering as she paced quietly to a wide clear expanse of hardwood floor. She had thought, setting forth that dust-hazed morn, that she might not return to her husband's estate.

She was, after all, Khir. And even though her husband might not be in the succession, it did not seem reasonable that Garan Sensheo would let him live much longer. Or her, for that matter.

The nights had cooled somewhat; bending her usual modesty, she hiked up the shift as she began the stretching that always preceded practice with the *yue*. What would she have done if the Golden came for her as well as the merchants? Submitted as a Khir woman should, or drawn her blade? She had been raised to obey, that central tenet of female behavior; she had also perhaps reached a summit of a noble Khir girl's dreams, for her red time was definitely late.

But all was ashes around her, like the breath of charring still discernable when the wind shifted from the direction of the Left Market. The world had decided to tilt off its course and plunge into madness. She had failed to protect her princess and betrayed her husband in the secret chambers of her liver, heart, and head-meat; while she was distinctly unimportant under Heaven, the punishment was still natural and pitilessly applied.

The unfortunate merchants' heads were mounted upon Zhaon-An's great city walls as if they were common traitors, and Yala had taken tea that afternoon with Garan Haesara and Gamnae with a frozen face and hands refusing to stay quite steady. The eyes of the entire court were upon her, or so it felt like; she was glad to retreat to her husband's estate though Haesara had remarked, apparently offhand, that with all the uncertainty she wished her young daughter-in-law was safely within the Palace.

She was Sensheo's mother, though. It could be a trap.

Yala stretched her legs wide and bent, her forehead almost touching the floor. A harsh exhale passed her lips; she stretched still more, muscles and tendons protesting.

Ashani Zlorih, the Great Rider of Khir, was dead. It was akin to the sun going out, or the rai refusing to grow.

Did Daoyan know? He was riding north; had he reached Khir? Had Heaven struck him down for his own deeds, laying him low in some anonymous ditch or upon a battlefield? Was he the new Great Rider, though many a clan-head might refuse to obey a merely legitimized scion of Ashani?

To not-know was a torment all its own, and no letter from Kai, either—of course, what could he say after the last one?

That was a selfish consideration. There were larger ones. By all accounts the new Emperor hated the head general of Zhaon; it would not take long for some charge of treason to be manufactured in that quarter.

For Yala found she did not quite believe Heaven's voice had spoken from thin air—not only because she was a modern woman possessed of some measure of common sense, but because Gamnae had known her brother was about to do something fatal, and her other brother was the target.

How terribly ironic, that she should find herself wishing Garan Kurin had not been struck down? It had happened so *quickly*; she had thrown herself over Gamnae without a second thought.

You protected me, the Second Princess had murmured to her just this morning. *And I'll protect you.*

It was laughable. Who could either of them truly protect, after all?

Yala's husband rode south, by all accounts across the path of the advancing Pale Horde. She straightened, pointing her toes, stiff muscles burning inside her thighs. She flowed through the preparatory positions—the archer's pose, the hawk in flight, the startled lizard, the lesser and greater wheel poses—and finally upright into the beginning stance like a mountain.

Her *yue*'s crosshatched hilt, warm from resting against her leg, clasped like a lover's hand. Now much of the poetry a young girl had to filch to read made more sense; some of the allusions required experience to untangle.

Where did her duty lie? To her husband, of course, and to his family. No doubt Mahara's shade would take vengeance upon her half-brother in some fashion, since Yala had failed so signally.

She should have known, somehow. The answer was in Takshin's hands all along, if she had simply been brave enough or intelligent enough to work it free—oh, and they called her *scholarly*.

The *yue* clove air, almost startling her. The buzzing, burning restlessness in her body *demanded* she move; she was drawn behind the singing blade as thread after a hair-fine needle.

Mountain pose became Hawk, falling upon an attacker from on high. The spinning-strike, the second hand locked to brace a lightning-quick stab, a twist of the blade to free it from cut muscle; she shifted to the River pose, fluidly evading an invisible attacker. Short huffs of effort, ending just past the strike, her breath coming high and fast, her ribs flaring and collapsing, her arms burning and legs trembling as she forced them to greater speed and precision.

The *yue* did not forgive inattention. Her concentration firmed, and there was no room in her head-meat for her brother's fierce, short, crushing hug before he left to fight at Three Rivers or Mahara's sweet round face, her father's quiet voice, Zakkar Kai's dark eyes fastened upon her, Takshin's touch upon her shoulder or his farewell in the entry hall of this very house.

I will return, her husband had said, and with the deep banked fire in his gaze, it was impossible to disbelieve.

And yet. How long had he known beyond doubt of the author of Mahara's death; when, if ever, would he have told her? She could have gone the rest of her life without—

A thin stinging swipe against her forearm as she turned, the *yue* singing as it bit. She parried the invisible attacker, giving ground slowly then lunging, bare foot touching down—it should have stamped, but any noise might alert a servant that their mistress was awake and presumably required care or watching. Spinning, a slight sound as her shift tore along a seam while her foot flickered, kicking—she would have to find some reason for it needing repair.

Her arms were heavy, her legs not quite as obedient as usual. And her red time was still late.

Fatigue blurred the crisp strikes. She came to a stop, cold metal flat against her pounding pulse, the *yue* held in the extremity position. Were she menaced with dishonor, this was the last step before turning her wrist and freeing her humors, a bright arterial jet like Garan Kurin's blood as his brother's sword sank between neck and shoulder.

Garan Sensheo had carried a blade to a festival banquet—oh, a princely prerogative, certainly, and Garan Jin had done the same. Gossip said Sensheo had suspected the First Queen's condition was unnatural, and possibly that he knew who had been behind the last efforts upon Garan Takyeo's life.

Could that have been Ashani Daoyan's work as well?

The *yue* had bitten her only once during this practice, when she deserved so much more. *You are Khir. This is your duty.*

"I am Komor," she whispered in Khir, though the words burned her mouth. "This is my pride." She was Garan now, was she not? And just that afternoon she had been used to kill a group of blameless men.

The warning was slight—the brush of an inhalation like the damp wind licking roof-tiles. Yala spun, the *yue* dropping to guard its wielder against new danger.

Anh stood just inside the partition; she had eased it open so softly Yala, lost in her practice, had not heard. She reached behind her, sliding the door shut; her eyes were huge in the dimness. She wore a kaburei's sleeping-tunic and short trousers, her small bare feet pointing outward.

"My lady," she whispered.

"Anh." There was no hiding the blade, but then again, the kaburei must have suspected. She did, after all, sew upon Yala's clothes.

The girl took two noiseless steps forward, then folded down to her knees and bowed, deeply. "I . . . I heard you, please, my lady, do not be angry."

"I am not." *Merely weary. And worried.* Yala tried for a smile, but her face would not let her. The rigid control necessary to navigate, to glide as if untroubled through court would not relax.

"Is it true? The Emperor . . ."

Pity broke the shell of Yala's own worries. What must the poor girl be feeling right now, listening to every swirling bit of rumor? "Garan Sensheo is the Emperor. I will keep us safe, Anh, never fear. It is what my husband would wish." *And yet I do not know how.* She was, in effect, powerless. What were a woman's weapons, even the women of Zhaon who discussed politics over tea and pounded-rai cakes? Even the women who, like the First Queen, had removed rivals and possibly . . .

"Oh, I know." Anh straightened from her bow, but her forehead was still wrinkled. "And I shall protect you, my lady. I may be only a kaburei, but I will do what I must."

"Women always do." It was a deep, unavoidable truth, and the instant the words left her a great peace descended upon the woman who had once been Komor Yala.

She was otherwise now, and not only was Anh depending upon her but her husband's entire household—for who would protect them in his absence? They were Garan Takyeo's servants, and that prince had been kind not only to Yala's princess but to Yala herself.

If Zakkar Kai returned from the North, he would need some manner of protection as well. Her husband, riding to Shan, was in just as much danger should he return alive.

She did not think it likely Garan Sensheo would leave an elder brother, even one removed from succession by adoption, alive to challenge him. And then there was Garan Jin, brave in the face of danger that terrible day Yala's princess had almost been kidnapped, and bringing Yala a packet of papers he could not know would rob her of peace for the rest of her life.

The *yue* found its sheath, and Yala approached her kaburei, beckoning slightly. The girl rose, and Yala held out her hands. "Women always do," she repeated. "And we are women, Anh. We shall endure."

"Yes, my lady," the kaburei whispered; her hands were almost clammy, cold against Yala's warmth. Of course *yue* practice brought all the humors forth, and stoked them as well. "I am frightened."

So am I. "There is no shame in fear," she said, and hoped it was true. She wanted to say *all will be well*, but who could promise such a thing? "Only in not performing our duty."

She tugged lightly upon her kaburei's hands, bringing the girl into her arms; it was not so difficult to offer comfort. Anh did not smell of expensive bath-additives but of fresh laundry and a faint sour edge of fried oil, but she trembled as Gamnae had against Yala's shoulder. Rain began, thunder retreating as thousands of drops tiptapped roof, street, and garden, and that night the kaburei slept deep and comforted upon the padded bench at the foot of her mistress's bed.

In the morning, smoke was sighted to the south as Khoa-An, a town accreting at a bend in the river where a wide stone bridge crossed, was fired.

The Pale Horde had arrived.

BELOVED SON

His mother's mouth was a raw red wound, her cheeks were eaten on either side, her throat was scorched, and her breathing a wet burble. Her long glossy redblack hair streamed across a rectangular bolster covered in blue velvet; her peach silk wrapper gaped at her chest in a way she would not normally allow. All Garan Jin's life his mother had been a tall, beautiful, polished spirit, all the lovelier because she was also warmth and intercession, sometimes stern and other times indulgent, and always his best audience when he discovered a new weapon, or the final arbiter of truth when he had a question he could ask no one else.

But now she was struck down, her eyes half-open and gleaming but so terribly distant. The physicians said the caustic burning poison had not breached her stomach and that she would heal, but the scars...they could not answer that. Her teeth were well enough, though her gums had suffered.

The partition was half-open, a Kaeje garden breathing under afternoon rain past a long wide wooden porch they had often breakfasted upon—Mother, Jin, and Sabwone, a tiny bowl of complementary things upon the bigger banquet-table of the royal family.

Sabi was irretrievably gone; not even letters would come to remind him of his pretty elder sister, who might have poked and teased and made younger children cry but also protected little Jin and held his hand during colorful, terrifying court ceremonials. The Pale Horde had stolen her, and now it was oozing ever closer to the city, burning as it rode.

Jin couldn't even scrape together righteous anger at the thought. He sat upon his knees beside his mother's curtained bed, the finely woven cloth meant to keep needle-nose bloodsucking insects from a queen's nightly rest moving as wet wind tiptoed restlessly into the bedroom. The autumn rains had arrived, sweeping in silver curtains under heavy-bellied clouds every afternoon; their downpours were brief this early in the season but it would not always be so.

Sensheo was in the red-pillared hall, issuing commands. Who cared? Let him. Jin watched his mother's chest rise and fall, the linen and silk of her undershift exposed.

Her hands lay discarded upon the counterpane, Sabwone's careful stitches tangling the *dae* and *boh* characters together in yellow against crimson satin. How strange that the fingers responsible for the work were gone now, either upon a pyre or rotting in black earth.

Jin shuddered. His mother's breathing paused, the candle upon her nightstand of ebon tancha wood standing straight and tall inside a blown glass globe-shield.

He hadn't protected her after all.

Mother made another damp sound. Her eyelashes fluttered. Even the rains couldn't erase the tinge of smoke—first from the Yuin, then from the fireflowers, and now from the barbarians circling Zhaon-An like hungry, mange-ridden dogs at an ox's bloated carcass.

He heard the rumors, of course; the physicians exchanged snippets of gossip in low tones outside their royal patient's door. There was a cough from the hall partition, a discreet knock, and Jin had to clear his throat before he could give permission to enter.

"Sixth Prince Garan Jin." Kihon Jiao, no longer quite so shabby, bowed properly before stepping through and bowed again. "I have come to offer my services once more; Princess Yala sends her regards."

That was another worry—he had replaced the papers in the Old Tower; would Takshin ever suspect? First, though, he'd have to come home. "Ah." Jin patted at his mother's slim, languid hand; the resin tipping her fingers was beginning to wear. Watching her apply it with the help of two close-servants after breakfast was always pleasant; he wondered if it would help her feel better. He should ask the physician today. "Mother, Honorable Kihon is here. Will you allow him to examine you?"

Her right hand twitched; Jin read the answer in her half-shut eyes.

"Yes," Jin continued. "Do come in, Honorable Kihon. How is Princess Yala?"

"In fine health; she is with Second Princess Gamnae." The physician bustled in, the strap of his ever-present bag diagonal across his lean chest. "Also in fine health, though very shocked by recent events. Third Dowager Mother of the Revered Emperor Garan Luswone," he went on, briskly, "may I take your pulse?"

Jin liked the man—it was easy to see why Kai had selected him, why Takyeo had and Takshin now trusted him. The physician's broad peasant face settled into its usual examining-expression, open and interested though listening to subtle things few could hear.

He set about a familiar round of examination—the multiple levels of the pulse under fingertips, the places where the subtle body touched the physical decorously but firmly tested with an ivory-tipped pointer to keep a woman's modesty intact, gentle viewing of Luswone's raw, weeping mouth. With that done, he nodded sharply and left the bedside, crossing to a hastily erected table crowded with paraphernalia—mortars and pestles, alembics fueled by flammable clear oil, bundles of herbs and other substances. As usual, Honorable Kihon cast a critical glance over the crowd, cleared a space with his fingertips as if he could barely believe he was forced to work amid such disorder, and set to without further ado, mixing and grinding.

Jin took his mother's hand again. It was cool and limp in his, heavier than it should have been. "Have they arrived?"

The physician's steady movement paused. He glanced at the partition, left slightly open so any passers-by could see him performing his duties under the watchful eye of a prince. It must have taken bravery for him to enter the Palace complex; at least at Takshin's estate he was relatively safe.

"Yes," the physician said finally, in his usual tone of dry fact. "Half the circuit of Zhaon-An is invested, though they do not enter the river-fen. The Emperor ordered the firing of much outside the city walls to deny the siege food and drink; there was time to foul some of the outer wells. The gates are closed; they have not tried them yet."

A little color crept into Luswone's face. Her gaze met Jin's, and though she could not speak, it was obvious she wished to.

"Shall I bring you a brush and paper, Mother?" Jin squeezed her fingers gently. He was all she had, with Sabwone gone, and the sword now constantly at his back was a reminder. It was not an item to be carried into a sickroom, but he would not leave her unguarded.

Not now. Not ever again.

Mother's breathing altered, a wet rasping noise. The physician halted, hurrying to the bedside. "Revered Second Mother, please be calm. Attempting to speak may cause further damage. I will have a soothing draught prepared in a few moments—"

Her fingers bit Jin's with surprising strength.

"Please, Honorable Kihon." Jin was surprised, once more, by how steady he sounded. In fact, he sometimes thought he sounded a little like Kai, or like Takyeo himself. "Mix your draught, I shall fetch brush and paper for my mother. Mother, see, I am doing it now." He had to free himself from her grasp, not ungently.

He knew where she kept inkstone, brushes, and a few sheets of heavy pounded-rag paper for quick practice or a beautiful, informal little note; the most difficult part was propping her upon several bolsters and settling the lap-desk over her knees.

Her breathing was tortuous by the time she was upright enough to write, and Kihon Jiao had the tonic ready. She actually lifted her other hand and waved it aside, a graceful, restrained motion.

Jin settled her fingers around the brush; she dipped it in the shallow dish of water filled from a jug upon the bedside—one tested by a servant in Jin's presence before being allowed to remain. Then across the inkstone with her particular swirl, gathering darkness in brush-hairs; she lifted her wrist at the correct angle and her half-closed eyes glittered even more feverishly.

The sound of wet brush against paper was lost in the tapering rain. Soon would come the gleams of westering sunshine, thick and golden under a pall of dark scudding cloud and the smoke from Zhaon-An's outskirts.

Two characters—Jin's name, and she gave him another meaningful glance. Then her hand moved again, the brush still carrying a heavy cargo of ink; a splotch on a downstroke was very unlike her and Jin's own throat was clotted with tears.

Jin.

Another vertical line, like the falling rain. *My beloved son.*

The last cost her a great deal of effort, but she brushed as beautifully as she could, for anything worth doing must be accomplished in as graceful a manner as possible.

Kill me.

Jin inhaled harshly, shocked. He subtracted the brush from her a trifle ungently, took the paper, and hurried for a brazier in the corner, meant for disposing of the rai-paper squares used to dab her weeping-damp chin at intervals. It took a short while for the writing to be fully consumed.

"I understand," Kihon Jiao said, very quietly. "Truly, I do. But, my lady—"

A slight rustle of cloth—she had made another peremptory gesture. She was brushing at the underlying piece of paper, too, and her eyes were fully open now, dark and terrifyingly focused.

Jin re-covered the brazier, casting a nervous glance at the hallway. He approached the bed step by step, Kihon Jiao averting his studiously set face, gazing at the hall partition too while holding the greenstone cup of tonic—the sacred material was held to repel poison and grant health—in a hand that was normally quite steady but now displayed the faintest of tremors.

The characters were hurried now, but still exquisite. *He will try again.*

Jin, my son, he will kill you.

You must do this.

"Mother," Jin whispered. "You mustn't."

She kept writing until he took the brush from her fingers and glared at Kihon Jiao. The physician was still turned away, granting what privacy he could; unwilling admiration mixed with deep fear and a bald edge of rage in Jin's gut.

He did not like feeling anger. He never had.

Garan Luswone glared at him, the spark in her gaze terribly like Sabwone's and her right hand outstretched for the brush, fingertips rippling, demanding.

"Mother." Jin shook his head, wishing his humors weren't trembling so inside his liver. "I will not *let* him; that is all. You must take your medicine. Honorable Kihon is to be trusted. You must listen to me, Mother."

She shook her head again, pointing at the crumpled paper in his fist. His palm was sweating and the ink might run. The burned, crimson hole that had taken the place of her pretty mouth, ever serene whether curved in amusement or relaxed in repose, moved angrily.

"Physician." Jin's voice did not quaver, though his throat ached. "Please, give my mother her medicine."

Kihon Jiao bowed, and leaned close. Luswone did not demur; she drank, and sagged against the bolsters. But her gaze, locked with her son's, did not falter, and medicinal bitterness filled his mouth, too.

The rain slowly, slowly faded; in its wake came not freshness but the scent of yet more burning.

Quite the Challenge

A campaign tent was always full of news both ill and good; still, each character in the falling lines of the proclamation brought at high speed from Zhaon-An was a fist to the gut. Zakkar Kai cursed, a term of surpassing and soldierly foulness, and Anlon looked up from his desk, the brush in his hand ceasing its steady movement.

There was little time to absorb the news, for Ashani Daoyan and a group of Khir noblemen were due at any moment. The new ruler of Khir—or the ivory pointer Kai was using to prod the remains of three Khir armies southward, balancing the risk of armed northerners in the heartland against the deep, unerring instinct rising from his liver—was too sharp a blade to be handled lightly. Tabrak was approaching and Khir's fangs were not yet fully drawn; a son of Ashani Zlorih was a useful implement indeed.

But bringing that tool to Kurin was one thing, and bringing it to Garan Sensheo was quite another. What, under Heaven or in the numberless hells, was *happening* in Zhaon-An?

And how had *Sensheo*, of all people, managed to overcome Kurin? What must Tamuron's shade think of this? One son killing another, then another—disgust curled through Kai's belly; he did not dare examine the sensation too closely.

It was not quite safe.

"We have a new Emperor." Kai heard the disbelief in his own voice and stared at the proclamation again; it would have to be read aloud by every cohort leader in the Northern Army. The pile of dispatches from the capital was sorted; he barely heard the squeak of a camp-chair as Anlon rose and hurried in his direction.

Everything is a battle, Kai. This is no different; simply consider the terrain and your forces. If Sensheo was upon the throne—where, under Heaven, was Takshin? At least he would insulate Yala, but it was his practice to slip an explanatory note into a sealed dispatch pouch, if only for a taunting aside proving he had, indeed, some idea of what was going on and was safeguarding what he could.

Or had Sensheo not only dealt with Kurin but also Takshin? *That* did not seem possible, but the distraction of a new marriage might make the Third Prince unwary.

And Jin's missives had halted too, their brief flowering giving Kai a very concerning picture indeed before falling like spent yeo-yan fleece.

Kai met Anlon's worried gaze. There was no need for speech, not with a man who had fought beside you for so long and brought your meals besides.

"Heaven smiles upon us merely to frown a moment later," his adjutant muttered, and refolded the proclamation with exquisite care. "Shall I tell the Khir you will see them in the morning?"

And show weakness? "No." Kai shook his head; the meat inside his skull suddenly held a different map than the one he had used to bring Khir to its knees again. Sensheo the sly, Sensheo with his habit of slowly mounting struggling garden-beetles upon bright needles filched from his mother's sewing basket while he smiled— it was a chilling thought. Bile whipped the back of Kai's throat. "It would not do to give Zlorih's son an inch of rein."

Zlorih's son had coolly, calmly maneuvered Kai into beheading his maternal grandfather, as well. As the first chess-move in a reign, it was an entirely traditional one, but the fellow seemed a bit young to be so ruthless.

Then again, he was an illegitimate son; such a creature in honor-obsessed Khir might well have long-standing and deadly reasons to be merciless. The greenmetal blade Yala carried was apparently a traditional item for highly noble girls, but Kai's indirect questions about it were met with sidelong looks and quick, polite conversational hints that it was a very ill-bred matter for men to discuss.

It was not even an *important* question, given what else he had to extract from the nobles left amid the ruin of Khir's armies, their swords held in the Rack and their attendance upon Ashani Daoyan at Zakkar Kai's request perhaps an intolerable insult they would seek to avenge in the chaos of a battlefield.

Many of them gave politely sneering replies to his other queries—direct or otherwise—about the death of Princess Ashan Mahara. Kai's feeling—shared by Takshin—that there was ultimately a Northern source for the ingots paid for a princess's misfortune was similarly deep and inarguable, though he admitted it was likely there had been several customers at that restaurant, and only the luckiest had gained a bowl and eating-sticks for his trouble.

What did Yala think? Could she even compass such a thing?

A damp wind tugged at the tent; the mirrorlight was fading after a long day of traveling southward. Grumbles of thunder rolled over distant hills; autumn rains would begin soon. The soldiers were glad enough to be moving instead of in battle or helping to bring and dry the rai-harvest; there were even reports of Khir and Zhaon infantry gambling together or raiding nearby farms for comestibles.

Soldiers, North or South, were the same. It was the nobles who were likely to be troublesome.

Anlon read the proclamation twice. "I shall have to make a copy. This...my lord general, this is very bad. If you will pardon my saying so."

"Hm." Kai riffled through the dispatches, searching for the note Takshin would have sent if there were any possibility of doing so. There were two fresh letters from Jin—he was mightily heartened to see those—and one from Gamnae; nothing from Yala.

Of course, how *could* she respond? He would be lucky to see her alone ever again; she would find graceful reasons to avoid him, certainly, and it might even be a kindness.

He broke the seals upon Jin's letters and read, his alarm mounting. Then Gamnae's, and it was there he found a description of a banquet interrupted by Heaven's voice—though very sensibly, Tamuron's remaining daughter merely reported what the voice had said, and that the Golden had found a brazen trumpet in the furniture-crowded rooms upon the second floor—and murder. His blood chilled as he read, and she made reference to Takshin riding south though the Tabrak were somewhere between Zhaon-An and Shan's capital.

Which meant Yala was left at court, unprotected.

And Sensheo was Emperor. It boggled the head-meat, and his revulsion mounted afresh.

It was dangerous for a general to grow weary of killing, though it was hideous for a man to enjoy it. And he was, he had to admit, thoroughly disgusted by this greedy display. His beloved warlord-father's shade might well be feeling the same.

"My lord?" Anlon's worry was such that he pressed twice, almost unheard of. "I must say something, and—"

"Do not." Kai brushed aside the warning with a peremptory gesture; better not to force subordinates to utter the obvious, though sometimes that was their function. "I am aware he hates me, Anlon. He has since childhood, with a constancy that would put a good wife's to shame."

"It may be time…" Anlon's gaze met Kai's, and it was both comforting to know he had at least one faithful friend at his side and disturbing to think Kai's position was so clear an onlooker would naturally think he must make some plans to hold his life, if not what his now-dead lord had gained, by warfare against one of that lord's sons.

I am sick of Garan Tamuron's children. It was not quite true—Gamnae, Jin, and Takshin deserved his protection. Was Makar truly dead?

It boggled the mind. Summer had not even turned into proper autumn yet, and how many of Tamuron's brood were left?

Kai turned his attention to the other dispatches. The rump of the Southron Army, falling back toward Zhaon-An, had finally reached some manner of safety at Khoa-An at least a tenday ago. Virtually leaderless and very close to the capital indeed, they were probably little better than a rabble; he should send someone to take control and fashion them into a shield, if there was enough time.

There was, he realized, probably not.

The Khir generals were announced; Anlon took the proclamation to his desk in order to let Kai break the news in the way he saw fit.

The Northern Army needed no reminder of its duty. And now Zakkar Kai was faced with the prospect of using it not just to defend Zhaon but also ensure his own survival.

"Here, and here." Ashani Daoyan, though illegitimate, had been trained for war as thoroughly as any Khir nobleman or Zhaon general. "Though if I were Tabrak, why would..." He did not finish the sentence, staring at the map upon the foldable strategy table, its surface missing the usual crop of small carved representations of Zhaon horse and infantry, not to mention artillery.

"It is strange," Kai agreed. He could admit he rather liked the lean, pale-eyed Khir; none even among his own generals had thought to consider *why* Tabrak had changed their traditional pattern. "They normally come here." He tapped at the map where the Westron Wastes narrowed—not enough to make passage easy, certainly, but eas*ier*. "And work their way south." Khir had attacked farther to the west, too, changing their traditional pattern, but given Three Rivers there was not much else they could do. They had fought the last battle, and Zakkar Kai had fought the one actually before him. "In every history, they have done so. Aro Ba Wistis has thought to do something different, and for that alone we should be cautious."

"An entire Horde." Ashani Daoyan smiled, rather mistily, at the map. His gaze moved avidly over inked lines. "Quite the challenge, and Zhaon does not have the cavalry though there are no shortage of pikes. And I find it difficult to believe the barbarians have cannon."

"The envoy made rather a point of asking about those." One of the provincial Khir, a smooth-cheeked lad with a bandaged left hand, shook his head. "They called them something strange— tubes-with-thunder, I think."

"They do not know how to build," Hazuni Ulo offered. "Only to destroy. 'Tis why Heaven allows them to wander about unbaked, pale as polished rai."

"They will have to fire towns as they come north; they must lay siege to Zhaon-An. 'Tis the only thing that makes sense, but this late in the season?" Kai glanced at Sehon Doah, who kept watch upon the Khir with almost unblinking suspicion. "What does this tell you, my son?"

"This Aro fellow wishes to winter in Zhaon," the tall, rawboned marshal replied. He was in leather half-armor, and his hand hovered near a swordhilt. Mistrustful looks cast at their guests were not quite as hidden as Kai might have wished, but it did no harm for some of the mistrust to be overt. "Or in Khir, but invading the north so close to autumn is an invitation to despair."

"Not to mention starvation and death." Ashani Daoyan tapped at Zhaon-An, a large intricate crimson circle with carefully brushed characters nestling inside. "Yes, I think he is right, General Zakkar."

"It still leaves a question or two unanswered." Kai met the new king of Khir's gaze directly. He did not quite believe Ashani Daoyan had left his homeland and traveled south solely in order to avenge his royal half-sister's death, then turned about and decided to ride back with vengeance unfinished.

The young man was entirely too purposeful for such a jaunt, no matter how honor-mad Khir nobles tended to be. And the nagging question of just why Khir would sacrifice a princess who brought peace could not be answered to Kai's satisfaction.

He did not like such unanswered questions.

The thought of Yala intruded as she never would in person, drifting through his head-meat like a wistful shade. What was she doing at this moment? Writing a letter to Takshin? Fending off Sensheo's ire, comforting Gamnae? Standing in a dry-garden, facing an assassin with her chin held high, only that slim greenmetal blade between her and...

"My lord?" Marshal Hurong Tai said, quietly. He looked mournful, and though he did not keep hand to hilt he flanked Kai's other side, careful to keep himself between his lord and the Khir.

"Nothing of any import," Kai said, finally. It felt a betrayal of Yala and her devotion to her princess, but he did need the Khir cavalry against the Horde, and afterward he could balance the northerners' army against whatever mischief Sensheo intended.

Assuming the Horde knew its place, and died upon the spear he was called upon to wield.

BROTHER MINE

Moving through countryside was relatively easy for riders; the infantry, confined to the roads, would still make good time. At least it was the end of summer, and they were not trudging through rain, or trapped by muddy fields upon the stone road-ribbons.

It was a fine thing to be among Shan bloodriders again, to ride with those who did not need to chatter or display. Kiron rode as always, protected by a hard knot—Buwon, Suron, Takshin himself, Taonjo, Buwon's retainer the mournful Ohjosi—all familiar, all men he was fairly certain could be trusted.

After all, the Mad Queen had not induced any of them to betray or kill him, and that was worth something.

Kiron rode with head upflung and gaze bright, watching the far horizon; Buwon rode sunk in profound thought, his round chin almost touching his chest. Suron was quiet, but then he was ever so; knife-marked Taonjo merry enough with Gaojun and Madauk—they were all as expected.

Only he was different. Takshin alternately cursed every hoof-fall that did not bring him immediately to his own door, and blessed it for at least moving him one step closer to his wife.

He did not altogether trust that Kurin would not use her in some fashion or another. The Horde was a smaller worry, for the city walls were strong...and yet it was that he brooded upon as

Shan's lords poured from the capital city, the infantry called from peasant farmholds south and east moving in maniple-files against a swelling tide of refugees who had decided, after all, to return to their homes.

The news that banners had arisen in every town square and the Awakened One's blessing invoked at piercetower shrines and temples had spread with speed to put even the dispatch riders to shame. Even men called from harvest-duty did not quite bemoan their luck, for that was backbreaking labor now left to wives, daughters, sons too young to fight, and grandfathers too old to march.

Kiron's horse edged closer to his upon the third day, and Takshin met his battle-brother's curious gaze. "You might as well ask," he said, and that was another relief—like Yala, Kiron did not take a flat tone of dry fact as a sharp reprimand.

The king of Shan had an easy smile, though it was often a mask over his true mood. "I am curious, of course." He was easy in the saddle, and his eyes were half-closed against sunshine-glare. Dust rose in choking veils both west and east—the infantry would be breathing it all day. "When you left, you were rather forceful in your determination not to place your feet within a matrimonial courtyard. And a Khir girl, too."

"You'll like her." *If she's alive when we reach the city.* The thought, quite natural, twisted a red-hot cord inside his guts; Takshin suppressed the urge to curse. Each time they halted, he was hard-pressed not to utter a short falcon-cry of frustration. "I hardly know what to ask you in return."

"Your sister was...high-strung." Kiron glanced at the horizon as a far mutter of thunder reached them; there were dark clouds coming from the east and more behind them. Autumn's downpours might strike before they reached the border, or Zhaon-An. "I did what I could to gentle her, Shin."

No doubt she thanked you roundly for the trouble. "She did as she should." It was all Takshin could say. Of course haughty, pretty Sabwone, ever mindful of her position as an imperial concubine's daughter of very noble blood, would lead even a king a merry chase. There was no time to mourn her, even if her letters had never faltered.

He was used to considering himself an unfilial creature, and the absence of deep grief at the passing of a girl who was, after all, his sister was simply another mark of how thoroughly he was marred. She had even, once or twice, flung the term *tradesman's son* at him, no doubt from the persistent rumor that his mother's clan had stolen their genealogy and painted it upon scraped goathide. Of course he had laughed at the insult, and she had stamped away in high dudgeon, cheated of a prize.

Still... her letters, when he was sent from home. Weightless but punctual, and given without grudge or thought of recompense— how rare, indeed, was that? Especially among nobles.

His battle-brother might have interpreted his quiet for grief, or perhaps not. "They have never started from Shan." Kiron's forehead wrinkled, a sign of deep thought. "I could not have known, yet—"

"There has never been an instance of them crossing the Westron Wastes so far to the south," Takshin agreed. "It makes me wonder what this leader Aro is thinking. He is driving north and the autumn rains are almost here. And he cannot expect Shan or Zhaon to forgive him, after sending a queen's..." The words failed him, and the irritation living as a steady stiff-bristle brushing in his liver turned into a blade slicing through.

Perhaps he was more filial than he thought. Sabi was petty, vain, and grasping, but she did not deserve... that. Her shade might wander the edges between the many hells and the Middle World forever, a head with long black hair howling without voice as it searched for its body.

They breasted a hill, pausing to take in the landscape. The trail of Tabrak's devastation was clear, vapor rising from fired farmsteads and tiny villages long after their passage, and harvests left for survivors to attempt to glean with bruised hands. The barbarians had even pulled down the towers for the dead whose carved tops made mournful music deep in winter when the north winds came. Takshin let out a low sound, not quite a whistle, seeing the path of destruction.

The Mad Queen would have admired it.

"Stunning, isn't it." Kiron had taken off his riding-gloves to stretch and dry his fingers; he slapped the leather carapaces against his thigh, a sign of decision. "We shall fall upon them like wolves, brother mine."

"Indeed we shall." If Zhaon-An's walls were breached, he could not see his Yala doing anything other than using that sharp green-metal claw to save herself from dishonor.

Then, Garan Takshin would have to kill every Tabrak he saw— man, woman, child, it made no difference. All the stinking, rai-pale barbarians would fall under his blade.

It was a response that might have satisfied *either* of his mothers.

"Indeed we shall," he repeated meditatively, and urged his horse down the slope. The two trade-roads running in tandem through the valley were alive with soldiers and moving peasants, a faint wailing rising from the latter and hard darts of sunlight arrowing skyward from the helms of the former. Another deep pall of dark cloud flickered with diamond lightning to the north, and there was the falling gauzy curtain of rain in its shadow. "But I would give much to know why the Horde has acted thus now, my brother."

"There he is," Kiron said quietly, his horse falling into step by Takshin's. "I have missed you, Shin. We need fear no barbarian. Shall I tell you what follows upon our heels?"

"Mercenaries from Anwei." A grim smile touched the corners of his mouth. The king must have sent for them upon the first intimations of Tabrak upon his borders being confirmed; they had marched long but leisurely to arrive with enough strength to fight. The Horde had arrived before, but who could have predicted this when they were behaving contrary to all history? "Did you think I had not noticed? Spending Mother's treasury; how she would rage at it."

"I find that whatever she would rage against is generally good policy." Kiron's lopsided grimace was too pained to be called a smile, and his gloves slapped his thigh again. "How strange it is, to have survived her after all."

"Do not be troubled." Takshin's own face was pulled into a similar mask. "The Horde may yet do what she failed to."

Kiron's left hand did not flash into the *avert* sign; truth itself was not ill-luck. "Not while we are together, brother mine."

Takshin nodded. His heart writhed within him. Each step brought him closer to Yala; he only resented the aching slowness.

Or so he told himself as they passed li upon weary li north, and the dark veils of autumn rain pressed from every direction to meet them.

MESSENGERS

The ring of barbarians closed tight about Zhaon-An, smoke drifting skyward as they settled to the business of destroying rick, cot, and tree with characteristic savagery under a fine, penetrating drizzle.

Two nights of pillage and rapine ensued, the walls of the city witnessing the desperation of a great tide of trapped humanity pressing against the south and east gates. Those gates, black-timbered and iron-bound, did not creak open under the pleading of mothers, elderly folk, or the wailing of children, and when the Tabrak finally turned their attention to clearing the mass they had trapped like pinchnose mice in folds of material, the slaughter took place amid a short but intense afternoon downpour. Mud splattered, hookblades flashed, horses and people screamed; the City Guard, Golden, and what remained of the Southron Army atop Zhaon-An's walls had to turn away from the sight.

The cries penetrated far into the city, and runners came four times every watch to the vermilion-pillared great hall of the Kaeje, where Garan Sensheo, in state upon the Throne of Five Winds, listened to reports with no discernable sign of unease other than a certain tendency to run his fingertips over silver-sheathed double hurai.

Upon the fifth day of the siege, a fitful quiet fell at the gates, and a group of three rode within bowshot, waving a bright truce-flag made from a hank of unbleached cotton.

The barbarians rode through streets hurriedly cleared by the City Guard and Night Watch, but no few of Zhaon-An's artisans or laborers banged upon a pot or pan from their window, expressing disdain and deep displeasure. Some few slops were thrown, but all in all, the two tall, rai-pale men with their massive blue-streaked beards and their stinking fur oddments passed largely unmolested through the city and into the Palace.

Their companion was much shorter and slighter; his coppery face was set with either distaste or the craftiness of a peasant, and he wore a snug leather collar, its pointed bottom disappearing beneath his linen shirt and fur jerkin both front and back.

The taller fellows refused to take their great furred boots off; while certainly rude, one junior eunuch commented in a low voice that it was probably to save their hosts the stink of their feet as well as the rest of them. The sally gained slightly more amusement than it warranted, delivered as it was in a moment of high tension, but Zan Fein's fan flicked and the young man hurriedly stepped back through the ranks of his dark-robed fellows until he was hidden from view.

The third fellow was much cleaner than his fellows, and removed his footwear with all propriety. He did not leave it outside, though, but thrust the glovelike leather boots into a bag carried at his waist for such articles; his barbarian foot-wrappings underneath were stained but at least freshly laundered.

He did not pay obeisance at the accepted stations, though when he and his two companions came to a halt before the Throne and a wall of wary-watching Golden spear-guards he bowed with the proper reverence. One of the big blue-daubed barbarians laughed at this, but the other elbowed him in the ribs, and upon the dais, at his enthroned brother's side, Garan Jin stood slim and tall, regarding the barbarians with quite uncharacteristically cold interest.

"Great Emperor of Zhaon," the peasant began in burr-accented Zhaon, "Etu, *scun* of the great Aro Ba Wistis, humbly addresses you. I am to translate for Daka Ba Wistin and Vasol Ba Senik, stirrup-holders of Aro Ba Wistis; please pardon my accent, for it has been long since I spoke Zhaon to one of such high station."

It was no great surprise that the Tabrak had Zhaon kaburei; a tide of whispering went through the assembled court.

Also upon the great dais, standing upon a lower step and peering over the heads of the Golden, was Mrong Banh. The astrologer did not look quite *nervous*, merely faintly apprehensive, and his topknot was pulled savagely tight instead of cheerfully rumpled as usual.

"A pleasant greeting. How long, precisely, has it been?" The Emperor's manicured hands lay in his lap; he examined the two large barbarians with much interest. "Were you taken in childhood? *Etu* is not a Zhaon name."

"Your pardon, great Emperor." Etu turned to his companions and spoke in the strange, atonal language of Tabrak, its consonants usually spreading a fine mist of spittle upon the interlocutors. The taller of the two nodded, and Etu faced Zhaon again. "I am given leave to answer, great Emperor. I was taken by the Horde as a child; my original home was three days' journey west of Fuzhao-An."

"Ah." The Emperor nodded as if this were the weightiest matter before him. "Are you here to give me your lord's surrender, then?"

Etu studied him for a moment, his dark gaze expressionless, then translated for his companions. He did not do so with Princess Yala's grace, as one of the courtiers remarked later that day—very quietly, of course, but the quip moved through the entire Palace complex with speed rivaling a cavalry charge.

The barbarians laughed, hooting through strong, slightly discolored teeth. The smaller of the two flour-pale fur-sacks was lacking a canine—perhaps he had been holding his reins in his teeth as some Shan horsemen were said to do while attacking—and it was he who gestured roughly for the kaburei to speak.

"Great Emperor, the son of Wistin says it is quite the opposite. We are here to accept *your* surrender."

"How very strange." Sensheo's fingers tensed, though he did not cease stroking at the hurai upon his left with a fingertip, a meditative movement. "You have no siege engines, no cannon, nothing but horses and fur. Winter comes, as well. Surely your lord Aro does not mean to spend it outside Zhaon-An's walls."

Etu translated; the taller barbarian made his reply at length.

"Great Emperor, your army has been defeated and the great city of the southroners has been laid waste." The kaburei shifted his weight, glancing at his blue-painted companions, and continued. "The northerners do not love you; their princess was murdered by your country. No aid will be forthcoming; besides, we have captured many of your thunder-speaking-tubes."

"We call them *cannon*," Sensheo corrected, with an avuncular smile. Garan Jin leaned forward, balanced almost upon his toes, staring at the taller barbarian. The hem of his dark scholar's robe quivered slightly, and the swordhilt poking over his shoulder was almost as rigid as the rest of him.

"*Cannon*." Etu bowed again. "This humble one thanks you. We have captured many of your cannon. Even now a battering ram or two is being prepared."

"Well." Sensheo made a low amused sound, as if watching a round of betting before a chariot race. "That sounds very exciting indeed." His glance rose over the assembly; one or two courtiers took the moment to laugh, but the sound died quickly upon strained air. Though the Great Hall's doors were open wide, the drizzle-mist did not send a cool breath through the packed interior.

Etu waited until a reverent hush returned before resuming. "Aro Ba Wistis is prepared to offer the Emperor of Zhaon an honorable position among his stirrup-holders. You shall rule Zhaon for the Horde." The kaburei glanced again at his companions, as if he expected some remonstrance. "We are prepared to be reasonable," he added.

"In other words, you have broken into a man's house, smeared filth upon the floors and hangings, violated his dependents, and now will graciously consent to live there as long as the man waits upon a table stolen from him." Sensheo lifted his right hand, his crimson sleeve falling at a very pleasing angle, and stroked at his chin much as Garan Kurin had his smallbeard not so long ago. "Truly a dizzying offer."

Etu's tone never varied as he translated. Now the two rai-pale barbarians did not laugh; the taller one growled another semi-lengthy answer.

"Great Emperor," Etu finally said, and a shadow of pained modesty crossed his expression. "The son of Senik says this is your last chance. Tabrak will winter in Zunnan's smoking ruins if they must, listening to the cries of your widows and children." His accent contorted the capital's name, and he winced as it did so.

"Elder Brother." Garan Jin turned halfway, bowing slightly and addressing Sensheo. "Why do we pass words with this filth? I should like to answer them with a sword."

"They are messengers, Jinjin." The Emperor lifted an admonishing finger.

"They killed Sabi. And Maki."

The smaller barbarian cuffed the translator, whose shoulders hunched as he accepted the blow. Etu spoke in Tabrak, a whining edge under the words. Clearly he was taken to task because he had failed to translate the words of the Emperor's brother, and he hurried to do so.

"True." Sensheo's smile dropped as if it had never been, and he spoke over the kaburei's attempts to perform his duty. "My Golden, seize the tall stinking ones and take them to the dungeons; Zan Fein, you shall question them closely."

"Your Majesty, I obey." Zan Fein's fan did not halt its steady movement as pikes lowered and the bright-armored Golden surged forward. "Yet I must apologize, for I do not speak Tabrak."

"That does not matter; there is nothing further I wish to ask them." Garan Sensheo's nose wrinkled once; perhaps some drift of the barbarians' odor had reached even to the throne. "Yet they must be questioned nonetheless, and I shall expect a full report of their agonies."

Suddenly at pike-point, the two tall barbarians stiffened. The smaller one hissed, sounding surpassing foul; Etu dropped to his knees, perhaps prudently wishing to be ignored so far as possible. The larger barbarian was slightly troublesome, but in short order both reeking flour-pale giants were wrapped with hempen rope and all but dragged from the crimson-pillared hall.

"This is not well," Mrong Banh said, faintly, the words akin to a single fiddle-leg's singing on an unseasonably warm autumn evening. "They are messengers, Your Majesty. Heaven might well be angered."

"When a guest shits into your rai-bowl, Honorable Mrong, he ceases to become a guest." The Emperor made a motion and Etu the kaburei was seized as well, though only with gauntleted hands instead of at pike-point. He was not wrapped like his fellows, and the two barbarians' imprecations faded as they were hauled outside with a little less care than trussed carcasses dragged by a butcher's assistants. "Now, kaburei, listen carefully, for you will take a message to your pitiful little horsefucking lord. Zhaon does not yield. Your Horde has invaded our lands; you will be sent back across the waterless waste in lamentation and despair. Tell him that. And you may add that he is a motherless son of a dog, as well."

"Yes." Etu was pale, and the pad of pounded rai in his throat moved as he swallowed convulsively. "I will deliver your message, great Emperor of Zhaon."

"Traitor," Garan Jin hissed.

"I have done what I must to survive, great lord of Zhaon." Even upon his knees, Etu had some dignity, and though one of the Golden holding him tightened his grasp upon the kaburei's nape, he did not seem to notice. "You may be glad of it yet."

"Take him away; send him safely back through the city and to his master." The Emperor waved a hand freighted with sacred greenstone and precious silver. "Zan Fein, to your work; Banh, to your charts. My ministers tell me the city is ready for a siege."

"Yes, Your Majesty." Honorable Zan bowed and hurried forth on feline-soft feet; his jatajatas would click upon garden paths and into the bowels of the palace dungeons very soon. The astrologer, looking somewhat greenish, gazed at Garan Jin as if willing the boy to come along, but the last son of Garan Tamuron pretended not to notice, and the astrologer's steps were very slow.

Tabrak's kaburei was escorted away, but not overly roughly. Jin waited until the man's shadow had crossed the threshold of the hall and turned fully to his elder brother. "Sensheo, you will let me kill them."

"Who are *you* to command me?" the Emperor inquired, frostily. "Be careful, Jinjin. Go visit your mother."

Jin stared at him for a few moments, but finally bowed. "Yes, Elder Brother." The honorific was as mutinous as possible under the circumstances; he strode from the hall, passing the court astrologer and fastidiously avoiding the streaks upon the stone floor from the barbarians' filth.

Mrong Banh hurried in his wake, his robe shush-fluttering. The Emperor's attention turned to Lord Hanweo, who hurried forward, restored to primacy and very busy. The burden of two ministerial positions fell upon him.

None could find Lord Yulehi even now. If he had retreated to his estate outside the city walls, it was perhaps burning at the moment; in the end, though, the members of his clan were merely grateful they did not seem to be feeling the lash of the Emperor's displeasure.

Yet.

A thread of smoke had worked in amid the incense and perfumes of the pillared hall, and the business of court life went on for the rest of the day.

That night, the fires of Tabrak spread, almost lapping against the great walls built in the Second Dynasty. Even the rain, intensifying as dusk fell, did not put them out.

And the thunder of Heaven was answered by cannon-booming.

STORM, PASSED

T hey took Daka and Vasol?" Aro Ba Wistis roared. "And you
did *nothing*?"

Etu, facedown against thick stolen carpets laid over pounded
dirt and scorched grass, pressed his nose into woolen pile and
inhaled sharply, gratefully. It could not have gone better, truly;
a sharp-eyed scun well used to gauging a master's mood with a
glance could very easily add a word here, a shade of meaning there,
and change the entire color of a translated phrase. He had not
expected the crimson-robed man upon his padded bench to be so
easy to bait, but Heaven—or the Burning One—had smiled upon
Etu.

Now his lord was without two trusted advisors who were also
mighty in the saddle and the Horde was trapped outside Zunnan's
walls as the autumn rains began. Even the kick the son of Wistis
directed at his hindquarters was not as hard as it might otherwise
have been.

I am a mere scun, what could I do? Saying it would avail him
nothing; it was best to let the greatest rider of the Horde spend his
fury. Etu's plan was bearing bitter fruit indeed, and his master was
forced to swallow every bite because he believed, after all, that it
was *his*.

It was so easy to lead a man who knew beyond a doubt he was
the master.

Aro raged for a short while yet, kicking at a mound of spoils brought just that afternoon. The women sent to his tent—scuni and prisoners both—cowered, making soft sounds of distress. Smoke filled the tent and rain slapped at the sides; those tending the fires tonight would have a miserable time of it.

Finally, Aro quieted, and Etu held very still. This was when the son of Wistis was most dangerous, when others thought the storm had passed.

Finally, he gave Etu's ribs another kick, but only a halfhearted one. "Only a scun, after all," he muttered, and Etu was thankful his face was hidden, for his mouth contorted in savage triumph.

"Never mind," the son of Wistis continued, striding for the tent flap. "We shall shatter their walls and take Zunnan. They have nothing left to gainsay us."

Nothing except an army to the north. The southron one was not nearly strong enough. But Etu did not say it; Aro assumed the army they had faced between Shan's capital and here to be the sum of Zhaon's might. No doubt Etu's implicit agreement had bolstered the assumption. Besides, Aro's own grand-uncle had led the last attack upon the clay people, and thirty summers ago they had not put up much resistance at all.

"*Get the thunder-tubes!*" Aro roared out the door, into the slackening rain. "Bring their scun to me, I shall give them orders!"

The most favored scun in the Horde lay where he was, as if still trembling from his master's ire. Most of those who knew how to tend the captured cannon had perished in battle, Aro's order to simply capture them not quite reaching his stirrup-holders in time for one reason or another. The few left could teach others, but not quickly. Even if the Horde managed to bring down the walls, there was still the winter to pass.

Etu had time.

CANNON OR THUNDER

There was no formal funeral, the pyre of Garan Tamuron's second-eldest son stacked in darkness, lit haphazardly, and fueled by mounds of imperial clothing tossed over his cooling body. Or so the rumors said, and no mourning was allowed for Garan Kurin, even an armband.

It did not seem right, but Yala lit incense before her husband's small ancestral shrine each day, hoping it would ward off ill-luck. She doubted she was the only one who did so, and after all it was relatively safe. If her prayers were quietly trapped within her head-meat, they could not be reported to Sensheo.

Her red time had still not appeared. The autumn rains had begun, and any relief in their relative coolness was outweighed by other considerations.

Brushed upon very thick paper, the summons was stamped with crimson ink and sealed with red wax. Yala accepted it with both hands, as protocol dictated, and glanced at Jin, who had delivered it to the estate and now sat bolt-upright at the table, a cup of Lady Gonwa's heaven tea cooling before him. He had touched his lips to the rim, which meant everyone else could drink, but he did not glance at Su Junha or blush when she looked to him.

In fact, he was unwonted quiet after his delivery and giving the news of Third Mother Luswone's health—precarious, since she was refusing even clear broth—and Gamnae doing as well as could be expected. And with his long nose and somber mien, he looked very much like his mother at the moment.

"I am summoned to the Palace," Yala said, in her usual clear tone, once she had read the entire missive twice. She was in very pale yellow silk today; it had become quite fashionable to dress in the lightest tone possible—without approaching mourning, of course. "With only a single maid."

"An insult." Jin bit off the edges of each word. "Takshin will be angry."

"Takshin is not here." She read the invitation once more to make certain no fraction of meaning would escape and refolded it with exquisite care, settling into her own seat now that imperial words had been witnessed. "We do not know if he met the Horde going south, either."

A faint scurrying in the hall halted the conversation; everyone in the room relaxed slightly when Mrong Banh appeared, his topknot askew, his robe slightly disarranged, and his eyes ringed with bruiselike dark. He brightened upon seeing Jin, and bowed in Yala's direction. "*There* you are. He's asking for you again, Jin."

"He can ask all he wants." The young man's chin jutted in a very decided manner; it was a look familiar to those who had attended his elder sister. "All he wants is someone to insult."

"There are barbarians at the walls; Zhaon needs you more than your pride does." Mrong clicked his tongue and settled at the table; Hansei Liyue, as the youngest present even though noble by birth, hurried to pour him a cup. "Thank Heaven there is enough water. The cisterns will be full ere long and the river is rising."

"That section of the walls is safe, then. And perhaps they will not try to sneak through the culverts into the Palace baths." Jin lifted his cup, sniffed it, and set it down as if surprised to find it was not sohju. "He wants Princess Yala in the Palace, Banh."

"Of course. If the walls are breached the inner complex may hold out some while." The astrologer nodded, and did not glance apologetically at the two young noblewomen, who might be understandably distressed at the thought of being left outside such safety. "Takshin would not like to return and find...well."

"If he was not met upon the road to Shan." Jin said it so Yala, as a good wife, would not have to repeat such a thing and, by repetition, imply she wished for it. "But he could not be," he hurried to add. "Our Takshin is too canny to be caught."

"May it be so," Yala replied, as tradition demanded. Her gaze lingered upon her hands while she set the invitation before an empty chair and poured a measure into a fine Gurai slipware cup, setting it before the Emperor's words to bring luck and health. "Honorable Mrong, I am most worried for my husband's household. What should I do?"

Su Junha, almost as pale as her well-mended green cotton dress, let out a small sound; the situation was grave indeed if even her patroness was deviating from the unbending rule of discussing tea, the weather, and various other small items before turning to business.

The soft exclamation caught Jin's attention; the Sixth Prince shook his head like a horse scenting fire. "Why, that's simple." He drew himself even taller in his chair, if possible. "I'll take them. With Mother...well, her household can hold a few more, to help with her care. Lady Su and Lady Hansei are invited to the Palace and will stay in the Iejo. As for the Steward and Lady Kue...oh, of course. It's high time I had a household of my own; I might as well borrow Takshin's for a short while. To become used to it, you see. There's more than enough room, especially...well."

Especially with my sister gone, he might have said. The words hung unspoken.

Yala nodded thoughtfully. "The invitation mentions I may bring a servant; it says nothing against another prince inviting the entire household. It may anger the gracious Emperor, though." If there was any sarcasm in the title, it was well-hidden. Her quiet look of gratitude, not to mention Lady Su's, fastened upon the young prince.

"I should think he has other worries." Banh lifted his cup, distractedly, set it down untasted. "They are firing over the walls; not only did this Lord Aro steal cannon but also had the intelligence to take at least a few of those who service them. It will not be long before they are working *upon* instead of *over*."

"A pleasant thought." Princess Yala picked up her own cup, her resin-dipped fingertips a pleasing contrast to the dry white Shan bonefire. She did not complain when Su Junha applied the warm, sticky, staining stuff each morning, though it was not an ornament a Khir wife would prefer. For one thing, it was a subtle way to show respect for the Second and Third Mothers. "There is still no news from the North, and none will arrive since—"

"That is what I came to tell you. Well, that and to find Jin." Mrong Banh poked at his topknot. "I heard from a Golden friend that pigeons from Tienzu Keep winged through the rain; Zakkar Kai's dispatches say he is riding south. But even should he arrive in time, all may not go well."

"That's wonderful…" Jin brightened momentarily, but sobered just as quickly as he continued down the chain of likely consequences. "But Elder Brother hates him. Tabrak is dangerous, and yet…" His expression plainly stated what he considered the larger danger.

Princess Yala's eyes turned sleep-lidded, a look of profound thought settling over her sharp-featured Khir face. "Then we must give some thought to saving Zakkar Kai." Quietly, as if it were the most natural thing in the world.

"Takshin will protect him." Jin folded his hands upon the table; a new light entered his dark gaze. His shoulders eased somewhat.

Su Junha refilled his teacup, pouring with her sleeve held gracefully aside.

"When Takshin returns. Which may or may not be before the walls are broken." Mrong Banh cast a nervous glance at Hansei Liyue, clad in very light sky-blue, who appeared sunk in thought as deep as her patroness's. Next he looked to Yala. "Princess, are you certain that everyone… forgive me, but perhaps not everyone at this table might care to hear what we are discussing?"

"There is nothing treasonous in protecting Kai," Jin objected, hotly. "Especially since Elder Brother did...what he did."

"Sixth Prince." Yala's tone was all gentle warning, though she did not glance at the door. "Please."

He subsided.

"In any case, Lady Su and Lady Hansei can hardly be kept unaware of anything passing in this household. And women hear things you may not, Mrong Banh. We hear things even a prince may not." Princess Yala gazed into her cup, her eyebrows drawing together. "Though often, not enough."

Sixth Prince Jin swallowed whatever he had meant to say. Instead, he laid his right hand upon the princess's, covering the plain greenstone band of royal rank upon her left first finger. The new princess's lash-veiled eyes were very bright, and she let her chin drop slightly, blinking hard.

"Princess Yala is our patroness." Su Junha sat very straight, and it was her gaze which lingered upon the doorway, alert to any passing shadow. "We did not abandon her when the Crown Prince suffered misfortune; we will not do so now."

"Quite right," Hansei Liyue added, with a decided nod. "It would not be noble."

"I did not mean to offer insult." Mrong Banh inclined slightly from the waist, a small bow taking in both girls. "Forgive me."

"There is nothing to forgive." Lady Su, as the elder, inclined her head in response. The colorless crystals upon her hairpin described a graceful arc.

Jin patted Yala's hand. "I shall need paper and brush to begin moving the household. Do not make arrangements for the furniture, simply bring everyone inside the complex."

"We have hardly finished unpacking anyway," Su Junha observed, her mouth curving into a slight smile. Still, both she and Lady Hansei were both pale now, and Junha had reached for Liyue's hand under the table. *"Bring only your robe, and a cup for our tea."*

"Zhe Har," Liyue observed, with a smile. "You have been reading."

"Who cannot, around you?" The elder girl rose, drawing the younger with her, and bowed to her patroness. "We shall begin immediately. Come, Hansei, let us fetch paper and brush for the Sixth Prince, and set about our arrangements. We should not delay."

"Indeed." Yala nodded, and was once again her usual calm, brisk self, though her pale eyes were still very bright, salt water welling against her lids. "Honorable Mrong Banh, is there anything we might do to ease your troubles?"

"My troubles are not worth mentioning, Princess." But the astrologer was unwonted grave. "I did not think to live long enough to see what I have seen this summer."

An uncomfortable silence fell, broken only by the ladies Su and Hansei making their bows and departing to fetch paper and brush for the prince. Princess Yala regarded Mrong Banh steadily; he returned the favor.

The rumbling passing through the air of the sitting-room could have been the thunder of autumn storms, or distant cannon. It was difficult to tell.

ANTS OR MAGGOTS

Upon the thirteenth day of the siege a soaking dawn rose red in the east; Sixth Prince Garan Jin stood above Zhaon-An's South Gate, staring at the mass of Tabrak below. The walls of Zhaon-An were old and strong; the Horde held the roads and massed before each possible entry point. The only place they did not gather was to the north behind the Palace complex's thick curtaining wall; the ground there was far too soft, especially with the river rising. They had fouled the baths and outbuildings in that direction before leaving a few guards to watch the marshy edges, though, and fired what they could. Some few peasants had perhaps escaped in that direction.

But not many.

Lihaon Baikan, part of the Golden's ruling triumvirate, stood at his shoulder. "So many of them," he said, softly. "Like ants. Or maggots in bad meat."

What would Kai say? Jin let the older man's statement hang in the wet, cool breeze like a standard just-raised. "Perhaps the rain will flood their barrow, and we shall be saved."

"Best not to count upon that." The Golden gave him a wary, sidelong glance. "Shall we?"

"Indeed." It was difficult to turn away from the spectacle—black dots of Tabrak tending unshielded cooking fires kept alive overnight despite the downpour, random cries rising from the fringes as the pale barbarians resumed the work of strangling the city and feeding themselves and their mounts. Smoke rose, torn to tatters upon the breeze. They carried no standards and did not move in cohort, or even maniple like Shan's army; the entire seething lot of them was indeed very like waxen maggots in a hanging side of spoiled curltail or ox.

Prince and Golden set off along the wall, more Golden flanking Jin. *Defend the city*, Sensheo said—well, Jin would. He had made certain Yala and Takshin's dependents were hastily settled in a part of the Iejo considered his when he had a household of his own; the quarters needed a little cleaning but were perfectly serviceable and as the new princess said, it would keep Lady Kue and Steward Keh occupied; he had also brushed a commission for Kihon Jiao, taking the physician into his own service as a precaution. Yala was visiting Mother, Su Junha and Hansei Liyue at Luswone's bedside when she could not be, so he didn't have to worry.

At least, not much. Gamnae was with Haesara; she had written him a small note before dawn that Second Mother was having trouble sleeping.

Well she might, as Sensen's mother. Jin wondered how much she knew, and when? But if she'd known, wouldn't she have done something about Maki?

He had little time to think about it; of far greater concern were the Golden surrounding him. He had never thought much before about where the bright-armored palace guards' loyalties might truly lie; what need was there, with Father alive?

His leather half-armor was a comforting weight. So too was the sword at his back and the dagger at his belt, and Jin's back prickled at the thought of others behind him carrying weapons.

Even the Golden, supposed to be ever-loyal. "Water we have, and to spare," he said. *At least for a while.* "What of the food supplies?"

Lihaon Baikan nodded, as if he was pleased at the question. "There was not enough time, but the granaries are three-quarters full. We may hold a moon-turn, maybe more, if the walls—"

Afterward, Jin was never quite certain if the wall had shuddered under his boots before he heard the explosion, or if his head-meat was simply shaken so badly he *thought* he had. He staggered; Captain Lihaon caught his arm, and a shriek of crumbling stone and sheared metal echoed across Zhaon-An. A great gout of smoke rose in the near distance.

Tabrak had halted the cannonade only because Aro Ba Wistis, after some thought, had decided there was a more direct way of solving the quandary of not enough artillery-soldiers to service the great brazen-and-iron tubes. The black powder itself, laboriously harvested from casks his people called *thunder eggs*, was serving quite a different purpose now, and though the walls were manned with bowmen there were hardly enough of them among the City Guard to keep every inch under view. The Golden mostly used pike and sword; the remnants of the Southron Army that had managed to reach the city's safety before the closing of the gates did likewise.

Jin grasped only that Tabrak had found some way of breaching the wall, and he shoved between two semi-dazed Golden staring at the rising plume with their mouths hanging open. Groaning and cracking lifted into a bright, fresh-washed morning sky along with the smoke, and a section of Zhaon's great stone city wall buckled. The South Gate was warped and half-splintered, and a massive cry went up from the Horde.

What would Kai say of this? For a moment Jin was too stunned to even wonder; then, quite naturally, the realization that Kai was not here and it was up to Garan Jin to do what needed doing struck him like a mailed fist to the gut. His hand flashed up, closing over the swordhilt at his shoulder, and behind him, alarm-cries, gongs, and trumpets sounded.

"*For Zhaon!*" he cried, his throat burning and the bellow too large for his still-boyish chest. "*We must hold the wall! For Zhaon!*"

TRAITOR AND WISDOM

The Great Hall's vermilion pillars were curiously uncrowded by courtiers that morning.

Garan Sensheo, Emperor of all Zhaon, denied the urge to make a fist. There were things to like about reaching the summit; he could, after all, do whatever he liked once the barbarians were taken care of.

Yet his back ached from sitting in state upon the padded bench, his head throbbed, he missed his archer's thumb-ring, and the woman before him, dressed in silk so pale green as to be practically mourning, was a deep irritant.

He'd given orders, but every court lady he saw was dressed like an angry shade. Which made him wonder if the barbarians had reached the new tombs, and if they were squatting in front of Father's memorial wall.

Even that thought couldn't cheer him. "What," Sensheo inquired, very mildly, "do my brothers see in you?"

"Your Gracious Majesty?" The Khir lady-in-waiting, Takshin's little whore, regarded him levelly. She hadn't looked at Kurin this way, no indeed, and of course she'd never been in Father's presence. Her entire country was treacherous, for all they mouthed truisms about *honor*—Khir had made some sort of agreement with a

Tabrak emissary, and this spying little bitch had probably known about it. "I do not understand your meaning."

Zan Fein was at Sensheo's side, his fan moving with babu water-clock regularity. "Your Majesty," he murmured. "Princess Yala has come to report upon the health of Third Mother Luswone."

Oh, that. Regrettable, of course, but the silly concubine had actually *drunk*, instead of waiting. Greed carried its own reward, wasn't that a sage Maki was quite fond of quoting?

Except Maki was dead. Sensheo had avenged him, but their mother would not even look at him. Haesara was perfectly polite, of course, but he'd seen her deploy that chilly formality before, usually upon tradesmen or the First Queen's little spiders. And she liked Takshin's wife, too, making a show of petting the woman.

So Sensheo was forced to incline his head slightly. "Well, *sister.*" Considering how she was dressed, it irked him to address her as family. "And how is our Third Revered Mother's health this morning?"

The Khir woman did not even glance gratefully at Zan Fein, which was disappointing. "Your Illustrious Majesty, the Third Dowager Mother of the Emperor has been refusing all nourishment, even broth and water. The physicians say she will recover if—"

Ah. Now that, I can use. "And why is she doing that?" he interrupted.

The Khir woman's gaze dropped to his scarlet-clad knees, rather guiltily. "Your Majesty, I do not know."

"Perhaps she fears what she might be fed, with a traitor at her bedside."

She said nothing. Her hands were hidden in her sleeves; should he order her searched for that greenmetal claw? She was even wearing an unmarked greenstone ring, as a princess. That would have driven Sabwone to outright cold rage; he wished she was here to see it.

"Khir received an embassy from Tabrak and raised their banners against Zhaon," Sensheo said, clearly and distinctly. "And you are Khir."

"My husband is Zhaon, Your Majesty." She kept staring at his knees. Even her hairpin decoration was pale; apparently the fashion was a chain or two of tiny glittering crystals. "Therefore I am as well."

She was *laughing* at him. And that kaburei of hers, squeaking and cowering, turning down his offers of manumission. Well, he couldn't do anything about the barbarians outside the walls just yet—winter would take care of starving them, and plenty of the useless poor within the girdle of Zhaon-An as well—but he could show everyone inside that he was strong, and treachery had consequences.

"Is that so." Sensheo glanced over the hall, gauging his audience. The pillars stood mute and bloody; only eunuchs and the barest core of ministers conferred amid the scribe-tables where just a few days ago the machinery of brush and bureaucracy transmitted policy into provincial directive. Many of the nobles were suspiciously absent today, no doubt supervising attempts to move what they could from their estates into the Palace complex. The ministers not occupied with such things were in a brightly colored knot to the right, conferring in tones of great seriousness and quite ignoring him.

"Yes, Your Majesty." And the pale-clad bitch had even tried to save her filthy countrymen. Takshin might be irritated if he returned to find her removed, but in the end he'd thank Sensheo for saving him some trouble.

Besides, wouldn't it be fun to see Takshin's face when he realized little Sensen was upon the throne? That sneering scarred lip of his would have different work to do.

Sensheo made another gesture, and four Golden, well-trained like the round little dogs some noblewomen fancied as pets, moved forward. Their pike-heads dipped; if she were to produce that greenmetal claw now he could have her flogged to death, princess or no.

Princess Yala did not move. In fact, the woman seemed not to notice the quartet ringing her, a tiny siege within a siege. Hands clasped inside long sleeves and her chin lowered, she was a scroll-illustration of a handmaiden waiting for a patron's direction. The hem of her silken dress quivered, though, and her sleeves stirred as if a stray breeze had breathed upon her.

Or a passing shade. Was Father watching this? Was Maki?

"Your Majesty." Zan Fein, a little louder. A draft of the chief court eunuch's umu scent carried a fan-breeze to Sensheo, and the Emperor wrinkled his nose. "It might be wiser to—"

"Wiser? To have a traitor in our very household, attending Third Mother?" Sensheo's tongue clicked, very much like Haesara's when she noticed a breach of etiquette.

"The Second Mother of the Revered Emperor sent Princess Yala to bear news of the Third Mother of the Revered Emperor's health." Zan Fein's neutral tone did not change. In other words, Sensheo's own mother had been taken in by this ill spirit in the shape of a Khir woman, and not only was Yala laughing at him, but Zan Fein as well.

Did they expect him not to notice, not to *see*? Jin had brought all Takshin's little helpers and lackeys into the complex without even consulting his elder brother. They had been Takyeo's dependents, certainly, but now they very well knew how their rai was seasoned. At least he could send Jin to the walls and hope for a stray bolt from a barbarian bow until he could arrange something more suitable.

Kurin was correct; it was lonely upon this particular bench. Elder Brother's pyre had been quick indeed, and added its smoke to the firing of Zhaon-An's skirts, but Sensheo had not carried the torch.

It simply wouldn't look right. Instead, the Golden had sent their erstwhile master skyward while servants bustled, bringing Rinrin's clothes to help fuel the blaze. Perhaps Kurin would meet his clan-uncle, whose corpse was quietly mouldering in a well just outside the city limits, near a burned-out shack overgrown with yellowed summer vines not yet juicy with the wet season's downpours.

No matter how many obstacles Sensheo removed, there were always more. Hadn't the Awakened One said something similar?

Makar would have known.

The time simply wasn't right for taking one of Takshin's toys. Especially since the ministers had noticed the Golden ringing the new princess and fallen silent, watching. "Go away," the Emperor told the Khir woman. "And be careful, my brother's wife. Treason will be punished in Zhaon, no matter *who* is at our gates."

She bowed, a subtle movement as she straightened including Zan Fain with impeccable propriety. Backing up three gliding steps, she bowed again, and the Golden moved with her since they had not been given leave to advance or to desist.

For a moment Sensheo toyed with the idea of barking another order and sending her to the dungeons, or having her body carried to the walls.

But there was time enough later, and she was only a woman, after all.

The Golden surrounded her as she made each required obeisance upon leaving the imperial presence, and their pikes did not raise until the third, when Sensheo magnanimously uttered the traditional *cease*.

"My mother should choose better handmaidens," he muttered, and turned his head to gaze at Zan Fein. "And you, Chief Court Eunuch, presume rather too much."

"This one apologizes to the Emperor." Zan Fein's fan snapped closed, and the beardless, umu-drenched councilor bowed deeply.

Sensheo might have said more, but a breathless Golden ran through the great double doors left ajar since the Second Dynasty, almost colliding with Garan Yala, who skipped nimbly aside and halted, her skirts swinging and the string of crystalline drops hanging from her hairpin's head quivering as she had not under the Emperor's displeasure. Mrong Banh, newly arrived as well and trapped in a knot of those summoned to wait upon the Emperor's pleasure near the door, hurried toward the princess, catching her elbow to steady her.

"*The wall!*" the newly arrived Golden cried, skidding to a halt. He had not even removed his boots upon the stairs. "*The wall is breached! The Sixth Prince sends word the city wall is breached!*"

Too Busy to
Think

I t was not like practice.

The hard knot of Golden and City Guard around him moved as a single unit, Garan Jin shouting march-time. His voice was almost lost under the chaos of screaming—both equine and human—and clashing metal, the barbarians ululating their glee and bloodlust, defenders desperately moving from point to defensible point along narrow-twisting streets the Guard and Night Watch knew almost better than the lines upon their own palms.

It didn't take consulting the Kai inside his head to see the hole in the wall couldn't be stoppered; bloody paste that had once been human beings dewed the tumbled, fractured stone blocks that had seemed so solid the many times he'd walked along their top. At least it had been quick; whoever had not died in the collapse was struck down by slip-scrambling barbarians and hoof-clattering horses straining through the uneven mess at the bottom of the gap.

How many cannonballs and casks had they plundered? Who had taught them such a thing?

It didn't matter, but even realizing as much in the clarity brought by utter disaster, Jin still would have liked to know.

"Pikes!" he yelled, and the four mounted barbarians deciding to charge their square could not gain enough speed to break through.

The horses screamed afresh, two foundering and a third refusing to be driven onto the points, rearing and beating the air with his front hooves. A Night Watch officer, his topknot falling half-free, lost a pike, torn from his hands as the great black beast whose chest it was buried in fell; he staggered backward and reached for the shortsword hilt at his belt. They could not afford to lose many more spears—but another group of Golden, seeing their cohort, hurried from a street-junction to the right, melding with Jin's party. Many of the Golden had spent time in Watch or Guard; Father had made sure Zhaon-An's peacekeepers and the imperial bodyguard were tight-knit and well-trained.

He was too busy to think of Father, of Ah-Yeo, of Rinrin and Sensen. Too busy to think even of Sabi or Mother, the lightfoot blooming in his calves and shins as he saw a possible avenue of escape only lightly blocked by milling, shaggy barbarians, wandering oxen dazed by their success.

It was no great trick to sail between two bright-helmed Golden, landing amid their pike-shafts, leaving them behind and running lightly over cobbles still bearing traces of last night's downpour and wet dirt in the channels between. His sword was a bright metal bar, blurring as he met the first too-tall, stinking barbarian-mountain, the blade biting deep as it never did in practice.

The first time he'd killed a man, the feeling had almost made him vomit. Now it was simply another sensation to be shunted aside in the chaos as he kicked, his good practice-boot forcing a barbarian knee in a direction the joint had definitely *not* been designed for. The stick-snap of breakage was lost in the hubbub, and time slowed down as it did whenever he was absorbed in leaping the palace complex's walls at night in search of drinking companions or driving an opponent across the great stone expanse of drillyard, his weighted wooden blade snap-hitting in quick succession.

All he had to remember was not to pull his blows at the last moment. He could not deny it was a fine feeling, all his skill and speed finally being called upon.

And yet the stink was massive, sprays of blood and fouler matter following the path of his blade, and the reeking barbarians sounded just like regular humans when they were injured, screaming in pain or fury. His mother would be horrified—any mess or unsightliness was not to be borne by a noblewoman of Daebo.

The thought of Mother propped upon her pillows, her mouth a red raw-eaten wound and her large dark eyes full of furious suffering like the horses' when their legs were snapped and all they could do was wait in the midst of their agony, ignited in his head-meat like sohju upon an empty stomach.

"*Follow me!*" Garan Jin cried in his father's voice, and fell upon the Tabrak.

FALSE HOPE

W e shall merely look in," Haesara said softly as they passed into the Iejo's bustle. Her gown was a very light sunshine yellow, brightly cheerful though the shade lingered very close to mourning. Her hairpin decoration was a fall of shivering golden leaves, catching the midmorning sun. "I do not think Princess Yala has returned yet."

"I should have gone." Gamnae's eyes were reddened and her nose pink-raw, but she held her head high and her hairpin's beads swung dainty instead of frantic as she tucked her hands in roseate silk sleeves. "I worry that..."

"I know." The Second Mother's hair was dressed very simply, as if her morning routine had been hurried. It was strange to see. "I think she means to save me pain. A good daughter-in-law." But she was pale, and her gaze did not quite meet Gamnae's, simply slid away.

What would it be like, Gamnae wondered, to know your son had done something so terrible? Takyeo had told his youngest sister to consider marriage very carefully indeed, and now she wondered if Ah-Yeo had seen some fraction of the future as the dying were wont to do.

It had been a summer of death, and now autumn promised to be just as bloody.

Gamnae kept her pace decorously slow, her indoor slippers

shushing along a familiar corridor. She had rarely seen the First
Concubine's private chambers before, but this hall led to a lovely
sitting-room where First and Second Princesses of Zhaon had
played at tea and conversation as children, attempting to imitate
their lovely, restrained mothers. Sabi was always better at it, of
course, but she was gone—and it was strange to think that now
nobody but Gamnae would remember those hours when they were
merely sisters, sometimes squabbling but also presenting a shield-
wall against many brothers who thought it great fun to torment,
poke, or tease.

Nobody else would remember their secret passwords or gossip.
Even if Sabi had turned cold and haughty, even if she liked to pinch
and make Gamnae's eyes fill with hot water at an injustice, she was
also *familiar*, and now she was irretrievably gone.

Like Father, and Mother, and everyone else. It would not stop;
Garan Gamnae was helpless to halt anything.

Haesara accepted the deep bow of Luswone's steward, the round
and often merry Turong Beh.

"The princess has not returned yet," Turong murmured, his
plump hands clasping very tightly before his belly as he straightened. He grasped himself so hard his pudgy knuckles whitened.
"Ladies Su and Hansei left a few moments ago to see if she may
be found, for my lady wishes her. Honorable Kihon and the two
physicians sent by the Glorious Emperor are with my lady, and her
close-servants."

Haesara nodded as if all this was expected, as if Su Junha and
Hansei Liyue did not have reason to worry and were merely making social calls. "Has she taken any nourishment?" It was faintly
outside etiquette to ask a steward such a thing, but a dowager
queen could do as she liked.

Not that it had done Gamnae's own mother much good, or satisfied whatever deep gaping *absence* had driven Gamwone to…
what she had done.

Attending Haesara was Gamnae's own private penance, even
though she had always liked the Second Queen. But if a mother

could be ashamed of her son—which Gamnae thought very likely, though the sages of course did not spend much time upon the question—a daughter could admit she had suspected her own mother of crimes even while supposedly too young to think of such things, and feel similarly helpless and baffled.

"Not so far as I know, Second Dowager Mother." For a moment Steward Turong's cheeks quivered; Luswone was well-regarded by her servants.

Not like Gamwone. Even Yona had disappeared from that part of the Kaeje, probably fleeing to some almost-forgotten family in a distant province; none of the frail, stick-fingered maids were left. They had melted into Zhaon-An or into the outlying fields even before Kurin's...before what had happened to Kurin; now they had to contend with the barbarians and a city under siege.

Haesara's sigh was deep and apparently real; never, in all her life, could Gamnae remember her father's second queen making that sound, like a peasant's maiden auntie expressing weary resignation. "Thank you, Steward Turong," she murmured, and the round man in his well-dyed brown cotton robe bustled away, probably relieved not to be asked for more specifics. "Stubborn," she continued, addressing empty air. "It served her well, though, these many years."

Gamnae could not find a reply

The bedroom was pretty and airy with the partition open, but the stink of medicines and the brown blots of robed physicians destroyed any peace Gamnae might have gained from the beauty. Haesara did not stop to greet even Physician Kihon—that was Gamnae's task—but glided directly for the bed, a maid hurrying to place the three-legged, cushioned stool the Second Mother used for her frequent visits. "Luswone," she said softly, and bent over her husband's first concubine, sliding her fingers under Third Mother's limp hand, the resin-stains on Luswone's fingertips fading. "Oh, my dear. You must try to swallow something."

"How is she, Honorable Kihon?" Gamnae hoped the once-shabby physician could hear the warmth in her tone. Ever since Kai had brought him to the Palace, she had liked his calm; he reminded her powerfully of Mrong Banh, but not so merry.

Banh was another worry. Sooner or later Sensheo would be upset with him, too. Kurin at least could sometimes be reasoned with—and how she squirmed at the thought that she did not miss her eldest brother as she should while simultaneously too much.

She missed Takyeo more, yet now it was too late. She suspected it would be too late for much more, and in a very short while, too.

The thought filled her with weariness.

"Fading, Second Princess." As usual, Physician Kihon did not bother with false hope. "Even with the cooling medicine to soothe the throat so she may drink, she refuses."

I might too, if I looked like that. It was an unworthy thought, and Gamnae had been having quite a few of those lately.

She could not seem to stop.

"You must think of your son," Haesara whispered. Gamnae almost hunched her shoulders, casting a guilty glance at the sickbed.

Third Mother stiffened, propped between pillows, and her dark eyes flashed. The edges of the wound twitched, but no sound came forth, just a small bubbling exhale.

I am *thinking of my son*, Luswone's eyes said, perhaps more clearly than an unmarred mouth could. Or at least, so it seemed to Gamnae, who realized, as if she'd known it all along, that the Daebo princess taken as a warlord's concubine knew very well she could be held hostage in the bed if Sensheo needed her son to behave in a particular manner.

Or if the newest Emperor wished her only remaining child to walk quietly to his own execution.

The chill pouring down Gamnae's back made her sway, and Kihon Jiao stiffened. "Second Princess? Are you faint?"

"No, thank you," she said politely, even though her head-meat did feel strangely stuffed with feathers. The sudden attacks of unworthy—but depressingly logical—thoughts seemed to stretch her skull from the inside each time. "I will try to convince her to drink a little, Physician Kihon. And don't worry." She could not tell if she was wearing a usual expression, and hoped she did not look wild-eyed. "You are... in no danger."

It was a singularly inelegant way to phrase Gamnae's willingness to protect a creature even weaker than herself at court; Yala would have had a better one. But whatever the physician would have said in return was forestalled by a deep throbbing toll, striking three times against ear and chest at once.

When the Great Bell was hit, the entire complex heard it. The closer you were, the more its heartbeat shocked your own. Instead of continuing, though, after three strikes there was a breathless caesura, then another three terrible heart-shattering knocks.

"What is that?" Gamnae did not mean to sound so squeaky-terrified. She knew what an uninterrupted tolling meant—yet another royal death, though it had not tolled for Kurin—but this pattern wasn't familiar at all.

"It's..." Second Mother Haesara clutched Luswone's hand; Third Mother roused herself and squeezed back, her dark eyes more scorching than ever. "Heaven save us."

"Well?" Kihon Jiao's tone was sharper than any Gamnae had ever heard him use, and with his eyes blazing he looked almost handsome. "What is it?"

"Yes." Haesara was so pale dark crescents suddenly rested under her eyes. "I have heard this signal once or twice, from smaller bells. The city wall is breached."

The wall? For a moment Gamnae thought they meant one in the room, and she glanced around instinctively to see what she had, as usual, missed. The bell continued, *jeong-jeong-jeong*, pause, *jeong-jeong-jeong*.

Then she realized what it truly meant, and not only was her back cold but all the rest of her as well.

Of course the Palace was beautiful and utterly familiar, especially this particular large rectangular garden. Yet Hansei Liyue's heart refused to settle properly inside her chest, hopping and throbbing in different places as if her humors were disarranged. Well, whose could not be?

Su Junha had spent more than one summer in the Palace's confines; Hansei Liyue had arrived a little later, of course, but neither noblewoman needed to pay much attention to their footing as they hurried in search of their restrained and quite noble, even if foreign, patroness.

"I don't know," Liyue repeated. "He has never been very nice, certainly." She glanced across a long dripping garden-vista, making certain there were no servants or Golden close enough to hear. Even though everyone with any sense was crowding behind whatever walls they could find, certain parts of the palace were curiously deserted the past few mornings.

It was unsettling.

"The Second Princess said once that he used to mount garden-insects upon pins, to watch them struggle." Junha kept a watch the other direction; her dresses had often been close to threadbare before finding a proper benefactress, but nothing in her head-meat needed darning. Many a more advantageously placed court lady had snubbed a kinless girl with a poor but very noble name before Princess Yala selected her for the Crown Princess's retinue; the ignored, though, heard much that others did not. "I heard from Lady Tsurai that he's driven more than one courtesan outside the city, too."

"Our princess says not to worry." Liyue's jatajatas made soft comforting sounds as they turned to pass under a vine-covered arch. The red trumpet-flowers were fading, though the rains had brought them to a last sad flush. Normally all the spent blossoms would be collected, but even the gardeners had other matters upon their minds at the moment. "Surely the Second Mother..."

"We can hope, I suppose." Junha's pace slowed; she glanced at the sky, gauging the prospect of more rain spotting their pale dresses—hers blue, Liyue's green. It was not quite wise to wear colors approaching mourning, but their patroness did so, and every other court lady besides.

It was the only real power a noble girl possessed, the choice of a garment. Sometimes not even that. And surely the Emperor could not punish them all?

But he might not have to, Liyue knew. He could make an example of just one highly placed lady, and soon enough the brighter dresses would emerge.

Men did as they pleased, especially the Emperor. Even a collective expression of remonstrance could be broken by such an august creature.

She tried, once more that morning, to fix her attention solely upon the matter at hand. "She must have come this way." It was not like Yala to be late. Were all Khir women so...of all the words Hansei had harvested from novels, she could not find the proper one. Of course their princess was scholarly and recommended one or two dusty old works from the Hundreds, but the novels were much more thrilling. Many were even brushed by women—once they were married, of course, but if Liyue found a good husband, it was a possibility.

She practiced her brushwork assiduously, after all. Look at the Third Prince, scarred and sharp-tempered, yet mild as a kitten when their lady was present. Perhaps Liyue *should* be more scholarly? But Su Junha, while perfectly literate, did not like the Hundreds and the Sixth Prince often looked at her, did he not? Nothing would come of it, but if something did that would be very pleasant indeed.

Liyue's head-meat would not settle, flitting from one worry to the next, halting at a fond hope, then circling back to troubles. It was rather like having a jewelwing caught inside her skull.

Her companion's steps were deliberately short to match Liyue's own, and Junha was occupied with more immediate concerns. "When we reach the Great Hall, we may say the Second Mother has sent for her." The taller girl's mouth was drawn tight; her hairpin ornament swung, glittering as the leftover raindrops strewing the gardens. "Perhaps she has not even seen the Emperor yet. He must be very busy."

With barbarians at the walls, certainly. Liyue could not repress a shudder. Everyone said that of course the Horde would be driven away, or starve over the winter. The city had stocks of food, there were springs in the Noble Quarter, and since the rains had begun the cisterns would be full. "Very busy indeed," she agreed, somewhat morosely. Winter would be cold, but there was furniture to burn, as in Lady Funai's *Episodes of Jen-ji's Life*. "If, though... Junha, if something has happened..."

"Then you return to the Iejo, to help the Third Mother and Honorable Kihon." But Junha slowed too, and turned away from her lookout to glance down at the younger girl. "I will go to the Second Mother, if she is not visiting. She will help. She has to." But Junha's voice quivered slightly. Not much disturbed her smooth copper complexion, yet at the moment she was almost ashen. "All will be well, Liyue. It will."

They went round and round like the sleeve of a story-lantern, dismally repeating the same scenes. Liyue opened her mouth to utter her own firm assent despite the fact that her palms were damp and her heart would *not* stay in its proper place.

A strange deep sound interrupted, and for a moment she thought it an odd species of thunder. Both girls halted at the edge of a long paved path leading up a broad flight of stairs, two gilded stone pards at the top standing frozen, snarling sentinel. There should be Golden there too, but most of those bright-armored men had been sent to Zhaon-An's ancient walls.

Three massive peals bounced from stone, echoing oddly, and Liyue's heart decided her throat was more congenial than her rib cage, leaping into it like an angry spirit and throbbing. The noise could not be thunder, and it wasn't her pulse.

"What is..." Su Junha almost staggered, clutching at Liyue's arm. It would be inelegant of them to land in a heap, and it was utterly unlike the taller girl.

She was always so graceful.

Liyue realized what the tolling must be when it paused. *Please don't ring again*, she thought. *I can't bear it.* "Lady Munau," she heard herself say. "*The Fall of Khao Cao.*" A positively thrilling novel, one no noble girl should ever admit to reading; she had snatched bits of it when she should have been sewing, or late at night by the fitful gleam of a candle in a blown-glass globe. "It's... Junha, it's the Great Bell."

Three more deep, wild strokes almost swallowed her words, trailing echoes in their wake like a great lady's retinue. Their princess had not yet had time to accumulate more ladies-in-waiting or clients; Liyue had sometimes wondered who Yala would choose while in her bed at night, a great warm feeling of satisfaction filling her as she thought of being one of the first in a princess's noble procession.

"Why won't it stop?" Junha whispered in the breathless pause. "Not again, please—"

The Great Bell, ignoring her, rang again. Liyue realized she was the one who must solve this mystery, and what they must do. "The city walls." She had to almost shout, unnaturally loud as a noblewoman must never be in order to pierce the next triple-clamor. "The walls have been breached. Come, back to the Iejo. We must hurry."

"But...the princess..." Wide-eyed, Junha stood frozen, like a stunned deer.

"He will be too busy to do anything now." If the city walls were broken, it was the equally thick—though not as tall—palace walls they must depend upon. The Emperor had Golden to protect him, of course, and the eunuchs and noble ministers as well. Liyue tugged at Junha's arm with one sweating hand, turning the older girl. "And she will want to look after Third Mother, she promised the Sixth Prince. She might go through the dry-gardens, we will take that route back. We must...come, Junha, *please!*"

Junha's hand settled over hers and clutched, the palm just as damp as her own; the two girls, the sound of their jatajatas lost under thunderous distorted bell-song, found they were both able to run.

CLAY SOLDIERS

A victorious army and a defeated one marched south in tandem for several days before a hastily scrawled dispatch staggering northward upon a half-dead horse met the forward guard near the keep of Tienzu. Hurried up the chain of command, it reached Zakkar Kai deep in conference with generals both Khir and Zhaon, hammering out a battle plan that had some chance of working against the Horde and—such was Kai's fond hope—would leave the head general of Zhaon placed advantageously enough near the capital to keep Khir from finishing Tabrak's work.

It would, he suspected, be well-nigh impossible. Still, there was some pleasure in learning more of Khir strategy and tactics, not to mention the personalities of the men he would be facing should they decide to become troublesome; no such knowledge was ever wasted. Tamuron would have enjoyed it too, both for the outwitting of one's temporary ally and for the company of like-minded men. It was almost an artisan's pride in his craft, but not quite, for the cost in ended lives and broken bodies was terrible.

The keep itself would have been better for this meeting, but instead they had halted in a small clearing, the folding tables standing upon yellowed summer grass—greening at its root from the strengthening autumn downpours—and wildflowers gone to seed. It would not rain for another watch or so, or at least it did not look likely to.

"—quite simple," Ashani Daoyan said, touching his right two fingers to the cup of his left hand to emphasize the point. "When one's hunting has not gone well, one approaches the ground differently. They mean not to raid but to settle."

"Perhaps they have not noticed the house is occupied," Hurong Tai commented with mock-seriousness, and a ripple of amusement at the old, well-layered joke ran through both north and south, just as a breeze freighted with green petrichor brushed every topknot.

Khir's new ruler—it was very possible, Kai thought, that he would hold the throne—contented himself with a tight smile. "It makes perfect sense. If he's not wintering in Shan's capital, then in Zhaon-An—which would be my choice too. He'll turn it into an administrative seat, if he can leave enough of the scribes alive. It's rather elegant, actually."

"You have given this much thought, Great Rider?" Hazuni Ulo did not sound quite sardonic, but his manner toward Zlorih's son had undergone an admiring change of late.

It was difficult not to like the fellow.

"'Tis not enough to merely survive, my lord Hazuni." The young man's pale gaze, very much like Komor Yala's but without her quality of serenity, remained fixed upon the map. "If one wishes success, one must *anticipate*. Which is how I stayed alive."

"Then he will be seeking to hold what he takes." Kai rubbed at his chin, a movement of deep thought. His fingertips scraped upon stubble; there was not time for more than hurried camp-baths during their short halts. Anlon, standing beside him, stared at the edge of this particular forest clearing with a worried air, a similar habit. "Not the Horde's strong suit." Nor was it Khir's, unless it was the defiles and high valleys of their dagger-shaped homeland, protecting the terraced mountainsides beyond.

Still, no need to point as much out with the guests at table.

"If he has no other course, he will be an animal at bay." Ashani's shrug was a swift, supple shiver; he was impatient with the world, a young wolf in autumn when the prey was slow and fattening for winter.

After a few seasons of cold starvation, Kai thought, he would learn to prize the easy catch a little more. This type of man, touchy about his own worth, usually flung himself after the unattainable.

As if Kai was any better. "And those are dangerous." Sometimes leaving a defeated foe an exit was preferable to spending the amount of blood necessary to crack a shield-square. "I wonder—"

The thought fled him when bootsteps approached at a gallop and a runner from the front bounded into the clearing, scanning frantically until he found the knot of armor that said *officers*. "Dispatch," the young Zhaon gasped, his cheeks gleaming with sweat and the morning fog. "From the front! Dispatch!"

The nights were becoming crisp, but the real rains were passing a breath to the east this year. Kai thought it an unlikely coincidence; someone in Khir had guessed this would be the case, or had a peasant's weather-sense. He had rarely fought this far west.

"He seems excited," Ashani said in soft, accented Zhaon, and if his hand twitched for a swordhilt, who could have blamed him? The rules for treating with a defeated enemy were stringent, for all they allowed a beheading or two if necessary, and Kai preferred to follow them until a clear breach gave him reason to do otherwise.

All in all, though, he was faintly disturbed that the heir to Khir—now their king, or Great Rider, or whatever the title—was proving so tractable. The young man must have reasons of his own, more than simple survival.

And Kai could not, under Heaven, discern what they were.

"Easy, runner." Anlon intercepted the package and brought it at a slightly slower rate to Kai, who broke the sloppily stamped seal. Someone had been in a hurry indeed.

He read, and knew he was turning pale. He could *feel* the humors leaving his cheeks, draining into his chest to hide. "You are a sage, my lord Ashani, king of Khir." The bitterness in his mouth was one they must be all too familiar with, though his heart had never been grasped with these particular bony fingers. Defeat was defeat, even if it did not involve a surrounded city. "Zhaon-An is besieged by the entire might of the Horde. They passed by the Southron Army in a forest fire."

"Ill-luck," Lord Domari Huzan said, his large bushy eyebrows moving dynamically to convey emphasis. He had a disconcertingly mobile face. "The prey is flushed, let us chase."

"Not headlong," Ashani said, gentle admonishing amusement in each syllable. "At least, not yet. *The eager horse is first to founder.*" It held all the quality of a proverb, and its musically accented pattern in Khir was pleasing.

"So is the weakest," another Domari, a lean dark supercilious man, muttered. Ashani affected not to notice, but Hazuni Ulo gave the fellow a sharp look.

"My lord?" Anlon knew the look Kai's face must have been wearing; his faithful servant's humors had drained too, but his eyes were bright. He expected his general to work yet another miracle; Kai had been hoping they could reach Zhaon-An before a major battle—if nothing else, to give the troops some chance of shelter when the rains truly started.

Kai did not hurry. What he decided now might affect the outcome of a battle far more important than any he had yet fought; Zhaon needed him. If Tamuron were still alive...

...but he was not. Nor was Takyeo; nor was Makar, nor Kurin. Takshin should have sent him some word by now, where *was* the man?

Had Sensheo done something to him? It seemed beyond belief, but perhaps the Third Prince was simply busy keeping Yala from danger. And though Kai was heartily sick of Garan Tamuron's sons—it was unfilial of him to even think such a thing, but there was no use in denying truth at the present moment—he did not wish ill upon Shin.

Except he sometimes did, at night, when he should have been asleep.

Anlon waited, used to this as well. Still, Kai was not thinking of what he *should* be, and it was an almost-physical effort to do so. The Zhaon generals, also used to their lord's silence before a spate of furious activity, were tense and waiting.

Hunting creatures ready for the leash to slip, the gongs and trumpets to beat. It was just past midmorning, a clear bright hot day with the dust washed from the air and mud drying to a hard crust upon the paved edges of roads.

Man and beast must reach the end with strength enough for combat. More haste is less speed in this case, and yet we must not delay.

"Raise the banners," he heard himself say, and his tone was reflective, not soft but not martial, either. "Infantry marching south with three days' ration and light packs; nothing superfluous. The baggage train will store everything but ammunition at the Keep; they will start toward Zhaon-An this afternoon as the roads clear. Cavalry will start at the same time, moving in screen." *With ribs of Zhaon between the Khir detachments, to keep them at their work.* He did not have to add that; Sehon Doah and Anlon would see to it. "We march to the relief of Zhaon-An, and shall crush the Pale Horde against its walls. Then the cavalry may hunt them all winter."

"Play kaibok with their heads," a provincial noble Khir youth with smooth cheeks and bloodthirsty gaze said; he was just as tense as the Zhaon. His armor was stamped with a flower, but a different kind than Yala's clan. She would know what it signified. "Let us cease talking and start *riding.*"

"Soon enough, my son." It slipped free, the affectionate general's term for an eager young soldier. His marshals waited, knowing better than to move before he dismissed them. "Do not send a pigeon in return, or a rider. Zhaon-An shall hold a few days; these pale bastards do not understand cannon even if they capture a few, and we have the newest designs. I want surprise; after tonight, cold camps."

"In the rain." Tall Hurong laughed, his hand falling to swordhilt and his sharp Daebo face lighting with familiar fire. His boots creaked as he shifted. "I can hear the cursing now. What else, my lord?"

"Send out the scouts and baton-wielders now—I want them at every crossroads and every twenty li, moving in diamond-pattern to keep abreast of the crowd. It will grow easier *and* more difficult as we approach Zhaon-An." More paved roads meant easier passage—although soon, whoever could escape Tabrak would be flooding said roads. And yet... "Do not yield the road for anything, even squalling peasants. We march like the clay soldiers of Niao Zheu." Those sage-wrought wonders stopped for nothing, crushing the unfortunate in their path. Though cruel, it was also necessary. "Go, and fear no enemy."

They chorused the traditional acceptance in return, bowing or saluting according to their station, and a few moments later Kai was alone in the clearing with the Khir contingent except for the two Zhaon soldiers on personal guard duty.

Ashani Daoyan's wry sidelong look said he knew very well no few of his noble generals might like him to seize the opportunity, no matter the breach of a surrender's terms. "It will be an honor to fight at your side, Zakkar Kai."

Will it? Very kind of you to say so, my fine young lord. "Likewise, Ashani Daoyan. What do your men need to move swiftly?"

"Nothing but the word." Khir's new leader cast a glance in Hazuni Ulo's direction; the other man's tight, wary smile also held a healthy respect. Of course the two of them had survived capture together, and such a thing taught you the true temper of a man. "Unless I am mistaken, my lords?"

The bare dozen grey-eyed men of highest Khir rank—only one had a dark gaze, though he was treated little different than his fellows—gave a peculiarly Khir salute, a bow with one hand cupped around the other fist. It looked like a Ch'han illustration; of course, the northerners had borrowed much from the distant, munificent land of culture and fabulosity. "Great Rider," the dark-eyed one announced. "If such is your will, Khir will accomplish it."

"Said like that, it sounds so easy." Ashani Daoyan accepted the homage with a half-bow that rivaled a younger Garan Tamuron's. His topknot was immaculate; some men had the gift of looking crisp under almost any circumstances. "They will sing of this in the streets of the city under the Great Keep, my friends. Come, let us look to our four-footed cousins."

The Khir lords trooped out in Ashani's wake; the young man was well on his way to solidifying his hold over them. The rest of the troops and perhaps the entire North would not be far behind, but that nagging sense—a critical missing piece of an enemy's motivations—was a torment, and it would not leave Kai be.

He was left with a clearing between two dark copses, hearing gongs begin to strike as news raced down the cohorts. Scouts, sutlers, quartermasters, and the soldiers currently assigned logistical duties were suddenly a-scramble, infantry sensing a hard march and the news of Zhaon-An's need not far behind the orders that would fly from throat to trumpet to gong to ear, settling in head-meat and forcing a man to his duty.

Zakkar Kai sank into an easy crouch, staring into the small smokeless fire some soldier had been ordered to build and leave behind for the officers. His half-armor creaked slightly, but hard use had turned it into a supple carapace.

Were he a sage, he could see some indication of Yala's safety or fate in the fire. And now, so far from the city and tasting the bitter liquid of uselessness, he knew he should never have left her there. He should have said something, *done* something, even challenged a man who had been more of a brother to him than Kai had any right to expect.

The Khir were obsessed with honor. Zhaon was more flexible, but not to the extent of compassing what was coalescing in Zakkar Kai's head-meat. And Sensheo, upon the throne? The more he thought of it the more Kai's disgust grew, until he was uncertain he could contain it.

He would do what he must, but then...who could tell? If Takshin were not still alive, did his shade know of the burning in Kai's rib cage, the way his hands ached, the hot cord tightening in his belly when he thought of a grey-eyed woman forced to choose between dishonor at the hands of pale barbarians or death by that stinging, slicing greenmetal blade held to her own throat?

"Live," he murmured, staring at flame eating small sticks and other fuel, a shimmer of heat over tiny, flickering, daylight-drained tongues. "*Live*, my lady Moon. Nothing else matters."

In a novel or a peasant's wish-tale, she would hear him speaking. But these were modern times; miracles were long gone.

All that was left was the killing, and the urge to begin it burned in Zakkar Kai's bones.

LAST FASTNESS

It was very bright outside the Great Hall, though the heavy sunshine had lost some of its summer weight. Mrong Banh had her elbow; Yala was glad of it, for her knees were not quite steady as she bent to slip her jatajatas on. She barely heard what the hurrying Golden yelled; the antechamber leading to the great pillared hall was crowded but her rank and Banh's glare—the astrologer was capable of quite a quelling glance when moved to actual wrath instead of just good-natured irritation—cleared a small path. It was like bronzefish swimming against a current; everyone was pressing closer to the doors and peering after the clattering, running Golden approaching the throne. A tide of news began to swirl from the august seat downward, but Banh's steady step did not pause until they passed through the Kaeje's greatest doors, left ajar most days to show the Emperor was willing to hear from his subjects but now flung wide. Banh halted them both upon the broad stone steps leading down to a wide, carefully flagged stone ground where the Lost Golden had been slaughtered to a man at the end of the Third Dynasty.

Their Emperor had fought among them, and died upon a warlord's spear. *That* part of Zhaon's history was spoken of in Khir with varying degrees of glee over a hated enemy's demise and grudging admiration for men who knew their honor's worth.

Banh let go of her arm, bending into a deep bow as he opened his mouth. Whatever he would have said—apology for grasping a silk-clad woman, an observation upon the new Emperor's behavior, an offer of aid or advice—was lost when a deep throbbing sound rent the air thrice. It paused just long enough for Yala to gather her breath to ask what, under Heaven, that terrible noise meant before commencing again. Over and over, the three strikes tolled, the space between each group just long enough for a thought to start before shattering it half-formed.

Banh staggered and might have fallen from the step had not her hand, with the thoughtless blurring speed of *yue* practice, flashed out to gather in *his* sleeve, righting him with a quick yank. They stared at each other, princess and astrologer, and she could swear age descended upon Mrong Banh all at once. She had read of men absorbing some blow that turned them elderly overnight without the slow accumulation of wisdom over long years; now she saw it before her in broad thick Zhaon sunshine.

"The walls," Banh said, blankly. "The city walls."

"Does it mean…" Yala's voice failed her; another trio of clangs from the massive bell in its red-painted pagoda at the other end of the wide paved space ate her words whole. The Golden shield-square responsible for guarding and servicing its massive brazen weight held to their work grimly, heaving a long, chained bar back in unison before letting go, catching it after each strike, their boots digging hard against stone during the pause.

"They are breached." Banh's palm closed over her knuckles, damp and chill. His humors must be taking refuge in his inmost caverns; he was certainly pale enough. "Come. We must…Gamnae, and the queens, we must bring them to the Tower. If the Palace falls it will be our last fastness."

Yala did not think it likely Luswone could be moved—but if necessary, she could be carried upon a back. Possibly even her own; what else, the proverb asked, was a daughter-in-law good for? "Come, then. Let us go."

It was not quite meet to run, but she snatched her hand from his sleeve and gathered her skirts. The astrologer wasted no more time with question or answer, but fell into step beside her as her jatas, not content to merely say their name, shouted it sharply over and over again.

Neither of them could know that not only had the South Gate been breached, but the East and West as well. The North Gate was left alone, for there was not enough black powder and besides, three was enough.

The Palace complex at the north end of Zhaon-An had its back to a blank expanse of city wall, the palace baths huddled there like a weapon slipped twixt a skirt and a woman's thigh; no barbarian wished to slog through the marshy ground outside the wall's curtain and the rising river, though they had fired the outbuildings hugging Zhaon-An in that direction and fouled every bath taking advantage of the water's nearness.

Instead, Aro Ba Wistis had cleverly given orders for the explosives to breach one side of the selected gates, shattering hinges and tumbling stone held together with ancient cement, its composition lost at the end of the First Dynasty.

Zhaon-An, at the end of long summer dryness broken only by a few downpours, had already begun to burn.

BATTLE-BROTHERS

Jogtrot and canter, holding fractious beasts and excited cavalry to the speed of marching infantry, two cold-camps spreading muttering through the ranks—it was every other forced march Kai had ever been on, except this time he was not alight with the fierce impatience of approaching battle to be met upon its own terms.

No, he was, instead, savagely frustrated with the slowness of travel. Each watch-gong brought no news from Zhaon-An *and* no relief from the terrible things he could imagine happening inside a city's walls if they did not hold.

Trickery, treachery, cannon; those were the three things all military theorists agreed could break a fastness. The Horde's leader might be cunning, especially if he had begun from the south in order to find his Horde a sliver of terrain to lodge for the winter like a splinter from a crossbow quarrel snugging in violated flesh, swelling with infection.

Yala had been wounded by such a bolt. If she had taken ill from it, what would Kai have done? At the time, he had been merely grateful for her survival.

Ashani Daoyan rode at Kai's side; the young Khir seemed to feel the same urgency. Of course, the sooner this was over, the sooner he could retreat to his country and begin the process of enforcing his rule with the noblemen who had fought under his command.

Such things tended to cement alliances between clans, if not rulers. The nobles, now led by Hazuni Ulo, kept their grumbling to a minimum; the Khir infantry had never been this far from home before, and gaped at the comparative wealth of the southron farm-steads and villages. Each door was barred and bolted; the peasants, warned of the army's approach, left the rai in the fields, foregoing a precious day or two of harvesting and drying that might be sorely missed if the rains swung west.

Had Kai not defeated the three separate-for-swiftness armies of Khir with the help of luck and his infantry's iron legs, he could have been called south to Zhaon-An's aid, allowing the western route—one Khir had not used before, both they and Tabrak were sewing new dresses this season—to bring an army upon his back.

The countryside began to be familiar instead of simply terrain; with Tienzu Keep behind them the roads improved and their pace quickened, though not by much.

On the afternoon of the fourth day, word filtered back from scouts who had reached the woods upon the last ridge before the approaches to Zhaon-An; quiet mutters had been racing down marching cohorts for at least two watches. Soldiers cheered Zakkar Kai as he rode by, but whisper-quiet, holding to the prohibitions upon both noise and cooking smoke. Surprise was not the entire art of war, as Huar Guin had noted more than once—but it was certainly an integral part.

It was a fine early-autumn afternoon, thunderheads gathering to the north and curtains of dark linen drifting beneath the leading edge of a storm. A handsome dilemma—attack when there was not enough daylight to be certain of scattering the Horde, or allow his army to endure a good soaking that might blunt their effectiveness after a night's fitful, feverish rest.

Ashani Daoyan kept pace with Kai as he moved briskly along-side the road, their mounts' hooves throwing up clods of good black earth. Several of the Khir horsemen they passed fell into place upon Ashani's side, guarding their lord; though they had been trained a-saddle almost since they began to walk they did not ride like Yala.

Nobody did. The Khir goddess of horses had whispered in a

single girl's ear. Kai hoped that celestial being was watching over the child she had taken such trouble with so long ago; Kai's urge to offer a prayer to that effect might not be looked kindly upon by such an august creature.

Still, it beat behind his heart and filled his lungs.

Anlon rode to Kai's left; cavalry marshal Sehon Doah did too, his beaky profile serenely untroubled. He would look the same if he was gutsplit, actually, so it was no comfort; the other marshals and generals were with their respective sections, keeping the army moving.

"My lord! My lord Head General!" A tiny scout upon a large, deep-chested bay appeared, working along the other side of the road; there were curses as he sent his beast across an orderly stream of traffic, timing it perfectly but also splattering nearby soldiers with clods. "Message from the front, sir!"

Enemy sighted. "Report, soldier." Kai's tone sliced through the mutinous grumble.

"Zhaon-An is invested, sir. The walls are breached at each gate; the city burns. They don't know we're here yet, but General Tsigau says 'tis a mercy of short duration." It had to be a direct quote; the scout's voice dropped into unconscious imitation of Tsigau's broad Gurai accent, a cousin closer to Zhaon than the Shan dialect. He was one of Hurong Tai's men and not very excitable, but the current situation would light a fire under the most stubborn of oxen. "Can't tell if they've reached the Palace. Orders, sir?"

"Return to Marshal Hurong Tai; the banners must signal our advance. Hold at the ridgeline."

"Yes, my lord Head General." A bow in the saddle and the boy galloped away. He had to be fast and vicious to survive as a scout; he was light enough the horse could bear him a great distance without tiring.

He even dropped into the beast's rhythm as Kai had seen Yala do, an unconscious fluid melding showing that perhaps the Khir goddess walked farther afield than her native land.

Let it be an omen, Kai thought.

"He rides well," Ashani Daoyan said, in Khir. "I take it the insects we must crush have been sighted."

One had to admire the fellow's dry humor. Growing up as an illegitimate son, turned suddenly into the heir and then the king—either he was much-beloved of Heaven, or meant for a truly crushing fate.

One could say the same for a foundling raised to an Emperor's head general, who was even now considering not only showing his banners in rebellion against a man he had been raised alongside, but stealing another man's wife like Khao Cao.

Let her be safe, and I will repent. It was the same as before every other battle, anticipation tightening his skin, a craving for sohju to numb him, his hand itching for a hilt. "The gates are breached. We fall upon their backs before sunset, Ashani Daoyan, though we might leave some alive to flee in darkness."

"I have not had a night-hunt for a while." The new king of Khir tensed; his mount sensed it and tried to sidle, was instantly controlled. "It will be diverting." He turned to cast a volley of sharp-spiked Khir at his new retainers. One peeled away at a gallop, keeping to the edge of a drained field and bearing for the nearest contingent of Khir. The cavalry would have to move forward and spread; he was intelligent to grasp as much, and very sure of himself to issue orders without waiting.

So he was eager for the fight. Maybe he was simply fey, prone to battle-madness. His father, an old wolf, had certainly seemed so near the end.

"The Khir are said to strike from darkness when it suits them," Kai noted, his own knees clamping against his horse's sides as the mount discerned a rider's restlessness. "And no doubt many of your countrymen will long for home once the spoils are divided."

"Or earlier? That is, after all, your hope." Ashani's laugh held an edge that had been missing until now. "Fear not, Zakkar Kai. In this battle, we are brothers." He touched his heels to his mount as Kai did, and both beasts swung into a matched canter.

Kai hoped it was true. But if not, he had plans for that occasion, as well.

He only hoped they were not transparent as those of his enemies.

Extraordinary
Shot

The major city-routes from the gates—breached or still whole—ended in the Yuin, but that smoking hole did not halt the Tabrak who galloped along the paved paths of least resistance. The vast Yaol slightly to the north would have held their interest more, had not the stalls been largely shuttered and carts pulled out of the main thoroughfares to provide the City Guard and Night Watch, not to mention the Golden, quick passage through. From the Great Market to the palace complex's gate the way was smooth, for none had expected *this*.

The first spray before the wave was a trio of barbarians who galloped up that broad, paved processional way to the palace's gates amid screams and scattering Zhaon—servants, some nobles who had decided the complex would provide more shelter than their estates, and artisans with the ill-luck to be caught bringing their wares to patrons or possibly to stock the warehouses of the Artisan's Home. Much of the city had not yet realized its peril, considering the walls safe enough against stinking barbarians who did not even drink tea; now, though, captives and barbarian kaburei were busy widening the gap so the Horde could flow in.

The Golden guards, brought to a high pitch of readiness, swarmed the unfortunate three barbarians, who were knocked from their horses by flickering pikes. The order to close the gates did not come from the Emperor, though it should have; instead, it was one of the two junior Golden leaders Kho Doah who shouted it, along with a cargo of obscene imprecations, as a shield-square in bright armor hurried to obey. The Great Bell was still ringing its frantic tattoo, its servants not given leave to silence and depart; the gates began to swing as more Golden poured from the barracks, brought by the cries of their fellows.

"*Sixth Prince!*" someone yelled from outside; Garan Jin with a streaming mass of Night Watch, City Guard, and Golden halting and re-forming every so often along winding Zhaon-An streets to push back a much larger group of howling, shaggy, blue-painted monstrosities upon their heavy-legged horses, came into view.

"Fuck *me*," Kho Doah breathed, in a tone of surpassing wonder, peering through the slowly slimming space between the two great halves of the Imperial Gate, red-painted ironwood banded with black metal.

He might have said more, but a group of Tabrak with their bows ready galloped from the right, where the Street of Zhaon's Delight met the great way issuing from the Palace complex. Their bolts sang, crunching amid the gate-pushers, and one—an extraordinary shot, fortunate or deadly ill-luck depending on who you asked, sank into the junior Golden leader's right eyeball. He was felled in an instant, and the resultant loss of a stentorian bawling of orders momentarily paralyzed the screaming, milling assembly.

The last soldiers of the Southron Army died upon Zhaon's walls, or in its streets. The City Guard were armed against insurrection instead of barbarian invasion, but they stood as the Night Watch—similarly armed—did, and the Golden closed about the youngest son of Garan. He was everywhere at once, the lightfoot hurling him over obstacles, his sword striking true each time, seeming almost to dance between his heavier, slower opponents' blows but always giving ground, stoppering a street or alley like a sohju-jug intended for travel just long enough for those under his command to catch their breath.

They reached the Palace gates, and Garan Jin's hoarse exhortations might yet have turned the tide had not a much larger group of barbarians arrived from the right as well—the West Gate, not facing the bulk of the barbarian onslaught, had been but lightly manned, and the Tabrak spilling through it, while not a large force, encountered practically no resistance upon their way. Those yelling, blue-painted shades of deathly ill fortune ran down the artisans and fleeing nobles in their way, hookblades flickering, and met the weary group that had fought step by step from the South Gate's destruction to this, the heart of Zhaon itself.

Even then, the exhausted men might have held long enough for the palace gate to shut, consigning them to the fate of those who had shown their loyalty and now must die to prove it. Yet a bolt flashing past scored Garan Jin's cheek, snapping his head aside and breaking his concentration upon the lightfoot, and he thudded to earth upon his back, dazed almost breathless.

Into the Palace the Tabrak rode, ululating in fierce delight. Smoke followed in their wake; many who could have added weight to their charge had stopped to fire street-stalls or buildings where some resistance was encountered. Autumn had come, but under the roof-tiles, great beams and partitions were still summer-dry, as the Yuin's devastation had proved.

Once begun, the flames spread with only token resistance. The Great Bell continued to toll.

THE GREAT BELL

Anh staggered, almost buffeted to the ground by a stream of bath assistants in their goldenrod cotton, many so hasty they had not caught up their shoes and consequently fled barefoot, every-which-way. The stack of freshly washed underlinen was knocked from her hands and trampled; her cry of despair was lost in hubbub as a double-file of Golden went by at a run, their boots pounding and their armor throwing blinding darts of noonday sun. The Great Bell's ringing meant disaster, but she had kept tight hold of the washing as if it could somehow save her, or clear her path to the Iejo.

The entire complex had erupted. It took so little to transform a nervous but intricate and tightly regulated dance into a seething heap of irritated shield-ants; now, as the Bell kept striking, Anh could see a thing that should not be, a thing she had never seen in the Palace despite spending most of her conscious life within its protective walls.

A lone, shaggy, mountainous rider upon a deep-chested, snorting, rolling-eyed horse galloped past, blue paintsweat streaking his face and his high-crested hair. His skin was the color of death and unbleached mourning; he walloped a running bath-girl—her name was Taia, Anh knew her slightly since she had been assigned to the baths for a brief stint as a child—with a gore-spattered hookblade. Taia's body, curling around the blade, almost wrenched it from his broad filthy hand, but his momentum shook her free and she fell with a sickening thump, blood rising in a high splattering arc. More screams, and another group of Golden clustered the fellow, their pikes flicker-jabbing.

Anh whirled, forgetting the laundry she had been carrying so carefully just a breath ago, and bolted.

She did not even know where she was going, but luck—or something else—was with her, for she spilled onto a little-used path between two dry-gardens and saw a familiar shape in pale green silk, hurrying along with her peculiar grace. It was Anh's lady, her hairpin's cascade of crystals shimmering. Behind her, Mrong Banh was at Kihon Jiao's side; the physician was oddly misshapen.

Then Anh realized he was carrying a frail figure in a blue silken wrapper upon his back, like the good grandson in Hurong Cao's story of the three pots and the snowy night. Second Princess Gamnae hurried along at his other side, attempting to keep Third Mother Luswone's wrapper from falling in any indecent direction; Su Junha and Hansei Liyue half-ran in Gamnae's wake, their hands tightly clasped like peasant sisters fleeing a fire. Two bright-armored Golden trailed the group, nervously trying to gaze everywhere at once.

"My lady!" Anh cried, and her feet hurt as her sandals slapped stone paving. The Bell was still tolling, its voice rapidly becoming ignored like a nagging costermonger. "*My lady!*"

"Very good, Anh." Princess Yala did not seem surprised to see her faithful servant; her grey eyes were large and very pale, full of terrible intensity. "I hoped to see you coming back from the laundry. This way."

It never occurred to the kaburei to wonder where Second Mother Haesara was, only to be deeply relieved. She had found her lady, and the feeling of safety was overpowering. Anh hurried along, now glad she hadn't stopped to reclaim the fallen underlinens, and dared to grasp her lady's skirt like a child afraid of losing a parent in the marketplace.

If her sweating fingers tore the silk, she would mend it later.

* * *

Second Mother of the Revered Emperor Garan Hanweo-a
Haesara, her head held high and her hairpin-decorations glittering
feverishly, glided between the Kaeje doors just before they thudded closed and were made fast. She passed like a mourning shade
through the milling eunuchs clustering a remote, pale Zan Fein,
his closed fan gesturing them into place; some among them fought
with dagger or fan-blade, or fists and feet as their god Two-Face
constantly drove ill spirits from Heaven.

They could not hope to hold a Horde for long, but none dared
quail or turn away from Honorable Zan Fein's dark, magisterial
eye as he placed them to die for the Emperor they had just recently
been brushing policy dictates onto rai- and pounded-rag paper in
service of.

None noticed her. Luswone had grabbed Haesara's sleeve and
gestured at the medicine-stacked table in her Iejo room; Haesara
had pretended not to understand as Kihon Jiao and Gamnae
discussed the best way to lift Third Mother onto a strong back
and carry her to the blue-sheathed Old Tower. In the middle of
that discussion Princess Yala and Mrong Banh had arrived, both
deathly pale and just a trifle disheveled. Then Hansei Liyue and
Su Junha arrived, gasping and ashen, clutching at each other. The
sudden appearances, underlaid by the throbbing of the Great Bell,
had caused enough of a stir that even the most exalted woman left
in Zhaon could walk away undetected.

None, indeed, would seek to stop her.

Through the antechamber and past the inner doors, where a
babble of ministers, senior eunuchs who had somehow escaped
Zan Fein's gaze, and courtiers crowded, gambling that the presence
of an Emperor would keep them safe and arguing with each other
in varying pitches.

But the Throne…

Haesara halted, staring at the low padded bench under the great
gilded sunburst, where her husband had sat in state for many peaceful years after Zhaon was welded into a single unit again. How

many times had she stood upon a dais at one court ceremonial or another, ignoring Gamwone's taunts and slights, keeping her gaze fixed where it should be?

The throne Garan Sensheo had bought with a caustic drink and a spray of blood was *empty*.

Her son, her only remaining child, had fled, even as his eunuchs prepared to fight unto death.

Of course there was a passage from the great pillared hall to a small room well-buried in the Kaeje's mass. The partition there was well-disguised, and gave out onto a hall of friezes; Zan Fein, as the keeper of the complex's architectural secrets, had shown it to Garan Sensheo the evening of his enthronement. *Sometimes an Emperor has found it necessary to be elsewhere*, the chief court eunuch had said, and such was his mien that Sensheo was uncertain if he was amused or displeased by the thought.

It didn't matter. What mattered was safety, and collecting his mother. She was probably in the Iejo, cowering with Luswone. Wouldn't she be glad to see him?

He hurried down the corridor, ignoring the Great Bell's stuttering heartbeat and tearing the greenstone pin from his topknot; the royal robe was a little more difficult to untie while moving at some speed. It was a mark of good breeding to let servants attend to one's tying, buckling, and buttoning, but at the moment he was wishing he had a little more practice with laces.

Silk ripped; he staggered into the small room Zan Fein had shown him behind the friezes and came to a halt, sweat prickling upon his brow, collecting upon his lower back, dewing his underarms. Even his stones were crawling northward.

Sensheo patted at his robe. First, he needed different clothing; servants brought the day's requirements or anything their august lord had expressed a preference for wearing to the Emperor's traditional dressing-room from the royal wardrobe. There would be something there. Everyone was likely to have fled; next he needed a weapon, then he could collect his mother from the Iejo. While he was there, he might attend to another loose end or two, like a seamstress snipping unsightly threads.

After all, the barbarians were only a temporary danger. Everyone else would attend to them, especially the Golden. What mattered now was reaching Garan Haesara; her mere presence would set all else right.

The Great Bell continued its pointless braying as Sensheo hurried through luxurious, deserted halls. It was strange to see the corridors naked of Golden and purposefully moving servants, strange not to be greeted with bows and downcast eyes. Wall-lamps burned, their tiny flames lost in drenching mirrorlight, and the sense that he had stepped into an old tale or upon a bare theater stage was almost overwhelming.

Someone had been at work folding and stacking in the Emperor's closet, to judge by the scatter of bright cloth upon the floor, trailing toward the doors. His usual wardrobe had been brought from the estate but not unpacked, and he lost precious moments digging to find a suitable robe. Fortunately, weapons were easier; the blade Father had given him upon Sensheo's reaching adulthood was in its own lacquered case upon a rack devoted to such things.

What would Father think of this? Was his shade watching, seeing how the son he had always ignored had, in the end, won?

Sensheo hoped so. His sweating fingers fumbled as he buckled the sword. The dual hurai would make his right-hand grasp uneven, but he was the ruler of Zhaon.

No barbarian could stand against an *Emperor*, could they?

In a dark though no less luxurious robe smelling of ceduan, somewhat inelegantly creased from storage and improper tying, the ruler of all Zhaon set out to look for his wayward dam. As he crossed the threshold of the imperial closet, the Great Bell's thumping halted between one stroke and the next.

Its tenders had either been struck down, or found they must fight.

Third Mother Luswone was making an awful gurgling sound as they hurried through garden after garden, cutting through an outbuilding, negotiating stone stairs with some difficulty, crossing the pretty colonnaded walk where the First Queen had often perambulated in autumn—mostly to keep it from being used by her rivals, it had often been said. Gamnae's jatajatas slipped more than they should and her head was stuffed with cloudfur, that terrible feeling of light airiness making it difficult to think. If she focused upon Luswone's blue silk wrapper she didn't have to.

Then the likewise awful stuttering pattern of the Great Bell halted, almost knocking the breath from her afresh.

"It's stopped," Mrong Banh said, blankly. The sunlight was pitiless, all the usual discreet laughter hiding in his expression had fled, and Gamnae realized he looked *old*.

He never had, before. He cast a nervous glance past the colonnade as a babu water-clock *thump-thock*ed nearby, and made hurrying movements with his hands.

"So it has," Princess Yala answered, quietly. She was breathless, too, and that was disturbing. "Were they ordered to, or..."

"Barbarians," her kaburei gasped, finally able to give her tidings. She clutched at the back of her mistress's dress; it didn't seem like the new princess noticed. "I saw them, coming back from the laundry. They are *inside the Palace*."

"Let us hope it is only one or two." Kihon Jiao grunted slightly as they left the colonnade behind and crossed a pretty arched garden bridge—why, just along the pond-bank there Kurin and Makar had played "duel" sometimes with hau-tree switches, and the gazebo floating over another pond lensed with the green leaves of padflowers had seen many of Sabi's sathron practices.

Barbarians didn't belong here.

"Shall I carry her for a while?" Mrong Banh hopped from foot to foot; his rope sandals did not quite match—one with a blue fabric twist across the instep, the other with dark brown—and his topknot was slipping sideways.

"No need," the physician said, shortly, conserving his breath. Luswone's breath bubbled again, and her eyes were half-lidded, glittering through her thick dark lashes.

I am sorry I thought it. Gamnae's throat filled with a sob; she glanced at Princess Yala, who drifted behind and a few steps to Kihon Jiao's left.

Yala's right hand was invisible, held low in her skirts, and her head kept turning. She was attempting to keep watch, Gamnae realized. The kaburei held her mistress's skirt like a child in a crowd, the girl's leather-wrapped braids knocked askew. Two bright spots of fever-color stood high on the girl's cheeks; a slim tendril of Yala's hair had come free of her braids and brushed the princess's cheek. Gamnae's own hair was probably disarranged too.

"Do you..." Mrong Banh's shoulders hunched. Lady Su and Lady Hansei took great sobbing breaths, clutching each other. The two Golden had vanished, where had they gone?

"Yes," Yala said. Her quiet tone did not alter. In the silence of the Great Bell's cessation came screams, alarums floating from other directions, and a persistent edge of burning. "Smoke. The Tower—its door can be barred, and the sides are tiled, yes? It may not burn." Her Khir accent rubbed through the words.

"There is a cistern upon the roof." Banh braced Kihon Jiao as the physician staggered, his sandals slipping.

Honorable Kihon made no sound, just settled Luswone more firmly against his back like an elder brother carrying a sibling.

"At least that," Yala said grimly, and halted so suddenly her kaburei ran into her back. "Perhaps you should help carry Third Mother, Banh." Her chin rose, and as the Khir lady half-turned, Gamnae saw a greenish gleam held against her pale silken skirts. "I hear hoofbeats."

Kihon's legs moved faster. Gamnae hurried alongside him, wondering if she should take his arm. Now that Yala had said it, she heard the hoofbeats too.

And they were growing closer.

Time to Kill

The sun became a bloody disc as it fell, thunder rumbling in the distance as an autumn downpour gathered strength to the northeast. The scouts returned with news harvested both from fleeing peasants and the sight of a pillar of smoke in the distance.

Zhaon-An was besieged. The Horde had invested the city except the northern fen-girdle; it was unclear whether the walls had been breached. There was much smoke from inside said walls, though; that had turned the sun's eye into the bloodshot gaze of a god who had drunk too much sohju.

Kiron and Takshin viewed the embattled city from the relatively high promontory near Jiyua-An, the ancient town that had collected upon the trade route south and west of the city itself. Even the belt of thread-creek marshes to Zhaon-An's north proper held a few columns of rising smoke, more from cooking fires than anything else; the wall there, cradling the back of the Palace and the baths with a protective arm, would be a daunting proposition.

He could hope the barbarians did not know about the culverts of the Palace baths.

Proud-nosed Suron, to Takshin's right, let out a long soft half-whistle of wonder, his head tilted as if he watched a play. "So many of them."

"A Horde." Kiron's face was alight; there was a gleam to his dark eyes Takshin knew well. Behind them, the forces of Shan and Anwei spread through forest and field, their way suddenly eased since the flood of refugees had eased considerably. "Where is the long-eye?"

Buwon, on his king's other side, produced the lenses and the cylindrical leather case; within moments, Kiron was scanning the battlefield in more detail. "They do not expect us," he commented. "All their attention rests upon rapine."

"The gates—south and east?" Takshin did not ask for the farlooker, but his hand itched for it and the wind brought a breath of burning to him. His eyes threatened to water, focusing hard to pierce the distance.

"I cannot quite..." Kiron exhaled sharply. "If that is the south gate, 'tis breached. I cannot tell how badly."

"The soldiers are eager." Buwon squinted heavenward, checking the angle of the sun. "Some had family in the capital, others—"

"Hist," Suron said, and stood in his stirrups, his head cocked. "Listen."

Faint noises rode the breeze.

"Gongs," Kiron said. "Trumpets. Someone is fighting to the north west."

"Probably Zakkar Kai." Takshin's heart leapt with useless hope; that was the price of caring about anything, the world took the opportunity to snatch and trample it. If she was harmed... "Perhaps he received word."

"I hope so." Kiron handed the long-eye to Takshin, who hated being robbed of half his sight while using the cunning invention, but put it to one eye anyway, closing the other with an effort.

As usual, there was a moment of disorientation; when he could make the images through the lens sensible the red-hot knot in his guts tightened another fraction. "The southron gate is indeed breached, and they work to widen it," he said. "When can we attack?"

"The field, there." Kiron pointed. "By the beginning of afternoon watch, I should think, if we use the gongs to tell the entire army. Perhaps they will meet us, though, so... I mislike attacking while daylight leaves us."

Takshin lowered the leather and lenses. It was, militarily speaking, correct doctrine. Night-hunting was for small groups, harrying bandits and other prey; a night battle without a full moon was an invitation to disaster. It would be a simple enough matter to slip through barbarian throngs into the city by night and find his Yala, though.

Simple, though not easy.

"Well?" Kiron's head turned; he leaned forward slightly, looking past Buwon to the silent, broad-faced man in tasseled leather half-armor, riding a dun horse ugly enough to be suspected of having some other quality useful to a fighting man lurking in his cob head and strong, inelegant legs. That mount looked, in fact, very much like the Tooth, and the knot in Takshin's belly wound itself into another ship-knot. "Honorable Keitan, what say you?"

The elected leader of the Anwei mercenaries—their method of dropping stones into piles to choose the general they would follow for a particular campaign was strange, but Takshin supposed any custom surviving from the Second Dynasty was bound to be—studied the terrain for a moment with his own farlooker. When he spoke, the soft lilt of the great harbor city and its rich hinterland turned the Shan dialect into a song. "If we may enter the city before nightfall, better chance the next day." He glanced to his own left, where an adjutant slightly younger but very much like Kai's faithful Anlon shrugged, leaning upon his pommel.

The rest of Kiron's bloodriders were either strung along the promontory or hurrying their particular part of the army along. It would take time to arrange them, but the roads this close to Zhaon-An were good, the farmland mostly level, and the field where they could weather any Tabrak charge enticingly close.

Kiron was silent for another few moments. Thin sharp sounds drifted from the battered city. How much of it was burning? Did Yala sense her husband close by? And Kurin, what was he doing?

At least his elder brother would fight to retain the city, and might even risk his own skin in the process. Yala would be brought into the palace complex; the walls there could hold for some while.

"The wind is with us," Kiron said. He did not look at Takshin; there could be no intimation that he was founding the decision upon his battle-brother's obvious impatience. "Raise the banners— no gongs, no trumpets. We aim for that field, but if they will not offer battle we shall fall upon their backs and drive into the city itself. We begin at the start of afternoon watch."

"My king." Buwon bent slightly in the saddle; his horse wheeled and he cantered down the rise to begin the process, the entire army fermenting like a pot of stiffened curd. The head of the Anwei mercenaries glanced again at his adjutant.

"We shall hold the left flank, or die," he said, formally. "Such is our contract, Suon Kiron, King of Shan."

"So it is, Honorable Keitan. May your horse be swift and your blade deadly this afternoon." Kiron nodded, and the leader took himself off much as Buwon had. "Can you wait that long, Shin?"

Why do you ask? I must, so I will. "Of course." The words stuck in his throat, but a little more waiting would gain a much greater chance of what he sought. Had he not, after all, won Yala in that fashion? *Let her be well, Heaven. Let her be alive, and unharmed. Or I swear...* "Surprise is an advantage, and should not be thrown away before its time."

"Indeed." But Kiron's brow had wrinkled. "The Horde has never acted thus. Perhaps they have gone mad."

"Who would not, living as they do?" Now that it was decided, a familiar chill settled over Garan Takshin. The cold was an old friend, and he welcomed it.

All he had to do was wait until it was time to kill.

BAR THE DOOR

I t was a group of three barbarians, their furry trousers melding into their horses so they appeared one single monstrous
being instead of a fourfoot cousin carrying a burden. Blue paint
streaked sweat-runneled over skin pale as mourning, and their hair
of strange, outlandish colors—straw, straw with a reddish tinge,
dark without the undertone of rich blue or red proper hair should
have—was pulled into high, clay-stiffened crests. They did not
pause upon seeing fresh prey, but spurred their mounts forward,
and everything within Garan Yala, once Komor Yala, shrank to a
single small point.

"*Go!*" she screamed, as she never had in her adult life—a noblewoman did not cry aloud so even during a hunt. She realized she
had spoken in Khir and cursed herself before repeating it in Zhaon,
again as loudly as possible, her *yue*'s greenmetal hilt cool against
her sweating fingers. "*Fly! Reach the Tower!*"

Third Mother Luswone made a terrible gurgling noise, Gamnae
let out a short piercing scream, and Kihon Jiao staggered into a
run, Mrong Banh forgetting his reticence and grasping the physician's burden from the other side, helping as much as possible. Su
Juhna and Hansei Liyue reeled after them; the younger girl had
lost her jatajatas and fled barefoot.

The riders charged, hooves clattering. Yala streaked forward
too, her skirt tearing free of Anh's fist. The *yue* was all but useless

against a rider on horseback—but she was Khir, and knew how to startle a fourfoot cousin.

Which would force the attackers to deal with her before pursuing the slower prey. Or so she hoped.

"*Hai!*" she yelled, darting at the lead horse—a fine deep-chested chestnut with a black mane and scars upon his withers, a sad intelligent gaze saying he deserved a better rider. The beast, used to fleeing creatures, was momentarily confused; Yala half-spun, jabbing her greenmetal blade—how ridiculously small it looked now, a tooth-cleaning splinter against the wide wicked hookblades—at the second beast, the large black gelding she knew she had to dissuade. The rider might be in command or not, but horses tended to follow others they knew and trusted no matter what the twoleg lords upon their backs demanded, especially in unfamiliar surroundings.

And she did not think the Tabrak often gallivanted through water-gardens.

She heard her own voice as if from very far away, screaming words she had no idea she could even pronounce without blushing, let alone hurl at armed intruders inside the palace complex of mighty Zhaon. A hookblade whistled down, and as it had before, the *yue* saved her.

Not the blade, too small to be of use. But she crouched, dropping into the lowest of the defensive postures, her skirt tearing even more as her left leg slid out straight and her right bent deeply, muscles used to stretching being called upon for even greater flexibility. "*Ahi-a!*" she screamed again, the cry for a hunter whose bolt had not gone astray, and the hookblade whistled over her head. Her hairpin skittered away along a paved walk as she surged upright in a rush, darting forward to jab at the black gelding's nose.

The horse reared, and she was vaguely aware of another shout, something whizzing past her.

It was a stone. Yala danced back, avoiding wild hoof-flails, and the thought that she was *attacking three Tabrak* threatened to overwhelm her.

Another missile streaked past. Once before, Anh had held off an
assassin by throwing tea-crockery; now she had scrambled to the
margin of the pond and was grubbing at ornamental stones, tearing
them free of sucking mud and hurling them with a peasant girl's
coney-hunting accuracy. A scrap of Yala's skirt hanging from her
hand made a crude but effective sling; the girl cried aloud again,
a fresh rock whirling over her head, clad in almost-mourning-pale
silk. The missile flew with a whistle, pelting the rider upon the
chestnut's other side.

Yala had no time to cheer or to command the girl to flee. The rider
upon the chestnut shouted something that sounded foul indeed, and
there was a curious blow along the outside of Yala's left shoulder.

It was the tip of his hookblade, digging just past her sleeve and
into flesh; she took the only move she could, throwing herself to the
left, almost *under* the black gelding, which let out a loud whinny
and reared again.

One of those hooves could shatter her skull, and she would never
worry about dishonor, Zakkar Kai, Zhaon, or anything else ever
again. Would her father's shade greet her, would she ride the Great
Fields since she had died in battle?

At the moment, Komor Yala did not care. She was only an eye,
a hand, a collection of limbs bent upon a single purpose—to give
Kihon Jiao time to carry his burden to the tower, to give Gamnae,
Liyue, and Junha time to gain that safety.

And give Mrong Banh enough time to bar the door.

The Iejo's great doors, normally familiar enough to be invisible,
were aflame.

Garan Sensheo spat a bright crimson wad; the hookblade hole in
his guts was a nail through a beetle's carapace. He enjoyed mounting bright-shelled things upon pins and witnessing their tiny dying
movements, but it was *not* fit for a man.

Or an Emperor. He had struck that torch-tossing barbarian
down, but the second one had pierced him and now he wondered if
he should have buckled on some armor.

He backed up the Iejo's steps, the hurai upon his right hand slippery with yet more hot blood, both his and others'. The barbarians were everywhere; did they not know whose house they were fouling?

You have not been practicing, little brother. It was Makar's voice, and the hole in his belly didn't sting as much as his brother's fist that morning—had it really only been that summer? So much had happened.

"Filthy beasts." His voice was a shriek. "*You killed Makar!*"

Oh, they had killed many more. Why, set next to their accomplishments, Sensheo's seemed rather paltry indeed. The fire breathed against his back, painted wood and hangings fueling it— they did their work well, these motherless, stinking dogs.

There seemed to be a thousand of them, but perhaps it was the veil over his eyes. His head felt empty, but paradoxically full of something fluffy and loose—cloudfur before it was spun, perhaps.

A barbarian ran from the flaming mouth of the Iejo, almost colliding with Sensheo. The bastard carried a brand, waving it aloft as he whooped with fiendish glee; the Emperor of Zhaon fell hard, his vision darkening.

He barely felt it when they ripped the double hurai from his fingers, one of them picking up his bloody sword and examining it closely. A whistle ribboned through the smoke—the signal for plunder or resistance, calling upon the Horde to congeal around it like the swelling around a splinter.

Moments later, a broken body rested alone upon broad stone steps before a burning palace.

CRY OF AN ASHANI

The rain had found Zhaon-An, battle-madness was upon Ashani Daoyan, and he did not care who he struck down. It was perhaps a mercy no Khir or Zhaon were before him, for his entire world had narrowed to the killing.

His second horse of the day, taken from a stinking Tabrak who had attempted to ride him down but was unprepared for a Khir lord full of fey wrath, reared. Hooves flailed, and a barbarian's skull splattered like a ripe aiju melon.

They painted themselves with blue clay and screamed as they streamed forth from Zhaon-An's great westron gate, their great ram-horn trumpets blowing wildly as Tabrak realized it did not have merely supine peasants and soft luxurious Zhaon to deal with. The other Khir lords were behind Dao, weight of horseflesh and skill shattering two attempts by the Horde to gather themselves for a charge at the pikemen.

It was Three Rivers again, except instead of marsh there was a thin penetrating rain, the sun dropping below cloud-edges to turn each falling water-needle into gold. It would have been a pretty sight except for the death, the blood, the bowel-tubes churned into foul mud by boot or hoof, the screaming, the *stink* of a battlefield rising around him in brassy waves.

His mount dropped back to four feet instead of two and answered the pressure of Daoyan's knees to drive forward, though every muscle of the beast was probably screaming at it to leave this mud-soaked nightmare of the Many Hells.

Another dismounted barbarian darted from his right—stupid, to approach the sword-side; Dao cut him down without a second thought.

When this was done, he would have an army, and Zhaon would owe him much. He would not leave this place again without the daughter of Komori Dasho upon his saddle. And he would teach her never, ever to—

A high, ululating barbarian cry rose. Dao freed his blade with a wrenching twist, half out of the saddle because Tabrak stirrups were very stupidly designed. But he was Khir, and righted himself with a savage effort that would pain him after the battle, when the body reminded a man how close it had brushed against death.

There was a banner, a crude symbol reminiscent of flames daubed upon its long vertical panel; under it, a knot of barbarians galloped. Daoyan screamed his defiance—a hunting-cry, or simply the rage of a nobleman balked at every turn of his life and captured just as he had escape within reach, a noble son who could not ever please a father, a noble *prince* who had been forced to smile, scrape, and bow entirely too often. The rage was kind—it nurtured, it soothed, and it allowed him to believe there was something in the world that would finally, inevitably, bend to his will if he simply pursued it hard enough.

The Khir behind him, hearing the distinctive furious cry of an Ashani upon the battlefield, answered with their own. Ashani Daoyan spurred his horse cruelly and galloped for the barbarians under the banner, and one of them—a wide-shouldered creature with stiff blue-crusted high-crested hair and a pair of inexpertly fastened metal vambraces once belonging to a Palace Golden— likewise spurred forward to meet him.

So it was upon the field north west of Zhaon-An that Ashani Daoyan, last of his mighty clan, faced Aro Ba Wistis of the Horde. The shock of their meeting tumbled the Tabrak to the ground, and the Great Rider of Khir wheeled his mount away, curving around a clot of struggling combatants and driving his horse back toward the son of Wistis, who waited with hookblade held in high-guard. At the last moment his knees bent and he pitched sharply forward, and such was his strength that the horse screamed, the hookblade nearly severing its front right leg. It was a mighty blow, but the son of Ashani was not done yet; he rose from a tangle of thrashing, dying equine with his own bright blade.

They met a third time, the Tabrak ululating to give their lord strength and Ashani Daoyan's cry piercing theirs like a silver needle as the Khir lords galloped for their Great Rider.

Continue the Work

It was not the almost-suicidal bravery of the Khir horselords nor the death of Aro Ba Wistis which broke the Horde. Rather, it was the riders of Shan coming from the south, arriving upon the main field of battle with Anwei mercenaries in their wake and charging repeatedly to break any formation the barbarians— swollen with plunder, expecting a long night of pleasant seizure and despoliation—could manage. The rain pelted down as the sun sank, a morass of blood and churning mud; Shan might not have even known of the battle upon the westron side of the city had not Garan Takshin recognized the trumpet-calls from that direction once the field upon the southron side was taken.

Suon Kiron, restraining his troops from filtering too soon through the shattered gates to hunt Tabrak inside the burning city, instead commanded them around Zhaon-An's girdle, slaying as they went. By the time the bottom edge of the sun had touched the horizon the battle was done.

It had not taken very long after all.

The westron sky was a lake of blood, Aro Ba Wistis's body was found with his head nearly severed. Ashani Daoyan, pierced and shredded by the hookblades of the stirrup-holders, breathed his last in clutching mud, and the keening of the Khir at his fall was terrible as they hunted fleeing barbarians well into the night—though most of the Tabrak attempted to retreat into the city, instinctively seeking refuge in the walls they had themselves broken.

Outside the walls, the barbarians who fled into the countryside also experienced the hospitality of terrified peasants with pruning-hooks and flails; the tall, stinking, death-colored monsters could not hide. Even Tabrak slatterns, kaburei, and cubs were slaughtered; Zhaon, Khir, and Shan faces were set with distaste whenever the event was referred to ever afterward, reaping a double harvest of rai and death.

Zhaon-An was lit with burning, terrified citizens too busy attempting to halt the fires to celebrate a victory just yet. Tabrak were found hiding in attics, in public parks, in stables and byres, in alleys and corners; what remained of the Night Watch and the City Guard hunted them as soldiers helped with the fire-fighting or turned to face yet another stray barbarian howling from the darkness with a hookblade aloft. The Golden, recalled to the palace, had similar work.

The great camp of Tabrak upon the edges of the marsh was set to fire and sword; surrounded and brought to bay the barbarians fought to the last.

But it was no use.

For some tendays afterward strays were caught in hayricks or copses, crushed like tiny blood-drinking insects between a maid's fingernails, and for many years mothers would frighten their children to bed by saying *Go now, or the white barbarians will take you.*

Zhaon-An burned for some while, yes. But Tabrak, the proud Horde, was utterly crushed.

THE MOON
WISHES IT

E ven a fool could see the battle was over. The last charge,
after fighting along the westron wall, across the south, and
turning northward, brought him to the East Gate itself; separated
from his companions, his helm lost, and with his armor terribly
battered, few noticed him. He rode through smoke and screams,
ignoring the chaos all around; the impatience in the very seat of
his liver spread through his bones. At least he knew the city's streets
well, and when a fire or a crush-crowd barred his way, there was
always another route to take.

The weariness was upon him, his arms and legs leaden, and he
was thirsty as a shade trapped in one of the many Burning Hells.

He did not care. Only one goal remained now, and he could not
rest until he accomplished it.

Through flickering flame and streaming smoke he rode,
and when he saw the great gates to the palace complex standing
open a single, weary sound escaped the man's lips. His mount
plodded through, and the fire was everywhere. The Kaeje stood
proud and inviolate, though its steps were starred with the bodies of dark-robed eunuchs; Zan Fein's last desperate defense had
held only because the ram-horns had alerted the Horde within the
city of trouble without, and called them to other work. The Iejo

was aflame, the Jonwa too. The fire at the Artisan's Home was in the process of being put out, and some few Tabrak were cut down as they attempted to escape the warehouses full of goods they no doubt meant to plunder.

Banh. Banh must have...

The rider turned toward the Old Tower, its blue tiles running with rain and wet firelight. The gardens were choked with dead and wandering, almost witless survivors; none of them were what he wanted.

If not for chance, he would not have seen it. As it was, he slid from the patient grey horse's back and landed with a jolt in a marred water-garden near the Tower, a bridge showing hoof-marks and a Tabrak body floating gently in the pond. More barbarians were scattered about; a battle had taken place here, too. The Tower, a mute sentinel, had witnessed it; but you could not ask stones to speak, or to cry aloud at injustice.

Not in this modern age, at least.

The man looked up, his eyes full of welling water to match the rain that would aid fire-fighting all through the night, and his hands were fists at his sides.

There, at the margin of the pond, confused marks showed a battle. Churned earth, scattered stones...

...and a kaburei, rocking back and forth slightly as she cradled a limp body in pale green silk almost the color of mourning.

His boots squelched in mud. He went to his knees beside the girl, who glanced up like a startled long-ear but returned to her rocking, singing very softly.

It was a peasant song, a child's rhyme for counting rai-seedlings. Her voice cracked, and she must have been like this a long while, for when he touched her shoulder with two fingers she slumped aside, the music halting and her dumb stare familiar from the aftermath of many battles. She had been pushed beyond endurance and could now only obey simple commands until she fell into the deathly sleep which followed such things, mind and body taking refuge in whatever surcease it could find.

Garan Komor-a Yala lay in her kaburei's arms, her right arm clamped across her bloody midriff, her left shoulder sliced and clotting, her lashes dark against coppery cheeks.

"No," the man husked. "*No.*"

And, amazingly, the new princess sucked in a tortured breath. Bright slivers showed under her eyelids, and a trembling passed through her body as the kaburei shifted.

Her eyelids lifted slowly, and she gazed wonderingly upon him. The wound across her belly—impossible to tell how deep it was; she winced in the dying rufous light, rain soaking her tumbled hair and mud squelching as her kaburei moved again.

The lady's lips were moving, and he had to lean close to hear.

"The Moon," she whispered. "The…Moon…"

Zakkar Kai, head general of Zhaon who had deserted his army at the moment of their victory to brave the burning city, bent over his mud-sinking knees as if he were wounded instead. He denied the wrecked scream rising from his very bones, and his lips skinned back from his teeth.

Instead, a harsh exhale carried words in Zhaon, accented like a sage's poetry. "*Then I will come to you,*" he said; Zhe Har the Archer's poetry in the mouth of a warrior faced with a Moon maiden.

Garan Komor-a Yala's chapped lips curved in the slightest of smiles, and she sagged unconscious in Anh's loosening arms.

WATCH FOR THE BLADE

B lood everywhere, and the golden needles of the rain turned to drab grey. No matter how many of the stinking bastards he killed, there were always more—until there were not, and the madness released Garan Takshin from its iron grip, leaving him standing amid heaped corpses, his dripping sword clasped loosely in an aching hand and the massive stink of death, shit, blood, and everything else he had been born to endure swamping him with weariness.

"*Takshin!*" Kiron bellowed, and the Third Prince spun aside, his sword rising in a brutally efficient arc, lopping the hand from the wounded barbarian approaching his back. The barbarian howled until Takshin's second strike took out his throat, and the blood-spray was a jet until it bubbled into a fine aspirated mist.

Another body, added to the pile.

The King of Shan pulled his lathered mount—not the one he'd started the battle with, of course—to a halt and slid from the saddle, landing with a grunt. "Motherless dogs," he snarled, and kicked at a corpse. "Are you hale?"

Takshin found his voice would work. "Hale enough," he rasped. "You?"

"We seem to have won." Kiron turned, scanning the battlefield.

The trophy-taking had begun, and the wounded were either being dragged in the direction most likely to have a physician or—if they were Tabrak—quickly dispatched, as one would crush a viper's head. "Have you seen Suron? Or any of the Zhaon generals?"

"Not…" Takshin coughed, a deep dry hacking. He bent to tear some rancid fur from a sprawled, head-crushed Tabrak, wiping his blade clean mechanically. "Not for some time. There are Khir here, too."

"Northern bastards." Kiron winced slightly as he swung his left arm, testing the muscles for injury. The two of them were perfectly placed to watch the other's back; it was a habit so old neither of them realized they had done so. The horse hung its head, shaking. "Probably come to pick some corpses clean. Are you certain you're not injured?"

Sometimes a man could not tell, as the battle-madness drained, what had been done to his own body. "Reasonably certain. You?"

"The same. I saw Buwon pursuing a group of these filth not too long ago." Kiron coughed, rackingly, and his gaze flickered over Takshin's shoulder, watching his battle-brother's back. "He wasn't smiling."

"When he's serious, watch for the blade." It was an old joke, but Takshin felt no amusement. Every Zhaon-An gate had been breached; the city was burning despite the rain. Was Yala safe in the Palace? Kurin would not let even a mildly valuable piece leave the board unless he was certain Takshin was dead; still, she might have stayed at the estate for the sake of the household, since her husband had consigned them to her care. "You're bleeding."

Kiron swiped at his stubbled cheek, scrubbing hard. A narrow slice at the king's hairline painted half his face with bright crimson, turning dark as it dried. "A scratch. Head wounds."

Takshin examined his blade. It would need whetting soon, but at least the beasts had not notched it. "I suppose we must find a few of the Zhaon."

"And whoever else we can—ah." Kiron's blade lifted, catching a last gleam of dying, bloody sunlight. *Ho there! Suron!*

Lord Suron's armor was battered, and his lean beaky face was set and bloodless. "My king. I am relieved to find you."

The Daebo lady he'd married would be glad of his survival. Takshin tasted bitterness; Yala *had* to be alive. Now he could look for her.

"Likewise, bloodrider." Kiron sheathed his sword after wiping the blade clean upon a handy corpse. Takshin followed suit. "Have you seen any of the Zhaon generals?"

"Over there." Suron cupped his hand, a nobleman's reflex to avoid rude finger-jab pointing. "They are organizing the physicians; the city is full of vermin but they will be rooted out soon. The Zhaon tell me they have yet another Emperor; Garan's fifth son. Sen-something?" He caught himself, glancing at Takshin. "My apologies, Garan Takshin."

Kurin was dead? A terrible cold sensation spilled down Takshin's back. *Sensheo? What under Heaven has happened here?* "None needed, Suron Haon. What other news?"

"Zakkar Kai rode south with a Khir—Ashani Zlorih's bastard son, it appears." Suron's throat must pain him; he spoke in a dry, quick rasp. "Aro Ba Wistis is dead, they say the new king of Khir killed him. There is confusion everywhere. All I know is that we hold the field, and the city is burning. If the Horde has more lurking somewhere it may go ill for us."

"Into the city then, and repairing the walls." Kiron rubbed his hands together, scraping away soot, dried blood, and dirt. "Where is Zakkar? I long to meet the man."

"They are combing the battlefield." Suron's shoulders did not sag, but his relief was evident. "Come, there is tea."

There was always tea, and it meant the battle was truly finished. Takshin turned, gazing at the walls of Zhaon-An. A blanket of smoke lay over the city, columns of firebreath underlit with gasping light. *Yala. Where are you?* "Suron. How did...my elder brother, how did he..." Was it the barbarians?

"My lord..." Suron shifted uncomfortably, a creak of half-armor. "There is much confusion. It was at a banquet, I was told. The Zhaon will be able to say more."

A banquet. And Sensheo? What happened to Makar? It boggled the mind; Sensen was too indolent. Not only that, but his cunning was a child's. "I see. Forgive me." It was rude to put Suron in a position to speak upon a prince's family matters.

Suron nodded; he scorned to hold any grudge. "Come along, my lords. Soldier's tea and counting our kills awaits us."

"There has been much slaughter today," Kiron agreed, and caught his weary horse's reins.

Takshin made a noise that could be taken for assent. Every muscle and bone in him longed to catch a horse of his own and gallop into the city to find her, to make certain she was safe.

If she was not, the slaughter would continue. His blood congealed at the notion, and the same restless anger making its home in his liver almost his entire life circled, a familiar discomfort.

He followed his battle-brother and his friend, leaving the corpses to those who would strip them. The remaining soldiers would be at burial and pyre duty for a long while; there was not fuel enough in any forest to burn the Horde. They would be buried in long trenches, caustic sweetener drifted over them, and the green howes might even be planted with crops in a few handfuls of years.

Besides, the purifying kiss of flame, lifting a shade to heaven, was only for those of Zhaon, of Khir, of Shan, of Anwei, of far Ch'han. The barbarians' shades could suffer and scream in papery whispers as they moldered.

Garan Takshin cared not a whit.

FREEDOM

The hardest part of removing the collar was not letting the knife touch his own skin; he already had Zhaon oddments in which to clothe the rest of him after this duty was attended to. Shivering and mostly naked, wearing only a rag clout and crouched in a charred peasant ruin, Etu sawed back and forth at the tough leather encasing his throat, listening to the faint cries in the distance, breathing the odor of smoke old and new.

This place had burned a long while ago, and its well was brackish and foul to boot. It smelled as if something dead was trapped in its stone throat, but he had seen—not to mention scented—much worse as a scun, and he could drink rainwater well enough.

If any of the Horde survived this battle, they would be far too busy to look for him. His Zhaon was accented, but he could travel south by night, eating whatever he found along the Tabrak's trail, until he found a congenial spot and some work that would keep him more fully fed.

The last sliver of leather parted under the knifeblade as rain dripped through a broken roof and fitful twilight gleamed with the glow of a burning city. Finally, he laid the knife—taken from the body of a Zhaon soldier, the fellow no longer needed it but Etu did—aside, and slipped his fingertips into the slice.

He closed his eyes.

All the kicks, the clouts, the buffets. Their terrible atonal language.

The casual cruelty, the smell, their hideous laughter. The arrogance, and the constant reminders that a scun was lesser, was unimportant, could be killed at any moment by a rider, for wealth was horses and horses were true wealth…all of it, years of it, over and over again, rising under his skin like water behind a rai-patch's dam.

Even if he had failed and Aro was still alive…and what was the aching in Etu's chest, the trembling in his hands?

Some caged beasts would not leave even when the door was open. He had always disdained such brute cowards, but now he understood their reluctance. He had been a scun of the Horde for most of his life; he knew their ways, their language, knew what his duties would be in the aftermath of a battle.

Was it really so bad?

With a short, grunting exhalation, he ripped the collar free. Cold air hit the skin underneath, filthy because Tabrak did not bathe with aught but dust or oil scraped from the skin by bone implements. He flung the sliced collar across the cottage's dirt floor, into a tangle of wet greenery poking through the wall.

Etu bent over, his arms crossed over his midriff, and only then could he allow the sobs. They poured through him in a tidal wave; he had not cried since that terrible day the Horde descended upon his village. The few who survived perished later; a scun's life was dangerous if they were not claimed by a rider. The only protection was a strong master, and a precocious child whose parents had scraped and scrimped to have the village headman teach their son precious literacy could have died writhing upon a bored rider's hookblade had not Wistis Ba Gavrok selected him for the Horde's great heir.

Aro had even been kind, sometimes.

The man who had once been Etu, who was now again Turong Lai, rocked back and forth, keening. The drenched night outside the shattered wreck of the cottage and its rancid well heard his cries, of course, but agonized groaning and lamentation were everywhere that day, and there was no answer.

Even victory has a price.

MOTHERLESS CHILD

The Iejo was still smoldering under a lash of midnight rain as Garan Jin hammered at the door to the blue-tiled Old Tower. "Banh!" His voice was a harsh croak; behind him, Golden in dented, no-longer-bright armor moved slowly through the dusk, stabbing the corpses of barbarians to make certain they would not trouble Zhaon further. Other groups of Golden and eunuchs were searching for Zhaon survivors—servants, nobles, court ladies, and the like—amid the wreckage; there were more than Jin had expected.

It seemed a miracle that anyone could survive the day. The scab upon the back of his skull was tender, his topknot had come loose, and he flicked long dark hair out of his face as he beat upon the barred door afresh. "*Banh!*" he bellowed. "Open, if you're there! It's Jin, it's me, we've—"

There was a wrenching sound from inside. Other small noises—they had blocked the door with furniture, too, a wise decision. Finally, with a groan, a slice of darkness appeared behind the heavy wooden door, and a lamp flickered in a trembling hand. "Jin?"

"Thank *Heaven*," Jin said, with feeling. "You are well? You are safe?"

"Safe enough." Mrong Banh's own topknot was far more

disarranged than usual. "Jin…oh, Heaven is kind. Gamnae is here, she is safe, but—"

Jin's knees threatened to give again, for the hundredth time that day. He held them grimly to their task. "Gamnae? And…and who else?" *Mother. Please, let her be alive.* Gamnae had been with her—but Mother had been abed, and the Iejo…

"Kihon Jiao." Banh's eyes were wide and frightened as a child's, but in a face suddenly ravaged. He looked positively *elderly*, but perhaps it was only a trick of the uncertain light. "And the Third Dowager Mother, but Jin—"

"Mother?" Jin surged forward, shoving at the door. It gave, and he plunged into a dry dimness. There was a jumble of furniture hastily moved aside; they had barred the door as best they could. It showed a certain presence of mind, and Jin was too relieved to notice Banh's slow dazed movements, the astrologer looking like a man caught in a nightmare there was no hope of escaping. "*Mother! Mother, it's Jin!*"

He took the stairs two at a time, despite his trembling legs, and burst into Banh's living quarters. Two halu lamps burned with welcome golden light. Gamnae was there, hugging herself as she perched upon her usual chair; only a few fantastical machines made of rai-paper and whittled-thin wood hung upon strings from the high ceiling. She burst into tears as soon as she saw Jin, her arms wrapped tight around herself and her hair a loose river down her back. Next to her, Su Junha and Hansei Liyue huddled on two other pulled-close chairs, clutching each other; Su Junha's hairpin glittered, knocked askew but still clinging to a coil of dark braids.

Kihon Jiao stood at the outer window, looking down into the night. He turned, and his eyes were dark, wounded holes like Banh's. He said nothing, but something in his expression halted Garan Jin's headlong gallop.

"Gamnae?" His sister's name cracked in the middle. "Gamnae, where is…"

"Oh, Jin." Gamnae gulped a deep breath. Her cheeks were chapped from weeping and she trembled violently, the chair creaking under her. Hansei Liyue reached out, clasped his sister's shoulder. "She…It is my fault, I was watching, but she went to the window and…Jin, oh, Jin…"

Jin's knees finally gave. They hit a stone floor he had played upon as a child, walked across as a boy, stood upon as a man while discussing some inconsequential problem or another with an astrologer.

"She would have survived," Kihon Jiao said, in the terrible silence underlaid with the murmur of rain. Lamplight painted his features; he spread his capable, medicine-stained hands. "The princess sacrificed herself for us to reach the Tower, and yet…What a waste. What a fucking *waste*." He turned back to the window and gazed down.

Jin knew what lay below that aperture—a pretty stone courtyard tucked between the Tower's blue-tiled side and the curtaining wall of the complex, stone-lipped garden boxes where Banh often attempted to grow vegetables. It did not have enough sun, but he still tried most years.

The paving below…well, the Tower was high. And if Garan Jin approached the window at daylight, he suddenly knew, without a doubt, what he would see broken in the middle of the courtyard.

Had she believed her son dead like her daughter? Had she thought the barbarians would break the door and…

Just like Sabwone, his mother had been besieged. And he had been unable to save either of them.

Garan Jin bent over. His forehead touched cold stone. The cry rising inside him was too large to be contained, but it was trapped by the pain. A boulder had settled in his chest, and he banged his forehead against the floor once, twice, thrice with increasing strength. He continued, making a low strangled sound like an ox in terrible distress, until Gamnae staggered to his side and folded over him to restrain the head-knocking, her griefstruck keening breaking the rock and setting his own cries free. Hansei Liyue and Su Junha burst into wailing as well.

He was the last remaining son of Garan Tamuron—Takshin

was, after all, adopted by Shan—for they had found Garan Sensheo's body upon the Iejo steps. And he was motherless as well.

Garan Daebo-a Luswone had stepped from the casement, falling like a star deciding to leave Heaven's great vault upon some incomprehensible errand. The next day, Garan Hanweo-a Haesara was found in the Kaeje, in her beautiful, luxurious apartments.

She had quietly left the vermilion-pillared hall, walked through the deserted palace of her dead husband, and hanged herself in her bedroom.

HONORLESS

Everything hurt. Even her hair. There was a soft crackling of fire, and for a short while she thought she was amid the wreckage of the Palace, wounded too badly to open her eyes or speak, waiting for the burning to reach her flesh.

"My lady," someone whispered, and there was a familiar arm behind her shoulders, lifting her slightly. Her middle gave an agonized flare of pain—the hookblade had carved through dress, skin, and possibly muscle underneath. Her left shoulder hurt as well, a faraway ache next to the greater pain from her midriff.

Garan Takyeo had been stabbed in the belly, and had borne it with much courage. Now Yala thought dozily that she admired him even more, for it *hurt*.

"Careful," a husky voice said. "I do not think a bowel-channel was pierced, but do not move her overmuch."

"I know." Anh did not sound grieved or impatient. Rather, her voice caught upon what had to be a relieved sob. "Here, my lady. It is tea; it is not very warm, but it will do you good."

The idea of tea was splendid indeed. Yala's throat was as dry as the waterless wastes the Tabrak rode over to harass those not of their kind. She accepted the cup at her lips gratefully; a breath of jaelo was not quite as strong as in Lady Gonwa's heaven tea.

She wondered if that redoubtable dame had found a bolt-hole to hide in while the barbarians raged. "Anh," Yala whispered, when the cup was taken away. "I thought us dead."

"I did too. But the General is here now, so all is well." The kaburei's face swam into focus as Yala blinked. Anh's leather-wrapped braids were neatly redone and she had washed her face, but soot lingered at her hairline and she wore an unfamiliar cotton tunic, its shoulder torn and flopping.

"Enough. Lay her down, gently." Kai's tone was harsh, but not with anger, merely weariness. "She tells me you held off no few Tabrak so others could reach Banh's tower, Yala. I told you not to risk yourself."

There was no other choice. She knew she was alive, for it hurt and she was being scolded. "I could do nothing else." She was glad of the tea; at least her throat did not ache now. "Kai? You are well?"

"Well enough."

Now she could see a banked fire in the middle of a raised platform; it was a small peasant's hut, its walls dark with neglect but its ceiling holding up admirably to rain she could hear. The terrible devouring heat was gone; Yala shivered, and Anh's fingers against her forehead were hot. "You will take a chill," the kaburei fussed. "Is there another blanket?"

"Not necessary." Yala blinked; more of the interior revealed itself. A single room, a raised platform over a winter-stove, a rotting modesty-hanging where a bulge told her a privy lurked—she had read of peasant lodgings, but never seen one this closely. "Thank you, Anh. Has the general had tea?"

Even here, even now, there were manners to display.

Kai was still in leather half-armor, but he lacked a helm. He had scrubbed his face as well, but the rest of him was filthy with mud and blood, or other things not nearly so pleasant. His dark eyes gleamed, deep-set coals, and he had redone his topknot, an iron pin thrust through its dark leather cage. He sat at the edge of the platform, regarding her warily.

"Oh. Yes." Anh laid her tenderly upon something soft. "There is no dinner, though. Are you hungry? I can perhaps—"

The thought of food twisted inside Yala's rib cage, and she shook her head, wincing as her shoulder twinged. "I could not, my dear one. You should have fled to the Tower."

Anh almost blushed, ducking her head. "All I could think of were the stones."

"You saved my life." A tremor passed through Yala. How had she survived? It seemed impossible. "The . . . the Palace, is it . . ."

"Still afire when we left." Kai shifted, and cast a meaningful glance at the kaburei. "I would speak with my lady privately."

"Yes. I see, yes." Anh pulled a horse blanket up, tucking Yala in like a child. "I shall be just by the door, you see?" She pointed into the darkness; the door was a hacked-apart collection of flimsy splinters, and outside the night was alive with the sound of falling water.

"Yes." Yala watched her kaburei's retreat, then turned her gaze to Zakkar Kai. "How bad is it?"

"I do not know." His shrug was slight; did he ache too? All told, the head general of Zhaon looked very grim. "Victory for Zhaon, I should think. The Horde is not a concern, but Yala, I told you not to risk yourself."

Victory for Zhaon? Then why do you look so . . . "Third Mother, and Gamnae, and Mrong Banh." She named them all, as an exorcist or follower of the Awakened One would count kombin-beads. "Liyue, and Junha. And Kihon Jiao. They had to reach the Tower, there was—"

"I do not *care.*" Kai made a sharp movement, stilled like a restless hawk needing flight. The uncertain firelight made his shadow dance, distorted, upon the wall. "I had much time to think, Komor Yala, and I have reached a decision."

You do sound very severe. Yala found herself alive, her heart beating, her blood and humors still in their accepted places, her bones all in theirs. Her belly hurt, of course, and her shoulder—but those were small matters.

Zakkar Kai was alive, too. The world had righted itself, catching upon him like a dress-hem upon a nail or a falling cup arrested by a fortuitous hand. And now she knew how deeply she had feared being without the knowledge that he was somewhere breathing, somewhere alive as well.

"I do not know if Takshin lives," Kai said, harshly. "I suspect he does; even a Pale Horde would not trouble him overmuch. But I am selfish, Yala. I owe my lord Emperor everything. *Everything*, do you understand?"

Of course she did. Life was about duty, about what was owed. So said the Hundreds, so said all her tutors, so said her father—and Komori Dasho had not only said so but lived it, daily. Her scalp crawled; so did the rest of her skin. There was roughened fabric against her belly—a bandage, pressing hard against the slice. "Yes."

"I am sick of the sons of Garan." Kai said it like a malediction, his gaze dropping. Color rose in his coppery cheeks. "*All* of them. I am sick of endless war in the North, of honor-mad Khir and court intrigue. I am sick of the killing and dying. I am leaving, Yala."

Her heart, treasonous thing that it was, threatened to stop within her. She could pretend the swelling in her eyes was from the pain of a wound honorably received. "I see," she whispered.

"Not yet." Kai half-turned, drawing up his knee and leaning one elbow upon it while he studied her. It was how warriors in scroll-illustrations of the Second Dynasty were often portrayed sitting upon the steps of their lord's house, though never so dirty or disheveled. "Tell me you wish to stay, and I will take you into the city. If Takshin is...well, a prince's widow is still a princess, Yala. Zhaon is not so bad for such a woman."

A pang went through her at the thought of Garan Takshin dead upon a battlefield. *He has had little enough*, Kai had said once, and it was true.

Balanced against that was the marriage endorsement in his elder brother's hand—well, she could suppose he had known the Crown Prince would die. She could even, were she required to, forgive him for the surety, and further forgive him for telling her the marriage was Garan Takyeo's dying wish.

It could, after all, have been true.

But the ledger pages covered in Khir writing—why had they been in the bundle with the endorsement? He had promised to bring the evidence to her, not once but over and over. Oh, he had told her he suspected Khir involvement in Mahara's death, yes.

And yet.

Yala closed her eyes. She could not bear to see Kai leave. Perhaps she could tell him to go and make her own way into the city, with Anh's help. Bury the tearing in her heart, bury her own treachery, her own honorlessness. "I hate Zhaon," she heard herself say, dully, as if from a great distance. "Zhaon took my princess." *And so much more. And yet it brought me to you, Zakkar Kai.*

"Anwei," Kai said. "A ship from there to far N'hon, once the winter storms are past. I can teach swordplay; they prize learning there, and you know enough of the Hundreds to tutor a noble daughter or two. We would not starve. And I am sick of it, but should I be called upon to win another battle, you would go with me, Yala. A general's tent is not a palace; nevertheless..."

For a moment she was certain she had not heard correctly, that she had slipped over sleep's border and was fever-dreaming. "I am honorless." She could not say otherwise. "For I would go with you, Zakkar Kai, though I am married to another. I would..." Her right hand twitched. "My *yue*," she breathed. "Where is it?"

"Ah. Well." He shook his head, ruefully. "I did not think to look for it. Another can be made, Yala. There are fine metalsmiths in Anwei, and in N'hon too."

Is it so easy? She did not dare to move or breathe. The pain was all through her now, from her breaking heart to her wounded shoulder, her aching legs and throbbing head.

All her life, she had done what she must. Was it truly honorless to wish for something different? Her father would be so disappointed.

But Komori Dasho was dead. Ashani Daoyan had killed his royal half-sister, and would rule in his father's stead. Nothing she could say or do would halt that, despite her duty to Mahara's shade.

And Garan Takshin? What would *he* do, did he still live?

"I let you go once before." Kai shifted, and her eyes flew open.

He was looking at the hut's soot-blackened wall, and his expression was terrible. "I do not think I can do so again. There is a very real danger of simply taking you with me, Komor Yala, whether you will or no."

What must it cost him, to admit as much?

"I called for you," she admitted, finally. "Every day you were gone, every night I lay in my husband's bed, I thought of you. I am *honorless*, Zakkar Kai, and you will tire of such a woman before long."

"Will I?" He scratched at his cheek, roughly, as if he still felt drying blood or other effluvia upon his skin. "*Over many li of silver grass he walked backward; to see his own footsteps was less lonely.*"

It was Zhe Har again, the penultimate stanzas of the Moon Maiden and the warrior who followed her through the Middle World and into the Many Hells, and finally hammered upon the doors of Heaven's greatest palace in search of her.

"*Until he reached the shore of the sea, and a ship there waiting, shining like his bride.*" Her throat closed, she swallowed dryly. "Kai..."

"I am honorless too." His chin dropped; his broad shoulders slumped. "I should stay, and serve whoever has survived. Especially Jin, he must..." Kai grimaced; his duty was as bitter as hers, whether endured or laid aside. "But I will not, Yala. And I would take thee with me."

She struggled for a long moment, then another. But there was no hope, and nothing else she could say. "I would go with you." A clear, low, fierce tone. "To far N'hon, to Ch'han itself, to the lands beyond if I must. If you will have me, Zakkar Kai."

"My lady," he said gravely, as he turned to face her, "I would have none other, in this life or the next."

Near the door, upon a pallet filched from a half-burned house during the terrible journey out of Zhaon-An in Zakkar Kai's wake as the general carried her lady, the kaburei Anh clasped her hands and smiled, pretending not to hear.

Until I Cannot

Two tendays after the Breaking of the Horde, autumn had truly fallen. The rains came regularly and the harvest seemed, despite all disturbances, at least sufficient for winter's requirements.

There were, after all, far fewer mouths to feed this year.

"I don't want to." Garan Jin scowled at the polished brazen mirror, a poor substitute for a window in this room deep in the Kaeje. A thumping pounded through the Palace, endless as the sea's reputed moaning, Golden and soldiers pounding their spear-butts against stone through the nightly watches. Come the dawn he would be enthroned.

There was nobody left, and his defense not just of Zhaon-An but of the Palace itself was spoken of admiringly in all quarters.

"You've said as much. Repeatedly." Mrong Banh cast a nervous glance at the doorway; Garan Takshin, in his usual Shan black but with a pale armband, said nothing. The gold hoop in his left ear glittered savagely and his silence was almost a living thing, cold as one of the dragons reputed to make their couch upon high snowy peaks; it was not known whether he planned to accompany his sister to Shan if Gamnae agreed to the marriage.

The Second Princess was taking her leisure deciding the question, as she had promised her eldest brother she would. Of course Shan had ridden to Zhaon's aid, and a marriage of the two countries was highly desirable—but Garan Jin would not allow her to be pressured, and once or twice Gamnae made a soft but entirely pointed observation very much in the style of a certain late Khir lady-in-waiting that made it clear she would not be rushed, either.

The remaining children of Garan Tamuron knew the value of stubbornness.

Khir's army had withdrawn northward under the command of Hazuni Ulo; it seemed likely that once another noble clan took the kingship of Khir more negotiations could begin. It would have to be a house with a marriageable daughter; in any case, the dagger pointing at Zhaon's heart was blunted for at least a generation and the new Emperor gave every appearance of being less concerned about Khir's rumored dalliance with an emissary of the Horde than about their future under Zhaon's benevolent gaze.

"I never have wanted to," Jin continued. He perched uneasily on a folding camp-stool his father had taken with him upon almost every campaign; it seemed Tamuron's martial spirit did not need such an object to infuse his youngest son with courage. "I wish someone else would."

Takshin stirred. "You are what is left, Jin." Flatly, with no inflection. He had spoken thus since his foreign wife's greenmetal blade was found amid a scattering of barbarian corpses downhill from the Tower; Banh winced inwardly. If only he had glanced back, if only he had *seen*...

But he had not, and Princess Yala had suffered for it. At least she was past any harm now, safe among Heaven's luminaries. Gamnae had taken Su Junha and Hansei Liyue under her royal wing, and the three found much solace in each other. If they spoke of a grey-eyed princess, they did so privately.

Elsewhere in the Kaeje, exorcists were holding vigil in a queen's chambers, though it was agreed that Garan Hanweo-a Haesara's shade had other business than to linger here. Her pyre, and Garan Daebo-a Luswone's, had burned side by side that very afternoon, and no rain had come from Heaven to interrupt the last journey of those two friends. Lady Surimaki, having survived the siege, was rumored to be at work upon a novel of their paired fates, though any hint of imperial displeasure would put paid to the project—or make it immensely, powerfully popular.

It was too soon to tell. And Garan Sensheo's pyre had been much more hurriedly attended to.

Despite the fact of his coming enthronement, the young almost-Emperor was clad in mourning, and would be for a few tendays yet. He refused to countenance that it might bring ill-luck. His mothers would be duly honored, and that, Garan Jin said, was final.

"*You* could do it." Jin's chin set stubbornly, and he glanced at his remaining brother. Then his face softened. "Forgive me, Shin. I am selfish."

"Then we are a pair, for I am as well." Takshin might have meant it kindly, but his tone robbed the words of any warmth. He peeled himself away from the doorway and paced into the room, laid a hand upon Jin's shoulder, and peered over him at the mirror, a black blot behind a pale one. "Zan Fein will help you, and Banh. There are many ministers, and they will be cowed some while. The nobles will be too busy repairing their estates to give you much grief, and if Gamnae marries, well." A Shan army at the call of an imperial brother-in-law was a powerful inducement to peaceable obedience. "But she may not," he finished.

"That's all very well." Jin exhaled sharply, and Banh was forcibly reminded of how young he was, after all. Still, Tamuron had won his first battle at that age.

And so had Jin, now. Banh shifted uncomfortably in his new padded slippers. Reports of stray barbarians still trickled in, most found starving and feral, brought to bay by peasants and their corpses dragged to local magistrates for a bounty.

"But will *you* stay, Shin?" Jin laid his hand upon his brother's. "Please? I know it is not...I mean..."

Takshin shrugged, with his usual feline suppleness. "Until I cannot," he said, as if it did not matter. But his fingers tensed, and he squeezed his baby brother's shoulder lightly. "You were kind to her, Jin. So was Naenae. For that, I will stay."

"I will need you." Jin's gaze met his in the mirror. "And Banh. I do not know what to do."

"No man does, Jinjin." Takshin's hand slipped away, and he turned sharply upon a slipper-clad heel. "That is what *man* means."

There was no sign of Zakkar Kai; his great horned helm had been found empty upon the battlefield. Men vanished thus in every war; already the peasants were saying the God of War had called his beloved avatar home, sensing Zhaon would have no further need of him. Small votives of Zhaon's great general had appeared in many a family shrine, despite the scars his battles left. Had he not defeated Khir fully, then flown south to relieve the capitol's siege? Shan's contribution, despite the opinion of military men that it had been decisive, did not weigh so heavily in peasant estimation.

"You should eat something," Banh offered awkwardly, in the tense silence. "Tomorrow will be long. I will send for tea, and a meal."

He bustled out into the hallway, passing between pairs of Golden every few paces. Upon the way to the kitchens—humming with activity both to feed the court and to repair damage wrought by fire and Tabrak—there was a shadowed corner where he could halt, and weep for a few moments in peace.

After all, Garan Takshin would not. Someone had to *for* him, and though Banh would not admit it, he was gladdened to have at least two sons remaining.

Even if they were not his.

IRONICALLY, SAFER
HERE

Two days after the enthronement, he could finally slip away.
The estate in the Noble District had not suffered too badly. Garan Takshin rode to its door upon a massive, ill-tempered grey called the Tooth—a strange name, but the prince adopted by Shan did what he would, and it were best not to gainsay him.

It was already apparent that as long as the young Emperor had this remaining brother's support, no minister or noble would dare anything less than unstinting, prompt obedience, whether the Second Princess married Shan's king or not.

The newly carved characters upon the gate-posts were deep and fresh. Takshin tossed his reins to a stable-boy who quailed under a princely glance and strode into his home, barely halting to remove his boots. Had he returned after a battle he would not have bothered, in his eagerness to see her.

His household—garnered from Takyeo's—was at Jin's service now; this place would not be inhabited. But Takshin could not bear to see it in disrepair, so Garan Luswone's steward and house-keeper were allowed a certain retirement. The latter did not have Lady Kue's quiet efficiency, but if he had seen familiar faces in these halls, Takshin's temper might well have snapped.

The dull, pointless, immortal rage in his liver made another

restless turn as he passed through the halls like an ill spirit. There
was the library; there was his study, unchanged since he left. There
was a window she had paused at to take in the view of the courtyard garden; there was a corner he had lurked in often, waiting for
her to pass by.

Yala's dressing room was unchanged as well. The Tabrak had
not had time to plunder this place; she might have, ironically, been
safer here than in the palace.

I should have taken her with me, he thought, as he did several
times a day.

Her private bedroom, unused except for changing dresses or
during preparation for the retreat of a woman's red time, was quiet
and still. There was a small table in one corner, with a stack of paper,
an inkstone, and brushes, arranged as if she meant to write letters
here instead of in the study that morning. The wardrobes were full
of what dresses she had not taken when summoned to the Palace.
If he pressed his face to one would he smell her, or just the ghost of
ceduan to keep moths away and the jaelo she favored in her bath?

He would never smell the small starlike flowers again without
rage threatening to blind him.

Takshin stood in the center of the room, his hands curling into
fists, releasing, curling again. It was as if she had just stepped away
to deal with some household matter or to attend a guest, holding
her sleeve aside as she poured. *Yes, my husband.*

He did not even have a pyre to mourn. She would not have
allowed herself to be dishonored; the greenmetal blade he carried
everywhere now—too short for a sword, too long for a knife, its
handle crosshatched instead of wrapped or hilted, easy to hide and
sharp as his regret—had probably tasted her own blood.

Her husband hoped, for her sake, that it had been quick.

Garan Takshin turned in a full circle. There was no relief, nothing to kill. Nothing but the silence.

He could rule through Jin, he supposed. Kiron had remarked as
much with a thoughtful look—not rudely, and not encouragingly,
but as a simple statement of fact.

What good is an empire? Takshin had snapped. *I do not want it.*

Kiron had clapped him upon the shoulder, a stinging buffet expressing apology and shared grief at once. *Do not wait too long to visit, Shin.* And then he was gone, riding south to attend to his own battered kingdom.

Takshin's eyes were dry and burning. The scar upon his lip twitched madly. He took two steps and went to his knees; he buried his face in neatly folded bedding. She had not slept here before he left, but maybe after...

He could not weep. And yet Garan Takshin, the Elder Brother of Shan and Zhaon, made a soft, harsh, hurt noise, a wolf wounded but too rageful to notice, muffled by silk and wool.

He did not know that within the mattress a packet of Ashani Daoyan's letters lurked, written in a hand recognizable upon certain other ledger-papers, neatly wrapped and tied with an embroidery knot.

Nor would he ever find out, for the mattress was burned two moonturns later, as was customary to avoid ill-luck after a death.

A Strange Pair

Four and a half moon-turns later

The great port city of Anwei, queen of both the southerly trade routes and her rich hinterland at Shan's rim, clung to the hills surrounding a deep natural harbor. The docks were a mass of heaving and noise, for the worst winter storms had just finished spending themselves and passage to N'hon and the eastern ports of Ch'han's vast coast were now open to all rather than merely the desperate who could not afford to wait.

The great broad-sailed ship *Archer's Folly*, crewed by straight-backed N'hon and smiling Anwei, was preparing for morning tide as dawn rose. Some passengers clustered at the prow, but those who knew their business gathered sternward, for the sea's restless turning would draw that part of the ship free first and the breeze would be fresher.

Passage to N'hon was cheap during the winter because the risk of foundering in a storm was so high; it was not too dear this early in the season either, for many a ship was carrying goods or people in that direction and if one captain would not take a certain cargo, another would.

Two tall grey-eyed Khir, speaking soft in their sharply musical language, were at the stern. Takari Hui and Takari Dao—either brothers or shield-married, and in either case best left to their own business—appeared not to notice one of their countrywomen aboard, for those who took ship in Anwei obeyed an old unwritten custom to leave each other strictly alone. Besides, the woman's husband—a man with a piercing, albeit muddy gaze bespeaking some noble lineage and a well-wrapped hilt protruding over his shoulder—was hovering, protective as the kaburei attending her.

And the Khir woman's hands hovered too over her middle, the posture of expectancy.

The pilot boarded and was treated to a ceremonial cup of strong smoky eong tea upon a small folding table near the ship's great wheel. Gulls, nafa-birds, wavecatchers, and zhariung-wings cried over the rasp of waves mouthing the shore. The breeze freshened as the grey eastern horizon reddened and the sun's first fiery limb stretched above the island at the harbor's mouth, mist upon its green tea-growing slopes. The bosun was at the gangplank, largely ignoring last-minute passengers attempting even cheaper passage by stepping aboard just before the ropes were slipped; finally, the order was given to unmoor and the decks were alive with hurrying, cursing sailors.

"I have never been upon a boat before," Anh said softly. "My lady, are you quite sure it is..."

"Safe enough, my dear one." Her grey-eyed mistress had gained some weight, and her smile was no longer so somber. "Our lord would not choose an unworthy ship."

"I should hope not." Zakkar Kai stood behind her, close enough for the heat of their bodies to touch but without an ill-bred display of affection. Despite that, the yearning between the two was palpable; *a hawk and a dove*, their landlady upon Anwei's Seventh Hill had remarked to her gossiping neighbors while they hung laundry to dry. *They cannot fool me, they have eloped from the far North.*

Indeed Zakkar Kai's Khir had improved beyond all measure; it was safer not to leave much trace, and he had not spoken Zhaon in some while. Anwei spoke the Shan dialect, and Yala had absorbed that tongue rather quickly; a winter's worth of translating classics for pretentious merchants while the man assumed to be her husband instructed petty noble boys in the rudiments of swordplay had given them both some facility.

Indeed, as he had promised, they would not starve.

Ropes were coiled, the wind freshened, and the breeze tugged at Yala's hair. A single rough pebble wrapped in silken, crimson thread at the head of the pin thrust through her braids dangled no bright adornments; many assumed she was a noblewoman marrying far beneath her. Others thought her husband a lord fallen upon hard times and escaping with an enemy's daughter; at least the couple had a kaburei, which denoted a certain station.

Finally, the ship took its first tentative swaying steps toward the ocean, like a girl uncertain upon her first pair of jatajatas. Yala sighed, tension draining from her shoulders as canvas and rope tautened. The sun mounted another few increments.

Who would care for her princess's tomb now? Perhaps Mahara's shade understood; Yala offered prayers daily at a small folding travel-shrine cabinet, knowing it was not enough but all she had left to give.

Zhaon had taken the rest. What little remained belonged to Yala's ancestors, to her princess—and to the man she should have hated, the conqueror of Khir.

"It is not a long passage, I am told," Kai said in her ear, leaning close enough that his chest briefly brushed the back of her shoulder. "How fares little Baiyeo?"

"Well enough." Her hands tightened over her middle. Her red time had not come again, only the gentle jewelwing brush of new life within her thickening middle.

It was better, she thought, for a son of hers—or a daughter— to be a general's instead of a prince's. And she did not think Kai would be disappointed with a girlchild.

Not as a Khir man would be, certainly.

The ship heeled, and Yala turned to face him, studying Kai's face as if it were a map she could not quite decipher. "We are a strange pair," she murmured, in her accented Zhaon.

A smile—half pained, half relieved—touched her husband's lips. "We always have been, my love."

Anh, slightly scandalized, looked away. The other passengers were too busy with the sea, the breeze, and the birds to notice; the crew had other concerns.

Sailors chanted, ropes tightened, canvas and wood creaked. The large craft continued its turn, and when the pilot was ceremonially ushered onto a smaller ship that had carefully shepherded the *Folly* into the proper lane, they were well under way. The last danger of pursuit faded with every swell the ship climbed, and with each drop into a trough a weight lifted from the hearts of all aboard.

Through a rosy dawn, the general and the princess sailed to far N'hon.

finis

ACKNOWLEDGMENTS

Thanks are due to Sarah Guan, who began upon the road, and to Nivia Evans, who shepherded a weary writer through the final gates. Another double measure must be poured out for various sensitivity readers who steered the story through many a rocky channel; any errors and missteps remaining are, of course, simply and solely my own. To the many historians and linguists whose passion and scholarly endeavors provided inestimable help, likewise thanks are given; the fact that any errors and inconsistencies are my own is vigorously restated. A great deal of gratitude is due my family, who put up with me during all this. For those anonymous by request, many thanks and undying gratefulness—you know who you are.

The last of this trilogy was written and ushered through the publication process during a pandemic and other terrible events; I wish to especially thank the Orbit production staff, the very patient production editor (to whom I am often an inadvertent trial, alas), the hard-pressed cover artists, the gallant and hardworking copyeditor, and many other unsung, honorable heroes along the way. Thank you, very much.

Last of all, much gratitude is due to you, dear reader, for your kindness and attention. The author hopes the story has provided you with at least some entertainment, and a reprieve from the many cares of our own Middle World.

meet the author

S. C. EMMETT is a pseudonym for a *New York Times* bestselling author.

Find out more about S. C. Emmett and other Orbit authors by registering for the free monthly newsletter at orbitbooks.net.

orbit

Follow us:

f /orbitbooksUS

🐦 /orbitbooks

▶ /orbitbooks

Join our mailing list
to receive alerts on our
latest releases and deals.

orbitbooks.net

Enter our monthly
giveaway for the chance
to win some epic prizes.

orbitloot.com